PLAYER MANAGER 5

PLAYER MANAGER 5

TED STEEL

Podium

THE STORY SO FAR
SEASON 2023/24

Max Best has used his football manager powers to get a job as director of football at Chester FC. Three weeks ago, he saved the club from relegation by winning three matches as caretaker manager for the men's first team. After the third match, Max was attacked outside the stadium.

PLAYER MANAGER 5

It's not what you know, it's who you know.

—Ancient Mancunian proverb

SYSTEM SHOCK

Someone tried to kill me.

As I left the stadium, on my way to save a man's career, someone tried to crack my skull open like a boiled egg.

As I rushed to do a selfless thing for someone who deserved and needed it, someone tried to hit me for a home run.

As I valiantly braved torrential rain to do a far, far better thing than I have ever done, someone tried to make mine the first head in space.

Bit harsh.

So, hospital. Tubes, machines, a flurry of activity, then quiet. A darkened room, for actual *ages*. There wasn't much pain. Mostly just boredom with moments of terror, rage, fear, and loneliness. Exactly like lockdown, then.

My initial worries were threefold. First, fear of catastrophic memory loss and mental issues associated with traumatic brain injury. Second, the fact I couldn't feel my legs, or much else. Finally, the lack of curse. All my screens were gone. Now that it wasn't there, I realised I had become addicted to it, opening the news screen once a minute, checking the squad screens to see if my players were improving, or even just using it to tell the time. And now it was all gone.

I longed to see the list of the latest transfers. I pined for the perk shop where I could plot my path through the upgrades. I even had dark moments where I longed for the curse to make me shout "FIFA!" in exchange for an experience point.

Losing my powers made me angry, but anger was unhealthy. Anger was a distraction from my primary goal, and my primary goal had nothing to do with football.

So every time anger coursed through me, I repeated the mantra I'd learned from YouTube: control your anger before it controls you. Which led me to another phrase that had become important in my football career: control what you can. I searched my body for my thumb and tried and tried to feel it, then to move it. My first thumbs-up came with a few tears of relief and joy. My first toe wiggle brought forth a flood.

I thought about the attack. It must have come from behind. A big sideways whack to the lower part of my head. Hard enough to knock me out. Hard enough to knock the curse right out of me, too. But if I could move my fingers and toes, I wasn't paralysed. I would heal quickly. Or would I? The curse wasn't giving me super healing *now*, was it?

I deduced that if I was in any real danger, there would have been a lot more activity around me. A lot more tubes and pipes and drips. With effort, I could remember past events, and with effort I could move my hands and feet. So the new thing that worried me was the feeling that I had a big hole in my skull and if I moved too much my brain would leak out.

I was bored, but I reasoned that I was being kept in the quiet, darkened room so that I wouldn't get overstimulated. If stimulation was bad for me, I wouldn't seek it out. I tried to enjoy the boredom; I had a goal.

I set myself little tasks. Tiny targets. How many ceiling tiles could I count? Time had very little meaning, but I suppose it took a few days until I could count them all in one go. Then the game was counting how many different nurses and doctors came to visit me. It was hard because they didn't always talk—sometimes they came in, did things, and exited, leaving few clues about who they were. Footsteps, a certain sigh, the one who wrote like she was trying to push the pen through the flipchart. I gave them names. Made up backstories.

Finally, the boredom became aggravating and I had to work hard to quash my frustration. But I had a goal, so if rest was what I needed, I'd rest. I'd rest so hard they'd detect my stillness on seismographs.

Then came the day I felt like opening my eyes when someone came into the room. A nurse in her blue outfit. I tracked her coming in, going out.

Breakthrough.

I celebrated with a little nap.

When I woke up, a guy in a white doctor's coat sat to my right. He was leaning back in a chair, with his feet up on my bed. He was snacking from a silver platter. I glimpsed caviar, blocks of feta cheese, things on sticks, a little glass of popcorn, and a Cadbury Double Decker chocolate bar that had been cut up into easy-to-eat slices. A silver lid was popped onto the platter, which was placed on a little wheeled table. The doctor slapped his hands up and down.

With some effort, I turned my neck a couple of degrees.

The "doctor" smiled at me. An enormous, angular smile framed by a wonderful, short, silver beard.

"Hello, Max," said Old Nick.

"Have," I said, but forming words was hard. Nick stood, straightened his white coat, and went around to the other side of the bed where my side table was. He poured some water into a glass and was about to rest his hand on the back of my head—to cradle me while I drank—but he saw the fear. My skull. Cracked like a jigsaw puzzle. There's a hole in my bucket. It was easy to tell myself I was fine, so long as I stayed completely still. But the idea of someone—especially him—touching me on the back of my head made me quite nauseated.

He loomed over me, calculating. Finally, he put his hand on the exact spot where I'd been struck—I squeezed my eyes closed, waiting for pain that never came—and he ever so gently lifted me to a comfortable drinking angle.

I sipped the water.

Nick waited patiently. I said "uh" to indicate that I wanted more, and he helped me. I drank a third of the glass before he eased me back onto the pillow. He wandered off, and I heard him go to the hand-disinfectant station. He came back rubbing his hands. Cheeky fuck! My annoyance amused him, and I realised he'd only done it to score a point.

He still had his mysterious accent—part cut-glass English, part highly educated foreign diplomat. "You were saying?"

I tried again. My voice was pretty rough. "Have you come to finish the job?"

Instead of replying, he took hold of a bed-mounted arm, the sort you get at the dentist, and pulled it so that the screen at the end was in front of my face. Nick checked the angles, then returned to his starting position and picked up his silver platter. I watched as he munched on a piece of feta.

"Today, Max, as reward for your diligence and hard work, and to aid your recovery, we are going to watch my favourite television programme."

Okay. Didn't expect that. Obviously his explanation was a load of bull, but it did seem like I'd get to watch some telly. Better than counting tiles . . . probably.

Nick didn't seem to expect a reply, which was good, because seeing him in my room, having him as my first visitor post-murder was disconcerting. Exhausting. I closed my eyes to steel myself and promptly fell asleep.

When I opened them, the light in the room was different. The subtle suggestion of natural light that came through in daytime was gone, and the general noise level suggested to me that the ward was less busy. I guessed Nick had come at 7 p.m. and now it was 11.

He spoke as though there hadn't been a four-hour gap. "Ready? Here we go."

Nick was able to play and pause without pressing any buttons. He resumed eating his nibbles. I stared at him—his face was back to being slender, almost gaunt, and he'd lost some of his muscle mass. He put his feet back on my bed—rude—and I noticed his shoes were scuffed and worn.

"Focus, Max."

I centred my head and tried to watch.

It was a game show called *The Traitors*. Twenty-four everyday Australians went into a big house surrounded by lush countryside. They met each other and made small talk. The participants met stranger after stranger in the space of a few minutes, had to learn their names, had to very quickly get a sense of who they were dealing with so they could outwit them later.

I closed my eyes and fell asleep, drained by watching an introvert's nightmare.

Nick really didn't seem to mind that I kept going AWOL. He'd finished his food, except for the popcorn. When I was ready, the show continued.

Four of the participants were chosen to be "traitors." The rest were the "faithful." Every day, two people would leave the game. One would be voted out in an evening ceremony, and one would be "murdered" by the traitors. Daytimes would be spent doing tasks to earn money for the prize pot, while the players gossiped and plotted about who was likely to be a traitor so they could be "banished."

"This is shit," I croaked. It was a big-budget version of the parlour game Werewolf, also known as Mafia. How is that a TV show? Have we tried literally every other format? "Have you got any *Peppa Pig?*"

Nick popped in some popcorn. His eyes danced across the screen, taking it all in. He was—not literally—in heaven.

Something like half an hour in, it happened.

The traitors, wearing masks and robes, gathered in their murder room. The first time they would learn the identities of their teammates. They took their masks off and there was a burst of glee and devilish excitement so strong that even in my weakened condition I pulled myself towards the screen.

"*How good's this?*" said the most interesting traitor. He was a lovely guy who, when he had taken his mask off, had smiled like a demon.

"*I just cannot* wait *to conspire to murder,*" said another, and his teammates laughed and clapped their hands.

They began discussing who to murder first, and again I was off my pillow. The planning, the strategy, the chess moves. *Should we kill a big personality to sow fear? Someone in the middle of the pack to really get under people's skins? Some abrasive types would get themselves kicked out in the evening banishment sessions. There was no point in us murdering them.* And so on. It was thrilling. I'd immediately identified with the traitors. It was by far the most interesting role in the game, and my head was spinning with moves, countermoves, and wondering if I'd have the wherewithal to back up my nighttime plotting with the daytime acting chops to blend in and not arouse suspicion.

That was the moment the concept of the show clicked. If you were one of the faithful you could never, ever truly trust the person you were talking to. And unlike a quick game of Werewolf, this one had stakes. Hundreds of thousands of dollars. Life-changing money. People were playing to win. They would be unscrupulous. They would murder and banish their closest friends.

Nick paused it.

"Humans do relish a spot of evil." He got up and pushed the TV away, and I was surprised by how much that disappointed me. "I prefer the Australian version of the programme, and so will you. There are fiendish characters in that one. It's interesting that the creators vary the format. This one starts with twenty-four contestants and there are four traitors. The UK version starts with twenty-two contestants and three traitors. Remind me, Max. How many play-ers are in the Chester first-team squad?"

A pang as I tried to bring up a screen that wasn't there. I concentrated. "Twenty-one."

"Is that so?" He walked around in a small circle, touching things. "The Australian version is very strategic all round. The UK one consists mostly of weeping Brits telling people they've known for three days 'You are my one hundred percent.' Touching, yet pitiful. If I know you, Max, you're wondering if you'd be good at the game. Everyone thinks they would be better than those in the production. But being good makes you a target." He dipped his head. "As you have discovered."

"The curse is gone," I blurted out.

Nick did something I couldn't see. An eye roll, perhaps. "Everyone in your position knows to call it a *system*. How did you settle on *curse*?" He came over to my side table. "More water?" He brought it to my lips, and this time when he placed his hand on my head, it barely registered. Nick replaced the glass, then sat. "Brain injuries cause humans to become agitated. Irrational. And above all, angry. Had you woken up in this dreary hole, unable to move, unable to communicate, you would have taken your anger out on me. You would have uninstalled your system. So I have hidden it from you until such time as you are healthy enough to make good, rational decisions."

"I've still got it?" I said.

Nick pressed his fingertips together. "Relief. Undercurrent of pleading. How very, very revealing. As I said, Max, the system is merely hidden. It will return when you are ready. For now, you need to recover. I understand it is the low season, anyway."

Low season! He still knew nothing about football. "Did Chester survive?"

"I neither know nor care."

"What about my mum? Emma? Ziggy?"

"I am not a town crier, Max. People will tell you all that you missed. I understand a decision was made not to tell your mother; do not fret. There, now we can put trifles aside. We have more pressing matters."

Ah. My nerves jangled. Nick was a powerful being, and in my reduced state I was almost as helpless as it was possible to be. I decided to play it safe for once. "Okay."

"Your first question revealed muddled thinking. The very suggestion that I would harm you is nonsensical. We're a team, Max. We're very much on the same side." He showed me his teeth. Very wolflike. "I'll tell you what's coming. First, you will have a brief reunion with Emma. We shall get that out of the way so you can make the decision that a great many people are relying on you to make. Which brings us to your second meeting. Jackie Reaper—delightful name—will inform you of his plan to resign as manager of Chester Football Club."

"What?"

Nick frowned and pointed his finger downwards. When it came to football or life, I didn't care much for his opinions. But in his doctor's coat, he carried a level of medical authority that subverted my defences. He was telling me to calm the eff down. I breathed in, then exhaled slowly.

"Jackie Reaper doesn't want to be the manager. You can do what you want, of course. One option is to throw a temper tantrum. A reliable standby. Another option, some might say, would be to respect the wishes of your friend." He smiled. "But what would I know? I've never had a friend. If you seem to be in full possession of your faculties, Jackie Reaper will summon Mike Dean, and he will offer you the position of manager. I assume you will be childish and difficult, but after needlessly tormenting your fellows, you will accept. Which is why I have scheduled the following meeting to be with William Barnes."

"*You* set my schedule?"

"I used your mobile telephone. I knew you wouldn't mind."

"I mind a lot. Never do that again." I closed my eyes, then pushed them open again. I didn't want to fall asleep and come back to an empty room. There was information I needed. "Who is William . . . ?"

"Barnes. Perhaps you only know him as Barnesy."

"Barnesy? The guy from the board?"

"Indeed."

"Why? Why him?"

"He was in your British army. You remember? He has contacts. You have asked him, via your telephone, if he knows someone suitable to be your assistant manager."

"How can I ask him that? I'm not the manager."

"Barnesy is not in constant contact with MD or the rest of the board. He doesn't know what Jackie Reaper is planning. But I see that I have been too subtle. The 'assistant manager' will, in fact, be your bodyguard. Big, strong, capable. A trained killer, no less. As your assistant manager, he will be able to follow you wherever you go. To protect you."

"The club can't afford a bodyguard for me."

"It can, but my colleagues assure me you will resist this common-sense precaution so you can invest in a 'box-to-box midfielder,' whatever that is. So here's what will happen. You will hire an assistant manager using the club's money. And a shockingly similar but not identical amount of money will later be injected into the club. Do you understand? I will finance the bodyguard, for the first year at least."

"He's a traitor," I said.

"Excuse me?"

"Like in the show. He's pretending to be one thing, but he's another thing. Is that why you wanted me to watch it?"

"He *will* be your assistant manager. Fitness training. Discipline. He will shout at the people you tell him to shout at. If anyone tries to stove your head in, he will stop them. He won't be a one-hundred-percent fit for the role, but he might save your life. What more do you need?"

My egg was scrambled, and it wasn't because of the murder. "I would want Jackie to be my assistant manager. This guy will have to be a coach."

Nick showed the first signs of impatience. "We have *thought* about this, Max. If it was possible the man could be a coach, we would have suggested that first. The man will be well paid. Very probably the highest-paid employee at the club. He cannot, then, be a mere coach." He waved his hands. "You will work all this out for yourself. Do not get bogged down in details. Let me remind you of the sequence. You see Emma. You are happy. You meet Jackie. You are unhappy, but you accept his decision like a good friend. You become manager of Chester Football Club. You meet Barnesy. He tells you he knows the exact right man for the 'assistant manager' job. You are free to focus on your health. You will start rehabilitation. Walking. Watching your new favourite TV show in ever-increasing slices. And so on. You will learn that there is very little for you to do this summer. Ah! Do not interrupt. There is much you *could* do. But not much you *must* do. It is perfectly feasible that your first day of work could be August fifth. That would give you two full months to heal."

"Heal," I said.

Nick walked around again. "Which brings us back to Emma. She will return, happy and proud that you have finally accepted the job you were born to do."

I scoffed. I hadn't been *born* to do anything except be a wage slave.

"And Emma will bring up the possibility of going on holiday. Spain, she will say. Some sun. Perfect conditions for an invalid."

"She's been trying to get me to Ibiza," I said, surprised that the memory had come so easily.

"Ibiza will be too hot, Max. The summer will be brutal all over the Mediterranean. You must mention Tenerife."

"Ugh, no." That was a name I associated with awful English holidaymakers—even more so than Ibiza.

More impatience. "Very well. Stay here and forever be weak and feeble. Or go to Ibiza and be baked alive. The choice, as always, is yours." He seemed to be gritting his teeth. "Another thing. Emma will offer to pay. I understand you have some resistance to the idea. You should accept more offers, Max. The last one worked out quite well, don't you think?"

"Yeah, until the murder."

"You can't blame me for *that*," he said, and I trembled as he clenched and unclenched his fists. He was *pissed*. "That was all you."

"Do you know who did it?"

He took a strident tone. "When Emma offers to pay, you would be a fool to refuse." He softened. "She will book something cheap in order to minimise your discomfort with accepting 'charity.' For my purposes, that's an acceptable compromise. The sun, the distance from home, the long lazy days, yes, it will, what's the new phrase? It will sort you right out."

"But—" I started.

Nick held up a finger. There was movement outside the door and for a moment I was scared. The murderer come to finish the job? Maybe a bodyguard wasn't such a bad idea.

The door opened and in walked a man and a woman. They were wearing suits with lanyards dangling around their necks. If they weren't police, my brain was more mashed than I thought.

"Max Best," said the man. "I'm Detective Inspector Barton and this is DI Rowan. We were wondering if you'd be up to answering a few questions."

Barton was around thirty, white, slicked-back hair, wide nostrils, very confident attitude. He came close, and would have taken a seat had Nick not blocked his path. I took such a strong dislike to him I wondered if it was a byproduct of all the meds. For some reason, I turned to Nick. "What do you think?"

The demon stepped towards the female officer, causing her to back away. That left Nick free to walk around Barton in a slow circle. "Max, are you quite calm?"

"Yes."

"I think you would find this man distressing."

"Why's that?" I said, already pushing myself onto my elbows. Fight or flight. Ready.

Nick came over and pushed me back onto the pillow. "You already won this battle, Max. Please be calm, yes?"

Already won? What? "I'm calm," I said, and it was true.

"I'd like to ask—" started Barton, trying to reassert himself in the situation. That might have worked on most people, but not on Nick.

"This one," said Nick, deliberately avoiding the word *man*, "was already at the scene of the attack, Max. Picking up overtime pay by helping fill the quota of police at the football stadium. Easy work. Easy money."

"How do you know that?" demanded the copper.

"This one *likes* easy money. The call came in. There's been a violent assault, come quick. He came quick, to be sure. Quickly came to the conclusion that Mr. Yalley, the man who stopped the attack, the man who called for help, was guilty. Call off the search. Send back the hounds."

"Mr. Yalley?" I said, stupefied. "Tried to kill me?"

"Is that your statement?" said Barton, whipping out a tiny notebook. I looked at him more closely. His air of confidence was utterly fake. He was a traitor trying to act innocent, and he lacked the mental agility to keep his stories straight. He was cracking under the pressure. But what pressure could a rando in Chester be under?

"Dear, oh dear," said Nick. "Your desperation is most unattractive." I couldn't see, but I think Nick flashed a sexy smile at the female officer. She swayed like a tree in a breeze. Nick sat on the edge of my bed. "I'm glad you're calm, Max. That's very good. You see, Mr. Yalley was, and was not, this one's typical victim. This one discovered, to his cost, that Mr. Yalley was not such an easy target as he seemed."

"He was by the body, covered in blood!" spat Barton.

"And where was his weapon, pray tell?" Nick was having a blast. "As I was saying, not such an easy target. You see, Mr. Yalley is under the protection of Max Best."

"I didn't do anything," I said, confused.

"You did. Who was in the stadium that day because of you? Sebastian Weaver, who turned the full might of his legal empire to the defence of a man he had never laid eyes upon. Bethany Alban, a rising star at this country's most popular newspaper. It is pro-police, of course, which makes its reporters tilt even harder at crooked cops."

"Hey," said Barton. "I'm not bent. And Yalley was *covered* in blood."

"To have a duty and to do the opposite is the definition of crooked. Of course, you thought you were safe. Who would believe *Mister* Yalley's version of events? Oh, no one. No one save for *everyone who knew him*. Bethany was fierce; Mr. Yalley is an honorary Beth Head. The Weavers bared their teeth. Allies heeded the summons. Dozens of players from Chester, from Manchester City, a coach from Altrincham, why, even his own pastor was in attendance. For ignoring a veritable United Nations of character witnesses, Mike Dean has banned this one from the stadium. The seven members of the board distributed a collective denouncement. And beyond the aid guaranteed by the friends of Max and by those who consider Mr. Yalley to be one of the faithful, he can also count on the unwavering support of anyone with enough brainpower to answer the simple question: if he is guilty, where is the weapon?"

I let this information settle. Nick didn't care about Mr. Yalley, or even the concept of justice. I got the feeling he was genuinely angry that Barton hadn't caught my murderer. Of course . . . maybe that's what he wanted me to think. "How did they know there was a weapon involved? Could it have been a punch?"

"Your physio, Dean, was summoned. After doing what he could for you—you might perhaps think about not sacking him in the near future; I like the idea of someone so calm in a crisis being near you at all times—he almost at once described what would have caused your wound. A heavy cylinder. Some building materials were found nearby. Metal rods. All the police needed to do, Max, was talk to Mr. Yalley. *Where did the attacker go? What was he wearing?* They might have found him. Instead, they decided to banish one of the faithful and the traitor is free to strike again."

I felt a surge of heat, but quickly got a grip. This Barton fuck was in deep shit. Sebastian hitting him from the left, Beth from the (far) right, Nick from below. Me being mad at him right now would add nothing, would only delay my recovery. "Nick," I murmured. He leaned closer. "Get rid of him."

Nick gave me a grin so sharp it could have sliced culatello ham. "Get rid of him? How would you like me to misinterpret that?"

I rested my head back on the pillow. If Nick murdered the guy and made me pay for it, I could probably have lived with it. But Nick seemed content to stick to our current arrangement.

He went over to Barton and clicked a button on a tiny cylinder that had appeared in his hand. He lifted Barton's eyelid and shone the light into his eyes. The dude didn't resist in the slightest.

Nick clicked off the light and mused. "What is . . . candyflipping?"

I didn't know, so Nick looked at the policewoman. Her eyes darted between Nick and her partner as she said, "It's when you combine LSD and MDMA."

"So many letters!" laughed Nick. "Whatever do they mean?" He stepped away, then put his hand on Barton's shoulder and turned him around. He gave him a little push and Barton started to fall. He seemed to come out of a stupor, jolted awake by his imminent fall, and stumbled towards the door. He hurt himself grasping for the handle. "This one will not be a problem, Max."

"What about her?" I said. I wanted my attacker to be caught. I would want to cooperate with the police for *that*.

"She is complicit," he said, and the officer turned white. "That one is this one's *one hundred percent*. Never fear, Max. Soon you will have access to other resources. Do you understand better now?"

I did. My assistant manager slash bodyguard would also be my detective.

I closed my eyes, knowing that when I opened them, I would be slightly more healed. And that there would be no demons. And no traitors.

When I woke, I was able to twist and turn to check if anyone was in the room—more progress. It was empty, and there was no sign of the silver platter or the extra table. There *was* a screen on the end of an arm behind me. If I turned it on, would Nick's show still be playing? I wanted to finish the episode. Reaching the arm and pulling it into place was beyond me. For now.

I thought about my conversation with Nick. He was the antagonist in my story, I was sure of that. But he wanted to help me heal and recover. It made sense—the sooner I was back grinding for XP, the better for both of us. And yet I couldn't help but feel like a contestant on *The Traitors*. I had to trust someone I didn't trust. But what benefit could there be *to Nick* of me going to Tenerife, soaking up the sun, and giving Emma exactly what she wanted?

It just felt too good to be true.

The alternative? Stay in England. In Henri's house in Darlington, while all my neighbours gawped at me and little kids asked their mum, "Didn't that guy used to be Max Best?" Shuffling around the supermarket, catching my breath in the cereal aisle, always looking over my shoulder, flinching at every bang and unexpected movement. Fleeing to Spain didn't seem so bad.

But what was Nick's angle? He'd given me water, kept me calm, banished a traitor, and yes, even given me a treat. A trashy Australian show that I couldn't wait to finish.

On the show, you had to make people feel you were on their side so they'd trust you so you could betray them. Which of the things he'd done hinted at which future deceptions?

And why had the conversation gone the way it had gone? I had twenty important questions I hadn't even thought to ask him. Why had he chosen *me* for the curse? Why exactly didn't he want me to be a player? What *was* he, and what were the imps? He'd called them colleagues. Does the curse have an expiry date? What happens when I retire? What happens to me if Nick dies? Can Nick die?

Was it my brain injury that had pushed those thoughts away, or was it one of his enchantments?

Mildly frustrating.

And Jackie. Mate.

Thinking about him made me tired. So I went back to my aggressive resting, and my incremental gains in movement, flexibility, and awareness. Getting myself in shape for when Emma arrived.

A nurse said, "There's an Emma to see you. Will I let her in?"

I gave him a thumbs-up.

He walked off and I had what, thirty seconds, to mentally prepare.

Emma would have been sick with worry. Three weeks of crying. Maybe she'd watched *The Proposal* on a loop because it was "our movie." There was simply nothing I could have done to make her feel better.

That didn't stop me feeling guilty as fuck. I'd put her through an ordeal. And now she'd see me like this, feeble, bed-ridden, and she'd only worry more. My goal, then, was to try to be normal. Calm. As much the old Max as possible. And, as with all our bedroom scenes, I wanted to last as long as possible.

She came into the room and blinded me with masses of long, blonde waves. In an instant, I saw that she'd done her hair, her nails, maybe spent the whole morning getting her makeup just right. She was wearing what I can only describe as a denim cardigan with more buttons than her leather jacket had zips. I turned away and closed my eyes. When I did that, her footsteps slowed. She got to the side of the bed, not knowing if she should sit or stand or what.

"Max," she said.

"Have you got a hat?"

"What?"

"You're hurting my eyes."

"Do you want me to go?"

"I want you to be less radiant. For a minute. So I can adjust."

"I'll try." She sucked in a breath, held it, and let it go. "Is that better?"

I half opened an eye. "I'm still feeling overstimulated."

"Sorry." She had placed her hand next to mine on the bed. We were touching, but there was a gap. A gap caused by however many days of separation, however many intense emotions experienced alone. Did she want distance, or was she hoping I'd bridge the gap? Whatever happened, I didn't want her to think of me as fragile. I commanded my hand to inch left, on top of hers. She flipped hers round. I was holding my girlfriend's hand. Like a real boy. I swallowed, hard. She must have felt something similar, because her attempt at low-key positivity failed. She croaked, "So how are you doing?"

"Mustn't grumble." Me talking like a pensioner made her laugh, but also brought tears. I closed my eyes. I didn't want to see that. That wasn't my goal. "I've been dreaming about football."

"I bet."

"No, I never dream about football. These . . . it must be the drugs. It's football that doesn't exist. Freeform football. No positions. Murmuration."

"I'll have what you're having."

I risked another look. Either it was getting easier or the light had shifted and wasn't bouncing off her so much. She was exquisite, of course. Flawless. But I knew her. "This has been hard for you."

"Yes," she said. "At first, I was in bits. I was here every day. Frantic. Desperate." A huge tear formed and started trekking down her face. She wiped it away with her free hand. "But they said it wasn't as bad as they thought. They had to pump you full of drugs for a while, but you made good progress, they said. And they moved you in here, so every day got a little bit easier. Every day there was progress. You weren't going to . . . you know. But there was always that worry."

"That I wouldn't be the same."

"Right." She sniffed, damply, but she smiled as she remembered something. "Then I got your message."

Hold up. Message? I hadn't . . . Nick! Of course he hadn't told me this part. "Oh. They had me on all kinds of meds. Remind me what I said."

Full smile now. Only positive thoughts behind it. "I was out in the little waiting area they've got there. By the vending machines. And a doctor came over with his white coat and his stethoscope and clipboard and all that and he said, 'Are you Emma Weaver?' And I said yes. And he said he had a message from Max."

"Go on." I wanted a description of the doctor, but I felt pretty sure I knew who it had been. The only question was, why hadn't Emma recognised him?

"He flipped up the paper and read it out. 'Tell the hot blonde I'm doing my best to get well but knowing she's out there is distressing and, like, totes the opposite of relaxing.'"

"Totes?"

"He read it word for word, he said. 'Totes the opposite of relaxing. So tell her she's not allowed to hang around whatever hospital this is like a weepy ghost and she's to go clubbing and find a huge guy with no neck and cheap tats and have a quick porking in a sticky-floored nightclub bathroom and I'll text her when I'm ready to hold court.'"

"That's insane," I said. "That doesn't sound like me."

Emma squeezed my hand. "It does. You always say mad things like that. So I knew you were all right. You know, inside."

A quick porking? How had Nick come up with *that*? "Did you see that doctor again?"

"No. I haven't been back. It was hard but I stayed away. Went to that hotel we go to. Got some sleep, finally, knowing you were going to be all right. Really all right."

So Nick had done me a favour, there. Told Emma what she needed to hear. Reduced her stress and worry by an order of magnitude. Thanks, dude. Or . . . was it another stratagem? I yawned and took my hand out of Emma's so I could put my arms over my face. This brief interaction had been draining.

"I don't want to strain you; I won't stay long. Listen, Max. They asked me to talk to you about Chester. I told MD and Ruth what the doctor told me—that you would need to heal and recover and do rehab, but that you're mentally sharp as ever. You don't need to worry about what's happening this summer. Everyone is chipping in. The jobs are getting done. Oh, and they got you a place to live. In Chester. They're going to make it really, really easy to get back to work, and there's no hurry. You can take as long as you need." She paused. "They're going to ask you to be Chester's manager. The men's team."

"Mmm," I said. "Bout Jackie?"

She shrugged. "He doesn't want to do it. Says he's not cut out for it."

"You think he's right?"

"He knows a lot more about being Jackie than I do."

"Do you think I should let him just walk away without a fight?"

"I honestly have no idea. I think it's hard for him."

"How?"

"You're much better than him. And everyone knows it. Everyone except you, he says."

I shook my head slightly, a gesture which led to me closing my eyes. I'm sure I fell asleep because Emma was suddenly reading something on her phone while holding my hand. I'm sure she was relieved that I was okay, that I was myself, but I had been pretty flat. There hadn't been a big, romantic kiss. No excessive display of emotion. It must have been disappointing, even if she understood why. I'd learned that being emotional drained my battery double-quick, and I hadn't worked so hard to get to this moment only to have one big sloppy kiss and then lapse into unconsciousness. But now that I was close to my limit anyway, I decided to ramp things up. To start with, I'd break Nick's timeline. Bastard had it all worked out, did he?

"Babes," I said, and she nearly dropped her phone from the surprise. "The dude said I'd be able to start my physical rehab soon. At Saint Cyril's, couple of minutes away. I'll be walking around in no time. And the doctor you met told me I should go on holiday. Somewhere warm. I think he said, 'bit of sun will sort you right out.'"

"We can go to Ibiza?"

"He was weirdly insistent about *not* going there. He said Tenerife."

She looked doubtful. "Those flights are over four hours. Can you manage?"

"I'm top manager. Jackie said." Another wave of tiredness. "If you're still offering to take me away this summer . . . Tenerife." I'm not sure why I decided to trust Nick on that. He'd messed my head up by showing me that *Traitors* TV show. Got me all paranoid, thinking about double- and triple-bluffs. I thought about asking Emma not to book something expensive, but Nick had already told me she'd go for the bottom end of the scale.

"Okay. I'll start looking for places in Tenerife." Hesitation. "When?"

"Oh. What is it now?"

"End of April. Nearly May."

May was the exit trials. Hundreds of talented kids would be there. Ones cut from other teams. I'd been so looking forward to those days, but it wasn't going to happen. I had to focus on my personal recovery. Had to. So May would be rehab month. Nick said I still had the curse. I still had super healing, then. I'd push myself hard, but sensibly. I'd use Dean, Magnus, and Livia (if she still worked for me) to augment whatever resources I'd get from whoever was paying for my treatment. I'd be able to walk in four weeks, surely? I only needed to be able to get on and off a plane. "June?" I suggested.

"That's quick, Max. Even for you. Look, I said, everything's being done. There's no need to hurry."

I covered my face again. I wanted to lift myself up, but I thought better of it. So I laid my arms beside me and settled down like I was in a coffin. I could be emotional, or I could say what I needed to say. I chose words. This was it. A lot of effort to get to this moment. I refused to waste it on gestures.

"Ems. Bebs. When I woke up here and realised what must have happened, I had a choice. To rip my tubes out and walk out of the hospital like heroes do in movies. Or to do what I yell at my players to do, which is to be a model patient. I tell them if you need to rest, rest. I'm normally a mad hypocrite. But this time I've been resting like an absolute legend. I'm a titan of tranquillity. I knew you'd be out there, worrying, crying, and I had to push that aside and focus on what I needed to do."

"Yeah, I know, course."

I swallowed. "It was hard. I must have been off my tits when I gave the doctor that message, because when I was alone with my thoughts, they were cold. Stay still. Don't move. Don't rush. Let your body heal. Don't get in the way. Let it happen. Slowly getting better as fast as I could. Because I knew," I said, and I had a sleep crisis that I snapped out of. "Because I knew *that* was the way to get to this moment the fastest. This is what's kept me going. This, now. Here with you." I exhaled, shakily. "It was scary. Wondering if I'd ever feel my toes again. Wondering what'd be wrong with me. Losing my . . . memories. It was a big shock to go from feeling all-powerful, to this." I closed my eyes, but not to sleep. Had to blink away a couple of tears. "And I'm scared of you and what you mean to me. I'll do whatever it takes to get on that plane. So you go ahead and book it. If I have to ignore you for a few weeks while I get my legs to work, I'll do that. But I promise you, I'll be next to you on that plane. And I won't pack a single hoodie."

That got her. She fell into bits. In a good way, I hoped. This scene was familiar—me immobile on a bed while Emma sat by me. Our date in Darlington, after I'd run myself into the ground the night before. I wanted to swear this would be the last time we'd be in this situation, but I couldn't promise that, could I? The traitor in the police had let my would-be murderer literally saunter off. Perhaps he would want to strike again. I needed a bodyguard. Perhaps I would finish the summer with one. But for now, I needed to be careful. Treat everyone like a potential threat until I could defend myself. If they came for me, they might get Emma, too.

"Babes," I said, eyelids desperately heavy. "Don't tell anyone where we're going. Or when."

"Why?"

Questions so tiring. Just trust. "Please."

"Okay."

One last burst of effort to hit my goal. Finish with a goal. He shoots, he scores! Gol gol goooool! Gol de Max Best! I was virtually motionless as I prepared to finish my speech. My team talk. Team. Squad of twenty-one. Three traitors. Players. Four-four-two, dissolving into a shape that can't be expressed through numbers. From 4-4-2 into a stanza, into a sentence fragment, forming and re-forming, a mist, moving according to rules only those inside the cloud knew. Fractal football. No! Don't sleep. *Emma.* Got to tell Emma. Got to tell Emma she's my one hundred percent. Got to. Got to. Do it now. But though I chased the ball with all my might, I was too slow. Too slow. Too weak. In despair, I fractured into many copies of myself, curving, sweeping, dancing. We surrounded the ball. The goalkeeper came rushing towards me. I put my foot on the ball and laughed. You fool! I was pretending. *I'm* the traitor. Now. Watch what I can do . . .

I didn't say much as Jackie told me why he wanted to quit. Nick had got in my head. *Respect the wishes of your friend.* Jackie didn't say anything I agreed with.

He couldn't handle the pressure. He was too slow, too cautious, too fearful. He couldn't do what I could do. The best thing for Chester would be for me to take over.

Wrong, wrong, wrong.

But he wouldn't listen to me. It was like the time I swore to him I wasn't a good player. You can't scout yourself, he said. And he was using his victory then to admit defeat here.

Respect the wishes of your friend. But Nick *would* say that, wouldn't he? He wanted me in charge of the men's team. I would get more XP per match, and there were forty-six league games for the men compared to twenty-two for the women. And impressing with the men would make it more likely I'd be offered prestigious jobs.

I had been staring straight ahead, which was borderline unpleasant, but it was the only way to keep my face from showing my true feelings. Now I looked at him. "The best thing for Chester is I keep doing what I'm doing and you keep doing what you're doing."

He shook his head, gripped it, rubbed his face, pulled his cheeks down. "I can't." Haunted stare. "I can't."

I blew some air out. I couldn't convince him, but maybe someone else could. "Is MD here?"

He didn't question how I knew that. "Yeah. Will I get him?"

I didn't reply, which he correctly interpreted as affirmation. While he was gone, I tried to do some slow breathing. Deep down, I understood this was hard for Jackie. Probably very hard. Nick had told me off in advance about making it harder. But come on, Jackie mate. Seriously, come *on. Fuck.*

MD came in, looking extremely nervous. I'd have to get used to that. Even the nurses—who knew better—treated me like I was made of glass.

We did a bit of small talk, but I pretended to be more tired than I was so we could get on with it.

"What do you think of all this, MD?"

He licked his lips. "It was incredible what you did in those matches, Max. I'd be very, very happy if Jackie stayed on. I'd fight to keep him if you hadn't . . . you know. In the most loyal possible way, you made Jackie's position untenable. The tactics, the sense of fun, the passion, the way you dragged the fans back onside, the way you saved the club from relegation. And made it all look so *easy.* I want Jackie to stay, but every time we lose two matches in a row people will call for you to take over. No one can work like that. Jackie has stayed on while you recovered, but he told me his intentions after the last game of the season. We've looked at it from every angle, Max. Either you take over . . . or we call Ian Evans. Sorry, that was a joke. We want you to be the manager, Max. There's no plan B."

"Great," I said, lifeless. In theory it was *my* job to choose the next manager, but I couldn't blame them for not trusting me to do that in my current condition. Letting Jackie go was a mistake, a huge mistake, but it wasn't mine to correct. I felt justified in making one last pitch. "Jackie thinks I'm a better football manager than him. Across three matches, sure. Let's agree to that. Bad news is, next season is forty-six games, plus cups. I can't improve players. The club can't replace Jackie's coaching. The chances of us getting a coach of his quality are zero. The men's team has three main assets: Pascal, Raffi, and Youngster. Next June, with me as manager . . ." I had a little think. Pascal had been just below CA 30 before my murder. I could double that, maybe. What's a CA 60 nineteen-year-old worth? What about the CA 70 he'd reach under Jackie? "With me as manager for a year, he could be worth thirty thousand pounds. With Jackie, at least fifty. Raffi?" I expected him to kick on even more. He'd start most games for either Jackie or me. "Under me, he might go for sixty grand. Under Jackie, a hundred. Youngster? Me, a hundred grand. Jackie? Half a mill. We're talking about millions of pounds of added value over the next ten years."

"If we can find the players," said MD.

"Which I can't do if I'm managing Tuesday, Saturday, Tuesday, Saturday. Guys! Think about it."

"Max," whined Jackie. "You only talk about what I can bring as a coach. I'm supposed to be the *manager.*"

"As manager, you can get us promoted," I said. "Easy. While I find players and run the women's team. The current situation is the golden ticket. Me as manager? I'll win games. Big whoop. What about the players? What about Youngster? What about Raffi's dreams? He can't have a season of bad coaching. Not at his age. I'll make more money in the next ten years from Raffi and Youngster if you're their manager for the next couple of years. That's a fact. So you're a cash machine. Do you want a pay raise? Let's talk. You're worth it. And managing? You've had an apprenticeship. Four wins, three draws, four defeats. In tough circumstances. Seven away games out of eleven! Why are you beating yourself up? It's fine. And it'll only get better. Jesus Christ. I got nine points. You got fifteen." I'd worked that out when Jackie told me how the last three games had gone. "Fifteen is more than nine. *You* saved the club."

"No one who saw the matches thinks that," said Jackie. "Without you, I'd have relegated the club and been sacked. Every other manager had my number, and I didn't twig until you pointed it out. But you know what it was? It was when Sam Topps got concussed. Everyone in football right up to the top ten managers in the world would have put Wisey on. Easy. Job done. Only *you* would use it as a chance to put Pascal on to mark a left back. Livia asked me what the hell you were thinking and I had to say, no fucking clue. Thank God Spectrum explained it on *Seals Live,* otherwise I'd still be scratching my head to this day. I can't do that, Max. I can't win a game with one substitution. And I can't walk around Chester like I'm top dog when I'm not. I'm not the right man for the job so I have to step down. It's that simple."

"Be a coach, then. Coach us."

Jackie looked away. I'd made a mistake—I should have said "be my assistant manager," but Nick had distorted my view of the future. If things panned out Nick's way, the assistant manager position was taken.

MD stepped in. "He can't go from being the manager to a coach. Come on, Max."

"Why not?"

"In my old company, if we did that to someone, demoted them but kept them in the same teams, they'd sue us for constructive dismissal. It's what you do to show someone they aren't valued. It's what you do to force someone to quit without a payoff. You can't ask someone to *volunteer* for such humiliation."

"We'll show what we think of him. We'll make him the highest-paid employee in the history of the club. He'll earn double what I get. Triple."

It didn't tempt him in the slightest. "Thanks, Max. But no."

"Fine. Great. You'll stay in place until the end of July."

More shaking. What the fuck had *happened* to him? "I can't."

So he was going to leave me with untrained, half-fit players? A player's CA probably dropped over the summer, and without Jackie, it'd be slow to recover. Guaranteed bad start to the season. Another mountain to climb. Another bad decision I'd have to fix. A surge of fiery anger went through me. Control. Emma. Holiday. Hundred percent. I made my lips relax from whatever hideous shape they had formed. I thought about asking what Jackie planned to do instead, but I was too angry at him. It wasn't treachery exactly, but I did feel betrayed. "MD. Am I allowed to fire him?"

"No, Max."

"Who accepts his resignation?"

"We can do it together."

"The Two Amigos," I said, resting my head back on the pillow. Jackie and MD got to their feet and tried to leave quietly. "MD, hold up."

I felt Jackie hesitate, wondering if I planned to say goodbye. I should have. But I didn't. With one last glance at me, he turned and left.

"What do you need?" said MD, quietly, because the room suddenly felt cavernous. Empty. Desolate.

"We've got loads of guys out of contract. I need to talk to some of them. The ones we need to keep."

"Ah." MD got shifty and slunk back into his chair. "Max, your injuries . . . we were told you were very badly hurt. And we thought you would need months to even get to this point." I blinked and he nearly jumped from his chair as if I'd shouted at him. He was acting guilty. Had he traitored me in some way? "The doctors *told* us, Max. Told us it looked bad."

"What did you do?" I said, with no heat whatsoever. He flinched anyway.

"We. *We* renewed contracts. So that you wouldn't have to rebuild the whole team," he said, pleading. I eyed him with amazement. He knew he'd fucked up but this reaction was weirdly intense. "And they won six out of the last seven, this team. But we've got more budget. You can still bring in a few hot talents. But, you see, this way there's no rush for you to come back. We could start the season tomorrow. It's all okay!"

I looked up at the ceiling. "Mike, will you calm down? I'm not mad at you. Just tell me you didn't renew Trick." Trick Williams, the worst human being in Chester. Apart from the one who tried to murder me and the one who tried to pin my murder on an innocent man.

MD's face told the story. The blood drained from his face. "He's our only left back. He's . . . he played well. Didn't he, Max?"

I blew more air out. Another year of Trick. Holy shit. "I know Len left. And we had twenty-one players."

"We had twenty-two," said MD. He was out of his depth when it came to football, but he was able to count. "If we include you."

Twenty-two. Just like Nick had been saying. The British version of the show had twenty-two players, with three traitors. "You renewed every contract . . . except three."

MD blinked. "How did you know that?" I didn't say anything. "Oh, they must have told you their intentions. Yes, Doug Walker and Chad Flintoff left." Three traitors. Just as Nick said! He wanted me on my guard. Wary. Less trusting. "But please leave the details to us, Max. I'm not doing this in a vacuum. I've had Jackie, I've got Vimsy, Jill, the whole gang. We're looking at everything saying, 'What would Max do?' Do your physiotherapy. Go to Italy." I gave him a sharp look. Emma had lied to him about where we were going. What a woman! My hundred percent. "When you come back, when you're ready, there's a little bit of budget and a lot of goodwill. We're ready to follow you, Max."

Emma had said people were banding together to make my return easy. Seemed she had heard right. I didn't need to think about Chester FC for a while. "Does Livia still work for us?"

"Yes."

"Can you get her, Dean, and Magnus to come here? Today?"

"I'll try. Why?"

"To start rehab. I've got a plane to catch."

I didn't have the curse. The *system*, as Nick wanted me to call it. Two items from its newsfeed, close together, would come as no shock to anyone. No shock to anyone except my murderer. If his motive was to stop me progressing my football career, he'd soon know he had failed. Would he try again?

Jackie Reaper has resigned as manager of Chester FC. Chester will now be looking for a replacement manager.

Max Best has been appointed manager of Chester FC.

HELL IS OTHER PEOPLE

We landed and there was half a round of applause. Half a round? A semi-circle of kudos. A crescent of claps.

I stayed in my seat with my sunglasses on and hood pulled down. The hood was a mild source of contention, but I had only promised Emma I wouldn't *pack* a hoodie. When it came time to pick a traveling outfit that could protect me from sun, rain, and attention, there was one clear winner.

The rest of the passengers shuffled along the aisle. I waited to make sure I'd be the last one—fifty percent less chance of getting pulled into a conversation, one hundred percent less chance of holding someone up—and inched along with my tiny, virtually empty travel bag. Emma was ahead of me, wheeling a bulging suitcase and gripping three plastic bags. The case she'd checked into the hold weighed more than she did.

The stairs down to the tarmac were okay, if I didn't try to go too fast and held on to the handrail, but then we had to get on a little bus that would take us to the arrival hall. All the seats had been taken, so Emma asked a guy if I could sit down. He said yes, of course, but we'd only been on the island for two minutes and Emma had already broken her promise not to talk to anyone, not to ask for help, and not to draw attention to me.

I pulled my hood even farther down and sulked.

The four-and-a-half-hour flight was at least an hour more than I was able to handle, so when we got to the hotel, I threw myself on the bed and drifted to sleep. I woke up, showered, and spent the rest of the evening under the sheets. When Emma fell asleep, so did I.

The next morning, I was in a much better mood. The worst was over. All the things that had made me anxious—turbulence, mid-air collisions, crying babies, stag weekends, hen weeks, airborne diseases, not being able to manage the toilet, getting sucked out through a porthole, terrorists, "Can anybody land this plane?," exploding engines, passengers breaking the rules, Emma being sat next to some overly handsome Spanish guy or—worst of all—her making friends with some Brits and offering to merge our groups for the holiday. Er . . . where was I? Oh yeah. None of that happened. Nor was the hotel one giant nonstop rave. Nor were the pillows too big, too small, too itchy. Nor was it unbearably hot, and nor did anyone try to make me eat anything I didn't want.

The forecast was two weeks of sun. Just sun, nothing else. Twenty degrees Celsius. Sixty-eight Fahrenheit. Acceptable! I went onto our balcony and took in the view. We weren't all that high and there was only one floor above us. In front, vegetation. Weird, alien plants. Rocks everywhere. Kind of a brown tinge to everything. Hell reclaimed by nature.

"You're up!" said Emma, who was wearing a white t-shirt and nothing else.

"Woke up feeling pretty good," I said. "Ready for action."

"Oh?" she said.

"Not that kind of action. Was I a dick yesterday?"

"Yeah. Big time."

"Huh. Well, they say hell is other people. And they're right. Good view, isn't it? But . . . where's the beach? Where are the other hotels?"

"I got us something a bit farther inland. A bit quieter."

I considered that. "I mean, yeah, great. Perfect. Let's do the tour." I'd put myself on a strict low-information diet so I could steer all my effort into my physical recovery. Emma had taken the concept a little further than even I intended, and postponed certain discussions—like which club Henri picked— until, quote, a more opportune moment. She certainly hadn't involved me in choosing the hotel. It would only have exhausted me—computers and phones were still very fatiguing, and Magnus had urged me to take the chance to do a digital detox. "Show me what you chose."

Emma smiled and led the way back into the room itself, sliding the heavy floor-to-ceiling patio doors closed behind me. "The master bedroom," she said. The bed was huge, and had that premium feeling you get from seeing crisp white bedding with a random brown thing lying across it sideways. I pinched the quilt cover and rubbed. Yeah, premium. Okay, so Emma got a deal. June wasn't peak tourist season, after all. Made sense.

"Bed's comfy," I said.

"Over this way is the shower."

"Yep. Great flow. Love those big square showerheads."

"And round this way . . . the jacuzzi."

Okay, hold on a second. "Jacuzzi?" I pottered around touching the towels, feeling the bathrobes, sniffing the shower gel. "Is this a spa?"

"It's a spa hotel. Is that no good?"

I looked at myself in the mirror. Nick had absolutely played me. Emma never had any intention of booking a cheap holiday, or if she did, such thoughts had gone out the window after my attack. Well, here I was. In the perfect place to continue my rehab, it seemed. "You have chosen . . . wisely." I touched my lips; a tiny sign that I was on the mend. Pointless movements were back. "Tiny potter around, then some breakfast. Good?"

"Good. Down in the dining room?"

The dining room? With all those . . . people? "How about on the balcony?"

"Sure. I'll go down and grab a couple of plates from the buffet."

"Top."

"But first, I got you something. Stand there."

I waited in a corner of the room. Emma came back with a football. She rolled it to me. "Do a tekkers." She meant a kick-up.

"I can't."

"Try."

I looked down at the ball. Really didn't want to kick it, but I didn't want to make a scene. There had been enough of that the day before. I tried to flick it up and couldn't. Couldn't move my feet anywhere near fast enough. So I bent, slowly, picked up the ball, dropped it, and as it bounced up, kicked it from beneath. The ball flew off to the right and hit the patio glass. When I looked up, I realised she was filming me. "What are you doing?"

"Doing a progress video so people can see what hard work can get you. Today, no tekkers. We'll try every day and edit it into a video. See where you are in . . . a while."

She had been about to say "a year" but sensed it would annoy me. I didn't want to be in a video documenting my inability to do basic tasks and my achingly slow improvement. And what if Nick had been so warm and chatty because he'd used my murder as an excuse to strip away my playing powers? I felt my face harden. "That's inspirational, is it? To whom?"

"To me."

I took a slow breath, got the ball, and tried again.

Tekkers: 0

A few days of the sun soaking into me. A few days of turning my brain off and just letting the time go by. Nice food. Short walks. Using the spa facilities when the other guests weren't around. Reading on our bed, my head on Emma's lap. Emma was devouring *Chocolat* by Joanne Harris. I read *The Da Vinci Code*. But Max, I hear you cry. I thought you'd read all the classics.

During my month of rehab, I'd spent a lot of time with Physio Dean, Livia, and Magnus. They were helping me relearn how to walk, and while they did, I was learning more about them. Trying to get an insight into who they were and what made them tick. Shortly before I was due to leave, I had an idea. They'd each buy me a book to read on my holiday. Dean chose the Dan Brown masterpiece.

As I read it, I wondered why.

We read with Chopin or Bach playing in the room. No Rachmaninoff. I wasn't ready for Rach n' roll.

Then, at breakfast, on our balcony:

"Bebs. Want to be my assistant manager again?"

"What's the pay?"

"Paid in kind."

"Yeah, but *when*?"

"When I can run."

"Why?"

"You have to run before you can pork."

She didn't laugh. "That makes no sense. That's not even the phrase. How long have you been waiting to use that one?"

"I'll 'use that one' as soon as I can. Believe me."

"Assistant manager. Fine. What do you need?"

I bit into a croissant. "What's the time in England now?"

"Same as here."

"What time's here?"

"Half eight."

"Can you call MD and ask what he's done with the under-eighteens?"

She sipped her Lady Grey and considered if I needed to know that or if it could wait. I explained that I understood why MD had given a contract to Trick, but if he was going to do the same with the eighteens and there was time to stop it, I should. She put him on speaker, and he said he had released all the older boys at the end of May. Panic came into his voice. "I thought you said there was no one good there. Did you want one? I can probably still get him. I'll tell him I misunderstood you."

"No, you did it right," I said. "By the way, where's Henri gone?"

"Bye, Max."

Emma stretched. "Henri's decision is made, Max. No point even thinking about it." She said bye to MD and hung up. That was enough work for the day. "Those poor kids," she said, almost to herself.

The previous group of eighteens had been a talent wasteland. This year, though, a few of last year's sixteens would be in there, lifting the levels. "Vivek's the best player in the eighteens now. That'll be a mindfuck for him." I yawned. "Right. Swim. Steam. Nap. Sauna. Nap. Dinner. What do you think?"

"I think that sounds like a plan."

I turned twenty-three. Emma had charmed the hotel's chef into making a special birthday cheesecake, the dessert we shared the day we met. I blew out the tiny little candle and made a wish.

A week in, I was noticeably better. Less physically stiff. Able to concentrate for longer. We'd started going to the dining room for breakfast.

"I'm ready to leave the hotel," I said. "Where are we, again?"

"Tenerife."

"Oh, yeah. That volcano thing up there is the highest point in Spain. Let's . . . let's have that as my target. The day before we leave, we go up there. Ideally I'd run all the way up and jump around like Rocky."

"It's about four thousand metres high."

"Okay I'll run the last . . . six metres."

She pretended to add a note to her phone's calendar. "Max . . . run . . . up . . . enormous . . . volcano. Done. I would like to choose what we do today."

"Oh!" I blinked. It struck me that I'd been extremely selfish, always choosing what to do. "Yeah, of course. Have I been a dick?"

"You haven't been *enough* of a dick. But there's something I want to do, and I want to do it before you get too much better."

What could *that* be? I rubbed my eyebrow. "Is it . . . something we do in the bedroom?"

"No. I'm not telling you what it is because you'll say no. Put your trainers on." She smiled. "I'm going to enjoy this."

Footgolf. The rules of golf but with a football. And obstacles. And three complete strangers. I kept Emma between me and them.

I didn't want to do it, but Emma pointed out that it was the one chance she'd have to beat me at the sport I was such a master of. I complained that playing football defeated the object of the holiday, which was a complete break from the game. She said I'd popped that balloon when I'd started trying to run a football club from a hotel balcony.

I was getting sick of losing every argument.

The owner of the footgolf place explained the rules to us. Our flight was me and Emma, plus a couple from Yorkshire and their ten-year-old boy. He kept staring at me, even though I was in my "outside disguise" of mirrored sunglasses and pulled-down baseball cap. Emma was wearing John Lennon sunglasses and a big, floppy sun hat, making her look like a Scandinavian pop temptress. When we got to the first tee, the little kid needed to know one thing before we started. "Are you famous?" His dad cringed, but the mother wanted to know, too. Disguise plus insanely hot girlfriend slash carer equals compelling mystery.

"I'm Cliff Baps, masseuse to the stars."

"Cliff Daps," said Emma. I grunted. Why had I picked a nom de guerre I couldn't remember? She turned to the family. "He's really called Max. I'm Emma. He's a football player but he's injured, so today I'm going to beat him at football, and there aren't many people who can say that."

"All three of these will beat me, too," I said.

"What, even the boy?"

"Especially the boy," I said. "Look how neat his shoelaces are."

The boy smiled at the praise and got ready to tee off. The balls were regulation size, but light. The first hole was straightforward—about thirty yards, then a dogleg, then a series of logs crossed the fairway so that you had to kick over or under them. After that were some sand traps, and in front of the green was a concrete tunnel.

"Do we *have* to kick through the obstacles?" I said.

"No," said the dad.

"So I'm allowed to kick from here to the green?"

"If you're good enough, yeah."

That depressed me. It would have been trivially easy not long ago. I would probably have made every hole in two shots. But now?

The kid kicked the ball too hard and it spun off into the rough. The mum did even worse. The dad hit a good shot straight down the middle, but left himself a tricky decision as to what to do about the dogleg.

Emma's turn. She got into position, wobbled back and forth, then did an abysmal toe-poke. Technique 1, passing 1, power 1, elegance 1, cringe 20.

Despite all that, the ball landed fifteen yards away, dead centre of the fairway.

I squeezed my eyes closed. I hadn't cared about losing until that moment. But wow. If she beat me kicking like that . . .

I stepped onto the tee and scratched my chin. Tricky. Attempt any kind of normal shot and I risked literally toppling. Proper technique involved putting my entire weight on one foot and striking with the other. Not quite ready for *that*.

I glanced at Emma. If her mad technique was consistent, she could actually outscore me. But she lacked experience. She'd never competed against someone like me.

I felt a familiar tingling. *Game on.*

I rolled the ball around under my right foot, getting a feel for it. Then I pushed it to the same spot Emma had teed off from, and mimicked her technique: half-kick, half-walk.

The contact went through my foot, up my legs and hips, and vibrated my neck. It was unpleasant, but no more. The ball dashed forward ten yards, slowed, and gently kissed Emma's, coming to rest behind it. The big spoon to Emma's little one.

Emma laughed. "Great minds dink alike!"

Dink is another way of saying "chip." Neither of us had chipped the ball, but I didn't want to ruin her joke. "Who taught you dink?"

"Henri," she said. I frowned. Had Henri and Emma been spending time together? Obviously that would be fine. Totally fine. Nothing to worry about there. Henri is a completely honourable, completely trustworthy . . . French . . . man. "He helped coach the boys' teams. He taught Benny about dinking."

"Henri coached the boys?"

"Everyone's been doing everything." She smiled. "People are starting to understand how hard you've been working."

In the second round of shots, Emma lifted my ball away—legally—while she took her next shot. Again, the hideous technique. Again, a decent outcome. She got to the curve, well positioned to get to the green in four shots. If her putting was good, she'd make par.

My turn. Again, I aimed to nestle my ball beside hers. I wasn't so accurate this time, but the shot was suspiciously similar to hers. She raised an eyebrow.

We did it again, and I got my shot close to hers again.

"Okay, what the hell are you doing?"

"Excuse me?"

"Why are you copying me?"

"Who said I'm copying you?"

She looked to the family for help, but they didn't know what she was talking about.

Emma's fourth—and mine—went through the concrete tunnel and onto the green.

She was suspicious. Four shots and I was in her head already. She knew I was up to something, and she didn't like it. "You go first this time."

"I go first on the next hole. The woman said."

"You go first now, Max Best."

I pushed my bottom lip out. Okay. No skin off my nose.

I calculated. There was a dubious patch of grass just in front of the ball, so I booped the ball a fraction off the ground. It rolled towards the hole, but at the last second it hit a bobble and went over. I'd get a bogey at best. Absolute joke.

Emma tried, but hers fell well short. We both sank our next shots. Level.

She glared at me as we got ready for the next hole. I went first, keeping to the same technique. Emma decided she needed to get distance from me so I'd stop copying her, and kicked it pretty hard. It sliced way off to the left, into the rough. She tramped away after it.

The dad had worked it out. "Mental disintegration."

"I would never do that to my hundred percent. No, it's not that. Never. Anyway, imitation is the sincerest form of flattery," I said.

He wasn't buying my BS. "Do you play for Tranmere?"

What a weird question. Tranmere was the third biggest club in Merseyside. I knew that about them, and almost nothing else. I'd met one scout from Tranmere. He'd signed a player from Chester's youth system. "Tranmere? No, why?"

"Oh. We saw them go into our hotel."

"Who?"

"Tranmere Rovers. Some of the squad. The vanguard. They said the rest were coming soon. Doing their preseason training here, I assume. Ah, but your girl asked us not to overtax you. Sorry."

He pottered off, and I was left alone, looking over at Tenerife's big volcano. I suddenly didn't care about running up it. Old Nick had been right about the weather in the Mediterranean—there was heatwave after inhuman heatwave the whole summer—but the weather here, with its incredible consistency and soothing Atlantic breezes, was perfect for my tastes and needs. That said, it was obvious he'd steered me to Tenerife for a greater purpose than just my recovery. Something about Tranmere. But what?

After I won the hole (against Emma—the dad and kid outscored me on every hole I played), I pottered over to my girlfriend. "Can you look up what division Tranmere are in?"

She was mad at me, though she didn't know exactly why, so she thought about refusing. "League Two," she said, shoving her phone away in a way that meant *no more questions.*

"Ah! Henri went to *Tranmere.* Is he here, now? On Tenerife?"

She blew air through her cheeks. "If I don't get any stimulation, neither do you. Henri is fine. He's happy. Please let it go. Focus on beating me."

"Babes, I already won. I know your weakness."

"What is it?"

"Oh, I could never *tell* you," I said. Which, of course, made her second-guess everything she was doing. She switched from kicking too hard to too soft. Sigh. Too easy.

I coped with most of the footgolf obstacles, but on the seventh, par four, the hole could only be accessed by a sort of basketball hoop suspended a metre off the ground. I needed to dink the ball up, or scoop it, and both felt a little too hard. I tapped out, and enjoyed unhurriedly walking around, sitting on boulders and blocks of wood and some benches where older customers could take breaks. As we said goodbye to the family, I asked what hotel they were at.

Emma gave me a very hard look. Strange question from someone who said he didn't want to meet another soul for two weeks.

She punished me for my mind games by filming me trying to do a kick-up.

Tekkers: 0

Quest accepted. Find Tranmere Rovers and surprise Henri with my detective skills.

I turned my phone on—hundreds of unanswered texts and emails; I was incredibly zen about letting everyone wait—but even with the screen dimmed, it was aggravating. No problem. Back to the digital detox, and maybe it would be fun to do things the old-fashioned way. Light bit of social engineering. While Emma did girl things, I slipped into my nicest, most summery shirt and took the stairs down. That was getting easier every day.

It was a guy at reception, but I tried to flirt with him anyway. I needn't have bothered—he was more than happy to help me with my weird request. He laid out a big map of the island and pointed to the hotel the footgolf players were staying in. "A training complex, you say . . . in this area . . . with football pitches. Jes, I think *here*. Here is a popular facility."

"Amazing," I said, rubbing my lips. "Now. What else is in this area? Something my friend will want to visit."

The guy smiled. He understood my intentions quite well. "Does she like animals?"

Sixty seconds later, I snuck back into the room. The perfect crime.

Emma came out of the bathroom, her hair swaddled in a fluffy towel. "Hey, bebs."

"Hey, bebs. Are you nearly ready? If we leave soon, we might be in time to see some dolphins."

The taxi dropped us off near the dolphin tours. Catastrophically, when the guy drove off, I had an attack of fatigue. Oh, no!

"Back that way a little bit," I wheezed, trying not to let my suffering show. "I saw a little café thing. The sign said they had Yorkshire Gold."

"Ooh, nice. Wouldn't mind a good cuppa."

So we walked towards the training complex. I mean, towards the little café thing. As soon as I saw a football rise into the air and fall out of view, I felt a thrill of accomplishment. I'd tricked my girlfriend. I was a master of deception. I would crush it on *The Traitors*.

Emma squeezed my hand. "Bebs. I think some people are playing football over there. Do you want to have a quick look?"

Wow. She knew. She knew and she'd gone along with it. Let me think I was outwitting her. Had she done that in the footgolf, too? My pulse quickened. Games within games! "If you don't mind . . ." I said, and found myself walking just a little faster.

Two grass pitches, one surrounded by a running track. To the north, outdoor swimming pools. To the east, a few low buildings housing gyms and a hydro-dynamic flume. To the west, tennis and volleyball courts. Up a slope, a massive outdoor CrossFit area.

This place was fucking top.

A handful of football players were doing some fitness work on one of the pitches. I glanced at Emma; she nodded. Permission to do my thing.

We walked on the running track, down the home straight, around the side curve, and back onto the other straight. I didn't see Henri.

A couple of coaches and a physio were on one side, along with a handful of equipment bags. No sign of the scout I knew. Why would there be? His last big job of the season would have been going to the exit trials, and now he'd be on a well-deserved break.

As I was.

So why was I hovering around Tranmere Rovers? Henri wasn't there, and I didn't have the curse. So what could I expect?

"Max. Promise you won't ask about Henri and Ziggy and the Man United takeover and all that."

I scratched my cheek. A lot of people had run to Mr. Yalley's defence. A lot of people were coming together to make sure the youth teams got training. In lots of small ways, an entire community was taking care of the club that represented it. And one hundred percent of those people wanted me to rest, relax, and recover. There were times it was hard, but this wasn't one of them. "Okay, just . . . Henri's not here, then?"

"Why would he be here?"

"If this even *is* Tranmere . . . League Two club. It's in Merseyside, pretty close to Chester. He could skip two divisions and still hang out with me all the time. Keep an eye on me. If I was him, yeah, Tranmere. Absolutely."

"Oh. Okay. He's not. Do you want to stay?"

I jiggled a nail in the space between two teeth. What did I want? "Can I do some football stuff?"

"As long as you don't tire yourself out."

"Can you look up who Tranmere's manager is?"

Emma frowned. Normally in this situation, I'd know the names of everyone in the area. Anything that hinted at memory loss or personality change was cause for alarm. "James O'Rourke."

"Right, yeah. Heard of him." If memory served, O'Rourke had stepped in as caretaker manager a couple of times, and always done better than the permanent bosses he'd replaced. As always happened in that scenario, he'd been given a chance to step into the big shoes. And, if history was any guide, he would crash and burn. Still, it wouldn't hurt to see what he was doing.

I walked towards the guy who was obviously O'Rourke. There was something familiar about the way everyone else orbited the manager. I'd seen it with Dave Cutter. With Ian Evans. Not so much with Jackie . . .

"What?" said Emma.

"Nothing."

Someone tapped O'Rourke on the shoulder. He turned and looked me up and down. He was in a black top with green sleeves. He was vaguely ginger, with pale blue-green eyes, small ears, a hangdog expression, and there was no hair at the front of his crown, except some strands he had combed over. He should have looked ridiculous, but I thought he was pretty attractive, all things considered. He had a kind of Marlon Brando vibe. Marlon Brando if he didn't know he was Marlon Brando. Marlon Brando if he had more opinions about play-acting than method acting. (Play-acting is pretending to be hurt. It's a good joke. Just go with it.)

So that was *his* look. Me? I was dressed very much with Emma in mind. Keeping my almost-no-hoodie promise. Nothing practical. Nothing black. The less comfortable I was, the more she cooed over how good I looked. Today I was wearing bright yellow shorts and an almost luminous pink shirt. I pushed my sunglasses up so they nestled into my hair. "Are you Tranmere Rovers?" The boss dude said he was. "I'm Chester," I said.

He looked me up and down again. Some memory clicked. *The kid who was attacked.* "Oh! Small world. I'm James."

"Max." We shook hands. "Tell me to piss off if you want. I'm just out here recuperating."

Kid who got attacked *confirmed*. "No, no, you're very welcome. Can we get you anything? Chair? Water? We're doing fitness with a couple of lads today. The rest of the squad's coming in dribs and drabs."

"How long are you here for?"

"Three weeks," he said.

"What's your process?" I said.

"We'll take those chairs," said Emma, with a big smile. A coach and a lanky goalkeeper type rushed to fulfil her request. She pulled me down into a chair and gave me a little shoulder massage.

I put my right hand on hers. "This is Emma," I announced. "My hundred percent."

I spent half an hour talking about preseason training with James O. Then I started to get fatigued. I apologised. He said to think nothing of it, then ordered one of his minions to take us back to our hotel.

A good nap followed.

I started getting ready for a balcony dinner, but Emma stopped me. "We're eating out."

The taxi tipped us out and we fell into some upmarket restaurant. To the left was a bright room with upbeat music. Emma pulled me to the right, and I floated, confused, to a small corner table. It was quiet and dark, as though they'd turned the lights and music down specially for me. Emma was to my right, James O'Rourke to my left. In front, a well-tanned older guy wearing head-to-toe linen, and a dolled-up older woman.

Everyone had drinks, including me and Emma, even though we'd just arrived. The table was a collage of tapas. It all looked and smelled amazing. Expensive.

I frowned.

What was happening?

James O nudged me. "Max. This is Mateo, our chairman. His family is loaded in two countries."

Mateo was a real silver fox. He was wearing a shirt with a jacket, but no tie. He was pretty tanned, pretty rugged. The smoothness of his hair and the cracks in his skin were a good contrast. He looked healthy. The kind of healthy you might get if you could look at your watch and say, hey, let's go for a quick spin in the yacht. "*Comfortable* in two countries." He reached over to shake my hand. "We've been researching you. No one can agree which Max Best you are."

"What are the options?" said Emma.

Mateo extended his thumb and touched it with the index finger of his other hand. "Rapid winger playing non-league who turned down a big-money move to Sheffield Wednesday."

Emma pointed at me.

Mateo added the index finger to the thumb. "Women's team manager who took his players off because a deaf girl was booked, and got the *Daily Mail* to spearhead a witch hunt against the referee."

Emma pointed at me, and didn't even seem to have any reservations about the guy's language.

Middle finger. "Rugby star?"

Emma pointed, but dismissively.

Mateo's wife spoke next. No one introduced her, but I later learned she was called Rachel, same as Emma's mum. She had the same exact nose as David Beckham. "The caretaker manager who saved Chester from relegation."

Emma pointed at me.

"And was sent to the emergency room after the decisive game," said Mateo, coming to his little finger.

Emma sagged, and reached her hand across the table. I took it.

"He's here to take it easy," said James O, with a hint of disapprobation.

Mateo nodded. "Of course. My way of saying you've done a lot in a short time. Trying to put together your story is like a thousand-piece jigsaw puzzle. Of the sky. Listen, my family has a stake in the training centre here. It's all booked out for Tranmere but please use it as you wish."

"What, really?"

"Yes. Definitely."

"Oh, wow. Top. You've got that wave machine thing."

Emma piped up. "I thought you didn't like wave machines."

"This one isn't evil."

Rachel said, "You mean the flume." She explained it to Emma. "You swim against the current. Big health benefits, almost no impact on the joints. It's expensive, but it's worth every penny. Shaves weeks off recovery time."

"Weeks!" said Emma, turning to me all excited.

I frowned. Traitors and faithful. Chickens, roosts. Karma, payback. "What's the catch?"

The cracks around Mateo's mouth spread. "How about you let us win when we play you next?"

"Oh, is that all?" I said. "Sure. I can do that. How about ten–nil? No, too much. Nine. Argh, that's obvious. Make it eight–nil so no one suspects."

I was glaring at the guy, but the more heated I got, the more of his teeth he showed. It was hard to tell what that meant, but I was sure no one talked to him like I was doing. To Emma, he said, "Is he always like this?"

"He's normally worse. He just spent three weeks in hozzie and a month in rehab. He can only just walk and he still beat me at football golf." This pronouncement was met with sniggers and mouth-covering. "What? It's annoying. He can barely kick the ball. He did the most basic shot every time. How did he win?"

"Well, Max?" said Rachel. "How *did* you?"

I leaned back. "I didn't *do* anything."

Emma pouted. "You did."

"Okay, I sort of . . ." I cut the air in a straight line, then pushed the line I'd created a few inches to the left, then mimed it turning into a circle. "I sort of guided you into a doom loop."

"A doom loop?" she said.

"Yeah. You were a threat to me, so I made you beat yourself. It's easier that way. I learned it from my buddy Sun Tsu. Doom loops are top. Except . . . that's what happened to Jackie. He's in a doom loop. I tried to drag him out but it didn't work. We have to let him burn out and then we can pick him up and dust him off. The prick."

Emma was aghast, and not because of my theory about JR. "You did something to me and now I can never beat you? Is that what you're saying?"

"Basically, yeah."

"Until this loop burns up?"

"Well," I said, hesitating like I wasn't sure if I should continue. "I programmed you with a trigger word. I can reactivate you whenever I want."

Emma was side-eyeing me, but not from aggression. There was genuine worry behind it. First, worry that I was joking, in which case, why wasn't I smiling? Second, worry that I was telling the truth. She needed to do something with her hands, so she reached for her glass of white wine and took a sip. "Oh, yeah? What's the trigger word?"

I waited until she took another sip. Maybe here's a good moment to mention a weird hobby of mine. I really wanted, with a well-timed joke, to get Emma to spray something she'd just sipped. To make it more challenging and funnier, I'd told her what I was doing, like when I'd told Jackie I was going to nutmeg him. The upshot was that Emma was always wary in formal settings. The interplay between us, the fun of trying to get the timing just right, the right word in the right place, not a word that's too funny, too crude . . . it had to be pitched absolutely perfectly. A couple of times I'd made her jackknife back on her chair, but I hadn't achieved spray yet.

So she took the sip, and suddenly understood what I'd set up. She was on high alert. I was going to say some unexpected word—no clue why but I'd chosen *mayonnaise*—and she was going to try not to react.

But it was so exhausting. So pointless. The complexity of it all gave me a headache. I rubbed my temples and said, "Never mind."

Emma's face fell. "Maybe we should go."

"No," I said. "I'm all right. It's really nice here. I might shut up for a bit, though."

James O filled my glass with still water, and told me I was welcome to pop by to any sessions I wanted. They were training before and after lunch every day, and next week they'd start on ball work and positional drills.

"We're leaving this Sunday," I said. "But I'd love to try that swimming thing."

"You're very welcome," said Mateo. "I was a player once. I know what it's like being injured. It's a lonely place. My physio always told me, 'Health is other people.' You don't have to do this alone, Max. There's pools, there's tennis, there's weights, but there's also coaches and physios. We can always spare a guy, can't we James? Get yourself healthy. Anything you want. I mean it."

"I mean," I said, then decided not to finish the sentence.

"Go on," insisted Mateo.

"Well, no. It's absurd." He made me spit it out. "It's just . . . if you're doing a mini game any time this week. Firsts against reserves kind of thing. If I could run the reserves . . . I know I'll be shit, but better to get back on the wagon a thousand miles away from base, isn't it? So *what* if I get dicked? When I'm back in Chester . . . they all think I'm pretty good. If I do stupid things, they'll think my head's wrecked."

Something flashed between the owner and the manager. James O put his hand on my shoulder and gave me a two-second massage. "I'm sure that can be arranged, Max. Now, get stuck into these tapas. Try that one. It's ham-on. That's Spanish for ham. Goes great with toast."

Next morning, Emma found me on the balcony with a pen and paper. She hugged my neck and tried to work out what I was writing. It didn't help that my fine motor skills were trash. Instead of writing whole words, I stuck to single capital letters.

"What are you doing?"

"Youth system. Everyone who turned eighteen is gone. So I'm thinking about which kids we've got. Up here, this V, that's Vivek. He's in the under-eighteens. The next five are eighteens, too. K is for Kian. Did you meet him? I guess you didn't. Vivek's got two years, then he goes up to the firsts, or he's out. I think he'll make it." I pointed at the next section. "The sixteens. We're well stocked there. B is for Benny. T is for Tyson."

"This is like the world's most specific 'learning to read' book."

"Most are new in the sixteens, but we already had a couple of decent fifteen-year-olds like Lucas Friend. He was a goalie I made into a left back. In here's Future, but he's much younger than the rest. In that group, there are *thirteen* players who are talented." I tapped some of the initials. "Goalie. Left back. We've got every position covered except right back. That team is exciting. Next there's the twelves. Seven good 'uns here. Two goalies, Stephen Watson is a DM. The best prospect in the entire system, but he's ten. Tadpole is the best goalie at the club, but he's ten an' all."

"Tadpole's a great name for a goalie."

"Right? You didn't notice I skipped an age group."

She slipped into the chair next to me. "The fourteens?"

"Yeah. If we have *these* guys with the sixteens and *these* with the twelves, we could disband the fourteens."

"Would that save money?"

"A little bit. I won't do it. There are still some kids in that group. None with talent. It's just an idle thought. The sixteens will be the most interesting group if I want to practice some weird new tactics or go to a tournament. But they need my help the least. I want to go round to all the schools like I said, find some players, beef up the numbers." I bit the pen. "I reckon in August I'll focus on the men's team. Do the matches, fill the holes in the squad. That might be exhausting enough. Transfer window closes on September first. I can scout school kids in September and October."

"Who's going to manage the women's team?"

"Good question." As it stood, I was Chester's director of football, first-team manager, and women's team manager. When the curse came back, I'd be able to keep an eye on both squads. If I appointed a full-time manager for the women, would I lose that screen? That was something I couldn't remember from before my attack—when, exactly, did the women's team appear in my page? When that memory came back, I'd be better able to make a decision. "Probably Jill as caretaker manager. I'll talk to her ted the team. Is Dani okay?"

"Dani is okay." Emma took the paper away, then gave me another head cuddle. "Right. The men are fine. The women are fine. The kids are fine. Let's get physical."

Tekkers: 0

The next three days had a new pattern. We'd go to where Tranmere were training (there were more players and staff every day) and I'd use the counter-current pool for as long as I could. I'd recover on a sunbed, then do a fast walk. That was hard—it felt like all my bones were slamming into each other, especially around my neck—but one of the Tranmere physios was with me at all times, and they pushed me to do a little more than I felt ready for. On the third day, I felt like breaking into a jog, and I asked for a second opinion.

"I reckon you can do it."

So I sped up. Not exactly the pace 20 I'd shown for Darlington, but to me it felt like the down section of a rollercoaster. I laughed, giddy from the discom-bobulated, almost forgotten feeling, and suddenly I was being force-cuddled by a weeping Emma.

"What? What?" I said, astonished. All I did was jog five yards.

"That's the first time you've even *smiled*," she said. A lot of pent-up emotion came bubbling out. Literally bubbling out. Ugh.

It's fair to say Emma was popular with the players and coaches, and a few came over to check on her. "Emma, what's up?" said James O.

She detached from me and gave him the same treatment. "Thank you. Thank you."

He gave her a squeeze. "You're all right. It was nothing." He looked around at the other coaches. He made a face like "aww." It was smiles all round. They'd done something nice for a fellow professional, and this was their reward. No good deed goes unpunished? Nah. "It's just a shame you're leaving so soon."

Emma detached from him, eyes wide. She took my hand, got fierce, and jabbed her finger at some invisible enemy. "We're staying! We'll be back tomor-row! If that's okay with you!"

Emma pushed our flights back, extended our stay in the hotel. I worried about the cost, but not for long. Another week and maybe I *would* be able to run up the volcano.

After lunch with a dozen Tranmere guys brave enough to try a vegan joint, Emma and I had our traditional bedroom reading session. Emma was under the covers, already on her third book—*Normal People* by Sally Rooney—and I finally closed *The Da Vinci Code*.

"That was terrible," I said, tossing the book aside. "I loved it."

Emma put hers down and gently fussed my hair. "You got faster. You were whizzing through the pages at the end."

"Yeah. I think that's why Dean chose it. At first I was all like, did he look up a list of bestsellers and pick the one at the top? Did he give it three seconds' thought? But no. I'm pretty sure he picked it because the chapters are so short. There's always an excuse to take a break."

"You're starting to like him more."

"We spent time together in Saint Cyril's. He's all right. He's got a big chip on his shoulder about something, but once you get to know him, he's really all right." I squirmed so that Emma could fuss with more of my head. She liked to feel around, trying to find my stitches, and she was so gentle it made me feel safe. "We talked it out. I asked what he wanted. He wants to do advanced research into sports injuries. Get funding and do trials and whatnot. I said we'd support him as much as we could, but for now he's the face of our medical team and I couldn't have him stropping around the place being all mardy."

"You said that to him while he was helping you learn to walk again?"

"What better time?"

"Almost any other time."

"Nah."

"He saved your life."

"About eight people saved my life. Anyway, I got three points against Chorley, so we're even. No, it was good. I'd said it all before, I think, but in that setting it was obvious I meant it. And when I said something, he had time to think about it before replying, and vice versa. He said what was on his mind, too. We cleared the air."

"You think he'll try to be a bit friendlier?"

"He already was. And you know what was good? One of the rehab people from Saint Cyril's was a bit of a dick. Quite abrasive. Didn't like Dean being there. Felt undermined or whatever. And after that sesh I did a big 'confession' about how horrible it was to be so scared and weak and to have people be mean to me. Which was not quite the case and Dean knew that, but he got the point. All right, fun book. Good choice. One relationship point to Dean."

Lap of the hotel, breakfast with a nice retired couple from Somerset, counter-current pool, light jog.

Now Tranmere were doing ball work, and James O let me get up close and watch the drills. Emma offered to take notes so I could use these drills in my coaching courses. During breaks, I sat on a ball and doodled ideas for tweaking the drills. That was good practice for my fine motor skills, too.

"What's that you're doing?" said a coach. Welsh guy called Colin.

"Oh. Just brainstorming. You're doing two v two that turns into four v four. It's a good drill. Great for preseason, isn't it? It's got some ball work, some sprints, defensive awareness, you're building little units. Yeah, I like it. But the players get the hang of it, don't they? I'm thinking of how to challenge their decision-making, too."

"Right. Like what?"

"Make a zone on the sides where one of the players has to stay."

"Ah, I'm with you. Most coaches do that kind of thing in the middle."

"I'm a winger," I said.

"Most coaches don't coach the way they played. Normally it's the opposite. Strikers make the most defensive managers."

"Is that right?" said Emma. "Why's that?"

"One of life's mysteries." The coach laughed. "I was a defender, but I love doing attacking drills." He looked at my sketch. "We could give that a try."

"No, thanks. It's probably gibberish. I'll try it on my youth teams, maybe.

With them I can say, 'Oh, that didn't work. Ignore the last twenty minutes,' and they accept it. If I said that to Sam Topps, I'm not sure he'd be very happy."

"I know Sam. Good player."

"If you ever want to buy him, let me know. We're a selling club. I want a counter-current pool."

Another drill I liked started as crossing practice. A guy on the side of the practice area played a long pass to a coach, who stopped the ball. The player sprinted and had the chance to hit a first-time cross. Meanwhile, two defenders and an attacker sprinted from the same starting line as the crosser. If the attacker ran fast, he'd have a chance to get on the end of the cross. If he was slow, he'd have to hope for a header. If he and the defenders were equally fast, he had to decide to dart to the front or far post and hope the crosser could predict which way he'd go.

So far, so basic.

But then, whether the attackers scored or not, the goalie would grab a ball and the defenders were now attackers. They'd dash back up the pitch and the crosser and striker would have to sprint back to try to defend. So two long sprints with decisions to make. Fantastic. Like in a real match.

In the break, Coach Colin came over, slightly out of breath, drinking from a thick plastic bottle. "Got any upgrades on that one?"

"Maybe. Another winger on the other side. Maybe."

That didn't make sense to Colin. "Why? What do you get?"

"More decisions. If you switch the play, you're allowed out of your zone. If you do it early, you get two v two competing for the cross." I bit my nail. "Needs to be a cost. Maybe if you leave your zone, you can't defend the next transition. Yeah. So you can increase your chance of scoring . . . No, that wouldn't do it. I want it so that if you take a risk, there's a cost. What could the cost be?"

"If you choose to switch, you can leave your zone, but the goalie can't leave his six-yard box. Easier finish for the other team."

I nodded. He was a good coach. "That might do it."

Emma was on the grass next to me, enjoying the sun. Whenever a conversation started, she popped her earphones out to check I didn't try to get "unhealthy" information. "But Max, why do you want that? You always want your players to attack."

"Not only. If we can attack, we should attack. If we have to defend, we'll defend. I've tried to set up my team so they have a lot of autonomy. Youngster, Sam, and Glenn set the tempo. These kinds of drills can let them practice that. And look, *I'm* comfortable if there's only three guys back ready for counter-attacks, but not all the players are so at ease. We *will* concede goals if we do things my way. I want the players to know it's worth it." I pointed to the pitch. "This is a physical challenge. It rewards positioning, crossing, heading, passing. I want another dimension. Football's a mental challenge, too."

Colin took another squirt of his drink. "You're in the National League North, right?"

"Yeah."

He didn't know what to do with his face. "Fitness. Heading. Tackling. Someone who can cross. A goalscorer. That's all you need."

"What Max Best needs," I said, "and what Max Best wants . . . are two very different things."

"You wanna win *and* play good football?"

"Yep. Yeah," I said. "I've got coaches for the basics." My new assistant manager would start in July. He didn't know much about football, but he knew about fitness. He'd train the fuck out of the team. According to Barnesy, if I was a player and he told me to keep running, I'd keep running. "Fitness? Tick. I suspect we'll be one of the fittest teams in the league." Then I had Vimsy for the shuffles and slides. The offside trap. Defensive spacing. Set pieces. "Dinosaur stuff? Tick." Emma and MD, seeing my improvement, had been drip-feeding me bits of news. All very carefully curated. Jude had been taken on as a full-time coach. He'd be a floater, covering gaps in schedules. One day the first team, the next the women, the next the under-twelves. Spectrum still had his hands full but would be available for some first-team sessions if I needed him. Terry was still almost exclusively doing the Chester Knights, but he could do a little extra if it was urgent. Family commitments meant it really, really needed to be urgent. "I need an elite coach who is willing to come to the sixth tier. Colin, who've you got?"

"Elite coach?" He laughed. "If I knew one who'd work in the lower leagues, he'd be here at Tranmere, wunnee?"

"Do you know anyone amazing who's unemployed?"

"No."

"Do you know anyone shit who's unemployed?"

"Yes."

"Do you know anyone who's . . . medium?"

He placed the water bottle down on the short grass and stretched. He turned his face to the sun and basked. "I'll have a think. And I'll keep my ears to the ground."

"Thanks."

He walked off. "How's your energy?" asked Emma.

I considered the question. "Good. Might do a few laps of the hotel before we read."

"How about we go to the dolphins like you promised?"

"To the dolphinarium!" I cried.

"Yeah in a minute." She held her phone up. "You know what I want."

Tekkers: 0

I got stuck into Magnus's choice of reading material—the seminal graphic novel, *Watchmen*.

I didn't have to think hard about why he'd chosen it. When Emma picked it up and flicked through, a card fell out from the back—I would have found it when I got to the end.

Max. This has your name on it. First, there are lots of pictures in case you get tired of reading. Second, the heroes are villains and the villains are heroes. Third, I thought you would appreciate the audacity. —Magnus.

"What do you think of Magnus?" said Emma.

"Amazing guy. Knows loads about loads. Stuff I've never heard of. Have you seen him recently?"

"Yeah."

"When I met him, he had huge gorilla arms from his weight lifting. Now he's more balanced. Looks like a footballer. Can't wait to see his profile."

I was lucky that Emma was only half-listening.

We almost always went for dinner with the Tranmere guys. The whole squad, plus coaches, physios, data guys, admins, and sometimes Mateo and Rachel. The noise and silliness and banter were draining, but when it got a bit much I'd go out onto the terrace and listen to the Atlantic. It was like my AirPods—ten minutes of recharging gave you an hour of use.

Emma was a hit, obviously, but now that Tranmere Rovers were turbo-charging my recovery, she was more charming than ever. I ate tapas and watched her work. She was incredible. It wasn't just that she was funny and smart, she also remembered all kinds of details about people. Trev Northcross wasn't just a CA 60, PA 80 reserve goalie (or whatever the real numbers were). He was a guy with two kids, and overnight Emma had come up with an idea for a birthday present for the eldest. Mateo wasn't just a guy who ran a football team. He was a linguist who loved telling stories about language, especially misunderstandings he'd gotten into. For example, in German, half eight wasn't half past eight, it was seven thirty! He'd once turned up for a date an hour late. Emma lapped it all up, making people feel good about themselves, giving them permission to keep talking.

While I watched her work, I had time to reflect. When I got back to Chester, I'd be able to ease into my new role. We had a team, and we had coaches. I didn't need to do a mad trolley dash throwing people into my basket. I could focus on quality. One amazing defender. One amazing coach. The kids were all right, and the club was financially stable. They wouldn't tell me about Henri, which suggested some decision I wouldn't approve of, but they'd also swore, multiple times, that he was doing great.

So the only thing I wasn't totally relaxed about was the women's team. I knew they'd been placed in tier six, but didn't know the levels of the other teams.

"Max," said James O, ending my reverie. "Our first game of the season's against Barrow. They play four-five-one. You play four-five-one with your lot, don't you?"

"With the women, yeah. We've only got one striker." We only had one striker because the best one I found had a hooligan boyfriend. He was the prime suspect for my murder.

"If you're up to managing a game, like you said, I'd love you to set up a four-five-one for me to practice against."

Five seconds later, Emma was enveloping James O. "Do I get a hug every time Max smiles?" he said.

"Yes," she said, kissing his head. "Yes, you do."

Two laps of the hotel, breakfast with five Irish sisters so I could listen to their accents, a new personal best in the pool, and a jog the full length of a pitch. One cool shower later, and I was in the middle of the thirteen players James O had assigned me. My assistant was taking their names, shirt numbers, and their preferred positions.

When I got the list, I put my baseball cap back on. It wasn't time to soak up the sun, it was time to see if I'd learned anything in the last year. Managing a match without the curse wasn't all that stressful. Losing was expected—I had worse players—and I was at far from full mental capacity. The Tranmere lot were super cool and chill. When it came to football, Tenerife was a consequence-free environment.

I stood and stared at the tactics board. It took me much longer than it should have, but I came up with a plan.

"All right, shut the fuck up," I said. "Your gaffer wants to have a go against four-five-one. So we'll start with that like the good and diligent professionals we are." I stuck my tongue out the side of my mouth. "But I like winning. So we're going to give him a little scare." I pushed all the magnets off the side, then brought them back one by one, naming the players. There were no surprises because I didn't know if they were capable of playing somewhere beyond what they'd told Emma. Chances are, one or two had some untapped skills but without the curse, I would never know. I gave some individual instructions based on what I'd seen of them in training. I told them I wanted four outfielders in the rest defence at all times, but the other six could go nuts. That news smacked a lot of eyes open. Normally they were much more rigid. James O'Rourke was another safety-first manager. "Now," I said. "I reckon we'll do this for twenty minutes. Then we'll slip into four-one-four-one. Carlos, you'll be the DM. No attacking for you. Total positional discipline, yeah? You'll be the playmaker. Set the tempo, pull the strings. Everyone got that?" They did.

"Max," complained Emma. "That's not four-five-one. James wants four-five-one!"

I pushed the DM magnet up two inches. "What's this, babes?"

"That's four-five-one."

"So you see. It's just a tweak. Tiny tweak. He might not even notice."

She wasn't sure she could trust me, so she turned to Trev, the reserve goalie she got on so well with. "Is he being a dick? I don't want James to think of us as *ungrateful*." She said the last word very much to me.

"It's fine," said the goalie. "It won't make much difference."

"Oh!" I said. I couldn't help myself. Trev thought of himself as a Tommy Tactics, did he? "Mate. You watch. Soon as we make that switch, we'll fucking slap."

I clapped my hands and retook my seat.

The match kicked off. The intensity was pretty good, and they didn't hold back much in the tackles. Trying to keep track of every move, every failed pass, every header won was tiring—I didn't have the tactics screens or the match ratings. I had to do everything for myself, like a pleb.

James had set the first team up in a 4-3-3, and in their all-white kit they looked awesome. The whites zipped around, being dynamic, trying to move my guys around with short, quick passes and then moving into space. But they were very central. Moving Carlos to DM would cut out a lot of danger. I had to wait a while, though. Emma was right about the ungrateful thing.

"Bebs," I said, and my assistant perked up. "See our four and six here? Go and shout at them to pass left." I couldn't do what I was doing *and* shout at the players. Shouting wasn't quite in my wheelhouse yet, anyway.

"Roger roger."

She did and returned. "Now go round to our five and eight and do the same but for the right."

"By your command."

I let that play out for a bit. The firsts were attacking very centrally, and the reserves were using the width. Both defences had been well coached, so there were few opportunities. Where could I make a breakthrough? It was hard not knowing the players that well and not being able to see their profiles. Some things were clear, though. My fullbacks were fast. "Bebs, tell the fullbacks to attack."

"Absolutely. What are fullbacks?"

"The left back and the right back."

"Why are there so many names?"

"There aren't. It's like brother, sister, sibling. Left back, right back, full-back."

"Oh! Good explanation." She strode away to pass on my instructions.

Our attacks started to look better. More dangerous. We'd often have two v ones on the flanks, forcing central players to come out wide to cover, leaving gaps. "This is fun," I said. "Tell Carlos not to go forward, though."

"*Sí, señor.*"

In a way, this was easier than having the curse. Sure, it was inefficient having to verbalise my instructions. But I could make bigger changes, like pushing players out of the strict formations they were in. I decided we were stronger on the left, and pushed the left back and left mid up one slot.

"So that number three," said Emma, trying to work out what my changes meant. "Is he still a left back fullback? He's more on the line where Youngster stands."

"Right. We call that a wingback. It's a hybrid of defender and midfielder. You can say defensive midfielder left, but I don't think it's very common."

"Why have I never seen wingbacks before?"

"You have. Remember you watched Arsenal versus Tottenham? Tottenham had wingbacks."

"Jesus, Max. I didn't know what the hell I was looking at that day."

"It'll be a while before I use wingbacks. Don't worry about it."

"You're using one right now!"

"Oh, right. Yeah. Good point. Basically, I want to push the whites back. I want to be the protagonist. So I'm making a defensive player less defensive and turning a left mid into a left winger."

"And this is risky, is it?"

"Yeah," I said and pulled my sunglasses back over my eyes. "Risky like a fox."

The match was only half an hour, and we lost 4–2. The players, glistening with sweat, laughed and joked their way to the showers. Well, some laughed and joked. Some looked thoughtful. Worried.

"Are you all right?" said Emma.

"Yeah. That was really tiring. In a good way, babes. But . . . It's weird . . . Look, which team seems happier to you?"

She scanned. "Yours."

"But we lost."

Emma shrugged. "I'm no expert, but I think it's more fun playing for you. And when Carlos went to the Youngster space, the whites didn't get many chances, like you said. You only lost because you were mostly sticking to what James wanted. Right?"

I scratched an itch on my nose. Did what she said make sense? Without the match ratings, I couldn't really tell, but I'd tried to come up with a grand tactical plan and then adjusted it to suit what seemed to be the strengths and weaknesses of every player. My team gradually got better through the half as I learned what was working for them and what wasn't. Hadn't James O been doing the same?

The man himself came over and did some light banter, teasing me about still having things to learn, but thanking me for sticking to a no-frills formation. Emma shot a glance at me—James hadn't noticed my tweaks, and that surprised her.

Before we went back to the hotel, she whipped out her phone and demanded a kick-up. I dropped a ball. It bounced up and I kicked it a little higher. As it came down, I kicked it again. The third strike it squirted away.

I blinked with surprise. Emma's jaw dropped open. Coach Colin came over and slapped me on the back.

Tekkers: 2

Another fancy restaurant. Another dinner with the Tranmere lot.

I didn't need to take breaks. I found myself smiling at James O's jokes, Mateo's stories, and especially Rachel's *corrected* versions of those stories.

Emma was much calmer, working less hard. Letting me pick up some of the conversational slack.

When we'd finished eating and were having a few cheeky wines, Trev Northcross came over from one of the long players' tables and sort of crouched to be more on our eye level.

"Sorry everyone, sorry gaffer. Quick Q. Emma, me and the lads keep wondering why you film Max doing one kick-up. Is it that thing where people pay you to record birthday wishes?"

"I'll take this one, honey." As I hoped, she was happy to let me explain, and she reached for her wine. I needed to time this to perfection. "Emma wants to film my recovery and splice together the clips to make an inspirational video. You know, never give up, that sort of thing. But it isn't going very well. She's actually getting quite frustrated with me." She had been about to take a sip, but she paused, wondering if she should deny it. "Ever since the . . ." I said, my voice quavering. Emma tipped the glass up and the pale liquid left the glass and went past her lips. It was something to do instead of bursting into tears. "Ever since that day, I haven't been able to keep it up."

I didn't get a wine spray, but it was a close-run thing. She half-stood, eyes bulging, cheeks puffed out, before she threw herself back onto her chair and smothered herself with a napkin.

There was lots of good-natured laughter. Emma's recovery was delayed by lots of little laughs. "Max!" she complained. "Don't do that."

"I'm going to get you," I promised.

Trev went back to his table, and I took a sip of wine and drank Emma in. She was amazing. Gorgeous, kind, funny. She was dabbing herself, drying her chin just in case, but her lips were moist. She felt my eyes on her. "What?"

"I'm ready for Rachmaninoff," I declared. Emma stood, thanked our hosts for a lovely time, grabbed my wrist and dragged me out of the restaurant, straight into the nearest taxi.

Emma extended the trip again—one advantage of working for your dad was getting as much time off as you needed when your boyfriend had just been murdered.

Time had lost all meaning. From hour to hour, I made choices. Walk around the hotel for ten minutes or jog on the treadmill for five? Wind down with a jacuzzi or in the salt therapy room? Big breakfast, small lunch, or vice versa? Tranmere or dolphins?

Every day was twenty-two degrees, cloudless blue skies, gentle winds. Tekkers two became tekkers three.

I ploughed through Livia's book. It was called *Please Give Jackie Time and Then Try to Help Him Like in Six Months or Whatevs*. Niche publishing was wild, man. Okay, fine, it wasn't that. She'd got me the autobiography of Alex Ferguson, the legendary Man United manager. Maybe she thought it was something like a manual of how to manage a football team. Maybe she thought I'd pick up a few tips. I wasn't sure why she'd chosen it. Unlike the book, Livia was hard to read.

My second and final chance to manage Tranmere's reserves came the day before they were going to fly home, two days before our departure.

James O gave me some players and let me put them in whatever formation I wanted. Since I knew he'd play 4-3-3, I did something I wouldn't be able to do when the curse came back.

Ten minutes into the game, Coach Colin strode over from the other side of the pitch. "Max. What the fuck formation is this?"

"Three-three-four," I said.

"That's insane," he said. By insane, he meant "delightfully unconventional." Having more strikers than defenders is not something that's often taught on coaching courses, sure. "Also, no one's ever going to do that in a real match."

Emma leapt to my defence. "Max would. Also, it's working."

Colin put his fists on his forehead and dragged them back through his hair. Like anyone on the island who moved a lot, he was sweaty. The temperature had risen to 24. Still very pleasant, but maybe Sunday was a good time to go. "Yeah," he said. He seemed annoyed. "It's working. But *why*?"

"Find me my dream coach and I'll tell you."

The mini-match ended 2–2, and this time my players didn't smile as they left the pitch. They *shone*. The reserves had ended their trip on a high. I'd done well, all things considered.

Emma rolled a ball to me and jutted her chin up.

Tekkers: 5

We said goodbye to the Tranmere squad—took a taxi to their hotel and everything. We hugged a few guys, fist bumped plenty more. One guy—a left back—winked at Emma and went, "Remember what I said." Cheeky fuck. Flirting in front of me! Left backs really shouldn't get in my bad books. But then they laughed and he hugged me. It had been a wind-up. Emma's invention. Payback for footgolf, she said.

They got on the team bus and headed off to the airport, with me and Emma waving at them like schoolkids. They turned out of sight, and I felt a twinge of disappointment.

Mateo had come to see them off, too. He was in his usual kit—open shirt, no tie, jacket, and today he was wearing sunglasses. He finished a phone call and wandered over.

"So," he said, "you're looking much better."

"Thanks," I said.

"I was talking to myself," he said, pointing at a mirrored window behind me.

Emma giggled, saying, "That makes no sense."

He put his hand on my shoulder. "Tell me, though. I heard you played three-three-four with the reserves yesterday. I've never heard of three-three-four. Why did you do it?"

His sunglasses stopped me guessing what his vibe was and why he wanted to know. "It's what I did to Emma in footgolf. Copied her."

No change in expression. "I don't follow."

"She kicked fifteen yards, so did I. She went through the tunnel, so did I. It's annoying. Puts you off. In the match, I man-marked every player. Every player! The strikers are used to it. Couple of the midfielders might have had it in the youth teams. But the defenders? No one's ever man-marked them. It's annoying. It put them off." I laughed. "I was just having fun. Embracing my inner prickness. And I'll tell any story if it means I can play with four forwards."

He took a few beats, then removed his shades. He folded them up and slid them into his jacket pocket. He reached out his hand. While I shook it, he said, "Let's keep in touch."

I looked up at the hotel. It was huge. I knew no one inside. There was no reason to stay, but where would we go? The island suddenly seemed empty.

Something popped up in my vision. I felt woozy, just for a second. Emma grabbed me, but with no real panic. "Max?"

"I'm okay. I was just overcome by an incredible desire . . ." Her eyes widened; she bit her lip. Rachmaninoff? *Again?* "We've only been to, like, four places. Let's rent a Vespa and ride around."

"Aww, canny! I'll ask at the desk. Wait . . ." Suspicion. "Where do you want to go first?"

I grinned. "Okay. Maybe one of the coaches told me he'd seen a good player. Maybe we could go take a peek. But after that . . . *second star to the left and straight on till morning.*"

She liked the sound of that, and scooted inside.

I still didn't have the tactics screens or the news feed, but one little part of the curse was back.

I was considered healthy enough . . . for Playdar.

3

PEP BODYGUARDIOLA

Chester Football Club Preseason Fitness and Mental Stamina Training

Final Module: Memory and Attention-to-Detail Assessment
Write your candidate number: Six
Write your real name: Six
Write eight thousand words to receive evening rations. Write nine thousand words to receive rations plus a bonus. Write ten thousand words to receive rations, bonus, and alcohol.

I have been kidnapped.

Send help. SOS. How many words is SOS? Could be one or three. Who makes the rules?

I've just asked Nine and he says in France they have a body that makes language rules. Don't think we have that in England. Yeah, Nine's here. So's Fourteen and Two. Fourteen is struggling physically but doing great emotionally. Two's the opposite. Who knows what Nine is thinking? Sometimes I ask but don't understand the answers.

Seventy-seven words.

Seventy-seven. That's Max's squad number. Does he know this is happening? Nine says *oui*. Fourteen says no. They're his clients and they know him better than me. I'm a midfielder, not a mind-reader. I reckon he knew about the first three weeks, but not the last three days.

Oh, God. I hate writing. The title where it says "final module" is another sick joke. Every time we go through some physical hardship and wind up in a godforsaken hut, we have to write an essay, and every time it says "final module." It's a mindfuck, plain and simple. We don't know when this will end. All we know for sure is we've got to write eight thousand words before we can leave the hut. It's a test of mental stamina. How well we notice detail. Stuff like that. Nine thousand words and we get extra rations. Ten thousand and we get some booze. I don't think I even want a beer. Tomorrow's going to be torture. Maybe torture for real, knowing these army fucks. I don't want a hangover while I'm being waterboarded.

The long and short of it is we underestimated the new guy. We didn't look after ourselves as a group over the summer. We've got too many subpar characters. Too many coasters. They don't understand that standards are higher. And now we're here, paying the price.

That's about three hundred words. If I stick to short words, I'll get more done.

Newsflash: Fourteen has found a note under his rations. He's the only one who thought about tidying up, so he's the only one who would have noticed it. Diversity in action. The note's got topic ideas on it. I'll use them as an outline.

Describe what you saw on July 3rd in as much detail as you can remember.

Right. I do remember that day. That was Monday. First day of preseason. Max was back from his . . . hold on, I'm asking Nine what the right word is. Okay now I'm asking him to spell it. Max was back from his SOJOURN in Croatia. Must have been absolutely boiling. Ah. Now Nine's saying it wasn't Croatia, it was Portugal. Also boiling. Fourteen heard it was Cyprus. Two heard Florida. Fucking Max. Everything's a game with him, and Emma encourages it. Maybe she said it was Florida because that's where Two is from? He's half-American. But then she would have told Nine he was going to France and Fourteen he was going to Ghana.

That makes no sense. We ate today but I'm still lightheaded. Snapping at everyone. Talking shit. Don't know how to stop myself.

So, just over three weeks ago. First day of training. Max was there. Maybe. There was a Max-sized guy in a baseball cap, shades, and the usual black hoodie pulled over his head. He had ear defenders wrapped round his neck for if things got too loud. I'm pretty sure it was Max, but you can never really know. He did the fake Jackies prank. Why not a fake Max?

Anyway, it was fucking good to see him. He was a bit shaky on his legs when he moved. But the guy had just come out of a coma. He's learned to walk again, he's come to work. It's mad. Mad stuff. I suppose he was just showing his face, except he kept it hidden. Was he checking on us? One thing: even though he was wearing all that clobber and I couldn't see much of his face, I'd swear on my life he was shocked to see Nine.

"Nine, why was Max surprised to see you that day?"

"Because I was out of contract. No one told him I would keep training here until I made my decision."

"Right. It's not long before the first match of the season, assuming we make it out of here alive. Who you gonna play for?"

"I need to talk to my agent."

"Your agent is Max, though."

"I decided not to retain his services."

"So who's your agent now?"

"I'm representing myself."

Fucking Nine! He's worse than Max sometimes. Good player, though. Looking around, we've got a defender, two midfielders, and a powerful striker.

We'd be a decent five-a-side team. Is that what this is all about? Nah. It's just teambuilding stuff. It's not working, though. There's a massive hole in this team, the way there's a hole in the number six.

Right, early July, Max is there, Nine's there. We're all thinking Vimsy's gonna do some fitness with us. Nope. There's a guy with Max. He's six foot odd. Very strange face. Blank. Not much going on in that head, you think. He's got that trench under the nose some people have. Very short, grey hair. Brown eyes. He looks a bit like Phil Parkinson, Wrexham manager, but Parky's a bit more . . . hang on.

"Nine. What's a good word to describe someone whose face is all wrinkly? But not wrinkly like old. With lines in it. Like a fisherman."

"Weathered."

Yes! Parkinson is weathered. This rando is smooth. At first we think it's because he's soft.

Nope.

Next to new guy are three more randos. One's maybe twenty-two. Next is twenty. Next is teenage. They look similar. Later we'll find out that Max has scouted them on his break and christened them "the Triplets." Rumour is only one of them's good but he's had to sign all three. No one knows why, or why someone as stubborn as Max would do that. He doesn't play by other people's rules. We start to come up with ideas, but that's all later. It's hard to focus on one thing at a time. That's part of the test, isn't it?

Vimsy gets us players in front of Max. New guy talks.

"My name is John Smith."

Hang on. I'm just asking the others if they think that's even his real name. Three votes for yes. I doubt it. I proper doubt it.

So he goes: "My name is John Smith. I am the new assistant manager for Chester Football Club."

That stirs the pot. None of us have heard a fucking peep about this. We all thought Max was going to manage a few games and persuade Jackie Reaper to come back. Something like that. He's mad on Jackie. There were loads of theories about how the season would go, but most of them didn't have Max as our full-time twenty-three-year-old football manager. Player-manager, I guess. When he's . . . you know. Available for selection. By himself.

Now, I'm thinking, if there's an AM, that means Max is set in stone. It's really Max as manager. For real. For proper.

Me? I'm all right with it. I'm more than all right with it. Can he set up a team? Yes. Does he get up the other dugout's noses? Yes. Will we bosh this league with him in charge? Yes.

Not all the lads see it that way. They thought Jackie was the man. I heard from Joe and Donny that when they were talking about extending their deals, Jackie straight-up said Max would be in charge next season, but they didn't believe him. They thought Max would be in hospital for ages, Jackie would stay until January at least, and if he got that far he might as well finish the season. Would they have signed their contracts if they'd known? Not sure. But why wouldn't you? This club is going places. Open your eyes.

They'll see sense. No doubt about it. Or maybe this whole John Smith thing will have everyone looking for the exit in January. I know it's crossed my mind. Then again, heading for the exit always crosses my mind. I wish it didn't.

John Smith continues. His voice is raspy, but it's not like crazy deep or anything. It's almost normal. Normal with an edge of posh. Soft southerner. "Mr. Best has asked me to get you fit in preparation for the new football season."

That struck me as dead odd. Why would he say football season? It's a football club.

"Today I will put you through your paces. Tomorrow the real work will begin. The work will be real. Mr. Best requires you to be the fittest squad in the championship."

Championship? We play in the National League North. Who is this joker? And who are the other three?

"If you have any questions for Mr. Best that can't wait, ask them now."

Nobody wants to say anything because we don't know what's going on. Like, this could be another wind-up. It would be just like Max to give us a week pretending this guy who knows nothing about football is the new AM, and then whip Jackie out. Probably disguised as a fake Jackie.

Fuck me, the way I think these days is twisted.

I stick up my hand. "We haven't heard about preseason friendlies. Normally we get told who we're playing and when. Glenn gets us tickets for our families and that. Preseason friendlies are a bit friendlier, if you get me. My mum won't go to a regular season game but she'll come to preseason."

John Smith leans close to Max. I guess he's whispering to him.

"No preseason matches. We go straight into the season."

Now that's worrying. That's not right. That's a bad move.

"Nine, what did you think when you heard we weren't playing preseason matches?"

"I didn't think much. It's obviously to spare Max as much as possible."

"But we need to get match sharp. It's one thing being fit; it's another thing using it in a match."

"I expect Max has the target of August fifth as his first major exertion. If you played a friendly and he wasn't there, only Vimsy, would there be much point?"

I notice he said "you played" instead of "we played." He's got one foot out the door. So why's he here? Anyway, he's wrong. We need matches. "Yes."

"Perhaps. The first match is against Bishop's Stortford. A promoted team. Probably rather weak. Max probably calculated it would be a sort of preseason friendly."

"I never underestimate a promoted team. They've got winning habits. Winning mentality. It's hard getting promoted. Takes balls. Then we've got York City. They were relegated from the National League. I know some of the players and they're handy. They shouldn't have gone down. New manager. They'll probably be pretty tasty. Could be our strongest rivals. I don't want to play them undercooked."

"I don't know how to reassure you."

Annoying. Him saying that made me realise I did need to be reassured. Which is soft. "Why do you keep saying probably? Don't you talk to Max?"

"I am considered too stimulating."

Fourteen has an opinion. "I trust in Max. If he thinks we do not need a preseason friendly, perhaps we do not."

"Great. But he's wrong. We do."

"Are you not excited about the season, Mr. Six?"

"I am. But we need to prepare right. And that means preseason friendlies. If it was me, I'd have three or four and each one would get a little harder. Like he did with the women's team! Yeah. Three friendlies. That's what you do. What you don't do . . . is this."

I just took a little break from writing while I tried again to get the fire to light. No dos. My wrist hurts. I haven't written this much by hand since I was in school.

Back to July third. John Smith. "New to the first team squad is Andrew Harrison." This Harrison guy waves. He's lanky. Very, very tanned. He's got one eye on us, one on his younger brothers, one on Max. We're all giving him dirty looks but it's accidental. We'll make him feel welcome later. The news of the AM has thrown us, big time. The fact we've got a new squad member is also out of the blue, but that's more in line with what we've come to expect from Max. I've been working with the kids and the women, and they say that every now and then there's some rando who's thrown into the squad. They're always shit, but they get good pretty fast.

Yeah, Harrison's welcome. No problem. Even when I find out he plays midfield. It's like Max said that time. If some rando off the street can take your place, what does that say about you? I'm not worried. I'm going to take Harrison under my wing like Max wants. Show him the ropes. And show him he'll never take my spot. I'm the number six at this club. The squad needs more bodies, especially with flakes like Nine, who's off to a bigger club as soon as he can pluck up the courage to tell his mate. And Two, who's signed a new deal but we all know his heart isn't in the club. His heart's not even in this country. It's in America.

"This is Michael. You may notice some slight similarity. Michael has agreed to join first-team training to make up the numbers. Finally, Noah is here to watch. He will join the over-sixteens."

No one corrects him, but that might be because no one can believe he's made that mistake. Over sixteens? Over?

Vimsy gets us warmed up while John Smith escorts Max to the building with all the credit card people. Half a minute later, the light goes on in the office. Then it goes out again. Someone closes the blinds. Every now and then I look up there and convince myself Max is watching us through the gaps.

He's such a strange person.

At least he's up and about. After the attack, people were saying all sorts of things and I didn't know who to believe. Fourteen said he knew Max would be all right. God told him. He was the calmest, that was for sure. Nine was worst. Took it out on Farsley. Didn't even celebrate his goals. I got that. Proper Max

Best football. Score, walk back, score again. Farsley were shitting themselves. We were like terminators that day. Cold, calculating, cruel. I want that. I want that every week.

The lads do, too, mostly, but they don't want to work for it. They think Max'll have a plan and we'll win every game. They frustrate me. Some exceptions: Magnus. Aff. And Raffi's been grafting like there's no tomorrow. Max threw him a lifeline and he's grabbed it with both hands. Fair play. Wish there were more like him.

But when the cat's away, the mice will play, and this John Smith guy has left the area. The lads are laughing and joking, being nice to Harrison, finally, who seems relieved. The Noah kid is begging to join the session. He's cocky. He's got spark. There's a lot of banter aimed at John Smith. It's like he's the new headmaster and we're thinking about all the shit we're going to get up to. He's a soft touch. A posh southern walkover.

Our new assistant manager comes back out, takes off his jacket, and we see his arms.

That's the first hint that we've misjudged him.

First, the size. They're long and muscular, but not the way Magnus used to look. This guy's more like a builder—bulk from being used. But what's he been using his arms for to get them looking like that?

Then the fact that he's wearing three watches on his left arm. That gets under my skin, big time. What the fuck does he need three watches for?

He gets everyone to line up. He walks up and down in front of us. Almost immediately, he chooses Trick, and that scares me, too. He's latched onto the biggest arsehole. He can smell the lack of character. Smith's face changes. So does Trick's.

"Name?"

"Trick."

Smith bristles. I think that's the right word. He puts his head all the way close to Trick and screams, "You will address me as Brigadier!"

"What?"

The Brig, that's what we've started calling him in the meantime, and he's come to allow it, does this thing where his muscles sort of twerk, one at a time, like a Mexican Wave. The flexes are getting closer to his knuckles, so Trick finally gets it.

"My name is Trick, Brigadier!"

"Squad number?"

"Three, Brigadier!"

"Very good. Run," says the Brig.

Trick runs across the width of the pitch and comes back.

The Brig touches one of his watches. "Was that your best effort?"

"Yes, Brigadier."

The Brig points to the grass. "Sit-ups until you can do no more. Count out loud. I will know if you try to deceive me."

He gets Gerald May to run. While he's waiting for him to return, the Brig makes a note of Trick's time in a black notebook. He gets May doing sit-ups, sends the next guy running, notes May's time. It's a masterpiece in organisation, and I think this isn't one of the first hundred times he's done this.

Oh, shit.

Max has found some army guy to come and drill us, and his drills aren't rondos. They're drills. He's a military dentist and we're in for a world of hurt. There's dread in the eyes of many. Vimsy, though. Vimsy's made up. He's been suspicious of Max since day one, but like anyone with a brain he's fallen in. Talent talks. But now Max has out-Evansed Ian Evans. We've got some fucking SAS guy yelling at everyone. SAS stands for Shouting and Sadism. Vimsy is the cat who's got the cream.

Not all that long later, the Brig's got a top speed score from everyone, plus how many sit-ups we can do.

He is unimpressed.

"We will now do an aerobic fitness test. Mr. Best requires that you outperform the Bangladesh cricket team."

My first thought is: that doesn't sound so hard.

My second thought is: oh fuck.

I knew where that was going. We all did. Someone made a noise and I followed his finger. The cones were all set out. Mother of God. The bleep test.

Describe your first week of preseason training in as much detail as you can remember.

Chester FC training so far in the 23–24 season has been quite different from at the end of the 22–23.

For example:

Under Jackie Reaper, we did a lot of complicated passing, possession, pressing, and counter-pressing drills. There was a lot of emphasis on individual skill and competition between our attackers and defenders.

Under Max Best, our sessions weren't so much about individual drills as they were about seeing a match as a single ninety-minute performance. There was a lot of emphasis on dancing, feeling who had a "hot hand" and feeding the ball to that person, and while there was a lot of incredibly specific opponent analysis, it was presented very much in the context of "we're top, they're shit, let's go slap."

Under the Brig, we mostly did running. Straight-line running, zigzag running, and as a fun change, hill running. There was a lot of emphasis on vomit.

"Nine, what single word comes to mind when you think about preseason training?"

"Vomit."

"Fourteen, same question, but you have to choose a different word."

"Sick."

"Two, same question."

"Pavement pizza. Sidewalk spew. Chester chuck-up."

"Thanks."

The second day, I remember looking around at all the cones and slalom poles and thinking this might be fun when the balls come out. But the balls never left storage.

We ran. We ran until we were sick. We had a break. We ran more. All the while, the Brig tormented us. He shouted, he questioned our manhood, he said we didn't deserve our wages, that we were cheating the club, we were swindlers, that we wouldn't pass the basic physical requirements for the Bangladesh cricket team. There was something about the way he kept talking about them that wound me up, kept me running past where I thought I could go. I'm sure they're great at cricket and that, but this is football. It's harder. We have to be harder.

Two was the first to burst into tears. He wasn't the last. I broke on Friday, but managed to keep it together until I got to my car. After the crying, I had to drive home and smile at Jane and little Tracy. I tried to pick her up and spin her round, she loves that, but I nearly dropped her into the fireplace. My arms were jelly from the push-ups.

My running times got worse. Somehow, I could do fewer push-ups on day five than day one. John Smith was a fraud. Not only a sadist, but an incompetent one.

There was only one good thing that week, and that was going with Max to the twelves on Thursday evening.

Hold that thought—I've just had an idea.

"Nine. You know the Brig?"

"Yes. Unfortunately, I do know the Brig."

"Erm. You know the way everyone thinks he doesn't know anything about football?"

"He is undoubtedly a rugby man, it is true."

"Right. He's rugby, he's military. I've heard on the grapevine that he's doing a coaching badge. Football coaching. So that he can be a real AM. When Max was in hospital, we all chipped in, didn't we? Going to the youth team training and all that. But it was all voluntary. Start of the month, I was forcibly 'volunteered' to go to a twelves. Brig wasn't there, and he's always with Max. Like, always. At the time, I thought I was there to sort of look out for Max and help him out if he got tired and all that. But what if I was there to be the Brig for the day while he did his course? Do you know what I mean?"

"No."

"Fourteen, Two, do you?"

"Not really, Six."

Hard to get my thoughts lined up. Been a long day. Long week. Long month. "I'm saying . . . I wasn't there in case he got tired. He only spoke for a couple of minutes at the start, then he watched. He was showing his face, is all. Reassuring the parents. No, I was there as his bodyguard. In case . . . you know. Remember those twats were after him before the women's match? That Thursday, Brig wasn't available, and Max trusts me. So . . . So what if that's what the Brig is? He's, like, Max's bodyguard?" I stop my knee jiggling—it's a waste of calories. "Our assistant manager. He's not the new Guardiola, he's Kevin Costner. He's the bodyguard, and Max is Whitney Houston."

Nine thinks I might be onto something. "Who else did the same sort of thing? Escorting Max that week?"

"Raffi. Glenn. Magnus." Strong lads you wouldn't want to mess with.

Two has thoughts. "Would you want Magnus on your side in a scrap?"

"Magnus would be my first choice from the entire squad," says Nine. We're allowed to use the real names of other people, just not from our little team. We got sloppy on the first day and it cost us rations.

"Really? Magnus?"

"He is formidable. Do not be deceived by the crystals and the love of humanity. He would destroy you before you had even planted your feet." Coming from Nine, that's something. We've been boxing each other—not by choice— and he's handy. Fourteen doesn't like punching a mate. Neither does Two. Nine wants his rations—when he's told to box, he boxes.

"I'm with Nine," I confirm. "I might pick Raffi first, though. He's intimidating. I fucking love playing midfield with that guy. He's strong, he's smart, he's streetwise. And he learns."

"Raffi brings out the best in you," says Nine.

"Do you think?"

"You trust him. That's why he's not in here with you. You don't need to learn more about him."

That's a low blow, not that Nine realises what he's said. "I trust all you guys."

"Apparently not."

"I mean . . . I do now. Even more."

Nine shakes his writing hand. I'm pleased to see he's suffering, same as me. "I will once more try the fire. Six, if it isn't private, would you tell us about Max's visit to the twelves?"

"It was mental."

"Oh! I think we have all earned a good story."

That's true. "Right. Before training, before I'm tired beyond belief, the Brig's given me very, very specific instructions. At exactly five past four, I drive to a certain spot, and no sooner do I park than Max slips into the back seat. I drive off. He's in full don't-look-at-me disguise, by the way. We get to the training pitch. Spectrum's there, and it's his first time seeing Max since the day. So he's all emotional and he wants a hug, and Max doesn't want one, but he doesn't want to disappoint his mate, so he suggests Spectrum stand next to him and gently wraps his arms around his waist and nuzzles into his neck 'like a lover.' And Spectrum blushes because I'm watching, but he sort of did it, without the nuzzling, and then I saw what Max was about. Spectrum got his hug, but Max making it weird made sure it wasn't too much, and there was something about the phrase that made Spectrum happy."

"It was a verbal hug," explains Nine. "It shows Max is himself."

"Yeah," I say. "That sounds right. Then Max gestures and says 'uh' which means let's get this over with. So the kids and their parents come over. A few are away on summer holiday, but it's a good turnout. And Max does his speech."

"Pardon me, Six," says Nine, inspired. "Talk a little slower and I will write this down. We all can. Bump up the word count. No one said anything about copying."

"I am not sure," says Fourteen. He's a stickler for the rules. "If we are disqualified for cheating . . ."

"Do we need to come to a united decision?" I say.

Nine sighs. "I suppose it's safer not to copy. I personally have no shortage of material." He wanders back to the fireplace.

"All right. No copying. Great idea, though, Nine. Keep that up. If you're still thinking straight after all we've been through, amazing. We'll need that to escape. Okay, so it's Max but you can only see his chin, and loads of worried kids. Max says, 'Hello, *mein kinders. Wilkommen* back in ze Chester training. As you know, I vas in ze ospital but now I am very better.' And little Adam puts his hand up and says why are you talking like that? And Max says, in his normal Manc accent, 'Oh yeah, I speak German now.' Most of the kids think this is amazing, but some of the parents are looking at each other. And Max goes, 'Once upon ze time, zere vas a little boy called Max.' And he starts telling the life story of, well, I think it was *Kung Fu Panda*. And Adam says, 'You're not German and you're not a panda.' And Max says, 'Prove it.' And Adam admits he can't. So Max says, 'Look, I only came to show you I'm all right.' And he pulls his hood back, takes his shades off, cap off. And I've got to say, he looked great. Tan, hair's grown back, looks chill. He's obviously not what he was, and he's not smiling as much and he's not as restless and dynamic and all that. But he looks good. I don't think I'd look that well a month after being in a coma."

"Two months after," says Nine.

"Sure. So he gets a football and tries to do a kick-up, but he can't. And that's the first mistake he's made. The kids look sad. Adam and John know him best and they really didn't need to see their hero reduced to this. Know what I mean? And he goes, 'Right, now you're all better at football than me. You should enjoy it. It won't be like that for long. And yeah, I'm not coming to work every day. My doctor said I need to eat loads of ice cream, pizzaburgers, and play with Lego.' Then came the craziest bit. He gets the ball again, and as he talks, he does kick-ups, but this time he gets past one. 'But not very long from now, I'm going to be able to do eleven kick-ups, and on that day I'm going to start going to schools in Chester to find superstar kids.' I'm not sure what his plan was, but he did nine kick-ups! And the mood totally changed. The kids were pushing each other, straining on their knees to get a better look, the parents were laughing, I thought one was crying. No group has ever been more impressed by nine kick-ups! I've got to say, I was buzzing from it, too. Nine kick-ups! I spent a week in April thinking I'd never see him again."

Nine doesn't notice how my voice quavered as I ended the previous sentence. "Me too, *mon ami*. Me too."

I press on before I draw attention to my mistake. "Max looks pleased with himself, but he's got a serious message. 'The superstar kids are going to come here, and if you aren't training hard, they'll take your place in the team. It's nice you were sad that somebody hurt me. But I'm back now, so you can stop being sad. I promise you I'm going to get all the way better. Soon there's going to be loads of new people, and they won't be sad. They're coming for your place in the team. You've got a few weeks of training to make sure you stay ahead of them. Know what I'm saying? You need to get your head back in the here and now. If you train right, you might keep your place. And if you're really, really good . . .' He puts his arm around my shoulder. 'Sam Topps will give you a private masterclass. What do you think about that?' And they go mental, like that's the best thing that could possibly ever happen to them." I fish some fleck of mud out of my hair. "I don't like being so easy to manipulate."

Nine sighs, but he's emotional, too. "I wasn't fulfilling the role of Bodyguardiola, but I did see him that week and I have a similar story. I told Jude I'd help him out with the sixteens, to check they had been practising their dinks, but after sharing the morning with the Brig, I regretted my generosity. I planned to go to the sixteens, sit on a chair, and smoke. I had a cigarette out and in my lips, and Jude was hiding me from view, pointing out I am too much a role model and within twenty minutes of seeing me in a cloud of delicious smoke every child in Chester would be irredeemably addicted to nicotine. We were negotiating when Max and the Brig turned up, and the young men entered a state of stupefaction. Max loves those boys—more than once he has very nearly blown up his career on their behalf. And they love him, too. It was very emotional, but a very frozen kind of emotion. It came out soon after, when Max had gone. His speech was like the one you described, Six, but he didn't say he was German. He claimed to be the first-ever zombie manager, lamented that the surgeons sucked the orange juice out of his head, and said while he was in hospital he invented a new formation. Tyson asked what it was. The reply was the word 'eleven,' accompanied by jazz hands."

Nine finishes messing about with the fire. He can't get it to go, either. He settles onto the bare floor, his back to the mouldy plasterboard.

"He also said that in hospital he had a vision of a beautiful blonde angel floating over him telling him he was special. Benny rolled his eyes and said, 'You mean Emma.' And Max said, 'Nah, it was me in a blonde wig.' As you've all seen, after the initial silliness he likes to get pensive. 'I've got bad news, lads. Bad news is, you lot fucking slap. If there's a better under-sixteens team between here and League One, I'll eat Henri's scarf. It's going to take me a bit more time to get back to my old level. But your new level is here.' He reached up to his chin. 'So if you aren't training hard, pushing each other, lifting each other, I'll know. If you think maybe I've mellowed, become kinder and more forgiving, you've got another thing coming. In fact, here's a demonstration. Henri? You're fired.' 'I'm not registered with Chester, Max.' He points. 'See? Proof. I'm back. Chester are back. Chester under-sixteens have teeth. Train like it.' And then he walks off. But he comes back, gives me the gentlest hug, smiles. The Brig leads him away. They drive off. The session is bad, at first, but gets better."

"Isn't it," says Two, but he shuts his gob.

"Go on," I say, daring him to continue. He doesn't get the warning.

"Isn't it all a bit childish?"

I grit my teeth. Nine helps me out. "He's having fun. He likes to be creative. But he's also building an emotional world for the young players to live in. You have read *The Wizard of Us*. Tyson was so close to leaving." Nine shrugs. "Tyson remains."

"I don't want to hear your doubts, Two, mate," I say. "You're lucky you got an extension. You've been dogging it since you got to the club. If you want to slag Max off, you better be as committed as he is. Otherwise shut the fuck up."

I've killed the conversation, which I didn't mean to do. I'm right, but I've shot myself in the foot. It's too damn quiet in here. There's the sound of Fourteen's pen scratching across the paper, and the wind coming through the cracks in the walls. My stomach rumbles. I want to kick something, but I don't have the energy. I think about lying down, but I know I won't get up. I curse the Brig, and Max, and Chester, and Two, and pick up my pen.

Write about the weaknesses of one or more of the current players in the squad.

Oh! I should have started with this. Here's an easy ten thousand words.

The goalies aren't agile, don't command their box, can't kick, and every time a shot goes at them, I get an ulcer. Apart from that, they're fine.

Glenn's a fucking rock. Proper captain. Leads by example. Weaknesses? Doesn't want to concede shots. He'd love a nil–nil with both sides keeping the ball in the centre circle. That'd suit him just fine. Jackie wanted us to attack and leave the other team to have long shots and hope to get lucky from set pieces, but he'd always want our defenders to outnumber the attackers. Max is happy to go man-to-man. We defend by attacking. It's hard for Glenn to get his head around. He says it won't work at higher levels, but I said, "Mate, we're not at higher levels." He does his job, though. It stresses him out, but Glenn is a Max Best player. He'll realise it one day.

Two is dogging it. He gets by on raw athletic ability. Just.

On the other side of the pitch, Trick, AKA Prick Williams. He's not even smart enough to hold his finger up and feel which way the wind is blowing. I am a hundred and ten percent sure Max would never have given him a new deal. Trick's decent going forward, I'll give him that, and he's consistent. But we had Jack Litherland in for one match—or was it two?—and he slapped. I'd be amazed if we didn't upgrade the left back this season.

Gerald is fine. Not very mobile, not a good passer, but then again, he doesn't try stuff he can't do. I don't worry about him.

That's the defence. Fourteen's a little gem. As DM, he gives them a lot of protection. I'm sure he'll have some bad games this season—he's only a kid—but apart from being young, what are his weaknesses? His long passing could be better. He snatches at shots. If he sticks to what he's good at, he'll have a proper career. If he gets better, adds a few strings to his bow, he'll play for a big club. And he's worked his socks off during this whole army roleplay.

Aff is quality on the left. We hope Max can play on the right. Imagine that! Teams in this league can't deal with him. They'd have to put two men on him. Aff would run riot in all the space.

The squad's a bit short, though. The two Triplets are nowhere near the levels. They're good lads, that's clear. But no chance Michael will ever play professional football. Andrew, maybe. A few minutes here and there in games where we're three goals up. Basically, no proper help from them.

We're really short up top. Len's gone, so we've only got Tony. What's Nine planning?

You know what? I'm sick of not knowing. We need to know.

"Nine! Why the fuck are you here?"

"Same as you. I was invited to Nando's."

"That's not what I mean. Why are you training with Chester if you aren't going to play for us? Why not sign with your new team already? We all know Max wants you to move on. But while you're here, the club aren't looking at strikers. When you fuck off, we'll have one fit striker for the first match. So what's your fucking plan?"

"My fucking plan is to survive tonight. My fucking plan is to write ten thousand words about a French footballer who is isekaied into a twenty-fifth century cyborg. My fucking plan is to cook the rations I earn and keep the wine to myself. So shut up and write if you want to eat."

I'm sort of standing over him, maybe jostling him a bit. "No, mate. No. I'm stuck here with you, needing you to have my back when shit goes down in the morning and I don't even know if you'll be here when the season kicks off. When you turn your ankle on the hike or get sick from drinking rancid water, I'm supposed to carry you to the extraction point? You're not Chester, mate. So why would I?"

He gets up and pushes me away, two hands, forceful. "It's none of your business, Six. Your job is to scamper around midfield. My job is to score goals. Max's job is to build a squad. My future is of no concern to the likes of you."

I bare my teeth. "Talk or I'll deck you."

He doesn't flinch, doesn't do anything.

I suddenly decide I have to take my frustrations out on him. He's to blame for all of this. I take a couple of boxer's steps forward, feint left, punch right. It's a move that's served me well. Nine falls for it—I think.

Next thing I know I'm on my arse. I wipe my mouth. There's blood. A lot. Fuck. I could wash it off, but then we'd have to take another detour to refill at the stream. Fourteen offers me his canister. I push it away. I've got tears behind my eyes. I've cost the team. I put my head in my hands and try to think. I'm low on calories, low on sleep. I'm making bad decisions. I don't know what to do.

Nine is behind me. I didn't hear him move, but he puts his hands under my armpits and guides me back to my spot. I slump and pick up my pen. I don't have it in me to slag off my teammates. I could write ten thousand words on my weaknesses.

Nine's back in his area. He's got the pen in his mouth like it's a cigarette. "Max wants me to play at a higher level. He encouraged clubs to make offers.

Good offers. I would like to stay at Chester, but they can't afford me. It will be easier when I can talk to Max. For now, plan A is to play the first six games of the season for Chester to give Max time to sign a replacement. Then, before the transfer window closes, I will move on."

"But if you keep the team that wants you waiting, they might sign someone else. You might lose your shot."

He shakes his head. "Then I will move in January. In a Max Best team, I will score bags of goals. I will be in demand. It does not sound so bad. Fire Chester to the top of the table, leave them in pole position for the last few months of the season. Can Max replace me? Of course not. But he spotted me in the warm-up of a match. During that match, Jackie introduced Max to MD, wanted Max to talk about his future, but he only wanted to talk about me. Yes, he has a remarkable sense for what is essential. Most men pursue pleasure with such breathless haste that they hurry past it." He's talking in his usual style, but now he pauses. The strain is getting to him, too. And when the shit hits the fan tomorrow, I'll need to rely on him most of all. So why am I throwing punches at him? "Max told me a hundred times he wants me to move on, but I want to help out. I want to be part of his story. I have an idea," he says, and his eyes close. He's that close to sleep. "It's the kind of idea Max comes up with. His love language is upturning convention. He might go for it." He spins his pen round and brings the nib to his paper. "Or I might punch him in the dick and never talk to him again. That is also an option."

Write about Nando's.

Okay. Ugh. Does writing "ugh" count as a word? It'd better. My fingers are numb.

So week one, the training was hard. We accept it because it seems like the Brig is trying to establish a sort of baseline of fitness and we'll expand from there with transition drills and six v twos and all the usual stuff.

But week two is week one with extra brutality. We have to throw a medicine ball while we're sitting down. He tells us only two have passed, but he doesn't say which two, and doesn't say what length is a pass. We're doing sit-ups, push-ups, weights, medicine balls, we're running, it's nonstop. There's vom, there's guys collapsing. I feel fitter, but my numbers don't show it. The Brig is constantly adding new demands. I feel like I start from zero in everything.

Max comes out, once, whispers to the Brig. We're all looking, hoping, praying it's him telling the bastard to calm the eff down, but he's only asking for Robbo to come out of the session. Livia, the physio, comes running, checks Robbo out. There's a consultation. Robbo later tells me he's given the choice of taking the rest of the day off or rejoining the group. He decides to stay. He regrets it.

Week three is a new level of depravity. We run, we jump, we sit, we squat, we throw medicine balls. We're taken to a swimming pool where we have to swim lengths in full Chester FC kit, we have to dive to the bottom to pick up a brick, we have to tread water for as long as possible and the first ten who can't hack it are punished.

Am I getting fitter? Am I fuck. I'm constantly exhausted, constantly drained.

That Friday comes the most intense moment yet.

We're brought to a lake and we have to climb up a shaky wooden platform. At the end—it's like walking the plank—we have to turn and let ourselves fall backwards, arms crossed, without being able to see where we're going.

A couple of guys go first and it's all easy. Piece of piss. Then Magnus, who's been around and done a lot of mad physical challenges, has his turn, and he's shaking. The Brig is there with him, says stuff we can't hear, and Magnus falls into the water.

Good for him, like, but seeing one guy afraid makes the rest of us realise how fucking scary this is. It gets harder and harder the more people freak out.

When it's my turn, I'm shivering like I've been in the cold water already. My teeth are chattering. Mind's blank. I've been pushed to a physical edge, and this is too much. I'm sure my neck will snap—I've seen the mad angles people hit the water at. I wonder what rocks and shit are beneath. There's one thought that sticks as all others ebb and flow—I know there's no way the Brig will let me climb down from that platform. I'll jump, or I'll stay there forever. I hit bottom—bad turn of phrase—and decide to just get it over with and if I die, at least I won't have these fears spinning me around anymore. At least I won't have to run up another hill wearing a heavy rucksack.

I fall, gravity takes revenge for all my soaring headers, I hit something, there's a mad panic, a wild feeling of having actually passed into the afterlife the moment I hit the water, but then I'm flying through clouds of my oxygen bubbles, and I surface, and I breathe, and it's the most exhilarating feeling. Like scoring a goal. Like when Tracy was born and she looked at me. I'm alive. I'm fucking alive, my girl. I'm dragged up onto a deck and someone wraps me in a towel. The squad's there. We've all been through something. We'll never look back. We've bonded as a team.

So when the Brig announces preseason is over and Mr. Best wants to reward us for our hard work with a trip to Nando's, we all believe it. We're buzzing. Nando's! The Brig says there will be a pub quiz later, so we should split into teams of four, remembering that Mr. Best values diversity and likes it when people step outside their comfort zone by spending time with people they don't know all that well. I'll credit myself with being alert enough—cynical enough?—to wonder why diversity would be mentioned there and then, so I tried to get in a team that was proper mixed up. I wanted Raffi, but he was determined to stick with Pascal. He loves that little German like a younger brother. I tried to get Joe Anka, because if it really was a pub quiz, he knows all about music, what with being a part-time DJ. But the team I end up in is pretty varied. Two gives us American stuff. Fourteen gives us Africa. Nine gives us France and useless trivia like philosophy and what long words mean. And I'm good on sport, I suppose.

So we get into five minivans, one per team, and that should have been the first red flag, but I genuinely don't think anyone in mine was worried in the slightest. We'd been through our ordeal, we were fit as fuck, we were on our way to Nando's. Life was good.

The van goes for ages, and suddenly the lack of windows becomes a topic of discussion.

It's a long, long drive, and by the end, we're scared shitless. The van stops, the back doors open, there are massive spotlights shining at us. We can't see anything. Someone puts a hood on my head and I get dragged into some building. The hood's removed and it's me, Nine, Fourteen, and Two, and we're shivering from the cold. We're in a room with rugged-looking, serious men wearing all black.

They make us change into army gear. We are told not to use our names at any point. We will be known by our squad numbers. We have to hand over our phones, our wallets, everything. For some reason, we're allowed to keep our analogue watches. I'm sure that will prove helpful, but the opposite is true.

We're pushed into four different rooms. I've got sheets of paper and a pen. I'm told to describe the trip from the lake to this location, in extreme detail. If my description matches the others', we'll all get rations. If not, we won't.

I do my best, but I'm disoriented as fuck. The army guys sneer at us. They want us to fuck up so they can fuck us up.

While someone reads our statements, we're made to wait in a cold room in silence. One of the guys comes to tell us we passed. We relax—we're hungry. The guy hands Two a map and compass. No one else is allowed to touch them. We have to get to the hut marked on the map as fast as possible. If we're the last group to arrive at our hut, the door will be locked and the rations inside will go unopened.

He suggests, from about a centimetre in front of my face, that we get a fucking move on.

We run through the door he points to, and we keep running. Eventually, Two stops and looks at the map. I yell at him to keep running, and call him a prick and some other names. He pushes back, saying he's not a midfielder and doesn't get paid to run around at random. That winds me up. He reads the map, looks for landmarks, yells fuck, tells us we should be running the exact opposite way. Fourteen can't believe the men would send us out the wrong way. That's me convinced—we turn around.

I don't completely trust Two with the map. We're on a quiet countryside road, so we make decent time, I think. It gets harder the farther we go, because the features get less distinct. There's quite a lot of frustrating backtracking, but we get to the hut. It's open. What relief!

We find four military ready-to-eat meal packs. They've got everything you need, including a heat source, but it needs water. There are four water canteens next to the MREs, but the canteens are empty. We have to go and find water! I can't believe it. I think we're all close to tears. We talk about splitting up, but Fourteen says that's a rookie horror movie mistake.

"Are we in a horror movie?" I say.

He points to a bundle on the floor. It's a rolled-up sleeping bag. "That is your bed for the night."

I look at the ceiling until I gather some strength. There's not much left. "Okay. We don't split up. Let's find water."

"Wait," says Two. "Let's make a plan."

His plan is good. Water flows downhill, so we follow the terrain. We find a stream relatively quickly, bicker about whether it's likely to be full of bacteria and sewage or not (Fourteen reasons there must be a way to filter it contained in our MRE packs, Two says that's not how it works), then retrace our steps exactly. When we get back to the hut, there are four huge plastic bottles of still water.

They are fucking with us. And there's more to come.

Describe in detail how much you enjoyed this training course and what recommendations you would have for making it even better.

We eat, we sleep. As soon as it's light, the army guys burst in and scream at us to get up. They kettle us in as we run. These guys are wearing heavy boots, heavy gear, and they keep up with us easily. They banter with each other, placing bets on which of us will crack first.

We get to a stream. We've got to get into it, totally submerged, then we're pushed to a log. We have to carry this log back over the stream. The four of us struggle, but we do it. It's another moment of joy. Two of the army guys pick it up and bring it back to where it was. One actually looks at his watch while he goes, it's so effortless for him.

"Again!" screams a guy. We do it again. It's so much harder. There's a crisis as Fourteen loses his footing, but the rest of us hold the log up, stop it from falling on him, and he scrambles to his feet. I yell at him to get out of the way. He insists on doing his part. I'm annoyed but relieved. We need all the help we can get. We put the log down, and I collapse, curling up into a ball. I'm done. If they ask me to do it again, I'm out. Proper out.

One of the army guys kneels and digs my arm. "Top man, looking after your mate." For a short time, I'm absolutely buzzing. But then I realise he was playing with my head. He knows I'm a fraud.

We're taken to a farm where a boxing ring's been set up. Three-minute bout, heavy gloves, win by landing the most punches. My team's fighting D-Day's team. I win, Nine wins. Fourteen and Two lose. Two–all. That means half rations for us, half for the other team.

We're led away, given time to eat, then a new map. At the end of the map there's a locked hut with some oil barrels outside. We've got to haul them next to the hut so we can climb in through the roof. Don't dawdle, we're told. The longer it takes, the less you'll sleep.

Two's good on the map. He did outdoors stuff every other year as a kid in the States, and it's coming back to him. We get to the hut, then it's a physical and strategic challenge to assemble the barrels. Fourteen tries to skip ahead, breaking the rules. He gets Two to lift him up to the roof, but the hatch is remotely locked. It will only open when the barrels are in place. No shortcuts.

It's hard. My arms fucking ache from the logs and the boxing. The barrels are proper heavy. I want to sleep but I can't until I do this. I miss Jane and Tracy.

Are they okay? Do they know where I am? Nine yells at me to concentrate. We push, we lift, Fourteen climbs in the hatch, opens the door from the inside. We pile in, unfold the sleeping bags, and I'm ready to drift away.

I'm so tired that sleep won't come. Fourteen's out, but the others are up. I chat to them.

We talk about all the stuff footballers talk about. The gaffer, the club, whose wife is fit, the latest hot goss, rumours about the Triplets, what we expect from the season, what we expect from the big teams.

Nine has a theory. When Jackie was around, Max was all about being super technical, all about sweeping passing moves. Now he's not got that. He's got an army guy, so he's pivoted. It's all about fitness. Outworking your opponent. Outrunning him.

Two says it doesn't sound much like Max. Nine says Max is deeply pragmatic. He won't make an omelette if he doesn't have any eggs.

It calms me down, and I get some shut eye.

Amazingly, they let us sleep in. I'm astonished to find it's eleven a.m., but Nine says it's ten. Two's watch says eight. They've snuck into our hut and changed the times. Why? To mess with our heads even more.

We find a box outside. There's a map. We have the choice to follow it to breakfast or to our first physical challenge of the day. No contest there. We go to breakfast, but when we get there, there's almost no food. A note informs us we're being punished for using our real names. All except Fourteen. He shares his rations, insists, but it's almost worse than if we had nothing. We've wasted all that energy getting there, and we have to retrace our steps and then walk on, stomachs growling, knowing there's some torment ahead.

It's a grim morning of physical challenges, a gruelling afternoon of large-scale puzzles, and a long, weary hike to the next checkpoint.

Which leads us to now. In the hut, writing it all up. I have absolutely no idea how many words this is. I'm nearly ready to pack it in, but Fourteen's got one last conversation for me to jot down. He's been deep in thought for a while, looking from Nine to Two to me. Mostly me.

"Six," he says. I note he's dropped the mister. "What is it you hate about me?"

"I don't hate you. Don't put words in my mouth. I don't like that."

"You have been put in a group with three players with uncertain futures. Nine is out of contract. I am on minimum-wage terms. Two regrets re-signing. I believe it has been done to provoke you. But it is more than that. You hate that Nine is not fully committed to the club. You hate that Two does not give a hundred percent in training. What about me?"

The little shit. Gets a few games under his belt, thinks he's Billy Big Bollocks. "All right? You want to know? Check this out, then. You ready? Want to write it down? Thing is, mate, we all know you're a big Christian. Got big beliefs. We were joking you'd start trying to convert us, one at a time, starting with the biggest sinner. We were wondering who you'd think that was. Not Trick, that'd be too obvious. So who? But it hasn't happened. You've kept your mouth shut. You listen, you stare, you see us misbehavin', but you don't speak up. So do you even believe it? If you aren't saying what you believe, what kind of belief is it? Have some fucking courage."

The whelp doesn't flinch, and after a delay he nods. "Yes. It works."

"What the fuck did you just say?"

"Mr. Best told me something once. We were talking about Tyson, the young player. Mr. Best went on something of a rant. Five ways in which Tyson annoyed him. Then he laughed and I asked why. Mr. Best said the things he hated most in others were the character flaws he saw in himself. I have often thought about that. And here we are. You train within yourself. You talk about being committed, but you have had discussions with other clubs. You would leave if a good offer came, as would almost anyone. And you have strong opinions that you never voice."

I don't like being dissed by a child. My knuckles are white, and I'm ready to go. Two and Nine are suddenly between me and the kid. He comes through them. Not scared of me in the slightest.

"What did you do?"

I deflate. He knows. No, he can't know. But he said about having talks with other clubs. I get the feeling I had on the plank. I have to fall in now or they'll never let it drop. "Okay. Okay. Confession time. When Max was in his coma, I was talking to agents. Teams in the National League testing the waters. Unscrupulous. Put my back up, to be fair. But I was flattered. In the end, I decided to stay and give it a go here. But I felt sick. All right? I felt disgusted. What do people think when they think about me? Teamwork? Loyalty? I'm no better than any of you. And these army guys know it. Every time they see me, they're giving it all 'Yeah, good teamwork,' 'Team player right here,' all that shit. To wind me up. Because they know what teamwork is, and I don't."

Two shakes his head. "Men like that don't give out compliments like candy."

Nine's got thoughts. "Six. It is not disloyal to look after yourself. Max wants and expects you to do just that. He is one of the most selfish and mercenary people I have ever met."

"How can you say that?" I'm genuinely upset. Nine's his best mate.

"Because I was there with him when he was plotting to leave Darlington! He told me the whole sick plan. When a chance came along to do it in a better way, he took it. But he would have burned a lot of bridges and hurt a lot of people. He thinks that's his job. And now he thinks it's his job to improve us as players. Starting with our fitness." He's saying "us." "Our." "I know for a fact he would love to sell everybody in this hut. Fourteen, obviously a fantastic talent. He has told you his plan, yes?"

"Of course. I do not want to leave. But Mr. Best will use the transfer fee to build a new training facility. To buy an X-ray machine. And so on."

"Me? I am a star striker. I have value. If I sign a long-term contract, he will still listen to offers in January. And Max thinks Two has a high ceiling."

"He does?" This is news to the American.

"*Oui.* League Two, he thinks. Possibly higher. And Six. You're one of the best midfielders in the league, but if he can get a good fee for you, he can replace you with someone like James Wise. Not quite as good, but cheaper, and he'll save on wages. And he'll use the income as Fourteen described. He's excited about selling players, provided you give him time to find a replacement. He does not want another Jack Litherland scenario. Which is why I am waiting to talk to him until he is ready. I have an unusual idea I would like to discuss with him. One that benefits me and the club."

I'm a little bit stunned. I feel like I've confessed to a horrible crime and no one heard me. "But he was in a coma and I was on the phone."

Nine bats it away. "I was not on the phone. I could not trust myself to talk. But I replied to emails from clubs who wanted to sign me. Yes, why not? It is no crime, Six."

Two props himself up in a corner of the room. If it's confession time, he's got a story, too. "My partner's a nurse in Florida. Much better place to be a nurse than here. I wanted to live out my dream of being a footballer. National League North doesn't pay the bills. I'm not doing well enough to really commit. I should probably go home. Grow up. Get a real job and start a family."

Nine repeats himself. "Max thinks you are good enough."

"League Two?"

"It is your life, *mon ami*, but if Max is right, and he normally is, you could be a starter in League Two. Have one amazing season, get a deal with a League One team. Double your wages. Finish your career on a high. But Six is right. You have been dogging it. You must train like the devil, or give up your dream. It is simple. I say go for it. As the Brig's tattoo says: Who Dares Wins."

I've got a lot to think about, and so has Two. "I'm going to write out this chat, then I'm ready to hand mine in. What about you guys?"

Two says, "I finished my text in thirty seconds."

"What? You've been writing the whole time."

He picks up his papers. There are sketches of places we've been. Bridges drawn from memory. A distant village. A farm and its field. Plus some attempts to recreate the maps we've been using.

"Is that your way of showing your attention to detail?" says Nine, while Fourteen boggles at the drawings.

"No," says Two. He's got a trick up his sleeve. He picks up the last piece of paper and shows it to us.

He's written, simply: TEN THOUSAND WORDS.

"Oh fuck me," says Nine.

Fourteen stares at the instructions before crouching and silently screaming.

I laugh. I laugh and I hug Two. "You smart little mother. Good for you, mate. Good for you. But you could have told us."

"Yeah. But then we wouldn't have worked it all out, would we?"

Final Module: Memory and Attention-to-Detail Assessment

Write your candidate number: Six

Write your real name: Six

Describe receiving your final rations.

When I was done writing, we took our pages to the drop-off point and put them in a box that was there. We trudged back to the hut and found four full military meals, new bottles of water, four Double Decker chocolate bars, and twelve cold beers. Someone had started the fire and provided spare logs.

A little note said, "Mission over. Well done. You can now use real names."

Fourteen pointed at it. "Is anyone going to fall for that?"

"Not me," said Nine.

We laughed and had one of the shittest and best meals of our lives.

The next morning the army dudes turned up and made us jog. It was an hour or so, but it flew by. I only started blowing near the end when the hills got really steep. Then we saw our destination—a plain, windowless minivan. We got in, unafraid, and were driven back to civilisation. We pulled into a gym, strangely, and used their showers. Hot water! Unbelievably good. Our clothes were there, washed and dried. We got dressed, got back in the van, and were driven somewhere else.

My stomach was rumbling by the time we were let out. Somewhere in Chester city centre. The army dudes gave us bags full of our last things—our phones, wallets, and so on. Then they hugged us and told us we'd done great. For the first time, I believed it.

"What do we do?" said Two, which was a step up for him. He'd only ever spoken to them when spoken to. "Where do we go?"

"Where do you think, map genius?" Army guy pointed to a familiar sign.

We crossed the road—strange to see cars again—and went into the Nando's. My wife Jane was there. My little girl. I embraced them. Drank in their scent. Lifted Tracy and spun her round and round.

"How did you get on?" said Jane.

"You knew about it?"

"Of course. You think I'm going to let Max Best run off with my husband? Not without a scrap, I can tell you! They said it'd be like army training and you always wanted to do that. So I said, great, sounds good."

I'm retrospectively twenty percent happier about the kidnapping knowing my wife was in on it. "We did . . . okay. I thought I'd do better on that sort of thing. Guess I'm not as tough as I thought. And we nearly killed Fourteen."

"Who?"

"Youngster."

"Oh, not him! He's a lovely boy."

"Yeah, he is."

"Sam Topps," said a voice. The Brig, dressed in civvies. Hint of a smile. "My congratulations. Very well done."

"Don't know about that, Brig."

"You caught the eye of the directing staff. They gave you an outstanding rating. Mr. Best was right."

"What do you mean, Brig?"

He doesn't answer. "How are you feeling? Ready for the coming season?"

Two groups come through the doors. D-Day's and Raffi's. They look how I feel—lean, fast, strong. "I'm ready, Brig. I'm ready."

4

FLAT

Thursday, August 3, 2023.

Aaaallll right.

I got murdered and so on and so forth. A lot of people chipped in while I was out, kept the place ticking over. But we had a match on August 5, so at the start of the month I decided I had to try to get back to the daily grind, even if I was far from ready. Even if my battery was flat.

People would understand if I got a bit tired or moody. People understood that all too well—most treated me like I was made of glass. The way people slowed down when they spoke to me was funny, until it wasn't. I liked when Emma fussed over me, made me cups of tea and opened or closed curtains based on her assessment of my needs. I didn't like it so much when a rando in Tesco offered to help me shop. The Brig was amazing in those situations—if I closed my eyes for ten seconds, the problem was gone and I could return to staring at cereal boxes.

I had a to-do list a mile long. I couldn't concentrate on anything for long. I couldn't sprint. I couldn't do a Beckham or a cannonball.

My physical improvement had plateaued. My bank balance was stagnant. As far as I knew, the agency I'd helped found was stuck on zero clients. And I hadn't earned any XP in four months. Four months!

All my forward momentum had gone. The wind had spilled out of my sails and the seas were flat. How had I got things going before? By stirring the pot with mad energy. What if I didn't have energy to spare? What then?

But even in my reduced state, I still had awesome firepower. The ability to analyse a football player in an instant. The power to shift formation at the speed of thought. And the power to improve—I had over two thousand experience points and as soon as the perk shop opened, I'd be spending freely.

Our first match was against a semi-pro team promoted from the division below. Not easy, but if ever there was a match I could sleepwalk through, it had to be that one. The week after was against relegated York City, and they were expected to go straight back up.

So one win, one defeat, and a whole lot of mental stamina training for me. I'd take that. By the time we played York again in January, Chester would be a much stronger team, and if my physical progress kept going the way I wanted, I'd be in the lineup. That assumed I could kickstart some progress. Make some numbers go up.

To that end, I was in the back of MD's car, temporarily alone with my thoughts, saving my strength until we got to Newcastle. MD was in the passenger seat, texting on one phone and reading on another. The Brig was driving.

The curse had been coming back to me bit by bit. First to return was Playdar. I'd used it to discover the Harrisons, AKA the Triplets. They were three orphans from Manchester, all midfielders who could play in the centre or on the right. One had PA over a hundred, the other two were decent. They came as a package, and I was happy to slightly overpay for two to ensure I got the one I really wanted. More on them soon.

After Playdar, the player profiles returned, apparently unchanged.

Then the Chester Men and Chester Women squad screens came back. My name was in the first, but Henri's wasn't. Proof that he'd moved on. Good for him! Except when I got back from Tenerife, he was still training with us and intended to sign a match-to-match deal. Help us out until the transfer window closed. And then what? He said the discussion could wait. Like everyone else, he was treating me like a balsa-wood toy. His player profile showed a two-point drop in CA over the summer. Better than most. Most players had lost three, four, five points. A couple had improved a lot. None were flat.

My player profile . . . was a ghost town. It showed my contract (five hundred pounds a week, month-to-month, no bonuses), this year's playing stats, and my data from Darlington the year before. But not a single attribute came with a number. Not my pace, my heading, and certainly not my CA or PA.

Fortunately, I knew exactly what my CA was: 1. But soon it would be 2. And I'd keep improving until I got back to my previous level, which may have been 140, or may have been 200. I planned to be terrorising defences by New Year's Eve. Even CA 60 would have me as one of the best players in the league.

Realistically, the only players who might be better than me at that point were Henri, Raffi, and Youngster. Possibly Aff. That, though, depended on me getting a top coach to replace Jackie Reaper. Which meant that unlocking Staff Search was my top priority. The perk shop hadn't reopened, though. There was only one upgrade I could currently buy. On August 1, I'd been offered the monthly perk, and it was the worst yet.

New perk available: Player Search patch (version 1.63)

Cost: 100 XP

Effects: This patch patches a thing that needs to be patched.

I planned to buy it during the match, provided watching Hibernian versus Inter, a team from Andorra, in the UEFA Conference League Qualifying Second Round gave me as much XP as I expected. If it didn't, I'd reassess. I got the feeling I had to buy this patch in order to get the shop back, and that annoyed me; I liked to think I was in control of this journey. Another part of the reason I didn't instantly buy the patch was that I was in no hurry. Even if I fully unlocked Staff Search and whatever else was in that upgrade tree, I wouldn't be doing anything with it just yet. On Saturday we had our first match of the season and that was where almost all my attention was going. If I got through unscathed, I'd go back to long-term planning. For now I was literally taking things one game at a time.

"How long to Newcastle?"

"Another two hours, sir."

"Going to have a nap."

The Brig woke me five minutes before getting to Emma's house so that I could wipe away the drool and so on. The exact right level of looking out for me.

It had been a long drive, and I took the chance to get out and stretch my legs. Emma's mum, Rachel, invited us all in for a cuppa, and we were happy to accept. While it was brewing, she gave me a tour of the garden, which I'd only ever seen in winter. I pottered around the flat bits, asking the names of the little flowers and shrubs and why each one was placed where it was. Gardening was like picking a football team. You put the big, thick things at the back, and the flashy, showy ones at the front.

It was the first time I'd seen Sebastian Weaver since the attack. He and Emma had been on the grounds that day—they'd snuck into the executive box, planning to surprise me. So he was on hand to charge to the defence of Mr. Yalley. Sebastian had defended me against the Football Association because his daughter asked him to. He'd defended Mr. Yalley because he was enraged by the injustice. He reached out for a handshake. I ignored it and gave him the best hug I could manage. I wanted to say something but words were inadequate. The best way to repay him was letting him go to his daughter's wedding.

We gathered around an island in the kitchen. Emma introduced the Brig (calling him "John," which irked me). Sebastian and Rachel treated me—surprise—like I had a huge hole in my skull.

"So, why Edinburgh?" said Sebastian, softly, with an encouraging smile.

I swallowed some mild annoyance. He'd earned a fuck-ton of goodwill. "Bit of concentration training," I said. "We've got our first match of the season on Saturday. Tonight I'm going to pretend I'm the manager of Hibs and see how long it is until I get dizzy."

"Hibs?" said Rachel.

"Hibernian," said her husband. "Why them? It's very far. Surely there's a closer match?"

"It's actually the highest level game going. Third most important European tournament." I was hoping I'd get 5 XP per minute. If the Champions League gave 7, same as the Premier League, and the Europa League gave 6, then maybe the UEFA Conference would give 5. Hibs versus this team from Andorra would be one of the lowest quality matches in that whole tournament, probably, but it was still *in* that tournament. There was a good chance I'd make out like a bandit. "I'm sure I'll learn a lot. Plus the fact the drive's so long means I get to spend more time with my favourite person." I hugged Emma. "MD."

My employer smiled. "I knew it! When I heard you wooed Emma by ig-noring her for weeks, I thought, *Oh! That's what he did to me.* Well, I'm flattered, but I can't say I don't deserve it."

"You do, mate. You've done what you set out to do: eased me into the start of the season. We need a few more players but it's not urgent."

"How's your mum?" said Rachel.

"She's great. Happy. Your daughter got her into *The Traitors*; she loves it."

"That wasn't me," lied Emma.

The Brig checked one of his watches. "Sir."

"Got to go," I said. "Thanks for the tea."

Outside, Emma pulled my elbow. "Can we do a tekkers clip?"

"No point," I said. "I'm stuck on ten."

"Oh. Are you all right?"

"Yeah."

She gave me a dubious look. "Health is other people, babes. Don't spend so much time alone."

"Why is John driving MD's car?" Emma wondered aloud as she settled into the back seat.

"I wondered the same thing," said MD.

"MD can't drive a car off one skyscraper onto another one. The Brig can. End of discussion."

"I'm happy to get some work done. It's quite luxurious, actually. Not that I'd want it all the time. I like driving."

I wiggled my arse until I was properly upright. It was time to catch up on all the goss. "Right. Let's talk about things. Rapid fire. The sale of Man United. What's up with that?"

Emma knew. She'd been keeping an eye on the story to see if Old Nick would appear in the background of more photos. She hadn't spotted him, but his fingerprints were all over it. "Three final bids were made. Qatar, a hedge fund, and the guy from Manchester. That was two months ago. Nothing's hap-pened since."

MD added, "The club's in purgatory. They looked at buying Harry Kane, but the price was too high. Too high for Man United! Imagine that. If the sale had gone through, the new owners would definitely have found the money."

Purgatory. Not heaven, not hell. If Nick wanted to spread misery, then leaving the players, staff, and millions of fans in an endless state of uncertainty would do it.

The idea of the league's best striker moving to the Red Devils stirred my loins. "Harry Kane at Man United. That feels right."

"He's going to Germany," said Emma.

"Come on," I said.

"Really! To Bayern."

"The England captain is going to Germany?"

"She's right," said MD.

"Okay so I went back in time. Roger Moore is James Bond. Footballers earn twenty pounds a week and spend most of it on cigs and warm beer. Got it."

"Is it so strange?" wondered the Brig. I was encouraging him to learn more about football. Primarily so he could help beyond fitness and man management, but also because once he learned enough jargon, I could make him do post-match interviews.

"The last time anything like that happened was Kevin Keegan going to Hamburg. What year was that, MD?"

"Oh! Before my time. Late seventies."

"Yeah. The olden days. Now, the Premier League is the only place to be, really. Apart from Real Madrid or Barcelona. Anywhere else is a big step down, to be honest."

"Except Saudi Arabia," said Emma.

I groaned. Her hometown club had been bought by Saudi Arabia, and now everyone in Newcastle was a propagandist for that petrostate. "Babes. Please."

MD turned round. "Max, the Saudis are investing huge money in the SPL." He saw I hadn't heard of it. "The Saudi Pro League. Looks like they're trying to create a Premier League rival. As you know, they got Ronaldo last season. This summer they've added Firmino, Henderson, and Benzema."

"Old guys near the end of their careers," I said. China had tried to do this a few years ago—a huge boom followed by a huge bust, and absolutely nothing to show for it.

"And Allan Saint-Maximin. Mahrez. Rúben Neves. Mendy, Jota, Malcom. They're on a spending spree. Crazy money on all sorts of talents, old and young. It's very serious."

Well, with those names it *did* seem serious. "Okay. I need a minute." This news was scrambling my brain. The Premier League had been slowly gaining in power, prestige, and popularity for thirty years, such that the centre of gravity of the entire sport was England, and that process had shown no sign of abating. Now . . . now there was a new challenger. And they weren't even in Europe. Wow. The contours of the entire sport were being upended.

What did that mean for Chester? For me?

It meant more money sloshing around. More chance I'd be able to grab some of it. But by the time I got to the top of the pyramid in England, would people ask if I could do it in a really big league? It was crazy-making to even countenance the idea.

"Is it bad news, MD?" said the Brig.

"Not for us. We're a long way from all that."

"Not as long as you think," I said. That was enough catching up for now.

Edinburgh, to watch Hibs, in their awesome green and white kit, against a team from Andorra in a nice red number. There were twelve thousand fans watching, leaving eight thousand empty seats. The locals clearly thought this was a low-level match, but as I'd guessed, the curse was giving me 5 XP per minute.

Nice.

Even better was the injury time the referee added in the first half—six minutes!

MD noted my surprise. "There's a new directive. Remember in the World Cup the referees added loads of time because of all the cheating and delays? They're doing it this season. There should be less timewasting. And there will be more bookings for bad behaviour. Yelling at referees and so on."

Right, so I'd get loads more XP for every match I watched, and the matches would have less shithousery and dicks would be punished? "That sounds fucking amazing."

He smiled. "I thought you'd like that."

The match itself was very one-sided. Inter, the Andorran visitors, couldn't defend. Their goalie had low bravery, and that's no good when teams are sending in gorgeous crosses and competing for headers. You do need a strong presence. The whole match (6–1 to Hibs) was a warning in what would happen if I focused all my attention on the front of the pitch.

"Let's talk goalies," I said. "I've told Ben Cavanagh he'll be our number one this season."

MD's eyes widened. The Brig asked why.

"Ben and Robbo are similar in terms of quality, but Ben is younger and has room to grow. We call it a higher ceiling." The Brig nodded. "Robbo's ahead of him right now, but Ben should catch up and then overtake him." Ben's CA was 35, one behind Robbo. But Robbo's PA was only 45, while Ben's was 67. "Next season we'll be happy we made the change."

Emma didn't like my tone. "That implies *this* season we won't be happy we made the change."

I shrugged. "It might cost us a few points."

"You don't seem worried about it."

"If we're doing things my way, we'll do things my way."

"Wonderfully meaningless." Emma always thought to ask about the people behind the numbers. "How did Robbo take it?"

"He wasn't super happy. But I told him I planned to rotate the goalies more than most managers would. He'll still get loads of game time. Right. The defence. If we play four at the back, it's Trick, Glenn, Gerald, Carl. It's all right. Not much room for growth. The only rotation option at the moment is Magnus. He can play anywhere in defence, and he's kicked on over the summer." His CA had risen to 36, taking him ahead of Trick and Gerald. "We need another centre back, ideally one who could cover left or right back, too. Let me take a tiny break."

Asking for a tiny break was a great way to get out of a difficult conversation, for example, and this is just hypothetical, if I was playing Monopoly with Emma and she asked why I suddenly had loads of cash. This time, it was because I'd decided to buy the stupid patch and get it out of the way.

After stumping up the cash and getting a pang of headache, I still had over 2,000 XP.

XP balance: 2,187

Debt repaid: 1,607/3,000

I went to the Player Search screen and it was, indeed, quite different. Instead of thinking a player's name and being brought to his profile, there was a list of every player I'd ever scouted, the club they played for, and their estimated transfer value. The last field was all question marks, but holy shit, I couldn't wait to unlock *that*.

I went through page after page of players, ranging from Conrad Etutu and Stephen McGough, to Ronaldo and Marcus Rashford.

A box called Filters let me refine my search. I could ask to see English players only—not as gammony an option as you'd think; the Premier League needed you to have a certain number of English players in your squad. I could filter by position, preferred foot, and more. The most intriguing was contract status. That one was not currently available, but would be when I unlocked the contracts perks. Would it show me players whose contracts were running down? I could accidentally bump into them in Tesco and suggest they hold off renewing until I was legally allowed to talk to them.

This was all amazing, but I dipped out quickly to see if the perk shop was open now. It was! Amazing. I'd been forced to use *my* XP to correct *Nick's* sloppiness.

But back to the player search. There was a weird filter that simply said: *Interested.*

I set it to *Yes* and went back to the list of players. It was much shorter now. Conrad Etutu and Stephen McGough were still there, but Ronaldo wasn't. I looked through the list. Most Darlington players had been filtered out, but Junior, the talented striker, was there.

So Junior was interested. Interested in what? Joining Chester?

Great, but we couldn't afford him. On the top-right of the player search area was my transfer budget. It currently read £0.

Mate. No need to rub it in.

I had a think, then filtered by defender.

The list got much shorter but was still pretty massive. Loads of defenders who would come to Chester! It made sense—this list was mostly Sunday league guys. Five-a-side guys. I looked for a way to filter by PA, but it wasn't available. I could filter by attributes, though. I set a minimum positioning skill of 10, and now the list was much, much shorter. Eight names. Ah. I'd scouted most of the defenders before I'd unlocked the positioning attribute. As you'll see, the fact that I'd have to keep re-scouting players and staff became something of a theme.

One of the eight defenders had a little *TRN* box next to his name. This guy was transfer listed?

"MD," I said, interrupting whatever conversation they were having. "You've got C-suite superfriends at Hereford, right?"

"I know people who work there, yes."

MD knew everyone in non-league. "Are you willing to humiliate yourself a bit?"

"Yes." That got him a big smile from Emma and a little nod from the Brig.

"Top. Will you call your dude and say you're in Scotland looking at a centre back and it's a disaster and you need to get Max some defensive cover and you're desperate and you've heard that Steve Alton is available?"

"Steve Alton? I've never heard of him."

Alton must have been an unused sub in a match I'd been to or played at, because I also had no memory of him. He was CA 30, not super impressive, but he had PA 53. He was a centre back who could play right back, too. And his positioning was 11.

"He'd fill the squad out very nicely."

MD dipped his head. "If I can say . . . Thing is, we sort of thought you'd be finding more players for free. Like Raffi and Youngster."

"But then you made me the first-team manager on my actual deathbed, mate. And we don't have time to wait a year for the next Raffi to get up to speed. We need a couple of lads who can play *this month*. So let's see about Alton Towers."

"Steve Alton."

"That's what I said." Emma showed me her phone. A picture she'd dug up of a footballer called Steve Alton. He looked like a Steve, and he was wearing a Hereford shirt. Almost certainly the guy. She showed MD. "Ems, will you check if he's a social media weirdo?"

"On it."

"Brig, can you have a dig around to see why he's transfer listed? That means his club doesn't want him. Is it coz he's a dick or coz they don't need him?"

"Understood."

I nodded at MD to signal it was time for him to do his part. He stared at his phone, bit his lip, then dialled. I gave him an excited shake. He liked it. The Two Amigos riding in tandem!

He went through his spiel, and ended up with a quote for twenty thousand pounds. I mimed slicing my throat. MD made some small talk and ended the call.

"Worth a shot," I said.

"They might get back to us with something more realistic. But Max . . . we don't have anything in the budget."

"MD, if we can get him for five K I'm going to be a total dick until you give me the money. Let's not bicker about it now. I'll try to find guys for free."

I went back to my Player Search tool and tried all sorts of other filters. I realised that for my current needs, my best bet was having some minimum attributes—positioning for a defender, finishing for a striker—and sorting the list by club name. This listed everyone who was currently under contract at Darlington or Hereford or FC United or wherever. But underneath all those were guys who didn't have a club. Out-of-contract players with good attributes. There weren't many, but there were some.

I clicked through into some profiles to see if any had high PA. My quick search didn't come up with anything. But it was a list of players who could come in and do a job, at the cost of taking up my wage budget. Basically, someone like Steve Alton but without the growth potential.

If I had mental capacity, I'd check it out on the drive home. For now I really needed to get all the XP this match had to offer. But if Staff Search was as useful as the new Player Search, I'd easily find the new Jackie and the season would be a huge success.

"What are you smiling at?" said Emma.

"Just being in Scotland with my honey."

"Liar," she said, with a smile.

"It is refreshing here," I admitted. "No one knows who I am. They're treating me like a normal, average, excessively handsome football phenom."

"Oh," she said. "So they *do* know who you are."

XP balance: 2,420

Debt repaid: 1,633/3,000

Saturday, August 5. Match 1 of 46: Bishop's Stortford versus Chester FC.

Bishop's Stortford is a nice-looking place in the south of the country. When I say south, I mean south. It's right next to Stansted Airport. It's basically London! Their team had been placed in the National League North after all the promotions and relegations of the previous season, but as the most northern of the southern clubs, they were sent, from their point of view, to the grim, frozen hinterlands. They appealed against the decision. They were a part-time club who didn't have the resources to travel all over the country like a full-time outfit.

For once, I had sympathy with the FA. There weren't an even number of northern and southern teams. What were they supposed to do? Bend space and time? Think how many seven-course lunches they'd miss.

I travelled in the Brig's passenger seat. (I was temporarily carless. Before the Southport match, I'd parked my Subaru on a random side street and couldn't remember where. It was either still there, right as rain, or had been towed and crushed into a little cube.) Not going on the team bus was better in terms of saving energy, but a long trip like that was a good time to have little chats with the players. Touch base with them all. Soon. Very soon.

In the stadium, I watched Vimsy warm up my players. Every time they sprinted towards the away team's dugout, they cast a worried glance in my direction. I sighed a long, unhappy sigh.

"Sir?" said the Brig.

"They all think I'm broken."

"They went through a trauma, same as you. They need to heal, too, sir. Now that you're here, they can start."

"Can you shout at them to heal faster?"

"If you wish it, sir. If I may be so bold . . . The rain is affecting how the ball travels. The rondo drills are not going well."

"Good spot. We're better than Stortford, but the pitch is a bog. It negates our technique and passing. It'll be a scrap. These guys are semi-pro. We should be much, much fitter. We'll battle and win in the last ten minutes."

"Very good, sir."

Stortford had an average CA of 39. Decent, then. They would set up in 4-4-2 with a gigantic, powerful striker who would be a nuisance. Unlike most gigantic, powerful strikers at this level, he wasn't a slow brute. He was surprisingly agile.

They also had a hulking centre back, but he, mercifully, *was* slow and cumbersome. Normally I would have considered some mad scheme like using Pascal to buzz around him like a mosquito. But the conditions put paid to any clever tactics. Today would be about duels.

We had Ben in goal, Magnus at left back instead of Trick, Youngster as DM, and a midfield of Aff, Sam, Raffi, and Joe Anka. The last of the eleven was Henri up front, meaning our average CA was 41.8. So despite the regression from the summer break, we were starting the season 0.5 CA ahead of the last match I'd managed. Okay! It wasn't much, but it was something. It cheered me up a bit.

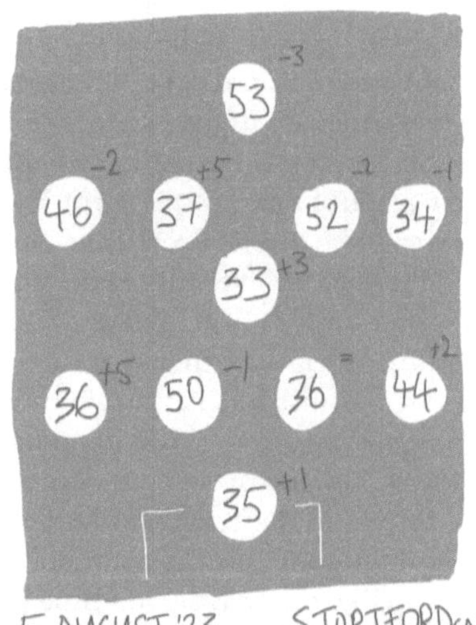

That summer regression was understandable, but annoying. Still, surely the players would add the points they lost very quickly? In the first couple of weeks of the season. Right? Or was the state of our coaching so bad that even that low-hanging fruit would be out of reach?

I planned to unlock Staff Search the following day, and really get stuck into that. If we could find a decent skills coach, could we get close to an average of CA 50 from training alone? We had quite a few high-PA players now. If just one of them put on a growth spurt, we could start to seriously boss this division. If we could get to CA 45, we could tilt at the title based on my superior tactics and optimisations.

As it stood, though, we looked very, very average.

I let Vimsy do most of the pre-match stuff and took my spot in the dugout quite early. I was in baseball cap and shades, and I was wearing my AirPods. I didn't want to get distracted by the noise. My job was to analyse the match and look for tweaks that would help us perform better. If I took it easy, I might make it through the ninety minutes.

I had some pre-match decisions to make. Bench boost? No. Triple captain? No. I'd upgraded the Fantasy Football perk so I could use those boosts once in the league, and once in every cup competition. But I'd probably save them for a must-win top-of-the-table clash later in the season.

I also had God Save the King. That gave me a once-per-season stat boost. Last time, I'd used it to boost Ziggy's finishing from 16 to 17. Ziggy, God love him, had decided to stay at FC United. I didn't regret using the boost on him, but I would almost certainly use it on Youngster from now on. He was my walking lottery ticket and by improving his attributes, I could improve the payout. It was a decision that could wait a few weeks, though.

I'd left Glenn as captain, and no one thought twice about it. Sam had shown a lot of leadership in the boot camp, as had Raffi, but Glenn was admired by all. Raffi's first pay raise had kicked in, making him one of the highest earners at the club. He was busting a gut trying to prove himself worthy. Youngster was still on a basic, minimum-wage deal. I'd sort that out in August, for sure.

The match kicked off. The tactics screens looked pretty identical to what I'd had last season, but now I had more detailed match stats for every player. Whether that was because of the yearly update, the patch I'd bought, or just the fact that I was the manager now, I didn't know. I suspected it was the update, because I couldn't remember having that data when the women played.

We took control. I'd deliberately kept things simple. The players knew this formation, knew what I wanted. Despite the boggy conditions, we were able to pass the ball around the defence and midfield. But we couldn't progress into the final third. Whatever we tried, something went wrong. We huffed and puffed our way to a lot of 6s and not many 7s.

Henri was putting in a 5 out of 10 performance. If I didn't know him better, I'd have said he was confused about which team he was playing for. Stortford had a chant—*Allez les bleues*—which in case you're not a top linguist like me is actually *French*. Why did this London club have a French motto? What the actual?

At halftime, I waited for a change from Stortford. They stuck to 4-4-2, so I left things as they were and again snuck into the dugout and hid there for the rest of the match.

After fifty minutes, Stortford got a corner and their enormous, lumbering centre back got his head on the end. One–nil.

Our players walked back to their positions. No one shouted any blame, no one looked especially angry. Huh.

Fifteen minutes later, Stortford got a free kick out wide. They loaded the area in front of Ben and aimed the cross there. Ben came rushing out, leapt, but was boxed out by the two huge players. It was a different guy who got his head on the ball, but he had an open net to aim at.

For a second, I thought Sam was going to rage at Ben for his decision-making, but he took a breath and walked back to his spot.

Two—nil, and we'd conceded from set pieces. After the boot camp, Vimsy had taken most of our sessions. We'd shuffled, slid, and practised these scenarios. We couldn't have prepared *more* for these situations. And it hadn't worked because how do you prepare to play in a bog against two actual giants?

I shook my head.

Non-league football. Holy shit.

The pitch dried off towards the end, but for the last twenty minutes, I was pretty spent. I'd barely done anything but it was still exhausting. I almost couldn't help but check the match ratings, read the commentary, think about tactical tweaks.

I asked Vimsy to suggest the subs we should make, and then did those. Trick on for Youngster with Magnus going to DM. D-Day for Joe. I also took Henri off and put Tony on. It hadn't been Henri's day. I hoped he wouldn't get all Henri about it; I couldn't face one of his outbursts.

We finished brightly. My guys fought, competed, ran, did everything you could ask of them, but we went back to the dressing rooms with a 2—0 defeat to our names. A sullen three-and-a-half-hour drive home awaited.

The Brig didn't ask me what had gone wrong. I wondered if he thought I was a fraud. He'd been hired to protect this genius, this boy wonder, and there had been zero sign I was anything other than broken. I could only imagine the mood on the team bus.

Sunday, August 6.

I woke up, had a tea, made sure I was feeling okay, and bought Staff Search for 500 XP.

It added a section to the search area. It was a list of all the coaches, scouts, and physios I'd ever met, plus their employer, where they were based, the job they were doing, and their current reputation. For example:

Phil Forster—Man City—Premier Division—Scout—Superb

I couldn't remember meeting Phil Forster. Maybe he'd been one of the hundred guys I'd shook hands with when Sandra and Kisi showed me around the Death Star.

The screen also showed managers and assistant managers I'd met who were now out of work. Poor David Cutter was there. I suppose the idea was that he might consider being my assistant manager, so why not show him on this list? He wouldn't come—when managers started getting sacked, he'd start getting calls.

Unlike with the player search, there wasn't a handy *Interested* option in the filters, so there were a lot of names that would never, ever, consider working in my staff. Ian Evans, for example. Clicking his name showed me that he was retired. Guys like him didn't stay retired, though. He'd be back.

I searched for Jackie Reaper. His profile was there. I swiped it away.

Back to Phil Forster, then. I could click on him to see his scout profile. Like with Evans and Jackie, it was all question marks.

Which led me back to the perk shop to see what new options had opened up. Still no Wibwob, but the one I really wanted *was* there. Staff Profiles was retailing for 2,000 XP. I'd be able to afford it very soon.

That would tell me how good my current staff were, plus, I assumed, all these guys on my list. An amazing advance. One of the biggest remaining jigsaw pieces. The end of my plateau.

Being greedy, what I also wanted was a list of every unemployed guy in the country who could come in and work for me. There didn't seem to be a way to get that. I'd have to introduce myself to every coach and physio I ever met to get them into the database. Then when their contracts ran out, or they got fired, I'd see them as available.

What else did I need in the coming months? The morale, injuries, and contracts perks. Plus 3-5-2. The latter was fairly urgent, in fact, because if I lost two of Trick, Carl, and Magnus, I'd struggle to field a coherent side. Three-five-two was my solution to having a small squad. And I had a bunch of talented midfielders. Yeah, 3-5-2 was probably going to be next on my shopping list.

I also needed to improve my own CA and mental stamina. So I closed the curse, replied to a handful of texts and emails—I was slogging through my backlog in small but increasing doses—and texted the Brig that I was ready to leave the flat. I checked my equipment bag. Swimming today, I reckoned. No. The pool was too flat. Maybe I'd go to the woods. Walk up, jog down.

Tuesday, August 8.

I used my new friendship with Eve at Wrexham FC to score two tickets to see their sold-out EFL cup match against Wigan. (The Brig had started his investigation into my murder and had looked into the Welsh club's youth coach. The prick had been with Eve the whole time and they'd heard about the incident in the car together. The Brig had ruled the coach out as a suspect and deemed it safe for me to travel to Wrexham.)

I had virtually no interest in the tie. It was just to get the XP I needed to unlock the Staff Profiles perk.

I got 5 XP per minute, and it went to penalties. Great for XP growth!

The Brig suggested we leave well before the decisive penalty. It's always frustrating to leave a match early, but he was right. We'd beat the traffic and there would be far fewer idiots in the car park. So we double-timed it to the car, and as I clicked my seatbelt closed, I bought Staff Profiles, leaving me with 700 XP. I had less than 1,300 to go on my debt, too.

All right! Things were very very incrementally going my way. I had to keep moving. Keep pushing, even if there were days when nothing seemed to happen.

While the Brig drove me back to Chester, I checked out what I'd bought. On the Staff Search page, I brought up whatsisname. Phil Forster.

Now there were far fewer question marks; the staff attributes were visible. Finally! Jesus Christ, what a slog that had been. The attributes were things like determination and working with youngsters. They changed from person to person, but it didn't take me long to work out why. Physios had an extra line: physiotherapy. Meanwhile, managing directors and owners had completely different ones.

But while I knew what the missing attributes were, every number was still a question mark. I knew just as little about Phil Forster as ever.

No please no give me a fucking break mate seriously come on.

Ah! But in the Chester squad page there was a list of our current staff. When I unlocked a new attribute for my players, I got to see them instantly in the squad screens. So surely I'd be able to see the profiles for my employees?

Yes!

BEHOLD, THERE WERE NUMBERS.

It had only taken seconds, at most, but I think I'd stopped breathing and then gulped in some air because the Brig took his eyes off the road to check on me. But I calmed down very quickly. The relief was incredible. I could see the numbers. No more working in the dark, holy shit.

	SPECTRUM
Adaptability	4
Coaching Goalkeepers	3
Coaching Outfield Players	11
Determination	5
Judging Player Ability	5
Judging Player Potential	2
Level of Discipline	3
Man Management	4
Motivating	6
Tactical Knowledge	15
Working with Youngsters	14
Coaching Style	Technique-based
Preferred Formation	3-5-2
Preferred Style	Patient play
Other	n/a

I didn't know what everything meant. Some of it seemed obvious, but sometimes the curse was obvious and sometimes it was tricky. Most of the numbers seemed to be out of 20. Spectrum's numbers felt low. If we averaged them, then yeah, probably low.

But what did I truly care about when it came to him? Adaptability? I wasn't sure what it meant but apart from asking him to go along with my mad schemes, his job was pretty unchanging. Coaching goalkeepers? He didn't do much of that. Judging players? I already knew he was shit at that. But choosing who to bring to the club was my job. I didn't care what Spectrum thought of players like Vivek.

Yeah, some of these low numbers really didn't matter.

But he was good with kids, knew tactics, and could coach outfield players. Eleven out of 20 seemed like something I could improve on, but I suspected there weren't many coaches in the National League North who were much better.

I turned to the Brig. Coaching style: Fitness-based. You don't say? He had 20 for adaptability, which was a big surprise. He also scored huge in discipline, man management, and motivating, and straight 1s in anything to do with football.

Vimsy was weak across the board. His preferred formation was 4-4-2 and his style was "cautious but direct play." His tactical knowledge was abysmal. Still, I was Tommy Tactics. I was starting to realise I didn't care about most of these numbers, and was honing in on one in particular. With a coaching outfield players (COP) score of 7, Vimsy wasn't very good at the main thing I needed him for.

Jude was better. His COP was 12. Seemed like our best coach. Talk about a lucky punch.

Angles had coaching goalkeepers 12. Seemed decent.

Jill was disappointing. Low numbers across the board and a defensive mindset. Not what I wanted for the women's manager. Upgrade needed ASAP—their season started in September.

Dean and Livia scored badly on most things, but had 20 in physiotherapy. I didn't want to rush to judgement, but it seemed they could easily be upgraded. Not that I'd ever "upgrade" on Livia. There was more to life than optimising numbers.

Finally, Magnus was a decent coach and had 20 in physiotherapy.

So the staff was . . . underwhelming. Probably what you'd expect from a struggling National League North side.

I went back into the staff search to see if I could see Jackie Reaper's numbers. Nope. I'd have to meet him again. Livia had hinted he was in hiding. Batted away my questions about what he was up to.

Ah, forget Jackie. He didn't want the job.

I bit my nail as I looked out the car window. I couldn't fire everyone on my staff. It was a community club and they'd all been doing extra work. Getting the maximum CA growth out of the players, though. That was paramount. That trumped almost everything.

How could I get rid of these guys in the nicest possible way?

Spectrum was fine where he was, for now, and one day I'd have the option of moving him laterally to some sort of data analysis role.

Vimsy. He wasn't all that close to retirement. Best case scenario, Ian Evans would get a job and try to get his old mate to join him. Yeah, that'd be amazing.

Jill. She'd have to go back to being a normal coach. The curse showed six coaching slots for the men's team, and six for the women's. Did that mean I could only employ six? I doubted it. But as I added more coaches to the women's team, Jill would get pushed down. When she was about to fall off the bottom, I'd have to move her into a new role. Some sort of general manager. She'd probably like that, and be good at it, too.

Yeah, the only one that worried me was Vimsy.

The last interesting thing about all the new data was seeing MD's profile. His attributes were business acumen, discipline, interference, man handling, patience, resources, and ambition. He scored highly in the first one. For once, luxury of luxuries, the curse explained what the number meant: *Astute business-man; will increase club income.*

Top!

A low number in interference was good for me. It suggested he'd let me get on with my job. Like, if I woke up one day and decided to buy three new goalkeepers, he wouldn't try to stop me.

His scores in resources and ambition meant he wasn't personally wealthy, which didn't matter since he didn't actually own the club, but that he wasn't aiming all that high. That could prove to be an obstacle one day. Say I needed to sign a player for three million pounds to make sure we got into the Premier League, and MD hummed and hawed about the expense and the wage bill. Yeah. Could be an issue. I wondered if I could plant ideas in his head and raise his ambition score?

It'd be interesting to do some tests on some of these guys. See if these numbers were fixed.

The club had got me a city centre flat. Someone was paying for it off the books, or the owner was a massive Chester fan who was happy to lose out on some income. As far as I could tell, it would normally rent for a thousand pounds a month. I loved it, but the Brig said the location was way too risky.

An alternative was being prepared, one that met the Brig's sense of security. I doubted it would be in the city. I'd always wanted to live in Manchester city centre: twenty-four-hour shops, transport links to everywhere, go watch a movie, get wasted, walk home. Chester city centre wasn't quite as buzzing, but it was still lively.

But there was a guy who wanted to kill me. I couldn't live like a normo.

While I was doing my late-night yoga, I had a great idea. The Brig was doing a coaching course. I'd see if his attributes increased over the weeks. And if I visited him in his classroom, I'd see the other participants' profiles and if there was one with good skills, I could snap him or her up!

My enthusiasm dampened. I needed to do everything in person. I could no more scout every coach in the country than I could scout every player.

Ah! But if I scouted some *scouts*, that would make my life a lot easier! Someone with judging player potential 20 was basically someone with Super Scout, right? If they had the ability to spot talent, they could tell me where to spend my time.

Yessss . . . that would be a big step forward.

I felt a little bit of the old excitement. Some of the old forward momentum. Yeah, I faced massive challenges. But my abilities were rising to meet those challenges.

Tiny, subdued roar!

Saturday, August 12. Match 2 of 46: Chester FC versus York City.

It was my first home match since the attack, and there was a big crowd. Loads of people who wanted to see me, talk to me. I hadn't written the manager notes. I hadn't communicated with the fans. They wanted to know I was really, really all right but I needed to focus on the match at hand.

When I walked past, they stopped talking. Turned their section of the stadium into a library. The hush spread quickly. Is he okay? Is he still broken?

I waved at them, but then sank into the dugout. It was the only way.

I'd decided to rest Youngster—he couldn't play every game of the season. So I'd gone for a 4-4-2, and if we took control of the match we'd switch to 4-2-4 and really attack.

With Trick and D-Day getting a run out, our CA was a meagre 40.7. The season was going to be long, though, and the sooner those lazy pricks got on the pitch, the sooner their CA would return to the levels from the end of the season. Surprise, surprise, they'd been the two players with the biggest CA drops over the summer.

As soon as I saw the York players, I knew we'd be in for a tough match. York City were a decent-sized club. They'd only been relegated because of a points penalty awarded for fielding an ineligible player, but they'd managed to hold on to their best players and were looking good for a quick return to the National League. Their average CA was 51, which by my guess put them in the top three teams.

So 40 plays 50. We had home advantage, but we hadn't had a preseason, and I didn't feel I could impact the game much.

It went badly.

For the first time since I'd been in the dugout, we didn't dominate possession. We struggled to pass, to connect with each other. Any sloppy play was pounced on, and York would soon be camped in our half. Our counter-attacking threat was nil.

I looked at my options on the bench . . . and pulled my baseball cap down.

One—nil down at halftime.

I switched to 4-5-1 to try to beef up the midfield.

It didn't work.

At the final whistle, we could consider ourselves lucky to only have lost two—nil. No one was to blame. We'd lost to a better, better-prepared, better-coached, better-managed team. We had lost this game the second some prick had decided to hit me with a metal bar.

At least I remained mentally sharp till the eighty-fifth minute this time, which was progress.

As I trudged along the touchline, something weird happened. I got a round of applause. I took my baseball cap and shades off, plucked out my AirPods. I looked into the stand. I retraced my steps a little. Six stewards copied me. I turned to the Brig to see if he had spotted it, but he was scanning around like a Secret Service agent. Of course he knew about the stewards—he'd set it up like that.

He wanted to keep a line of bodies between me and the fans. To shield me from their emotion the way I'd shielded myself from the noise. I looked behind me. The players were trudging off the pitch. The shield had worked too well. We'd played okay. The players had done their jobs as well as they could. But we'd started the season without emotion, without passion, and we'd been outplayed twice.

Now here were the fans telling me it was all right. They were still onside. We had some credit in the bank. How many defeats would it take for them to get restless? Not many. Four or five. But it wouldn't come to that. Something inside me was stirring.

A thought struck me. I went back to the York dugout and shook hands with all their staff, making sure all their profiles were added to my database. Their physios seemed much friendlier than Dean, but had similar profiles to his and Livia's. Shit at everything but with 20 in physiotherapy. Weird.

Their coaches were slightly better than ours, but only slightly. They didn't have an advantage there, and anyway, they didn't have any players with PA over 80.

Okay, good. We had a lot of ground to make up, but it didn't look like York would be massively improving in the meantime.

I went into the dressing room and stopped Henri from going into the shower. It was time for a talk.

Before I could get my thoughts in order, though, thumping music came from the away team's dressing room. It was about two percent too aggravating for me to ignore.

"Brig."

"Yes, sir."

"I'd like to address the troops. Would you ask York to kindly shut the fuck up for five minutes?"

"Very good, sir."

Henri and the rest of the players waited, not sure how to feel apart from beaten. The mood was flat.

Next door, the music stopped, restarted, and stopped again. There was a loud murmur of conversation, then a crash. Shortly after, the Brig returned. "They were more than happy to accede to your request, sir."

"Top," I said. I looked around at my guys. Some very talented ones who needed proper coaching to progress. Some journeymen who would do us a job across the season. And one talentless armpit stain whose sole contribution to civilisation was having a decent left foot. "All right. Honesty time. We've lost the first two matches and that's quite a comedown from last season." Some heads popped up. I hadn't talked much to them since the attack. "We're flat. But last season was the end of a story. Today was the epilogue. You expect me to scream and shout like anyone else would do. Yeah, well. I'm still a few weeks away from giving you the hairdryer. And you don't deserve it. You worked hard. You put a shift in. You did."

I went on a lap of the room, checking everyone's mood.

"I realised something in that second half. I realised that it was always going to be like this. I'm not ready. You're undercooked. The fans were quiet. We've all been through a hell of a trauma. We put it all on the line at the end of the season, and now we're all a bit spent. A bit empty. You're fit, some of you have spent the summer working on your skills. But collectively, emotionally, we're paying the price for how we finished the season. We flew too close to the sun and now we're back to Earth." I smiled. "I'm all right with it. Better this than the alternative."

I rolled a ball under my foot.

"I say we draw a line under it. Those two matches? That was our preseason. Our season now is forty-four league games. Tuesday we've got Chorley at home. After that, I've got some work to do. You need a great skills coach. The squad needs a few more bodies. Let me just say I'm optimistic about finding them."

I pushed the ball away. It hit the far wall and rolled back towards me.

"You're all treating me like I'm broken. You're worried about me. I get it. But you've got to stop. We've got to look forward now. You're worried I don't know what's going on? That I've lost my edge?" I stopped next to Glenn. "Ryder. Four headers won from six. One interception. Decent performance. Quiet, though. Let's get back to organising. I want noise complaints about you." Next to him was my client. "Raffi Brown. Sixty percent pass accuracy. Miles off your usual. You were trying too hard to make things happen. Aff. Six dribbles attempted, one completed. Their right back's good, but he's not that good."

I wandered back to the front.

"See what I'm saying? I'm watching. It's all going in. If you're spending more time worried about what I'm doing than what you're doing, you're playing with fire. You're going to find I've signed your replacement. *I* can afford to lose a couple of matches. *You* can't afford to play like that again. Not if you want to be in my team." I left a pause. "Does anyone know what the last match of the season is?"

Two hands went up. Youngster's and Pascal's. They smiled at each other; Youngster put his down. Pascal said, "Darlington."

"That's right. Listen, guys, I've been flat, you've been flat, it's been tough, but it's a new season. A new storyline."

I thought about my new powers. Imagine being so overpowered that adding a huge new area of expertise still felt like being "flat." Like I was stuck on a plateau. The thought raised my pulse. I felt my smile get cheeky.

"I'm going to mix things up. Fresh faces, fresh coaches, fresh ideas, weird and wonderful new tactics."

I looked at my high-potential players. I was going to hop on their backs and ride them to glory. They were young. Conventional wisdom suggested young players made more mistakes.

"I'm sure there will be bumps along the way. Who gives a shit?"

I thought about my own playing career. Playing bog-standard league matches (sometimes on actual bogs) didn't much appeal. Ten matches to get my medal, sure. But the cups?

"We're going to go full tilt at the cups and see what sort of fun we can have there. I, er, might treat myself to a few cup matches. I want to get to Wembley before Dani does."

I thought back to all the stuff I'd told them about storytelling. About looking beyond the next pass to consider a match as a complete, ninety-minute event with a beginning, middle, and end.

"The story of this season isn't written yet, but I know how it ends. It ends here, in this stadium, at home to my former club. And Pascal's. And Henri's. I'm not saying I'm going to be a dick and rub it in their faces. Just the opposite. I really like most of those lads. I'm saying we will lift the league trophy here, in this stadium, in April. And it'll be the exact opposite of last season—I'll be surrounded on all sides by my *mates*." Little wobble on the last word. Stupidly, I looked at Henri. He'd gone all damp. I steeled myself. "That *will* happen. The women will win their league, and the under-sixteens are looking amazing. This is going to be the best year in the history of this football club." I nodded a few times. "That's the story. Chapter one is on Tuesday night against Chorley. Get some sleep. Relax tomorrow. Next week, the fun begins."

5

CHESSTER

"Football is like chess, only without the dice."

—Falsely attributed to Lukas Podolski, 49 goals in 130 games for the German national team and owner of the world's most famous kebab shop

Monday, August 14. Transfer window: 18 days remaining.

The day before a match, training is normally a bit less intense. It's certainly shorter. But *normal* wasn't a word that I heard much in relation to Chester Football Club, unless it was preceded by *ab*.

Why were we doing a full-length session? Because I was testing my new staff profile knowledge; I'd put Jude in charge of first-team training. The curse said he was my best coach of outfield players, so instead of having him float around filling in gaps in schedules, he was my new main man. Boom. Take a pawn, promote him to a golden pawn. That's how chess works, right?

Vimsy was still the most senior, most visible coach. My bishop. He'd be the one helping me on the touchline, the one who'd yell at players when they were late, and all that kind of thing. I'm sure his demotion from the guy leading the training sessions would have been slightly awkward under normal circumstances—that word again—but when Jackie left, I'd used all my coaching resources in a mad whirlwind of drills and mini-drills. Asking more from Jude, if anything, was a return to *my* kind of normality.

The players responded—we had a few bits of green, a couple of bumps in CA. Jude!

Maybe Jude and one new guy could replace Jackie. How could I do tests that would provide concrete answers? I could use the Triplets, maybe. The older brothers were pretty similar in terms of their profiles and starting points. I could give Andrew one coach, and Michael two coaches, and see who'd improved most after a month. Was that science? Maybe. It seemed pretty weird, though. They were human beings, not chess pieces, and I needed them both to improve as fast as poss. I'd have to guess for now and hope to find definitive answers eventually.

As I strolled around, Jude ran a transition and pressing drill. We didn't press much as a team, certainly not in the coordinated, precise way elite teams did. But it was a drill that was also good for passing, technique, and stamina, and

89

engaged players' brains more than most. Jude blew his whistle, and that was the end of the session. The players looked tired, but happy.

I blew my own whistle, but not so loud it would hurt my delicate ears. The players rushed over to form a semi-circle around me. I wasn't sure if that haste was because they didn't want to keep me waiting or if it was because the Brig was wearing a blank expression—his scariest.

"Good sesh. Thanks, Jude. Lads, I want to have chats with you all this week. Give you some targets and talk about your hopes and dreams and all that. Today I need to see Youngster, the goalies, Raffi, and Henri. Henri's going to take his usual hour-long shower, so by all means hang around and come talk to me until then. It won't take too long. All right? James, let's walk."

I chatted to him on the way to my little office. The Brig followed, not to keep me safe, but to learn about football.

Once in my office—my office! Jackie's stuff was still on the walls—the first couple of minutes were me asking about James's dad. Was he okay? Had he been very stressed? Is there anything he needed? James asked me to stop worrying.

"It's pretty hard, mate. Your dad saved my life."

"Saving people is what we long to do," said James, smiling into his lap.

"Sir," said the Brig. "I've been to see Mr. Yalley. I'd say he's in rude health."

"Indeed he is!" said James.

"When have you seen him?"

"Visiting him was the second thing I did as part of my investigation."

"You know I'm going to ask what the first was. Don't make me waste energy."

The Brig nodded. "The CCTV footage. I didn't find anything useful, but I ensured there were copies. A lot of places overwrite the drives. Or, in the case of the Deva Stadium, the tapes. I also sourced footage from nearby shops, the car showroom, and so on. Sometimes when I have a spare twenty minutes, I look through them."

I thought about making some joke, but the guy was my only real hope of finding out who attacked me. If he was being diligent about it, great. "Thanks." James had been very still during that little chat. I remembered why he was here. "Bro. First of all, you were right about Moisés Caicedo." He looked panicked. "You don't remember? In the World Cup. We watched Ecuador against . . ."

"Qatar."

"Of course! And I had that question about the player with the highest transfer value. And today he's going to sign for Chelsea for a British-record fee. A hundred and fifteen million! You weren't just right, you were really right!"

James beamed. "You should write to the organisers and request a bonus point."

"That's not the worst idea. Hey, I've just had a brainwave. Find some time to sit with the Brig and explain to him what factors are involved in transfer fees."

The idea of spending time alone with the Brig horrified James, and he struggled to keep his emotions contained. "Of course."

"Oh! And since you've shown some potential in player assessment, I'd like to sign you up to a scouting course."

"A scouting course?"

"Yeah. Quick intro into how to be a scout. Maybe I can send you to watch a certain player for me. The club will pay the costs of the course and any travel we make you do." This was a genius idea. I had loads of players—male and female—and the chances were high that two or three of them would have great coaching or scouting stats. Normally people started looking into post-playing roles late in their career. But if Youngster did this course, the curse would have to give him a scouting profile, right? And I'd see, fifteen years ahead of schedule, if he had any talent.

"Is this voluntary?"

"Of course. It's completely voluntary as long as you agree to do it. If you refuse, it will stop being voluntary."

"I understand."

"Top." And if he was a shit scout, I'd send him on a coaching course! "Now, then. You've been more than generous in playing for basically free. It's time to sign you up to a proper contract. It's obviously pretty weird that I'm your agent and your manager, but I've got a solution to that."

"Oh?"

"Yeah. The solution is that I don't give a shit what anyone thinks. You need a good wage, but I need to keep some budget so I can sign more players."

My new weekly budget for player and staff salaries was £16,000. (The women's team had their own funding.) Including the £95 a week Youngster was getting, the combined £850 the elder Harrison Triplets were on, and the £800 a week we were (under)paying Henri, I'd used £13,320. Giving James £500 a week or so would leave me with just over two grand. Four average players. Two good players and a good coach. One Henri.

"Okay. Of course I will do as you say."

"Wait wait wait. I'm being flippant but this is a serious thing. This is your life. Your future."

"I have faith that you will not guide me wrong."

"Look, just choose a number between four hundred and six hundred."

He grinned. "Six hundred."

"Top," I said, writing that down. "You get six hundred chances to say the number that's in my head."

He tutted and looked at the ceiling. "Five hundred."

"Deal!" I said with a slight smile. "Here's the thing. We're a small team. The facilities are . . . what they are. You've been to Man City. You've seen where Kisi is learning. We can train you to a certain level. And next season, we'll be playing against better teams so you'll be able to improve a bit more. The thing is, even if we get promoted every year all the way to the Prem, very soon we'll be holding you back. I'm not sure when the best time for the club to sell you is. One year, two years. I'm not sure yet. But no more. I know you'll make friends and you'll want to stay, but it's not your destiny. I'm serious now. We can't have a thing where I'm expecting to sell you in a year or two and you turn round and say God told you to stay. We've done that bit, and it worked out great for me. The best thing for you, me, and the club, is that you let me move you on at the right time."

He fussed with something on his training top. "It will be hard, Mr. Best."

Leaving and starting somewhere new wasn't emotionally challenging for me, but it was for most people. "I know." I sighed. "I know. But it has to be this way. We'll give you a three-year contract. Five hundred a week, and if you keep improving I'll give you a raise next summer. All right? Any questions?"

"Can I have a goal bonus?"

"No. I don't want you shooting. You're terrible." His finishing had climbed to 7, but I suspected there was an attribute called long shots. From his DM position, Youngster wasn't normally close to the goal, and sometimes he'd get carried away and shoot from thirty yards out. He was definitely long shots 1. If I could get him to never shoot again, that alone would add five million to his eventual transfer value. It was unlike him to ask for more, though. Greed was a sin. "Is five hundred not enough?"

"With all the travelling . . ."

"What? Are you still in Manchester? You need to move here. I moved here when I was in a coma. It's easy."

"Is that another voluntary order?"

"No, mate. It's common sense." Common sense would have told me that he could hardly move out of his parents' home when he was on minimum wage. "Ugh. What am I talking about? Okay, scratch that. But start looking now, yeah? You work in Chester. Start looking at options, okay?"

"Yes, Mr. Best."

The goalies came in next, along with their coach, Angles.

"Ben, two games under your belt. Nice. But I want Robbo to get one soon. Get his season started. Get match fit, ready to come in at a moment's notice and all that. So Robbo, we've got Chorley tomorrow night and Banbury on Saturday. You can choose which one you play."

"Oh!" said Robbo. His new boss was being weird again. Ab, meet normal. "Okay. When do you need to know by?"

"Now. Choose now. What the fuck."

"Oh. Are you serious?"

I let my face do my talking.

Robbo looked at his hands. "So . . . Chorley."

"Why? Because we beat them last time?"

"It's home. Bigger crowds. I like a big crowd."

"That's it, then. Job done. Ben, you're Banbury. Any questions?"

"What about next week?" said Angles.

"What am I, some kind of floating chess brain who can think three moves ahead?"

"Yes," said Angles.

"Okay, fine, you got me. But I've just upgraded from thinking one match at a time to one week at a time. I trust both these pricks. That's all for now."

They left.

"That was clever," said the Brig.

"Was it?"

"I would have expected you to pick which match suited which goalkeeper. But letting Robbo choose shows you meant it when you said he'd play matches this season and doesn't feel like you're dropping Ben."

I nodded. I felt good about it. "Yeah. I'm not quite thinking three moves ahead yet. But I'm starting to see some very obviously good ones, if you know what I mean. Open goals. Tap-ins. Easy wins. I'll see Raffi next."

Raffi and I had a quick, easy chat. Catching up. Checking in. He had a good contract, negotiated by yours truly, and was now on 750 pounds a week. Decent money. That wasn't what I wanted to talk to him about.

"Bro, I notice you've come back fitter and sharper than ever."

"I trained the best I could over the summer. Tried to get some mates to do drills with me, that sort of thing. My first season nearly ended in relegation. When it was sure we were staying up, that I was going to get another season for sure, I was like, I can't let this slip. I've got to be on it from minute *one* next season."

I spun a pen around my fingers—fine motor skills training. "Well, I noticed it. I feel a breakout season on the horizon. It's my job to make sure you get top coaching, top players to play with, and minutes in the team. But to really leave no stone unturned, I'd like you to do a coaching course."

He bowed his head. "You sure?"

He'd had a quick go on a youth team and in his mind, it had ended in disaster. "When you did that match—was it the under-twelves?—I noticed you the next week. You were more thoughtful. You weren't just doing the drills, you were wondering why we were doing them. Starting to think like a coach. I want that from my players even if you don't do any coaching. Believe me, if you're shit, you're not taking any sessions at this club. Don't worry about me asking you to do things you're not good at. But that mentality, that way of thinking about the game. That's worth the course fee, and that's worth a bit of your time." I paused. "Do you need to think about it?"

"No, Max. I'll do it."

"Top bins."

He stood and turned a fraction towards the door. "Are you really all right?"

"I am now," I said, giving him the biggest smile I could manage.

He left. The Brig gave me a nod. I was on fire!

Henri came in, leaving a wispy floating trail of mandarin and white musk. He swished a light scarf around his neck, spreading the scent even more.

"Is that Old Spice?"

"No, Max. It is not Old Spice."

I invited him to sit down, but not in front of my desk. At the back of the room, I'd got two short chairs and a small table that almost matched the height. On it was a chess board. It was one of those ghastly cheap plastic monstrosities, but it was the best the Brig could do at short notice. He suggested that if I wanted better quality, I should choose my theme for the week with a bit more alacrity.

I sat in front of the white pieces.

"I see," said Henri. "Your injury has improved to the point where you are able to imagine yourself capable of beating me at chess."

"Not only will I beat you, but I will tell you how I'm going to beat you and in how many moves."

"Indeed? Then let us decide who plays as white." He picked up a white pawn and a black pawn. Chess people hide them in their fists and you choose one and the one you get is the colour you play.

"No, I have to be white. I only know the rules for white."

"The rules are the same."

"Look, I don't have a chess tutorial butt plug, all right? I only know how to play white. I'm white." I moved my king's pawn two spaces forward. "How was training?"

He moved a pawn *one* space forward. Jesus. He was one of *those* guys. "It was good. I like Jude's sessions."

I moved a bishop. Very big, sweeping gesture. Top wing play. "Let's talk about why you're still here."

He pushed a pawn to block the most likely line of attack from my bishop. "I have a scheme. One that suits all our needs."

I moved a knight out into the world. "Pray tell."

He moved another pawn. His defence already looked impenetrable. "Short-term, you need a goalscorer. Long-term, you need transfer funds. I will sign a contract here. You can sell me in January."

I moved the other knight. "Go on."

He moved *another* fucking pawn. "I could earn a higher wage at another club. But I want to stay here. I want to win games for you on Saturdays and thrash you at chess on Sundays."

I tried moving a pawn. It seemed to be a good thing. "You'll play here for a low salary? Is that what you're saying? I can't have that. You already lost thousands letting me stay in your house."

"One cannot lose what one never had." He moved a bishop, like, three spaces. What's the point?

"So you want to stay here for eight hundred pounds a week? No way. I won't do it."

"You're not my agent anymore, Max."

"I'm a football fan. I want to see you at the highest level you can play at."

He shrugged as he took one of my pawns. "If I score, say, fifteen goals before January. How much could you sell me for?"

I made some random move. I couldn't see through the layers of pawns and bishops he'd created. "I don't know. Let's say fifty thousand."

"That seems low."

"If you've got six months left on your contract, why would someone pay more?"

"I could sign a three-year contract. Could you get a hundred thousand?" He took one of my knights somehow.

"If I get the right coach in to lift you up to your old level. If we go on a cup run and you boss it against some bigger teams. If you cut out the wrestling. Sure."

The number of ifs didn't bother him. He moved a piece backwards. I finally had him on the ropes! "So we split the money. The club gets half, I get half."

I frowned. "That's weird. Is that a thing?"

"I doubt it. If the club owns the player's registration, why would they give up half? If the player is out of contract, why would *he* give up half? But if we work together, we can increase the pot. It solves many problems. I get to stay and play vivid football, you get money to improve the team, I get compensated."

I looked away from the board and considered the idea from different angles. "It seems to be absolutely bonkers. I love it. What's the catch? What am I missing?"

His lips twitched. "When you see how vital I am to your title charge, you may reconsider selling me. I will be a prisoner here."

"I can live with that," I joked.

"Yes," he said, and with a start I realised he was attacking my king from multiple vectors. "Yes, perhaps I could, too. That image you suggested of us holding the trophy surrounded by our friends, the opposite of how the last story ended. It is compelling. Why *don't* I stay for the rest of the season? You can sell me in the summer as easily as in January. Perhaps for an even higher fee."

I picked up a pawn and looked at it for a minute. Trying to calculate. Failing. For some reason my thoughts kept drifting to the possibility of using God Save the King to improve Henri's finishing attribute. It would help with this season and any coming transfer, but it was dumb when considered over a ten-year horizon. I needed to be very careful not to make short-term moves simply because I could only think one move ahead. I put the pawn down and slid it one space forward. "Checkmate in seven moves," I announced.

"No, Max."

"Pardon me?"

"I already checkmated you four moves ago. I give you the benefit of the doubt for obvious reasons, but . . . I do not think you were ever very good at chess. What made you think you could beat me this morning?"

I shrugged. "I just assumed I'd be good at it. Huh. Lesson learned."

He chuckled. "Oh, Max. You are incorrigible."

"You encourage me, too, mate. Thanks." I stretched. "Have you rented out your place in Darlo?"

"I sold it."

"Oh." That hit hard. "What about the crab apple tree? I wanted to see it alive."

"You saw it alive, my friend. But I know what you mean. We can go on a pilgrimage, if you wish. But I will buy a new house. When my future is decided. And we can choose a tree together, and plant it there."

I was getting a bit tired. I was on the verge of talking absolute shit. "You should buy a place in Chester and rent a room to Youngster. Oh, and Pascal."

"I should become the unofficial digs? Ho. What a thought."

"There's going to be more and more super talents. Someone could make a killing renting to them. I'd do it if I had a few hundo." Time to wrap this up. I got up and went to my desk, found my pen. I spun it around my fingers and tried to summarise the discussion. "So I can plan around you being here until January. For eight hundred a week. And we'll sell you, or not, and either way is great."

"Succinct." He offered me a handshake. I accepted. "Perhaps one day I'll teach you how to play chess."

"Sure," I said.

He looked back at the far side of the room. "Perhaps it will take more than one day."

The Brig suppressed a laugh and Henri strode to the door—it was a fucking amazing exit line. I hated that I had to ruin it. "Wait," I cried. "Soz. It's just that I need you to take a coaching course."

"I will do as you ask," he said, swept his scarf around him, and left.

And I was even more astonished. He'd topped his own line! "John," I said, forgetting the cool nickname I'd invented. "Is it just me or was that cool?"

"It was the coolest thing I've seen today."

"Tough crowd. Okay, no more brain work for a bit. I'll do a jog, lunch, nap, then this evening I have a surprise for a lot of women."

The women's team was gathered around, full of pent-up energy, ready to work off the stresses and frustrations of the weekend. But first, they had to listen to me. To be fair, they didn't mind. I hadn't spent much time with them recently.

"Ladies and ladies," I said, in my speech voice. "The grandmaster is back, and this time my positional play is better than ever." I paused. Hadn't I been dreaming of a way to evolve past rigid formations and prescribed solutions? Did I really want football to be played like chess? Short term, I had no other choice. I pressed on. "This is my assistant manager, John. I make the men's team call him Brigadier because he was in the army and in my opinion, *Brigadier* sounds cool and no one knows what level it actually is."

"I know what level it is," said the Brig.

"You don't count."

"Very good, sir."

"First item of bizniz. I'm sure you've been told but just in case, the men's team and the back-office staff are going to watch the Women's World Cup semifinal on Wednesday lunchtime. England's Lionesses against the Matildas. How awesome are those names, by the way? It's not too late to rebrand you. Something mighty: Chester *Warrior Queens*. Or something sure to get us a juicy sponsorship: Chester *Coke Fiends*. I'm just saying. So, the semifinal. Any of you who can make it, you're more than welcome, and your partners or a friend. Unless they're Australian. Sicilian defenders *are* most welcome, and there will be food. Pawn cocktail sandwiches. Gambit and eggs on toast. Fianchettoed beef. And, of course, there will be plenty of forks."

Pleasantries done, I looked at my former team, who were still technically my current team, but not really. They'd have a new manager soon enough.

In terms of talent, most were pawns, and always would be. There were three players tied on CA 14 as the current best in class, and there were six who were talented enough to come with us to the next level after we got promoted. Bonnie, Lucy, and Bea Pea were knights. Pippa and Maddy had enough talent to be bishops. What's a female bishop? Not a bishopric. Ah! high priestess. And, of course, there was one grandmaster. Wait, *I* was the grandmaster; Dani was the queen. Ugh. Anyway, whether they were pawns or queens, they'd all, every single one, worked their arses off, and they'd all kept my promise to Dani that we'd have a proper team.

"So it's got all weird and awkward because of all the mad stuff that happened. I didn't want to wait too long to come and tell you that you are still my special little chess pieces and I promise never to sacrifice you to take a rook."

Bonnie, the powerful centre back with great leadership qualities, said, "Max, you're accidentally talking shit again. Is it true you made the men go on an SAS boot camp?"

I looked to the Brig. He replied, "The men's team took part in a two-and-a-half-day corporate team-building event. SAS selection involves a sixteen-mile trek across the Brecon Beacons carrying four stones of weight in a rucksack. The course must be completed in eight hours forty-five minutes. If you believe the processes to be comparable, I should like to hear more of your fresh and unique perspectives on life."

"Stop being sexy and intense, please. Thanks. That's my job." I looked up at the floodlights. "Right. Season starts in September. It's weird, isn't it, the schedule? One match every two weeks. Sundays instead of Fridays. Since you're playing semi-pro football, some of you are going to be offered semi-pro contracts." There was a little buzz of excitement. "That's going to be fun for me. I like the idea of rewarding you for your hard work and talent. But look, let's be real. Most of you will carry on the same as last season, with a bit of a pay bump. It's really not a fair reflection on how hard you worked and how fucking badass you were last year. But that's football. It's my job to be cruel. So . . . soz. I mean . . . sorry." I blew air out of my cheeks so I wouldn't start tearing up. I rubbed my lips hard. "The good news is I exploit the men even worse, so for this season at least, the pay gap won't be that bad."

I looked around. Dani, reading the text as it appeared on her phone. Pippa, looking tanned. Maddy, with a new punk-inspired trim.

"I'll talk to you all individually over the next few weeks but until then, I want you to know that I'll be checking on you this season. Watching you closely. Making sure everything's laid on that you need. To that end, I'm in the market for a really, really good coach slash manager. Sort of a Max Best replacement with more focus on coaching and less emphasis on, you know, soap opera. Basically, someone to make sure you improve as much as poss this year. Watch this space. If I'm a bit slow on that, no probs. We've got Jill, and you all know how to play. I reckon you lot would do a good job with the league this year. You'd have a good stab at it. But there's no doubt you need reinforcements.

A bit of competition all over the pitch." I tried to repress a smirk. "So I've got a surprise for you. In chess, you get your pieces and that's it. But in footy, you can just go and recruit a load of new cannon fodder. I mean, players. It took a while because I've been slow replying to all my messages, but one email I found recently was from a trio of former Man City players. They'll be coming to training on Wednesday. I don't want to hype them up or anything but . . ."

I smiled. My silence did the hyping for me.

"I'll see you on Wednesday!"

"That was interesting," said the Brig, as we jogged around a spare pitch. I was finding it possible to do multiple training sessions a day now. "Do you think they'll train harder today because of the way you made them fear for their place in the hierarchy?"

"I'm sure they will," I said. "But plus ten percent effort for one session is meaningless. No, I was uncomfortable announcing that there would be a split . . ." I waited to catch my breath. Jogging and talking was hard. "A split between the amateurs and the semi-pros. Bringing in some talents from City explodes that whole debate. The squad . . . the squad will see there's a whole different level. Three-quarter pro. I'm hoping the City ladies will seriously raise the bar. Dani will strive to catch up. Pippa and Maddy, too. And the rest won't feel so bad . . . about not being paid the same."

"If the new players are so much better, then yes."

"Well, quite. We'll see."

"You're uncomfortable with the contract discussions."

"Partly. Almost everyone works hard. Sacrifices. So I'm basing how much they get paid on how afraid I am of losing them." I was starting to pant. The Brig stopped jogging so I could catch my breath. I already knew him quite well—he'd let me finish, let me recover, and then we'd continue in silence. "So it's based on my personal assessment of their talent. Which is unfair. If I were one of the unlucky ones, I'd resent it."

"I understand. I will monitor for unhappy campers."

"Bit more jog, then I'm done for the day. Do you think we can drive around and look for my car?"

He checked one of his watches. He was down to two now. "Yes. But I won't say what you want me to say."

"Come on, it's easy. And fun. I say, 'Dude, where's my car?' Now you say . . ."

"I don't say the D-word. I'm too old."

"How old are you?"

"That's a state secret."

I knew how old he was, thanks to the curse. But telling this particular man I knew secret things about him would be absolutely insane. I didn't need to think three moves ahead to imagine where I would end up, or what would be tied around my ankles.

"How are you enjoying the job so far? Good, innit? Are you having fun?"

"I've had *more* fun."

"When?"

He smiled. Pretty rare. I knew what he was going to say, so I helped him say it. "That's a state secret."

I got a text.

MD: Do you still want Steve Alton? Hereford have come back with a lower price.

Me: Yes. £5,000 is our limit. Absolute limit. Any more is a joke. A sick joke. But our real limit is £8K. Talking of transfer fees, we need to discuss a mad, crazy, insane idea. It isn't one of mine.

I pressed send and felt a presence at my side. I got a mild shock of fear, but it came and went. The Brig was much more aware of our surroundings than I was. The terrifying newcomer was . . . Dani. She had her phone.

Dani: If you're training here, why don't you train with us?

Me: Because I'm shit.

Dani: So's Maddy. Come on.

She dashed back to the sesh, where Jill was putting them through their paces. Unlike the men, almost all the women had improved over the summer. From a lower starting point, obviously, but it hinted at a lot of excitement about the season ahead.

I showed the text to the Brig. "Health is other people," he said. So Emma had gotten to him. They were in cahoots! Training with others was tempting. The only real downside was letting everyone see how poor my movement was, how quickly I got tired.

While I was biting my thumbnail, I glanced at the Brig. "Aren't you going to shove me over there or something like that?"

"We don't have that kind of relationship, *sir.*"

"If I was Sam Topps what would you do?"

"I'd make you quit football and join the army. Plan B, take up rugby. But if you're asking my opinion, I think you joining in is a good idea."

"They'll lose respect for me."

"Are you sure?"

Just then, Jill whistled to start the first rondo. Three players in a small triangle trying to keep the ball away from two defenders. It was one of Jackie's favourites. I locked on to the nearest ball, followed it as it zipped around, and like a dog tracking the path of a plate of meat from the oven to the dining room table, I found I was very, very hungry.

Thirty seconds later, I was on the outside of a triangle, along with Maddy and Pippa. Dani and Erin were the defenders.

I lost the ball as soon as it got to me. "Guys," I said. "Can we slow down a bit? Just while I remember how to do this." I tried to sign this to Dani, but the Brig stepped forward and held his phone in front of her. She gave me a thumbs-up.

Maddy and Pippa passed the ball to me and I practised the two main types of passes needed for this. First, the instant return, which I could do no problem, there was almost literally nothing to it. Second, the half-turn and pass. That was hard. It involved a precise first touch, a good decision about who to pass to, and the need to maintain technique under intense pressure. In the past I had solutions for every obstacle—feints, disguises, annoying little hops, first-time passes disguised as instant returns, no-look chops, even dinks and lobs. In this mini-game, I'd gone from being a queen, able to move rapidly in any direction, to being a pawn, shuffling straight ahead, fearful, as the important pieces smashed into each other around me.

I did a thumbs-up. Ready.

Maddy passed and I instantly touched it back. I'd survived the first two seconds!

She passed to Pippa, who dinked a spinning ball between the defenders. Towards me. Oh, shit! I reached out a foot and was amazed to find I controlled it perfectly. I smiled at the ball—must have looked pretty goofy—as Erin pounced and took it off me. I didn't care. That felt so good.

Into the middle I went. I was supposed to run around putting pressure on the three ball players. I did what I could, but to zero effect. I couldn't compete on physical gifts; I needed to think ahead. If Pippa passed to Erin, she'd hit a wall pass to Pippa, who would spin one of those dinked passes to Maddy.

I realised everyone had stopped. Had Jill ended the drill? No, the other groups were still darting around, laughing, grunting with frustration.

"What?"

"Are you okay?" said Pippa.

"Get on with the game!" I commanded. "Jesus Christ."

I had to run around for ten seconds, to let everyone relax back into their grooves. Then I stood next to Maddy so that Pippa would pass to Erin. Erin's shaped to play the wall pass, so I went back to where Maddy was. On autopilot, Pippa played the pass I'd expected, and I intercepted the ball. Not quite the silky-smooth touch as a second ago, but my overall scheme worked.

I went to the edge, and Pippa into the middle. Dani slammed her fist into her palm. I guess it meant she wasn't going to take it easy on me. I mimed playing my bottom lip like a piano keyboard. *Oh, I'm so scared.*

Her face hardened.

The ball zipped around. I did a one-touch pass back the way it came. Then I deflected Erin's pass on an angle to Maddy. That was satisfying.

Then another pass from Maddy that I wanted to return. But Pippa could play rondo chess, too. She launched herself in the path of that option. So I opened my body and pointed to Dani's right. *Erin, I'm passing that way!* Dani stretched out a leg to intercept . . . and I nutmegged her.

Our rondo stopped. Everyone apart from Dani came to celebrate with me. I raised my fists and looked up at the heavens. My first nutmeg since the attack!

Dani stood and fumed at the scene, which made it way too funny to stop. We celebrated harder. Finally, she cracked. With an annoyed smile, she signed: *Done good job.* And then something like *Let's get on with the training.*

I was pretty terrible for the rest of the session. There were some parts where I was able to use my brain, my anticipation, or even my tactical knowledge to slightly close the gap between me and the women. But generally, I was shit. I felt like a normo—one good moment in an hour was enough to keep me motivated.

When Jill had finished her post-sesh talk, I put my hand up.

"Can I do this again?"

Match 3 of 46: Chester FC versus Chorley.

Kick-off for Tuesday evening matches was 7:45 p.m. and the under-twelves trained from 5 till 6. My new plan was to gatecrash as many training sessions as my body could handle. Starting with the women, who wouldn't kick me simply to prove how tough they were, and the under-twelves, who were one-tenth my size. When I started to feel comfortable, I'd work my way up to the fourteens. Top plan!

Spectrum was moderately appalled that I was joining in. I think he was worried I'd find the sesh too basic, but it was just what I needed. We started with a very simple passing drill. Three lines of players, the first one playing a ten-yard pass then running to the back of the next line. Even from that drill, it was shocking to see how much better Stephen Watson looked than the others. He was the PA 146 defensive midfielder I'd found while waiting for Jackie in Liverpool. He just oozed class. In the break before the next drill, I went over to rave to his dad about how good his kid was. Like all the parents, he found it weird that I was training with their sons, but I needed to train, and my enthusiasm smoothed a lot of potential bumps.

After a tiny break, my fellow children and I did the same routine but with our left foot, then with a one-two before the "long" pass, then with really long one-twos. Then Spectrum said, "Double triangle!" and the kids ran around moving the little cones. The drill was perplexing. Spectrum tried to explain it to me. I didn't get it. I wondered if I'd pushed myself too far, but the Brig suggested I'd pick it up faster from the inside. So I joined in, and made such a mess that the kids laughed at me.

Then: click. "Oh!" I said. "Only the outside triangle changes."

"That's what I said," complained Spectrum.

"You didn't."

"He did," said the Brig, the traitor.

Another good workout under my belt, a nice, warm shower, then a quick drive to the stadium. I wanted to walk but the Brig wouldn't have it.

I was feeling good. Not one hundred percent, but I felt I could see one hundred percent way off in the distance. The best thing, I thought to myself, had been intercepting Pippa's pass. That meant I still had my superhuman anticipation. I used to be pretty good at making those sorts of predictions in the old days, the pre-curse days, but the ease with which I put myself in the right place suggested I was still maxed on my mental attributes. The patch hadn't reset me, the player. In other words, every little step in my physical recovery would add to my CA.

The stadium was starting to fill. Fans loved a late home game. Many locals could walk to the stadium, have some beers, and walk home. Even more were in range of a single bus ride. What better way to spend a warm, summery evening than boozily singing on a bus after a victory?

I walked up to the director's box. MD was there with Steve Alton. He'd come to check out the vibe. Check me out. See if he was even interested in a transfer to this crackpot club.

Steve Alton was twenty-five. Born in Warrington, near Chester, he'd scrambled around non-league hoping for a big break that had never come. His time at Hereford had been a disaster—he'd barely played, and when he asked to leave, the manager froze him out. I could get him for free at the end of the season, but there was no way I'd be signing someone with his limitations in the future. He had one shot to become one of my pawns. If he agreed, I'd push him to the far side of the board and turn him into a pawn in a bishop's hat. Turn him into Glenn Ryder. Maxing his PA would make him as good as my current best defender, which was great.

I gave him the quick spiel. *Hi, I'm Max. I'd love to sign you if we can make it work. We're a community club, fan-owned, but we're ambitious. Aren't we, MD? We're ambitious and I want to win the league this year. We don't do pranks and bullying. We like players who help out with the youth teams and so on. To that end, we'll support you if you take a coaching badge. That's good for you as a player, too, because I like people who can think on the pitch. You won't come as a starter, but if you kick on like I know you will, there are spots in the lineup that are up for grabs.*

He was cautious. The fact that we'd been dicked in our first two matches worked against me. As did the fact that I was a brash twenty-three-year-old. He had one main question. "What makes you think I can improve like you say?"

"Data analysis plus the eye test. Data analysis—we've got one of those AI computers. It says you've got good positioning. The eye test—you've seen me play? I know a good defender when I see one. We've done some poking around and what we hear is that you're very professional, very determined. You need coaching and game time, and you'll get that here. Oh," I said, standing up. "You'll also get a league-winner's medal."

I laughed, gave him a friendly pat on the shoulder, and went to the manager's room to prepare for battle with Chorley.

"I want to personalise this," I said, looking at the bare walls. This was the innermost of the inner sanctums. And it was mine. "Photos of me everywhere. That kind of thing."

The Brig took his seat. He had a newspaper under one arm and a notebook and coffee in his hands. He laid everything out.

I held up my hands. "Mate. Is that the *Daily Mail*?"

"Yes. I like to stay up to date with events. You never know when a job opportunity might arise in one of the world's many trouble spots."

"We don't like that particular publication in this stadium."

"Oh? A lot of people told me you worked with the *Mail*."

I sighed. "Look, read what you want. Just don't let me see any headlines about 'brown people.'"

"Very good, sir." He opened the paper, carefully put finger and thumb together, removed two sheets, and threw the rest into the bin. I grinned. The Brig had a sense of humour! He saw that I'd enjoyed his joke and opened his notepad. "Can you guide me through your thought process at this point?"

"About Steve Alton?"

"No, I understand that. You need an experienced player who can come into the team, first as strategic reserve, then as vanguard. I meant the starting lineup."

"Oh!" I said, leaning forward, pulse jumping. He'd given me full licence to show off. "Right. Well, you'd think this time would be really intense, all smoke and mirrors, feints and counter-feints stuff where me and the other manager tried to disguise our intentions from each other. Lying about which players were injured in the media. Arranging to be papped by journalists testing out a custom four-three-three you have no intention of using. But it's not like that."

"You seem disappointed."

"I want to win the league and it's good if the other managers are lazy and unimaginative. But yeah . . . I do respond to a challenge. So Chorley. Pretty typical opponents in this league. We played them in my second match as caretaker manager. They went four-four-two, on paper a slightly stronger squad than us, good goalie, two good CMs, a good striker, and a fast left back. They had a slow and old right back. They've upgraded the right back but lost one of the two central midfielders. And in the last match, their fast left back didn't attack much because we took a grip on the game after eight minutes." Chorley's average CA from last season had been 43, now it was 42. We'd started the previous encounter with a CA of 40.8. Today's lineup would be 40.2.

"Robbo's in goal—as you know, I want him to get a run-out. Get his season up and running. I think it'll help him train. If he out-trains Ben, he'll get his place back.

"Today's defence isn't the strongest I could field. Trick's still working off his summer boozing, the prick. Gerald and Glenn are a bit off the pace, too. Carl's actually improving, which I despaired of ever happening. I've got Magnus on the bench—he can cover all those positions. Oh, Trick's in because he's left-footed. When we get our attacks going, it's ideal to have a left-footed player in that role. But he's by far the worst player in the team. I'm tempted to switch to three-five-two soon so that I don't have to even look at him.

"But it's four-one-four-one, and that means Youngster's in as the DM. My aim is to play him in half the games this season. Other matches we'll use Magnus as DM—which is why we need another defender. Or we'll use a different formation. Four-one-four-one gives us a lot of control and lets us attack down the wings. And if we've only got one striker, players don't kick the ball long hoping the strikers can do something with it; he's outnumbered four to one. It sort of forces us to play the way I want us to play. So that's our default, but it does mean we rely on James and Magnus being fit.

"Then Aff and D-Day on the wings. D-Day's annoying, but he's flexible. If I want to switch formation midgame, he lets me do it. Chorley are a load of wind-up merchants, and when teams are trying to distract me and cause a bit of chaos, I like to switch our formation. We can easily shift to four-four-two but no one on their bench will notice when they're doing their antics."

"This is the chess part."

"It's chess if one player knew the exact value of every piece and could make five moves to every one from his opponent, who also didn't even know that he had a left castle playing at right pawn. All my players are in the right positions, by the way. Sounds simple, but you'd be surprised.

"Sam and Raffi are the midfield. Sam will compete and do a lot of invisible dirty work. Then Raffi will get on the ball and look good. He's really blossoming now. He's starting to play eleven-a-side the way I saw him play five-a-side in Manchester. It's exciting. We play great together. When I'm fit, we'll annihilate this league. Me, him, and Henri.

"Henri's on his own up top. When we give him a lot of chances, he doesn't dick about trying to start fights. When we don't involve him in play—which is a big risk with this formation—he can get angsty. Referees at this level don't normally go straight for the red card, but his temper does make me anxious.

"So that's the basics. I'm also trying to balance winning this match with giving players like Joe Anka game time. It's a long season and I need to use all my pieces. Apart from Robbo, the only player who hasn't had any minutes so far is Pascal."

"Does that mean he will definitely come off the bench today?"

"I'm leaning towards not using him. He was shocking against these guys last time. I'm not sure of his psychology. He'd probably overcompensate. He's my fastest player, my best presser, but he's still not connecting well with the other guys, which is weird given how much Raffi loves him. Pascal's too smart for most, and the pitches are too shit for the intricate passing moves he initiates. I'll be handling his career very carefully. When I'm fit, that'll be good for him. He'll be a key player when I'm around." And by the time I was naming myself in the team, Pascal's CA should have risen from 30 closer to the 40 that was really the baseline for a Chester player. A thought that irritated me, since *six* of our starting eleven were under 40. "Don't worry about him. I'm on it. What else do you want to know?"

"There's no place for the Harrisons?"

"Not for months, no. Think of them as ornate chess pieces you ordered and they're in the post. From . . . where's the place in the world it takes the longest for post to come from?"

"Belfast." He looked at his notes. "You say Chorley like to cause chaos. Wind-up merchants. How would you like me to behave?"

"Can you do a one-inch punch?"

"Everyone can do a one-inch punch."

"Can you punch someone, from an inch away, and send them flying across a stadium?"

He wrestled with his answer. Finally, he said, "No."

"All right. So just keep our guys calm. If they get angsty, make them stay on the bench. If they're reacting to something on the pitch, let them vent. Like a bad tackle or whatever. You can't stop someone getting worked up about that. It's actually bad if they *don't*. But if they're being worked up by what the other manager is doing, calm them down or fuck them off."

"That would be falling into the enemy's trap."

"Right. If I ever need a spontaneous reaction to something, I'll tell you in advance so we can plan it."

"Understood. By the way, is Neymar a player of particular renown?"

"Yes. On talent alone, probably the third best in the world. Top five, anyway. Paris bought him for a world-record fee. That was a real statement of intent from them."

"Since I took this position, my friends and family have been trying to engage me in football-related banter. Today my nephew wrote to suggest Chester, ahem, place a cheeky bid for Neymar."

"Is there some Neymar news that I've missed?"

"He is joining the Saudi Pro League for one hundred million Euros. Rather a lot of Steve Altons."

Neymar to the SPL? Mind. Blown. I tried to work out the ramifications. More attention and hype for the SPL. Less for the French league. If Henri was around, I would have said "even less attention for the French league." What did it mean for Chester? For me? What would happen next? I couldn't get my head around it. My chess skills weren't up to the task of understanding how the Saudi Pro League would reshape my sport.

The tactics board still had Chorley at 4-4-2. I wandered along the side of the pitch, wearing my baseball cap but no sunglasses. The AirPods were in my pocket for if I needed a break from all the stimulation. I listened to the crowd, waved at a few kids, and wandered back to the dugout.

"Max," said someone.

I blinked. "Chad!"

Chad Flintoff. I'd named him in my very first lineup as a professional football manager. He'd given me the option to switch from 4-4-2 to 4-3-3, but his low CA meant he wasn't someone I'd have used very often this season. Fortunately, when I'd been in hospital, he'd left Chester. I hadn't thought about him since classifying him as a traitor in my Nick-induced state of paranoia. Now, here he was, standing awkwardly next to me.

I held out my hand; he shook it with relief.

"Oh, Max, I felt like shit leaving like that. But what could I do?"

"Don't sweat it. It's natural. You were right to."

"It's just . . . you never replied to my text so I thought maybe . . ."

I whipped out my phone, showed him the hundred plus unread messages. "Blue light still fucks me up. I'm answering a few a day. Getting better. I'll get to yours soon enough!"

"Oh," he said, scratching his cheek. "Sorry, I didn't realise . . . I shouldn't have . . ."

"Mate, relax. So you're at Chorley now? That's crazy. You're not on the bench, though."

"Got a little ankle thing. But . . . Look. I don't want you thinking I'm a Judas or anything. But I told the gaffer a few things. He was dead interested. I . . . didn't think anything of it till later. Thought maybe I shouldn't of."

I did a quizzical grin. "What did you tell him?"

"Like, just how you know what formations teams are going to play and stuff. How you look at a bench and guess what changes they'll make. You know . . . Max stuff."

I still couldn't quite work out what he was saying. It was like someone had moved a chess piece off the left of the board and it had reappeared on the right. But I had just enough about me to open Chorley's tactics screen. And they'd changed formation!

I gasped. I sucked in air so dramatically the Brig shot to my side, ready to catch me if I fell. "Sir?"

"I'm all right," I said, as my lips pulled themselves out and up. I might have some work to do after all! "Seems like Chad here taught his boss how to play chess." I gave him a high-ten, and jogged to my technical area, impatient for the match to start.

Chorley's manager—I'll call him Charlie—had obviously had a big old think about what I'd done to him and had come up with a 4-1-4-1 smasher. A block-busting tactic to negate my advantages!

I have to say, I was impressed.

The problem of having a single defensive midfielder—a single pivot—is that he could be closed down. And if you lock down the pivot, you stop the team from turning.

You guessed it—he was going to man-mark Youngster!

Charlie had gone for a 4-4-1-1 formation. It was basically the standard 4-4-2, but with one of the strikers dropping one zone to be more like a CAM. But the player chosen for the role wasn't attacking by nature—he was a midfielder with good stamina and tackling.

There was so much fun I could have had with this if I had complete freedom to move my players anywhere, but I didn't. Still, I—

I paused, turned, and checked to see if the imps were in the same seats as last time. They weren't. Why was I thinking about imps? Wibwob. The tactics imp wanted me to buy Wibwob. Maybe Wibwob was the key to complete tactical flexibility.

Anyway, limitations could be liberating, as a famous French chess player once said. I needed to learn formations, step by step, even if it cost me a bit of time and effort.

I switched my team to 4-4-2, with D-Day joining Henri up front, and Youngster playing right mid. Youngster in the Max Best role! He was deeply unsuited to it.

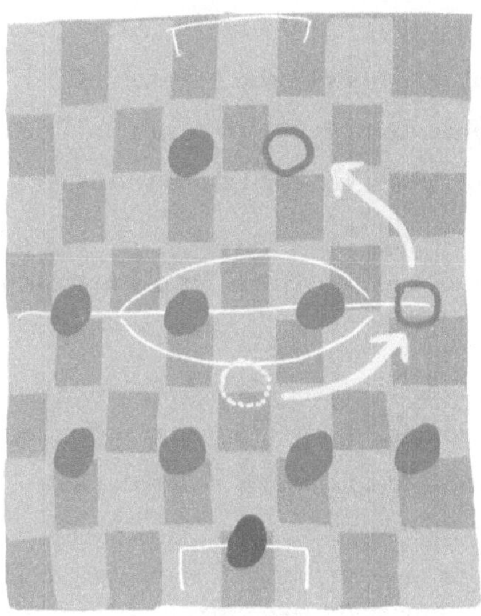

But if I understood the marking instruction, Chorley's CAM would follow Youngster over to his new position. The CAM would get in the way of his own left midfielder. It was a trick I'd tried a couple of times before; the other team's manager normally ended their man-marking experiment within minutes.

I bit my nail—I didn't want this mistake to be corrected. I wanted the CAM to play double left mid for as long as possible.

So I mixed-and-matched two of my oldest tactical innovations. I reset the team to 4-1-4-1. I would disguise what I was doing. At every break, I'd get Youngster to drift back to his DM slot, and once the match had restarted, he'd wander off to the right of the pitch, taking his marker with him.

I set Aff as playmaker and instructed everyone to pass left.

My fullbacks wouldn't have much defensive work to do, so I set them to make forward runs.

The match kicked off. I wandered up and down my technical area, trying not to give the game away by grinning too hard. "Brig," I said. "Can you stand next to me and look worried?"

"Here?"

"No, the other side. I don't want them to see me laughing."

"Very good, sir."

The match quickly fell into an absurd shape. Exactly as I wanted. It was so abnormal that even my rugby-loving assistant could see it. "Sir . . . this isn't what we practised."

"No, mate. This is what chess would look like if you could stack three pieces on one square. Fuck, I'm about to cackle. Cover me." Saying "cover me" to the army guy made me nearly lose my shit, so I went back to the dugout. I peeked out from the side to see what Charlie was doing. He was going absolutely ballistic. And quite right, too.

Trick receives the ball. He pushes forward.

Raffi takes control. He nudges the ball to Aff.

Aff shapes to dribble, but plays a pass out to Trick.

Raffi takes a square pass. He has two options to his left.

He chooses Aff.

Trick takes a defender away with a lung-bursting run.

Aff swings it in.

GOOOAAALLL!!!!

Henri powered through two defenders to head home!

Chester are playing like they have an extra man.

My players celebrated—our first goal of the season! The Brig's job on goals was to stand in front of me and make sure no players came anywhere near me. Footballers are always breaking their necks doing somersault celebrations. Or take the case of Steve Morrow—he scored the winning goal in the 1993 League Cup final, and during the celebrations he was dropped to the floor and broke his arm. He watched the rest of the party from hospital.

Yeah, go over there and celebrate with the fans, you idiots.

When the stupidity had subsided, I switched back to 4-1-4-1, but this time I let that stick for five minutes. When I felt that Charlie had relaxed, I switched it all back again, and the fun continued.

We dominated down the left to amusing proportions, got into prime slapping position, and a defender fouled Aff. Yellow card, free kick in a dangerous position, and Max Best used that famous chess move called "mashing the Free Hit button."

I didn't really have a direct free-kick specialist, apart from me, obviously, so we generally treated free kicks in shooting positions like angled corners. This time, Aff hit his cross a bit softer, which I wasn't a big fan of because it meant the guy on the other end had to generate more power with his neck muscles to beat the keeper.

Aff with the free kick.

He approaches the ball.

Sent into the corridor of uncertainty . . .

It's onto the head of Gerald May . . .

GOOOAAAALLLL!!!!

A magnificent header.

More celebrations—even wilder. May didn't score too many, even though he was tall. The curse told me his heading wasn't as good as the naked eye said.

We were 2–0 up and our key player, our pivot, was on 4 out of 10.

I peeked and saw Charlie gesticulating at the CAM who'd been set to mark Youngster. I was pretty sure that experiment would soon be over, until halftime anyway. Maybe Charlie had another trick up his sleeve. Maybe he'd even be stupid enough to try it out.

I reset my team. 4-1-4-1, normal instructions, no extra help from me or the curse. Youngster would set the tempo, we'd try to slap down the sides of the penalty box.

Next to me was the most powerful piece—the Brig. To the side, Vimsy, Dean, Livia. Jude was in the executive box making notes. Tips on how to improve in the second half.

On and off the pitch, the team was following my plan.

A chant echoed around the stadium, followed by a round of applause as Robbo sprinted out to clear a long pass. The fans were enjoying it. Up in the box, MD would be mumbling to members of the board that he needed to put eight grand on the company credit card.

Yeah. I'd done well.

I put my AirPods in, pressed play on some Chopin, leaned back so I could almost fall asleep, and let my pawns do battle for me. Sometimes it felt good to be the king.

DUDE, WHERE'S YOUR CAR?

Chester Check Chorley Charge; Boss Best Boosts Blues

Chester FC got their season up and running with a cool 3–1 win over high-flying Chorley today at the Deva Stadium. After losing their first two matches, the Seals looked more like the team that finished last season in rampant style, particularly in a fast, energetic first half. After the break, Chorley improved and pulled a goal back, but Donny Dorigo scored after a goalmouth scramble to settle nerves and settle the match.

A healthy 2,100 fans turned out to witness good individual performances from Diarmuid Dubhlainn and Raffi Brown, while teenage star James Yalley struggled.

Manager Max Best looked much healthier, continuing his remarkable recovery from life-threatening injuries, and was in his usual belligerent mood in the post-match press conference.

Max, it was a tough second half, but you scraped through with a win. How do you feel?

Scraped? Wow. Okay. Yeah, I feel fine. Thanks for taking the time to discuss feelings with another man. If we all did a little more of that, we'd be a lot happier and healthier. How are *you* feeling, Gary?

The referee made some questionable decisions.

Questionable decisions? How about we start with your haircut and this French tuck thing you're doing?

Who was your player of the match?

You have to give it to Aff [Dubhlainn] for his two assists, but Raffi Brown caught the eye. Chorley have a good midfield so I think that was Raffi's best performance yet.

James Yalley struggled.

No, he didn't.

He barely touched the ball in the first half.

He created two goals with his movement. It's fine you didn't notice, but don't tell me he played badly. That's annoying. He did exactly what I told him to.

You dropped Ben Cavanagh. Is that because he conceded four goals in two matches?

Referees, scapegoats, dropped players. Come on, Gary. I'm not doing this for the next ten months. I'm paying twenty players to be ready to play football matches, but I can only use eleven at once. Who plays is based on a superabundance of factors including how much they laugh at my jokes. Using words like *dropped* is reductive. The modern football fan understands rotation. Why don't you?

Players play poorly sometimes.

Not my lot. They play badly when I ask them to do things they can't do. That's on me. My players are sweet as.

Sam Topps hobbled off. How serious is it?

Famously, I have X-ray vision so I already know the answer, but I've sent him for a scan just in case. I doubt I'll use him against Banbury, if that's the question you were trying to ask.

Banbury beat you in the same fixture last season. What are you hoping for this time?

Maybe it's my traumatic brain injury talking, but I seem to remember after that narrow 1–0 loss, you declared us "as good as relegated." But we finished fourteenth. It's almost as though you don't have the first clue about football. That's weird, isn't it? It's also weird that I have to talk to you or the club will get a fine. That doesn't seem right, does it? Almost un-British. What am I hoping for from the match? I think I'd like a 90–0 win. With all ninety goals being scored by someone you scapegoated or said I dropped.

You're clearly on the mend. Is there any chance of seeing you in a Chester shirt this season?

I hope to be physically able to do it, yeah, but as the manager, I have to be very careful. We've got great team spirit; it's a good group. Introducing a volatile character like Max Best to the playing staff could be incendiary. If he wants a place in the team, he needs to work a lot harder on his attitude. That's all I really have to say about that guy.

Good win today.

Thanks.

Wednesday, August 16.

Training was pretty chill. It was more like an extended warm-down, with some chats about what went right and wrong the night before. I stood to the side and kept an eye on the lads while thinking about Sam. His injury was small but left a big hole in our midfield. After thinking about my options, I called Magnus, Jude, and Vimsy over and said I was interested in using Magnus in central midfield on Saturday, so could they please plan the rest of the week with that in mind. They fucked off, discussing it.

"It's good to have someone so flexible," said the Brig.

"Yeah, he's ace. I keep waiting for him to hit his ceiling but he's showing no signs of that."

"What makes you think he has a ceiling?"

"Everyone has a ceiling." But unlike Sam, whose PA was 60, or Glenn, who was all too close to his PA of 54, Magnus's was -2. What did it mean? What could it mean? If the best player in the team had CA 100, could Magnus get to 98? The only way to find out was to keep using him, keep pushing him, until he stopped growing. Maybe then I'd find out what -2 meant. "He's hard to read, in terms of talent. But he's reliable and intelligent. If I start him at left back in four-four-two, I could switch him to right mid in a three-five-two. Amazing. I want to use him as much as poss, but if I keep throwing him all over the place, there's a chance he won't ever learn a position."

"Is that bad?"

"Not too sure, to be honest. When I started playing, I didn't really know the nuances of any role. I played and trained enough at right mid to do well there. It wouldn't stop *me* learning another position, but as we move up the leagues, generalists might have less of a role. We'll need specialists . . . I think. For now, Magnus is a bit of a secret weapon."

"You often mention three-five-two but we don't practise that, do we?"

"The lads know it from Jackie Reaper's time." The main reason we didn't practise it was that I hadn't unlocked it yet. I was 1,000 XP short.

XP balance: 1,348

Debt repaid: 1,791/3,000

The 3-5-2 perk was 2,200 XP. That was a pretty essential formation for me to have with the men's team, and would be perfect for the women's team if the Man City newcomers were as good as I hoped. But I had to consider other options.

Morale was 2,000 XP. It would show me a player's state of mind. "Brig, what do you think of the mood, generally?"

He swept his eye across the pitches. "Very good. Everyone has had playing time, except Bochum and the Harrisons, who understand their exclusion. The players believe they will be given chances to show their skills and get playing time. They believe you when you say their improvement is your top priority. Between you and me, sir . . ."

"Go on."

"They like that you substitute Henri when he isn't playing well. And that you use Trick. You have favourites and . . . anti-favourites, but that doesn't seem to come into your footballing decisions. It's more like a meritocracy than at other clubs."

"They've told you this, have they?"

"I have been trying to get to know the troops, sir."

"Do they talk to you?" I said, surprised.

"I am very personable, sir," he said with a hint of a rebuke.

"Mint."

If the Brig was going to help monitor morale, me buying the perk could wait a minute. Going down the contracts route (Contracts 1 was 1,000 XP) could supercharge my transfer market activities by telling me what other teams were paying their players and who had how long left on their contracts. Also, as a tiny side bonus, if I unlocked it fast enough, I'd finally be able to solve the mystery of whether Ian Evans had been trying to line his own pockets when he'd suggested we recruit a player and pay half his salary.

Then there was Injuries for 3,000. It seemed absolutely essential, but on the other hand, I had a medical staff. Whereas if I bought Condition for 2,000 XP, I'd start getting fitness data from players, and knowing that could help me prevent injuries from ever developing.

And I needed to keep unlocking attributes! I thought of myself as having judging player ability 20, but that wasn't true, was it? If I only added two attributes per season, it wouldn't be true for years.

I was starting to get frustrated, but Vimsy ended training and a bunch of players came over to ask me to explain why I'd moved James to right mid and switched to 4-4-2. They knew my changes had given us two goals, but they couldn't work out why. I was about to explain in the most show-off way possible, then thought about Chad Flintoff telling his new manager how I worked. Did I want more of that? In two seasons, virtually no one in the current squad would still be at the club. If I spilled the beans, there would be twenty managers who knew about my man-marking trick.

I batted the enquiries away with a knowing smirk, and after showers and whatnot, we went to a bar we'd rented to watch the lunchtime World Cup semifinal.

I tried to mingle, to give time to all the little groups, and partly succeeded. But while England dominated and looked comfortable for most of the match, Australia's Sam Kerr appeared out of nowhere and equalised with a thunderbolt. So I retreated to my assigned spot in an area with MD, Henri, the Brig, Vimsy, and Jill.

The entire men's team were there, including Sam, whose injury had come just as I was about to make a sub—he got kicked at a helpful time, what a pro— and all the physios. Wives and girlfriends had turned up in numbers, which was good because they were the only ones drinking. I was astonished to see Steve Alton—it turned out Glenn had invited him. That's why Glenn was the captain. I loved that people were thinking of details like that and not relying on me to do everything.

A fair bunch of the women's team had come. Not Dani—she lived in Crewe and they were away on their summer holidays anyway. But Bonnie, Robyn, Maddy, Pippa, Lucy, and Bea Pea had all cancelled some plans or swapped shifts. We also had Inga, Secretary Joe, Ruth, Bulldog, and Sumo. The last three weren't members of the board any longer. Their terms had ended and they couldn't stand for re-election for another year. I'd have to get to know seven new people.

It was good to see Ruth. First because she was smoking hot and a thing of beauty is a joy forever. But also because I hadn't seen her (except at a distance) since the attack. We needed to have a private chat and talk about the women's team—she'd financed it—and our nascent agency.

The match was too tense to really enjoy. Every time I convinced myself England were in control, Australia had a chance that they probably should have scored. Sam Topps and Tony had bonded with the women's team and from the start were just as into the match as me. The rest of the squad got sucked in through the quality of the play, the narratives, and the tension. After an hour, the vibe was identical to watching the men's team.

Finally, finally, England scored a second, then a third. Near the beginning of my footballing journey, these women had set the country's imaginations aflame by winning the European Championships, but what if they won the actual World Cup? Holy shit. They'd got to England's first World Cup final since the men won it in 1966. They were ninety minutes from eternal glory.

I annoyed everyone—especially the women—by demanding to see replays of Lauren Hemp's sublime double-spin and reversed pass that led to the third goal. Everyone else wanted to see the celebrations. Celebrations? Who cared? I'd just seen someone do something impudent that both took the piss and led to a goal. And she'd done it in the biggest game of her life. Who cared about people running around taking selfies? Show me the skill. The talent!

While most of the English people sang and danced, MD and I, along with Henri, stood in front of the main TV. I watched Hemp's brilliance one last time and sighed.

"What are you thinking?" said MD.

"Last night we competed with Chorley. It was an even game. For a while, my tricks allowed Aff to strut his stuff, and we got two goals out of it. Second half was one–all. So far this season, we've been relying on those little moments of magic to create opportunities. At the end of last season, we had this . . . thing. This vibe, that led to chances. It was like . . ." I closed my eyes, trying to remember. "Like a car-assembly plant. Every pass was a little conveyor belt pushing the ball closer to goal, then a tiny Frenchman would drive the car out of the plant and into the world. That's a metaphor for scoring a goal, by the way."

"I am not tiny," whinged Henri.

"You're not? You're good at chess so I assumed you were a tiny dweeb."

"I'm average at chess. You, Max, are tragic."

"As I was saying, MD, we had something, we lost it, I don't know how to get it back. This England team are impressive. They have a way of finding a collective solution."

MD scratched his nose. "I don't think I totally understand what you're saying."

"I'm saying . . . we need an identity. And we need to keep in touch with the top of the table for the first half of the season. If things go to plan, the second half of the season will be like that." I pointed to the screen. "Our players finding ways to win. Taking my ideas and turning them into actual, real-life moves. We did the boot camp . . ."

"Which was crazy expensive," whined MD. The army guys had actually done it at cost price as a favour to the Brig.

"I wonder what else we can do? Simple team-building shit. Or maybe our improvement will bring its own morale?"

"Max, what the fuck are you talking about?" said Henri. "You are gibbering. The team is fine. It is playing in an identical way to the matches you managed last season."

"No, we're off it."

"You're off your 'ed."

The Brig checked his watch. The only watch on his left wrist! I was excited to think he'd gone full civilian, but noticed he was wearing one on his right wrist, too. "Sir, are we done here?"

"Er . . . yes. What? Do you think I should thank everyone for coming or something?"

"Perhaps I might say a few words."

Weird. "Absolutely." I couldn't wait to hear this!

The Brig stood in the centre of the space and tapped on a glass. Someone turned the volume down on the conversations. "It's time," he said.

Something crazy happened—the players from the first team gathered in little groups. It didn't take long for me to realise it was the same groups they'd been put in during boot camp. Glenn grabbed Steve Alton and Bonnie. Defenders unite! Other groups absorbed the women's team and the physios.

The Brig cleared his throat. "Operation D Where's Your Car? will now commence. Remember, if you find it, do not post the number plate to social media. Group captains, you've got your routes. Keep in touch. Group One, initiate."

Glenn led his team out. Their WAGs followed. Sam's team went next, then Raffi's, and so on. Soon the bar was almost deserted. "What the shit?" I said.

"It's a nice day," said the Brig. "We're going to find your car. If we split up, we can cover the entire city centre. I've given each team a route that will cover virtually every street. The rest of us," he said, looking at MD, Ruth, Inga, Joe, Sumo, and Bulldog, "will remain and coordinate."

"Wait, why are they doing this?" I said, meaning the players. "Did you volunteer them?"

"No. Didn't have to. They think it's fun."

"What do the winners get? The dudes who find my car?"

"Immunity from being kidnapped, was Glenn's suggestion."

I laughed. "All right but fuck this. I want to walk around, too."

The Brig looked at Ruth, who glared at him and handed over what looked like ten pounds. "We thought you might say that. I've saved a few streets for you."

"Good. What's the name of the operation again?"

"D Where's Your Car?"

"What does the D stand for?"

"I'm not sure, sir. I can look into it and get back to you."

"Lead the way, then. Let's go find my car."

We went slowly, chatting, talking about the England match, or Chester, or all sorts of other things.

Ruth said Bark, the young right winger from Darlington, was "poised" to sign with our agency later in the season when it was time to start considering his options. Until then, he wanted to focus on his football. Dani was still too young to sign anything. Everything else was on hold until I was fully back, finding players. She asked about the Triplets. I looked around—I'd been keeping everyone in the dark about how good the Harrisons were. "Great for Chester, not for the agency," I mumbled.

Inga told me she had missed my mad requests when I was gone. I promised a swift return to madness. She put her arm through mine—Emma would be furious!

Bulldog complained about Noah Harrison. He said I needed to get to the sixteens and do to Noah what I'd done to Tyson. When I asked why, Bulldog described a player who was cocky, arrogant, and disruptive. I tried not to smile too hard—he was describing Tyson from a year ago. I assured him the progress of all the kids was constantly monitored and the sixteens were no exception. He said, yeah but Noah's *really* a prick. I replied that I'd heard he was fast, direct, always looking to make things happen and if, sometimes, his teammates weren't on the same wavelength as him, he was hardly to blame. Was he? "In fact," I said thoughtfully, "from what I hear, this Noah kid is the future of Chester Football Club." Bulldog fumed so hard I had to laugh, and when he realised I was winding him up, he nearly boiled over. When I moved away to talk to Joe, Bulldog was shaking his head with a rueful grin. I was his kryptonite.

Ruth and MD had a good chat, and a sneaky glance as I pretended to look in a shop window showed that he was just as into her as ever. Ruth, as always, gave him zero encouragement.

Sumo had heard that the Brig was ex-military, so of course he wanted to discuss tactics he could use in his four-v-four deathmatches, or whatever you did in those multiplayer games. I preferred to go solo.

We'd already bumped into two of the boot camp groups, and when we turned a corner and saw a third, I stopped and pulled the Brig aside. "What are you up to?"

"Sir?"

"You've got our route overlapping all the other routes. You want me to see the lads out and about, on this wild goose chase. But why?"

"I'm sure I don't know what you mean, sir. It's possible I made a mistake with the route plans."

"My arse. You planned this to within an inch of its life."

"As you say, sir."

His face gave nothing away. "Huh," I said, and that was the signal to move on.

Across the road, Glenn's unit was smiling and laughing with some shoppers. Posing for selfies, answering questions, all the stuff footballers did. They usually did it inside or just outside a stadium, though. Sometimes in a hospital or school. I looked around. The vibe in town was awesome. Word had spread that loads of footballers were milling around. People were excited and Bonnie was just as big a hit as Glenn. I still didn't know what her initial objection to joining us had been, but she was all the way in now.

This is it, I thought. *This is it.*

"Is this it?" said Secretary Joe. He showed me a photo on his phone—one of the other teams had spotted a car that mostly fit the description of mine.

"No, but it's close. Mine's in much worse condition. The more rust, the more likely it is to be The Duchess."

"Okay." Joe tapped away on his screen.

"You're enjoying this," I said.

"Oh? Well, yes, I am. It's old-fashioned, isn't it? Like a scavenger hunt, but there's only one egg. It's a nice thing to do for you, and everyone's having a nice time in their groups. Connecting with the community as they go. Helps that the sun's out." He smiled. "I'll admit I thought John Smith's salary was excessive, but we've had one good round of publicity, and this will be another."

"Publicity?"

"Fans loved the boot camp stuff. There was a child who did his own boot camp. Slept in his tent. Carried a brick from one side of his garden to the other. And so on. Very cute. MD was happy. The sponsors love that stuff."

"And you think this will turn into something? I didn't have the Brig down as a marketing genius."

"That's the point. It's authentic. If you try to make things like this happen for PR, they tend to fall flat."

"Max! Max!" Ruth dashed over, big smile, many teeth. "Is this your car?"

She pressed into me, showing a photo of Raffi doing a Maxy Two-Thumbs next to a shitty brown Subaru. "Yes! Holy shit! Dude, there's my car!"

We got the location and practically skipped towards it. The other groups headed that way, too.

Ten minutes later, twenty employees of Chester Football Club watched as I confirmed that yes, that was my car. It was a joyous moment. I didn't remember parking it here, had no memory of this particular side street. I would have found it eventually, but how much better was it like this? My team, my team, my actual football team, my mates, my comrades, had banded together to help me out.

It felt like winning a trophy. I couldn't stop smiling. I hugged all sorts of people. Indiscriminately hugging everyone within arm's reach. I'm pretty sure Ruth took a step closer, while MD took a step away. It didn't matter; he got enveloped.

I felt energised and ready to take on the world. Health is other people. Wow. True story.

I'm the king of the world! Whoo!

"Bagsy shotgun!" said Maddy. She was reserving the right to go in the front passenger seat on my triumphant first drive.

I tapped my trouser pocket.

Suddenly I let out a wail. A moan of anguish. All the phones that were being held up to record the moment "for the socials" were trained on me. "Dude!" I called out to a cold, uncaring universe. "Where's my car keys?"

I rested in my flat while the Brig went to the hospital to find out where they'd put my valuables. They claimed to have given everything back, which I thought was bad news. But the Brig's eyes were darting around, calculating. He was *fizzing.*

"Sir, according to Mr. Yalley, the person who struck you bent before running away. It's possible he picked up your keys. You could have had them in your hands, the faster to open your car door, which in your agitated state of mind you had forgotten was parked elsewhere."

I couldn't remember if I'd taken my keys out or not, but it was very possible. So the guy clubs me over the head, and as Mr. Yalley rushes towards him, he picks up my keyring and scoots off? "He would have got my house keys, too, but that place was in Darlington. And I didn't have anything worth stealing. Just a load of weird post-it notes. The whole idea is crazy."

"People behave strangely under stress. I can't imagine stealing your keys was the main motivation for the attack. But if he did steal them, he might still have them. A trophy."

I scratched the back of my head. It felt absolutely normal. "So . . . we have our suspects. We ask to check their houses. Try to find my keys. Something like that?"

"A wonderfully novel approach." His lips twitched. "However, on this matter, it might be better if you remain in the dark, so to speak."

"Do you know how to break into a house?"

"Of course not. On an unrelated note, I drove your car to a garage and they are going to change the locks and so on. They have to order the parts. They are, ah . . . no longer common."

Guy was dissing my car! Not acceptable. "How did you unlock the car, John? How did you start the car, John?"

He put his index finger to his bottom lip. "You know, those are good questions. I find I can't quite remember." He checked one of however many watches he was wearing. "Are you ready to go?"

"Yep."

"What do we expect from the new players?"

"Massive boost in standards. A squad-building shortcut like no other. Guaranteed promotion. We should try to make a good impression."

"Ah. Perhaps not the black hoodie, then."

I put my hands on my hips. "Wow. Emma did a number on you, didn't she? Our relationship doesn't extend to you complaining about my hoodie, which is all the rage in Darlington, by the way, or my car, which is extremely reliable. Are we totes clear on that?"

"Excessively clear, sir. I shall refrain from commenting on the item."

The way he said "the item" put my teeth on edge. I picked up my kit bag and strode to the door.

Training was good. I'd asked Jude to take the session to show us at our best. Dani was away on her summer holiday, but everyone else turned up. Lots of interest in the newcomers.

The three girls were exciting. They were all from Greater Manchester. The first two had Chloe Kelly-style bleached blonde hair in a long ponytail. The third had an awful, boyish, K-pop sort of trim. Really puzzling. She was shy and timid, until she got the ball to feet.

Gail was a twenty-two-year-old striker. CA 29, PA 122. Big talent! She'd fucking crush whatever goalscoring records the sixth tier had.

Mary was a twenty-one-year-old left back. CA 24, PA 99. A stupendous addition to the team. I could move Lucy to left-sided centre back, maybe. But as far as I was concerned, Mary was our locked-in starter. She was so good it was tactically problematic—we would *have* to play four at the back. It would limit the new manager's options in the best possible way.

Charlotte was the shy one. She was twenty-one, central midfielder, CA 23, PA 101.

We did half an hour of Jude's best drills—shamelessly copied from Jackie Reaper—then did a short-sided match at the end.

I joined in, and whether it was the life-affirming wholesomeness of the day or the thrill of seeing three high-quality players drop into my lap, I couldn't tell you. But I found my body was more willing to obey me. In the match, I played DM behind Charlotte, and found she was as good as her profile suggested. I went back to my old standby—one-touch—and anytime the ball came near me, I deflected it to her.

She was rusty—the three of them had tried to stay in shape but I could imagine their CAs had been on a slow decline ever since they'd left Man City and found themselves training with third- or fourth-tier outfits. But despite her ring rust, Charlotte was a luxury model. Forget the haircut, the introverted way she held herself. She was a baller.

Gail, the striker, was absolutely lethal—she punished any mistake, made runs, was strong with great technique. Bonnie couldn't deal with her. Meanwhile, the connection between Mary and Gail was one of those telepathic ones like Raffi and I had. Mary would play a seemingly pointless pass, only for the defence to realise Gail had started sprinting to collect it.

By the end of the match, I was already thinking about next season. This season was *done*. Next, though, we'd need a top goalie. Another centre back. The season after, we'd need to upgrade Bea Pea.

We showered and I hung around waiting to take them to a bar to chat them up and get them to sign. They would raise the standard so dramatically it wasn't even funny. And they'd take the pressure off Dani. Allow her to blossom at her own pace without being the player we looked to every time we needed a bit of magic.

The Brig drove me in his car while the women followed in theirs. The Brig was already a fucking five-star expert in Chester's hospitality scene, and he recommended a place that was both cool enough to showcase Chester's delights to women from the big city while being cosy and friendly enough to promote conversation. And, he added, there were clear lines of sight.

"That was sweet as!" I said when we were all settled with our drinks. "Gail, your movement is fantastic. Top technical quality, badass attitude. It's obviously not something you can really *see* but knowing you were coached by Sandra makes sense. You've got that Man City vibe to a tee. You're way better than the strikers I saw her with, though. It was bad enough playing her with a squad that didn't have forwards. I bet *your* year fucking smashed every competition you were in. Mary, talk about vision! If you can meet short passes and long and treat those imposters just the same. Wow. Natural fitness. A fullback with the heading of a centre half! Fuck me. And Charlotte. Mate. Man City love to churn out a midfielder and, shit, you're just class. I'm absolutely buzzing."

It was true. I couldn't stop smiling. I took another few seconds to enjoy imagining the final league table. Played 22, won 22, goals for 122, goals against 4. Something like that.

"We'll smash this division. Add another three like you next summer, smash tier five. My problem then will be trying to convince you to stay. We can't get promoted every year, you'll say." I leaned forward. "But we will. There's absolutely nothing to stop us going straight to the WSL." The Women's Super League, the equivalent of the Premier League. "I reckon we'll be able to start having a go at cups in the third tier. It's possible Dani will be unplayable by then." I nodded. "And that's assuming I can't find more superstars. But I don't plan to miss another whole summer." I smiled at my bodyguard. He flicked his eyes towards the women.

I'd been so enchanted by their player profiles and the way they'd played that I hadn't noticed that something had changed. In the car drive, they'd compared notes and they'd . . . something.

I opened my mouth to ask what was going on, but shut it. I'd already said more than enough.

After hundreds of tiny "no, not me, you tell him" type glances, Mary, the left back, spoke. "Sandra spoke highly of you, and we trust her. She was our rock, and when she said we should check you out, we thought, why not? We aren't getting a deal at City, and semipro at an ambitious club sounded interesting. But . . ."

There was an endless pause. Literally endless. Universes died and were reborn, like, eight times before she spoke next.

"I mean, we know you had the accident and all that."

"The murder," I said, striving for maximum accuracy.

"And you used to be good and whatever but it's . . . We didn't expect to see you in the session."

"Right."

Gail spoke. "It's like, you're not serious about the women's team. You wouldn't do it with the men's team, would you?"

I was a tiny bit confused. "Do what?"

"Gatecrash training."

"I would, actually. But the women are a lot less likely to break my ankles proving how tough they are."

"I just think it's not serious."

I frowned. The Brig wasn't giving me much help; I was on my own. Not serious? Was I supposed to respond to that? "It was their idea, but okay."

The ice had been broken. Mary had lots to say. "And, like, when we wrote to you, you were the women's team manager. Now you do the men and you're looking for a new manager. We've heard all about how you're a magician—"

"Wizard," murmured Charlotte, who must have read Beth's article.

"And that's exciting. To think we'd be in tier six but still learning the game. Couple of years going sideways to go forward. We could deal with that. But it's not even going to be you."

"I hope to get someone amazing, but it will be a step down from me. That's true."

"So it's like you've used the women to get a men's job. And now what happens to the women? We all know."

"Seems you know a lot about me."

"It's not just you, either. It's the facilities. They're . . . basic. To say the least."

I didn't blink. She'd gone from criticising me, which I usually felt was fair comment, to complaining about Chester. "You knew that before you came. We aren't owned by a country. We're owned by our fans." I worried I'd snarled on the word *fans*, but no one seemed to react too strongly. I tried to get a grip. Slippery, like that agent who may or may not have tried to kill me.

Gail took over. "Okay, but it's one thing to know it, another thing to see it. D'you know what I mean?"

I turned to the Brig to explain. "See, at Man City, whenever they score a goal, they fill an Olympic-size swimming pool with crude oil and set it ablaze."

Mary tutted. "Come on. You don't have a gym. You don't have ice baths. You train on a pitch and there's some pensioners' team ready to come on. No chance to do an extra few reps."

The bar was full of young people. The Brig had chosen well. Young, optimistic, no time to think about getting old. I'd had plenty of time to think of that in hospital, especially during my rehab when I tended to be sharing a room with oldsters who'd just had hip replacements or bad falls or whatever. They were tedious conversationalists and wouldn't know a meta joke if it slapped them with a Best 77 shirt, but a few had worn me down with their unremitting optimism and positivity. I'd done a complete one-eighty and now thought the fact we had to get off the pitch to let a bunch of retired dudes on was fucking *top*.

That was when it struck me. That was when I knew. I'd never sign a player from Man City. Nor from any other big team.

These women were working class. They'd worked hard to get their chance at City, had grafted, had put in the time. Amazing. Showed character. But getting there had ruined them. Every session had eight coaches, every swimming pool was triple Olympic size, every presentation was delivered by a not-yet-disgraced TED Talk speaker. Chester, to these three, was like something squishy they'd found stuck to their soles. It would be wrong, probably, to jump to the word *entitled*, but they were talking like entitled nepo babies.

I used my palm as a head rest and groaned. "Kisi," I said. "No." I needed to get her out of there before it was too late. Unless it was too late already. "Shit."

"What?" said Mary, but I didn't reply. My world was in tatters. If I'd ruined Kisi through my ignorance . . . Yes, I'd tried to give her a shortcut. A path to rapid CA growth. But what does it profit a girl to gain CA but lose her soul?

Gail said, "The standard isn't as good as we'd hoped."

I lifted my head all the way up. Stared right at her. "What?"

Gail shrank, but Mary was unbowed. "The standard isn't as good as we'd hoped."

"What does that mean?"

"The other players. They aren't that good."

I found myself licking my lips. Some kind of precursor to spontaneously combusting from anger. I hadn't been angry for a while, I didn't think. Even in hospital. Nick had hidden the curse from me in case I got unreasonable, and that was probably a good idea. I'd had some dark moments. But I hadn't lost my shit. Even when my rehab stalled, I'd vented with one enormous scream of rage, apologised, and got on with trying to make my leg go forward two inches.

The Brig was watching me with interest. I guessed he'd been warned about my temper, and since he hadn't seen it yet, he was curious. That thought calmed me just enough.

I spoke to him. "Dude. When you were training a squad and people talked shit about them, how did you react?"

He scoffed. "Oh, in my early years, sometimes violently. People learned not to badmouth my men."

"Yeah," I said. That was how I felt. I wanted to defend my women. They were fucking mint. All of them. An image came to mind of Maddy tagging along with Raffi's group, looking for my car. Instead of getting wasted celebrating England's semifinal win, she was doing team things. For the team.

"See, Max," said the Brig, startling me. He never used my name. He looked right into my soul as he said, "No one knew like I did how much those boys suffered. How much they sacrificed to get to where they wanted to get. Yes, they fucked up. They fucked up morning, noon, and night, some of them, but no outsider had the right to talk about them with anything other than respect. And I'm proud to say I never let any of them down. I did my level best for each and every one. They didn't all make it, but by God, we tried."

I shot to my feet, causing my chair to fly into some other group, which provoked a chain-reaction of chaos. I didn't track it. I was in an absolute fury. A whirlwind.

I felt hands on my shoulders. I cocked my head and realised it was the Brig, pushing me down onto the chair that he'd recovered.

"But these ladies have travelled to be here today. You must treat them with dignity, sir."

"Really?"

"Yes, sir."

I couldn't look them in the eye. Maybe the Brig was right, but I didn't have to look at them. I stared at a spot on the table. Some whorl in the wood. "Thanks for coming. You're not interested in playing for Chester, and I'm not interested in signing you. My team is incredible. They're immense and I can get everything I want from them. We can win, win with quality, and keep our to-getherness. You're a shortcut. You're me playing this league on easy mode, and that's not what I need or what this club needs. We need to suffer and sacrifice, to leave it all on the pitch for every single point we get. To make our fans proud, and represent a community of people who this country has forgotten. I understand now we can't take players from above. We have to get them from below, and bring them up with us. Find players willing to suffer and sacrifice. There's talent here. Untapped talent. This way's going to be slower. It might take us an extra season. But once we get going, we'll be unstoppable. City have a fucking Death Star to train in, but no one there will ever have a day like I had today. I guaran-fucking-tee it. My players are fucking unbelievable and if you can't see that, I don't know what to tell you."

I checked the time. 8:30. There would be loads of matches being played.

"Brig, I want to get back into scouting." For security reasons, he'd "banned" me from randomly traversing the city. As such, I'd barely used Playdar since leaving hospital. What was the point if I couldn't follow the beams of light? And how could I explain to the Brig what I was doing? Tell him I was getting tips about players *every single day of my life*? But so fired up was I, let me tell you, that I did not give a single shit. "Like, right now."

That was a rare moment of disorientation for the Brig. "Now?"

"Yes."

"It's not safe."

"I don't give a shit. There's a thousand girls out there playing football right now, pretending to be Millie Bright, Mary Earps, or Ella Toone. They might never kick a ball again. We've got to go right now."

"Sir . . . it's not safe."

"Then you'll fucking have to deal with it. All right? Let's fucking go."

He blinked, then stood. "Sir."

We strode towards the door, but some stray thought made me go back. "Charlotte. When you half-turn and pass to the right, it's way too slow. You need to fizz that pass. Put some fucking energy into it."

And *then* I left.

I told the Brig to drive for a while, then made him pull over just before a roundabout. He had this paper map that was on the one hand super quaint, on the other super useful since I could stare at it without getting the blue light tiredness I got from my phone.

I asked him to point out any football pitches or local parks in the area, and since he had map reading 20, he was absurdly good at it.

Normally, when I pressed Playdar, I went in a mad rush towards the target. With the Brig, I felt a sense of calm that was soothing beyond belief. When I felt ready, I clicked the icon. In the distance, a giant yellow pillar of light appeared. I pointed to the direction and the Brig scanned the map and said there was only one possible location where outdoor football could be going on.

We drove there, and sure enough it was a small park with some football goals. A few kids—three boys, four girls—were walking away, carrying a football.

"Whoa!" I said. "I'm legendary football scout Cliff Daps. I got a phone call saying someone here was fucking top at football. Can you go back and play for, like, eight more seconds so I can have a look?" They seemed uncertain. "All right, fine. I'm not Cliff Daps. I'm Max Best." Absolutely nothing. The Brig stepped forward and showed them the "As It Was" video.

Instead of going back to their game like I'd quite reasonably asked, they demanded to see me do some live tekkers.

I waved for the ball and started doing kick-ups. "The thing is, I can't really. Some douche tried to totes murder me. I'm waiting for a bionic head." I got a message and pulled my phone out, but immediately put it away. I needed to get these kids back playing their game so I could scan them again with Playdar. "How old are you lot?"

They told me their ages. They ranged from eight to twelve, which is why they were going back home before they got in trouble. Eight to twelve. More players that wouldn't hit the first team for at least six years, probably ten. But talent was talent, and I wanted all of it. I only needed them to get back to playing Headers and Volleys.

"I played for Darlington," I said. "Scored, like, a billion goals in three games. A fascist wrote a viral article about me. Did I mention I'm the manager of Chester Football Club? I'd love to see you do two more minutes of your game. Just so I can see you doing your thang." I realised there was a weird vibe. Weirder than normal. "What?"

"You said you can't do tekkers," said the, like, third littlest kid. He was the one most worried about getting into trouble for going home late.

"Yeah. So?"

The Brig stepped forward—pointed at my foot. "Sir."

I was so stunned I nearly let the ball drop, but I kept going. I'd smashed my post-injury kick-ups record. With a puzzled look on my face, I tapped the ball up, and up, and up, rolled my foot over it, let it hit my standing foot and bounce up. Finally, I kicked the ball high in the air, and without looking, crushed it dead on the half-volley.

"Sir!" said the Brig.

I pointed at the worried boy. "Dude, where's your da?"

The kid pointed to one of the houses that backed onto the pitch. "My friend's going to tell him you'll be home in five minutes. All right? You won't get in trouble. You're my team, and I look after my teams. Now let's play some football." I grinned, remembering what you said just before you started a game of Headers and Volleys if you didn't want to be the goalkeeper. I hadn't said the phrase since before these kids had been born, and now I said it with relish. "Bagsy not in net!"

DAVID AND GOAL-IATH

@ChesterFC

Here we go! Chester are pleased to announce the signing of defender Steve Alton from Hereford on a two-year deal. Manager Max Best says, "Steve is an exciting addition to the first-team squad. He's experienced enough to slide right into the team, but has a high ceiling, too. It's my first transfer with a fee and as my own boss I rate this a ten out of ten bit of business. I'm happy, Steve's happy, and my boss is happy."

Excerpt from Deva Victrix, the only Chester FC podcast made by idiots, for idiots

Huey: All right, let's talk social media. It's been a busy time for Chester on the old socials. Can either of you remember a busier week?

Louie: When we beat Southport and Best got attacked. That was wall-to-wall.

Huey: Yeah. That was hectic but that was all the same story. This week's been so random. We've had the win over Chorley, the team live-tweeting the World Cup semifinal, walking around the old town looking for Max's car, a mad new signing, shaky footage of Max Best training with a load of kids, then yesterday was all about Simon Black.

Dewey: I've still not seen the first video.

Huey: So you'll be the last person in Chester, then. I'll describe it quick. So it's this guy, this dad, and he's in his kitchen recording himself going, "I can't believe this, Max Best has just been here playing Headers and Volleys with my Simon, and he wants to sign him." Dad's *buzzing*. And his wife's on her phone, on speaker, and she tells her sister and there's just a big scream. And they're hugging each other and laughing and crying. So happy their kid's signing for Chester. It just got me, I don't know. It's raw. They're just *happy*. And they finally turn the camera to this little kid. Little Simon.

Louie: He's tiny.

Huey: He's sooo tiny it's unbelievable. And his dad says, "Hey, you've been scouted by Max Best, what do you think about that?" And the kid is, I don't know, shy, and he says, "It's okay I guess." And his dad says, "Hey! You'll go to training and play games every week, isn't that good?" And the kid *almost* smiles, says, "Yeah but Max says I need to work on my heading so I'm allowed to jump on the bed." And that sets them all off laughing because it's so funny. Big joke. So it's a great video, just really sweet. It starts getting traction this morning. And after a while, the club's official account leaves a comment. Goes, "Max says that wasn't a joke. We asked him to stop telling kids to wreck their beds, and he's agreed. He's bought Simon a mini trampoline instead."

Louie: Next thing, the dad posts a picture of a cardboard box.

Huey: He's bought a little trampoline with his own money.

Dewey: Who has?

Huey: Max!

Louie: Has he fuck. That's marketing. It's good marketing, but it doesn't fool me.

Huey: You're so miserable. You're really starting to get on my tits. Why *wouldn't* he buy a kid a trampoline? It's only a hundred quid.

Louie: You saw his car. It's a piece of crap. He's not rolling in dough. We heard from our mates on the board what he's paid. *So unless he's got some secret source of income . . .*

Dewey: You need to be careful what you say next, mate. His girlfriend is gunning for you. I heard she wants to grab you, turn you upside down, and shake you until your last penny has fallen out. But what's your issue with Steve Alton? He's your common-or-garden sixth-tier defender. How is that a "mad signing"?

Louie: It's not. That's the point. *That's* what's mad about it. One week he's signing three lads he met on holiday. That's what we expect from him, right? Someone says, "Guess who's done a madness?" and you say, "Oh, shit, what now?" Three total randos. Not on trial, either. No experience? No problem. Straight to contract. Then it's a proper defender. Someone who's actually played professional football. Someone who can perform at this level. It's not his style. It worries me.

Huey: I'm not worried in the slightest. We were all stressed about his clients, right? Well, Youngster's being scouted left, right, and centre. We know that. Raffi Brown's one of my favourite players already. Henri Lyons—we were promised goals, and he scores goals. Absolutely no way he's still at the club if he isn't mates with the boss. And this Simon Black kid, someone's dug up footage of him rampaging through his school teams, scoring ten goals a game and mad shit like that. My question is, why wasn't he *already* a Chester player? Best is out there throwing our weight around. Like we should have been doing for the last ten years. We're fucking big at this level. Why is no one acting like that?

Louie: You've been brainwashed. We're not big. We're small. Literally. You heard what Spectrum said on *Seals Live* last match. They've stopped tracking the kids' height and physical data. If you don't know how tall a kid's going to be, you're going to be investing a lot of time and money creating a team of Pascal Bochums.

Dewey: What was the reason for that? Did he say?

Huey: Said Max doesn't give a shit. Kid's going to be as tall as he's gonna be. Why make them feel bad about it? Right, that's enough of that. Let's talk upcoming fixtures. Two tough away games on the horizon. Banbury, then Scarborough. What do we reckon?

Dewey: Banbury's all about Chris Beaumont.

Louie: Goliath.

Dewey: Shut him down, it's an easy win. But give him too much attention, they'll hit you somewhere else. Jackie Reaper couldn't thread the needle. Best's good on the old tactics but this sort of thing might be a bit basic for him. Not sure if he gives giant strikers a lot of thought. Could be a tough day down there.

Louie: I'd be happy with a draw. Two–all. Pride intact. Beat them at home. Four points from six, good stuff.

Dewey: Agree. I'd bite your hand off for that.

Huey: A point? Against *Banbury*? [Heavy sigh.] Yeah. I suppose.

Spectrum put the Steve Alton tweet out on Thursday morning. Nice bit of news for people to read on their way to work, and most of the replies were positive.

Just what we need! Good to see the club doing the business. I've been crying out for this kind of signing. Good stuff, love it.

There were a couple of negative ones, but they weren't complaints about Steve Alton, per se.

Steve Alton is why my season ticket went to the moon? Hang on, this nobody is why I can't afford to go to games? This guy better be 15% better than the others.

I hadn't seen MD on Thursday to ask him about it, but he popped by on Friday to see our new defender in Chester gear for the first time.

I showed him one of the tweets I'd saved. "What's all this stuff?"

"You're on Twitter!" he said, surprised. "The app formerly known as Twitter."

"I'm not. Cliff Daps is. It's easier than asking Emma all the time. But looks like I've joined at the wrong time. It's falling apart."

"What isn't?" He read the tweet, unbothered by its tone. "Ticket prices were increased."

"Were increased? By a warlock? By a rogue AI? You mean *you* increased the prices."

Still unbothered. "Yes, Max. I increased the prices. By fifteen percent. After full and frank deliberations with the new board."

I ran my fingers through my hair. I wanted to get it cut really short. Summer buzz. New season, new hair. Put the past where it belonged—in the barbershop hairbin of history. "I went back to look at the club's tweets after the first games. The replies are all like this. *Losing to Stortford, this is why prices have shot up?* And so on. This feels like a wedge between the club and the fans. I'm sort of trying to do the opposite of that. Remember?"

"I know, and I love it. I'll support you as much as possible, including finding eight thousand pounds to buy a player shortly after I told you the transfer budget was zero. But the survival of the club is paramount. Don't look like that, Max. Bills have shot up."

"We're going to start generating income this year. Trust me."

"No. I have placed a lot of faith in your hands, but I have to act as though you might quit tomorrow."

"I won't."

"You might. And then what? Pascal, for example. You believe in him. No one else does. Not even Jackie did. So if you go, that investment goes with you. Raffi's a more obvious talent, but if we sell him, do you know what we get?"

"Eight hundred thousand pounds." That was Raffi's release clause. High enough to do a lot of good for Chester, low enough to tempt some Championship or League One sides into taking a punt on him.

"If we get something astonishing for this level, such as fifty thousand pounds, that will pay the *increase* in our electricity prices."

"The increase?"

"Last year, our electricity bills alone went from fifty to ninety thousand. Joe and I spent hours calculating if playing Saturday matches earlier would save money. Pro: save a few hundred pounds per match on floodlights. Con: lose money from hospitality lunches. The bills we pay are increasing, so the prices we charge are, too. There's nothing we can do about it."

It was hard to argue with his point, except I knew this club would soon be a cash machine. Income from matches would be a drop in the ocean compared to transfer profits. I made little clicking noises from the side of my mouth. "Right." I scratched my eyebrows, triggering a once-per-week perk called Super Patience. "I'm going to generate a lot of money for this club. A lot. Most needs to be reinvested in the squad but we need to make sure fans can afford to come to games." He wasn't quite listening. I got a bit heated. "I want a full stadium, MD. I want to give Crackers the atmosphere I promised him. I don't want fans moaning and complaining. I want them cheering and singing. It helps us win, too."

"I also want a full stadium. Bring in money and you'll get a say in how it's used. If you want new players, it can go to new players. If you want to keep tickets cheap, great. But I promise you, it will always be a choice between one or the other."

He wandered off.

My jaw had tensed up. I tried to rub it loose. Getting an extra fifty quid a season from a fan was meaningless in the grand scheme of things. All it guaranteed was bad publicity and ill-feeling. I wanted happy faces around me. Smiling little kids, excited to train. Fans walking around in blue-and-white scarves. Optimism. Excitement. Feeling like the club was on the way up.

If electricity prices had doubled, there was an obvious solution—generate our own. Solar panels and batteries. How much would it cost to become self-sufficient? Half a Raffi? And the savings . . . I worked it out on my phone. Ninety thousand a year was £1,730 a week. Three new players. Or a ticket price freeze.

I needed money.

I scanned the pitches. We had some decent players. Some that would eventually turn into real assets. But nobody worth selling before the window closed on September 1. And probably no one who'd fetch their peak price in January. If things went great, Raffi would be catching the eye by next summer.

A year from now. Too slow. Too late.

I was so deep in thought it took me a while to realise the players had stopped training.

I went over to investigate and found there was a heated discussion going on. Not a crazy one like you sometimes got where players would start beating the shit out of each other. This was Trick and Gerald versus Glenn and Carl. My defence attacking each other.

"What's all this then?"

"Max," said Glenn, relieved. "Trick's . . . we're talking about Beaumont."

"The match is tomorrow," whined Trick. "We don't know the team. The plan. What do we do about Beaumont?"

So, a little background to explain what I did next, maybe. Remember, I was feeling aggrieved. Annoyed in general. Annoyed by MD raising the ticket prices. Annoyed that I was going to have to appear in public and defend the decision. Annoyed that the Man City women couldn't see this club for what it was—a sleeping giant. Yeah. The mismatch between what I *knew* and what the rest of the world *believed* was getting to me.

But nothing grated harder than hearing the name Chris Beaumont. This was literally the hundredth time I'd heard it said since Monday.

You might remember that I had given Jackie Reaper a verbal dressing-down when I drove him to the clinic in Liverpool because he'd treated this Chris Beaumont guy like he was prime Zlatan Ibrahimovic. Suffice to say the two players were *not* comparable. Jackie took my rebuke well, quitting shortly after and leaving me knee-deep in shit. The prick.

"Oh, you're talking about Chris Beaumont," I said. "The striker who plays for Banbury."

"He's enormous," said Trick.

"Oh, is he? Is he an enormous, unstoppable striker?" I was being sarcastic. Incredibly, no one picked up on my tone. They were *that* afraid of him.

"Boss," said Sam Topps, who was taking part in non-contact training. "I know you're busy and still getting up to speed and all that, but if you've already decided on a team and a plan, it'd be good to hear it early like you did last year."

"Right," I said. "But back then I thought naming the team early was smart, but later Vimsy pointed out that the guys who knew they weren't in the team trained like shit for a week. So that fucking pissed me off. If I had my way, I wouldn't tell you the lineup until ten minutes after a match had kicked off. I need you all to train flat out, all the time. We win this league in training, not on match days."

"I'm with you, boss. I get you. And Vimsy's right about that week. But Beaumont's a nightmare, he really is. If you've got the answer to it, we should start preparing that. Practising it."

Even fucking Youngster was afraid of this neanderthal. "He is *extremely* large, Mr. Best. Truly, he is the Goliath of the league."

It just so happened I knew a thing or two about the David versus Goliath tale. I was about to launch into an epic rant, but I stopped myself. Did I have the skills to handle this maturely? Probably . . . if my head was clear.

But my team's CA hadn't been increasing as fast as I wanted. I thought it was because we'd played a Tuesday-night game but now I was wondering . . . Were these pricks so busy fretting about Beaumont that they weren't even concentrating on their own improvement?

"Brig? I need you for a minute. Lads, I'm popping inside to get something from my office. Now, when Henri was at Darlington, he gave an interview that got him in a lot of trouble, but all he was saying was that managers should listen to their players more. So split into your boot camp groups and I want each of you to come up with a solution. David versus Goliath. We're David, obviously. So how do we win? All right? You've got five minutes."

The Brig and I strode away, and once we were inside I took him into the break room and gave him a paper cup of tap water. I had one, too, which I drank while staring out of a window trying to process my feelings.

"What's your plan, sir?"

"Not sure. Think I might try and vent some of my frustrations. It might blow up in my face. What do you think?"

"I'm afraid I don't know the issues, sir."

"The team we're playing have a very large object playing as a striker. A small moon with his own gravity, attracting the ball. It's hard to win a header against him, and that causes chaos."

"That does sound problematic."

"Nope. We know exactly what Banbury will do when they get the ball. They have one weapon. One way of playing. It's hard to talk about this without sounding dismissive or disrespectful . . . but it's small time. It's beneath us. It's one thing to mention it as something to look out for. I mean, that's just being professional. But it's another thing to obsess over the guy for a whole week. Have fucking training ground bust-ups about it."

"And you have a plan to stop him?"

I eyed the Brig. It felt like he was winding me up, but that was just because I was on edge. "My plan is to say happy birthday to that cute girl at reception."

"How do you know it's her birthday?"

"Didn't you see all the balloons?"

I left the credit card building alone and went to collect the ideas the players had been dreaming up.

Before I did, Jude jogged over to me.

"Just how tall is this guy?" he whispered.

"What would you guess based on their reactions?"

"Oooh . . . based on their reactions . . . twelve foot?"

I finally cracked a smile. One little joke was all it took to boost my mood by twenty percent.

The first boot camp squad suggested that Glenn should man-mark the giant. Minus four percent to my mood! Footballers are so fucking stupid sometimes. They'd literally *just* seen that tactic fail.

Raffi's group—Pascal's group, in this case, since he had the best tactical brain—suggested getting tight to the wide players to stop crosses coming in. Fine, but Banbury hit long balls from *everywhere*. It wasn't only crosses that were a problem.

Henri's group proposed a "Max Best Special." Flooding the midfield to gain complete control of the ball, denying Banbury any possession whatsoever, and having Youngster play just in front of the ogre. Henri explained. "It would have the dual effect of making Goliath waste energy trying to press Youngster, while also being another body in the area for knockdowns and second balls. Youngster will block, intercept, and annoy."

"All right," I said. "Some interesting ideas there. I find that I'm so intimidated by this guy's vast enormousness that I can't think straight. So I've come up with a way to put all your ideas to the test. To the sword, you might say, since we're talking about David versus Goliath." I waved, and the Brig emerged from the credit card building.

He marched, upright, dignified, while holding by its string a shiny helium balloon.

I studied the players. There was some amusement. Some retreated behind blank poker faces. This sesh had taken a turn for the weird and they didn't want to get embarrassed.

"What we're going to do now is replicate the experience of playing against Goliath Beaumont. We don't have a massive hulking brute we can swap into the party—actually, that's a good idea, someone write that down—but I think we can approximate it. So listen. Goliath is tall and has too much bulk to move or grapple. So what do we do? Easy. We devote all our focus and attention to him. We dream about him. We have nightmares about him. Fear is tremendously helpful. Much better than worrying about silly old passing drills."

The Brig passed the balloon over. It was in the shape of a rabbit coming out of a magician's hat. "Dude," I mumbled. There had been a unicorn one. The Brig shrugged.

I tied the string around my wrist so it couldn't float off, then gripped the hat and held it in front of my forehead. "Right, I'm holding this balloon. It's about the height of Chris Beaumont, yeah? Someone come and compete for this header."

No one came, so the Brig volunteered Michael Harrison, the eighteen-year-old Triplet.

He stood next to me. I gave Vimsy a nod and he threw a ball up. "My ball," I yelled, pushing the balloon into it. "Have it," I grunted, as the ball blopped away. "Oh. Let's get someone taller. Glenn, get over here."

"I'd rather not."

"Brig, yell at Glenn."

Glenn sighed and replaced Michael. Ryder made no effort to jump for the header, but I barged into him as I won the ball. "Banburyyyyy!" I yelled in an overly deep impression of a caveman. "Well up, Chris. Get in!"

"Max, come on," said Angles, who'd brought the goalies over when he'd seen the balloon.

I released the balloon, trusting my knot to keep it tethered, and waved my arms around like a managerial octopus. "No, you missed it, mate. Big chat about Chris Beaumont over here. You know him, right? Banbury and England striker Chris Beaumont. Top scorer in every league he's ever played in. Three billion followers on Instagram. You know. Chris Beaumont! Nicknamed Goliath. We've got to do something about Chris Beaumont!"

The players were unhappy I was mocking their fears, but this was my first real outburst since coming back from hospital, so there was also some interest. No doubt some of it was morbid curiosity—was I more damaged than I seemed?

Sam still had belief in me. Enough to challenge me. "Max! He's good. He's dangerous."

I frowned. I knew everyone's CA and PA. I was acting the way I was because my players were being stupid. Fear of Beaumont, whose CA was in the 20s, was completely irrational. But it was rational to them. I couldn't discuss this in terms of CA and PA. But there were other numbers. "Sam. Guys. He scored six goals last season. Six league goals in forty-six games. That's shit. He's not good at football."

"He wins headers," said Glenn. Losing aerial duels was rare for him. So rare it frazzled his brain when it did happen.

I took a few seconds to compose myself. I'd tried words. Now something for the visual learners. "I know some of you think I can pull a rabbit out of the hat. No? Nothing for that? But honestly, lads, I'm all out of ideas. David versus Goliath, there's only one winner. Big old Goliath, every time. Am I right?" Surely even the thick ones—which I was starting to suspect was *all* of them—knew who won that particular fight. "I did have one small idea. Not quite a rabbit from a hat, but maybe a . . . mouse . . . from a sock. Let's run a simulation since you're not in the mood to do the actual drills I wanted you to do today. Aff, over there. Henri." I pointed to where I wanted them to stand. Aff walked to the left of the penalty box. Henri in front of the near post. "Joe." I sent Joe Anka over to the right, but farther away than Aff. "Aff and Henri, you're Chester. Joe, you and I are Banbury. Round one, Chester. Try to score a goal."

Aff looked suspicious, but he passed to Henri. Henri jabbed the ball into the empty goal.

"A classic Chester goal!" I said, eyes blazing. I would have clapped but my hands were full. "High-percentage chance, expertly tucked away. One–nil to Chester. Joe, swing in a cross." He frowned, but then did as I said. The ball flew right at my face. I dodged inelegantly. "What the shit, man?"

"What?" said Joe. "You said cross it!"

I nodded to the rabbit. "My head's up there, you dick. I'm not ready to smash balls into my *own* skull. What the fuck. Good cross, though. Do it again but higher."

There were plenty of murmurs of complaint from the rest of the squad—they weren't enjoying this game—but Joe sent in another cross. I tried to push the balloon into it but missed.

"Argh, no good. Hard to score that kind of chance. Okay, Chester, your turn."

"Max," said Henri.

"Chester's turn!" I said, louder than I'd meant. They went through the charade of passing and scoring again.

"Great goal! Two–nil! Joe, here we go."

Joe sucked in some air, looked away, then clipped a cross in. This time I got good contact on the balloon but the ball bounced off at a crazy angle.

"Oh, so close!" I said. "Chester."

"No, Max," said Henri.

"What?"

"You've made your point."

"I've made my point?" I said, turning and looking everyone in the eye, one at a time. "Made my point? What's my point?"

He sighed. "That we should play our game and not worry about Banbury. Our style is more effective than theirs."

"But that's not it. That's not it." I gestured at Joe and Aff, telling them to come join the main group. When they were close enough to hear, I continued. "David versus Goliath. You think we're David? Nobody understands the point of that story. David sees this gigantic guy who's taunting the army his brothers are in. David listens, goes 'Let's go kill him.' And his brothers are like, 'No, dude, he's tall. Look how tall he is. Look how many headers he wins!' David says, 'Mate. I killed a lion. I killed a bear. Let me go sort him out. No big D.' King says, 'You sure?' David says, 'Yeah but let's hurry this up I've got to look after these sheep and that.' He gets his stones, walks up to Goliath, swings his little whatsit, boom. Headshot. Tall guy's got a big head. Easy target. David? David turns any little stone into a fucking railgun. He's killed a lion. A bear. Why's he gonna be afraid of some one-mile-an-hour dude? The absolute worst thing that can happen is Goliath falls onto one of David's sheep as he's dying. Collata-wool damage."

I waited to see if Youngster was going to complain about my framing of the story . . . and he came through. "Mr. Best. That story is about having faith. David won because he believed in God."

"Sorry, bro. Not having it. He killed a lion and a bear long before he ever saw Goliath. It's not a story about faith. It's a story about being so skilled winning is inevitable.

"I'm struggling here. I do want to encourage you to give me ideas. Genuinely. But when footballers talk about David and Goliath, they're talking about small clubs playing against big clubs. *We* are the big club. This week I met three women I wanted to sign who don't get how big this club is. They'll end up in some tier-three, tier-four team, and we'll zoom right past them. I need you to get this into your heads. Imagine me writing this all down on a little stone and sling-shotting it right into your brain. We have the skill of David. We have the size of Goliath. Banbury is some blank space on the page where we tell our story.

"What do you think Banbury have been talking about this week? Think they've been going, 'Oh, Chester, who get triple our attendances? Chester, whose manager is the only one in the league who can count to ten without using his fingers? Of course we'll smash *them*.' Think that's what they've been saying? Have they fuck! They're having these same conversations you've been having, but about *Henri*."

I walked over to my star striker and circled him. "Henri's ten times scarier than their guy. Henri can head, shoot, shoot with power, left, right, first-touch finish, unbelievable movement, penalties. The only person who's watched more videos of Henri than Henri in the last five days is Banbury's manager."

Henri grinned. Sam was nodding. He understood my point. Not everyone did. I reinforced it.

"Chris Beaumont and Henri Lyons do *not* belong in the same conversation. So what the fuck are we doing here?"

I let the scene breathe. Changed my tone to wistful.

"You don't understand what's happening. We're here, we're training, to win the league. To win. The league. The fact you're even thinking about some *dude* from *Banbury* worries me a hundred times more than the dude. You need to get your head around this. I'm plotting our path to the *title*. We've got the best tactics, the most flexible manager. If we aren't the fittest team in the league by the winter, there's going to be one less Brigadier in our ranks. The *five* best players in this league play for *us*!" I smacked the nearest ball into the goal. It might have looked more impressive if the floating rabbit hadn't bumped into my head six times in two seconds.

I sighed. My vision for the club wasn't aligned with anyone else's. How could it be?

I handed the balloon back to the Brig, then vaguely wagged a finger at the squad. "It's not your fault. It's not my fault. We didn't have a proper preseason. We never talked about what was going to happen. I didn't tell you my expectations. We'll have that talk soon.

"I'm going to tell you tomorrow's team. Anyone who uses that as an excuse to slack off for the rest of today will fucking regret it.

"Four-one-four-one. Ben. Trick, Glenn, Gerald, Carl. Youngster. Aff, Raffi, Magnus, Joe. Henri.

"We won't be marking Chris Beaumont. He brings chaos. How do we fight that? With order. Glenn? Order. Organisation. Concentration. Yes? Youngster at DM mopping up, like Henri said. Aff and Joe closing the wide players down, stopping them getting quality on their crosses like Pascal suggested. That's it. That's the plan. The under-twelves could do it. The rest is about what we do when we get the ball. Our quality. How we attack. We're better than them, so I want relentless attacks. Left, right, centre.

"I want Andrew on the bench for the matchday experience. And I want a comfortable lead so we can get Steve on. We need to load some minutes into those legs. It's going to be a long season, lads, but it's going to end with you as champions." I cracked my neck left and right. "So you'd better start thinking like champions. We've killed a lion. A bear. What's left to fear? A slow, predictable striker who wouldn't get in our *squad*?" Quick look around. Mixed response to my words. Hard to tell if anything had hit home. "Get yourselves warm again, then we'll do eleven on eleven to finish. Trick. A word, please."

I pulled off to the side. The Brig automatically came with me. Trick didn't seem happy about being singled out, but this wasn't about Chris Beaumont. Not directly. This was about his CA being stuck. "Max?"

"You came back from the summer break off the pace. Not too happy with that, but it's understandable. I'm not a complete dick." Silence. "This is where you agree that I'm not a complete dick."

"Right, yes. I mean, no."

"You struggled at boot camp, and you haven't kicked on." His CA was flat on 27. His PA was only 31, but there was a hell of a difference between a weak player who was maxed out and one who wasn't even living up to his shitty potential. I fucking hated seeing that number 2. Every time I thought about Trick I saw a giant, steaming pile of number 2.

"I feel fit, Max. I feel good."

I glanced at the Brig. A signal that I wanted his help. Something along the lines of good cop, bad cop. "I'm not enjoying my Friday, mate. Let's skip to the bit where you tell me why you're not doing the basics."

I caught his micro-expression. Annoyance. "I am."

With an annoyed tap of the foot, I turned away. Carrot or stick. My first instinct with this guy was always stick. I wanted to *try* to treat him like any other player. "Have you ever won anything?"

"Won? Yeah. Stuff. Loads when I was a kid."

"You need ten games to get a league-winner's medal. You'll have that by January, then you can move on."

"Move on?"

"You're not happy here. You thought you were getting Jackie. Thought I'd be in a coma for a year. I'm picking you. I'm trusting you in big games. But you're not giving me anything. I don't have the experience needed to get that last ten percent out of you, so let's just front up here and we'll agree you can move in January and instead of finding another forward player like the squad *actually* needs, I'll spend my extremely limited and precious time replacing *you*."

"I've been playing well."

I leaned close to him. Bit of bad cop. "You don't listen, mate. It's so frustrating when people don't *listen*. I'm asking you to train harder. I'm asking you to train. Harder." Leant back. Reasonable cop. "Magnus can play left back, but I prefer having a left-footed player there; the attacks are way sharper. There's no one in the under-eighteens. Right now, I don't have money for a transfer. I might find some rando to come in, but it'll take a year to get him up to speed. So it's you. But you don't want to be here. See my problem?"

"I want to be here," he mumbled.

I pretended I hadn't heard him. "Left back's my Achilles forehead. I could switch to three-five-two and that'd be the last time I ever think about left backs. Sucks for the team, sucks for Youngster, sucks for the fans, sucks for you. But I could do it." I'd gone from carrot to stick so fast I almost didn't notice I'd done it. "Or you could give me an extra ten percent. Get back to where you were at the end of last season. That's all I'm asking. Be a valuable member of the squad who plays most games and bails me out when my tactics run away from me."

The Brig judged that more stick was needed. "Sir, I've heard *you* can play left back. Perhaps if Mr. Williams doesn't *fancy it*, as you footballers say, you could step in."

"Of course I can play fucking left back," I snapped. "But why would I want to?" I pretended to hesitate. Got thoughtful. "If MD sees me playing in defence, shuffling and sliding like a good little boy instead of scoring a goal every thirty minutes, he'll find me some transfer budget." I let that hang in the air, then turned to Trick. One last try. "Or Trick could play there, like he was born to do."

Mic dropped, I walked towards the offices. Time would tell if I'd made things better or worse. The Brig fell into step beside me.

"Was that all right?" I asked.

"Sir?"

"Pretending to bite your head off. It felt right but maybe it's bad to undermine you."

"You're the boss. You're the football expert. You can bite my head off." He looked behind us. "It was my intention to suggest there is more competition for his place than Trick suspects. Perhaps it wasn't the best move to imply he was safe."

I nodded. "It felt like a fifty-fifty. Not every formation needs a left back. He knows I'm flexible."

"But he knows you want to play Youngster in the defensive midfielder position, and that's best achieved with a flat back four."

I laughed and slapped the Brig on the back. "Listen to you! You sound like a real boy." Don't ask me why, but him using the jargon cheered me up.

"I shall take that as a compliment, sir." He hesitated. "Can you really play left back?"

"Yes."

"Will we ever see it?"

"Perhaps not. I can do all the bits—the passing, the tackles, whatnot. But keeping in line, being disciplined. It's not my nature."

"I understand. And you prefer a left-footed player on the left."

I glanced at my assistant. It wouldn't do to tell him all my secrets, but I felt I could trust him. "My left foot's as good as my right. I like to hide that fact."

He stopped. Rare confusion. "But why?"

Why indeed? "One day . . . I'll have a free kick in a big match. I'll stand there, all lined up to hit a right-footed Beckham. And I'll pretend to get annoyed by something, and I'll step to my right to point and gesticulate at a teammate, and then when the goalie is relaxed I'll dab the ball over the wall and into the net, left-footed."

"You'll hide your talent for years with that one, theoretical, moment in mind?"

"Yep. Absolutely. It's not like I'll *never* hit the ball left-footed. But if I score an amazing goal with my left, I might spend the next half an hour making it seem like I got lucky that one time. You know, like shanking three crosses in a row out to touch. Play like Trick Williams for a bit."

It was interesting watching his eyes. They locked onto some spot, then made a small jump, then another. It was like watching a clock hand travel in increments of two or three hours. Finally, he looked at me, back to his most opaque, unreadable blankness. "But then you're serious."

"About what?"

"About winning the league."

I wasn't sure what equations led him to that conclusion. "The playoffs are a lottery," I said. "We have to win the whole thing."

His lips twitched. Not with amusement. No, it was his version of James Yalley's savage grin. I imagined him in an underground fighting pit, sawdust everywhere, tossing a knife from hand to hand. "Indeed," he said, and the twitch of triumph moved from his mouth to his eyes.

But my heart sank. Even the Brig, who spent more time with me than most, wasn't listening. Not *really* listening. But why? If the Brig told me he was going to cut off my legs, I'd believe him. What was I doing wrong?

I had to talk to the squad. Tell them how the season would go. But that wouldn't be enough to make them really believe it. How could I make them believe something that would be true tomorrow, but was not true today? How could I make MD start acting like we were drowning in transfer income? How could I make talented players see beyond the bumpy pitches and frayed corner flags?

I pushed my thumbnail into the gaps between my teeth. It didn't help.

Still annoyed by dozens of small things, I went to evening training with the women.

It was pleasing to think that my body was starting to obey me more. Had I shot from CA 1 to CA 3? I knew it was likely that after one good session I'd be absolute dogshit in the next, just as night followed day. I could deal with that—the memory of not being able to push my feet forward a couple of inches was still present. Still vivid. A failed dribble, a mis-hit cross, a bizarrely poor first touch—it was all such a bonus.

And if the session was so bad I couldn't even laugh at how bad I was, I'd go out and hit Playdar again. I'd watched the Simon Black video twenty times and it never failed to make me feel better. And it wasn't just a happy moment for that family. Simon was a fast little striker. PA 77, same as my squad number. He reminded me of Michael Owen. If we trained him right and showed him in the best possible light, teams would definitely overpay for him when the time came. Those Man City women had irritated me into finding a valuable asset. They didn't understand the story. They wanted to play for Goliath, but David was the only one with a future.

Fuck 'em. I'd outwork them, outthink them, outperform. Anyone who doubted me would end up in an unloved heap.

I thought all that as I did my own warm-up, separate from the women, with the Brig jogging along next to me, so at first I didn't notice anything weird. But when I decided I was ready to join the main sesh, I saw her.

Charlotte, the PA 101 midfielder who hadn't made it at Man City had turned up to training.

My mind boggled. "Brig, are you seeing that? Didn't I do a big monologue and flounce out of the bar?"

"It wasn't quite a flounce, sir, no. An abrupt exit in three acts, perhaps. But I confess, I'm surprised to see her."

I'd already Whatsapped the squad informing them that the City girls wouldn't be coming. I had blamed myself for it. Said I hadn't been persuasive enough. Hadn't mentioned the whole they-think-you're-shit thing. "The others?"

"It's just her."

I took a second to compose myself, but it didn't help. Why was she here? I wandered over and there must have been something about my face that made Jill defer to me before I'd even spoken.

"Charlotte." I squeezed my eyes tight while I tried to formulate my question. "Er . . . what?"

She swept her fringe to the side. Glanced around. I think she didn't like being the centre of attention, but the rest of the squad shuffled closer. This had the potential to be a good scene. "I've come to continue my trial."

I took a minute. I had to be careful here. Did I want to tell the squad that these Man City fucks had been bad-mouthing them? It would certainly be motivational. Something like that could see us through a difficult first season. Keep us warm during long winter nights. Or should I mention their complaints about the facilities? Didn't seem the right energy. Better to stick to diplomacy. "I thought we decided I wasn't the right person to help you get your careers on track."

"Sorry, Max, but I didn't agree to that. I liked what you said."

"What did he say?" said Bonnie.

Charlotte was also wondering how much to repeat. "It's not what he said, it's how he said it."

"How did he say it?"

"Intense." There were some chuckles. Some nods of recognition. Charlotte spoke to Bonnie and the players near her. "He challenged us. Said he was only looking for players who'd suffer and sacrifice like what you done, which, by the way, hello? I didn't get into Man City by pressing snooze on my alarms. And then he goes, 'Fuck you spoilt brats I can go find a player like *that*.'" She snapped her fingers. "And by the time I got home, there was all this stuff on Chester Twitter about some kid he'd found in a park." Charlotte shook her head, nearly laughed. "I've done my research. There's a buzz about this club. This team. I liked what I saw on Wednesday. I want to be here."

"Well, it isn't up to me," I said. "If you want to join the squad"—I'm sure she noticed I didn't say team—"you need to prove yourself in the crucible of competition."

"All right. What do you want me to do?"

"Easy. Take a penalty. Score and you're in. Miss and you can do one. Robyn, you warmed up?"

"Enough to save a penno, yeah," said the goalie.

Every single person shuffled over to the penalty box. Charlotte put a ball on the penalty spot. Robyn danced around, waving her arms, pushing the crossbar.

Charlotte centred herself, took three steps towards the ball, and rolled it, gently, towards the middle of the left half of the goal. Robyn watched the ball, then dived theatrically . . . the other way.

"Goal," said Charlotte, simply.

I frowned. "Robyn. The fuck?"

She got up, dusted herself off, and shrugged. "She's quality. We need good players."

I looked down, nodded a few times the way people do when they're really angry. "I loved everything about that. You're in. Get hyped, you're about to get your first league-winner's medal." The ladies reacted hugely positively— they were ready to celebrate. It was obvious to all that Charlotte had leap-frogged everyone and was now by far our best player. Chester Women were on the move again, after a long plateau. I forestalled the party. "One thing, though. This . . . *this* is how you take a penalty."

Robyn got set, proper determination on her face. I breathed, exhaled, stepped forward, and blasted the ball closer to the moon than many rockets get. If I was David, Goliath would have chopped my head off about two seconds later.

"Well, fuck," I said. "A few months ago, that would have been *so* cool."

"Sir," said the Brig later, when I was taking a little break from the sesh. It was getting more intense the closer we got to the first match of the season. I was playing better. CA 3 for sure. Jill was near me, as were Lucy, Pippa, and Bea Pea. "What would you have done if Miss Charlotte had missed the penalty kick?"

I shrugged. "Then she would have been out. We need winners here."

The Brig smiled. He didn't believe me, but I didn't mind. This time he had good reason. "Sir. You were so excited about those newcomers. Before, during, and after you saw them play."

"You think I got to this point of my life without sticking to my word? Score and you're in. Easy."

"Sir," he complained.

"Fine," I said, getting to my feet. I was ready to do a few more minutes. Push myself the way Trick refused to. "But even you know enough about sports to deal with that situation. You simply say, 'Best out of three.'"

"Ah!" he said, satisfied. "Of course." He grew thoughtful. "Didn't work for Goliath, though."

"This is sport, mate. It's not a matter of life or death. That's what's great about the league. Forty-six matches. You can lose your first two. Some giant can make you drop points. Some ref might send a goalie off after five minutes. But you win the next three, you're right back in contention." I jogged onto the pitch and took my orange bib off. "I'm switching sides. I want to be team Goliath. Charlotte, get ready. I'm coming for you."

Match 4 of 46: Banbury Pygmies versus Chester FC.

I went into the dressing room to reassure the guys that I was there. I hadn't travelled with them; I'd spent the day with Emma on a romantic walk along Oxfordshire's canals. I got their attention. "Banbury are four-four-two, as always, so we do our thing. Back in a bit."

A few minutes making sure Emma was okay in the tiny, off-centre, 250-capacity stand that was the only seating area Banbury offered. Emma deserved better, but the shitter the stadium, the more she seemed to enjoy being there. What was it? She wanted to suffer and sacrifice? MD was late, which was unusual, so Emma took his seat—it was slightly less obstructed by the three large metal pillars at the front of the stand. He would sit in her spot and not complain about it.

I was chatting away, trying to be charming and funny and mostly succeeding, but then I noticed something weird—I was getting profiles from a couple of guys who were standing way over behind the fence that surrounded the pitch. They were just behind the floodlights opposite the mini stand.

"Babes, will you be all right? I've just seen some people I might want to talk to."

"I'm grand. You go do your Max things."

I didn't like to leave her there—like Chester, Banbury sometimes had idiot fans who caused trouble. Not before the match though, surely? I didn't want to have to think about it. I phoned the Brig and got him to sit with Emma for a while. I knew they'd compare notes about my hoodies and how best to protect me from myself and all that, but I also knew that if someone started something, the Brig would finish it.

The two men I'd spotted had scout profiles and were from teams in the division above ours. One was called Jack. According to the curse, he was employed by AFC Fylde and had a judging player ability rating of 9. Tom was from Newport County, and had judging player ability 7. Both had negligible scores in judging player potential.

I introduced myself—they were taken aback that I knew they were scouts, but I said I was sure I'd seen them around, and they agreed it might have been possible. I asked if they were there to scout Chris Beaumont. They laughed—correctly—and said they had their eyes on some of my lads. They wouldn't say who, though, which was infuriating.

Scouting the scouts, though. I needed to do this at every match. Build up my database. If I ever found someone with a scouting rating of 15 or more, I'd try to poach them.

Talking of building up databases, Tom asked when I'd be playing again because he wanted to scout me for Soccer Supremo. I told him to give me 77 in everything, winked, and walked away.

As the team prepared for kickoff, I bit my nails. We'd had a weird week in training. I still had confidence in Jude, and blamed our lack of improvement on Beaumont-mania. Both goalies had improved, and they were off in their own sessions, not working themselves into a frenzy.

Youngster hadn't gone green in anything. It could have been the fearful mood, or the way I'd shifted him around the pitch against Chorley. We won because of it, but if getting a low match rating affected training, I'd have to be very careful with my tactical innovations. I could lose a match here or there. I couldn't summon up another hundred-million-pound player.

Raffi had improved, as he seemed to every week these days. Trick, D-Day, and Joe Anka hadn't. They'd had game time in their preferred positions but still hadn't even caught up to where they'd finished at the end of last season. Trick and D-Day were thirty-three years old, past their prime, but Joe was only twenty-eight. No need to worry just yet, but it was one of a hundred tiny details that weren't going in my favour.

What it all amounted to was the sobering fact that our average CA was 39.6. Diabolical. But how could I get it higher if I didn't rotate the team and give everyone the best chance to improve?

Banbury's was 39, so in theory it should have been a close match. I felt that we were much better, though. Banbury's players had lots of strength and heading, but they were slow with poor technique. If we got the ball on the grass and passed it around, we'd slap. If we fell into their trap of playing caveman football, we'd struggle.

Kickoff, a few minutes of blood and thunder, a few tackles the referee would have handed out yellow cards for if they'd come later in the match.

Then a long ball was sent towards Chris Beaumont. Glenn Ryder was behind him, ready to compete for the header. Youngster was in front, trying to block the guy, ready to pounce on the second ball.

Beaumont won the header. It bounced straight up, took an age to come back down. Beaumont had spread his arms, trying to hold Glenn off. But Glenn had dropped back five yards, organising the offside line. Surprised, Beaumont tried to trap the ball. It was a heavy touch, and Youngster darted towards it, nudged it away, and that was that.

"Whoa!" I said, surprised and delighted. I looked around, beaming. Vimsy was sitting, calm as a monk, not getting involved with the other dugout. "Vimsy. Who came up with that?"

"Carl," he said. "He called it the Meatball Sub. We practised it this morning. How was the canal?"

"Slow," I said. So Carl was stepping up. That had been a long process. If I had been conscious during the summer, I might have cut him from the squad. Good reminder, there, maybe. Patience. And Vimsy had taken Carl's idea and worked on it. Made it concrete. "Brig?"

"Sir?"

"Will you join me in a ceremonial quadruple thumbs-up?"

"Aimed at whom, sir?"

"At Vimsy."

"Very good, sir."

Vimsy blushed.

In the first half, we dealt with Beaumont well. Banbury's "attacks" normally ended with Youngster scampering away from the danger zone, bringing the ball with him ten yards before playing a simple pass into the midfield.

Great. We were, miraculously, able to contain the league's slowest, least technical player.

But the midfield wasn't clicking. Magnus was doing well in place of Sam, but he wasn't impacting the game going forward. He wasn't even *going* forward. I triple-checked his instructions, wondering if I'd somehow prevented him from making forward runs. I hadn't—in fact, I'd *encouraged* him to get up the pitch. It was key to the whole plan that he joined attacks. Him staying put in midfield meant Joe was isolated on the right. Sometimes Carl would make a run and we'd get overlaps, but not overloads.

I complained about this to the Brig.

"At the risk of sounding like I haven't been doing my homework . . . please remind me of the difference."

I was a little bit surprised because the guy seemed superhuman sometimes. But football wasn't his game and he'd had to learn a lot in a short time. Not all of it was sticking. "The left is functioning pretty well. Aff's the left mid, and he's the main weapon. He gets forward, crosses, we score. The other team knows that, so they have someone watching him. So we send Trick forward. He runs to the left of Aff, even closer to the touchline. He runs past Aff. That's the overlap. Now they need *two* defenders over there or we'll get crosses in whenever we want. So now we get *Raffi* to join those attacks, too. Three on two, that's an overload. They bring another defender across, we get Sam to help out. Or Magnus today. And we do that same stuff on the right. The top teams will keep switching from left to right until the overloads create a gap or there's a really purposeful overlap. We can't switch left and right like that, but we also don't need to because these aren't elite defenders. We just need to attack one part of the pitch with enough numbers until Aff or Joe get a chance to cross."

"Yes," said the Brig. "But that's what Banbury are doing. Crosses, I mean. So it's more effort for the same result."

I pointed to a spot ten yards away. "Banbury's crosses are from this sort of zone. When you cross from here, it's much easier for the defence to clear. And harder to score even if you make the header." I pointed much farther down the line. "We do all our dicking about to get to the penalty box, because crossing from *there* is much deadlier. Especially from someone like Aff. But I don't even *want* crosses, really. Crosses are low percentage. I want the lads to keep playing, keep passing, and cut into the box from the sides. From there, it's havoc. It's headshots all the time." I sighed. "We're not getting anywhere today. It's awful. I hate almost everything we're doing." The curse agreed with me—almost every Chester player was on 6 out of 10.

The Brig put his finger on his lips, and we stood there for a moment, watching the match. We must have looked like a pretty glum pair.

Finally, he said, "And it doesn't cheer you up that we've scored two goals?"

At halftime, the lads were buzzing. They'd worked hard in training—their opinion, not mine—and this lead was their reward.

I briefly considered letting them enjoy the moment. But rewarding this mediocre performance would bite us on the arse. The bite might come in the second half or be delayed until some future game, but it *would* come.

As always, I gave them a couple of minutes to talk to each other. In that time, they often mentioned players who were giving them problems, talked about moves that worked and moves that didn't. This time, there wasn't much of that. They weren't worried about the second half. Max had been proven right, Max was back, and all was well with the world.

"All right," I said. They settled. "You seem pleased with yourselves."

The mood dropped in a second. Went cold. Henri had scored a neat goal; he was one of the only players on 7 out of 10. One of the only ones sure not to be in my line of fire. "We're winning, Max. The Beaumont Sandwich is working."

"It's the Meatball Sub!" called Carl, and there were a lot of laughs and counter-arguments. The sub versus sandwich debate, I later learned, had been a big feature of the coach ride down.

I rubbed my temples. I was angry enough to start shouting, and they deserved it. But the idea of traumatising my own brain made me get even quieter. I spoke in something like a growl. "I feel a headache coming on." The Brig stepped close to Carl; the American shut up. Sam Topps smacked his mate Tony on the back of the head. Resting Topps was common sense, but I wished I had him on the bench, at least. I'd named Andrew Harrison as a sub to see if that would give him a CA boost. Logical, long-term thinking, but it came with the cost that my options were limited. "I'm not happy with that performance. Henri's scored a great goal from nothing, and they've panicked and scored an own goal from a good cross. Okay? Take those moments out and the rest was pretty dogshit."

I rubbed my eyebrows, hard, trying to get positive, but the memories of shit moves, shit passes kept filling my head.

"Magnus, you're not joining attacks."

I waited for him to reply. "Sorry, Max. I'm trying to make sure I last the whole ninety minutes."

"You don't think you can last the whole match?"

"I can if I don't sprint into the box and back once a minute." He glanced around the dressing room, almost ashamed. "I haven't played a full ninety minutes, Max. I thought it was because you knew. I'm working on it," he added, downcast.

I looked at the tactics board, absorbing this new data and applying it to my system. The real value of Sam's ability to get box-to-box, up and down the pitch, many, many times a game had just become clear to me. Without that, we lost a lot of attacking thrust. Magnus knew his body well, and the way he was playing was smart. It gave me *most* of what I wanted, but not the last part, the last part that I craved. One less body in the box. One less attacking weapon. But there was no point asking him to give me something he couldn't give me, and there was no point reminding him I wanted him to lose some of his upper body bulk and do more cardio. He was already doing that. This scene would only make him more determined.

"Okay, this is my fault, then," I lied. "You're right to pace yourself; you'll play the whole match today. So, wingers. Lots of crosses. I seem to remember asking you to get into the box from those positions, too. Remember we talked about slapping? Remember I played an awesome song and danced around? And we do the Art of Slapping drill once a day? You think we do those drills for fun? Let me say it for the hundredth time. I want you to grow a pair, stop taking the easy option, and get the fucking ball into the side of the fucking penalty box, like I constantly, constantly ask you to. You didn't do it *once* that half."

Aff started to speak, but I stopped him.

"Sorry, mate. Nothing personal but I'm done with this. Watching my team play like shit is depressing. Magnus, give me ten minutes of overloads, please. We're going to play my system, properly, for ten minutes. Anyone who doesn't feel like doing things my way, we'll find out in the next ten minutes. Ten minutes, please. Then we'll switch things up, get more conservative, see out the match. You've got ten minutes to play some Max Best football. That's it. Get out."

They got up, one by one, and walked out onto the pitch in silence.

When they'd gone, Vimsy's face changed. He'd been as subdued as the rest of them but now he perked up. Now he reminded me of Jackie. "Fuck me, Max. Talk about motivational halftime speeches!"

I managed a thin smile. "I don't have it in me to really let rip."

"Oh," he said, with a chuckle. "You let rip all right. No volume, but that was fucking devastating."

"How will they take it?"

"No clue. I'd say we'll see what they're made of, but we know that, don't we? We saw it last season."

I clambered onto a bare stretch of bench and closed my eyes. Confrontation was draining. "Would you two like to stand on the touchline and scream at them for the next ten minutes?"

Vimsy's smile broadened. "I thought you'd never ask." He put his hand on the Brig's shoulder. "Let me teach you how we do it in non-league. It's not as sophisticated as what you're used to in the army."

They went off, happy as clams, while I thought about what I'd done. If I'd smashed morale and turned a 2–0 lead into a draw, or, somehow, a defeat, it'd do more than push us a few spots down the table. It could seriously mess up the whole vibe of the club. The togetherness, the belief in each other, the belief in me.

A noise startled me, and I snapped my head in a panic—the Brig had left me alone for once. It was Livia; I relaxed. We hadn't talked much since I'd returned to work. I didn't know what to say. There was an elephant in the room, and the elephant was wearing Liverpool shinpads and refusing to come to work. Livia got something from her coat pocket, hesitated, then left.

I spent the rest of the halftime break alone.

Nerves. I didn't get nervous as a player, and almost never as a manager. But here I was, mouth dry, blood pounding against my eardrums. Why?

In the past, I had almost always asked players to do something I knew they could do. Telling Ziggy to be a striker. Moving Beth into defence. This, though, felt different. It felt like the players might say no. And if they did, if they wanted to play like they had in the first half, what would I do about it? What *could* I do? Replace them all in the summer. And what if the next lot didn't want to play Max Best football?

Yeah. I was nervous.

I slumped into the dugout. I must have looked fierce, because the subs stopped talking, and the chat didn't start back up.

The match resumed.

Again, the first interesting moment of the half was a long ball struck towards Chris Beaumont. This time, though, Glenn Ryder had his eye in. "Ryder!" he yelled, marking his territory. He sprinted from five yards away, leapt like Michael Jordan, and headed the ball so far it went for a throw-in deep into Banbury's half. My captain had smashed into Beaumont on his follow-through. The giant took his time getting up.

From the throw-in, we waited, waited, then suddenly swarmed all over a midfielder. He turned the ball over, and both Trick and Carl instantly sprinted forward, full-pelt, trying to get close enough to help the attack. The ball came to Raffi. He ran, holding onto the ball until a defender neared him. He played the ball to Aff, who burst past the defender. We were flying forward from all angles now.

Trick finally got on the overlap, Aff found him, Trick played a simple square pass into the box—like we fucking *practised* nonstop—and Aff cooly took a touch, looked up, saw Henri zooming to the front post, taking the two centre backs with him. Aff pulled it back to Magnus, who had also been sprinting to support the move. The second centre back recovered his position well and flung himself at the ball, but Magnus simply played it diagonally forward five yards to a spot where Carl was slightly ahead of Joe Anka. I worried they'd get in each other's way, but Joe let Carl take the shot.

Bottom-left, keeper no chance, 3–0.

Vimsy hugged the Brig. The bench went nuts. The players ran to the away fans.

I was dizzy; I wanted to sprint around like a madman. That goal was mint. It was fucking thrilling. Fantasy football. Fearless play. But I kept it all bottled up. I'd told the lads this would happen if they played my way; I could hardly jump around like it was unexpected, could I? It would show that I didn't believe in myself. Vimsy came over. "Max?"

I showed him the time on my phone. "Six more minutes."

He blinked rapidly. Three–nil. He didn't understand what I was unhappy about. But he flicked his tongue around his lips, reset his face, and returned to the sideline. He shouted at Joe. "If Carl's underlapping like that, he should have stayed wider." The Brig picked up the tone, and he barked out complaints, praise, urged the guys to keep at it.

The next six minutes were enjoyable, but I didn't let that show. We took risks, we spread Banbury, attacked from all angles, and their defence got deeper and deeper until Youngster put his foot on the ball and started trying to lead them back into our half. The plan was to annoy them into wasting their energy and moving high up the pitch, leaving gaps. Like we'd *practised*. But they didn't. They let us pass the ball around, almost without contest. The game was over.

The relief was incredible. I'd been so tense, and now I could relax. There was something I was doing, or not doing, that was making me trip up over my own feet. But we could still win football matches. We could still play the football I wanted. The team were still with me. We'd get the machine working smoothly again. I'd find the magic oil.

I got up from the dugout. Vimsy went to sit down, but he'd been doing great ignoring the wind-up merchants on the other bench. I let him stay.

Time for squad rotation and fresh legs.

I took Trick off, replacing him with Tony, who became our second striker in a no-frills, energy-saving 4-4-2. I moved Magnus to left back, Youngster to central midfield. Then five minutes later, I swapped Carl for Steve Alton. Cosy debut for the new signing.

With twenty minutes to go, I swapped Joe with Pascal. The little German's first minutes of the season, and he flew out of the blocks trying to impress, trying to make things happen. At a break, I called him over and I smiled. Showed how calm I was. "Let it happen," I said. "Relax. We've got ten months of this." He played less frantically. More like the real Pascal. Another positive step.

Banbury left Chris Beaumont on until the end, which was weird because we'd totally nullified him and he was on 5 out of 10. But I got another lesson in patience.

In the last minute, Steve Alton and Pascal, two guys who'd never played together before, got into a misunderstanding and Steve had to make a foul to stop an attack. Yellow card. I kept Pascal and Tony on the halfway line, hoping for a fast break.

But the free kick was taken from the very spot I'd pointed to when I'd told the Brig about low-quality crosses versus good ones. The delivery was virtually perfect. An invitation. Chris Beaumont skittled our defenders and thumped a header past Ben.

Three—one. Final whistle. Three points and lots for everyone to think about. But our fans would go home happy, and drink themselves into oblivion on the coach ride home. They'd sing our songs, and talk about our goals.

I'd added a few hundred XP, bringing my total to 1,680. Most things I wanted to buy were around 2,000. I'd have a decision to make soon.

In the dressing room, I was calm. Forgiving of their abysmal first half. Said the second half was much more like it, and I'd see them the next day for the World Cup final, but if they didn't mind I would rush into the arms of someone who'd give me more than ten minutes of pleasure.

I also told them not to plan anything for Monday afternoon. "I'm going to teach you how to play football. Again."

"Will it be a different song this time?" said Vimsy.

I laughed. He didn't like the song I'd chosen last time. "They know how to play for ninety minutes. They'll learn how to play for ten months. They'll learn why Andrew was on the bench today. Why I'd like to bring in a couple more players even though I'm happy with this squad. And you'll learn why I'm one hundred percent sure we can win this league. And why I'm sure there's no one who can stop us."

That was intriguing enough to wash away any resentment at me suddenly annexing their free time on Monday. But it wouldn't be all one-way traffic in that meeting.

My players would learn a lot, sure.

But I was going to learn something, too. I was going to learn the name of my main opponent for the season. The only dude with the skills to stop me achieving my goals. A person with a massive grudge against me. Just because I'd, like, got his dad fired or some shit. He was the angry son of the slain Goliath. And I'd never even met him.

It was totes unfair.

SCARBOROUGH UNFAIR

Chester Men, Chester Women. Twenty men, fifteen women, companionably squeezed into a downtown sports bar. Midfielders playing snooker, defenders playing pool. The goalies playing darts, Robyn holding her own. Trick nursing a beer, waiting for me to see it before he could really enjoy it. Raffi tucking into a burger, feeding fries to his daughter when Shona wasn't looking.

And on the big screens, any second now, the World Cup final! England versus Spain. Probably the two best teams in the tournament.

We had a bumper turnout of wives and girlfriends. WAG culture hadn't touched me yet, and that day was my first taste of it. The social undercurrents, the glances, the jealousies and rivalries. To take one example from many, Robbo's wife absolutely loathed Joe Anka's girlfriend. How on earth had *that* happened? The men barely ever hung out. Barely even trained together.

I wondered if these social events could do more harm than good. Robbo refusing to pass to Joe wouldn't crash our tactics, but I couldn't deal with that sort of shit on top of everything else.

Or maybe I was overly worried about Emma. The rest of the WAGs were cautious around her, being the boss's girlfriend. Kept a bit of a distance. Scoped her out. Emma was charming and friendly to absolutely everyone, and didn't do any of her weird jokes. Still, I saw one woman look her up and down with a big sneer. She caught me looking. I stepped towards her to ask what the fuck was going on in her tiny little mind, but suddenly Gemma was blocking my path. I thought Gems had come to re-seduce Henri, but he wasn't coming, and I'd told Emma that. Didn't want to be in a room with "a hundred happy English," he said, but he might pop by if Spain won. So then I thought Gemma was checking out who else was available; she loved a footballer. But in that moment I realised she'd come to provide moral support for her best mate. Protect her from the wolves. And protect me from me.

"Did you see that?" I said.

"I did, Max. I'm impressed you caught it. Most men are oblivious."

"Why aren't you as enraged as me?"

"I am. Look." She smiled.

"I don't see it."

"That's right, Max. Very good."

"You think I should . . . what? Ignore it?"

Gemma fussed with my shirt. "Emma's smarter and fiercer than any of these women. If they start anything, they won't know what hit them. When she needs something from you, she'll ask." She finished adjusting me. "She won't ask. You've got the Brig. Emma's got me."

I shook my head. "I always get you wrong. What's up with me?"

"I'm enigmatic," she said, and her eyes danced. It was the first time I'd ever been attracted to her. She looked around the room. "You're pretty good. You knew it wouldn't work with me and Henri." She sighed. "Who would you set me up with?"

"Andrew Harrison," I said, without hesitation.

She hadn't been expecting that. "The Triplet? Why him?"

"He's outstanding."

"As a player?"

"As a man."

"He's pretty young."

"He's almost the same age as me."

"You're older than you are. Go on, then. What's the sales pitch?"

I hesitated. It wasn't really my story to tell. But she could have gotten the details from Emma. Why hadn't Emma suggested Andrew to Gems? Emma had been there in Tenerife when I'd scouted the Triplets. The five of us had hung out in bars and restaurants together, had a whale of a time until it was time to fly home. "He's been raising his brothers. Parents died. The guy scraps every day to give them the best life possible. Noah, the youngest, said he wanted to go abroad this year, so Andrew's been doing extra shifts, side hustles, overtime, to make it happen. He's beyond determined."

She smiled. "Love that."

"He's from Bolton. Greater Manchester, right? Basically a Manchester lad, swimming against the tide, putting in the hours. No one's ever given him anything, not that he's asked. First day of training, we make him run. Second day, run more. Couple of weeks of that, we put him in a van and make him sleep in huts carrying bricks around. He didn't sign up for that, but he gets on with it, never complains. Does his best. The army guys who ran the boot camp picked out a few lads they'd want in the trenches. Andrew was one." For the hundredth time, I wondered how I would have done in the boot camp. Probably shit. Too rebellious. Too analytical. But I felt a kinship with Andrew that went beyond superficial details like place of birth. "Emma's worried I've got sentimental, helping him out because he reminds me of me."

Gemma closed her eyes, trying to remember some snippet of something she'd heard. "You had to sign all three to get the one you wanted, but no one knows which is the good one."

"Oh, someone knows," I said.

"Who?"

I smirked. "Me."

"Still a prick, I see." She smoothed out my shirt. "A well-dressed one, for a change."

My smug grin left and I grew embarrassed. Emma and I had made a deal that she'd put knives away when she'd finished using them. Seems absurd to say it, but she always left them dangling off every kitchen surface, and I had a morbid certainty that if one fell, I'd stick out a foot to stop it hitting the floor. Dave Beasant, a really good goalkeeper, had injured himself once when he tried to stop a bottle of salad cream. The story had stuck with me. Emma thought I was utterly bonkers, but she'd agreed because in return . . . "Emma's allowed to choose what I wear once a month."

"And the rest of the time you wear any old shit. What a lucky girl."

The match was hard to watch. England huffed and puffed but couldn't build attacks. Spain had incredible technique and beat England's press with superb one-touch passes, then drained England's energy by keeping the ball for long stretches. England were pretty solid, but the one time a defender lost her position, Spain scored from that very zone.

It reminded me of Man City's toddlers against the Beth Heads. One team had a lot of heart and passion. The other were cold, ruthless, untouchable. Belief versus science. Emma gently rubbed my arm; I'd been grinding my teeth. I hated to be on the wrong side of the equation.

Science > belief.

With the Beth Heads, I had overcome City's technique. What did we have that day that was missing from England's performance now? A tactical platform that allowed players to make good, quick decisions. England didn't seem to know their system and their players were doing wild, inexplicable things. A pointless backheel that ended an attack and gave the ball to Spain. A shot from forty yards when there was an overload on the far post. Players caught offside in places where it made no sense. Everyone thought the boot camp was about team building and fitness, but it was really about making good decisions when tired and stressed.

So a clear tactical plan that helped tired, stressed players make good decisions. What else did my best teams have? The ruthlessness to see the plan through to the end.

Science < belief + good decisions + ruthlessness.

Great. But I didn't want to have to choose which elements I wanted. I wanted it all.

Science + belief + decisions + ruthlessness.

The team I would one day assemble and manage would combine all those elements. What about when I was fit enough to play myself? What qualities would I bring?

I realised Emma was holding her phone up so she could snap a photo of me. "What?"

She turned the phone round, showed me my face. I was doing a Youngster-style savage grin. "What were you thinking?"

"I want it all. With a sprinkling of stardust. Soak it all in razzle-dazzle. Belief plus science plus *art*."

"Oh, right, then. Good. Let me know when you're back in the room."

England's best moment came when Spain were awarded a penalty. The handball rule is supposed to stop outfield players using their hands to gain an unfair advantage. The football haters who are in charge of modern football have warped that rule, bent it backwards over itself so that almost any contact between hand and ball is given as a penalty.

Sometimes when a patently unfair penalty is given, the player taking it subconsciously takes a few miles an hour off their shot. That's what it felt like in the final—the Spanish player struck it, not all that hard, to her right.

Mary Earps, England's goalie, later named the best in the world, didn't just save it but caught it, which is pretty rare. Everyone in the bar went tonto—a guttural roar, flying beer, chairs pushed over as their occupants jumped for joy.

But it got better. Earps got to her feet and as the camera zoomed in, she screamed, at Spain, at the referee, at the universe, "FUCK OFF! FUCK OFF!"

Possibly the most English thing that's ever happened. Earps was instantly catapulted into top spot for Sports Personality of the Year. Her skill and defiance struck a nerve. The players and WAGs doubled down on the celebrations. Somewhere in the north of England, Henri was turning in his grave.

I pushed my way through the mob to the biggest screen and yelled, "Goalies! MD! Ruth!"

We formed a huddle in a corner with a view of Chester old town, right there in the middle of the second half. My head was spinning from the excitement, the sense of opportunity. My blood was pumping, and it was hard to keep calm enough to even speak. "Did you see that? So did ten million others. Every little girl in Cheshire is going into her back garden right now to see if she likes saving penalties, too. Right? We've got to seize the moment. There are five superstar goalies out there and four will never be interested again. We've got to get them, right now. Right now! Angles, get onto the goalie academy guy. I want to do an open day. Fill the place with tiny goalie girls. Free training from every Chester goalie. Selfies, photos, whatever. I'll be there. I'll get Smasho and Nice One. Is everyone with me? Ruth, MD, I want to go hard on this. No dicking around. Don't talk to me about money. This is massive. This is worth it. Pick an evening. Put out the tweet. We'll get all these pricks to spread the word, too." I scanned the members of the huddle, picked my champion. "Ruth, you're in charge. Let's go!"

I paced around, glaring at the screens. I wanted to get onto a pitch. Do some drills. Put my ideas into practice. Summon something. Reshape something.

England couldn't get any pressure going. The cumulative effect of lots of details. I was obsessed with Chloe Kelly being caught offside all the time in right midfield. I'd never been caught offside. Not once. So why was that happening in a World Cup final? I needed to watch the footage a few dozen times to work it out. Emma came up to me. "Babes. We need you."

"Yeah?"

"You're going to talk to camera for the socials."

"No, I'm not."

"For She's a Keeper!"

"What?"

"That's what they're calling it."

"She's a Keeper."

"With an exclamation mark."

"Oh, the goalie thing. Talk to camera. Right, sure. Great. Now? Why are *you* asking?"

"Ruth says I know how to make you look good." She fussed with my collar, the way Gemma had done. "It's going to be tomorrow from five to nine p.m."

"Tomorrow? The goalie school guy's motivated, then."

"Oh, he can't believe his luck."

"I bet. Right. I'm ready."

Emma tapped her phone and pointed it at me.

"Hey, Cheshire! Max Best here. Everyone at Chester FC is watching the World Cup final. Mary Earps just saved a penalty and we all lost our minds. Do you want to learn how to save a penno? Come to JM Goalkeeping Academy tomorrow from five to nine. Free goalkeeping lessons for girls and boys, all ages. It'll be fun, and maybe, just maybe, it'll be *you* saving a penalty in the next World Cup final! See you there."

Monday, August 21.

The lads had gathered for my big speech. My preseason speech that was happening three weeks into the season. We'd got every coach, the physios, plus I'd invited MD and the new board. Two randos showed up; I guess that was two of the seven.

There was a lot I wanted to say, so I didn't waste time with pleasantries. Many of the guys were clearly suffering from hangovers. After their supervised pint and a half, they'd gone to have six and a half more. In case I couldn't see it from the bags under their eyes, or the ginger way they were walking and talking, their player profiles had red attributes. Minus one jumping, finishing, technique. Most of the women's team had similar drops.

"Couple of sore heads in here. I'll let it slide because I like seeing you treat the women's team like part of the gang. Which is what they are. And World Cup finals don't come round very often. But that's your party this season. Okay? Any questions about what I've just said?"

Some head shakes.

Henri said, "I was not drinking, Max. Does that mean I retain my party joker?"

"Yes."

"You are as wise as Solomon."

That reminded me. "Did I ever get you tested by a psychic dog?"

"No, Max."

"We'll go soon. You can meet my mum." I lost confidence. "If you want to."

"Of course I do, my friend."

"Right. Good." Things had gotten out of hand already. Better stick to what I had prepared. "All right, listen up, you worms." I closed the door. We were in the meeting room at the credit card company. It had super bad feng shui, but today I didn't care. Today was the ultimate expression of substance over style: Max Best was going to talk football. I jiggled the flipchart into place. Ideally this presentation would have happened in a VR world where I was a six-hundred-foot floating megabrain, but you can't have everything.

I rubbed my chin, then stretched. Turned to the first page of my presentation. It simply said, *Last season versus this.*

"Last season was bad. You flirted with relegation. You stank the place up. I did a survey and found that four percent of the population of the British Isles will never again watch this sport because of what you did to it. But you pulled through. Some people call what you did at the end a miracle. The Great Escape and all that. Not me. I knew you. I knew your levels. I'll take some credit that I reminded you how good you are. But I wasn't on the pitch, was I? You did it. Nineteen points from the last twenty-one.

"What about this season? Where are we? I'll tell you with incredible precision, but if you'll indulge me for a second . . ."

I picked up a little printout I'd made from a Wikipedia page.

"Ahem. I've been listening to an album recently. Albums are, like, bundles of songs. In the old days, you'd listen to a whole album in one go. Joe, am I saying this right?"

Joe Anka was our biggest music buff. He had a machine that played music from large plastic discs. A grandmaphone, I think it was called. "Yes, Max."

"Check this out. This is what people thought of the album when it came out." I started reading. "'Initial critical response towards the release was negative. Metacritic . . . average score of forty-two out of one hundred . . .' Some quotes now: 'bizarre' . . . 'big-budget disaster' . . . 'an exercise in misguided ambition that makes no sense outside of pure theory.'"

Joe was eating it up. "Are you going to keep me in suspense for hours like you did last time?"

I shook my head. "I'd love to, but I need you to pay attention during the football bit. This is what people said about *Scream* by Chris Cornell. He was a grunge, rock dude, and he wanted to do something a bit different. He collaborated with Timbaland, hip-hop guy, to make this weird album. No guitar. His fans hated it. I didn't know any of that. I found it, listened to it, went right back to the start. I love it. It's been on repeat for days. It's ten out of ten for me.

"So this is the first thing to say. We don't look at Metacritic in this football club. We don't read our reviews. Don't care about the press, Twitter, Facebook, or anything. I don't care what your girlfriend says, your boyfriend, your kids, your former managers. There's one critic in this world, and it's me. We're going to make some fucking weird music this year. People are going to freak out. They're going to give us all kinds of shit. And we won't be listening. Because there's only one opinion that matters. Mine.

"Now, this album probably isn't exactly like our season, so I didn't make it the theme of the presentation, but it starts weird, quickly gets into its groove, and the end is nonstop bangers. Every song . . . *match* . . . sets up the next one, clarifies the previous one. So . . . maybe it *does* fit our season."

I took a sip of water. Joe was on his phone, which players weren't normally allowed during these meetings, but I knew he was buying the album and would give me detailed feedback a week from now. I was struck by a wave of nostalgia for this very moment. *Deja vu* for the first time. *Deja preview.* I would remember this again and again, replaying it, re-experiencing it for years to come. If I lived to be an old man, I'd remember Joe Anka, keen to listen to every piece of music someone else loved. He had his preferences, but never looked down on anyone else's tastes. Maybe when I was old, I'd have learned a lesson or two from him.

Probably not.

On my handwritten flipchart page, I circled the word *this*. "Summary of slide one: *L'État, c'est moi.* Henri, did I pronounce it right?"

"No. But I fell in love anyway."

"Would you like to translate it for the two people with sub-par French?"

"*I am the state.* Max is the Sun King. Our absolute monarch."

"I am the state." I let that thought permeate all those pickled minds. "When I say you played well, you played well. If you're winning two–nil and I say you're playing shit, you're playing shit. If I say you're not playing on Saturday, accept it. Don't waste my precious time and energy by complaining. I'll explain most of my decisions for the whole season, right here today. Because I'm not writing songs, I'm writing an album."

I turned to the next page. It said: *Actions > Words.*

"There's going to be a lot of words today. Three months from now, you might have forgotten a lot of this. So look to my actions. Are they consistent with what you remember me saying? You'll find they are. And when they aren't, I'll explain."

I turned the page: *Money = Action.*

"We're Chester Football Club. We don't have loads of resources. So when I spend money, it's meaningful. There's a lot of resource here." I pointed to people as I named them. "Vimsy. The Brig. Jude. And me.

"We need Vimsy. We need to be solid. We need to know our defensive roles. Gaps, distances, lines, offsides. I'd love to talk about slapping all day. I daydream about fast counters, overloads, pressing weak spots. If it was just me doing the coaching, we'd lose every match five–three. It'd be incredible, and I'd get sacked. That's why my first signing was a defender. That's why Vimsy's still part of my fantasy football laboratory. Defence wins titles. I've put money into that statement.

"The Brig. Fitness. This year's going to be a long old slog. We're fit and getting fitter. I've noticed we're fading at the ends of games. That's the price for what we'll start seeing soon—those last five minutes will feel like walking down a hill. Do I get up in the morning and lick my lips at the thought of watching you lot run until you pass out? No. But we've put money there because it's important.

"Any questions so far? Good.

"Jude. He's our skills guy. I want to get another Jude. Twode? No, cut that. That's terrible. You saw Spain yesterday. You saw what technique can do. We're never going to do tiki-taka on these pitches, but the better our technique, the more we can slap. I'm saving some money for another coach. Someone like Jude with a different perspective. More challenges. More variety. We'll win ten matches this season just because we've mastered more of the art of football. We can battle in a four-four-two; we can be sophisticated in a three-five-two. That's not wanky garbage—that's points on the board.

"So we've got loads of bases covered. Defending, fitness, skills. But I want more. I want decision-making. I want to be able to use whatever mad tactic I come up with. Counterattacks. Pressing. Overloads, overlaps. Shuffles, slides, pivots, double pivots. We will do it all. You think that's overly ambitious for a National League North team? Then get the fuck out. Those things aren't even hard."

I spun a marker around my fingers. I was getting to the point where I rarely dropped things.

"An aside, on the topic of resources. On match days, we've got limited mental and physical energy and when we put all our effort into playing football, we do well. When we get distracted by opposing managers, opposing players, shit referees, we play shit. Some of you like a fight. *I'd* like you to stop. Focus. Use our resources where they can be effective."

I laid the marker at the base of the flipchart and turned to a page that said, *Play; facilities; coaches; opponents; shouty shouty.*

"The word of the year is *improvement.*

"How do players improve? Six main factors. By playing matches, the quality of facilities, the quality of coaches, the quality of the opposition, and being shouted at by Vimsy and the Brig.

"As long as your attitude is right, you'll play. Proof? Four games in and everyone's had game time except the Triplets, who aren't ready. The rest is what it is. Could be better, could be worse."

"More shouting can be arranged," suggested Vimsy.

I smiled and turned the page. It said, *Training.*

"And the sixth thing. Training.

"Training is everything. You dicks are obsessed with match day. Who gets picked, who gets left out. That's not even twenty-first-century thinking, lads. That's *Victorian.* I want you to completely change how you approach your job. I want you to train like you're being paid to train and there aren't even any games. Do you know what I mean? Forget who gets picked against Scarborough. Believe me, that is not how this club measures your worth. Your worth is entirely based on what you do Monday to Friday on the training pitch.

"As an aside, that's why I got so worked up about all that Goliath shit. You were so focused on that guy, you weren't training. You weren't improving. There isn't a minute to waste. As you'll see."

I turned the page. The next one was a simple chart with an X and Y axis. X was time; there was one dot for every league match we'd play. The dots were evenly spaced. Y was team strength.

"The league is forty-four matches. James, put your hand down. We agreed to forget the first two. What did Pastor Yaw say about being pedantic? In a second, I'm going to tell you how good every team in the league is. But let's take Banbury." I took a green marker and drew a horizontal line close to the bottom. "They're not that good, and that won't change. They'll be about the same until January, and unless they buy Messi in the winter transfer window, they'll finish the season at the same level. They don't have much ability to improve as players, and therefore, nor as a team."

I took another pen.

"Blue for Chester. Let's do a dotted line. We're about here. Better than Banbury. Now, yellow. Yellow for York. We played them and we all saw how good they were. They're definitely one of the top three teams in this league." I drew the yellow line a good few inches above the line of blue dots. "Thing is, York are better than us today, but they're also not going to change too much. They have good young players, but they won't get much game time. So they're not going to get better, are they? And their best players are maxed out on talent. What you see is the most you're going to get.

"Chester, though."

I put the markers down and walked left and right, staring into the eyes of my dudes. They were engaged. They were listening.

"Hands up if you think Raffi Brown is done improving."

No one budged.

"Hands up if you think Henri's reached his limit."

Nothing.

"Hands up if you think MD can never play at a higher level."

Most hands went up. MD shook his head and folded his arms.

"Just checking you're paying attention," I said, walking back to the flipchart. "This is why I've got such a bee in my bonnet about training. Treat every session like it's a cup final and we're going to improve. There's massive potential in this squad. We've got Premier League, Championship, League One players. It's an unfair advantage." I took the blue pen and drew a thick line on a slightly upwards trajectory. "I'm not sure the exact dates, obviously, and if we stress about this too much it'll stop it happening. But let's say we overtake York by January. That makes us the best team in the league already. Then we keep going, keep going. March, April, May, we're really smashing everyone. Did we drop a few points at the start of the season? Sure. But we're the only team that can go on a twelve-match winning streak. We'll more than make up for a slow start."

I paused. Checked a few key faces. Henri. Glenn. Sam. Trick. Were they buying it?

"It's my job to make sure this improvement happens. I'll do everything I can. New coaches. Better facilities. I'll beg, steal, and borrow to get you equipment. You'll self-report injuries and tweaks so you don't miss too much time. When you're not playing a match, you're thinking on a ten-month horizon. Like me.

"I'm going to repeat this because I don't want anyone saying they didn't hear or didn't understand. Your future as an employee of Chester Football Club is one hundred percent linked to how you train. How committed you are to improving as a player. If you are less motivated by your own improvement than I am, we have a big problem." I slapped the chart. "Because when it comes to this, there's no negotiation or compromise. I'll listen to your opinions on how we should do it. If you think there are better drills than what we're offering up, I'll listen. We all will. But the basic principle that we finish the season as the best team in the league—that's not up for debate. If you don't have it in you to be better tomorrow than today, come and see me and we'll ask Banbury if they want to take over your contract."

Pause for water.

"Let's talk about our place in the food chain." I turned to the next page. There were some numbers that I circled as I said them. "Despite being dogshit for most of the season, we had the *fourth* highest attendance in the league. *Three* times higher than clubs like Banbury. If we start playing our football, we'll shoot up to *first*. You know our fans. They're noisy. We'll turn the Deva into a fortress. Last season we finished with *fifty-seven* points. The winners got *ninety-five*. *Sixty-eight* got you into the playoffs, but that's the last time we're ever going to mention the playoffs. They're a lottery. I play the lottery when there's a rollover. This football club isn't a lottery ticket. We win the league. End of. Including me, we have *twenty-one* players. That seems like enough, but it's not."

I turned to one of the most important pages. The players sensed it, too. They all leaned forward.

"Who's who in the National League North. Some of this is educated guess-work, obviously. But let's be honest, I'm good at this. Teams might be out by a place or two, but not more." I sucked in a breath. "Last season, Fylde and King's Lynn got promoted. We've seen the best team to come down—York. They're good, but nowhere near as good as the two who went up. The promoted teams are not good, apart from South Shields. So overall, the league is much weaker."

I'd made a mistake in turning the page so early. People were reading instead of listening. I flipped the whole thing closed and asked Trick to repeat what I'd said. He *had* been listening.

"Perfect, thanks. So let's take a proper look."

I'd divided the league into four groups: title contenders, playoff hopefuls, mid-table floaters, relegation fodder.

"Title contenders. York, Kidderminster Harriers, Darlington. Any questions?"

There were none. Everyone agreed with me.

"Best of the rest: Alfreton, Gloucester, Scarborough. I've got South Shields next, based on what they've done so far. We play Scarborough this weekend, so that'll be very, very interesting. Because you'll notice I haven't put Chester on this list. That result will give us much more of an idea of where we are.

"Interactive time. Turn to the person next to you. Make groups of three if you want. Discuss where Chester go on this list. Be honest. We're not number one. I'm not looking for stupid answers. York dicked us. We lost to a team I've got down as the nineteenth best. So discuss it properly. Three minutes, go."

I stopped them after ten seconds.

"MD! Brig! Livia! You're part of this. Join the fuck in."

Soon the entire room was abuzz. The only person who had absolutely no clue was the Brig. Everyone else had seen a lot more non-league football than me. Except Youngster. I wondered how well he'd do.

"Top," I said. I'd been eavesdropping and the chats had been good. I wanted to do a lot more of that sort of thing. Engage their brains. "Right, hit me."

I pointed at the first little group. They called out the number. I kept going round the room. Most had us around eighth. Only one person had the same answer as me—fourteenth.

"Vimsy, explain yourself."

"That's where we finished last season. They say the league table never lies."

His reasoning was old-fashioned, but hard to argue with. My conclusion was slightly more scientific—our average CA was a weak 42 and there were thirteen teams with 42 or higher, based on the last time I'd seen them and a bit of analysis of the season's results so far. Some clubs had refreshed their squads to a greater extent than others, but I doubted there would be huge changes.

I wrote Chester in the gap between Boston and Buxton.

"Fourteenth is honestly about right . . . with caveats." I flipped back to the progress timeline. "It's very temporary. By the end of September we'll be what? Seventh? Why not?

"Bit of an elephant in the room, now. Best seventy-seven. I'm starting to feel good in my body again. Will I be on the bench against Scarborough? No. I'm ages away from playing. But what if I start getting minutes in November, say? That's realistic, I think. Dean's shaking his head. We'll see! Then twenty minutes in the December games. First eleven in January. It's like a new signing. Sorry to be all Max about it, but if I'm back to my best . . ." I closed the flipchart. "None of that shit matters. I will go on a rampage like the world has never seen."

"Whoo!" said Youngster, to a chorus of sniggers and affectionate chuckles.

"Thanks, bro. Obviously, we have to act and plan like I'm not going to play even a minute this season. Dean's shaking his head again. Make up your mind! What I'm saying is, we keep in contention. Be near the top of the table and at the end we'll go on a hell of a run. Either from your relentless improvement, or from me playing on God Mode. Or—get this—*both*.

"I one million percent know you can all give me at least ten percent more. It all comes down to you. Your mental state. Do you believe you can play better? Are you willing to stay in the gym another ten minutes? Can you leave off the sauce when all your mates are on? Maybe you cry off a stag party. Maybe you switch to cold showers. I don't know, do I? *You* know. I'm asking you to do what you know you need to do.

"Okay, last thing." I grinned. "This . . . this is where it gets weird. Gets a bit Max Best, maybe." I flipped to the last page. It was another progress timeline, but without the dots representing matches.

A few guys sat up straight, including Sam, Aff, and Joe. I took it as a sign they liked when I got weird.

"We don't have a lot of money. And we have a lot of matches to play. And over the winter, there are bound to be postponements. So if we assume you train like champions and all that . . ." I drew our progress line, trying to keep it the same as the one I'd drawn earlier. "Something like that, right? We're so, so strong in the last weeks of the season." I looked around and encouraged someone to join the dots. Dots—I drew a few months' worth, and then stopped. "Winter . . . Postponements . . ."

Pascal jumped up. "If matches are postponed, we'll play them when we're stronger!"

"Right," I said, pacing around, starting to get excited. But I had to calm myself. I went to my little pile of papers and rummaged around, emerging with a printout. "I've printed the fixtures, and tried to work out when all the cup matches will be. Now, humour me for a minute, and let's assume we win all our cup games . . ."

The fixtures covered seven pages. I stopped at the third page. "October seventeenth is our first Cheshire Seniors Cup match. They're always on Tuesday nights. It doesn't clash with a normal fixture. Fine. Bosh. Win that."

Something was up. The energy had changed around the Brig. Right. He didn't have any context for this stuff.

"Brig, you're lost. Okay so we play the league. But we're also in three cup competitions. There's the Cheshire Seniors. Teams from Cheshire and Greater Manchester. It's the least important cup, but we're the big dogs in Cheshire. I want to show that.

"Bit of a bigger deal is the FA Trophy. That's a cup for non-league teams. The final's at Wembley.

"Then there's the FA Cup. You know that one. Oldest cup competition in the world. If we go far in that, we'll play Man United and Chelsea and all that.

"They're all knockouts, very exciting, all that jazz. But the main thing for right now is that cup matches take priority. If there's a scheduling clash, we play the cup match and the league one gets pushed back."

The Brig nodded. I shuffled the first couple of pages to the back of the pile.

"January thirteenth. Ready for this? FA Trophy fourth round. We already have a fixture for that Saturday. Peterborough Sports."

I turned the flipchart back to show the ranking of the teams. Peterborough were rated tenth, four spots above us.

"February tenth. FA Trophy fifth round. Scheduled fixture is Scarborough at home." I pointed to the rankings. Scarborough were sixth. "If we're in the FA Trophy fifth round, that match will be moved back.

"Next page. March ninth. FA Trophy sixth round. Home to Curzon that day." Curzon were twelfth. "They're decent. Tricky match if we played them tomorrow. But if we get to the sixth round of the FA Trophy, we'll play them in fucking April. When we'll be the slappingest team who ever slapped! And here's another one. FA Trophy semifinal, April sixth. Away to Gloucester. The fifth-best team in the league, and we can get that pushed back, maybe all the way into May!"

I turned to the last page and added some dots to show our league games, with a big cluster coming right at the end of the X-axis.

"We get cup glory, we get to play difficult matches at a time when they're not so difficult. Any questions?"

Henri nodded. "We'd have a lot of games to play. Three a week sometimes. Yes, we can move some tricky ones to the end, but only by replacing them with high-intensity cup games. So we will be exhausted."

"Yep, normally. That's why I'm rotating the team. That's why I don't want to hear complaints about being 'dropped.' You're not dropped. You're rotated. I want to win the Cheshire Cup. Chester should win that every year. I looked on Wikipedia and we're barely even in the top ten winners. I want to win the FA Trophy. And have a pop at the FA Cup, too. See if we can't get to the third round. Pit my wits against Pep. So you see, there will be enough minutes for everyone. If we lose a couple of fullbacks, we'll switch the formation. If we're short in central midfield, we'll play diamond. And so on. We'll keep things fresh. We'll roll with the punches.

"By the way, this insanity is why Andrew was on the bench last time. He needs matchday experience. We all know he's not ready for proper action, but if we can get him up to speed for the last month of the season . . . You think that's not much but we could play ten games in April, plus some in May. It could get bonkers. Good bonkers, but if Andrew can play four of the last ten, it could be the difference between winning the double and getting nothing. Do you know what I mean? I'm thinking long-term. And when you start seeing Michael on the bench, that's when you know I've started to think about *next* season.

"Right. Really, really, the last thing.

"Cup wins come with prize money. I haven't discussed it with MD or the board, but if they go against me, I'll throw endless tantrums until they cave. When we start winning cup matches, we'll be guaranteed prize money. A few thousand here and there, rising to decent amounts for semis and finals. And my pledge to you now is, if you train, *hard*, eat well, cut out the drink, all the things, I will take that prize money and put it right into the facilities. Example. FA Trophy fifth round win comes with five thousand pounds. More weights, more machines, more whatever we need. You can start telling Glenn what's lacking and when the dosh starts rolling in, we'll get right on it."

MD didn't seem opposed to the idea of motivating the players with the prize money they would earn. He was looking thoughtful.

I stretched. "I think that's enough grand strategy for one day. That's the season. That's what's ahead." I smiled. "The rest of the league is not going to see this coming."

I pushed the flipchart out of the way and started collecting my papers. I looked up, surprised. No one had moved an inch.

Glenn Ryder, club captain, said, "Boss, can we ask questions?"

I blinked. I thought they would have been sick of my voice. "Sure."

"I was just thinking," he said.

Henri interrupted. "Forgive me, Glenn. Before we lose the moment." He smiled. "Am I the only one thankful to have been present for this? At last," he sighed. "At last I know how it would have felt to live in the Three Kingdoms. Yes, it's the Three Kingdoms but Max is both warlord *and* advisor. The Crouching Dragon has spoken."

"Jesus Christ," mumbled someone.

Henri stood tall. "Now that I have Max, I am a fish that has found water. I intend to stay at Chester. MD, prepare a five-year contract."

"Thanks for the feedback on my presentation," I said. "But no. Now sit down."

"I would also like to offer feedback." Pascal, pushing his black hair away. "The analysis is impeccable. Almost as good as what we get in Germany."

"Someone punch Pascal," said Glenn. Raffi obliged. While Pascal rubbed his arm, Glenn continued. "I'm with Henri . . . I think. Sometimes I don't understand if he's for or against. But boss, if . . . Thing is, it all depends, doesn't it?"

"On what?"

"On whether we can improve like you say. If that's not true, then we're, you know . . . *not*." Not going to win the league, he meant. Not going to finish as the best team by far. "We joke about the Cult of Max. But this is a bit . . . we need to believe, don't we?"

"No," I replied. "No. This . . . Imagine a Venn diagram. Fuck it, I'll draw one." I did. "Three circles: art, belief, science. We're slap bang in the middle. To me, football is science. Technique and passing are nine-tenths of the law. Okay, so there's more to football than that. Duels and shit. Great. Everything can be improved. You *will* improve all aspects of your game, individually and collectively, and I'll be able to prove it with facts and figures. Pass accuracy, running stats, shots per game, expected goals for and against, points per game. All that shit will rise nonstop through the season. We don't have *great* data but look at any metric you want from the time Jackie Reaper took over. Right? It *can* be proven.

"But sure. Belief. If you *believe* it's going to happen, it's going to happen *faster*. So trust me. And why *wouldn't* you trust me? Think where Raffi and Youngster were a year ago. Henri will tell you I spotted him in the warmup of a Darlo match. I saw he was amazing from the fucking warmup! Wait, MD was there. MD, you remember you were trying to give me a job and I kept asking about Henri?"

"It's true, lads. He didn't know the first thing about non-league. He thought we were called Chester City. Hadn't seen four-four-two in a live match before. He was a non-league novice. But he wouldn't shut up about Henri, and you can check, Henri didn't play a minute that day."

"Right. So, look. I'm not going to lose my shit if you ignore me and train like you always have. It's not a cult." I laughed. "Why do I have to keep saying that? But it's like religion in one way. Do what the book says and if heaven's real, you get in. There's no downside, is there? Do it just in case. That's what religion is all about, isn't it, Youngster?"

"No."

"Exactly."

"What's the art?" said Joe.

"The Art on the Venn diagram? Different things. First, the beauty. One of Aff's crosses. Glenn's thumping header. A flying save. But let's talk about improvement. It's hard to know exactly what works and what doesn't, right? Sometimes with the kids I try for ages to get them to learn something, then one day I do something totally different and suddenly they've understood the first thing. Progress is scientific in that it's measurable and repeatable, but it's art in that you don't know exactly what works."

"I have thoughts about this," said Henri.

"Amazing. Please email them to me. Is that the end of the questions?"

Apparently not. Carl said, "Are you all right?"

I knew what he meant. "Yes. And I'm going for an MRI this week. They're going to look at my brain and that. I'm not worried." It was true. Surprisingly.

D-Day. "You said you want more players? Like what? What positions?"

"Another forward. Someone like you, to be honest, Donny. If I had two of you on the pitch, I could get really freaky with sudden formation changes." I battled to stop myself cackling. "Or a pure winger. And someone else just for the numbers. Anyone with a bit of upside. Ideally who can cover two positions."

"Have you got anyone in mind?"

"Not really. The free transfer market is slim pickings. There are some guys who could play, they're decent, but I want more."

"What about loans?"

"Only in emergencies. Don't like them."

Tony. "Are you still going to manage the women?"

"For now, yes. When I find someone good, I'll step down. But I need to improve, too. I'm far from the finished package. Isn't that right, Trick?"

"Er . . . what?"

"I need to improve my man management skills, don't I, Trick?"

His eyes narrowed while he tried to plot a safe path through. "No," he said, and that got a few chuckles. He smiled with relief.

Raffi. "You want us to become coaches to help with all this?"

"Yes. It'll make you a better player, too. And anyone who wants to stay in football when they retire but isn't sure about *coaching*, there's a scouting course, too. One big problem we've got this season is that our rivals play at the same time as us, so I only get to check them out when we play them. It's not ideal. If you're injured, I'd love to send you to watch Kiddie or Alfy or whatever. Help me, help the team, even when you can't play. I don't know, maybe I'm crazy, but I'd prefer that than being miserable in the stands."

Sam. "What else can we do?"

"Fuck me, mate," I said, beaming. "Eleven out of ten question. You're already doing what I most wanted. There's loads of knowledge in this room. Don't wait for the coaches to ask you to pass on what you've learned. Teach each other. Talk about things you notice in other players. Sam, you've been teaching the kids and the women some of your tricks. It's great. They love it and they love you. I turn up—me, the boss, the big star—and they're like 'Hi Max. Is Sam coming?'" Sam pretended not to like this praise. "Anyway, we've got players here who could learn a lot from you. Youngster, Pascal, Raffi. And me. I'd love some tips." I looked up at the ceiling lights. "Not sure how you want to do it. Casually after a session or more organised with the coaches backing you up. Whatever you want. Some of you don't want to help your rivals progress because it means less game time for you. But if you're making players in your position learn fast, I'm going to want to keep you around a season or two beyond your use-by date. Think about it. Just saying.

"Oh. Another thing you can all do. If I tell you you're not going to play the next two matches, that's me giving you two weeks where you can do extra. Sulking and whining is not helpful. If you've got a problem, train like a champion then come and talk to me."

Aff. "Can we ask about you?"

"What do you mean?"

"When you were in hospital, me mam was worried sick. 'That poor boy,' she kept saying. She was asking after your family, and I had to say we didn't know much about you. MD came and talked to us. I asked about your mam and he told us they'd decided not to tell her; it was best like that. Okay, that melted my ma's brain but it was something to say, at least. And you're the boss, now. I . . . I suppose I don't *need* to. But I'd like to know . . . something."

"Oh. I mean . . ."

"Not if you don't—"

I scratched my nose. "Nah, it's—"

He put up a hand. "Forget I said anything."

Awkward pause. "Go on, Aff. I didn't think . . . didn't expect . . . but okay. We're going to be spending every day with each other. For literally ever. Go on."

"Tell us about your da?"

I looked down. "Nothing to say."

It was crazy, but everyone was absolutely riveted. Why? "What about your mammy?"

"Well, you know she's not well. We, er . . . try to keep every day the same. Routine's good. And she's got her best mate there. And a psychic dog. Raffi, you've met him, haven't you? Dog said Raffi was a good egg. Said I was a prick. He's never wrong." Aff had asked about my mum, not who she lived with. "Er . . . she's . . . she likes trashy TV. *Love Island*, *Fuckboy Island*, anything like that. I tried to get her into *The Traitors*, which is top, but it didn't take. Not enough slutty young people."

Henri. "Do you think she likes those shows because they remind her of you?"

I gave him a middle finger on one hand and flicked Vs at him with the other.

Aff. "So . . . But she doesn't know about all this?"

"About what?" I was calm, but I felt something inside me start to bubble. A chemical process getting underway.

"That you run a football club. That you're a genius. That you're an amazing player."

Eyes starting to sting. "No." Slight lip tremor. "She thinks I'm still in the call centre."

Aff shifted. He was uncomfortable, now, but he ploughed on. His own mum had given him a mission, and he wouldn't let his discomfort—or mine—get in the way. "And . . . that must be hard, so."

I wiped something from the side of my right eye. I wasn't sure what I disliked more—the people who were looking at me, or those who couldn't. "A bit." I pushed my rear teeth together until I had control of that whole region. "I'd like to tell her. But I won't. It'd do more harm than good. It's enough for her . . ." *Oh, shit. Don't even try to finish. Why are you trying to finish?* "It's enough for her that I'm happy."

Suddenly, Henri was by my side, pulling me into him.

The Brig coughed. "I think that's enough for now."

I wiped my eyes some more. "No, John. It's all right." I waited and took a few breaths. Nodded a few times. "Life's not fair. No news to anyone in this room. I'll leave the philosophy to the taxi drivers. And the French. All I know is football. We're going to win the league. And I'm going to get rich. I'm going to find a care home that looks like the house my mum grew up in. All eighties stuff. Sofas wrapped in plastic. Phones with pig tail wires. Those music things, Joe. What are they called?"

"Albums."

"Albums. Made of plastic. All right? I'm going to take care of her. Aff. You tell your mum not to worry, yeah?"

"Yes, boss. I'll do that."

"Great. Fuck off to lunch. Back in an hour. Run off those hangovers. Tomorrow we start our season for real."

Henri bundled me out of the room, dragged me along a corridor, pushed me into his car. The Lotus Seven was back. I hadn't seen it for ages. He dropped me into a chair, and when I came to my senses, I realised I was in Nando's.

After a while, Henri came with two plates. He'd ordered my favourite: piri-piri chicken.

"Why are we here?"

"There is comfort in the routine, Max. Even for a warlord."

We ate for a while. I warmed up. Felt better. Good enough to be honest. "That was a disaster."

Henri mumbled to himself in French for a good ten seconds. "I wonder sometimes. Are you infallible or is that a load of old bull?" He waited for a reaction, got none, and sighed. "Max, you are very stupid. That was not a disaster. You gave us all something we needed. For Pascal and myself, the education. For Glenn, the shot at glory. For Sam, the pursuit of excellence. For Joe, the creativity. But for all of us, the emotion. The humanity." He shook his head. "Aff's mother may have just won us the league. But listen. I wanted to dispute your analysis. In private, I thought was best."

"You'd have Kidderminster ahead of York?"

He put down his cutlery and wiped his lips. "Max. The real danger in this league is Darlington."

I frowned. They were the team I knew best. "I don't think so." I had them as solidly third, and last season they had underperformed their CA.

"Things have changed. They have a new manager." He eyed me. "Player-manager."

I shrugged. Being player-manager was hard. It was even hard for me when I had massive CA. "And?"

"Do not dismiss me, Max!"

"I'm listening!"

He did a dramatic show of controlling his temper. "His name is Folke Wester."

I laughed. He said it so portentously. "Oooh!" I said, like a child showing he's not afraid of a ghost.

"The name isn't familiar?"

"I mean, I've obviously seen it on the lists and that. But it doesn't mean anything to me. Some four-four-two caveman, I'm sure."

Henri nodded. "Do you remember your last game for Darlo? Against Scarborough?"

"Vaguely," I said, spearing a stray slice of red pepper. "I assume I slapped."

"You slapped very hard. You slapped Poul Wester out of a job."

"Paul?"

"Poul. The manager. Scarborough were heading for the playoffs. Your antics led to a crisis of confidence throughout the team. Humiliation followed by humiliation. They sacked him, hoping the replacement would pull them back into the playoff race. Poul's son, Folke, followed at the end of the season."

I scanned my database. "He's a player? I've never seen him."

"He was injured at that time. And now he's bitter about his father's treatment. He took the Darlington job. Switched to a new formation. Four-one-four-one."

"You're kidding."

"I am not."

"Darlo don't have a DM."

"They do. Folke Wester. He plays your system, but with more brutality."

"They've scored a lot of goals."

"That is why he's a problem. He's not defensive. His teams attack. He's Ian Evans with a brain."

"Copying my system."

"What could be more intelligent? A hard-tackling, defensively capable Ian Evans team, but always attacking, and using *your* tactical ideas. And . . . he does not like you. He will be extremely motivated to defeat you."

"How do you know?"

He didn't want to say. "I know what he says in the dressing room. I have some friends there, and so do you. They do not wish to see you come to harm on the pitch. In public, Wester is charming and personable, but if you play against Darlington, he will see it as an opportunity to hurt you. Physically. Take you off the chessboard, so to speak."

I knew exactly when the Darlington fixtures were. And it seemed like I knew when I'd be using Triple Captain and Bench Boost. "November eleventh. Away. I reckon I might be able to play the last twenty."

"Please do not be rash! The man is serious. He's not to be trifled with."

I smirked. "Wester can go Folke himself." I laughed at my own joke.

He held his hands out, pleading. "At least promise to stick to the wing. Stay away from him. Do this for me." So said a man who wasted nine-tenths of every match butting heads with cavemen. If Henri was an animal, he'd be a ram. A ram in a scarf.

The problem was, he'd accidentally set me a challenge. One I knew I wouldn't be able to resist. "You know, I think against four-one-four-one, I'd play four-four-two diamond." I laughed at Henri's expression. He knew what I was saying—that I'd play as our CAM in that formation so that I'd be in direct confrontation with this Wester guy. "Henri. I heard you. I'll check him out. See what he's up to. And I promise," I said, with maximum sincerity, "not to do a no-look backheel nutmeg on the twat. Okay?"

Henri fumed. It was almost as though he didn't believe me. "I was going to treat you. But you can pay for your own lunch."

I let him steam for a bit; he seemed to enjoy it. But then I genuinely asked for help. "So . . . I check this guy out. In a couple of weeks, I say, 'Lads, my rankings are holding up but there's one change. We've got to look out for Darlo.' Something like that? Or do *you* want to tell them?"

"It should come from you."

"It would make you look good, knowing more than me."

He lifted himself up. I imagined peacock feathers spreading as he went. "I do not need their admiration to preen my ego. I have no ego, Max."

I smiled. "Skip training tomorrow. Let's go see what the psychic dog makes of you."

He eyed me without humour. "No. Tomorrow will be the best day of training in the history of this football club. And I," said the man with no ego, "will be the best of the best."

The goalkeeping tryouts were absolute mayhem. Little kids everywhere, frazzled coaches trying to create some semblance of order, dozy parents wandering into drills asking where the toilets were. In terms of publicity for the club and the goalkeeping academy, it was an undisputed win. In terms of finding talent, it was only a moderate success.

When the number of participants was at its peak, I hit Playdar and was swamped with data. Very few of the wannabe goalies were actually goalies, and most who had potential had less than 20 PA. But I did pick up an eleven-year-old goalie girl with PA 33, and two decent boys: an eight-year-old centre back with PA 35, and a tricky winger with PA 44.

The turnout of girls was a bit disappointing. We'd pitched it as a girls' event with boys welcome, but it was seventy percent boys (and one optimistic forty-year-old P.E. teacher who claimed the reason he'd never made it as a pro was pure jealousy and conspiracies against him. He was PA 1). I hoped that when the women's team got going, people would realise we were serious about the project.

For the men's team, training intensity went up a level. Whether it would pay off with sustained CA increases remained to be seen, but this week's improvement was nothing short of spectacular. Green almost across the board. I suspected that at some point—for example, CA 60—our facilities and coaches would hold us back, but if effort from players was one potential bottleneck, I had stuck a knife down the opening and rammed the cork out of the way. For now, at least.

The main problem, which a more experienced manager might have predicted, was that the most determined players went *too* hard. Henri, in particular, ran around like his feet were on fire. Perhaps booting Glenn Ryder up the arse would help? It didn't the first nine times, but perhaps the tenth . . . ?

We spent the week having increasingly fractious interactions where I suggested he focus more on playing football and less on trying to establish dominance over his markers. He insisted that roughing up defenders would open space. I said it was pointless and risked a red card. I wasn't *totally* sure I was right; Henri had always seemed to need the jostling, the wrestling, to bring out the best in him.

One thing I was sure of: he and the rest of the team were motivated as fuck.

Match 5 of 46: Scarborough Athletic versus Chester FC.

The schedule was pretty weird in that we had a tough Saturday away trip to one of the better teams, followed just two days later by a 3 p.m. home game against one of the weakest. Monday was a bank holiday, which is UK speak for "public holiday," which meant a bumper crowd.

The trick was managing our levels of fatigue across the two matches. I decided I could play my strongest team against Scarborough, and then field a weaker team against Farsley. Farsley were also playing two games in three days, and they wouldn't rotate as much as I would. If we didn't dick them, I'd probably just quit and become a music critic—I couldn't be any worse than the ones who had savaged my new favourite album.

So I went for our usual 4-1-4-1 with Magnus playing DM instead of Youngster. Sam Topps was back, boosting our average CA to 42.1.

Scarborough were 4-4-2. Average CA 46.

First half, they battered us. Ten shots, seven corners, one goal. I tried to tweak things, to use tactics to change our fortunes, but no dice.

It was because we were effectively playing with ten men. I'd just witnessed a brainless performance from our resident intellectual, who had spent forty-five minutes smashing into defenders, grappling, arguing with the referee, and offering absolutely nothing to the rest of the team.

My halftime team talk was cool. I pointed out a few weaknesses in the Scarborough team. If Aff was closing down the right back, he might like to notice how he tended to cut back and clear with his weaker left foot. Raffi could push a bit higher when we broke because his opponent was lazy and didn't do his defensive work. And I suggested to Henri that he might want to try moving into positions where he might receive a pass. You know, to help the team.

If looks could kill, I would not venture across the English channel, which Henri probably called the French channel.

The second half started much the same. I looked at my options on the bench. "Tony," I said, looking at my second striker. "Take your socks off."

"Sorry, boss. Didn't quite catch that."

"Socks off, please."

He didn't argue, but simply started untying his laces.

"Henri!" I called, as I used the tactics screen to drag his icon off the pitch. Doing that didn't trigger a substitution, which I'd learned in the Dani yellow-card match. He came over with a curse-powered blank look on his face.

Off the pitch, he woke up. "Max, what the fuck?"

"Stand there."

"No. Put me back on at once."

"Why? So you can get a red card? I hate how you're playing. It's shit. You might as well watch from the stands because you're not helping us. Everything you're doing is shit. I can't watch it anymore. Tony, are you ready?" I turned and saw, to my shock and horror, that my second striker was tapping the bottom of his upturned football boot. He wasn't even wearing socks. "Tony, what the fuck?"

"Got stones in my socks or summat," he said.

"Put your kit on, you twat! Fuck me."

"I won't get a red card, Max!" yelled Henri.

I pushed him in the chest. "What the fuck is wrong with you? I've told you fifty times to cut that macho shit out. Fucking off-the-ball nonsense, fuck that, fuck you. We both know you're only doing it because their number four has you in his pocket."

"He does not."

"You can't compete with him. Can't win your duels, can't beat him on speed or quality. So you get yourself sent off, have a big old whinge, complain about how unfair life is. Pathetic. *Tony!*"

While I was looking away, I slipped Henri's icon back onto the pitch. Henri waved at the referee, asking permission to return, and sprinted to his position. He spent a couple of minutes sulking, but noticed Tony—who got a huge, cheeky grin from me and a quadruple thumbs up from the management team—vigorously warming up, fully shod. Henri nodded to himself a few hundred times, then suddenly he dashed away to the right of the pitch. He latched onto a loose pass, touched it to Carl, raced back towards goal, doubled back, held the ball up again, brought Sam into the move. While Sam played it out to D-Day, Henri circled around, getting tight to the number four. D-Day squared the ball behind Henri, who took a touch, dropped the defender on his arse with an outrageous shimmy, powered forward, and slipped the ball into the bottom-left corner.

One–all!

Henri, veins throbbing, neck tight, ran up to me and gesticulated, one might say, rudely. The rest of the team, shocked, pulled him away. Henri glanced back, and I mimed a big yawn. He stopped in his tracks, and even from that distance I saw one eyelid twitch.

He walked around, apparently catchly disinterested in the match. Was he sulking? Suggesting that if he couldn't fight, he wouldn't play? But then he sprinted over to the left, even before Magnus won a defensive header—one of the benefits of having him as DM instead of the faster, more mobile Youngster. Trick took the ball, passed to Raffi, and hared upfield.

Brown plays a neat first-time pass to Lyons.

Lyons holds off a challenge, skips past another, and plays a square pass to Topps.

Topps pushes the ball to D-Day.

Carlile overlaps. He cuts back into the penalty area.

He picks out Lyons with a simple pass.

Lyons shapes to shoot . . .

But passes left.

Williams is running onto it . . .

He cocks his leg . . .

GOOOOAAAALLLL!!!!!

A devastating counterattack!

Wait! The referee is consulting with his linesman.

They're checking for an infringement in the buildup.

The goal stands!

Scarborough are behind, after dominating for so long.

I punched the air, jumped around with Vimsy, Tony, the Brig.

When we played, when we *just* played and nothing else, we were fucking *brilliant*. We could play far better football than the quality of our team should allow, far better than anything else I'd seen in the division. I'd done this somehow. The curse helped, of course. The curse was the starting point. But it needed more. The formation needed someone like Henri, and needed him to play the way I wanted him to play, not the way he wanted to play. Somehow, I'd been able to get that change, and now I was getting my fantasy football and the Chester fans were making all the noise. The Brig nodded at me. I felt . . . proud.

I don't know what it was, but Aff's words from Monday morning thundered in my ears. *Does your mammy know about this?* I fled to the dugout, hid, pulled my baseball cap on for the first time since my recovery had escalated.

It was dreamlike. We were beating one of the best teams, away. Yeah, we'd ridden our luck, but as the saying goes, sometimes you make your own luck.

Henri was reborn, literally. He'd played like a worm, but now . . . Now he was playing with ice in his veins, making scientific decisions, linking up with the others, fluttering from Sam to Aff to Raffi like a beautiful little *papillon*. Playing like the artist he thought he was. He was so good it was unfair.

A Scarborough defender passed the ball to his goalie, who took a heavy touch. The ball bounced away from him, near enough to Henri to make the Frenchman think he had a chance of getting to it first. He ran, ran, and, realising he wasn't going to make it, hopped out of the way. As the goalie slid past Henri's dangling foot, he cried out in pain, writhed around.

He wasn't acting; his attributes went all kinds of red.

The referee went red, too. Red card for Henri.

The rest of my players didn't even complain—it was such an obvious foul. And they didn't rush to protect Henri as he was jostled and sent on his way by the angry Scarborough guys.

It was cut and dried.

There was just one problem—Henri hadn't touched him. The keeper had caught his studs in the turf and twisted something in his knee.

As Henri strode across the pitch, head high and haughty, I got as close to him as I was allowed. I didn't want him jumping into the crowd doing kung fu kicks like French players sometimes did.

He tried to push me away as I put my hand on his back, but I stuck with him all the way down the tunnel and into the dressing room.

He kicked our bag of footballs, kicked a bench, then sat on it.

"So. You were right. Are you happy now?"

I crouched in front of him. "I am happy. More than happy. Can I ask a favour?"

That disarmed him, briefly. "A favour?"

"Can you always play like that, please? That was phenomenal."

He swallowed and looked up. "I got sent off, Max."

"No you didn't."

I'd disarmed him, and now dislegged him. "What?"

"You didn't touch him. I know that, and I'll get the card wiped out. The ref made a mistake. That's unfair. That's football."

He looked doubtful. "Why are you so sure I'm innocent?"

I laughed and sat next to him. "I'm not the best player in the league any-more. But I'm still the best referee." We stared ahead for a minute. "Mate . . . If you play like that, we'll win the league. You've got to believe that."

"You want me to join the Cult of Max?"

I laughed. "Sure. Yeah, okay."

"You should go back and manage the rest of the match."

"What? You think I can't do it from here?"

He smiled. "If anyone could . . ." He pushed me away, so I stood and waited, enjoying the moment. The home crowd were roaring their team on, urging them forward, but I thought I could hear the Chester mob. Another little surge of pride. Henri had gone through some process of his own. He bowed his head. "Thank you."

"No, man. Thank you. You took my sketch of a tactic and turned it into a masterpiece. You're the science *and* the art." I held out a hand.

He clapped his into mine. "And the belief."

I nodded. That was the moment I stopped believing. Belief is when you *think* something's true. But the fact that we were going to win the league wasn't something I needed to believe in; it had become the water in which I swam. I smiled at the striker. I'd seen him in the warmup on my first visit to Chester and I'd been right about his talent. But MD had been right about him, too; Henri

Lyons was a total nutjob. "Good news is, if you start your shower now, you'll be finished at the same time as the rest of the team."

"You greatly exaggerate how long I spend in the shower," he lied.

"Actually," I said. "We might be late back in. I think it might be a good time to give my presentation to the fans. Don't you think?"

"You don't have your flipchart."

"I don't need it."

I got Vimsy to hang out in the dressing room so that Henri wouldn't get into trouble.

Scarborough equalised, and pushed, and pushed, and my guys fell back, and back, but held firm. Two–all. An unfair result, but both teams were unhappy not to win, so maybe that's the *definition* of fair.

At the final whistle, I ignored the other manager, who had been a total dick when he thought Henri had hurt his goalie, and gathered my players, dragging them across to the little band of Chester fans. A couple of hundred had travelled, and they applauded our efforts, sang some of our songs.

The wrong songs, though.

I motioned that they should be quiet, first by making the universal "lower the volume" gesture of pushing my hands down, then by holding my finger over my lips. The squad—sans Henri, sadly—were looking at me like I was crazy. Most managers didn't ask fans to be quiet. Most managers didn't stand on the advertising boards in front of the away terrace while being propped up by his central midfielders.

But I wanted to start a new chant. Remind the Chester fans of a song they hadn't sung in ten years. They'd need it this year, that was for fucking certain.

I sucked in a breath and prepared to bellow. It could have been interesting to track which of my players joined in, and when, but fuck it. This wasn't a time for art or science. This was a time for pure, insane belief. Time for an exercise in misguided ambition that makes no sense outside of pure theory.

I locked eyes with one fan. Just one fan—if he joined in, more would follow, and those who didn't sing today would sing on Monday.

I needn't have thought that hard. As soon as they realised what I was doing, half my team, and most of the nearby fans, raised their voices alongside mine. And by the second line, everyone was in.

To the tune of "For He's a Jolly Good Fellow":

"We're gonna win the league!

We're gonna win the league!

And now you're gonna believe us,

and now you're gonna believe us

and now you're gonna bel-ieee-eve us!

We're gonna win the league!"

9

SILENT BUT DEADLY

"Tranmere Rovers may never be able to compete with Liverpool or Everton. They are big liners like the Queen Mary. However, I see Tranmere as a deadly submarine, attacking them silently from beneath with a torpedo."

– Johnny King, legendary Tranmere manager

Sunday, August 27.

Mr. Yalley saved my life. I wanted to parade him in front of the fans at a home game, maybe even give a very short speech in his own language (read slowly, phonetically, after much practice). That idea was torpedoed—he didn't want to be the centre of attention like that. But he couldn't stop me doing something even more socially thunderous—sitting next to him in his church, giving him a billion social proof points.

When I told Emma my plan, I had intended it to trigger a rational assessment of the logistics of her weekend. Did she really want to go from Scarborough to Chester and back to Newcastle in the course of about fourteen hours? Or did she want to take a break from my weird old world and have a girls' weekend? It seemed obvious what she should do. The last thing I expected was that she'd insist on coming to church with me. To *church*. That hadn't even *occurred* to me.

So there we were—sitting through the entire service while loads of Ghanaians clapped and sang and listened to Pastor Yaw. My little section went me, Emma, then Kisi.

Kisi was an old hand at navigating the boredom—the trick, she'd told me once when I'd asked how she could stand it, was having a tube of chewy sweets and unwrapping one every five minutes. The best brand, she had insisted, was Fruit Pastilles. First you could spend half a minute sucking the sugary coating off, then you chewed as slowly as you could manage. Then you'd get a while of exploring the backs of your teeth looking for remnants. If you did it right, you'd only have to wait another minute before the five minutes were up and you allowed yourself the next one.

Kisi handed Emma a Fruit Pastille, and my girlfriend chucked it in her gob, chewed once, and swallowed.

Kisi's face crumpled, but when Emma held her hand out to ask for another, she got one. Such a good kid.

I wasn't bored, though. That's because I wasn't listening to The God Stuff.

I was taking the chance to review. To strategize in a situation where I couldn't get distracted or check my email or Cliff Daps's Twitter.

It was strange, being the manager of a football club. While I tried to keep a long-term view, there was always a match looming that tried to suck in most of my attention. And my situation was stranger than most—I also had the women's team to manage, plus all the age groups. An endless stream of blips on the sonar. Friendly ships, enemy submarines, you never knew what was coming, but there was always something. I'd been so busy, my days had been so relentless, that I hadn't really taken a minute to reflect on my voyage. So I waited until Kisi quietly unwrapped one of her candies and popped it in her mouth. I knew I'd have about five minutes.

Yeah. Quite a time. Mad.

All right, that seemed like enough looking back.

The next blip on the sonar. That was tomorrow's match against Farsley. They had been the opponents in the first game after my attack, and Henri had gone psycho and scored a hat trick in a 5–0 thrashing. This time I wouldn't have Henri. He'd conf called me and MD that morning saying he didn't want to appeal his automatic three-match ban. He'd looked at the footage of the incident and there wasn't a good angle that proved he made no contact with the goalie. The risk was too great, he concluded, that the decision would not be overturned. Failed appeals were normally punished with longer bans (to discourage frivolous complaints). He said he would take the time to redouble his efforts in training. Take a ten-month view of the season.

I'd be relying on Tony Hetherington for the next three games, then. He was a great guy and a good player. He wasn't outstanding in any particular thing, but he had a good balance of skills that matched our style. I hoped he'd do well for many reasons, including the fact that this would almost certainly be his last season at the club. He was CA 40, PA 44. Perfectly good backup for this league, but when we got promoted, he wouldn't be able to hack it. I imagined him playing a third of the striker's minutes this season, with Henri playing the rest. In that time, Tony should easily score fifteen goals, what with being the focal point of an attacking team like ours. Fifteen goals was good; he'd definitely get a new club next season.

My thoughts turned to what Henri had told me about Darlington and what I'd found in my research. I'd spent some time reading Bingo's match reports and watching clips of the new-look Darlo. New Darlo was very similar to the old one, but with less stardust. Less Max Best razzle-dazzle. The new signings were grizzled veterans, and while they had improved in the centre and right of midfield (compared to Webby, the mediocre right mid I had usurped in my time there), they were using Chumpy and TIM (The Invisible Man) on the left-hand side of their stolen formation. The player-manager, Folke Wester, looked a very good DM, I had to say, but nothing like my class. There was no doubt he was a good manager. New Darlo scored more than under David Cutter, and looked very, very tight at the back. They would definitely be near the top of the table by the end of the season.

But champions? Contenders? Nah.

I'd dug up their lineups for every match, including their preseason ones, and found that Bark, their talented half-Jamaican winger, hadn't featured. At all. He was PA 130, had turned seventeen in July, and was surely ready to make the step up into the first-team squad. I'd have loved him at Chester, but I didn't have any money and I suspected this Folke Wester clown wouldn't do business with me. But if Bark was to be our agency's first client, it looked like the best thing we could do for him was move him out of Darlington. I'd texted Ruth asking if she was still in touch. She'd replied yes, with more chats being initiated from his side, hinting that things weren't going well for him and he'd be open to letting us guide his career.

Darlington, then. Decent team. Still not good at identifying talent.

And I definitely planned to play in the November 11 fixture. I was even more motivated than when I'd talked to Henri about it.

I'd found some scuttlebutt going around the internet. Someone had leaked some of what happened in the Darlington dressing room during the Kettering game when we'd had two players and our manager sent off. I'd taken over, reorganised the team, given us a tactical plan to work from. I'd left absolutely everything I had on the pitch that evening, and we'd managed to draw 4–all. It was an amazing night. But the leaks were saying I'd refused to play the second half.

Sad to say, I understood it completely. Dirty pool. Skullduggery. Tarnishing the old "mystery winger" legacy. Folke Wester was digging up dirt about me and was getting it out there to turn the Darlington fans against me.

Now, that might have been helpful when it came to securing his own position, especially if Darlo fans were calling for the club to make an effort to get me back as player-manager, as they'd done after a couple of bad results in preseason friendlies. But don't rile me up if you've got Chumpy and TIM on the same side of the pitch as I normally played!

Emma put her hand on my elbow. I looked at her and she gave me a little eyebrow raise. Had I been cackling? Breathing heavily? Swearing?

I moved on to a less provocative topic than me dribbling at Chumpy, one of the group of cavemen who had tried to bully me out of Darlington. The league table. We'd lost two, drawn one, won two, giving us seven points from five games. That put us twelfth, slap bang in the middle of the table. At the top, Darlo had fifteen points after five wins from five. York and Kidderminster had thirteen—they'd played each other and drawn.

We were eight points behind the league leaders. There was still plenty of time, but we couldn't afford loads of slip-ups. We had to win the majority of our games for the rest of the season. Two of the next three were very, very winnable, even without Henri.

My thoughts drifted to our formation, 4-1-4-1. Solid defensively. A good platform to build attacks. The flaw was that our striker would be outnumbered—we couldn't hit long balls to him and hope for the best. If we followed my plan, we'd create lots of high-quality chances, and any half-decent striker would put enough of them away for us to win most matches. Easy.

Yep, we were in good shape, all things considered. Which was a welcome thought, because the transfer window was closing in a few days, and we wouldn't be able to get players from other teams until January.

I glanced at James Yalley. He was happy I'd come to church, but I think disappointed *he* hadn't been the one to convince me. I was still planning to use God Save the King on him. With that perk, I could increase his finishing, strength, heading, passing, or some other attributes by one point. But the more I thought about it, the more it seemed like a waste. His finishing, for example, was 6. His normal training would take it to 7 fairly fast—he was probably due a pop. So why bother? Henri's finishing was 16. It could take years to get it to 17. It was possible 16 was the maximum he could naturally get to. From that point of view, it made sense to use the perk to increase a number that was already very high. But financially, it only made sense to use the perk on James. Ugh. I was really stuck on that decision. I had the rest of the season to worry about it. Sometimes the right decision was a quick decision. But when in doubt, I liked to wait. Making mostly good decisions would make me, and Chester, stand out from the crowd. Making mostly good decisions would let everyone achieve our goals, even our backup players like Tony Hetherington.

I reached into a pocket and pulled out a tube of Fruit Pastilles. Kisi tracked it—only her eyeballs moving—as though it was a million-pound coin. I ate one, gave one to Emma, and handed Kisi the rest of the pack.

Cost: Sixty-five pence.

Reward: Plus eight thousand reputation points.

My week was off to a great start.

Match 6 of 46: Chester FC versus Farsley Celtic.

It was my first time since the attack writing the manager's notes for the match day programme. Since I had absolute power, I changed the name of my section from "In the Dugout," which I thought was a bit agricultural and didn't speak to my station or abilities, to something a little more regal. I took a programme from the stallholder—the Brig took one too—and I quickly scanned it to make sure the printers had left all the jokes in.

From the Desk of Max Best: A Proclamation

Greetings and salutations, people of Cheshire! (Also greetings to any away fans who bought this programme. You're from a beautiful part of the world. I'm guessing Birmingham way? Somewhere south. Got to be. Farsley. Far. Because it's far. Nailed it.)

Because of the tight schedule around this bank holiday weekend, I've had to write this before knowing the result of the Scarborough game.

But I think I can safely assume that everyone is happy/sad/distressed with what happened/didn't happen and that the team fought hard/fought medium/ fought just right and our win/draw/loss was deserved/undeserved. Also, a special shout-out to our player of the match: Ben/Ken/Ren/Sven. We hope to do better/worse/the same in today's match. (Delete as appropriate.)

This is the first time I've been able to sit at a computer and write a Proclamation. It took me a while to reply to all the kind emails and texts I got while I was in hospital, but I've caught up now. For everyone else, for all the people who did small things that went unnoticed, or contributed without making a fuss, or clapped harder or wore a Chester scarf with a bit more pride, I'd like to offer a blanket THANK YOU.

And I'd like to say that your financial contributions to the club at that time were unreal. Believe me when I say the money is being put to good use. THE GOLD WALLPAPER WAS ALREADY THERE.

Apart from nearly dying and having to do months of rehab to walk again and the fact the police, to put it diplomatically, botched the case and my assailant is still at large, the MAIN thing I regret about what happened is that the under-eighteens left the club without hearing it from me. Releasing players is awful, but it's my job, and I hope it's not too arrogant to think that our young players will respect the football decisions that I make, even if they don't like them. Those young men didn't get the chance to play for Chester's first team, but they represented the club and the club's values in every match and every training session. I wish them all the best.

(On the subject of my murder, I note with interest that Detective Inspector Barton is still employed by Cheshire Constabulary. I know what you're thinking. You're thinking: THAT'S WEIRD. The guy who tried to frame the man who saved my life and has shown no interest in pursuing the case . . . is still *employed*? By the *police*?)

Today's match, then. We know all about Farsley Celtic. I mean, my players do. I don't, because when we played them, I was in intensive care and DI Barton was typing out a confession for an innocent man to sign. They're a hardworking team—Farsley, not the detectives assigned to my case—but with the home fans cheering us on, we hope to get the three points.

Three points. That's how many points Jackie Reaper took from Farsley in that match. He's obviously off work at the moment, recuperating, and we all wish him well. But when he's up and about, why don't you go to him, say, "We know what you did for our club. There's always a job for you at Chester FC, mate." And then buy him a pint, and whisper in his ear, "Come on home, Jackie, lad. Come on home."

I rotated the team as much as I could. We had Robbo in goal instead of Ben, Magnus at left back, Steve Alton making his full debut in the centre of defence, Youngster, Joe Anka on the right, and Tony as the lone striker. Average CA: 41.1. More than enough to deal with Farsley's 37.

Sure enough, we roared into a two-goal lead within the first fifteen minutes. Aff burst through, and slotted a low shot past the goalie. Then Joe tried to hit a cross, but he caught it wrong and sliced it onto the crossbar. It bounced onto the goalkeeper and went in. Comical piece of luck going our way, for once. Two–nil up and the players relaxed, playing their version of fantasy football. Outrageous long shots, cheeky chips, ambitious long passes from the defence—it was all going on, followed every time by appreciative applause from the crowd, and slaps on the back from teammates. Around me on the bench, our subs gasped and laughed. They thought all the weird things we were doing were wonderful.

Vimsy was shaking his head. "This is the best we've ever played," he said, amazed.

"Who needs Henri Lyons?" said Henri Lyons.

Only the Brig caught my mood.

I was seething.

He gestured that I should talk to him. He brought Vimsy, too.

"What's up?" said the oblivious coach.

"Mr. Best is not happy."

I unclenched my jaw. "I want to scream at these idiots but I did that a couple of games ago. How much shouting is too much?"

"There's no such thing as too much," said Vimsy. He didn't know what I was upset about, but he'd swung all the way into angry right-hand man. Good sidekick. It was right I was picking his brains instead of flying off the handle. I was inexperienced; checking my decisions was solid technique.

"I don't want to keep shouting at people, though."

"Then you're in the wrong business, Max." Vimsy gripped my shoulder and gave it a little shake. "You are a state," he said, trying to be helpful.

"I am *the* state."

"That's what I said."

In the dressing room at halftime, I tried to keep it off my face, and listened for a minute as the players talked amongst themselves. I kept an eye on Farsley's tactics, but they stuck to 4-4-2 and didn't make any substitutions.

Aff in particular was ecstatic. He was chatting a mile a minute in his Irish accent, saying everything was deadly, which meant good. "That pass was deadly, Magnus! It was deadly, that move after their corner."

Finally, there was one too many laughs and I knew I'd explode if I didn't get started.

"Tony," I said, and the players ended their conversations, leaving the dressing room quiet except for the sound of studs on concrete, the fizz of sports drinks, the snip of scissors as guys re-bound their socks. "Tony, there's a little lad out there in the stand. I promised you'd sign his whatever. Or a selfie. I don't know. Go and do that so I can stop worrying."

"Right," he said, uncertain. "Am I . . . ? Am I playing all right?"

"You're perfect," I said. "Just indulge me. Don't like leaving threads loose. Weird little mania of mine."

He picked up some paste and a drink and went through the door. I assumed he would wander up and down the main stand looking for kids who were hold-ing pens.

The Brig waited five seconds, checked Tony had left the tunnel and wasn't eavesdropping, and jammed the door shut with his big boots.

I slapped my hips. "Right. What the fuck was that?"

The team had been pretty jubilant. From their point of view, they'd con-trolled the game for forty-five minutes and were slapping. Some guys stopped dead, mid-action, like we were playing musical chairs.

I held my clenched fists out in front of me. "Why do you hate Tony?"

Lots of confused looks, especially from Tony's best mate, Sam. "I don't. We don't."

"Is this because I shot instead of passing?" said Aff. "I scored, Max."

I shook my head. "The shot was a thirty-percent chance. Passing would have been fifty. But it's your decision, there. I would have passed, but that's not what I'm in-can-DESCENT about." I tried to count to ten, but got to three. Thanks to the bank holiday, it was a Monday that felt like a Saturday. The fans were hav-ing a great time, we were winning, and this should have been a joyous occasion. "Right. Let me tell you a story. Once upon a time there was a model professional called Tony Hetherington. He played football and was good at it. One day, a wizard took over his team and summoned a combo target man slash fox-in-the-box with the heading ability of Goliath, the movement of a ballerina, and the bone-headedness of a skeleton. And the wizard decided to play with one up top, so Tony became, to his surprise, a backup player. And Tony fucking crushed it in training, came back from summer fit and ready, and never once complained."

I paused for breath. I was getting worked up to the point there was a danger I would start smashing stuff.

"One day, events transpired so that Tony would get to play three games in a row. And his wizard didn't worry because he trusted Tony to do the job and had massive respect for him. But what the wizard didn't know was the rest of the team were a bunch of fuckwits who didn't value Tony as a person or a player. So they cut him out of the match completely, and at the end of the season when Tony's contract wasn't renewed, no other clubs were interested. And so Tony couldn't feed his children."

"He doesn't have kids," said Sam. I *think* he was trying to be helpful.

"Tony told his wife he wasn't a footballer anymore and couldn't *afford* to have kids."

"He's not—" said Sam, deciding this was a good time to update me on Tony's marital status. His decision-making matrix kicked in, and he shut his gob. Maybe one of the factors in his decision was the way all the veins in my body were straining on their leash, waiting for the signal that I should attack.

Henri was by my side, calming me with a hand on my back, and on my arm. It helped. "What did you see, Max?"

"Is that a joke?"

"No. I swear. It looked like our normal football."

"Oh. Right. Okay." I walked around, glaring at my shitty players as I went. "So here's what I hoped. I hoped Tony would bag a bunch of goals in these three games. Six, maybe. Imagine being a striker and getting six goals to your name in the first week of September. Takes the pressure off. Makes you look good to other teams. That's good for his future. His future family, too. Right? And it's good for us. When Henri has a knock, we put Tony in, no drama. But what do we get instead?"

I looked backwards and followed my glance to loom over Raffi. I gave him the stink eye.

"We get Raffi Brown who decides to start chipping Hollywood passes into the penalty box. Oh, the crowd loves it. I bet it looks *amazing* on camera. But it's nothing we've ever practiced, is it? It's nothing Tony can do anything with. I've never seen you try that shit, ever, and you choose to do it today. Why? To make Tony look bad? I want to get the ball wide so we can slap our way into the box, but instead you're slapping Tony in the face."

I took a few strides and bellowed at Youngster.

"And the fucking James Yalley long shot is back! Tony's in the penalty box, moving around, being a handful, working openings, doing his job as a professional football player. But you think it's funny to blast the ball out of the stadium. Out of the stadium! And what do we get? An apology to Tony for ending his career? No. We get a fucking cheeky grin. Oops! Silly me! Well, your career won't be ended if you never score, but *his* will. So good job showing your true colours, mate. All that shit you gave me back in your house, remember? Well, that shot is one of the most selfish things I've ever seen. It makes me sick to think you'd laugh after doing that to your teammate."

His head dropped. I was far from done.

"Aff. You sent all your crosses to the far post. That's where Henri lives, mate. You're got a brain, you've got eyes, so you must've noticed that Tony likes to stay in the centre. So what are you thinking? Carl, Magnus. How many times have you punted long balls down the centre? Look at the fucking tactics board. He's on his own against four defenders until we work the ball up the pitch! What the fuck are you doing?

"Why is everyone doing whatever the fuck they want? We have a plan. We have a system. We train in a specific way. You don't get to choose to do whatever you want. It's like the fucking last day of school out there."

I went over to the tactics board and plucked the striker magnet off. Stared at it. I wanted to threaten to buy a whole new team to replace them, but they knew I had no transfer budget.

My energy had all drained off. I was barely audible when I spoke next. "I'm done begging you to play the way we train. I'm done begging players to respect their teammates. Football shows character. I didn't see any in that half. I don't want to be in the same room as any of you. Get out."

The Brig opened the door. Almost everyone fucked off.

Henri waited near me, solemn, until the Brig closed the door behind him. Henri's eyebrows shot up. "You really hate being two–nil up at halftime, Max! Is this your secret? Two–nil is the most dangerous lead. Make sure the players aren't complacent. Something like that?"

"Don't you think I have a point?"

He shrugged. "Of course you do. You have a point like a torpedo has a point. To be clear, I agree with everything you said. I'm not sure it's healthy to get worked up about it. Torpedos don't usually survive the explosion they create."

"I've changed my fantasy."

"Oh? You're off the flight attendant thing?"

Despite my mood, I laughed. We had NOT talked about that. "When we play Darlington, I'm not going to go on a rampage. I'm going to give an insanely perfect, disciplined interpretation of the role I assign myself. No frills. The correct decision, every time. I'll show these fucks what teamwork looks like, and what happens when a cog in the machine starts to function exactly as intended." He was smiling at me. "What?"

"You're such a fundamentalist."

"Is that good or bad?"

"Oh it's good," he said. "And bad. But Max, players make terrible decisions all the time. Defenders like to shoot. It makes them happy. Why do you take it so personally?"

"If Tony scores a lot of goals, we can sell him in January. *We* raise a bit of cash while *he* gets a juicy, long-term contract. Or he leaves at the end of the year with twenty goals to his name and has eight offers from clubs." That face again. "What?"

"So it's really about Tony? I thought you were using him as one of your MacGuffins."

"Don't you get it? We are all Tony."

"Ah, yes. That's clear now."

At the start of the second half, Farsley came at us like a steam train. My speech had knocked the stuffing out of a few players, especially Raffi and Youngster. Farsley won duels. Forced us back, got shots.

Robbo made a couple of saves. Glenn threw himself into a block. Sam put in a thumping challenge.

When we snapped out of the funk, we snapped hard. We worked the ball through our diagonal patterns. We were patient. Youngster brought the ball backwards to lure Farsley into our half, then with a quick pass-pass-pass, we'd have the ball with Aff on the left or Joe on the right and we'd probe for overloads or overlaps.

Again and again, we got the ball to the side of the penalty box, and someone would either try to get into the box, or cross.

Magnus got to the byline, but had to cut inside on his right foot. Too slow. His cross-cum-pass was intercepted.

Carl got past his man, but didn't feel good about his crossing angles. So he played it back. Joe leaned and whipped in a lovely cross. Tony got a good head on it, but it went wide.

Raffi exchanged a few passes with Magnus, but couldn't move Aff's marker out of position. So he burst into Aff's zone himself, faked a cross, and dribbled into the box. Raffi hit a low cross, there was a scramble, and the ball was in the net.

Three–nil. Tony wheeled away in celebration. The other players didn't celebrate very hard, still stung by my surprise attack.

A minute later, Youngster moved forward, moved forward, found no one was coming to press him. Farsley had sunk and split to protect the wings, from where we'd been doing all our attacking. For a second, I was sure he would shoot and I would be forced to either murder him or substitute him. But he waited, and waited, and when a defender finally came at him, he played a one-two with Tony, ran faster than I'd ever seen him, surging with the ball into the penalty area. Youngster drew the keeper towards him, then cut it square. Tony had an open goal. Four–nil. Much bigger celebration this time.

I got up from the sulk zone and went to the edge of the technical area.

"You're satisfied with the response," said Brig.

"That goal isn't what we practice, but it fits the principles of the team."

"I have to say, I don't really see the difference between the first half and this."

"Really?" I said, frowning. I tried to see things from an outsider's point of view. "I suppose it's hard to explain some of it. Just so you know, those players know full well what they did. Right, let's take two things. First, Youngster's shot versus this dribble. The shot is selfish, annoying, zero-percent probability. He might as well hand the ball to the other team."

"Why don't you ban him from shooting?"

"I did! I've told him a hundred times. Fuck. Right, compare that to this dribble thing he did. So, he shouldn't really do that because he's a permanent part of our rest defence. But we had plenty of players back. And the other team weren't expecting it, and as you saw, he didn't do anything hard. The percentages were all good, and he did it because he really, really wanted to make it up to his mate. So it's fine. It's good. It's Max Best approved. Vimsy?"

"Yes, boss?"

"Let's add that to our repertoire. Work on who stays back when Youngster goes on a run like that."

"Got it."

I let them play another five minutes, then made a double change. D-Day and Pascal replaced Aff and Joe. Pascal's first act was to skin the left back and rocket towards the goal. The fans got up on their feet—fans love fast players—and Pascal very nearly found Tony. That was Farsley's cue to drop back into a low block. Men behind ball. Not trying to get back into the game, just trying to stop us running up the score.

So I threw Andrew Harrison on for the last ten minutes. Giving him match time was a bit premature, but we were winning 4–0, and maybe it'd accelerate his development. He kept things simple—simple passes, no tricks. Perfect. Ten more players like that, please.

Near the end, we got a free kick in a good position. D-Day stood over it. He wasn't allowed to take penalties—that was a permanent ban, but based on the testing I'd done in training, he was our best bet for a goal from free kicks. I used Free Hit, D-Day struck it well, and that was that.

Five–nil.

I didn't want to go back to the dressing room. While they'd played well in the second half, the shit they'd done in the first half was lingering like a radiation leak on a nuclear submarine. Also, I was very slightly embarrassed by my outburst. I needed to do *something*, but surely there was a way that didn't involve a five-minute collapse in morale? I gave myself a break. I was twenty-three. I had skills but no experience. I'd work on it.

I went in and turned off the victory music. Everyone stopped what they were doing.

I rubbed my forehead and looked at a spot on the far wall. "Forget the goals. Is there anyone who prefers how we played in the first half to how we played in the second half?"

No one spoke.

"Is there anyone who thinks we'll beat Spennymoor away playing like a load of clowns?"

No one spoke.

"Double training on Wednesday. Double training on Thursday."

I pressed play on the speakers. Thumping victory music came out. It felt somewhat sarcastic.

I went to find Gary, the newspaper prick, to get the interview over with. I praised Tony Hetherington to high heaven. I think I called him Two-Goal Tony at one point, called him a sharpshooter, praised his teamwork, decision-making, and professionalism. I probably went a bit overboard, but my relentless positivity infected Gary, and we ended up having a decent chat. He even forgot to ask me about the referee.

I went up to the executive lounge where MD was entertaining a handful of sponsors. They wanted to meet me, and even more than that, MD wanted them to meet me. He said it was both urgent and important.

Important I got, but urgent?

The sponsors were three men in suits, and they'd invited a handful of friends each. MD helped me understand who I needed to impress by only telling me three names. It wasn't very diplomatic of him, but I later learned he'd warned them I got worked up during matches and wouldn't be firing from all missile tubes.

I was not very charming, at first. I was still stewing from the first half "performance." The three rich dudes and their most outgoing friends soon turned into my therapists. "Max!" they'd say. "We won five–nil! It was one of the most one-sided, dominant performances in this stadium in years."

"Do you accept mediocrity in your companies?" I said.

"But it was great!" they said. "You're fantastic."

I hadn't been drinking much because I was taking my recovery very seriously, but I treated myself to a big German wheat beer—Pascal taught me about that stuff—and after a few mouthfuls I conceded that maybe Raffi *had* played well and Aff *had* been a constant nuisance and Youngster *had* played like a much more experienced player with one blip.

The whole thing then took a surprising turn. MD clinked on his glass of white wine.

"Max. You've met the sponsors. I'm sure it was quite educational for them! Only Max would be fuming after a five–nil. Welcome to the new Chester, ladies and gentlemen!" Some cheers. Some laughs. "I've been telling them about your plans for the season. That you want to win everything."

"Why wouldn't I?"

More cheers.

"Did you find any free transfer players to bring in?"

"No." There were options on the player search pages. Guys with CA 30, PA 40. Plenty of that kind of thing. It was all just a bit . . . Ian Evans. If I couldn't find anyone who got my pulse racing, even just a little bit, I'd use the money to hire another coach (on top of the other coach I wanted), or a scout, or start buying new equipment. "What we need is someone to add something to the squad. Something we don't have."

"What?"

"Oh, I didn't mean I had something in mind. I meant generally. Give me a new toy to play with. Like a really fast winger. You saw what Pascal did when he went on near the end—scared them to death. Imagine that with a more powerful player. Or a forward who can play loads of positions. Or someone who can take a good corner as well as do his job to a high standard."

MD got me to stand up and rehomed me at the front, facing the three VIPs like a teacher. "Max. I lied to you about Steve Alton."

"What?"

"You're substantially under the wage budget I set you, and if you multiply that by the number of weeks since the start of the season, it basically pays for Steve Alton." He didn't want to say the numbers in front of the outsiders, but I had a quick think and yeah, I was probably under budget, cumulatively, by about eight thousand. In other words, when he'd made a big song and dance about finding the transfer fee for me, he'd actually been using the existing budget. The cheeky fuck.

"Right," I said, confused about where this conversation could possibly go. The sponsors had the air of men about to witness the launch of a new type of battleship.

"We're excited. Me, the board, everyone in this room. The fans backed you over the summer by putting their hands in their pockets to give you more budget. I put the sponsorship rates up, and there was no shortage of interest. But we want to do even more. It might be a dream, it might all turn sour, we've all had our fingers burned in the past. But we'd like to push the boat out. Tell us about a player you'd like to buy, and we'll try to find the money. Something like thirty thousand should be achievable."

"Wait . . ." This was a head-scratcher. This wasn't like MD. His ambition score hadn't increased. "Hang on. Okay. You're saying . . . I pitch you on a player I want to buy . . . and you'll buy him? So I should, what, pick someone dynamic? Someone who scores goals? Does dribbles?"

The oldest sponsor, a thin, wiry guy with silver hair, spoke. "MD says you've got unique ideas. You're right to say that if we were choosing, it'd be someone flashy. That's right. But you choose freely, young man. If you need a boring player, you choose that and stick to your guns. Max knows best." He cackled. I wondered if he had a grandson in the youth system. "I like you. I think you've got it. And I'm willing to put my money where my mouth is."

"Hear, hear," murmured some of the hangers-on.

"Wow. Okay. This is wild. This is blowing my mind. I thought my squad was settled, more or less."

MD blinked. "Didn't you want to bring in a couple more bodies?"

"Yeah but free transfers I can sign any time. Don't have to stress about the transfer window closing. Okay, so it's Monday. Last day for deals is Friday. Erm . . . you're not giving me a lot of time to choose."

"Darlington drew, so we're two points closer to the top of the league. And five goals loosens a lot of purse strings, Max."

"Yeah? Next two home games are against Hereford and Bradford. What do I get for ten goals?"

They loved it. Loved me being cocky, being positive, talking the club up.

MD opened his mouth, but I raised my finger, sat down, and tipped some beer into me. I stared into space while I went to the player search area and filtered by guys who were transfer listed. There wasn't actually a transfer list. No website where clubs could say which players they wanted to get rid of. When I'd asked MD to see "the transfer list," he'd laughed, but quickly apologised for mocking me. He said some guy had tried to make an app with all that kind of data, but it had failed. So clubs told agents and agents told rival clubs. The more contacts you had, the more opportunities would come your way.

The curse, then, was being *very* helpful in showing me a pool of players whom clubs wanted shot of. As I scouted more and more teams, I'd have the most complete list. *I* would have the only transfer list!

Because we didn't have any transfer budget, I hadn't spent much time looking to see who was available. Window shopping was something I could do when on the toilet, or bored in church, so I *had* taken a look at a few guys, but only half-heartedly.

I raced through fifty player profiles in around ten seconds and picked out a couple of possible candidates.

I decided it would be motivational to the sponsors to be in on the decision, to some extent. It was their money, after all.

"All right," I said. "Two guys spring to mind."

MD looked stunned. "I thought you'd need a day or two to think about it and then we'd scramble to get a deal done on deadline day."

"Yeah, you love the deadline-day drama. Making calls, rushing around, feeling like a real boy. I'd rather get it done and get him into training ASAP. Right. Player one. Dan Jones. Fast winger at Altrincham. He's twenty-eight, had a few injuries, lost his place in the team to a younger model. Can play either wing, so he'd give us cover for Aff, which we're a bit short on." He was CA 50, PA 70. "He'd come here, I think. He'd rip up this league and he's got room to improve, too. Like I said, a fast winger could do a lot of damage in our system."

MD made a note. "Dan Jones. Got it."

"Option two is Josh Brown. Wrexham centre back." CA 55, PA 63. "Decent technical qualities. Very, very good in the air. He'll massively help out at set pieces. At both ends of the pitch."

"We've got Gerald May," said MD, who still thought May was a top defender.

"May's fine. Brown would be an upgrade."

The silver-haired sponsor nodded. "So it's attack versus defence. You already strengthened in defence. Ah, but the winger is injury prone. How many games would he actually play?"

I rubbed my lips. "I hope we'll take better care of him than his other clubs. Players get injured; I'm not stressed about a guy with a few minor setbacks on his CV. I rotate the team anyway. And the system is the star. Know what I mean?" I brought the beer to my lips and hesitated. "Unless I'm playing. Then I'm the star."

MD was loving my performance. "Max, I didn't expect you'd pluck two names out of the air like that."

"Then why did you do . . . this?"

"Because *I* want to pitch a name to *you*."

"Oh." That was absurd, but I think I kept my face neutral enough. I didn't want to discourage MD from having ideas. Or giving me money. "Let's hear it."

He got excited. So excited the name burst out of him. "Ryan Jack!"

Not sure if he was waiting for applause or what, but there was an agonising silence. "Please do continue," I said helpfully.

MD paced around making unusually large gestures. "I had him in mind even before today. He played with Jackie Reaper at Everton and he's been, you know, ageing his way down the divisions. Jackie always talked about signing him. He's at Rochdale, and I've got mates there. Ryan Jack is available."

"But what is he?"

"He's a central midfielder. He's not the fastest, but he's got a brain. You've been complaining about the players today. Well, maybe it's because they're too young."

"There's no such thing as too young."

"Of course there is. York beat us with an average age of twenty-eight. Every man on the pitch knew his job inside out. Kiddie have an old team with a couple of stars. Very good balance. We started with an average age of twenty-six today, and by the end it was twenty-five. We're getting younger and younger. Which is the Max Best way, I get it, but you're going to have days like these, and too many could cost us."

"You've put a lot of thought into this."

"Not really! It just seems right! Maybe we need an old head. A bit of experience to balance the young tearaways. You shouldn't rely on Youngster to set the tempo. Let him learn from someone more seasoned."

I scratched my chin. Some good points here. "How old is Jack Ryan?"

"Ryan Jack. He's thirty-five or something. I know you'd never buy a player like that. No resale value. No long-term upside. Which is where we come in. We're fans! We want instant success!"

He was getting really hyper. It was charming. Made him look young. "You know I need to see players in the flesh. Can you get him down to training?"

"I think so. Tomorrow?"

"I won't be there tomorrow. Wednesday or Thursday. The afternoon, though. The morning will be fitness work."

MD frowned. "Double sessions? Two days in a row? Are you punishing the team?"

"Yes."

The main sponsor said, "Du duh!" and I twisted my head in astonishment. What? But everyone else knew what was happening. They joined in. "Duh duh, du du duh." They were singing the Great Escape chant, which ended with the two-syllable shout: Ches-ter!

I downed my beer, joined in for a chorus, then went to find my bodyguard.

Tuesday, August 29.

The Brig was catching up on his coaching course—he was taking it a lot more seriously than I'd expected. To minimise my danger, we swapped cars. Anyone tracking a brown Subaru would end up face-to-face with a fearsome killing machine . . . being driven by the Brig.

I was cruising in his extremely comfortable Volvo S90, on my way to Birkenhead. The Volvo was so, so quiet. Like driving a Typhoon-class submarine with the caterpillar drive engaged.

I docked at the Tranmere Rovers training ground, known as The Campus. There was a full-sized pitch, three slightly smaller ones including an all-weather 3G, and two baby ones. One side of the space backed onto some houses, giving it an air of being for use by anyone. Slightly amateur, but also friendly. I wasn't sure if I'd want this for Chester's new facility. Something more isolated might be more impressive, but there was a danger of disconnecting from the local community. Leicester City had invested a hundred million in a new training ground, and everyone hated it. It was more serious than what they'd had before, but players stopped bumping into the friendly club staff who always gave them a smile and a few kind words, and I'd read more than one insider blame the new facilities for their relegation.

I was there to hang out with James O'Rourke, Colin the coach, and my holiday friends. To keep in touch. To be a good person. Also: to spy on them and steal their drills.

The training was fascinating. First because I finally got to see the player profiles for these guys. I did some quick maths and worked out that the first team had an average CA of about 77. That seemed on the low end for a League Two team, but it made sense. Tranmere had only recently moved up from the National League. The lowest guy had CA 55—Henri should have been in this squad, competing for a spot in the team, pushing himself, instead of wasting away in the National League North. The dick.

Next, I got to see the coaching and physio profiles. As I suspected, Colin was really good. Coaching outfield players 15, coaching goalkeepers 10. There were five first-team coaches taking the players through some drills. Their numbers varied, but the overall effect felt good. I'd need to come back in a month to fine-tune what "good" meant.

And, of course, I got to see James O'Rourke's profile. There he stood, in his long Tranmere coat, looking like a ginger Marlon Brando. I was dismayed to see that his numbers were pretty weak. His motivating and man management were fine, but his tactical knowledge was 7, and his judging player ability was 4. His preferred formation, as I knew, was 4-3-3.

I kept wandering around, pretending to be taking in the sights and sounds, but really, I was finding it hard to compose myself. James had been so good to me, but it was like he was heading straight into a torpedo that only I could see. Unless everyone in League Two had similarly weak profiles, he wouldn't last the season. How could I look him in the eye? I wished I had a way to help him out. Throw him a life jacket. Teach him to swim. Drive my submarine in front of the torpedo that was threatening his.

By the time I finished my circuit, I had calmed enough to be able to treat him more or less as normal. Our handshake turned into a three-slap hug.

James asked how I was getting on; we chatted about our teams' mixed starts to the season; we shared our dismay at seeing the fires that had devastated Tenerife. Once we got going, the old bonhomie came back. The ease, the lack of friction.

Still, I was relieved—ecstatic—to see Mateo, Tranmere's owner. He'd been just as generous as James, letting me use his special swimming pool and making his club's physios and coaches take care of me. He'd really gone overboard on a guy who was basically a complete stranger.

He was in his usual outfit—jacket, shirt, no tie. His tan looked slightly less vivid than in Tenerife, but that might have been because of the clouds above.

I jogged over to give him a hug. He was taken aback—I'd improved rapidly during my time on the island but had never shown such energy. I did a little dance in front of him to show how much I'd recovered.

"Fuck me, Max. Look at that. Amazing. I'm delighted! Yeah, I'm absolutely made up." We eyed each other, enjoying the moment. Then he turned to a couple of guys I hadn't noticed. "This is Tristan. Football agent. And one of his clients, Jo Brimstage. Guys, this is Max Best. Chester manager. Bit of a star player, himself."

We shook hands, but neither my name nor Chester's provoked any interest. I was some rando, forgotten already. Mateo led us towards the training session. The drills had abruptly ended and now a small-sided match was taking place. Making training look fun! It was obvious that Tranmere were keen to sign this Jo guy. Jo stood watching, eyes darting around. I wondered what position he played—until I saw him kick a ball I wouldn't know. But his current club wouldn't allow him to join in Tranmere's training session—what if he got injured? I thought of a way I could repay Mateo and James for their incredible generosity.

I pulled Mateo aside. "Can you do something weird for me?"

"Depends what it is."

"Get this guy to take some shots or do some kick-ups."

"Why?"

"Humour me."

Mateo gave me a long, cold look. We wandered away and I thought Mateo had dismissed my ravings. But during a lull in play, Mateo went onto the pitch, bringing Jo and the agent with him in his wake. The Tranmere players looked on, politely interested, like seagulls. Mateo was suddenly gregarious, laughing, suggesting Jo might want to take a couple of penalties against the first team's goalie. "We've got a cup match tonight," he said. "Could go to pennos. Let's see how our keeper does against someone he's never played before."

The agent didn't sense anything wrong, and Jo was competitive. He wanted to test himself.

Jo lined up a shot, and I hit Playdar at the exact moment his foot made contact with the ball.

It worked! He was the best player in the area who was currently playing football. I got his profile. It said he played for Partick Thistle. CA 59, PA 61. Almost maxed out.

He was a perfectly decent forward. I'd have bought him. But I was two divisions below. He wasn't good enough for Tranmere.

Jo took another penalty. He scored again, and he enjoyed the shouts of approval from what he thought were his future teammates.

Mateo led him back to the side of the pitch, where Jo stood flushed with pleasure. He'd enjoyed the shit out of that.

Five minutes later, Mateo looked at his watch. He had places to be. The agent took the hint, grabbed Jo, and left.

When they were out of sight, Mateo came over to me. "Well?"

"Have you done the deal?"

"It's not finalised."

"How much is it?"

"That's private," he snapped. Then almost immediately, "Hundred and ten."

"No," I said. "No way. That's crazy."

"We're upgrading our arsenal. More firepower. He's going to push us to the next level."

"Who says?"

"James."

"No. He's supposed to go right into the first team? He doesn't improve you, doesn't even have a ceiling. No, you have to get out of it."

"You're basing this on two penalties?"

"I had a look at him last year," I lied, reading from the history tab of Jo's profile. It only showed me data from the previous season. This was a rare demo of why unlocking more of the History tab could pay off. "Partick Thistle. Thirty-three appearances, fifteen goals, two assists. He's totally functional. He'd do for us, but trust me, he's not good enough for you." He didn't seem to be getting it. "Matty, you're *Tranmere*. You're the deadly torpedo. You can do better."

Mateo's face went blank. He stared at something, or nothing. "Understood."

"What? You're going to back out of the deal?"

"Yes."

"Oh."

"That's what you said, isn't it?"

"I thought you'd ignore me, then a year from now you'd see I was right, and I could save you from a disaster *then*."

"In my family, we trust our gut. My gut's saying you'd know a striker better than anyone here." He scanned the players and staff, focusing on one guy for a moment. James? Colin? I couldn't tell. "James will be pissed. We need a striker. Know anyone?"

I scratched my scalp. "Junior Howland at Darlington. He's fast, got good movement. He'll do well in this league. Not at first. You'd have to train him up. But you've got good coaches here. It won't be an issue. I played with him and I rate him. Darlington won't sell to me, otherwise I'd be all over it. We could maybe afford him, too, since he's third-choice striker now. He doesn't fit the way they're playing. *I'd* make him work, and he'd work in your four-three-three. Yeah, this would be a good move for him. Six months from now, he'll be better than Jo. Absolutely."

Mateo adjusted his cuffs. "Is he one of your clients?"

"Junior? No. There's a kid in the academy there who might join my friend's new agency. You should sign him, too. Right winger. Doesn't really fit the four-three-three you're doing, but the next manager will be glad he's here."

Mateo gave me the longest, hardest look yet. Finally, he said, "What's his name?"

"Calabash Barkley. We call him Bark. He's a big talent. If you sign either one of those two, I'll pat myself on the back and say I've repaid your kindness."

"Two players who can't go straight into the team. The opposite of what we need."

I shrugged. "Jam tomorrow."

"And if I could only sign one, which would I choose?"

"Bark."

"Your friend's client."

"The bigger talent."

He stared at something. "Are you coming to the match tonight?"

"Wouldn't miss it. Emma's leaving work early. She loves you guys," I said, smiling. "'It's not like going to football,' she said. 'It's like going to a mate's house.'"

Mateo cracked a smile at that. "See you later, Max."

He strode off, whipping his phone out as he did. I went over to James to complain about my rabble disobeying me. He was more than happy to join in the whingeing. We concluded that football would be amazing if it wasn't for the players.

EFL Cup Second Round (North)—Tranmere Rovers versus Leicester City.

Prenton Park, Tranmere's lumpy stadium, was one-third full. Over to my right was The Kop, Tranmere's biggest stand. It doesn't look proper when the biggest stand is on the width instead of the length, but overall, it was a great stadium. Great place to watch football of an evening.

I was in the executive boxes along with the owners, Emma, and the Brig.

The match kicked off and I found I was getting 6 XP per minute. Nice! Leicester, having been relegated, had sold a couple of their star players, including the dream-weaver himself, Tielemans. But they still had Jamie Vardy (Chat Shit Get Banged) and a fifteen-million-pound defender whose name, ominously, sounded like farce.

The first half was lively—lots of good play let down by a poor last pass or a player running left when they should have gone right. The Brig asked me about a piece of news.

"Roberto Mancini has taken a position as the manager of Saudi Arabia. His salary will be twenty-five million euros per year. I saw his name in another story recently. A few days ago, he quit his job as the manager of the Italian national team. Am I right in suspecting the two stories are linked?"

"What, are you saying he quit his dream job, the job he'd wanted since he was a little boy, the job every Italian wants, simply to multiply his salary by a factor of seven? No. I'm sure he quit the national team for unrelated reasons. He is famously unmotivated by money, that guy."

Saudi Arabia throwing its money around again. They'd been picking off top talents from all over Europe for their league, and now they were hosing cash onto the national team, too. It was unreal. Like they had a bottomless pit of money.

Bottomless pit. Why did that make me think of Old Nick?

At halftime, while the Brig made good use of the buffet, Mateo and Rachel gave Emma and me a tour. Down to the medical rooms, mercifully devoid of freshly injured players, and into the home dressing room. Normally I wouldn't have interrupted a halftime team talk, but I suspected the players would be happy to see Emma. A little motivation boost, perhaps?

Sure enough, they cheered when she went in. There was a one-tenth echo when I followed, and a louder one for the owner.

"Wow, it's so big," said Emma, checking out the space.

"Oi!" I said to a cheeky left back who was opening his mouth. He'd been outrageously flirting with Emma in Tenerife, and he was pretty good at it. Good-looking, bubbly, funny. His problem when it came to a woman like Emma was that he was as thick as two short planks. He smiled at me now, pivoted his joke.

"I was just gonna say, this is Tranmere. We're not the biggest, but we're a deadly submarine." He licked his lips in anticipation of delivering the punchline.

I knew where he was going. Ninety percent of nautical jokes have the same ending. I bent down and got eye to eye with him. "What's inside the submarine, mate? What's inside the submarine?"

He hesitated. "Sailors," he mumbled, and his team mocked him for losing his nerve.

"Good choice of words," I assured him. I reached out for a fist bump and got one. Guys flirted with Emma all the time. This dude was way better than most.

Emma said hi to her holiday superfriends, and was astonished to find that Tranmere had hot and cold water piped right into the dressing room. Two sinks! They didn't have to go into a nearby bathroom to give their gear a quick wipe. Such luxury!

"Any tactical advice, Max?" said Coach Colin, bringing the focus back to the matter at hand.

"Yeah. When they break, Vardy drifts to the far post. You've got to cover him."

"That'll open a big gap. The ball carrier will dick us."

I shrugged. "It's Vardy. You've got to." I sensed James wasn't a billion percent happy with the interruption, so I pulled Emma away and waved everyone goodbye.

On the way back up, we went through some of the back-office rooms, and into the media suite. Emma was fascinated. This was where the commentators prepared, where the press could write their match reports. I stepped through a door and realised the media dudes could sit out here like normal fans, albeit in amazing seats, then pop inside and work in relative quiet. I crabbed along the walkway, unseen, with an aquarium view of what was happening inside the room.

There were a couple of guys my age there. One was in a tech bro beanie, a super-premium hoodie with extra zips that did nothing, and had a wispy, untidy beard that took hours per day to look so untidy. He looked like the sort of person who has to read the last chapter of a book before he reads the rest. The other guy was less obviously slappable. He had glasses, a beard, a stained t-shirt, and the hooded eyes of a guy who *only* read the last chapter of a book. Tech Bro and Stalker.

Tech Bro noticed Emma and slapped his mate on the shoulder. *Check this out.* Dislike times infinity. Stalker looked, raised his eyebrows, and leaned forward to whisper something to his mate. Of course, they both pissed themselves laughing. I went back to the door and slunk behind the guys. I wanted to get through and out without more conflict; I'd lost my temper enough for one month.

Finally, Mateo led us into the boardroom. It had the usual heavy wooden table and luxurious furnishings. They'd seen better days, but the overall vibe was still very classy. Very elegant.

"Emma," said Mateo. "You'll love this." He sat his arse on the edge of the table, looking completely at ease. It was as if he owned the place, which, of course, he did. "Your boy comes to training this morning. We've got a new signing having a look at his new teammates."

I opened my transfers screen—the number of transfers was increasing exponentially as we neared the end of the window. There was nothing about Jo, or Partick Thistle, or Tranmere.

"Max says, let me have a look at him. I get him to take two penalties. He scores both. Max says nah. Bin him off."

"Max!" complained Emma.

"What?"

"I don't know!" she said, in the same strident tone.

I laughed. "I was trying to be nice. Save them from a bad decision."

"Oh." She thought about it. "That's fine, then." She looked in the direction she thought the pitch would be. "Which one is he?"

Mateo knew what she meant. "He's not here. I cancelled the deal. Made up some excuse."

A slight chill crept up my back. Another agent with motive to hate Max Best. "Is there any danger the agent is going to blame me?"

"Danger? No." Mateo frowned. "No, your name didn't come up. He's such a narcissist!"

"I know," said Emma.

"He recommended two other players. Junior Howland and Calabash Barkley."

"Oh, I know them! From Darlo. Max raves about them as players. He'd know. All I know is they're lovely people. Dead nice. I shouldn't say more; I'm doing the paperwork for the agency that signed Bark."

Mateo nodded. "Stand by your recommendation, Max?"

"Course."

Rachel spoke. "This is you repaying our generosity, Matty said."

I gave Emma a squeeze. "We had the best time in Tenerife."

Rachel looked dubious. "It's a risk signing non-league players. No guarantee they'll be able to play at this level."

"No guarantee," I said. "Lots can go wrong. But in these cases . . . the talent is right, the personality is right. It's a ninety-eight percent chance. Jo was a hundred percent chance of a dud, so at least I helped you out there." I laughed. "Watch him go on a goal spree now!"

Rachel's eyebrows flicked up. She turned to her husband and they communicated nonverbally. He smiled, reached into his pocket, and clicked the top of a pen. He walked to the head of the desk, bent, and signed a piece of paper. He stood, satisfied. "Our new striker. Junior Howland."

My spirits lifted. I'd launched my friend out of non-league like he was a surface-to-air missile. I'd gone ballistic, for once in the right way. "How much?"

"Sixty." He looked at a pile of papers next to the one he'd just signed. "Plus fifty for Barkley. His agent is holding things up."

Emma and I turned to look at each other. She laughed. I went out, closed the door behind me, and called Ruth.

"R.E.M. Enterprises," she said. "We never sleep."

"Howdy, pardner. I hear you're holding up my carefully constructed deal."

"I have some concerns. I'm worried about my client, Max."

"Are you worried he's rotting in the reserves of a club that doesn't value him?"

"I'm worried Tranmere play four-three-three and don't need a right winger."

I felt a surge of frustration that turned into a laugh. "I talked to a top football expert and he says based on the training facilities, the coaching, and the exposure to players of a higher standard, Bark will thrive here and by the time he's ready for the first team, the first team will no longer be using four-three-three."

"You don't know who the next manager might be. It could be some . . . buckaroo." (She didn't say that. She said they might hire someone who also plays 4-3-3. I prefer my version.)

"Statistically unlikely. But two years from now, if that happens, Chester will have money. I'll buy him."

She was quiet for a moment. "You've got your motivations. You're friends with the owners. You're trying to do them a favour. I get it. It's good of you. But my only interest is my client."

I looked around, checked no one was within earshot, and murmured, "Our client." Louder, I said, "How's he taking it?"

"He's bouncing off the walls. He can't believe his luck."

"That's right. Because this is an unbelievably good move for him. He'll be in a more elite environment. Trust me, his talent will shine to the point even James O'Rourke will be tempted to change formation. Bark is that good. How's the money?"

"Acceptable. He won't be buying any horses anytime soon."

"Right. Call Tranmere. This is a rare win-win-win-win-win."

"Is one of those wins Darlington?"

I smiled. "Depends how they spend the money. It's a win if they use the money to get better players. Spoiler alert: they won't."

I hung up, and went back into the boardroom.

Mateo's phone rang soon after.

He said a few things, then: "Great."

He put his phone down, signed the contract. He picked both documents up. His club secretary would fax them off, and that would be that. I'd brokered two deals on a day off! And got my agency up and running.

Most of all . . . "Emma. I've repaid my debt to society. Are you proud of me?"

"Very." She leaned up to kiss me.

Rachel smiled. Now that the decisions were all made, her demeanour switched from suspicious to wildly optimistic. "I have a very good feeling about this, Matty. Max, have you got any more tips for us?"

"Whoa!" I said. "You get two top talents in the name of friendship. Everything from now on costs."

"How much?" said Mateo.

"What?"

"How much to find us more of these prospects?"

I laughed. "Mateo! We're competitors! We'll be in the same division soon."

He got a steely look in his eye. "You think we're going down?"

"God, I hope not. No, we're coming up."

His phone pinged. "Second half's starting. Let's get back to your, ah, assistant manager."

Emma asked if she could visit the media room while the match was going on. She was super interested to see what went on in there. Rachel handed over her badge so she could access all areas. "*Mi casa es su casa.*"

The match continued to be entertaining. Tranmere were outclassed, of course, but competed as well as they could.

Mateo asked what I thought of the match on a tactical level. The Brig leaned in to hear my answer.

"It's interesting. James is sticking to his four-three-three. I have mixed feelings about it. From one point of view, you could say it plays into Leicester's hands. Or James could say that's the formation we know, we're good at it, it's the formation I understand best as a manager, so let's stick to it. He's got a point. They've had chances. Score them and he looks like a genius."

"What would you do?"

"I'd be tempted to do three-five-two. Try to swamp the midfield. That'd give Leicester a lot to think about. They'd probably reshuffle, put more bodies in there. Then I'd try four-two-four, go direct, bypass midfield on our attacks, see if we could exploit all that space they leave on the wings."

"You'd do that in one game?"

I laughed. "I'd do that in one minute. Why not? You only need one or two flexible players. Where's Emma got to?" I frowned. She'd been gone far too long. I looked at the Brig. We both stood at the same time. "Back in a second, Matty."

"Take my badge," he said.

Before leaving the executive area, some instinct made me put on my shades and baseball cap. The Brig put some sunglasses on, too.

I beeped my way through, scanning every corridor but moving fairly quickly. I paused at the door to the media suite and peered inside. There was a little sofa thing, and I knew from the composition of the occupants what had happened. Emma had started chatting to the reporters, or whatever they were, and they'd invited her to sit, and now they were sort of trapping her on the L-shaped couch. She was wedged into the corner, while Tech Bro was next to her, his legs stretched out like a fence. Stalker was on the edge of his seat, to Emma's right, a closed gate. He'd taken his glasses off.

It took me all of zero seconds to take all that in, and when the red mist cleared, I was ready for anything. Mostly ready to beat the living shit out of some creeps. But also ready to accept that this was less gross and shitty than it looked.

I forced myself to stand there and take another look at the scene.

Emma was hunched into herself. She seemed really small. Tech Bro had draped his arm across the back of the sofa, and his hand was dangling just under her hair.

As I watched, he brushed it. Emma leaned away and made a vague slapping motion that the twat found delightful. In a total, brain-consuming rage, I pounced, but didn't get anywhere. The Brig had grabbed my arm. An iron vice. He didn't want me to go in there and batter the twat.

I gave him a look that may or may not have been hidden by my sunglasses. "What would *you* do?"

"If I were you, sir, I would ask *me* to take care of it."

"That isn't your job."

"One is always happy to straddle the bridge between duty and recreation."

I fumed for a few seconds, then thought, *fine*. Making good decisions under pressure. That's what I wanted, wasn't it? I was the fucking manager of Chester. I couldn't go smashing faces in the media room of a rival club. I handed over the badge.

As he was about to enter, he paused. "What's the name of the stadium?"

"Prenton Park."

He mumbled it under his breath, then went in. I slipped in behind him and walked over to a tea-making area and pretended to be brewing up while checking my phone.

"Excuse me, sir," said the Brig to Tech Bro. "May I see your credentials?"

"What?" said the twat, humming with twatty defiance.

The Brig didn't repeat himself. Tech Bro, now that he'd got out of the trapping-a-hot-blonde mindset and had stared into the inhuman, reflective lenses of the scary army man, lifted a lanyard over his head. The Brig took it, touched his ear, and said the name aloud. The guy sat up. Things had got very serious, very quickly.

"Yes, I thought so," said the Brig, to absolutely no one. He took his finger away from his ear. "Sir, we would ask you to leave Prenton Park immediately, by mutual consent."

"By mutual consent?" spluttered the media prick.

"You can ask your solicitor what consent is," said the Brig, and I was suddenly glad I'd let him do this. My way would have been catastrophic. His way would leave a longer-lasting scar, was much less stressful for Emma, and in its own way, was funny. "It would be more *agreeable* if you consented to leave, sir. The alternative is murder on my shoes. Escorting you all the way down, I mean." The Brig took a couple of steps over to a desk with a view of the match. "You missed a goal." Stalker shot to his feet and went to one of two laptops. Emma took the chance to escape the sofa. She noticed me, and relaxed. I put my finger to my lips. Emma nodded and waited behind the sofa.

The Brig had been lying about the goal, but now he knew which laptop was Tech Bro's. He unplugged it and folded it up. "We'll need this for the investigation."

"Investigation?"

"Into the allegations," sighed the Brig, now bored. He pulled his sleeve up, revealing that he was wearing two watches. Tech Bro's eyes nearly popped out. "That will be all." He settled into a very military pose.

"But . . . but my laptop," whined the wannabe Lothario as he got awkwardly to his feet.

"I'll post it when I'm done," said the Brig.

"But you don't know where I live."

My assistant manager tried to contain his amusement. "Oh, dear."

"But—"

"Time's up," said the Brig.

The twat looked for moral support from his "mate"—who was bright red and hunched over his laptop, pretending to be writing. Tech Bro looked at me, but I was slouched over the counter, looking at my phone. With a bit of luck, he wouldn't remember my face. He'd remember Emma's, though. And one day, he'd see the Brig on TV, standing next to me in the dugout. Would our disguises be enough? Would this bite me on the arse? Did I care?

Tech Bro was slinking towards the nearest exit. A button would allow him to leave, but without his badge he wouldn't be able to get back in. He was about to make one last effort when the Brig touched his ear and said, "He's on his way. No, not this time. But turn camera four off, just in case he gets lippy."

The twat left. I moved into the centre of the room. "What about that one?" I said, pointing to the accomplice.

The Brig held out his hand. The guy gulped and handed over his lanyard. The Brig stared at it, then handed it back. He nodded at me, and that seemed to be that. It seemed inadequate. Yes, the Brig would probably torment this guy in some way, but I needed something more immediate. I had so much frustration building up in me, and this guy was a worthy vessel for some old-school venting.

"Actually, you know what? Let's divide and conquer," I said. "You do twat-face. I'll do this one."

I approached Stalker, turned him to face me. I saw my sunglasses in the blacks of his eyes. Cool effect. I thought about punching him in the gut, but Emma coughed. I turned. She did the sign language for *in this world, it's just us.* I didn't totally get why, but it was obvious she didn't want me to do anything violent. So I used my words. "I don't like your decision-making. You need re-education. I'm a guest today; I don't want to embarrass anyone by getting stuck in." I glanced at Emma; she approved. "But next time I see you, I *am* going to hit you in the face." I gave him a couple of friendly slaps on the cheek. Four o'clock shadowing, I think it's called.

We left. In the corridor, I stopped my little team.

"Do we tell Mateo? I vote no."

"Why?" said the Brig.

"I like the idea that I know where this guy's going to be."

"I agree if Emma does."

"I'm okay," she said, which worried me. That hadn't been the question. Maybe it's what we should have been asking, though. I calmed all the way down. Retribution could wait. I took my sunglasses off and gave her my full attention. She continued. "I was asking them about their work. They were friendly at first. Then it was weird and I wanted to leave, but I just froze. I felt at home here. My guard was down. I'm sorry."

"What do you want? Go home?"

"No way! I'm not going because of them. No chance. I want to stay. With my mates." She stuck her jaw out. "I've been looking forward to this. I want to enjoy it."

I smiled. "Then let's do that."

I tried to keep my spirits up, to be fun, to give Emma what she wanted. But it was hard.

So many terrible, inexplicable decisions. Torpedoes in the water, destroying what they touched, setting off chain reactions. I'd saved Mateo from one—the Scottish striker. Saved him a hundred and ten grand that he'd used to invest in two great prospects. But I was powerless to stop my players doing crazy things they'd never done before. And powerless to stop two doughy nobodies feeling absolutely free to harass Emma.

And as I watched, yet another piece of utter mindlessness.

Leicester had a corner. A Tranmere defender got his head to it—it flew high in the air, just outside the penalty box. A very, very difficult volley. Peak Max Best would have lobbed it back into the danger area. Messi could have shot but would have been too smart—it was too low percentage. No, Messi would have controlled the ball and passed it back to the corner taker. Messi was the best decision maker in the history of the sport. So be like Messi. Yes?

No.

The last person in the world who could have scored from that position was the Leicester defender. Taking shots was not in the defender's wheelhouse. So, naturally, he took an ugly swing, made some sort of contact, and the ball flew high into the stand, where it nearly hit a Leicester fan in the face. Fifteen million pounds, this player cost.

Henri got a three-match ban for nearly touching a goalkeeper. I would have banned this defender for a month. People had paid to watch him perform, his team's fans were pinning their hopes and dreams on him achieving his mission, but instead of piloting his submarine through tricky rock formations, he was shooting bullets at his own missiles, trying to blow them up.

I shook my head. This wasn't fun, but I was racking up XP. Soon I'd have enough to buy 3-5-2. Then I could start to look at Injuries, or Contracts, or whatever. Or maybe I'd wait to see if a monthly perk dropped at the start of September.

Tranmere had a rare attack—pushed numbers forward to try to make something happen. They lost the ball, and Leicester broke quickly down the right. Tranmere's rest defence moved across to where the ball was. The ball carrier sent a long, curving cross to the far post, where the deadliest counter-attacker in recent years was totally unmarked. Jamie Vardy leapt and powered a header downwards. The goalie had no chance, and Vardy took three short strides towards his fans. He celebrated.

Eventually, Mateo finished swearing. "Max. Didn't you warn us about that very move?"

"Yeah."

"Christ!" He ranted to Rachel for a while. He seemed able to shake off unpleasant incidents much faster than me, though. "I appreciate the warning, anyway." He laughed. "What happened to us being competitors?"

"No harm giving you advice you're not gonna take."

"We took some of your advice today. We'll see how it turns out."

I gave him the brightest smile I could manage. I wasn't worried about the Scottish guy turning into a deadly goal machine, or Junior or Bark not living up to my hype. I was, though, slightly worried about Emma. "Babes?" I said.

"I'm okay," she said, which was even more worrying than last time.

I put my arm around her, and she sank into me. She'd had a shock, but the Brig had dealt with the sitch like a boss. Seasoned. An old hand. Conflict barely touched him; he made good decisions. Yeah, he'd battered Tech Bro without using his fists.

I could learn a lot from him. Maybe I could learn to stop my team doing stupid shit *without* demotivating them. But maybe in the meantime I could get some on-pitch help.

I got my phone out and left a voice note. "MD. Do your best to get Jack Ryan down tomorrow. I think you're right. We need some more salty sea dogs onboard."

Emma pulled her head straight. "Jack Ryan? Isn't he from that movie you always watch?"

"Ryan Jack, I said. Hey! That's a good idea. After this, let's go home and watch the greatest movie of all time. I've got some ice cream in the freezer."

"Okay!" she said. Cosy movie night sounded perfect. "One thing, though."

"What?"

"Absolutely no clue why, but I'm mad craving Fruit Pastilles."

"All right. Fruit Pastilles, Sean Connery Russian accent, submarines. What else?"

"Tekkers video. And a mini prosecco to celebrate."

"Celebrate what?"

"We launched our agency today."

"That's right! We'll need two. One to smash against the side of the fridge."

She laughed. A beautiful laugh. Uninhibited. Natural. "You're so strange. You're lucky I like you." She slipped her arms through mine and squeezed.

As I looked into her eyes, I checked my mental sonar. There were no blips, no beeps, no pings. No decisions to make, no torpedoes to evade. Just a quiet night in. Netflix and chill. That sounded . . . that sounded . . . what was the best word? Aff's favourite came to mind.

That sounded *deadly*.

10

BAD BOYS

Football glossary: *Running through on goal. The act of sprinting with the ball towards the opposing goal, often during a counterattack. Often leads to a one-v-one situation between forward and goalkeeper. Famous players who mastered the art of running through on goal: Eduardo, Michael Owen, Max Best.*

Wed Aug 30—Junior Howland—Darlington—Tranmere Rovers—£60K

Wed Aug 30—Calabash Barkley—Darlington—Tranmere Rovers—£50K

The curse confirmed the transfers in the morning, and I was intrigued to note that Mateo had told me the right fees. I seriously doubted I'd get the truth from most football insiders and I seriously doubted I'd have told him the true figures if our situations had been reversed.

It made me think of Mateo as a man of his word. Someone I could trust more often than not.

The Brig and Vimsy put my players through their paces. Fitness shit. Caveman shit. While my guys ran, and ran, and ran, I plotted.

I had 2,757 XP. Unlocking 3–5–2 would cost 2,200, leaving me with about 500 to put towards Injuries or Morale. Those were absolutely essential for someone in my position, but I felt that 3–5–2 was even more urgent. Every formation I owned used four at the back, meaning Trick Williams would feature heavily in the rest of the season.

Since I'd challenged him, Trick had been training better, but would soon hit his maximum CA. Even Pascal, who I could barely use, was already on CA 31—Trick's maximum. Trick hadn't let me down in a match so far, but he was quickly becoming our weak spot and mixing formations up would stop rival managers developing plans against him. No point spending a week aiming to target our left back if we might play without one!

Our next match was against Spennymoor, who I rated as the ninth best team in the league. If I used 3–5–2 against them, we'd have an average CA between 41 and 42 depending on how training went. With Henri suspended, D-Day would have to play up front. Our usual 4–1–4–1 would have the same average if I picked Youngster to start. I wanted to play him every other game, but after I'd yelled at him, I was tempted to play him against Spennymoor and rest him in the (easier) home match against Hereford. He wasn't some thirty-year-old prima donna whose sense of self-worth came from being named in the first eleven, but he was still human. Being told off and left out of the next game might have been overly demotivating.

From what I'd seen and heard, the group had taken my latest rant fairly well. We'd see if there were any lingering effects, but Henri said that while there was more grumbling than usual, most of the guys accepted I was right. Notably, Raffi and Youngster didn't complain at all.

I saw the first signs of the group flagging and blew my whistle. I gestured to Vimsy. "Lunch," he called. "Back in an hour."

As they walked towards the credit card building, hands behind heads, blowing hard, I picked up an enormous bag of cones and went to lay them out according to my session plan. Many heads turned to see what I was doing, but the layout was nothing like any drill we'd ever done.

MD turned up as the squad returned. He had a guy with him—had to be Ryan Jack.

He was ready to train, apart from being in flip-flops. The drill wouldn't involve contact and Rochdale trusted him to make professional decisions. His boots were slung over his shoulders. He was short, thin, and scrawny, but had oversized thighs. Being old, his curly hair was receding, but only at the sides, above the temples—the rest was intact. He was one of those guys who would end up with a wispy, central, cotton-candy patch, an oasis of joy on an otherwise lifeless, barren moon.

"Max, this is Ryan."

We shook hands. "Ryan, thanks for coming."

"Yeah, no, delighted."

Two things. First, his expression was the exact opposite of delighted. He had a morose look about him, which was understandable if he'd started life as an Everton player and been reduced to *this*. Second, he was Scouse.

"Heard you're big mates with Jackie Reaper."

"Jack's sound, yeah. Good lad. Good crack. Kept an eye on him coming through. Kept in touch."

These few sentences seemed to exhaust the guy. I half-expected him to fall to his back and raise his leg for me to push on.

"You've not played much recently."

"Nah. Dale got some kids. Tyros. Little tearaways. Never stop running. It's like that cartoon. It's all pressing these days, innit? Never been much for pressing."

MD chipped in. "Ryan was planning to see out his contract, see what came up in the summer."

"Coaching?" I suggested.

"Not me."

Hmm. Annoying if he wouldn't even do the basic course so I could see his coaching profile. But there was no point making a big deal of it before I'd even seen him kick a ball.

MD continued. "Basically, Max, Ryan doesn't want to step down to the National League North. But he will for a two-year contract. For job security."

I looked at Ryan. "And for the thrills and spills of playing in front of an adoring crowd, of course."

"Not much thrill at my age," said the guy, and I realised his morose mood wasn't a mood. It was who he was. "Plenty of spills."

I laughed. This guy's humour was so dry we could slash our towel budget. Personality-wise, he was the opposite of Jackie. How had they ever become friends?

"Can we afford this, MD?" I was asking what the wages would be.

"For a two-year deal, he'll take what our top earners are on." That was 750 a week. A lot for a guy with no legs, and locked for *two* seasons. It'd still leave me with about a grand a week to bring in two inexperienced coaches . . . or one experienced one. I wondered if signing Jackie's mate made it more likely that he'd come back to work. "It's a pay cut, Max," MD said, like that's what I was worried about. "We're very lucky on this. Also, Chester's a bit closer to home than Rochdale. I think this could work out well for all concerned. If, of course, he passes your tests."

He was talking about football tests. Like everyone, he wanted to know what my new drill was. (Out on the halfway line, Jude was explaining it to my players. There seemed to be a lot of pointing and asking him to repeat things.) But there's more to being a footballer than being a footballer.

To Ryan, I said, "I've had some basic research done on you. No red flags so far. Mind if I ask you a few questions?" I wanted to weed out some of the nutjobs who infested the football world. There were plenty of dressing rooms where they were welcome. Mine wasn't one of them.

"Go for it."

"What shape is the earth?"

"What are the choices?"

"Round or flat."

"Round with flat bits."

"I decide to turn the club vegan. What do you say?"

"Two quornburgers, please. Extra ketchup."

"What do you think of the *Daily Mail*?"

"Max!" complained MD. "You can't ask things like that. It's not relevant, anyway. He's allowed his own beliefs."

"What do you think of the *Daily Mail*?"

"Not much."

"What do you think of women's football?"

"Love it. Have you read *Unsuitable for Females*?" That was a book about the Football Association's shameful ban of women's football in 1921. "Women's footy was getting too big, so they shut it down. They were unfit to govern then and nuttin's changed."

This guy was all right! A bit dour, but I liked him. Maybe he'd cheer up with a ball at his feet. "Ryan, you're an experienced pro. I'd say you've forgotten more about the game than I know, but that would be bullshit. My coming was literally predicted by Nostradamus. There's a TikTok about it. Still, you deserve better than to wind up here playing in a business park for some baby genius, but it is what it is. It'd be more respectful for me to go and watch you in a match but there's no time."

"I get it. And I'm here, yeah? Been a while since I had a trial, like. This," he said, nodding to the pitch. "Doesn't look like a match. Jackie said you do things different."

I perked up. "Jackie's alive?"

The hangdog expression didn't change. "Yeah. Said to ask you not to mention him in the match programme again."

I tsked. "Sorry, no can do. I need him back. If I have to get the entire population of Chester begging him, that's what I'll do."

"He said you're a prick."

"Why are you here, then?"

"Because he was smiling when he said it," he said.

"All right," I said, clapping my hands, starting to walk towards the halfway line of the pitch where my squad were stretching out. "Bit of an experiment. New drill."

"MD said it's double sessions because you didn't like how they played."

"Right."

"In a five–nil win."

I stopped and put my hand on his arm. "Ryan, mate. This isn't Everton. This is Chester. *We* have standards."

He nodded. "That's funny."

It *was* funny, but you wouldn't have known it from his face.

The drill was simple. Describing it . . . not so much.

My entire squad, plus Ryan Jack, lined up on halfway. Half wore blue bibs, half yellow. In one goal was Robbo. In the other, Ben.

I'd choose an attacker and a defender. The defender would start ten yards inside the half he was defending. The attacker would dribble at him.

Good so far?

As the attacker got going, the Brig and Vimsy would unleash two more blues and two more yellows who would race along "cone valleys" to help or hinder the attack. Every cone valley was a different length, and as you started dribbling, it was practically impossible to keep track of all the lengths. This was to replicate the chaos of a real match, where players wouldn't run where you hoped they would, at least at first. Once outside the valleys, players could do what they wanted.

So it was a three-on-three attack, but starting *in media res*, and with an arbitrary restriction that no one liked except me.

When the blue team scored, or didn't, we'd do it again, attacking the other goal with different players, so everyone got practice on both sides of the transitions. Teams were rarely the same twice, by design.

When I took Ryan and a fascinated MD to the starting point, Joe Anka called out, asking what this drill was called.

"Bad Boys," I said.

Long pause while everyone tried to work it out. They gave up. "Why?" said Joe.

I sang the theme from the Will Smith movie. "Bad boys, bad boys, whatcha gonna do? Whatcha gonna do when you're running through?" There were a surprising number of blank looks, but I didn't feel like explaining.

We started in earnest, attacking Robbo and ten seconds later attacking Ben. It became a whirlwind of limbs, a frenzy of sprints and shots. The gaps between moves could be counted in milliseconds. Left, attack, right, attack! Left, right!

An example of doing the drill well.

I threw Pascal a ball, and he dribbled towards a yellow. He feinted to surge on the outside, but passed square to Henri who had just stormed onto the pitch (through a short tunnel) with a yellow five yards in front of him. Henri passed left, to Ryan, who emerged from his long tunnel in slow motion as Henri whizzed around him. Ryan took a simple touch that somehow bamboozled two yellows into stepping away from their men towards the ball. Ryan feinted to pass left, back through traffic, to Henri. That was a pass most of my idiot players would have tried. Flashy. Look at me! But Ryan leaned back and hit a simple, but glorious, thirty-yard pass on the diag to Pascal. His first touch was perfect and he had the choice to shoot or wait for support from Henri.

As Pascal always did, he played the percentages by passing. One day, that would become a weakness. For now, I didn't give a shit. What he did in the box was up to him; it was everything leading up to that last, decisive moment that I cared about.

"Very good," I called out as Henri applied the finish. "Bad Boys!"

And now an example of the drill done badly.

D-Day got the ball and immediately started doing stepovers. No point doing them when the defender is ten yards away, but it seemed to make him happy. To his left, Raffi and Aff were surging forward. D-Day decided to bypass Raffi and hit a beautiful, chipped pass out to Aff. The beauty was all in the execution, not in the planning; the defender read it and had plenty of time to intercept.

"Sad Boys!" I called, and a few watchers repeated it in tune with the song: "Sad boys, sad boys!"

At first we had more Bad Boys than Sad Boys, but my assistants were ruthless in choosing who should take part in each round. Anyone who was struggling would get picked to defend after doing a big attacking sprint. All too soon, our guys were tired and back to doing inexplicable things. It really frazzled them when we sent four defenders, or five, breaking our own rules. Once, we only sent two defenders out, and that somehow caused an even bigger meltdown.

I was trying to improve their decision-making. Whether it was working or not, I couldn't say. I was in charge of the session, which meant there were no changes in attributes and no movement in CA. That was one reason I barely did any coaching—it was a waste of a session. But I thought it was important that I did these special events every now and then. Nothing could signal my demands more strongly than me showing the players out on the training pitch *exactly* what I valued and *exactly* what was important to me.

After a while, I began weeding out the worst performers. I cut D–Day, the Triplets, Steve Alton, and a few more. In the next round I cut Youngster, Tony, and Trick. With only smart players on the pitch, the quality got seriously good, before plummeting—the guys were toast.

I blew my whistle—my players needed time to catch their breath, and I needed time to think.

It came as no surprise (to me) that Henri, Pascal, and Aff nailed it. Henri was shaky (but surprisingly willing) on the defensive side, but made ruthlessly good decisions when going forward. Pascal knew what to do defensively, but would sometimes be knocked down by our more cut-throat players. Aff was probably our best all-rounder—he was top three in both attacking and defensive phases.

No, the main surprise was how fucking good Ryan Jack was.

I'd been all set to smash Playdar to get his details. After all, Scottish Jo's profile hadn't shown when he joined training up at Tranmere. I had needed to use Playdar to get his deets. But Ryan was in our session in a way that Jo wasn't, and the curse offered up his profile with no superpowers needed.

Anyway, as soon as he'd joined the session, his profile had appeared, and it was not awe-inspiring. As usual, I first looked to his ability scores, and they *did* get the old ticker pumping. He had PA 151, which made sense if he'd once been thought good enough to play in the top division. His CA was 60. I could get a CA 60 central midfielder for thirty thousand pounds! That seemed like a hell of a deal.

But then I took in the rest of his profile, and I understood why he was available, why he wasn't playing for Rochdale, and why there wasn't a bidding war for him.

Mostly, it was the speed. He had acceleration 4, pace 6. I knew it'd be something like that because I'd watched clips of him playing and when I set them to double speed, he didn't get faster.

But it was also the strength and tackling: 10 and 7, respectively. In the hurly-burly of non-league football, central midfielders needed a bit more about them or they'd get bounced and buffeted all over the place.

And it was the heading. Actually, his heading was fine, but his jumping was 6. Not much help at a set piece, this guy.

Except he'd be *taking* the set pieces. His passing was 17. His technique was 16. And to perplex me even more, his finishing and teamwork were both high—13 and 16.

This guy . . . was confounding. He was half of an amazing player, but most non-league stars had the *other* half, the physical half. What could I do with him? He was a luxury player. A passenger. When we were winning, he'd be great. But I needed someone for the games where we were the underdogs.

All those doubts and misgivings vanished as soon as he got going.

Running at one mile an hour, looking like his boots were made of recycled ship anchors, arms flailing like windmills trying to help him get up to his top speed of two miles per hour, he was nothing like my dream footballer. But the first time he got the ball, he made the exact pass I was willing him to make.

Same with the second, same with the third. It was uncanny, like the curse was controlling him more directly than with most players. But the tenth time he made the right decision, it struck me—he *was* my dream player simply because he was hyper-rational. He'd float around the midfield, keeping us on track, making the right choices—shit! I could make him playmaker and make my idiots give him the ball! If they stopped thinking for themselves, we'd increase our team's IQ by, like, a factor of ten!

An on-pitch floating megabrain. Who cared if he was slow? The youngsters could do all the running. Put him in the middle of a 3-5-2 with Sam and Raffi doing all the donkey work. I started to salivate. I wasn't thinking clearly—I was dizzy. This was why I still didn't have a credit card.

I went for a little walk. What about the fast winger or the dominant centre back I'd seen on the transfer list? They'd be worth thirty thousand pounds, too. They'd help us.

I looked over my shoulder. Ryan Jack was explaining something to Pascal and Raffi. The morose Scouser was slapping his arm and pointing. Explaining how football worked. Pascal was mooning over him. The German yearned to learn more about this game, and he had seen enough in the last half hour to show him that Ryan was a master. Little Pascal Bochum was ready to sign up for an apprenticeship; he knew extraordinary talent when he saw it. After all, I said, standing tall even though no one was watching and no one could hear my thoughts, that's why he had come to Chester.

I'd already made up my mind when I saw Dean and Livia on the sidelines. There was always a buzz when a new signing first arrived. They'd missed the action, but seeing Livia there made me smile.

Back in the middle of the pitch, I waved everyone in. I'd barely talked to them since the Farsley debacle. But all that was more or less forgotten. Forgive and forget, as I sometimes say. When it suits me.

"Lads, I hope you made Ryan Jack feel welcome. Because if he signs for Chester today, you can have your afternoon back tomorrow."

I grabbed Ryan and MD and herded them, double-time, to Dean. Sent them off to do the medical, ASAP. I wanted Ryan in my dreams that night and in full training in the morning.

Livia smiled. "This guy's cheered you up."

"I just love Scousers," I said. "So bubbly. So alive. So very, very positive."

She looked down to hide an even bigger smile. "I like him."

"Me too," I sighed. "Now you and I have got one more thing in common."

"What's that?"

"We've both fallen for older men."

That got a little eye roll. "He's got a few years in him yet."

She meant Ryan, but it became clear to both of us that I would deliberately misunderstand and make a joke about Jackie. We both sort of almost-laughed, and that was enough. "There's one thing that worries me, though. Ryan's still in great shape, still a valuable asset. But his level is above the level of our facilities, if you see what I mean. This guy played in the Premier League, for God's sake." I shook my head, performatively, but Livia knew me too well to buy it. I ploughed on. "I'm just worried our poor coaching will take its toll and his career will be over even faster than if he'd stayed at Rochdale." She gave me nothing. "Poor guy. If only we had an elite coach," I sighed.

She finally blinked. "Am I supposed to pass this on to Jackie? What's the plan? Emotional blackmail?"

"What's he doing today? Sitting on the sofa, drawing hair on his head with a ballpoint pen, watching *Antiques Roadshow*? When was his last shower? He's earned a few weeks of moping around the house. Earned a break. But that's not his destiny. He should be here, now, telling me the eight things that were wrong with my drill design. I'm going to do everything in my power to get him back here. Proclamations, post-match interviews, constant, obnoxious name-dropping. And now I've got his mate here, you'd better believe I'm going to use that, too. I've kept some budget back. I'd pay him full salary to come and do one day a week. Don't tell him I said that, but I would. If it's money, if it's status, if it's respect, I'll make sure he gets it."

She blinked. I realised I'd got a bit worked up. Hadn't really spoken about Jackie for ages, not even to Emma.

"Livia," I said, and though I tried to be calm, my words came out with heat. "There's another thing we have in common. You never gave up on him. I never gave up on him. And I never will. I'm writing a new story: The Prodigal Scouser. I'm going to weave a dream—Max and Jack, the genius fist in the bald glove, beauty and the beast, Fred Astaire and Brendan Rogers—I'm going to make people delirious at the prospect of what we could achieve together. I'm going to build the pressure, build the tension, and the day Jackie walks back into that stadium will be electric. The fans will go fucking mental."

She gave nothing away. Nothing. "What if he joins some other club?"

"Then I'll stop." I smiled. "I'm famously *very* reasonable."

She put her hand on a little post, gave it a shove to see if it would wobble. It was unmoved by her efforts. I knew she was about to ask me to stop. To leave him alone. Would she be able to move *me*? "It's *Cash in the Attic*."

"What?"

"Not *Antiques Roadshow*. He watches *Cash in the Attic*."

She walked back inside, ready to assist players who came in with a strain or a knock. I took her last statement to mean she wholeheartedly, unreservedly approved of what I was doing and how I was doing it.

@ChesterFC

Chester are delighted to announce the signing of Ryan Jack from Rochdale. The 35-year-old midfielder's experience will be a valuable addition to Max Best's squad. "Ryan played with our very own Jackie Reaper," said the Chester manager. "If Ryan has half the impact his old mate had on this club, we've just made the signing of the season."

Friday, September 1. Transfer deadline day.

New perk available: Preloading

Cost: 100 XP

Effects: This patch allows the SYSTEM to preload new content, minimising deleterious effects.

I woke up to an underwhelming monthly perk option. It seemed like this patch would stop me getting headaches every time I used a new formation or tweaked the user interface to be the way I liked it. It didn't really help me in terms of progressing as a football manager, but I bought it right away. The headaches were legit unpleasant. And since that seemed to be that for extra perks in September, I went ahead and bought 3-5-2.

It unlocked a weird formation—it was simply called "Sweeper." For 1,900 XP I could have a sweeper behind two centre backs, two attacking wingbacks, three central midfielders, and two strikers. I'd have to buy it one day, if only to get the next one. But would I ever use a sweeper in a meaningful game of football? How would it work with the offside trap? Also, how many players could even play as a sweeper? You'd need amazing positioning and outstanding technical qualities. There weren't many Franz Beckenbauers in the modern game.

I knew one thing—I was done buying formations for a long while. My next dilemma would be whether to buy Injuries or Morale.

Friday morning's training was a match where we practised our formations. The first team did half an hour of 4-1-4-1, then half an hour of 3-5-2, while the seconds did 4-4-2 to replicate what we expected from Spennymoor.

One bonus of Henri being banned was that he played on the second-string team—a big test for Glenn and the other defenders. In the first section, Raffi lost his place to Ryan, while in the second, Youngster did. Adding their energy and dynamism to the reserves meant the first team had to be on their toes. The matches were ten percent sharper than normal.

It felt to me like the squad was starting to get really good. The average CA across the whole squad, including Angles, the ancient goalie coach, and the Triplets, was 37. Better than some first teams! My stated goal was to have the best first eleven in the league by the end of the season. But what about my seconds? How good could *they* get?

It was an excellent session, wrapping up a good week of CA pops. Most players were at least back to their levels from the end of last season, while a few had improved markedly.

So I was in a good mood when Livia came to get me. I followed her to the medical room and felt my heart sink. What *now*?

Dean came out of his little room, smiling. "Oh, Max!" he said, and his smile dropped. Fake smile for the patients! That was progress. "We've got you a present."

"A present?"

"Yeah. For your recovery. It's going well, isn't it?"

"Yep. Think so, anyway. I'm going for my MRI after lunch."

Dean nodded, then reached into a shitty plastic bag. He glanced at me, realising his mistake. He should have made an effort with the presentation! It didn't bother me—I was shit at wrapping Christmas presents. I was also shit at remembering to buy them.

He handed me a little box. It was red and black and the logo said Airofit. The product displayed on the front looked like the part of a snorkel you put in your mouth.

"It's a breathing trainer," he said. "There's an app. You follow the instructions, breathe in and out when told, and it should, over time, increase your lung capacity. Build your inspiratory muscle strength and flexibility."

"Wow," I said, starting to open it. "That's weird."

Livia laughed. "Dean loves his gizmos. He's hoping you'll love it and buy one for all the players so he can make a little spreadsheet and track everyone's numbers."

Dean didn't look embarrassed. "Yep."

"Mate," I said, "This is exactly what I want from you. How much are they?"

"About two hundred and fifty."

"For the whole squad?"

"Each."

That'd be about six thousand pounds to equip the entire first team. "Fuck me. Don't set up your spreadsheet just yet, Dean."

"I know. But you said you wanted us to start thinking about where we want our future riches to go. So I've started. There's a subscription model with added features but I don't think we need that."

"Dean, I'm very happy with this," I said, feeling the box's weight. "Yes. This is exactly the kind of thing I want us to be doing."

"It helps with snoring, too," said Livia.

"Huh. Top Christmas present idea for MD, then." I looked at the thing. It was a chunky piece of plastic with two dials on the sides. I got the app, paired it up, and took my first lung test. I had to breathe out to empty my lungs, breathe in as hard as poss through the mouthpiece, then blow as hard as poss. Dean and Livia crowded round, watching the results on the app. "Three point three litres," I said, slightly light-headed. "That feels shit."

"But it'll get better," said Dean. He looked at his laptop in a vaguely desperate way.

"Go on, you weirdo," I said. "Write it down." I looked at the packaging. "Ten minutes a day? I can do that. I'll text you my numbers, what, once a week? Oh, look!"

"What?"

I was pointing to an image on the box. "Red when number goes down. Green when number goes up!"

They looked at me like I was mental.

The MRI went fine. Being in the machine with its insanely loud clacking noises is a horrible and scary experience, but I went into my screens and tinkered with formations and tried to optimise in terms of CA. When Henri was back, we'd potentially have some very sexy average CA numbers.

The specialist talked me through the images. Said I was all good. I asked him if I had what my mum had. He said there was no evidence of that, but there wouldn't be. I said I needed to know so I could decide if I would have kids or not.

He got still, went internal, and finally said that my mum getting it early did hint at a type that might be passed on genetically. He said it wasn't his place to say such things, but that the percentages were massively in favour of my children having long and healthy lives, and if not . . . he shrugged. It meant life's a bitch.

I left with mixed feelings. Yes, I was in good shape. My brain was not full of holes, and I felt completely confident about buying and using new formations and perks.

But while I wanted my footballers to make rational, percentage-based decisions . . . it wasn't so easy when it came to starting a family. My mother hadn't known about her condition before she'd had me. I *did* know. I couldn't ignore it.

I decided I would sit down with Emma and have a very serious chat about our future. When would be a good time to do that? I checked my calendar and decided to pencil that in for the year 2030. If we were still together in seven years, maybe the relationship had legs.

I trained with the women's team. Their first match of the season was coming up on Sunday—a preseason friendly. The week after would be an FA Cup qualifying match against Nantwich Town, who were in tier seven. I was treating it as a preseason friendly because if we weren't miles better than Nantwich, we were seriously fucked.

We seemed to be in good shape in terms of fitness and morale. Dani was back, and while her CA hadn't improved, it hadn't regressed, either. She was looking at Charlotte—our new midfielder—the way Pascal had looked at Ryan. Massive respect, ready to learn.

Overall, I was optimistic, but our CA was behind where I probably would have wanted. I was hoping that our first real, competitive match would kickstart our growth, and we'd get another bump from playing our first league match. Both events would signal that we were a real team.

The contrast between the men's team, with its CA 60 star and the women's, whose best player was only CA 23, made me even more painfully aware that we really needed a great coach and another striker. As always, I'd have more time to find them when the transfer window closed.

"Max," called Jill.

"Huh?"

"Duels," she said. I looked up and saw I was standing in front of Dani. She had a ball at her feet. Looking around, I saw we were doing simple one v ones. Try to dribble past the person in front of you.

I gave Jill and Dani a thumbs-up and took a few steps forward, trying to get my defensive balance right. What I wanted was to be able to move left or right with equal ease. Most players had a stronger side so you could defend against their weaker foot, but Dani was two-footed. Not that she'd been playing like that . . . I fractionally turned towards her right foot.

She came at me, hesitated, and I kicked the ball away. Abysmal. Worse than D-Day. I held my arms out. "What the fuck was that?"

She didn't look at me.

"Your turn, Max."

We swapped ends and I dribbled at Dani. When I got close, I did a shitty trick, got it all wrong, yet I was past her with the ball safely at my feet. Jill was watching. I said, "Did she even try to stop me?"

"Not really."

I pinched the bridge of my nose. Training with the under-twelves had been great, but I was starting to find it too easy; next week I was going to promote myself to the fourteens. The women were way, way better than me and I'd been enjoying the challenge of trying to compete. While they hadn't gone trying to smash my shins off, this was the first time one of them had gone easy on me.

"Switch," called Jill.

"No. I stay with Dani. She's not switching until she beats me. She's not doing any other drill until she beats me."

Jill typed it out and showed Dani the text.

Dani's head dropped. She wasn't into it. Well, she'd get into it. What the fuck was it with her? She was the weirdest person I'd ever met, and it was nothing to do with her being deaf.

She came at me. I snuffed her attack out in seconds. I went at her; I drifted past like she was a ghost.

For the first time since learning to walk again, I had done two successful dribbles in a row. It had been something I was looking forward to, a landmark of my recovery. To get it like this was infuriating. I threw a little tantrum.

Bonnie and Maddy were the next pair—a very interesting battle, there. They stopped what they were doing and came to calm me down.

"Max, what's up?" said Bonnie.

"Didn't you get your afternoon nap?" said Maddy.

"What's up with Dani?" I said.

"Nothing. She doesn't want to hurt you."

I sighed. "If she doesn't step it up, I can't join in the training. This makes no sense. *She* was the one who invited me to join in."

"That wasn't duels, Max."

I looked up at the darkening skies. I'd been enjoying these sessions, enjoyed feeling my improvement. It's hard to explain how motivational the sessions had been, especially when I got my body to do things it used to be able to do. One of the women would notice and make a fuss, and I would pretend not to like it. Yeah, losing these sessions would be a downer. But it was over; I was a liability now. "Fine. I'll get going."

Maddy stepped in front of me, blocking my path. "Let me handle it."

"What?"

"Man up, Best. Watch me fix your shitty broken superstar." She walked away, backwards, jagging her head from side to side. It was pretty awesome.

Maddy squared up in front of Dani, and rolled the ball to her. Dani, noticeably more determined, ran. Maddy sprinted forward, got into a good defensive stance, then stepped across Dani's path. The collision left Dani flat on her arse—and Maddy with the ball.

Maddy punched the air, turned to see Dani still on the grass, and gestured *Get up!* Not sure if it was proper British Sign Language, but what it may have lacked in grammatical accuracy, it made up for in clarity.

Dani, slightly dazed, got to her feet, and before she was up, Maddy was haring towards her. Dani stuck out a leg, Maddy did a spin move to go the long way round her opponent. This had the bonus effect of sending Dani tumbling.

Maddy dribbled to the end cones with her hands aloft.

Dani slapped the surface of the pitch and got up. *What are you doing?* she signed.

Maddy made a boo-hoo crying gesture, then slapped her fist into her palm, like Dani had done the day we'd stolen Maddy from her former team. Dani fell into a hunch and slapped her fist into *her* palm.

"How does this end with Dani dribbling at me?" I said.

"It doesn't," said Bonnie. "It's not always about you, Max."

"This time it *was*," I whined.

She pushed me. "Why don't you pick on someone your own size?"

I looked her up and down. "Because you're shit."

"Ooh, bad boy!" she laughed. "Come on, Best. Do your worst."

Henri: Some activity in Darlo. Looks like they're about to spend the money you gave them.

Me: Stop trying to make a rivalry happen. It's not going to happen.

While the women played a training game with Dani up front in a 3-5-2, I pottered around the touchline with my phone in hand. I was tracking the transfer rumours, while fielding calls from hopeful agents and even a couple of out-of-contract players.

The amount of money being spent continued to boggle the mind. During the summer, the Premier League spent a combined £2.36 billion on new players. God knows how much the Saudi Pro League spent, but in addition to that, they also made a £150 million bid for Liverpool's Mo Salah. Now *that* would have been a hell of a coup, but if they really wanted him they wouldn't have left it to the last minute. Liverpool wouldn't sell Salah if they couldn't replace him, and they couldn't replace him within a couple of hours. Maybe the point was to destabilise the player so they could get him in January.

The BBC, Sky, and the rest weren't very good at tracking non-league transfers, so I was glad of the constant updates from the curse. By the time of the next window, I'd have seen almost every player in our league and this information would be even more useful.

As it was, there was only one team on my mind. How would Darlington spend their money? Would Folke Wester even see any of it?

The answer came pretty definitively.

Thu Sep 1—Jonathan Hurts—Ebbsfleet United—Darlington—£70K

Thu Sep 1—Christian Dicks—Dagenham and Redbridge—Darlington—£40K

All right! Talk about a statement of intent. I was able to find out that Hurts was a left back and Dicks was a left mid. Darlo had upgraded their weak left-hand side of the pitch. But were these big-money signings actually upgrades? I didn't know anything about these players, and the problem was that I wouldn't get to see them until we played Darlo in November. We'd always be playing on the same dates.

Unless . . .

Match 7 of 46: Spennymoor Town versus Chester FC.

Spennymoor is in County Durham and so they are one of Darlington's rivals. They played at The Brewery Field, a cute little stadium where all the stands had been painted black, making it seem modern and low-profile. There were loads of small details that I liked, such as a place to eat a burger and have a pint that had astroturf as flooring. Pointless, but fun stuff that added to the matchday experience. I was into it!

The pitch was incredible—from looking at it, I was sure it was more astroturf. But no—it was grass. Proof that the groundsman had excelled. Very well respected in his field etc etc. It was an absolute carpet.

Moors had an average CA of 44, and I knew from last season that they had a lethal striker, Taylor. He'd finished second in the goalscoring charts with a very healthy 23. They also had a tricky right winger. You might remember he had dicked us when Ian Evans was in charge, just after the Jack Litherland loan fiasco.

For that reason, I knew I wanted the defensively solid Magnus at left back for this one, and that meant starting with 4-1-4-1.

I had a strange compulsion not to start Ryan Jack. He was our best player, but he had barely played this season. I'm sure every other manager in the league would have thrown him straight in, but I was taking the ten-month view, and that meant easing him into the squad.

So: Ben, who had finally edged ahead of Robbo in terms of CA; Magnus, Glenn, Gerald, Carl; Youngster; Aff, Raffi, Sam, Joe; Tony.

That gave us an average CA of 42.5. With Henri out of the team we were down to two "gold" players (CA 50+), but we had four silvers, including Raffi, who'd crept up to 40. Ben and Magnus were close to moving from bronze to silver, and Aff was very close to gold.

It was happening!

I pottered around, taking in the sights and smells—one of the pies smelled unbelievable; I really wanted one of those bad boys—and was struck by how friendly everyone was. The opposing manager, the referee, the Moors directors. They were all happy to see me. I asked MD about it later, and he said I didn't realise how big a story my murder had been. It'd probably stop when I led my team to too many wins, but for now I could be assured a warm welcome almost everywhere in the National League North.

The match kicked off, and I knew from the first five minutes we were in for a classic.

Spennymoor liked to play football and on their day felt they could beat anyone. The question was, how many "days" would they have? They'd lost their first match 4–1 and won the next 5–1. Their strength was their weakness—they had three outstanding players—striker, right mid, centre mid—and there was a bit of a drop-off to the rest of the team. I felt that if we could gain control of the midfield, we'd take their striker off the table.

Nah.

He scored after three minutes.

But we stayed on course, playing mostly Max Best football, mostly fearless football, even if it was all a bit frantic. Then Sam fed Joe Anka, who whipped in a cross that Tony threw himself at. Diving header! Gorgeous angles, but the cross had done most of the work, and the celebrations were rightly centred around Joe.

One–all, and that was the trigger for a real ding-dong battle. Proper end-to-end stuff.

The Spennymoor manager, who had been really gracious and welcoming before kickoff, turned into a monster as soon as the match started. He never stopped screaming, and everything needed to be repeated. "Our ball! Our ball! Here we go! Here we go! Ref, that's red! Ref, that's red!" When he tried to get in my face, the Brig was there. "Mr. Best is not currently receiving visitors."

I have no idea how we got to halftime at one–all. It could have been 4–3. Christ, it could have been 7–6.

Both keepers were having blinders. Ben was on 8 out of 10, and the Spennymoor guy 9, which to me hinted that although Moors had had more shots, ours had been higher quality.

The lads were buzzing at halftime but got subdued when I decided to speak. I reckon they thought they'd get a bollocking.

"Dudes. That was incredible. The effort, the teamwork, the togetherness. Ten out of ten. What's the opposite of double training? Half training? That sounds like a punishment, too. Er . . . yeah, look. I'm happy. Now, it was all a bit frantic. A bit harum-scarum, and I'm not writing a harem story." I paused. "No reaction to that? That's a good line. Okay, please give me the same in the second half. The same effort and intensity and whatnot. But we are going to switch to four-five-one."

That surprised them. They'd been expecting a change to 3-5-2, but that would have meant putting D-Day up front, which I wasn't keen on. He wasn't bad there, but he wasn't good, either. Four-five-one would let me get Ryan Jack in the centre of three CMs, which was my heart's desire.

Taking off Youngster and putting on Oldster improved our CA to 44.7. These were dizzying heights! A couple of changes from Moors slightly lowered theirs. We were now the stronger team!

Of course, they had home advantage. Any reasonable manager would have been happy with a point.

So I went bonkers in the first ten minutes. I ranted, I raved, I waved my arms, I demanded more, I demanded higher. I got what I wanted.

But it was very little to do with me and my antics. It was Ryan.

Good work from Magnus to knock the ball out for a throw-in.

It goes long into the penalty area.

May and Taylor climb.

May wins it.

The ball bobbles around—Brown knocks it out of the penalty area.

Jack collects it. He's got Spennymoor players all around him.

He turns away from one challenge, turns more, keeps turning.

A simple forward pass . . .

And Brown is away!

He hits it wide to Aff.

Aff sprints down the wing.

Great cross!

Hetherington was so close to it!

A stunning counterattack.

And so it went. Spennymoor tried to press my new signing, tried to deny him time and space. But he was far too good. He was CA 10 physically, and CA 100 between his ears. It was unreal watching him.

And it wasn't just fancy footwork, neat and tidy passing. Twice he sprinted—yes, sprinted!—and launched into fierce tackles. In those moments his expression changed from one of boredom, indifference, to one of pure savagery. *My ball! That's my ball!*

He turned the tide. We were starting to dominate—the possession stats shifted our way. We added three shots to every one from Moors. Our passing got slick and rhythmical.

Then, disaster.

A little hamstring tweak for Joe Anka. He self-reported early, so no more than a week out, but he'd been playing fantastically well. I had both Donny and

Pascal on the bench. Half an hour to go. I liked the idea of using Pascal for the last ten minutes when the other team was as tired as they were going to get, but for thirty minutes plus injury time? Ryan Jack was shorter than average. With *two* short guys, Moors would loom over us at set pieces.

I can't explain it, but I threw Pascal on. Maybe it was how great the pitch was. Maybe it was the way the match had been played in a good spirit and it seemed no one was going to try to break his legs.

There were the usual laughs as he ran onto the pitch. It did look like we'd sent a ball boy on by mistake.

And for five minutes, we were forced back. All our hard work clawing our way into a dominant position, gone.

Had I made a terrible mistake?

Five more minutes of scrapping and battling and fighting for territory and keeping it tight. A time of dread—every set piece seemed like a death sentence.

And then:

Topps with a good tackle. He plays it short to Jack.

Jack plays a quick one-two with Brown.

And another!

Spennymoor don't like that; they're moving in.

Jack hits a forty-yard, outside-of-the-foot pass.

Bochum hurtles forward. He's got the beating of the fullback!

Bochum pushes the ball towards the corner of the penalty area. The left back swings a leg.

He misses; that could have been nasty.

Bochum looks up. Hetherington steps toward the near post, then checks his run.

Hetherington is in space!

Will Bochum pick him out? The ball is on his favoured right foot.

Bochum points to where he will pass the ball—every defender moves to intercept!

Bochum taps the ball left-footed.

GOOOOAAAALLLLL!!!!

Bochum swept it into the empty net!

An impudent finish.

He's swarmed by his teammates.

And a yellow card for the defender. The referee played a good advantage there.

I celebrated like I'd scored the goal. Scratch that—when I scored, I didn't normally dance around. Let's say I celebrated like a Chester fan. Joyously bouncing around, high on the stakes and the disbelief. So many things about that goal had been amazing. The midfield control, the pass out wide, the first touch that skinned the defender, and everything that happened in the penalty box. Everyone knew Pascal would pass—it was just a case of him guessing where Tony would go and if the pass would be accurate enough. Absolutely no one expected him to simply *roll* the ball into the net.

So, so satisfying.

Spennymoor switched to 4-2-4 with direct passing. Pretty sensible—we were crushing midfield so there was no point competing there. Instead, they'd try to bypass it completely.

I took another risk and switched to 4-3-3 with Aff, Tony, and Pascal as the three forwards. I set most of the players to no forward runs and our team mentality to counterattacking. Aff wasn't the most natural fit in the role, but it was a seriously rapid frontline.

It worked—we scored a third through unselfish play from Tony. He laid the ball off to Aff, who was in a better position than him. Three–one. I exhaled; I'd spent minutes second- and third-guessing myself.

But Spennymoor hadn't even realised we'd switched formation, so they stuck with what they were doing. Maddeningly, it paid off. Their star striker touched the ball to a mate and got it back in the box. His finish, as they say, was unerring. Three–two, and the last five minutes were agonising. Pascal pressed like a hydraulic machine. Glenn leapt for headers. Ben brought out his Octoman moves—slapping away shots and crosses like he had eight limbs.

The last word fell to Ryan Jack. Carl Carlile rose to head a cross away, and Jack was in the right place to get it, as he so often was. He took a touch, looked like he was going to send a long pass to Aff, waved his arm, instructing Aff to go wider and higher. He was really going to leather this pass! But this whole scene took so long a Moors player came up behind him, ready to tackle. Jack cocked his leg and found himself on the pitch in a heap, writhing in pain. Howling in agony. The Moors player had already had a yellow card, and out came another. Two yellows equal red, and he was forced to leave the pitch.

I knew from his profile that Ryan was fine, and before he'd even gotten up I'd switched back to 4-1-4-1, with Trick replacing the old man, who hobbled off, supported by Dean and Vimsy.

When I asked him if he knew the guy who was coming behind him was on a yellow, and *that's* why he took so long to get his pass away, Ryan gave me a sad look. "How would I know *dat*, boss?"

Scousers. Never believe something until they deny it.

Three–two, then. Good win, away from home against a strong team. It showed what we were capable of. I liked how we played.

The victory music was playing. Vimsy stopped it.

He brandished his phone like Neville Chamberlain waving a peace treaty. "Darlo lost! York lost! We are going up, say we are going up!"

That chant went well, but I wasn't satisfied. A couple of minutes later, I stopped the music again.

"Henri, get back here. Jesus Christ, you're always in the shower when I want to talk to you. Holy fuck." I looked around. The dressing room was small, with a central bench dividing the space in half. "Everyone on this side. Pascal, stand on that bench. Joe, stand on that one. Come on! Everyone in here." I looked around, plotting. "Right. What we do is, Joe, you film me starting the chant. I'll be here, and I'll move back into the mass. When I turn around, everyone else joins in. Yeah?"

"What's the chant?" said Sam.

"Fucking listen!" I said. I cleared my mind, got my social media face on. I was nearly ready to go when something occurred to me. I looked over my shoulder and saw Henri still naked except for a small towel around his waist. "Put a fucking top on!"

He rolled his eyes, but pulled a Chester shirt on.

"Joe, tell me when."

"You go when you're good. I'll edit it."

"You know what I'm doing, right?"

"Think so."

"Make sure you put subtitles on."

"For Dani, I know."

"For everyone! Jesus fuck!"

"All right, Max. Go when you want."

I pinched the bridge of my nose, got calm, and remembered what I was doing and why. Put simply, it had taken me a while to realise what Pascal had done. He'd done the Bad Boys Challenge . . . in a match. At speed, with a defender trying to ruin him. He'd made a decision under pressure that had led to a goal, and in the end, a win. He'd done everything I wanted. And now I wanted the fans to stop mumbling "blunderkind" under their breath. I wanted him to have his own song.

I nodded at Joe's camera lens, and got a cheeky grin on my face.

"Bo-chum! Bo-chum!" I said, splitting the name into its component syllables as I jiggled my shoulders. "Whatcha gonna do? Whatcha gonna do when he's running through? Bo-chum! Bo-chum!" I turned, and the brighter slash more musical players caught on quick. "Bo-chum! Bo-chum! Whatcha gonna do?" Pascal didn't know what to do—he turned red and floundered. But we were singing to him, and he was a footballer, so he folded his arms and tried to look tough. "Whatcha gonna do when he's running through?" The players loved it, which meant the fans would love it, too.

At exactly the right time, Joe changed the chant. He yelled, "Chess-ter! Chess-ter!" and we went nuts on that.

Later, when Joe sent me the link, I saw that Henri had stripped his top off in the half a second between him putting it on and Joe pressing record. See what I have to deal with?

Also later, when I looked at the Darlo match in closer detail, I spotted that neither of their new players had played, or even been on the bench. That seemed odd. Most managers would have thrown them right into the team.

I did some digging and found—and this blew my mind—that both players were currently suspended for picking up a red card in a game for their previous clubs.

Darlington had signed a couple of bad boys.

Henri had said something about them getting harder, dirtier. Looked like Folke Wester was reshaping Darlo in his own image.

And I'd given him a huge push.

Sunday was all about the women's team and their first friendly of the season.

I'd asked Inga to set us up against the Puddington Pirates—the first team we'd ever played. They'd dicked us 7–0. It wasn't that I wanted revenge as much as closure. Not just for the women, but for me. I was ninety-nine percent sure Ian Evans had quit after that match so that it would be impossible for me to become the men's team manager.

Well, lookee here. See who had the last laugh on that one.

Another reason to play Puddington: their manager. I'd nicknamed her The Owl. From my point of view, she'd done something remarkable with her local village team. They were way better than they should have been; I desperately wanted to see her manager profile. Would she take a job at Chester? No clue. But I wanted to get those digits.

She turned out to be disappointing. Her superpower was judging player potential—she had 11 out of 20 on that one. Her man management and motivating were decent, but everything else was 5 or less. Shame.

We lined up in our usual 4-5-1 with an average CA of exactly 12. The Pirates had 8.

With Charlotte set as playmaker, we controlled the match from start to finish. Easy street. Bea Pea scored one, then another, allowing me to experiment with 3-5-2 in the second half.

I wanted to see if Dani could play as a second striker. Her profile said she could play as an attacking midfielder. Ideally I'd have dragged one of the striker icons back one slot, but I couldn't do that yet. Maybe when I had Wibwob. Anyway, Dani did fine. Not great, not terrible. I suspected I needed to be careful about playing people in the wrong positions, but using 4-5-1 every match was fucking annoying. I needed options, even if it was for a ten-minute burst.

Next, I moved Dani back, put a rando on as a second striker, and experimented with the best placement for Charlotte. It seemed logical to put her in the centre of the three, putting her really in the heart of everything. But there was also the argument that putting her next to Dani would give us a stellar combination on the left, like I'd tried previously with Pippa. I tinkered with the formation pretty much nonstop, but didn't reach any concrete conclusions.

We won 3–0. The third was a powerful header from a Dani corner. Bonnie was a real handful at set pieces.

All in all, it was a ten-goal swing from the last time we played Puddington. The women played it cool, but after a respectful delay, they let loose. Dancing, singing, more dancing, more singing.

As for me, managing two games in two days was very, very decent for my XP growth.

I got 360 in total from the men, and 180 for the women because it was a friendly. I expected to get 360 from their league matches, same as for the men's team. Some quick mental maths suggested I'd get 3,000 XP a month if I stayed in charge of the women.

Tempting, but I needed a proper succession plan. I went to talk to The Owl. She didn't have any tips for me about out-of-work elite coaches, but when I suggested I thought she had a good eye for a player and would love it if she sent any decent prospects to us for a trial, she got weird. It was only when Jill stepped forward to give her a hug that I realised she'd got emotional.

"What did I say? I'm sorry," I said, aghast. I thought I'd been doing better at not annoying people.

"It's not that. It's just so nice to get a compliment. So rare."

"Come on," I said. "You're killing it. You're top. You beat me seven–nil. Me! If you're not getting praise, it's because you're too good. It's just become normal."

Jill liked that—she gave me a little nod. And The Owl liked it as well. She promised to keep an eye out for hidden gems.

Monday, September 4.

The best thing about being the boss is making your own rules, and the best thing about having a Brig is being able to plan your own capers.

I sent out a text blast delaying Monday training till the afternoon—guys with parenting duties etc could negotiate with Vimsy.

We drove to Henri's place, essentially kidnapped him, then headed east.

Henri didn't speak for twenty minutes—I wondered if he was mad at me, but he was just waking up. His first word was "coffee," so we had to make an emergency stop to get one for him, which then turned into a whole drama when the Brig said he needed a tartlet. So that was yet another detour, during which we spent five minutes spitting the word tartlet at each other.

The idiots finally got the coffees and pastries they quote unquote needed, and we finally pulled into the car park at the Eastbourne Sports Complex. I put on my disguise: baseball cap, big sunglasses, fake moustache, and told the others to stay in the car.

The thing I'd realised is that I *didn't* need to wait for November to see Darlo in the flesh. I knew full well you could just walk into the training centre! Why had I not thought of this before?

I cut myself some slack; I'd been in a coma not long ago.

So I strolled around, calm as you like, my piping-hot Earl Grey tea proving a useful prop for blending in and giving my hands something to do. I walked past the training pitches, just another guy, and re-scouted the players I knew so well. I also got Folke Wester's playing and management profile, plus the profiles for their two new signings.

While I watched, their new left midfielder, Dicks, found himself through on goal, all the time in the world. Their new left back, Hurts, appeared out of nowhere, steaming towards the sitch. Dicks unleashed a sickeningly powerful shot that Hurts blocked. Dicks rebalanced, then hit another shot, this time with his right, yet somehow Hurts was in the way of that one, too. Dicks got the ball a third time, nutmegged Hurts, and was taken out by Folke Wester. The three of them ended up crunched into a pile. As they unpeeled themselves from each other, they were all grinning from ear to ear. This was the new Darlington. Fast, fierce, committed, skilful. And the CA . . .

I sipped my tea.

Then, apparently more interested in my phone than the pitches, I turned right, cut through the reception building, waited in a toilet for ten minutes to make it seem like I needed more than five seconds to scout an entire squad, went out a doorway most people didn't know about, and was back in the car park before my tea had got cool.

The perfect crime.

The Brig didn't wait—he'd turned around so that we could drive off, just as though I'd robbed a bank. He wiped a bit of tartlet from his lips and accelerated away.

When we were clear, I removed my disguise. I grinned so hard I had to bite my lip to stop. I tapped the bottom of the window.

Henri, now awake, tilted his head. "What did you discover?"

I looked at him and raised my eyebrows.

"What, Max?"

"Tell us, sir," said the Brig.

"It's good news, isn't it?" pleaded Henri. "Tell me I was wrong."

"No, my friend. Your instincts were bang on. We . . ." I laughed. "We are in big trouble."

11

THE END

"This is not the end of the season, nor is it the beginning of the end of the season. But perhaps it is the end of the beginning. Of the season."

—Winston Churchill

Before heading home, we took a detour to Henri's old house. Henri and the Brig were desperate to know what I'd seen at Darlington's training session, but I didn't want to waste energy by explaining it to them and then again to the rest of the squad. In the end, Henri's whingeing became unbearable, so I told them about Folke Wester and the two new signings. I said we all had a lot to think about, that the war would be long and bitter, but that in the end, we would surely triumph. Then I suggested they shut up so I could concentrate on what I was going to say to the new homeowner.

A woman peered from behind the net curtains in the front room—she'd heard the car crunch up the drive.

"It's almost certainly the mother. I should do the talking," said Henri. "She bought the house from me."

"You never *met* her, did you? It was all done through solicitors. You have no more relationship with her than I do."

"If I may be so bold," said the Brig. "I should do it. I effuse a soothing air of trustworthiness. My popularity with housewives is the stuff of legend."

"Right, but I'm Max Best," I said, and they didn't like that. Henri and the Brig decided they'd knock, then wait to see which one of them the woman spoke to.

The door opened and a woman poked her head out just far enough to check us out. We were hovering a couple of yards away from the door so we'd be slightly less intimidating. Henri gave her a crooked smile that I guessed was supposed to be sexy and mysterious. The Brig was smiling, too, in his own way. I think—pretty sure—he was trying to make his eyes twinkle.

The woman's slight frown of suspicion vanished when she saw . . . drum roll . . . me.

"Max Best!" she cried.

I stepped closer—WINNER of the contest, boo-ya!—and offered my hand. "You must be Mrs. Green."

"You used to live here. We found out after we moved in. The neighbours told us."

"Oh?" I said, confused. I looked at the houses around us. "No one ever spoke to me. I thought they were worried I'd have mad parties all the time."

"No, they wanted to leave you alone," she said. "You wanted to keep yourself to yourself, they said, and that was understandable what with you being a big football star." Henri made a noise like a sigh.

"We couldn't come in, could we?" I asked.

"Oh! It's an awful mess. You didn't leave anything, I don't think. But we've kept your mail."

"I have mail here? I didn't think about that."

"Of course you can come in. But why *did* you come?"

"I buried something in the back garden. Want to dig it up. I'll need to borrow a big spoon."

She smiled. "You *did* come for the mail. How about a tea?"

We went through, into the familiar space. They'd put all different furniture in. I preferred how Henri had it.

The mum kept chatting away. "Yeah, they're lovely, the neighbours. And I know you. You're Henri Lyons. The vendor."

He was ludicrously pleased to be recognised. "You're the buyer. Your signature is very charming. Very elegant. I'm something of a graphologist," he added, as though that would make him irresistible.

"And this is John Smith," I said. "Assistant manager of Chester Football Club. Listen, when I was here, the tree in the garden was all dormant and that. I never saw it with leaves on. Can I go look at him?"

The familiar moment when my weirdness met a normo's expectation of convention. "The tree? Oh, of course. I mean, why not?"

I waited for her to open the patio doors, and we stepped through. The garden looked the same, but there was a small football goal and several balls scattered around. I smiled at them, then went to the tree.

It looked very tree-y. It had started to shed its leaves, and the little fruit things had turned brown. The shade on the grass was dappled—a word I learned three minutes into the first gardening programme I ever watched and had heard in every gardening programme since, but never in the real world. With a bit of wind moving through the leaves that were clinging on, it was very peaceful. Very pleasant.

"Good tree," I said eventually. "I love how craggy it is."

"Is that the right word, Max?" said Henri.

"I mean . . . it's like a tree in a fairy tale. Not just with a straight trunk. It's grown the way it had to grow. For example," I said, bending under it to show one twist of a branch. "This is where someone tried to murder it, and it's had to, like, re-learn how to walk but it's coming back stronger and smarter than ever. And *this* branch is its relationship with its star striker, which is nice and placid now that he's promised not to get sent off for doing dumb shit. And these roots here are the months of work he did turning the team into a winning machine."

"Is this tree your picture of Dorian Gray?" said Henri.

"Dorian Gray?" I said. "Who does he play for?"

Henri smiled, but the mum wasn't sure to what extent we were joking. The Brig came out with four cups of tea. "I took the liberty of finishing, Mrs. Green."

"Oh, lovely," she said, clearly not used to men helping out around the house.

We sipped tea and I sighed, pretty happy. Yeah, Darlington had massively strengthened their team and were a major, major threat, but I'd been planting trees in the wilderness and they were coming into bloom—Raffi, Youngster, Pascal. My tree of knowledge was growing—soon I'd buy either the Injuries or Morale perk. What else did trees symbolise? Family trees? The guy had said I could have kids. My mum was doing well. What else? The dappled shade was . . . the atmosphere in the Deva stadium? That was a step too far. The tree theme was done. Close the thread, archive the chat.

"Tree," I said, which was intended to draw a line under our visit. Signal that it was over. Inexplicably, the others didn't understand that.

"How did you recognise Max so quickly?" wondered Henri.

"My son Tommy's a big Darlo fan. He used to be for Newcastle but he's off them now. He's got posters of you on the wall; he cried when you went to Chester. But he's stuck with Darlo. His dad's made up, takes him to every home game. It's been amazing for their relationship. We're not sure about this Folke Wester. There was a rumour you were coming back to take over as manager. When the old one, I don't know his name, was let go, you turned up that morning. People said you were there to take the job, but you didn't. Wester, I don't feel sorry for him, not really, but he's living in your shadow."

There was one less Newcastle fan in the world because of me. Had I heard that right? Suddenly I was buzzing. In the mood for mischief. Folke Wester wanted people in Darlington to talk shit about me. Think the worst of me. Good luck with that! "Your son. Is he at school?"

"Yeah."

"Which one?"

"Max," said Henri, in a warning tone. "Whatever you're thinking, stop thinking it."

"What?" I said, finishing my tea, face full of innocence. "I'm just politely interested."

Five minutes later, I was peering into a school classroom but couldn't see the target. The Brig had a look. "There he is. Right aisle, back. Class is in alphabetical order, no doubt."

"Top," I said, knocking on the door and entering. About half the kids gasped.

"Yes?" said the teacher, who was the only person who didn't enjoy what followed.

What followed was perfectly normal. Football star makes unannounced visit to boring lesson. The usual.

Fifteen minutes later, I relaxed back into the Brig's Volvo, sighed happily, and explained what I was thinking. Henri blew air through his cheeks and looked away, but the Brig seemed impressed. He got thoughtful.

I sent Emma some video files and a request. Could she match this footage to a script I'd write?

Emma: Can it wait till the weekend? Dad's got me doing extra to make up for staying longer on hols.

Me: I can get Sumo to do it.

Emma: You mean you can ASK Sumo if he has the TIME and INCLINATION to work for free. Again.

Me: That's what I said.

Emma: I would like to do it.

Me: There's no hurry. Before November is all.

Emma: Sigh. Before November 11?

Me: What a strange thing to say. So specific. Remembrance Day? We're not at war.

Emma: I know that's when you're playing Darlo.

Me: Is it? Anyway, thanks babes!

Whizzing back to Chester, I opened the mail the Brig had remembered to take. Half was junk, because half of everything is junk, but there were a few letters from well-wishers. Randos, mostly, but one was on Man City stationary. I skipped to the end, expecting it to say *from Sandra* or *Meghan*. But it was from a dude called Patricio. I had a player profile for someone with the same name as him, but it took me ages to remember why.

We'd met the day I'd toured the Man City Campus. Patricio had been tickling free kicks into the net, top bins every time, and I'd done some light showing off. I hadn't thought about the guy since, but apparently I'd left more of an impression on him.

"What is it?" said Henri, noticing my shift in mood.

I explained it to him. Said these Man City fucks always made it hard to hate them. "But I don't get why he sent it to Darlington."

"He got your address from Kisi," he said.

"That's it. Amazing. You really would make a good detective. We should do an escape room. Me, you, the Brig, and . . ." I tried to think who the optimal fourth member of the group would be.

"Emma," said Henri.

"Why? Little hands?"

"No. If we don't escape the room within an hour, at least we spent an hour with Emma."

"Good point."

"That was a smooth line," mused Henri. "Next time we do a dual date, bring up escape rooms so I can say it again. With my date's name, of course."

The Brig spoke. "I have to withdraw from the team, sir. I don't do well locked in confined spaces. There's a high risk the scenario would trigger another lethal psychotic episode."

Bit of a nervous silence. "You're joking," said Henri. "He's joking."

"Very good, sir."

"Henri, I think what he's saying is, he's shit at escape rooms and would be ashamed to flounder and fail in front of us."

"Regretfully, the opposite," sighed the Brig. "Escape rooms are yet another avenue of pleasure I may not drive along. My skills and training mean puzzles designed for the average member of the general public are no more challenging than simply opening the door and walking out."

"Come on," I said. "You're not that good."

Another sigh. "I wish that were true." He pursed his lips. "I'm better suited to designing such puzzles." He tapped the steering wheel a few times, uncharacteristically. "The world of football has been more challenging than I anticipated. There is much to learn. Many variables. Formations, types of players, the impact of pitch and weather, the caprice of the referees and even the game's administrators. And now the meta-game surrounding the game itself. Today I have seen disguise, espionage, and the social media equivalent of dropping propaganda pamphlets on disputed territory. I didn't realise we were engaging in total war."

"We're not," I said. "Darlo is my house. I've popped out for a minute and some prick is in my fridge eating my fruit corner yoghurts. I'm allowed to give him a slap. That's the law."

"It's not," said Henri. "You should be careful, my friend. People might think you're *really* interested in a return to Darlington. Darlington *Football Club*," he added, since I'd played for the rugby version, too.

"I wouldn't want anyone to think that, would I?" I laughed. As long as I was massively popular in Darlington, Folke Wester would never feel secure in his job. And insecure people made mistakes. For once, a bit of bear-poking was in Chester's best interests. If playing Mario Kart had taught me anything about football management, it was that the best way to slow the leader down was to throw some banana skins their way. "I like the idea of destabilising my enemies, though. John, tell me more about total war."

Back in Chester, after their late start, the guys did a simplistic session—some fitness stuff, couple of rondos, passing drills, then small-sided games. Henri ran to join in, having missed the beginning, but not the end of the beginning. Quick showers all round—Henri was furious that I sent the Brig to get him after a mere ten minutes—and into the war room. I mean, the meeting room.

The team was intrigued—why all the intrigue?

"All right. Let's whizz through this. I've just been to Darlington to spy on our rivals and their two big-money signings. Long story short, they've gone from having the worst left-hand side in the league to the best. Bloody Tranmere giving them a cash injection," I said, shaking my fist at an imaginary cloud. MD had come, and he dropped his forehead into his hand. He strongly suspected I was involved in the transfers—both of Tranmere's new players had been at Henri's house when MD and I had watched the "As It Was" video for the first time.

I turned to an invisible flipchart next to me. "Based on what I've seen and the data and all that, I'm moving Darlo from third in the power rankings . . ." I pretended to slide their name plate up. "To first."

"How good are the new players?" said Pascal.

"Very good. Hurts is the best left back in the league. He is potentially, temporarily, the best *player* in the league. Dicks is excellent, but Aff will overtake him soon." The left back was CA 65, and the left mid CA 60. They brought Darlo's average CA from 48 to almost 54. "Folke Wester is a good DM. He's got good positioning, passing, all that stuff." Wester had CA 50, PA 101. Decent lower league player, but judging by his career stats, which showed he'd played more than forty games a season for most of his career, he had worked hard to maximise his ability and stay as important as poss for as long as poss.

He was a good manager, too. I'd only seen a few managers since I'd unlocked the staff profiles, but he was by far the best. High in motivating, tactics, and judging player ability. He didn't seem interested in judging player potential, and his preferred formation was 4-4-2. That was interesting—by copying my idea, he was stepping outside his comfort zone; 4-1-4-1 suited him as a player, but not so much as a manager. I wondered if that would be a factor in the final reckoning. The league could come down to small details like that.

I continued.

"But most of all, they're aggressive. They're going to go in hard, every match, and they're going to get away with it because the refs are shit. So it's a clash of styles. They are an old team. A win-now team for a win-now manager. In a couple of years, they're going to fall off a cliff and we'll never hear from them again. They're physical, so it's all about duels, and when they've smashed teams up, they'll overpower them in the last twenty. All right? That's them.

"We, Chester, are a team of artists. Of artisans. We are a band of brothers. We—"

"Max," said MD, looking at his watch. "Can you hurry up like you promised?"

"I'm just saying we don't waste our windfalls on guys with no resale value. We trust in youth, believe in youth, and that's why we signed Ryan Jack." A good mix of guffaws and snorts followed that. Pleasing. My cheeky humour was defusing the bad news. The guys were with me. They were showing me on the training pitches that they were soldiers. Why had Old Nick made me think of traitors? "The season's going to be harder than I thought, but only slightly. We're lucky that September has loads of winnable matches. We can go on a run now. We *need* to go on a run now.

"Last thing. Football experts will say we've got too many young players and there will be mistakes and we'll drop points. Not sure about that, but whatever. Darlo are going with experienced hot-heads." I glanced at Henri, thought about making a joke, but his pained expression was already funny enough. "They will get red cards, they will miss games, the backups are shit, they'll drop points doing their strategy, too. Glenn, you're unhappy."

Glenn nodded. "No, Max, I was just thinking . . . But it doesn't change anything, right? We try to win every game and we train hard, that's the plan."

"Absolutely, and let me say that you've all been training like bosses. Trick—I see it; you've stepped up. Well and truly noted. Ben, superb. Raffi, tireless.

"So I thought it'd be interesting for you guys to hear all that, but mostly I wanted this meeting because I realised I could just go and watch Darlo whenever I wanted. If I can scout teams on a random weekday morning, that's huge." I looked at the league table on my phone. "There are still teams in this division I've never seen. Hands up if you ever played for South Shields. No one? Warrington Town? Gerald, you did? Amazing. Is training there like this one, where you can just walk in?"

"Well, there's no fence or anything," said my overpaid centre back. "But . . . you're going to *spy* on them?"

"Spy? Like in a baseball cap and false moustache? Please be serious. I want to watch them for ten minutes. Get a feel for the levels. See what the facilities are like, too."

"You could look at the facilities *after* we play them," he said. I got the feeling he was upset by my idea.

"What's the problem? This is public land here, and it is in Darlington, too. What if I wanted to go see my old mate on reception? Diana. Maybe Dana. Dinah, at the outside. What if I want to go see my close friend Dinah? Am I not allowed?"

MD stepped forward. "You remember Spygate, Max. Leeds sent a guy to spy on Derby County. He was caught in a bush, there was a big fuss about it. The EFL made a rule that teams aren't allowed to watch training sessions from other teams within seventy-two hours of a fixture."

The EFL started with League Two. We were not subject to EFL rules. "Are we in the EFL now? Did I get isekaied into my own body, two years in the future?"

MD wasn't amused. "I don't want that kind of drama around Chester, Max."

Some of the players were nodding. "What the shit," I said, maturely. I frowned and glared at something. "Fine. I've seen York, I've seen Darlo. Kiddies will be tough but I'll go in blind if it makes you clowns happy. Turn off the radar! Fly straight into the thunderstorm!" I glared at the flipchart that wasn't there. "York, Darlo, Kidderminster. Everyone else we can slap." I bit my thumbnail. I wanted to go and watch teams not just to find out their latest CAs and devise tactical plans for our match, but to scout their staff and flesh out my database of players. If I went to watch every team in our league train, I'd get to see all their reserves and maybe some youth team players, not just the first eleven and subs. In the summer, when contracts ended, I could snap up all the talented ones while the rest of the league was on holiday. "What about the National League?" I said.

"What about it?" said MD.

"Is it 'cheating' to go and scout those teams and see how they do training?"

"Of course not. We're not in the same league as them."

"We will be next year."

"Yes, but . . . But it's not cheating. How can it be?"

"Great. Hands up if you've ever played for a team currently in the National League?" Some hands went up. "Top. Talk to the Brig. Describe in tedious detail how you drive there, what the car park's like, do you turn left or right at the pitches, where do the goalies train, where's the medical room. All right?"

I was about to change the topic completely when Ryan Jack spoke. "What about other teams? Do you want to watch dem?"

"Other teams?"

"Everton."

"I'd love to see Everton training, yeah. That'd be amazing. But I doubt I can just walk in off the street with my baseball cap and fake moustache. I've seen documentaries. They've got those little boxes in the car parks and there's a man and you have to tell him the password and then he raises the barrier. The password when I went to Man City was *Hail Hydra*, but they've probably changed it by now."

Ryan was shaking his head, which for him was the equivalent of uproarious laughter. "Get yourself invited."

I put my phone to my ear. "Hello, is that Everton? Can I come and watch you train, please? Sorry, where should I stick it? How far up?"

More head shaking. "I'll get you an invite."

I pointed at him. "Get me into an Everton training sesh and I'll give you . . . a joker. That you can use to get out of one session, media duty, or kidnapping."

"All right."

Henri spoke. "Can I have the same if I get you into Reading?"

"Absolutely. Offer is for everyone. Talk to the Brig." The players were buzzing. Most hadn't played at big clubs, but many knew someone who did. They could try to set something up. "I should tell you about tomorrow night's game. Hereford, at home. Four-one-four-one, control the midfield, control the tempo. Second half bring on our young whippersnapper for his home debut. Ryan, I was thinking if you scored a goal you could, like, touch your toes as a celebration."

"I can touch my toes, boss."

"Top. Prove it. Saturday's home to Bradford Park Avenue. They might be the weakest team in the league and we'll have Henri back, so you might as well go full-out tomorrow. Run up the score, put some miles in your legs. Final lineup TBC, depending on certain injury updates and whatnot. I'll text you later."

I looked at the notes I'd scribbled in the car. The Brig's Volvo was very smooth, but still. "Erm . . . trying to read my handwriting. I think this says, who wants to volunteer to spend time with a hot blonde?" Most hands went up. "This session is being livestreamed to your girlfriends." Some hands went down. "Too late now, you dicks! Right. If I can volunteer Ryan, Henri, and . . . huh. Angles, did you ever get a boot sponsorship?"

"Gloves, yeah," said my goalie coach. He'd been at some biggish clubs in his youth.

"Ah, mint. I'm going to add you, if you don't mind. You're allowed to cry off, but you'll enjoy it. My friend Ruth, former board member. You know her. She's got her first client his first move, and now he's all hyper about getting a boot deal."

Henri exploded. "He hasn't even played a minute of professional football!" There was a lot of laughter for that. Our older players thought the young 'uns were ridiculous.

"She can handle him. But at the same time, she wants to be prepared. So you three handsome gentlemen are going to give her an education in sponsorships and boot deals and glove deals and all that. If you have an old contract you don't mind showing her, that'd be top. Basically, she's going to start schmoozing these companies so she's ready for when she has an actual star on her books. And it's good for us, because maybe a few spare boots will find their way down here."

There was utter delight at these words. Ecstasy. Even fucking Pascal, the most level-headed kid of all time, lost his shit. Free boots! Swoon.

"Jesus Christ," I said. "That was odd. I think I'll be talking about that moment in therapy. More volunteers, please."

"What's it for?" said Aff.

"Just fucking volunteer," I said. Half the hands went up. "Put your hands down. Look, I'm pretty busy. I'm managing three competitive matches this week. Is that sustainable? Of course it is, it's a piece of piss. But the other four days I want to focus on me and my needs. I'm still in recovery mode, even though it doesn't feel like that because I'm absolutely killing all aspects of my life, including flossing, which I remembered this morning. Okay? But I haven't been to a Chester Knights game, and I haven't been to an under-whatevers match. You know I've been training with the twelves, and next week I'm going to the fourteens. So those little shits have been basking in the sunlight of my attention, but the older groups, not so much. I'm with the women in some godforsaken part of the country on Sunday," I said.

The Brig interrupted. "Nantwich."

"Yeah. Christ knows where that is. Fucking Mexico or somewhere."

"It's in Cheshire. Half an hour."

"Oh! Nice. So, look. If you're going to the zoo with your kids, could you pop by and watch the Knights first? Or go to the sixteens at full time and pretend you were there for the whole thing. If just one of you went, that'd honestly be super relaxing for me."

Glenn said, "Someone will be there, boss."

"Thanks." I rubbed my hands through my hair. "That's it."

"Boss," said Glenn. "Er . . . we have things to say."

"To me? That's awfully uppity." It wasn't uppity, but I did like saying that word.

Ryan Jack spoke first. "The Bad Boys drill. Some lads said they didn't always know what was a Bad Boy and what was a Sad Boy. We should film training so we can review things like that."

"Totally," I said. "But when I asked Spectrum to cost me a plan for proper cameras around the pitch, he said it'd be like ten grand, minimum. It has to wait."

Ryan nodded. He knew we were poor. "Sometimes a phone on a pole is good enough."

"Sure but I still need to get Spectrum to cut things together. He's already working a hundred and ten percent. But video of the sessions. Got it. Noted. We can talk about spending some of our prize money on some cameras and a work experience kid. Oh, there's more?"

Sam said, "You said we could say if we didn't like the drills and that." I glanced at Vimsy and Jude, and Sam noticed. "No, it's not that we don't like what we *do*. It's set pieces. We don't train them enough. We should do much more than we're doing."

I looked at Vimsy. He nodded. He and most of the players agreed. "All right."

I scratched the back of my neck. My approach to set pieces was to take them and score. And if we followed my tactical plans to the letter, we'd win every game 10–0 and wouldn't need to worry about set pieces. But in the real world, dead-ball scenarios were a little more important than I wanted them to be. It was undeniable that I'd neglected an important part of our training mix.

"Get together in groups and talk about your favourite set pieces. Talk about how we attack and defend. Let me give you a couple of basic defensive principles— we never have everyone back defending. Ever. If Pascal's playing, I want him on the halfway line ready for a break. I want Ryan just outside the box so he can send long, deadly passes or use his Scouse wiles to get someone sent off. Everything else is up for discussion. When your mini-groups are done, get together as a whole group, talk through what you want to practice. Don't make final decisions until you've spoken to Spectrum. He loves a bit of data munching. If you want to have defenders on both posts from corners, he might dig up a stat that says it's pointless. Maybe you still want to do it that way, but I want it discussed and debated. Er . . . when you've got good routines and everyone's happy, get me little diagrams. I need to know who's up and who's down."

Henri stood up. "Max, are you giving control of the set pieces to the team?"

I shrugged. "I guess? Yes. Power to the people. To be honest, I'm not that interested. One day we'll have a specialist set piece coach. Until then, I can't imagine being that bothered. When I'm playing, I'll just shoot most of the time." That reminded me that I currently had no objective way of knowing who should take my free kicks and corners. One thing I had always wanted to do but never had time for was a proper set piece trial. "Ryan's our default set piece taker now, but let's do some data mining. Put a fucking . . . melon on a stick by the penalty spot and see who can hit it the most. Tell me who's better than Ryan, or who's next best or whatever. Forget what you think. Let the melon decide."

Henri spoke again. "So who is in control, Max? Us or the melon?"

"This is an art slash science slash belief thing, dude. If you can't hit a melon from thirty yards, why are you asking to take my corners? Know what I mean? Just go with it."

Vimsy shuffled forward. "But Max! You want us to do all that today? I don't know how to choose a melon! Is it the same as an avocado?"

I laughed. "No hurry. You can have . . ." I glanced at Henri, looking for help. He raised two fingers. "Two years?"

"Two weeks, Max."

"Two weeks to give me a ranking of who should take corners, direct free kicks, indirect free kicks. At the same time, you can have one of my skills sessions per week to do set pieces until I get bored and change it back." That was actually perfect—it would let me release Spectrum from first-team coaching duties and let him get back to his actual job. "But if we're going to do this, let's do this Chester style. Is everyone willing to donate an afternoon a week to do extra set piece shit?" No complaints. "All right. Vimsy, what do you think? Thursdays?"

"Yep."

"Done. Thursdays for the rest of the month." I hesitated. "I need a catch-phrase for this. Jean-Luc Picard had 'make it so.' Hmm. 'Get to work, you slags!' No, you're volunteering for extra sessions. Should be nice. Classy. Let's go with an old faithful. *So let it be written, so let it be done.*"

As I'd told my players, matches were going to come thick and fast, so I had a choice to make. Did I want to take care of my physical well-being or go nuts on XP growth?

Growing my abilities as a manager would be helpful, of course. But the squad was fixed, probably for the whole season. I had seven formations and I could see match ratings and what my opponents were doing. I was pretty over-powered for the sixth tier.

Any match was a potential banana skin, but there were only a few we'd start as genuine underdogs. Two against Darlington, two against Kidderminster, and one more against York. If I could play in those games, and play well, we'd run away with the league.

I needed to be able to *play*.

So I didn't go looking for extra matches to watch—there were fewer options because of the international break, anyway. I would use my free Mondays, Wednesdays, and Fridays to train with the women, and Tuesdays and Thursdays with the under-fourteens. I'd re-evaluate in a couple of weeks, because the sooner I could get to the under-sixteens, the better. There was a big drama going on between two camps. The first camp included the Wizard of Us alumni and the other players who bought into the team-first ethos. The other camp was Noah Harrison, who was apparently considered so obnoxious that even Future didn't want to hang out with him. It surprised me—Noah had been sound in Tenerife. But I resisted calls to go and intervene. I couldn't do everything. Spectrum, Tyson, Benny, or someone needed to step up.

On Monday night I trained with the women—staying away from Dani, who was weird and annoying and not improving anywhere near as fast as her talent would have implied.

I was still miles off where I used to be, but the basics were all in place. Long jogs, short sprints, running on a diag, defensive crabbing, hops, accurate short passes, decent medium passes. Still lacking accuracy and power on shots, and Beckhams and cannonballs felt like months away. Headers? Pencil those in for 2030.

After I'd showered, dressed, and had a long chat with Jill about the upcoming cup game, I got in the car and let the Brig drive me home.

"Your next accommodation is nearly habitable," he said.

I laughed. "You make it sound like it was a wreck." He didn't reply. "John. Tell me it wasn't a wreck."

"I already used my amusing misdirect for the week, sir."

"What exactly is this place?"

"It's . . . secure. It's what estate agents call . . . spacious and full of potential."

"Where is it?"

"It's secluded."

"Is it full of ghosts?"

"I'm sure the reports of chains rattling and incessant whispering are merely foxes at play."

"Well. Sounds absolutely charming."

Match 8 of 46: Chester FC versus Hereford FC.

From the Desk of Max Best: A Proclamation

They say James Joyce exhausted the limits of the English language when writing Ulysses. And I, too, having written a few of these programme notes, feel that I have exhausted the limits of the medium.

Welcoming our guests is futile. Yes, we wish Hereford well in a general, non-footballing sense, and hope they have a safe journey home. But they ain't leaving here with no three points, so they might come welcome but they goin' home hopping mad, let me tell ya. So why even write that they're welcome? For word count? I'm the manager and the manager's boss. I set my own word count. Those uppity typesetters down at the printers can complain all they like about the "negative space," but I don't care! I'd rather have a big, ugly white gap than pretend to welcome a team, who, while they ARE actually welcome, are also going to leave upset and miserable.

Review of recent matches? Yeah, we beat Farsley and Spennymoor, but you knew that before you bought this programme. Sure, us getting six points from six is new information to the guy from the printer, who I know for a fact is a Derby County fan. He doesn't care about Chester, and why should he? But if he's the only guy who didn't know the scores, why write about them? I'm struggling here, lads.

Oh! How about some news you can't get anywhere else? That'll help shift some programmes. Apparently year-on-year sales are already up twenty percent.

So we signed Ryan Jack from Rochdale. But did you know that the idea for the transfer was actually suggested by Mike Dean, our general manager? He'd seen Ryan in one of those old British Pathé newsreels and showed me a cigarette card with a lithograph of Ryan on the front and a short biography on the back. I didn't know he played in Rhodesia and Siam! Ryan came down to our training ground, impressed us all with his long shorts and ability to play in formations ranging from W–M to 2-2-6.

(Those are all jokes about him being old, by the way. That's how desperate I am for content. It's interesting that the ancient W–M formation is, apparently, back in vogue, being used by none other than Pep Guardiola.)

The women's team are playing their first competitive match on Sunday! It's an FA Cup tie against Nantwich. It's just down the road. Come and watch! And the men's team are playing the FA Cup next week. The magic of the cup! A double dose, please.

I think I'm ready to wrap this up now, especially as I need to write AN-OTHER one for the Saturday game and the printer—who thinks I work for HIM—wants the text today. I'm starting to wonder if this printer is related to another person who doesn't quite understand his role in society—Detective Barton. Still being assigned new cases, if you can believe it. I got quite a lot of communication from Cheshire Constabulary since my last Proclamation. Funny, that. None of it was about the case. CCTV footage? What's that? Interviewing suspects? Too busy, mate! Threatening to sue because I insinuated that Barton tried to frame an innocent man? Ooh, that gets the old juices flowing! Plenty of capacity for *that* kind of work.

There's no good segue from Cheshire's worst inhabitant (second-worst, I suppose, after the guy who actually smashed me with a metal bar) to Cheshire's shining light. A man who puts the "ooh" in shell suit. Who looks better the balder he gets—and believe me, he's very bald. A man who doesn't need a five-dollar app to remind him to floss. Sing it with me, now: *J-A-C, K-I-E, Jackie is the man for me! With a knick-knack, paddy whack, give a dog a bone, why don't Jackie come on home?*

Excerpt from Deva Victrix, the podcast by people who think they could do a better job than the manager for people who think they could do a better job than the manager

Huey: All right, we're on. Recording. We're here in The Warehouse with a whole lotta happy Seals after the Hereford match. I'm on the Staropramen. Dewey's on Erdinger. What's that you've got, Louie?

Louie: Timmermans.

Huey: So. Hot takes in five words or less. How are you feeling? Dewey.

Dewey: [Audibly counting on his fingers] I. Fucking. Love. Raffi. Brown.

Huey: Louie.

Louie: Good. Win. Now. Go. Again.

Huey: All right. I'm going with *no right mid no problem*. We've got a few lads in the chat, there. Some familiar names, always good to see. Go ahead and leave your own five words, and any questions you've got. Onto the lineups. Any surprises for you there?

Louie: It was 4-1-4-1 again, so that means Hetherington on his own up front. Ben Cavanagh in goal. That's not a surprise anymore.

Dewey: Seems like he's properly number-one choice, now.

Louie: Robson will play the next game. I've worked it out.

Huey: Go on.

Louie: Cavanagh plays two, Robson plays one. That's the sequence.

Huey: Huh.

Louie: Slight surprise in the defence with Steve Alton replacing Gerald May. Alton's second start. Those two are much of a muchness so whatever.

Dewey: Midfield, Joe Anka had that hamstring strain, so Donny Dorigo played. The only decision that made me go "huh" was Ryan Jack on the bench again. Club record signing, not in the eleven. Why do you think he did that?

Huey: Jack hasn't played much for Rochdale. He's fit but he's not match fit. Easing him into the team. I'm fine with it. He came on early, anyway.

Louie: Right, let's get into that. Ten minutes gone, team's looking good, Best is mouthing off to his assistants. Five minutes later, he hooks Donny Dorigo. Thoughts?

Huey: Had to be an injury.

Louie: See, I don't think so. I've been watching Best. Forget the first couple of games. We all know that was too soon for him to come back.

Dewey: Jesus, will you give it a rest?

Louie: I didn't mean it like that! I'm just saying forget that guy sitting stock still in the dugout, white as a sheet. That's not him. I don't blame him for that at all. Club shouldn't have asked him to do that. Let's not go into it again. Look, when you watch him in most games, he's either bored, like he isn't even watching, or psycho. He's almost never . . . moderately animated. Know what I mean? I promise you something today—Dorigo was getting on his tits. We know they've got previous from when Dorigo took that shit penalty against King's Lynn and Best drove from Darlington to rough him up in training. I think today, Donny wasn't doing what Best wanted, so Best was ready to hook him.

Huey: After ten minutes?

Louie: Absolutely. I think he was *ready* to do it after ten, but gave him five minutes to turn things round. He didn't, so bam. No messing.

Huey: Okay. Maybe. But we saw Dorigo with ice packs and he hobbled down the tunnel at halftime.

Louie: That's theatre. Best's not out to humiliate the guy so he does the whole ice pack thing. I bet you anything he says Dorigo got a knock, took him off as a precaution. Then he'll batter him in private.

Huey: I don't know.

Dewey: I think it was an injury. Donny's been getting minutes. He's played a part in almost every match. Anyway, he comes off, Bochum goes on. I was all right with that. He played well against Spenny, and his song is class.

Huey: Spenny was with Ryan Jack feeding him passes, though.

Dewey: Yeah but Raffi Brown can do that, too. Got to say, I'm really loving the whole Raffi Brown thing. He's as physical as Sam Topps, but he's got more passing range. Apparently he's top mates with Bochum, but we've not seen that on the pitch, have we? Today they combined a few times. It was much better. It's like Ryan's calm has rubbed off on a few lads out there. The whole Bochum thing is starting to make *sense* to me now. He's fast and you put someone like Ryan Jack in the team, it starts to click. Together they stretch the pitch. Make teams retreat. Don't you think?

Louie: He's too small.

Huey: I never thought we were going to lose, did you?

Louie: Not really, but I started to have doubts when Bochum got himself kicked after, what, ten minutes? Halfway through the first half and we've used two subs already.

Huey: If you weren't at the match, Best took Bochum off, put Trick Williams on, moved Evergreen to right mid. From that point, it was like we only attacked down the left and kept the right solid. Makes sense, but I thought we could have been a bit more ambitious.

Dewey: Right, well, you've got Joe Anka injured, you've got Dorigo disobeying instructions or injured, you've got Bochum injured. Who've you got to get up the right?

Louie: Swap Evergreen and Carlile. Carlile's a much bigger threat going forward.

Huey: I like that. That's smart.

Dewey: Can we talk about those guys? Carlile—I was watching him today—he's always been fit and strong and all that. He's still got a mistake in him, but he's really starting to look good now. Don't you think? They've always talked about his quality, how well he trains, all that stuff, but now we're seeing it as fans. Half English, half American, all action. And Evergreen. Is he the only player apart from Brown who's played every game?

Huey: Aff.

Louie: And Ryder. But I know what you're saying. It's like he's first on the team sheet.

Huey: That's why, though, isn't it? You play him anywhere. Imagine if we didn't have a player who could move from left back to right mid. What would we have done? Gone 4-3-3 or something? No, we don't have enough forwards. Anyway, without Evergreen's flexibility, I don't think we're getting Ryan on the pitch today. We wouldn't have seen that second half.

Dewey: Right. Second half, let's get into it. It's nil–nil at halftime, but we're on top. Hereford look very ordinary.

Huey: They beat us at the back end of last season!

Dewey: That's what I'm saying. We're making good teams look rubbish. They didn't know what to do. So halftime, Youngster comes off, on goes Jack Ryan.

Louie: Ryan Jack.

Dewey: Ugh! That's the hundredth time today! I wasn't sure about that move. Youngster was doing fine. Forty-five to go, plus injury time, no subs left. It's a big, big risk.

Huey: Yeah, that got my palms sweaty. Five minutes later, we're in so much control that I forgot. But then Hereford get a break, Cavanagh comes rushing off his line, and it looks like he's taken the player out, red card, penalty.

Dewey: Who are you putting in net, there?

Louie: I've got a feeling Raffi Brown could do it.

Huey: Got to be Evergreen. Man for all seasons, innee?

Louie: Yeah, that's it. Evergreen. But it doesn't come to that, thank fuck. Was the guy offside? Something happened, anyway. Ref didn't even have to make a decision. We can all breathe again! From then, Ryan takes over the game, doesn't he? Man of the match for you?

Huey: No question. Tore Hereford a new one. Two assists, then they took the foot off the pedal. Which was a bit disappointing because Hereford really didn't turn up, but it's understandable.

Louie: Yeah, no complaints from me. We know Best wants to live out his mad *Soccer Supremo* fantasies with us, but it was professional today. Get the points in the bag. Put pressure on Darlington and York.

Huey: Darlington left it late, didn't they? Lucky bastards.

Dewey: Don't sleep on Kidderminster. They're dangerous. I'm worried they'll give us a punch in the nose when we play them. We've got a lot of young players. Things are going well now. How are they going to react when we have a bad spell?

Huey: Guys. Listen to us. Talking about who's going to win the league. It's good, isn't it?

Dewey: Comment from Splendid_Isolation in the chat. *We couldn't, could we?* Anyone know what that means?

Huey: That's his five words or less.

Louie: [laughter] He's saying could we win the league. What the fuck.

Huey: Well, why not? Three points in the bag. Sixteen points from eight games. Fourth in the table. Three points off the leaders. We're playing good football, Henri Lyons is back from suspension, there's three good teams who'll take points off each other. If Max Best comes back into the team, who's going to stop us?

Louie: Okay, hang on. Hang on a second. I'm excited about this season. I am. We *are* playing great football. Players *are* improving. The atmosphere gets better every match, not that you'd hear it the way they keep turning the music up. We've got Bradford on Saturday and I've never been more confident about winning a game of football in my whole life. All right? Best is a weird guy. I'm never going to like him, I don't think. But I reckon we'll finish fourth, get into the playoffs, have a proper bash at that. And that's amazing, when you think how we were last season. It really is. But guys. He's never going to be the same player. There's no chance. You slag me off because I'm negative, but you need to wind your neck in, here. Asking him to come and be the player he was for Darlington, that's not fair on the lad.

Huey: I'm not asking him to. I'm *hoping* he will. Football's about hope. I think fourth or fifth is about par for this team. But can we get first place and stay there? I reckon, yeah.

Dewey: Look at the team. Glenn Ryder. Top class. Sam Topps. Topps class. Raffi Brown is miles too good for this level. Dubhlainn is amazing. Henri Lyons is a goal machine. Ryan Jack's amazing. No other team has six players that good. No way.

Louie: Not you an' all. Right, check this out. We're top of the league in Jan, Feb. Right? Best case scenario, no pun intended. Say Stockport County are having a bad time. Struggling at the bottom of League Two. They get on the phone. Next day, they unveil their new manager. Max Best. He's got history saving teams from the drop. That's what's going to happen. Yeah, enjoy days like today, but winning the league? Even if he's the reason all this is happening, which I doubt, he's off.

Huey: Come on. That's crazy. He's not leaving till he's played for us. There were those rumours that he did a team meeting, said he wants to win all the cups. He's motivated. He's not leaving in January. Get real.

Louie: You sure? Then why won't he sign a contract? Why won't he talk about his future? Why won't he commit? Why is Henri Lyons on a short-term contract? We had those lads on from the Darlington podcast. They want him back as manager and as we've seen, they've got deeper pockets than we have. You mark my words. Max Best will not be Chester manager by the end of the season.

Huey: Splendid_Isolation, in answer to your question . . . yes, we could.

XP balance: 803

Debt repaid: 1,986/3,000

Cost of Morale perk: 2,000

Cost of Injuries perk: 3,000

Match 9 of 46: Chester FC versus Bradford (Park Avenue).
Saturday, September 9.

We were playing at home to the worst team in the division. The kind of match known in the world of football as a "banana skin." You're stomping along, talking about winning the league, and oops! You go flying, land on your back, smack your head on the concrete.

Yeah. I was done smashing my head all over the north of England.

I would send out a strong team. Rotated, but strong, with the most dominant midfield the National League North has ever seen (I assume) and with a hungry Frenchman leading the line. Hungry Lyons? No, cut that. That's terrible.

As I filled in our team sheet, I thought about training.

We'd had another top week of attribute and CA growth, even though we had a Tuesday night game, which meant fewer sessions. I put it down to the addition of Ryan Jack. He'd actually added a point of CA himself, rising to 61. He was so good, I had to find a word to describe the 60+ CA band. Something above gold. After many long, sleepless nights, I happened upon a little-known metal called platinum, and decided that fit the theme quite well. So bronze remained 30–39 (Trick Williams had finally clawed his way up into this band), silver was 40+, gold 50, and platinum 60. Training with a platinum talent energised the others.

I knew these gains were probably one-offs, and I really needed to add another coach into our mix to keep the improvement going. I hadn't had any luck finding one so far, even though I'd been using my mornings sneaking into training sessions at Altrincham, Rochdale, and York City. There were decent coaches there, but no one transformational. And if I did find that guy, what would happen? Why would he leave one of those clubs to join us? Everyone in this industry was competitive—they liked to move *up* the pyramid.

I decided I had to start visiting the league below, too. After all, Jackie Reaper had been in tier seven with FC United. Surely if I found another Jackie, he'd be willing to make the step up?

I looked at my wall clock. Still half an hour before kickoff. Strangely dead time—I'd done everything there was to do to prepare for this fixture. For some reason, I thought back to the Hereford match. As easy as a fixture as you could hope for, yet there was a time when we were 0–0, had used all our subs, and it looked like our goalie would get sent off. The thought nagged at me, but it had all turned out all right. These simple wins, though, were rarely simple. Things could blow up in your face. All I could do was play the percentages and use my time well.

Time management was everything. From five weekday mornings, I prob-ably needed to spend two in Chester, looming over the squad, keeping them on their toes. One morning spying at a club higher, one spying on a club in our division or lower. If I kept that up for the rest of the season, I'd have a massive database of players, physios, and coaches. The fifth day I would probably take off to avoid burnout.

In the afternoons, I was back on the plan to go watch school sports days or inter-school matches. Anything to do with schools was weirdly hard to arrange, but Inga assured me that "school scouting" was going to start happening soon. I was sneaking into some Footy Addicts matches, too, with a focus on through balls, dribbling, and general ball control.

Evenings I had my training sessions, followed by spending time with Henri, Raffi and Shona, and even MD. Avoiding football chat. Just being social. Being a real boy. My resolve never lasted—I was starting to fixate on certain dates on the calendar. The November match against Darlington, of course, but also one in October against title rivals Kidderminster that felt almost important enough to make me want to use Triple Captain and Bench Boost. Many times, someone would be talking to me and I'd space out. I was always thinking the same thing—if I stumbled upon my dream coach *now*, I could get six weeks of better training before the Kiddies game. Time enough for Carl Carlile to hit gold and for Henri to hit platinum.

But what more could I do than go spying on teams, building my staff database?

I had one idea, but it was weird, even for me.

With a sigh, I opened my laptop, went on the Jobsinfootball website and left an advert. This would definitely bite me in the arse, but it had to be done. I showed it to the Brig.

He pulled a face. "Sir. That is not very . . . dignified."

"I need a coach more than I need dignity."

The bell rang, and the Brig and I made our way down the tunnel to the dugout.

Robbo was there, in his big training coat. I'd given him the option of playing this league match or in the cup next week. He chose the cup.

The next decision was moderately complicated; there were three things I wanted.

- I wanted to use Trick, to reward him for training well.
- I wanted to play my three amazing central midfielders in central midfield, which meant 4-5-1 or 3-5-2.
- And I wanted to use both my strikers; I wanted goals and Bradford wouldn't take risks by pushing bodies forward.

There was no way to get everything I wanted, so Trick lost out. I explained it to him and said I'd almost certainly start him in the cup match. He was disappointed—his last start had been against Scarborough and he'd got 8 out of 10.

But with 3-5-2, I was able to field almost my strongest team. Joe wasn't quite fit and D-Day had pissed me off big time with a 4 out of 10 performance that made no sense whatsoever. He was either injured so slightly it didn't show on his attributes—which meant buying the Injuries perk was a priority—or he was in such a bad mood he couldn't concentrate—and I'd need the Morale perk to spot such times. I planned to buy both ASAP, but the dilemma was, which first?

I picked Pascal at right mid. His CA of 31 was by far the lowest in the line-up, but despite that, our average was 46.7.

Poor Bradford's starting eleven had an average of 36.

This would potentially be our last home match for almost a month, so I was happy to run up a big score. Lay down a marker. But ideally, I would have put Trick on for the last twenty—a reward for his improved effort; D-Day for a chance to unshit the bed; and either Steve Alton or Andrew Harrison, depending on how the game was going.

As kickoff neared, I pottered around in front of the main stand, in a pensive mood. Things were going well. Very well. Too well?

I spotted some scouts and went over to talk to them. They were ones I'd never seen, a little batch of three, representing clubs in higher leagues. One had judging player potential 14, which I found quite sexy.

"Gentlemen," I said, smiling at them. "I didn't spot a lot of scouts at Chester matches last year. What's going on?"

"You've got more talent," said one. Older guy. Big nostril and ear hair, but friendly.

"Is that right? Go on, put me out of my misery. Who are you looking at?"

The guy in the middle glanced at the scout to his left, then to his right. "Raffi Brown."

"Oh," I said. I should have been expecting that. If I'd been more switched on, I would have asked who had recommended Raffi. That might have saved me a lot of grief down the line. "Huh. Well, he's amazing." I thought about the club that scout was working for. "Not going to let him go cheap. You might want to tell your bosses to look elsewhere."

"There's Youngster, too."

"Henri Lyons," said Scout 2.

"Carl Carlile," said Scout 3.

I shook my head, resting my weight on my right thigh. "You've got good taste, I'll give you that. Look, we've got the whole season to talk about my players. Let's talk about you. You're out there, driving all day and all night, watching teams, watching players, writing reports that get ignored." I knew all this from my brief time as a scout. "Imagine there was someone really interested in your work. Some young guy who's been overpromoted and he's scrabbling to catch up. And say he wanted to send you, for example, fifty quid a week to see your reports. How would that conversation go, do you think?"

"Not very well," said Scout 1. "If one team is paying for the report, they probably don't want any other teams reading them."

"What if they weren't in the same division? I mean, none of you work for clubs way, way down here. But I'd love to know what's going on at a higher level. Love to know what I'm supposed to be paying attention to. Might make me a better manager and all that."

The scouts looked at each other. I knew what they were thinking: we couldn't . . . could we? Scout 1 shook his head. "Count me out. It's not worth it. If I got caught doing something like that, I'd be sacked. Forget it. But seeing as you're here, I was hoping to leave a business card with someone. My wife is doing a sponsored swim. Raising money for the local library. Maybe we could talk about that?"

"Yeah, one sponsored swim as a test," I said. I didn't want to commit to buying every report the guy ever wrote. "I'm mostly interested in young players I could get cheap, train up, sell on. Find me someone as good as Youngster and I'll sponsor a lot of swims." Suddenly two more cards were being held out. These scouts were not well paid. No reason to turn down free money. It wasn't *that* unethical to let me see reports about teams in higher leagues. It was about on par with food companies who call sugar "crystalised fructicle" or "languid galactose" or some shit. "By the way, I wasn't planning to use Youngster today. He needs a break." Scout 1 nodded. He didn't mind—it meant more petrol allowance for when he came again. "Raffi and Youngster are going to the top. Henri needs a club with a story. Everyone else is available, but not for cheap. We're gunning for the league this year, so I can't imagine wanting to sell in January. Needs to be a good offer, ideally in summer. Tell your bosses, yeah? That said, I do want to upgrade the facilities so I'm not going to be a dick about it if they want to throw in a cheeky offer. Just don't wait till the last day of the transfer window. Nice talking to you."

"Wait," said Scout 1. He was highest in the food chain. "What about you?"

"Your club wants to buy *me*?" I laughed. "My girlfriend listens to this Chester podcast run by *twats*. They reckon I'll be off at the end of the season to save some club from relegation. Doesn't really appeal to me. I'd rather win the league." I turned my head. Based on something Emma had heard, I'd told the hospitality manager to stop blasting music before kickoff. We weren't a disco; we were a football club. Fans would sing, or not, as they wanted. Today, they wanted to sing. "Hear that? That's the sound of hope." I grinned and leaned closer. "I'm telling a story here. If I'm going to leave, the story needs to be just as good. And my next club needs deep pockets; I'll be doing a lot of sponsored swims." I laughed again. "Keep your eyes on Carl Carlile. He's got the X-factor. Equally comfortable in a three or four. Physical, smart, brave." And easy to replace.

I walked back towards the dugout, smiling to myself. Sometimes being a football manager was even better than advertised.

The match was so one-sided it was unbelievable. I'd expected a red card in the first minute, or three injuries, or something mad to level things up. But no. We were on top from the first minute, and all the luck went our way.

The first half was a monumental battle . . . between Ryan and Henri to lay down an unanswerable case to be considered man of the match. Henri was lithe, fast, dynamic. Being out of the team for three matches had sated his thirst for violence. Instead of trying to hurt his direct marker, he was entirely focused on kill shots. He scored twice and barely celebrated. He was in a sort of trance.

But I would have pinned my rosette onto Ryan Jack. The guy didn't put a foot wrong, dominated the midfield, sprayed passes to Aff and Pascal, and when Bradford had the nerve to attack, launched into savage tackles or poked the ball away with timely interventions. Plus, his delivery from set pieces was fantastic. I hadn't bought him for that because I didn't know his set pieces score, but he was really a step above everyone else in the squad. Except me, obvs.

Yeah, the first half verged on perfection. Four–nil, and I had a strange dilemma. Should I change things, put some fresh legs on, let others in on the fun? Or keep things the same and let the first eleven run up the score?

I decided to keep things as they were, and was fairly horrified to realise that the first eleven were content with what they'd done. You'd hope they would be equally motivated in the second half as the first, but no.

It wasn't like I could be mad at them. They were crushing the match. After sixty minutes, I swapped Pascal for D-Day. Donny put in a 7 out of 10 performance, meaning I could select him in future matches after his abysmal 4 out of 10 showing last time out. But he didn't push us towards a more emphatic scoreline.

So with twenty minutes left, I switched to 4-4-2 with Trick coming on for Ryan. Trick didn't seem motivated to bomb forward, though, so that didn't help.

I couldn't explain it. My guys were happy with 4–0 and there was nothing I could do to change it. Bit annoying.

With five minutes to go in normal time, I took Raffi off and put Andrew Harrison on. This was all about letting Raffi get a round of applause from the fans, and absolutely nothing to do with football.

He finished with a match rating of 8, bringing his average rating for the season to exactly 7. His CA was 41, his attributes were improving, he was becoming the player I had always seen.

Now the Chester fans were seeing it, too. They rose as one and applauded him off the pitch. He waved at them, gave me a high ten, and went to the dugout. I turned and smiled at him. He had put in the fucking work and it fucking showed. He gave me a shy, lopsided grin, and looked away. He knew.

I wondered if I should tell him there were scouts watching him, but then there was a rough tackle and I forgot all about it.

The match closed with Andrew Harrison trying to do an impression of Ryan Jack and failing by about 54 current ability points. Still, it was his second appearance as a full professional. I wanted more goals—goal difference could be a factor—but in terms of giving minutes to players who needed them, the match could not have gone better.

The players didn't celebrate too hard, which I took as a good sign. We were supposed to beat Bradford, and we did. No big deal. Routine win. Take it seriously, yes. Win your duels, yes. But we were Chester. We don't lose our minds over these wins.

Not anymore.

I went to talk to Gary, the newspaper guy. I felt we'd had a breakthrough the week before, when I'd had an agenda. I wished I still had Miss Fox in my life to check my workings, but basically, if I ignored the questions Gary asked and gave him a fully formed story, he'd go with it. He was incredibly lazy.

Last week, I'd gone overboard about Tony Hetherington being a top dude, great teammate and all that. That had been a message to my players. Now, what did I want to say, and to whom? How did this battle fit into the overall campaign?

I decided to continue undermining my main rival, Folke Wester. It probably wouldn't lead to an implosion in Darlo, but it'd be entertaining. And who knew? Maybe he was one of those tough guys who lost his mind at the slightest pushback. There was only one way to find out.

Good win today, Max.

Thanks. Good belt today, Gary. Very chunky. Masculine. And it matches your shoes. Go get 'em!

Chester really dominated. I don't have the stats—

We had sixty-six percent possession and eighteen shots to Bradford's three.

I'll have to check those, but—

Yes, sounds like a great use of your time and your company's scarce resources. Write this down, you ready? The attendance was 2,372, which shows a nice upward trend. Man of the match was Ryan Jack, but Henri ran him close. We've "scored" three own goals this year. So our opponents are our third-highest goalscorers! Alongside Aff. Tony has four, Henri five. Today was Aff's fifth assist.

Chester are fourth in the table. What should fans think about that? What can be achieved this season?

You know those questions make me Churchillian. Can you stop getting me hyped up? Thing is, we don't have hundreds of thousands of pounds to spend on new players. We bought a player late in the window and someone said he was our most expensive signing since the club was re-formed, and I was like nah be serious. And he said no bro that's right! And I said yeah but that's like cheaper than a Volvo S90. Our most expensive player is cheaper than a second-hand car, so if you're out there spending hundreds of thousands, you're definitely going to win the league. I mean, that's Wrexham money. That's Ryan Reynolds money. [Laughter.] If you're dropping a hundred K in the National League North, anything less than winning the league by twenty points has to be considered an abject failure.

But what about Chester?

We're just trying to get to fifty points, because that's when you start to feel safe from relegation. We've got great fans, the groundsman is well-respected in his field—wow, you need to tell me why that's funny—but we're not at the level of other teams who can smash sixth-tier transfer records for a left back. Teams like us have to improve players through coaching and, you know, nurturing and supportive comments. We can't just buy the finished article and let them get on with it. It's all hugs, here, all the time. We finished fourteenth last season, so I'd be delighted with thirteenth, especially considering my limitations as a manager. Did you know I'm only twenty-three?

Max! Last week you were getting the away fans to sing "We're going to win the league!" You can admit you have ambitions.

Oh, I'm very ambitious. I'd like to see Chester get into the top four leagues in the next, say, thirty years. Is that crazy? That's crazy, isn't it? I shouldn't have said that. Look, we can't compete with teams who spend seventy thousand pounds on a defender. The other day, I thought to myself, gosh, maybe I could try 4-3-3 in a game. And someone said, "Max! You've got two strikers and one's suspended!" Suspended for nothing, I might add. The top clubs in this league don't get red cards even when their players really aim to maim, as a certain manager's got tattooed on his knuckles. I've seen footage of certain players in this league and it's more like thingy. MMA. Two-footed challenges, leg breaks, wrecked knees. If you play for certain teams in this division, you can do whatever you want.

Are you saying teams get preferential treatment?

Of course not! That would be actionable. No, I'm just saying, I said to the specialist who's overseeing my recovery, maybe I could play against "Team D." And he said, whoa! I've seen them. Nary a minute goes by without them separating someone's bone from the soft tissue surrounding it. He showed me hours of footage, all taken from *this month*, of cruel and unusual tackles that went unpunished by referees. Long story short, he said I could think about playing a few minutes against teams with decent, honest, fair-minded managers like the ones at Tamworth and Buxton. But not against . . . others.

I'm confused. You're talking about referees? What did you think of the referee today?

All I'm saying, Gary mate, is that with great expenditure comes great responsibility.

But what does that mean?

There's one elite referee in this league. You'd better not try and turn his matches into a warzone. I wonder how the rest of them will react to the sudden, grotesque increase in aggression? I just want to feel safe getting back on the pitch. I hope the referees in this league get together and, like, realise what's happening.

Fans are worried you won't sign a long-term contract. Do you have any news about that?

Darlington? Why do people keep linking me with the Darlington job? They have a manager. From what I hear, he's even better than his dad was. What was the question? Oh, long-term. What's more long-term than a tree? Thing is, Gary, if you care for a tree, it'll keep growing long after you've left. Where will Chester finish this season? I don't know. It might be one place above second, or two places above third. But will Chester be bigger, more splendid, more dapply next year, and the year after? Absolutely. And that vivid imagery is worth much more than any piece of paper.

Thanks, Max.

Yep.

		P	PTS
1	Darlington	9	22
2	Kidderminster	9	20
3	York	9	20
4	Chester	9	19

I was feeling pretty good. Six points from six in the last week, great progress on all fronts.

My tree was growing fast. Fans were starting to really believe in us. Scouts were taking notice of our talent. Numbers were going up.

And now that beating most of the teams in our league was becoming normal, I was thinking more strategically. Sure, this league was all about winning forty-six battles. But there were other ways to fight a war than just fighting.

I was sure my interview would be read by Folke Wester, and it would make him livid. The reference to his father, especially. That hadn't been planned, but I couldn't help myself.

And now, Emma had sent me another weapon to add to my arsenal. The Brig had called it the social media equivalent of dropping propaganda leaflets, but it was simply a video. A video aping the vapid social media "news story" style—short clips or photos with chunky, short text appearing at the top or bottom. They were so, so annoying, yet so compelling. The people of Darlington would lap it up, there was no doubt about that.

I clicked the file, waited for it to download, then watched it more closely than I'd watched our last two league games.

First, I saw me and Henri walking along a nondescript road. When we turned, the camera turned a little farther and zoomed in on a school sign. The beginning of the name was blurred out, but everyone at the school would recognise it, and it would spread around Darlington social media, no problem.

As we walked, sombre music played. White text on a green background said, *Max and Henri used to play for Darlington FC.*

Then there was footage of me scoring a couple of goals, but Emma had found some good Henri moments, too. It was only a few seconds, but it was clear we were amazing players and the fans loved us. *They played their hearts out.*

The music changed. Got discordant. The images were of me in hospital, face bandaged, tubes in my mouth and shit. I got upset, and paused the video. But then I thought . . . impossible. Who had taken that footage? And, slightly calmer, I rewound. It wasn't me! I think it was from an American TV show. *Max was attacked at his new job.*

That was good. Emma had changed "new club" to "new job." Yes, Henri and I had been motivated. Yes, we had cared. But guys—it was just a job. We were allowed to leave. Same as anyone.

The music got more upbeat.

Henri and I walked into a classroom, and the kids went nuts. *When Henri sold his house in Darlo, he couldn't have imagined . . .*

Cut to Thomas Green, the little kid who had a poster of me on his bedroom wall. *That Max's biggest fan would be moving in.*

Cut to me signing a black and white shirt. *Max found out, and had to bring Thomas a signed Darlo shirt.*

Cut to me helping some kid with her maths equations. *And a message. Work hard in school, kids!*

Cut to me staring wistfully at the Darlo badge, as I finally handed the shirt over to Thomas. *Darlo will always be in their hearts.*

The scene ends with me, Henri, and Thomas, posing for a photo with the kid holding a signed Best 77 Darlington top. *They didn't leave. They just moved away.*

Closeup on Thomas's goofy smile. *And a new generation wonders what the future will bring.*

The images faded to black, and a chunky font appeared, white on black. *#AlwaysBelieveItsDarlo.*

I watched again, laughed, and put my phone down.

Folke Wester could spread snide rumours, but I could spread joy. The people of Darlington would lose their minds over this video. Max Best, the conquering hero, had returned to Darlo to sign a kit for a fan? What a legend! While Wester went low, I'd go high.

What if . . . what if Wester lost a few games in a row, and someone from Darlo contacted me? Sounded me out just to see if I'd be interested? Would I hint that maybe, just maybe . . . ? Then they sack him, I decide to stay, they reach out to Ian Evans.

I rewatched the video and laughed even more. It had come out perfect, almost exactly how I had imagined it. Everyone in Darlington would think it was lovely, sweet, unplanned, unstaged, and uncynical.

Everyone except Folke Wester.

My beginning had ended. But his end . . . was just beginning.

12

THE TRAGIC OF THE CUP

Football glossary: *The Magic of the Cup. A phrase used to summarise everything that's good and holy about English football: the romance of small teams competing against (and sometimes beating) bigger rivals, the fact these minnows often feature plumbers and electricians in their first eleven (leading to a media frenzy), the collective memory of past glories, the fact that Sir Alex Ferguson's career was saved by what today would be considered a meaningless third round FA Cup match. Just mention Ronnie Radford, the white horse of Wembley, or Mark Robins, and football fans of a certain vintage will be transported to a former time, a better time. (Imagine the Jamaican bobsleigh team, but every year since 1871.)*

Sunday, September 10. FA Cup Qualifying, First Round. Nantwich Town FC Ladies versus Chester Women.

Did you ever have one of those days where everything turned to shit?

I woke up, happy as a clam, and immediately started daydreaming about FA Cup glory. I texted Emma, whose interest in attending football matches all over the country had diminished somewhat. I thought if I could get her hyped about the cup, she might come to watch the men's team the following Saturday.

Me: Today, magic will be made.

Emma: In the first Harry Potter book, he doesn't cast a single spell.

Me: I know. I told you that.

Emma: Go ahead. Tell me about magic.

Me: Put every team in the country in a big hat. Pull out two names. They play each other. TO THE DEATH. Straight knock-out, no group stages, no Swiss models, no seeds, no coefficient rankings. Simplicity is beauty.

Emma: Gosh. So if you win today, you could play Newcastle next.

Me: They aren't in it yet.

Emma: Did you know the things you call simple . . . aren't?

Me: The whales get released into the tournament step by step. First it's us tiny fish trying to eat each other. Today, all the teams are like Chester, or even smaller.

Emma: Today it's the Nemos.

Me: It's loads of local village teams with a fisherman goalie (picking shots out of the net, boom!), IKEA employee defenders (set up in a flat pack four, badum-tiss!), and Conservative MP far-right winger (no joke needed, lol).

Emma: Maybe you should get another hour of sleep.

Me: Too excited.

Emma: I don't get it. It's just more football. It's the same as all the other football.

Me: It's not. It's got 30% more magic. Today it's the women. Next week, the men are playing Tadcaster Albion. They're in tier nine. Ziggy would be by far the best player in that league! You could beat some of them in footgolf!

Emma: I'll come to the final.

Huh. Obviously we wouldn't get to the final. Not of the main FA Cup. We were a good few years from doing that. I dropped my phone onto the bed and pottered around my little city centre flat. The chat with Emma put me slightly on edge. I looked out of the window to see if there was a group of sinister men waiting to get me.

Nah, fuck that! It was FA Cup day. I intended to stay positive.

The phone vibrated. It was the Brig.

Brig: This FA Cup. I get the sense it's an irritant to most managers. Will you pick a weak team?

Me: Why would you say that?

Brig: It interferes with the league. Managers who get knocked out seem pleased. They say they can "concentrate on the league."

Me: Those managers don't like football, and I don't like those managers. Even Ian Evans went hard in the FA Cup. The women's league is only 22 matches. It will be incredibly boring without a couple of cup runs. I will pick a strong team every round.

Brig: I see. So we can win it?

Me: Of course not.

Brig: I see. Then why expend so much effort?

Me: Why do short people wear lifts? Why do bald men wear wigs?

Brig: Please enlighten me.

Me: Glory! Eternal glory! We play for the heritage. A link on Wikipedia. Prize money. It's also my only chance to pit my wits against managers from a higher level.

Brig: I am not sure every player shares your enthusiasm.

Me: They will share my enthusiasm or they will share my WRATH.

Brig: Understood. I will pick you up and bring you to the team bus. I will drive separately to the match with a VIP.

Me: Very Intimidating Person?

Brig: Just so.

I threw my phone back onto the bed and got a football and did some tekkers. Strange that Emma and the Brig didn't have massively positive sentiments about the FA Cup. To me, it represented everything that was good about this sport.

Why was I bad at conveying my passion? I shrugged. I supposed it didn't matter.

Feel free to take ten seconds to conjure up an image of a small or large dog biting me on the arse. That visual might come in useful. Pawshadowing, they call it.

When we got to Nantwich, I was pleasantly surprised by the venue. We'd be playing in the Swansway Stadium, where the Nantwich men's team played. There were two small covered stands, and lots of standing room on the rails around the pitch. The capacity was 3,000, with 300 being seated. Someone told me it cost £4 million, which was a little bit depressing. Four million didn't stretch too far, it seemed.

Still, it was great to see the club treating their women's team well. Playing where the men played was pretty basic, really, but lots of teams didn't even do that. Including, sadly, us. Our women's team would only get a few matches at the Deva this season, because I didn't want the pitch to get ruined by playing too many games on it. As we moved up the divisions, I'd invest in the pitch—undersoil heating, top drainage, more groundsmen, all that jazz—so we could put a bit more strain on it. For now, Nantwich were well ahead of us in that respect—or they didn't care about the kind of free-flowing football I wanted my teams to play.

In the dressing room, my players were buzzing—most of them. Well, some of them. A few were hunched over, concentrating on their studs or shoelaces, not looking at me. We had played a few friendlies in the Deva stadium, but this was a competitive fixture. This was the FA Cup! There were TV cameras filming the action. Ah. They were avoiding eye contact because they didn't want me to see that they were nervous. Fair enough. But some of them, like Charlotte, couldn't stop grinning.

"Hey," I said. "You're looking hyped. Didn't City eat games like this for breakfast?"

"Well, yeah," she said. "But I didn't play, did I? I was like a ball girl for most of it. This is real, today." I held my fist out for an affectionate bump. I loved making dreams come true.

"Ladies, listen up," I said, and they stopped fussing with their boots and whatnot. The changing room was a bit bigger than those at the Deva, but ours looked better. A fan had spent 400 hours rebuilding them from scratch based on what he'd seen from Premier League footage. There had been a presentation about him at halftime in the first match of the season, but I hadn't been aware of it—I'd been doing my vanishing act. "As you all know, my favourite movie is *The Prestige*."

I normally started team talks like that, and there was normally a roar of friendly abuse. This time, almost zero. *The nerves*, I thought.

Pippa shook her head. "Max, you mention more movies than we have time to watch. Skip to the meat, please."

"Ugh. *The Prestige* is legit amazing. Seriously. Ugh! Be like that. Nantwich Town Ladies. Note that they've gone for Ladies instead of Women. That's very psychologically interesting, don't you think?"

"No," said Bonnie.

"Yeah, me neither. The Chester Prestidigitators? No? I genuinely don't get why you enjoy having a boring name. All right. Magic of the Cup. Nantwich are in the tier below us. Got some okay players, focus on physical strength, couple of fast ones, but they're inconsistent, judging from the results. And they're not technical. So if we play to our best, and they play to their best, we win. Simples." Nantwich actually had a CA of 15, which was fractionally higher than ours, but we had way better passing. "We go four-five-one, loads of bombing forward, loads of dribbles from the wide players. Good? Robyn in goal." She had CA 10, PA 14. Like a few players, she would max out her talent very soon. Lots of squad-building needed, but it was harder to simply turn up to other clubs' women's training the way I did with the men. It wasn't always obvious where or when they trained, and I couldn't think of a way to ask.

"What's that? Is that the number one?" said Robyn.

"Yes! I've spent some of Ruth's money on fancy magnets. Do you like them? They're a bit bigger, shinier, and they've got your squad numbers on."

"Oh, amazing!" said Robyn. I really fucking wished I had the Morale perk, because I was sure she'd just increased a few points.

"Yeah, now that we're all serious and whatever, I have to give you a squad number and that's your number for the whole season. League rules." This innocuous announcement got a similar reaction to when I'd hinted the men's team might get some free boots. "What?"

"Do we all have squad numbers?" said Bea Pea.

"Yes. You're number nine."

"Yes!" she said, like she'd scored a last-minute winner. Another morale boost! Management was a piece of piss.

"Dani says, what am I?" said Mo, one of the defenders I needed to upgrade.

"She's seven seventy-seven. That way her army of fans have to buy three sevens to press onto the back of the shirt and the club can make triple the money."

Dani did her special laugh. How granular would Morale get? If it was a score out of 200, I'd probably see a few numbers go up when Dani laughed.

"Can I get back to naming the team now? Sake. Er . . . Lucy, Mel, Mo, Bonnie. Bonnie's captain." I moved four magnets into position, with the numbers 23, 22, 15, and 4. The gently ascending balloon of happiness went crashing down to earth. I blinked. I could literally *feel* the . . . the what? The anger? I glanced back at the whiteboard. Then I nearly smashed myself in the face.

So stupid.

(If all that follows is absurd to you, just keep in mind that being given the number eleven or under is like winning at three-card monte.)

In giving Mo the number 15, I'd signalled to her that I planned to sign a better centre back, and that woman would get the number 5.

In giving Mel the number 22, I'd told her that I planned to sign a better right back, and that woman would get the number 2.

Lucy, 23, better left back, who'd get the coveted 3.

I'd done it this way because there had been a four-month gap in my squad-building. In my numbering system, I'd left space for the *real* first-teamers to come in. Well, it made sense to me, and it very much made sense to the squad. Problem was, it told them all exactly who I thought had a future, and who didn't. Why couldn't I have just given them all random numbers?

Because I was a football purist. What Emma had called a *romantic*. I wanted my first team to have the numbers one to eleven.

If I'd done that, a tiny rational voice said, I'd only have postponed this bad feeling until *next* season, when the better players would have asked for better shirt numbers.

But mate, said the same rational voice. Don't dump this shit on the players just before the first match of the season!

Well, yeah. Good point. But it was done now.

I slid the number 16 magnet to the side of the defence. "Erin, you're defensive backup." She nodded, but she also seemed slightly more downcast. She was CA 9! What did she want? A fucking six-month run at the Pantages theatre? She didn't have star quality! I hesitated before continuing, knowing there was more pain to come. Not as much—the midfield was where most of my talent was. "Gracie, Maddy, Pippa, Charlotte, Dani." Magnets 14, 11, 6, 8, and 7. Gracie had CA 12, PA 17. I think she knew she wasn't as good as the others, and 14 was better than she'd feared when this whole ordeal had started.

The mood was so sombre, I nearly burst out laughing. The whole thing was so mental. I wore fucking 77, for Christ's sake. Grow up!

But I didn't laugh. I'd chosen 77 for myself, and that was totally different from being given a high number by someone who despised me as a way to make me feel less valued. Stupid as it was, I totally understood the reactions, and I should have seen them coming.

Our only other midfielder of note was Susan, who was CA 12, PA 21. She got squad number 12, which, again, was better than she'd feared.

Bea Pea already knew she was the 9, so I slid that across.

Some of the women had seen a shirt on their spot, laid out by Jill, and gone to the bag to get one with a number they liked better. Those women peeled off the wrong shirts, and put the right ones on, in the process, shrinking. Then they sat, staring forward like they'd just been sentenced to actual death.

My lineup had an average CA of almost 14, with not much progress having been made in the last month. I expected a big push in the coming weeks as we started to feel like a real team. I suspected, though, that there was a link between Morale and how well players trained. Had I just cost us a few weeks of progress with my thoughtlessness?

"*Seriously*. Okay. Nantwich, straight four-four-two. Physical, no technique. Let the ball do the work, pass it around, they'll get tired, we'll crush them second half. Any questions?"

I regretted asking for questions as soon as I'd said it—I really didn't want to talk about why I valued Maddy so, so highly but thought Susan was so, so shit. The difference in their squad numbers was one, but it was the difference between being on the life raft, and dying just next to it.

Fortunately, no one wanted to be the first to speak.

I clapped my hands. "Great. Let's go win a cup. Abracadabra."

The players ambled out, their buzz shot to pieces, their boots not smacking onto the concrete but slipping along.

I stayed back for a moment. Jill and Livia hovered around. Jill knew I wanted to bring in a really amazing coach who could also manage the team. It can't have been a nice feeling, knowing I didn't think she was quite good enough. Livia was the opposite—in case we'd fallen through the relegation trapdoor last year, I would have sacked Dean and made her the head of a much reduced medical department.

This was something I'd struggled with—these moments where I'd let slip to a player where exactly I saw them in the pecking order. How good I thought they could be. It was one thing telling Raffi Brown I thought he could play in the Championship—he could try to prove me wrong by making it to the Premier League. It was something else to pick Mo ahead of Erin, or Gracie ahead of Susan. There could be single-match tactical reasons for that. But seeing me leave the best squad number *blank*? In the *hope* that I might sign someone better?

"The magic of the fuck-up," I said.

Livia zipped up her medical bag. "Was it a fuck-up, or were those the right squad numbers for those players?"

"They're the right numbers," I said. "If anything, I was charitable in a few cases."

"So you didn't do anything wrong."

Jill didn't completely agree. "The timing could have been better. We could have done the squad numbers on Monday, let them have a week to get over it."

"Get over it?" said Livia. "It's a number on a shirt. Wait till they're in the medical room with their knees shattered, or they do an ACL." She bent and rapped her knuckles against the nearest piece of bench. *Touch wood.* "Then see if they still care about their shirt number. Let's make sure they're warmed up properly."

That last comment was aimed at Jill. The older woman was surprised, but she hurried out. Livia nodded at me, heaved her bag, and went to the dugout.

Nice to have an ally. Nice to get a sense of perspective. Amazing to see Livia back to her old self—that meant she'd stopped worrying about Jackie.

But I fretted. As we got more serious, more professional, I'd have to be ruthless. How could I do that while making the women's team what I'd promised Dani it would be?

It took me a minute to decide what to do to make sure we won this match. I *ingenieured* a plan. A sort of *woman sawn in half* approach. One side of the woman—the head, I guess—would be me tweaking every player's individual instructions according to the needs of the match, getting really granular in a way I sometimes didn't bother with—*pass left, no forward runs, pressing yes, offside yes, man marking no.* The other side of the woman—also the head, because I hadn't thought this image through—would be a vigilant watch for weaknesses in Nantwich's temperament or tendency, which I'd lay out in a thunderous, detailed, handsome, halftime team talk.

The two halves of the woman would then be magicked back together by the stagecraft called victory.

That was terrible. Cut all that.

I stormed towards the dugout, ready to get to *work.* Blood thumping in my ears, only a narrow cone of vision. Nantwich's all-green with a black slash versus our blue and white stripes.

Fuck your morale, you pricks! You'd better win, or I'd give you something to really be unhappy about. I'd learned that there was a name for unfit footballers being snatched away and forced to do a military boot camp—beasting. *The beastings will continue until morale improves.* Great line.

In my new, hyper-determined mood, I nearly smacked Triple Captain and Bench Boost, but I held off. I wanted to use them in the first round of every cup competition, because if we got knocked out there was no point keeping it in reserve. It wouldn't roll over to next season! That would be amazing, though. *Perk perk perk!* I thought, trying to convince the curse to give me that option.

No, if we couldn't beat Nantwich, we had big problems. I swiped the options away.

"Max," said someone, on the edge of my awareness. You know how this bit goes. I stewed and ranted and raved some more, and the person kept saying my name.

Eventually, I realised there was no sign of the match starting. That made me breathe properly and my field of vision widened. "Oh, what the shit? What now?"

It was fucking Beth. How did she always find me when I was at my lowest? She was by the side of the pitch with the referee and the Nantwich manager, Chrissie Priest. There was also some rando and a photographer. Beth waved me over. "Max!"

I actually turned away and grabbed onto the top of the dugout, held myself there for a few seconds. I didn't deserve this. I didn't deserve to be knocked out of the FA Cup in front of the *Daily Mail*. To have my unhappy players turn traitor and tell Beth all the mental things I'd been doing.

Yeah, I was a bit of a dick, but the universe repaid me tenfold for anything I got wrong. I dangled for one last second, one last second where I felt like I had some choice in how my day went, then tried to sort of swing myself into a good mood. My arms disobeyed, refusing to defy gravity on my behalf. I let go, turned, and pulled my hood over my face. It was *something*.

"Hi Beth," I said. "How's the Death Star?"

"I don't work for FIFA, Max. Stop moping around. What's wrong with you?"

"A busful of women are mad at me because I got overly romantic."

Her eyes darted around, crazily, while she tried to guess what had happened. Was this a hot scoop? "Go on, I'll bite."

I pushed the hoodie back a bit. "If we lose today, it's because they didn't like the squad numbers I gave them."

The response to this statement of OBJECTIVE FACT was annoying. The referee sniggered into her hand. The Nantwich manager turned away and did a quiet bobbing motion. The rando and photographer laughed out loud. Beth tried to be like the referee, and mostly succeeded.

I bit my bottom lip, then let fly. "Squad numbers have rules. First choice goalie is number one. Backup is thirteen. Third in line is twenty-five. Anyone disagree?"

Beth rubbed her smile away. "No, Max. There is only one way to do football. The Max Best way."

"Quite right. Please tell them that." I gestured to my shitty players.

"Does that mean I can talk to Dani?"

"No. Stay away."

"Well, this is about her," she said. She turned to the rando and he stepped forward with a fluffy white sweat band and a referee's whistle.

He spoke excitedly. "It's a whistle!" I wanted to step away, like I did from all crazy people, but it wasn't a good look in my new role so I was trying to get better at that.

I checked my phone. We were two minutes overdue to start the match. "Guys, this is the *FA Cup*. What the shit are we doing?"

Beth shook her head, grabbed the sweat band, and pushed it up my arm, towards my bone-dry, neutral-smelling armpit. "Captain of the ship," she said, and just for a second, while I was the only one who could see, there was a bit of flirty heat in her expression. I opened my mouth to complain. She snapped, "Fuck sake, Max! This is important!" I looked around. That had given me a big jolt of deja vu.

I fiddled with the sweat band. It wasn't touching my skin but it still felt itchy.

Beth took the whistle and blew it, right in my face.

I backed away, pretty pissed off, but then I realised what was going on. The sweat band had vibrated!

I took it off, had a look at the inside. There were a few bits of electronics. The rando stepped forward in something of a panic. I dared him to complain.

Beth was in control of the situation. "This is Raymond Richardson, inventor and *Daily Mail* reader." For some reason, everyone followed Beth's gaze to my scowl as she said the last part. "And like most *Daily Mail* readers, he was moved by the story of little Dani and her shockingly unfair red card."

I gave this Raymond guy more consideration. Now that I knew he was an "inventor" his look fell into place. Oddball, had a shed full of wrenches and tiny screwdrivers, knew a lot about waveforms, forgot to pay his water bills.

"So he set about solving the problem."

Raymond took his cue. "The deaf girl wants to play sports and she should be allowed!"

The unfairness stuck with him more than her name. I didn't mind that. He was clearly a nutjob, but my kind of nutjob. I closed my eyes for half a second so I could calculate. Beth had obviously done a number on the ref and the Nantwich manager. She only needed my go-ahead. I didn't like being forced to pick the card the magician wanted me to pick, but this wasn't about me or my distrust of Beth.

"Bea Pea," I called. "Get Dani." Bea Pea was in the best position to get her attention.

Dani jogged over. The photographer acted like someone had just flicked his switch. He went full pap, pushed his camera to his face and kept it there, somehow able to navigate the world with his vision several metres in front of the rest of him. Dani saw Beth and smiled. *Shit.*

Beth gestured that I should put the armband on Dani. "Do the honours, Max."

I glared at Beth. She was sailing close to the wind. I imagined this scene turned into a newspaper article. "Raymond should do it. He's the star of the story."

"We'll get one of him and Dani if the armband actually works in a match situation. For now, a picture of you and Dani in happier times. It'll pay off the previous picture where it was all a bit intense. It'll be thematic. I know you love that stuff." She said it sniffily, as though she hadn't written "The Wizard of Us."

I was keen to get on with the match, so I pulled the armband off. Beth wanted me and Dani in her hero image because it would get the most clicks. I didn't exactly mind, but my goals were slightly different. "No, Beth. I want the referee and Chrissie, err . . . Miss Priest in the photo. The story isn't me and Dani, or Chester and Raymond, it's the whole football community welcoming a new member."

"Oh, I like that," said Priest. "Call me Chrissie, by the way."

Beth glanced at the photographer—tried to communicate with him nonverbally. Something like, frame it so we can cut out the spares. "Beth, I swear to fuck."

"Fine," she pouted. She blew air out her cheeks. "Fine," she said, brighter. "You're right, Max. That's the story."

That earned her a suspicious little frown, but with the referee and the Nantwich manager behind Dani, I slipped the armband past Dani's elbow and up to the short sleeve of her top. "It's a bit loose," I said.

Raymond stepped forward to check. "I had to guess how thick her arms were. I can do it a bit smaller."

"Should be fine for today," I said. "Let's try it out. Dani has no clue what's happening."

Beth handed me the whistle. "You do it."

"Absolutely not," I said, a bit louder than the rest of the conversation. I wasn't totally stupid. "I mean, the ref should do it."

The ref took the whistle, and I made sure to step back so the photographer would be forced to focus on those two. The ref blew, Dani looked at her arm in absolute astonishment, and three seconds later, all Beth's dreams came true— the biggest smile in the history of smiles.

Dani signed, wildly.

"What's she saying, Max? And to whom?" said Beth.

"Why, Beth, she's talking to you. She's saying that this will make a wonderful story. She's saying it is lovely, sweet, unplanned, unstaged, and uncynical."

"Aw," said the referee.

"She's also saying let's get on with the match because Max's naps are carefully timed and if he misses one, he gets grumpy."

The ref laughed. "Right. Let's make some FA Cup magic!" She looked down at Dani again, blew the whistle, and smiled in response to Dani's smile. "Some *more* magic."

I shuffled into my technical area, not knowing what to expect. Half my team were throwing girl-sulks, but my most talented one was far beyond the highest morale it was possible to get, and my current best player, Charlotte, looked ready to put on a show.

Beth had followed me. She looked good in the technical area. I wondered what her manager profile would look like.

"What do you think, Max?"

"I think you're way too good at your job."

"Do I get something?"

I turned my head, amazed. "What? What?"

"Access to the next Das Tournament. The inside scoop on your new adventure. Access, Max. An interview. Maybe one in a few months that explains why you left Chester and went back to Darlington. Put your side of the story out."

She was fishing. "What makes you think I owe you something? You've got two great stories out of this unfortunate incident."

"One was simply reporting the facts. This one is a little feel-good tale. Everyone who reads it will go *aww*. But I've saved Dani's career. She can play without fear now."

"Until some ref refuses to use the special whistle."

She scoffed. "You hand the whistle to the ref before the match. If she refuses it, call me. There will be hell to pay. I might have a word with the referee's boss for Cheshire."

"See *that*," I said, "would be an example of you *really* doing something for Dani. And not for yourself."

"Okay." She punched me on the upper arm. "Fair comment. But I still want something."

"And what? I get protection from the *Daily Mail*?"

She laughed. A free, lighter-than-air laugh. "You're the wizard, not me; I can't do magic. No, no one can save you from yourself. You're fair game. You know the British media. We build people up so we can knock them down." The match kicked off and Beth's expression changed. She wasn't a reporter now, she was a footballer. She eyed the action with something like hunger. "Four-five-one again? It doesn't strike me as a Max Best formation."

"Is this the interview?"

She snapped out of her analysis of the match. "What?"

"I owe you an interview, you think. Is this it? You want to waste it on the Women's FA Cup Qualifying First Round?"

Her attention flickered from the pitch, to me, to the pitch again. She started to wander away, towards the inventor and the pap. She paused. "I'll need a quote after the match. About the armband."

"Nah," I said. "Busy." Smiling sweetly, I said, "Make one up, Beth. I trust you."

Good play here from Chester.

Gracie touches the ball to Pippa.

She helps it on to Charlotte—the debutant is really catching the eye.

It keeps going right, this time to Maddy.

Maddy plays it first time to Dani, who lays it off and sprints away.

Maddy sends the ball down the line.

Dani hares after it!

A patient move, and a surgical through-ball! These two are operating on another level.

But it's given offside.

What a pity.

I'd never seen anyone more delighted to be given offside. Dani, unable to stop smiling, gave the referee a big Dani two-thumbs.

Now that referees were adding time stolen from the viewing public by *cheats* onto the ends of matches, making that kind of cheating futile—on an unrelated note, Newcastle United were suddenly, inexplicably struggling to win games—I had a new bugbear. The biggest crime in football, apart from the usual things like bad tackles, was a right midfielder being caught offside.

It really shouldn't happen; from that position you are looking down the line of the other players. How can you not *see* that you're offside? It had cost England several good opportunities in the World Cup final, I'd seen it on TV when watching Premier League games, and now Dani was doing it.

I wanted to let her enjoy her day, but I also needed to win.

We'd started to bring A5 sheets of white card and marker pens so we could give Dani some simple instructions. I bent and wrote:

If you are caught offside again

I will get the Brig to kidnap you

And make you watch French movies

For a week

When we got a throw-in vaguely near me, I raced to stop it being taken quickly and showed the message to Dani.

She rolled her eyes, did her laugh, and nodded.

I walked back to my technical area, staring at my screens. The demotivated players were on 6 out of 10, some flirting with 5s. Dani was on 7, touching 8. Charlotte, the former City player, was the best player by miles, absolutely crushing the game. She was different gravy, and her 9 would hit 10 if she scored or assisted.

I'd been leaning on the match rating screen ever since I'd got it, and it was a fantastic tool. Like all tools, it had its limits. It was quite biased towards attacking play. Goals and assists would bump a player's score up no matter how badly they did everything else. I supposed I was fine with that, since goals were the game's only real currency.

But the match ratings over-rated activity in general. For example, the kind of work Bonnie did, the organising and talking to her teammates, scored her bugger all, even though it meant the other team got fewer chances. For Bonnie to go from a 6 to a 7, she needed to win headers, win tackles, and complete passes. Being so well-positioned, she stopped an attack without getting within ten yards of the ball? Curse didn't give a shit.

So I couldn't just sit in the dugout reading Dan Brown books. And on a day like today, when small things were going wrong all over the pitch, I could actually influence the game. Get players to focus on the details.

I spent fifteen minutes yelling at the defenders, trying to get their lines right, get them more solid. But it wasn't working. They wouldn't listen.

For the next five minutes, I gritted my teeth, scowled at them. Three of the four defenders were sulking, including the vastly experienced Lucy, who was forty-two years old! Imagine being forty-two and still getting upset about tiny slights. I planned to stop overreacting to every little thing that ever happened by age twenty-five.

What were my options here? I could sub off Mo and Mel, put Erin on, and go to 3-5-2. That'd mean the only really sulky player on the pitch would be Lucy, who had the best chance of snapping out of it during my halftime tantrum.

"Erin!" I called. She came, reluctantly, next to me. "I gave you shirt sixteen, same as Roy Keane. Same as Michael Carrick. Anything you want to say about that?"

"No, Max."

"I need someone for the second half. Someone with a clear head. Someone who wants to play. Someone who gives a shit about the FA Cup."

She scratched her eyebrow. "I want to play."

I pointed to our other young defenders. "If you play like that, you're done here. Do you get me?"

"Yes."

"Do you still want to go on?"

"Yes."

"Aight."

Erin swung herself away from me, but turned most of the way back. "Why are you so into the FA Cup?"

"What?"

"The league's the most important thing, isn't it?"

She seemed genuinely confused, which genuinely confused me. "Are you saying you don't care about the cup?"

She shrugged. "I thought it was all about the league. We get promoted, it's bigger crowds, better opponents. The manager will give more of us contracts. Get promoted again, we'll play in the Deva every week, train every day."

"That's very rational," I said.

Something in my voice made her reluctant to keep talking, but she had a high bravery score. "*You're* rational," she said. "You want to go to a bigger club." She pointed to the number 16 on her shorts. "The squad numbers are rational. I wish I was number five, but I'm not. I'm not good enough."

I shook my head. "You're good enough to win this game for me. Go and loosen up."

She walked behind me. I heard the moment she stopped. "Did you mean Roy Kent?"

"What?"

"Roy Kent from *Ted Lasso*."

"I did not."

I shook my head. Some of these ladies needed a history lesson.

At halftime, Dani smiled as, for the first time ever, she was able to walk to the changing rooms at the exact same time as everyone else. It's the little things.

The score was 0–0. We'd dominated, and some of the play between Maddy, Dani, and Bea Pea was causing anxiety for the home team. But Nantwich had caused us a few problems, too. I felt that if they scored just one goal, we'd be heading out of the cup. Next goal wins.

The proximity to disaster was getting to me. Making my neck hot. It didn't help that Beth was here, writing it all down.

And what was worse, it seemed like half my players wouldn't give much of a shit.

Erin knew Roy Kent but not Roy Keane. What did the cup mean to these players? The heritage, the glory? Probably nothing. They were trying to win because they were competitive, but that's where their motivation ended.

As usual, I let them talk to each other for a couple of minutes. Everyone went to check out Dani's new toy, and the invention plus Dani's smile undid some of the morale damage I'd caused.

"Right," I said, and for the first time in my management career, that wasn't enough to get their full attention. If the Brig had been there, he would have shouted, but he was in the main stand with Ruth.

Bonnie had to get everyone quiet. I shook my head, trying not to get too angry. First I would try to *communicate* our way out of this hole. Rage could be plan C.

"Right," I said again, in a sarcastically jolly tone. I switched to something like normal. "That was . . ." I swallowed the word *shit*. "That wasn't your best work, ladies. At first I thought it was because you were demotivated by the fact that I want to improve the squad and need premium squad numbers available to entice elite players to join us. But then I remembered you were strong, modern women and wouldn't let yourselves down with that kind of primary school 'She took my coat hook!' bullshit. And then I remembered, I've already told you millions of times it's my ambition to bring this team to the top. So you know there will be churn and change and, of course, you know that playing like sulky brats will accelerate that churn. And change."

Good start. Nicely passive aggressive. I pottered around.

"But then something occurred to me. I've told you I want us to take the cups seriously, but maybe you thought I wasn't being serious. Maybe you've seen the new Tottenham manager. He *said* he'd take the cups seriously, but he made nine changes for his first cup match. Tottenham lost. So now his team can't win anything this season. And he might say that finishing fourth in the Premier League is worth more than winning a cup. And he's right, financially. But football, ladies, is about glory. It's about memories. It's about playing in a cup final at Wembley, the home of football. It's about the last game of the season, Chester Men versus Darlington, and after we win eight–nil, we parade our cups and shields and plaques and medals. I want a fucking mountain of silver there, all the men, all the women, champagne, ticker tape, confetti, vegan hotdogs all round.

"So if you're playing like dogshit because you're not motivated to play in cup matches, then *I'm* not motivated to invest time and money teaching you to play this game. If you don't think the cup is magical, I suppose that's fine, it's a free country, but you better get it into your thick skulls that *I* do. Let me be super honest with you. Brutally honest. What I saw out there was three players writing a resignation letter. Three players flying little planes over the stadium with the words *I don't want to play for Chester* trailing behind. You've got ten minutes to save your career. Show me that you give a fucking shit. Then I'm switching formation and bringing Erin on."

Livia was on chat duty. "Dani says, why are you so thirsty for the cup?"

I checked the time. "I'd need more than five minutes."

"Give us the executive summary."

I clicked my fingers. "That's it. It's the difference between sport as sport and sport as business. The league is business. That's your bread and butter, as the saying goes. You have to go hard at the league to feed your kids. The cups? The prize money is shit—for the big teams, anyway. But you go to Wembley and you win a trophy. When you're old, are you going to say, 'Oh we finished fourteenth in the National League North one year, let me find the photos of that'? Or are you going to say, 'Hey! We got to the third round of the FA Cup and we were beating Birmingham with ten minutes to go. We were so close!' You've all met Smasho and Nice One, yeah? What stories do they tell? Cup games, mostly. Giant-killing.

"This is a *business*. Your job is to train. But this is a *sport*. Your dream is to win.

"My first match as a professional was in a cup. The FA Trophy. Alfreton, four-five-one. I put in a ten out of ten performance that no one who was there will ever forget. You've seen my goals from that game. An otherworldly eighty-yard dribble and a free kick known in some circles as 'The Transported Ball.' The word of the day in the papers and online after my feats? *Magical*. League games aren't magical. They're a grind. Maybe at the end of the season you get some of that feeling, because there's no more room for mistakes. All your chips are on red; it's all or nothing. But every cup match is like that. I am a football romantic, and every cup match is Valentine's Day."

The bell rang.

Maddy stood up. "Great speech, Max. I love the cup now." Sarcastic little shit! "I'm playing to win because I hate losing. And because their number eight keeps elbowing me. But you're missing the point."

I was incredulous. "*I* am missing the point?"

"People aren't playing shit because of the squad number or because it's the cup. It's because you're leaving."

"Leaving. Leaving what?" For some reason, I patted my pockets. Had I left my keys somewhere?

"Leaving the club."

I had no clue what she was talking about. I racked my brains thinking of a club that I had joined. She *couldn't* know about my five dollar a month subscription to Chess for Overachievers on Patreon. "What club? I'm not in any clubs."

"You said you were going to Darlington," said Livia.

"No, I didn't. When?" I said, but the bell went off again. The players filed out, motivation lower than ever.

Worst. Team talk. Ever.

Some of the ladies had, at least, been paying attention.

Mo Walsh had taken my "ten minutes to save your career" thing to heart. In the first minute of the second half, she crunched into a tackle. She got the ball, but followed through, wiping out her opponent.

The ref, amazingly, didn't give a free kick.

I thought Mo was trying to intimidate that particular striker. Defenders often did that, and it often worked. That was one great thing about Dani, by the way. She was so used to being kicked in her old pan-disability matches that she barely noticed it happening. She certainly didn't take it personally.

Mo, however, was either self-destructing to punish me, or her motivation had gone into overdrive to prove how badly she wanted to stay. She thundered into another reckless challenge, this time missing the ball completely.

And this time, the ref had no hesitation in brandishing the red card.

Before Nantwich could take the free kick, I subbed off Mel, our right back, and put Erin on. I switched to 3-5-2 with the missing player being the second striker. We would still be solid, would still dominate midfield, and if we played with a bit of spark, we could nick a winner.

A Nantwich player with mediocre technique and finishing blasted the ball towards the left-hand-side of the goal. It hit our defensive wall—Erin, of course—wrong-footed Robyn, and squirmed, apologetically, into the bottom-right.

One–nil to the home team.

I rubbed my face and scrubbed my fingernails through my hair. What could I do? The only decent player I had on the bench was Susan Butler, a CA 12 central midfielder. Useful if we got an injury or to replace tired legs, but she couldn't change the game. I had no options, except the very, very mediocre one of pushing Dani into attack, making a 3-4-2. From what I'd seen, Dani was more likely to score bursting from midfield than being stationed up front and marked closely.

The only card left in my deck was Free Hit. If I was desperate, I'd use it on a late corner. But the odds we'd score, even with the ten-percent boost to the probability, were long.

For the first time that day, I sat on the bench. Powerless. At the mercy of the players on the pitch. Players whose morale had been shot before the match even started, because of the mind games I'd been playing with Folke Wester. What I'd thought was nerves was resentment and only a few players had been buzzing with anticipation.

This defeat was my fault, because I hadn't thought about every possible consequence of my actions, and not my fault, because this particular outcome was absurd. Regardless, I had no rabbits, no hat, and now I was about to be dumped out of the FA Cup by some nobodies.

I stared ahead, face blank, with an XP counter overlaid on my Match Overview screens. At least I'd get something from the day. Watching my XP grow by four XP per minute. The magic of the cup.

I could have wept.

All the setbacks, all the morale swings, all the nerves, the fact that our meltdown was being filmed and would show up on some compilation of sporting disasters and "cupsets" . . . It was too much. We were toast.

I sat forwards, gloomy, then sat all the way with my head resting against the plastic. Gloomier.

But then I leapt out of the dugout, rushed to the side of the pitch, heart pounding.

Nantwich were going men behind ball. Shutting up shop. Holding on for a famous victory!

I laughed. I couldn't believe my luck!

All they had to do was keep going, maybe even attack us harder. But they retreated.

I ranted and raved until I'd locked eyes with Bonnie, Pippa, and Lucy. The senior players. I threw my arms towards the other team's goal. One; one; one two three! Attack; attack; attack attack attack!

Nantwich fell further back, let us move twenty yards up the pitch without having to work for it. Now, Maddy and Dani were twenty yards closer to Bea Pea. They started to get their combinations going. Little, dancing triangles. One-touch layoffs, ambitious scoops and chips. Trying to conjure a little piece of devilry.

I knelt and pounded the grass. How many times had I *told* them? I got a marker and sheet of white card. I wrote:

LET IT HAPPEN

I danced around the side of the pitch showing it to anyone who'd look.

Charlotte saw me with, from her point of view, a tiny postcard, came closer, read it, sprinted to Dani. She made some hand gestures that were too distant for me to follow. Dani nodded. Charlotte ranted at Maddy, at Bea Pea.

I stormed around, fuming, furious, desperately screaming at everyone to relax. Just chill! I screamed, calmly.

The next few minutes made it all worthwhile. Our right side, the three young guns, supported by Charlotte, whirled and rotated and glided across the pitch, a lava lamp of movement and countermovement, keeping it simple, keeping the defenders reacting, giving them decisions to make. Once we settled into our patterns, stopped letting the ball go out of play, once we sustained the pressure for more than ten seconds at a time, Nantwich looked like the team with one player fewer. They could keep their shape for a time, but then Charlotte, schooled in the Guardiola style, would switch the play to the left. Nantwich had to slide all the way across, but then Charlotte would bring it to the right again, and we'd probe and pass and feint and go on overlaps, but we'd keep the ball, keep the ball, and then:

Dani receives the throw-in. She holds the ball up well.

She passes back down the line to Erin.

Erin sweeps the ball left.

Charlotte fakes to pump a high ball to the wing, but turns back and plays it to Maddy.

She exchanges passes with Dani.

Dani sprints down the line ready for a pass . . .

But the ball is played between the centre backs. Bea Pea will get there first!

She dinks the ball over the onrushing goalkeeper.

The goalie gets a hand to it . . .

But she can only push it onto her own defender.

GOOOOAAAALLLL!!!!

Disaster for Nantwich! It's the unluckiest own goal you will ever see.

Chester are back in the game. They've equalised with only ten men!

I sagged—all the anxiety and fear I'd been trying to keep myself from feeling came flooding over me, but then came the gigantic, absorbent sponges of relief and pride.

Jill tried to hug me, Livia too, but I was pretty drained.

And then, when I was wondering if the curse would ever update its text commentary with more modern versions of phrases like "down to ten men":

It looks like Nantwich are taking a more attacking approach.

Game on! Bring it, Chrissie Priest!

I'd learned it was hard for teams to switch their mindset—once they went defensive, their attacking play had less potency. At the levels I dealt with, anyway. I could imagine an elite counterattacking team being exempt. *My* teams seemed to be more flexible than most. Either it was the curse, or the way my players knew defensive periods were part of an overall plan to attack as much as possible.

I moved Dani to the vacant striker position and Maddy to the right. It was shit, but it was all I had. I was playing chess without a full deck of cards.

I need more players. Urgently.

Nantwich tried to build up a head of steam, but our defenders hadn't been busy for the last ten minutes. It had given them time to clear their heads, or Bonnie had talked them into a state of calm, or something. Whatever it was, we stamped every Nantwich attack out with gorgeous efficiency, and with a couple of neat passes, Charlotte would be on the ball.

Her match rating hadn't touched 8 for some time—it was a solid, solid 9. A high 9. And with two minutes left, while I was looking at the Match Overview instead of the pitch, it jumped up to 10.

My attention snapped over, and I just caught the end of the move. Charlotte was dribbling at the centre backs, which was unusual for her. She'd been trained in the Man City style—plans A, B, and C were passes. But Nantwich backed away, on their toes for the inevitable pass to Dani or Bea Pea, who were making opposite diagonal runs. Nothing we'd trained, but the moment they crossed paths, the defenders suddenly didn't know what to do. In that moment of pure chaos, Charlotte let the ball roll onto her right foot, then curled it from the edge of the penalty area around the goalie and into the bottom-right of the net. Two–one!

I collapsed to my knees and put my head on the grass like I was about to pray, then felt unsafe having the back of my head exposed like that. But what could I do? I wanted to run onto the pitch. I wanted to whip my top off and whirl it around my head while I sprinted the length of the pitch. I wanted to explode in a giant fireball.

When the final whistle went, I still hadn't cooled down. I thought about asking if I could do sprints around the pitch for half an hour to burn off my surplus energy, but for once decided the thing that came into my head was *too* weird to say out loud.

I shook hands with the Nantwich manager, thanked the referee, and found myself in the dressing room, in front of the victorious Chester Women squad. They were all looking at me, waiting for me to speak.

"Football is a business," I said. "Nothing more. The winners of this match, us, got eighteen hundred pounds. That's all that matters."

They jeered, they booed. As I'd hoped, victory had brought us closer.

Livia came forward. She had her medical gloves on while she administered post-match massages and stuff. "Enough shit, Max. We want to know if you're staying."

"You do or Dani does?"

"We all do."

I raised a hand. "You know I'm looking for a top coach to take over. Are you saying you won't . . . play for someone else?"

"No," said Bonnie. "But I came here, God help me, because I wanted to be on the Max Best train." She shook her head. "Christ knows why. You don't have to drive the train. But you . . ." She faltered. Her metaphor had led her down a tunnel. "You have to be the director of football of the train."

Quite a few nods. "So if I get offered a billion pounds to go to Saudi Arabia, you're going to what . . . hate me?"

Pippa finished taking her boots off and stood up. "I won't hate you. But we've made a commitment to this club, in our own way. You believe in us, and we want to believe in you."

I tried to hide a grin. This conversation was serious, but I couldn't help myself. "Sorry, Pippa, it sounds like . . . it sounds like you're asking a sexy twenty-three-year-old international playboy to whisper sweet promises in your ear."

"Pippa can get in line," said Maddy, but I wasn't sure if she was talking about herself or teasing Dani. Or someone else. "I won't hate you if you go to Saudi. Or a big team. But I *will* hate you if you go to Darlington."

"Right!" said Bonnie, and several others.

I held both hands up. "All right. I've heard you. You want certainty in an uncertain world. Totally understand it. But that would be a hell of a magic trick, wouldn't it? If I could do that." I smiled, then tilted my head. "Who's texting Dani?"

"Me," said Erin, who had already showered and changed. I put my hand over the screen. "This can't go on record. This can't go in the chat history." I crouched in front of Dani and mimed texting and then *no-no*. She was puzzled, but gave me a thumbs-up. "Someone explain it later. Listen, I don't want to go to Darlington. I didn't think I'd have to explain that to you. I didn't have to explain to the men, and they're thick as pig shit."

"So what's going on?" said Gracie.

"I am *fucking* with Darlington," I said. "It's going to be a long season and I'm going to be fluttering my eyelashes at Darlington as long as they're rivals. Okay? I'm fucking with them. Tying them in knots. Mental disintegration. But I'm not very good at it, because I've accidentally disintegrated my own team." I slapped myself on the cheeks. "Just relax, okay? If our relationship is going to change, I'll tell you to your face, not via fucking . . . oblique references on TikTok. Right. Don't tell anyone any of this or it's a world of shit for nothing. Maybe you should act worried that I might actually leave. Yeah. Let's go with that for now. Drop hints that team morale is shot and you're winning despite me."

"I don't get it," said Bea Pea. "What's it supposed to do?"

I spread my arms wide. "Look at the fucking chaos in here today because you read some out-of-context quotes in your shitty Facebook groups! It was absolute bedlam. And we nearly lost because of it." I bit my lip. "Now imagine what it's like in *Darlington's* dressing room." I laughed. "Actually, fuck that. Darlington's not your story. You focus on your own progress. You made a little bit of FA Cup history today. Be proud of that. Maybe I'll put together a little video of some of my favourite FA Cup stories and we can talk about them after training. Before the next cup match. Anyone up for that?"

Most hands went up.

"Top. Erin, back on the chat? Thanks. Listen. You've won your first real match. Achievement unlocked. You're in the next round of the cup. Can you feel it? You're one step closer to Wembley. And you know what that means?" They didn't. "It means you get a song."

I took the phone from Erin and typed out a chant. I only did the first half, so it didn't take long, but it took long enough that a bit of tension came back into the room. *What's he doing now?*

I finished typing, but didn't press send. I looked around at these women I'd found, and trained, and who'd repaid me with one of my best moments as a manager.

I threw my arms wide, sucking in breath, and bellowed:

"Wem-ber-ley!

"Wem-ber-ley!

"We're the famous Chester Women and we're off to Wem-ber-ley!"

I thought the backlash was over, but there was more to come. The Brig drove Ruth and me back to Chester, which I didn't think was weird until things started blowing up and I wondered how the situation had come about.

At first, the car was pretty quiet. The Brig said, "Well done, sir." I mumbled something back. Ruth should have been buzzing—her team was up and flying, but she wasn't. I didn't think twice about it—she wasn't a mega football fan, after all—so I took the opportunity to decompress and look at some of my stats. This thing called Manager Points had been quietly updating in the background after matches, and was one of the most stupid and baffling parts of the curse, which was saying something.

I simply couldn't work out the system. I got 4 points for a win. Then 4 points for the next win. Then 27 points. Then 60 points. Then 5 for a draw. So frustrating. The win today gave me an entry in the Women's Team Managers section—reputation unknown, manager points 4. I couldn't spend manager points, and the ones I got last season had vanished when the midseason update had happened. So what was it all for?

Sighing, I turned to my achievements. I got a new one called Tragic of the Cup, which was for knocking a lower-ranked side out of the competition. One XP. I also got Red Red Whine, which was awarded because I'd complained about the red card. Which, by the way, I didn't. It was a nailed-on red, and I blamed myself for winding my players up too much and not spotting the warning signs that my player had gone tonto. No XP. So why bother?

Shaking my head, I thought in general terms about the team. We really needed some more quality, either on the first team or on the bench. I was pretty sure we'd have an amazing week of training, but we'd just played a match where we had the same average CA as a tier-seven team. Rapid growth was needed so we could win the league this season, and I needed bench options so that managing the matches would be rewarding for me, personally.

"John," I said, after a while. "What's the latest with Welly?"

"He's still prime suspect. Hasn't been seen since that day. Which doesn't prove anything, but . . ."

"Yep. He had this girlfriend that triggered the whole thing. Julie. Really good striker. I didn't want to deal with the drama, but I've dealt with the drama. So . . . can you find her?"

He squirmed. "I know where she lives, where she goes. Are you sure she's a good idea?"

"No. But she's local, she's talented. We'll talk to her. If she's got her head screwed on, we'll give her a chance. And if it drives Welly insane . . ."

"Yes, sir?"

"You'll be there."

He sighed. "Unless I'm not."

"I order you to be there," I said. "And if you're not, it was nice knowing you. Avenge me."

"Very well, sir."

I tapped the base of the window a few times. Giving Julie a chance felt right. I'd be careful before and after matches, and maybe I'd be able to hire another Brig type next season to get even more bodyguard coverage. The next one could be disguised as a physio, maybe. Or maybe be an actual physio.

What about other positions? I needed some defenders. Ideally some with at least CA 20. Ruth's investment wouldn't stretch to transfer fees. I closed my eyes. I needed to be able to spy on training sessions. Maybe then I could—

"So you're going to bring a disruptive player in, and then fuck off to the northeast?"

"Excuse me?"

I turned—I almost always sat in the front, even though I would have preferred to have a better view of Ruth. Henri had shown the Brig how to calibrate the passenger seat so it would put less strain on my hamstrings, and the Brig insisted I sit in the front. For the first time, I saw that Ruth was unhappy. Deeply unhappy. "This Julie girl. You ruled her out once before. Now that you're planning to leave, she's suddenly okay to sign?"

"Who's planning to leave?"

"Always believe it's Darlo," she hissed.

It hit me. Another one who put two and two together to make 666! "No! Not you as well. Come on."

"So you're not going? Not interested in moving closer to Newcastle? So, what? You're kicking up a storm so we offer you a pay raise?"

"Pay raise?" I said, impressed. "Oh. That's a good tactic. Talk about leaving, get a raise. Love it. That's properly Maxiavellian."

She punched or kicked the seat. "Don't be a dick. We've looked after you!"

"I know," I said softly. Then, progressively less softly: "But don't *yell* at me when I haven't done anything. Whatever you're mad at, it's all in your head. All right?"

"It's not all right. John, tell him."

It took me a second to wonder who she meant; I was quite tired. The Brig bent his head slightly. Adjusted his grip on the steering wheel. "Perhaps it would be better to tell Miss Ruth what you are plotting."

"The players need to know. I see that now. The coaches, the staff. Parents of star players. MD, probably. But everyone else? It might work well for me to keep them guessing."

"Miss Ruth should know, sir."

"Oh, should she? Why's that?"

"For reasons that will become clear, sir. After you have told her."

I stared at him for a while, trying to work out what he could possibly mean. Then I shrugged and decided to trust him. So I turned and told Ruth everything, starting with my assessment of the men's team and their chances of winning the league.

"So while I can only promise," I said, wrapping up my little speech, "to do *what* I want to do *whenever* I want to do it, I can almost totally rule out a return to Darlington. The drama might make me seem to some people like a whiny, ungrateful brat, but the last match of the season, I plan to be walking around the Deva stadium carrying more silver than you've got in your posh cutlery drawer. All right? Now stop getting mad at me. Even if I'm not angling for a raise, I *am* underpaid, even considering I'm not paying rent."

The Brig cleared his throat. "Excellent timing, sir."

"What?"

"Do you know where we are?"

I looked around. "No. Wait. Near Ruth's mansion, isn't it?"

Ruth was most of the way back to normal. She didn't like my idea, but she accepted I was doing something I thought was good for the club. "I don't have a mansion, Max. I have a small house with a moderate stable attached."

We turned onto the road that led to Ruth's house, then onto the smaller road that *only* led to Ruth's house, but then we went a little farther and turned right instead of left.

We got out—the Brig opened the back door for Ruth with typical class; it hadn't even occurred to me—and stood in front of a building. I say building, but it was more like some rotten wood that had fallen onto some crumbling stone in the vague shape of a house. I'd seen cosier dwellings in *Minecraft*.

Ruth came next to me, her high heels sinking into some newly flattened mud. She didn't seem to care. "Promise you'll stay at Chester," she said.

"No."

"Promise you'll stay for the whole season."

"No."

She tutted and held her hand out. I put mine under hers and she dropped a key into it. I raised one eyebrow. I took a few squelchy steps forward, put the key into the door, turned it, and walked inside.

Ruth's home looked like something you'd see in *Country Life* magazine. This . . . *this* place you'd see featured in the pages of *Shithole Quarterly*.

I rummaged for a light switch and couldn't find one. Ruth flicked a sticky-outy lever that was about a foot lower than switches were supposed to be. I let my eyes sweep the place. There were two main colours—dark wood and darker wood. "I live here now, do I?"

"Yes, sir," said the Brig.

I pulled a face that was a genuine attempt to not be an ungrateful dick. "Before you go off on one," said Ruth, spreading mud all over the hardwood floor. She walked around the space that I guessed was the living room. "This was my grandfather's house. My father grew up here. He loved it. But when he married, his wife said she wouldn't want to raise kids here. So they built," she waved towards her mansion. "And that's where I grew up. But I spent lots of happy time in here, Max. Dad would take me to Chester City matches, then after we'd come in here and tell Granddad all about it and eat Jammie Dodgers. That was my favourite part—the talking, though the biscuits helped. Grandad loved the stories. My dad complaining about referees, describing the goals, saying what he'd have done instead of what the manager did. Which players he'd get shot of."

I kept still. So did the Brig. It felt like a private moment that we were trespassing on.

Ruth swept her hand along a stretch of wood. "They loved the FA Cup, same as you. They were crazy for it. Grandad used to try to get tickets, whoever was playing. Bolton. Wimbledon. Crystal Palace. Didn't matter, did it? The FA Cup Final. That was the highlight of his year. There's a box, somewhere, of his old Cup Final programmes." She stopped. She was far too still.

"Sounds like I would have liked him," I said, daring to speak. Bravery 20, mate.

"Oh, and he would have *loved* you. You cocky little shit." She turned away and wiped her eyes. "Every time you pull some fucking dumb stunt, Max Best, I think about what my dad would have thought. What he'd have said to my granddad. Those times I spent in here were magical. You've put some magic back into my life. I know it's just an illusion, but . . ." She wiped away more tears. "You can stay here as long as you want. Don't take the piss on electric. I've got someone coming to get the wi-fi good." She took in one last, sentimental breath. Talking about wi-fi speed is a good way to bring yourself down from an emotional high. "But if you go to Darlington, I'll dump all your shit on the side of the road and have the locks changed before you've even finished sending out the tweet."

With that, she strode to the door, pausing with her fingers around the ancient handle.

She looked at the Brig. "When you find that Julie girl, let me talk to her first."

"Yes, miss."

"Wait, wait, wait!" I said. "I give the orders around here." There was a bit of a pause. The time after an axe leaves the magician's hand, but before it slams into the Wheel of Death. "Johnnnn," I whined. "Who's in charge here?"

"Most definitely you, sir."

The two oldsters looked at each other. The Brig was not smiling, in a way that made me think he was smiling inside. Ruth did something similar, then she flounced out. Ten out of ten exit.

"See what I have to put up with?" I said.

"Time to go, sir," he said, looking at his solitary watch.

"What?"

"Forgive me, sir. I thought you might like to spend the night in a space that contained an actual bed."

"If my bed's not here, why are we here?"

"Miss Ruth wanted to impress upon you, sir, her desire for you to stay in Chester. A property like this could be rented for thousands. She has spent a considerable amount restoring it. There's more to do, of course, but it is a tremendous show of faith."

"What do you think I should do? Stay here forever, earning peanuts?"

"It is not my place to say, sir. But your recent moves have provoked no small amount of consternation. From what I've seen, you could achieve your goals with a lot less . . . ambiguity."

"Yeah?" I said, walking around the living room. I poked my head through a door into a small kitchen. I paused on my way up the stairs. "What would be the fun in that?" I raced up, nearly falling over because the stairs weren't the right distance from each other. I laughed as I took a painful whack to the shin. "Fuck! That'll take some getting used to." I had a quick peek into the two bedrooms and the bathroom. I went down the stairs much more slowly.

All right, I thought. *It's not my dream house. But it's quiet. It's safe. There's a hot blonde next door and I can learn about horses. And it's free.*

I tried to think about fundamental things, basic things, like which room would I take as my bedroom, could I fit a home gym in here somewhere, stuff like that. But my thoughts kept drifting to one of the other challenges the day had brought up.

How could I convince my players I wanted them to go fucking hard at the cups?

Saturday, September 16. FA Cup Qualifying, Second Round, Tadcaster Albion versus Chester FC.

"All right, listen up, you worms." I jiggled the whiteboard into place and started shuffling magnets around. As I feared, the men's CA improvements had massively slowed. Only a handful of guys had gained a point. Raffi, who seemed to improve every week, was now CA 42. Youngster (37) and Steve Alton (34) were the only other guys to get an increase.

All conversation ceased. I'd told the players privately who was in the team and who wasn't, but there was always a chance I'd changed my mind at the last minute based on new information I'd gleaned, i.e., me seeing the other team's profiles.

Tadcaster Albion was in Tadcaster, obvs, halfway between Leeds and York. Probably a nice place, most of Yorkshire was, but I couldn't give a shit. I was there to knock them out of the FA Cup and get level 2 in my Tragic of the Cup achievement. And that was almost inevitable—Albion were a tier-nine team. Nine! When I saw a few of their players wandering around, I realised their average CA would be around 9, too.

This was a big day for Albion, and potentially an even bigger day in the history of Chester FC. Most of our guys had changed on the team bus, and we were now stuffed into this tiny dressing room like handkerchiefs in a performer's jacket pocket.

"Robbo's in goal," I said, sliding his magnet across. He was squad number one. No drama there—these numbers were ancient history. "Trick the trainer!" I announced. Williams was on CA 30 out of his possible 31. I'd keep praising his improvement until he peaked, then I had other plans for him. "Magnus the right back holy shit this kid can play everywhere! Gerald and Steve oh my God does that mean he's giving Glenn a rest yes it does even though Glenn is fucking pissed about it."

There were a lot of laughs about that, and Glenn stuck his tongue out the side of his mouth. He hated being left out of the lineup, but it just proved I didn't have favourites. Which was strange, because I did have favourites.

"Ryan Jack, FA Cup legend! He was riding that famous white horse, I believe. Raffi Brown! That's the entire midfield. What!"

I moved the next two magnets to the wings. We were playing an ambitious 4–2–4, hoping to absolutely blitz Tadcaster in the first half.

"Bad Boy left wing! Donny the redeemed right wing! Henri and Tony the strikers! What a team!" I said, standing back to enjoy my work. It only had an average CA of 40.3, but come on. I couldn't remember being part of a bigger mismatch.

"Subs! Ben!" Cheer. "Carl!" Cheer. "Topps! Aff!" Double cheer. The noise died down, and I moved away from the whiteboard. All done. Presentation over. Nailed it.

"Max," called out Henri.

"What?"

"That's only four subs."

"Is it?" I said, confused, picking up my notes. I'd already handed in the team sheet, but I'd scribbled the team on the back of a massive Nando's receipt, which got another chuckle from my easily amused players. "Right, one more sub. Who is it? Let me see. Huh." I walked around, looking confused, then leant down to peer at Youngster. He blinked at me, which made his eyes bulge. What was I doing? I got closer, then reached behind his ear and came up with a magnet. "Don't do that, mate. These were expensive."

"Mr. Best," he complained, exhaling in a happy way.

I went back to the whiteboard and took one last look at the magnet before I stuck it on the right of the pitch, under the other subs, but with my hand covering the number. The set of magnets I'd bought only went up to number fifty, so I'd had to make my own with correction fluid. It said, in very shit, shaky handwriting: 77.

"Ah, yeah. The last sub . . . The last sub is me."

13

PROPERTY MAGNET

Saturday, September 16. Tadcaster Albion versus Chester City in the FA Cup.

Three–nil up. Tadcaster were a good bunch of lads, friendly, doing their best, so we went about our business in a good way, passing the ball around, getting a few goals in the bag, then taking it easy. I hadn't told my lot to ease up. I worried the curse was somehow limiting our maximum score—we'd recently had that match where we'd scored four goals then stopped putting the work in.

"Why have they stopped?" I asked Jackie.

He grinned. "They're waiting for you, la. It's all about you now. Your return. Your *triumphant* return!"

"You're right," I said, then ripped off my hoodie, revealing a glowing blue-and-white Best 77 kit. Unusually, mine didn't carry the name of the sponsor. Instead it said, *I'M BACK*, which was funny because it was on the front.

I stepped forward near the touchline, but when the referee saw me, he blew the whistle. Like everyone else in the stadium, he knew what today was all about. No need to wait for the ball to go out of play naturally—let's bring on the star.

My players and the Tadpole guys sprinted to the side of the pitch, forming a yellow and blue guard of honour. Everyone in the stadium stood and applauded. I shook Henri's hand—he was weeping so much he kept having to relight his cigarette. I shook the ref's hand—his assistants had posters of me they wanted me to sign. "Later," I said, amused by their impatience. "We've got a match to play!"

It had taken months—rehab, a sun-drenched holiday, a lot of humiliating grinding—but now I was back. I was like a tadpole turning into a . . . I want to say frog? My glance swept across the pitch. Tadpole Albino were pretty rubbish, but there was no point humiliating them. I changed us to a conservative 2-3-5 formation, with me on the right wing.

As I went to my station, every fan in the stadium rushed from where they were sitting or standing and began following me up and down the space between the halfway line and the corner flag. There was only one show in this town. "Max!" screamed a leggy redhead. I waved at her; she fainted.

Magnus fizzed a pass to me. The Tadpole left back ran at me, but he was so, so slow, and I was so, so Max. I let my body twist so that my right foot would hit the ball while my left leg was already halfway through a line sprint. The ball touched my foot, obeyed, span seven feet high, came right back down to earth on the other side of the defender. He was tracking the ball, saying "huh?" in slow motion.

But I was away!

I dashed fifteen yards in the blink of an eye. But who to pass to? I checked my mini-map. It showed me the location of every player on the pitch. Henri was there, on the shoulder of the left centre back. But as I cocked my right foot, he peeled away, between the two cavemen. Yes, mate!

I hit a sensational, eleven out of ten cross. Henri leapt, took the ball facing away from goal, on his chest. It bounced up, Henri landed, filled his leg with elemental energy, and trampolined himself back up. He acrobatically played the ball over his head—it sailed over the goalie and nestled into the back of the net.

We celebrated by forming up in a four-by-ten grid, including the Tadpoles, and line danced to Cotton Eye Joe.

"Max," said the referee, in a panic. "The scoreboard is broken." We turned and looked at the ancient, hand-cranked scoreboard that had suddenly appeared over the goal. "If we can't update the score, the goal doesn't count."

Jackie ran around, head in hands. "There are no ladders! There are no ladders!"

"I got this," I said. A button floated down my vision, and settled. It said *WINGS*.

I clicked it, and my famous white, feathery wings emerged.

"Yes!" said Youngster, punching the air.

I smiled, flew up, turned the three to a four, then circled the stadium. But instead of landing, I kept going. Where did I want to go? Should go home. Where was that, again?

A flash of hair caught my attention. Smirking, I flew back to the stadium, picked up the redhead, then carried her, not home, but away.

Eeee! Eeee! Eeee!

I leapt out of the bed, enraged. I found the lamp switch but mashed it so violently the whole thing toppled and shone sideways. Good enough to find my weapon. I picked up the old-fashioned broom that was leaning against the wall and whacked it into the ceiling again and again.

"Fuck you!" I cried. "Get fucking fucked, you fucking twat!"

The screaming paused, and for a time there was dead silence, save for the hundred-decibel pounding of my heart. There was something in the attic, or in the floor above my bed, and several times a night it would make incredibly loud, incredibly close screaming noises. Murdering a mouse, perhaps. Or its version of sexy time. It was at least a hundred and ten decibels, and somehow was always timed for when I was in the deepest phase of my sleep cycle.

Maybe this time, I'd finally convinced it to—

Eeee! Eeee! Eeee!

I smashed the broom into the ceiling and the exposed wooden beams, screaming, "I am the apex predator! I am the apex predator!"

This went on for a while until the thing stopped of its own accord. Mouse eaten, wife porked.

I fell back onto the bed, lightly sweating, heart rate returning to normal.

What the fuck *was* it? I'd complained to Ruth, but she was away flying planes. I'd complained to the Brig and he checked the area and said there was no immediate threat to my person. I accused him of mocking me, an accusation he denied.

I took my phone and used its screen glow to creep downstairs. I killed the light and peered out of the windows but it was pitch black in all directions. I needed some garden lights so I could see what was out there.

What could it be? Some kind of fox? Did foxes move into abandoned dwellings? I would if I was a fox. One difference between me and this guy was that *I* wouldn't scream at the kind-hearted human who had moved in and was trying to enjoy a rare football dream.

Still fuming, I went to the stairs and sat there while I fired off some angry texts.

To Ruth:

We need to talk about the coven of foxes that have an altar one metre above my head. They do nightly summoning rituals powered by the bodies of freshly killed rats. The weight of a hundred years of corpses in the cavity will soon come tumbling through the plaster, burying me in bones and viscera. Perhaps you have a less satanic house I could live in. You know where doesn't have NIGHTLY MURDERS just above my head? DARLINGTON.

To the Brig:

Please source me some night-vision goggles and enough infrared cameras to cover this house and its surrounds from all angles. Maybe a claymore mine or two. Spare no expense. Ruth said she'd take care of it.

I exhaled and turned the big light on. No more sleep tonight, I didn't think. I put the kettle on and got my new toy—a second-hand iPad Pro I'd got for a hundred quid. It was very much yesterday's model, but it had a bit of life in it, still. I enjoyed reading about myself on the big screen. I switched tabs to the match report from the Tadcaster Albion game, and poured hot water onto a ginger and lemon tea bag.

Magic of the Cup! Sensation as Max Best Makes Chester Debut!

by Gary Beswick

Chester FC's FA Cup Qualifying match against Tadcaster Albion should have been a non-event, and indeed, for seventy minutes it was. Goals from Dorigo,

Hetherington, and May eased the Seals into a 3–0 halftime lead, and from that moment the only area of intrigue was if Max Best would bring himself onto the pitch—a mere four and a half months since the attack that left him paralysed in intensive care.

The team sheets were passed around the Ings Lane media room with a palpable sense of disbelief. Best had named himself as a substitute. Mistake or prank? Insiders knew Best had been training with the under-fourteens. The news spread; two hundred were tuned to the match on *Seals Live*. By the start of the second half, the audience numbered two thousand. The property magnate who owns Tadcaster Albion can only dream of attracting such numbers.

There was no sign of Best warming up, and the excitement began to fade. All at once, the assistant referee was holding aloft the number 77 and Best exchanged a simple high ten with Donny Dorigo and walked to the right midfield slot.

Best was called into action immediately, as a pass was sent forward by Magnus Evergreen. Tadcaster's number 3 didn't know whether to press or stand off, so he did nothing. That proved a wise choice. Best tried to flick the ball in some overly ambitious way, resulting in him falling, stumbling like a drunk, and knocking the ball from his knee onto his other knee—putting the ball out for a throw-in. Best thought this was hilarious, and so did his teammates. One wondered if Dorigo would be extended such latitude.

Best's next involvement was to play a simple five-yard pass to Raffi Brown—to celebrate his achievement, Best knelt and motioned like he was trying to start a pull cord lawnmower—a gesture last seen from the winner of the US Open.

His next two touches involved him immediately losing the ball to the left back, followed by a mis-control that led to another throw-in, and a contested sprint that Best lost comfortably.

This reporter took no comfort from the abject performance, and with extreme reluctance began to pen a savage hit piece that was in no way recompense for Best's withering belligerence in post-match interviews. Three incidents happened in the last ten minutes that resulted in the hasty deletion of 500 words of scathing, hilarious, cathartic retribution.

First, as Pascal Bochum cut inside from the left midfield position, Best sprinted square across the pitch offering himself for a pass. Bochum fired the ball into Best's path. The burst of acceleration that followed brought hundreds of spectators to their feet, but Best ran over the ball, bringing the entire right-hand side of the defence with him. The pass went straight to Hetherington, who touched it first-time to Lyons, who fired wide.

Next, Best embarked upon a grand tour of the pitch, wandering around, playing one-touch passes with his defenders, creating triangles, moving all the way to the left of the pitch where he stayed for some five minutes, leaving the right-midfield spot vacant. Best waved his team back, towards his own goal, infuriating the away fans. The stratagem encouraged Tadcaster forward, and the left back, with nothing to do, ran forward to add pressure to a rare attack. When Chester's goalkeeper, Robson, caught the ball, he boomed a long punt towards the right of the pitch where Best had appeared, as if by magic. Best chased after the punt with no opponent within thirty yards. Chester's director of football appeared to be laughing. But his glee turned sour as he was flagged for offside. Best, who famously never criticises referees, sprinted back to where he had been standing when the kick was sent his way—comfortably in his own half, from which spot he could not be offside. He spent a full minute receiving passes from the same spot, every time spinning to check whether the assistant referee's flag had been raised, feigning surprise when the decision was made correctly.

But the final moment was perhaps the epitome of the Max Best experience—puerile, imaginative, and effective.

Chester were awarded a free kick in a dangerous position a few yards outside the penalty area—perfect for a right-footed free-kick specialist. As soon as it was given, the hundred or so Chester fans standing behind the goal rearranged themselves to be in line with the path of the ball, all the better to witness a piece of sporting history. Dubhlainn, another second-half sub, came over to ask if he could take the free kick with his left foot. Best openly mocked the Irishman, who tried to walk away with his tail between his legs. Best forced him to stay and watch, finger pointing down like a pompous headmaster.

What Dubhlainn saw went something like this:

Best got down on his hands and knees, smoothed out the grass, and searched the ball for its nozzle, which he placed just so. He clambered to his feet, sucked in a couple of restorative breaths, and lined up his shot, all sidesteps and hand chops and deep, performative breaths. This endless, farcical process culminated with Best "sat" in a Johnny Wilkinson rugby kicker squat. Best wiggled his behind, took one step toward the ball, swung his right foot at it, missed completely, and crashed onto his back with his leg pointing straight up. In the quarter-second of confusion that followed, Dubhlainn caressed the ball over the motionless defensive wall, past the dumbfounded goalkeeper, and into the net for Chester's fourth goal.

Cue pandemonium—on the pitch, in the stands, and even in the press box.

Chester's name will be in the draw for the next round, and Max Best now cannot play for another team in the FA Cup this season.

The Chester fandom has recently been up in arms following comments Best made that hinted he may not stay in his post for long. Spreading consternation seems to be his stock-in-trade, whether the victim is a ninth-tier football team, a hardworking sports reporter, or his club's own fans. But while his physical recovery has some way to go, Best's talent for mischief and entertainment remains gloriously undimmed.

This reporter has decided to enjoy the ride, however long it lasts.

I smiled. Gary had blown off some of his cobwebs and put a bit of effort in. He was pretty pompous, though. I knew for a fact that this crowded press box he kept hinting at was him, Boggy from *Seals Live*, and a guy from Tadcaster.

Yeah, safely through to the next round and I'd made my Chester debut. Until the fox had shaved a year off my life by screaming bloody murder at me, it had been a pretty perfect day. Only 2 XP per minute when managing, and half that when playing. But a good twenty-minute runaround, and lots for people to talk about.

XP balance: 1,639
Debt repaid: 2,078/3,000

I'd probably fall just short of getting to 2,000 in the women's match tomorrow, but I'd be able to buy the Morale perk soon enough. I was also pretty sure I would use one of my discount codes to buy the Injuries perk. A ten percent discount would bring the cost down to 2,700 XP. Sure, I could save more XP if I waited to buy something more expensive, but getting my teams to higher leagues would generate more XP per week, and Injuries would surely boost my chances of getting promoted.

Seeing Tadcaster had got my head spinning. They averaged CA 9. My first thought was that I'd never get a better chance to get some game time against opposition who were probably around my level. As it turned out, I'd slightly overestimated my own CA. I skimmed Gary's match report again. Maybe I was closer to CA 1 than I thought! But if my players got big boosts from returning to competitive action, why shouldn't I? And the women's team had got a big boost from playing in the cup, so why shouldn't I?

My second thought was—huh. Tadcaster were playing in the ninth tier and had players ranging from CA 5 to 20.

When I was scouting five-a-sides, Sunday Leagues, youth tournaments, or used Playdar, I found loads of players in the CA 20 to 40 range. Players I generally wouldn't bother bringing to Chester. But what if I had a relationship with a club like Tadcaster? I could send them all the players I scouted from that level. They'd smash their league! They'd smash tier eight, too. But why bother? It wouldn't get me anything.

I checked what other tabs I had open.

One was a link to a story about a bunch of British YouTubers who had played a match at the London Stadium. The match sold out, and was streamed live, and since the top divisions were on a break, it was the most-watched football match of the entire week. Sixty thousand spectators, tens of millions watching online, two million quid for charity, absolutely no players I'd ever heard of. Absolutely bonkers, but good luck to them. I swiped the tab away, never to think about it again.

A few tabs were about a former Tranmere player, Danny Prince, a dashing young left back. His contract had run out in the summer and he'd been snapped up by tier-two Blackburn Rovers. For older players, that would have been the end of the story, but because Prince was under twenty-four years old, an independent tribunal would decide on a fair price for Blackburn to pay. (The tribunal system was intended to reward clubs for developing young players, and to stop their prized assets being poached for free.) Mateo had heard on the grapevine that the amount was likely to be much lower than Danny Prince was really worth, and he'd asked what I thought about it.

My thoughts were many and varied, but after the previous fox encounters, I had been up all night watching clips and poring over all sorts of data. The main thing that would tell me about Danny Prince's true value was his PA, and to get that I'd have to get into Blackburn's training ground. Which they probably wouldn't be too happy about, at least not before the tribunal had made its decision.

One YouTube video showed a row of houses that backed onto Blackburn's training pitches—all I needed to do was sweet-talk some old biddy, go into her back garden, and I'd be able to see the profiles of all or most of the Blackburn players. Unless Danny Prince was injured, I'd see him, and no one at Blackburn need ever know.

The Brig was usually up for anything slightly illicit, so we'd gone together on Wednesday morning, and I discovered that the Brig hadn't been joking when he said he was a housewives' favourite. A woman who described herself as a "football widow" had been more than happy to let us into her garden when we'd explained we were from an insurance company and we thought one player was lying about an injury he'd picked up and we wanted to see if he was training or not.

Long story short, Prince was a hot prospect, PA 162. If the rumoured tribunal fee was correct, then Tranmere were getting dicked. I asked Mateo to bring me to the tribunal—maybe I could help out, but mostly I wanted to see how the process worked. Better now than when it involved one of my players!

Another iPad tab had the *Northern Echo*'s match report for Darlington's FA Cup win. Bingo was positive about the performance and the result, but when I looked at the lineup, I saw a lot of rotation. Players like Chumpy and Tim got a game, which either meant Folke Wester trusted them to get the job done, or he didn't care about the cup. My suspicion was the latter.

The next tab had the advert I'd posted to the Jobsinfootball website. I read the text again, laughed, and decided I was in a good enough mood to get some sleep after all.

I lay down, turned the light off, and two seconds later, the ritual recommenced.

Sunday, September 17.

Three unhappy people stood outside the so-called house that had brought so much so-called joy to Ruth and her family.

To her credit, Ruth had left her week of flying her stupid little planes to drive all the way back up north to deal with me and my latest tantrum. It might have been her being a good landlord, or it might have been the threat to quit Chester and blame it on her if she didn't do something.

I explained what was going on with calm words followed by a banshee wail as an attempt to imitate the sound.

"It's actually *worse* than a murder," I said. "I know what murders sound like. Murders are quiet. This . . . this is beyond anything you can imagine. Let's swap houses and see how it feels when someone tells you to ignore it."

She inhaled. "Max, I'm sorry."

That threw me. "What?"

"I'm sorry. I should have taken you more seriously, but . . . it's hard to tell when you're being a drama baby for attention. No one's slept in there for years. The workers have been in, but no one at night."

Just the fact that someone was listening calmed me. A lot. "What do you think it is? A fox?"

"A fox would love it, but it would have to be a pretty big hole. You didn't see one, did you John?"

"No, miss. But it's possible there is one."

"It's more likely to be birds. Bats. Rats, maybe. Relax. I don't think it's rats. More likely mice."

"Squirrels?" said the Brig.

Ruth nodded. She took her house keys and unhooked one. "Max. Stay in my guest room tonight. In the main house." She sighed. "We'll, er . . . deal with the squirrels."

"Yeah. Murder the bastards," I said, remembering how they had wronged me.

"Well," said Ruth.

"Whoa, now hold on. I was joking. I don't want you to murder a squirrel. Just block up the hole so he can't get in."

"Right," said Ruth, and she flashed a look at the Brig.

"What?" I said.

"Er . . . it's just . . . if there are any young in there. A family."

"We'd be trapping them in," I said. "Well, then, that's obviously not an option. What the fuck?" I kicked a stone.

"We'll find out what it is, then we'll decide what to do. But if it's a family of squirrels or the like, we'll have to wait for the spring. They'll go into the woods and return in the autumn. By which time we'll have found the hole and stuffed the cavities with insulation."

I nearly laughed. Spring was a long time away. The satanic squirrels were evicting me. "I'll find somewhere else."

"Safe houses don't grow on trees, sir. Especially not rent-free ones." Even with not paying rent for months, my bank balance was a mere six thousand pounds. Enough to splash out on a second-hand iPad. Not enough to live somewhere safe from Welly and his ilk. "Certainly not ones where you are free to show your face in the local stores." I'd started to have more unpleasant encounters when in supermarkets. Idiots hassling me, asking for selfies, begging me not to leave the club. Some enthusiastically annoying, some borderline Wellies. The customers in the shop where Ruth lived didn't know who I was, and if they did, were tactful enough to leave me alone. If I wanted to live centrally, I'd have to stick to online shopping. Forever.

I paced around, ready to tear my hair out. "Why am I such a magnet for this crazy shit?"

"If I may, sir? My understanding with magnets is that opposites attract. If my surmise is correct, you attract 'crazy shit' because *you* are solid, stable, and most definitely uncrazy."

Ruth laughed, but put her hand on my arm. "We'll work this out. I promise. And really, I'm sorry."

I sagged, sort of defeated. Being mad at Ruth was stupid. "You didn't do anything."

"I know. But I'm sorry anyway." She rubbed my arm. "We're a team. To-gether we can achieve anything. Team," she repeated.

I smiled. "What the fuck is happening?"

She checked her watch. "Emma told me that always worked on you. Right, I'm off. Not spending the whole day ground pounding when there's clear skies and great visibility. Help yourself to what's in the fridge."

The Brig was supposed to have the morning off, so I let him dump me at the sports hub early so he could fuck off to do whatever people like him get up to. It wasn't the worst thing, because I got to watch three teams before my part of the day's entertainment started, which meant I'd be able to afford Morale by the end of the day.

First, the Knights had a friendly. I hid until the end because the players had a habit of rushing off the pitch to hug me mid-match. I needn't have both-ered—half the team were players I'd never seen before. Terry told me some had aged out of the programme, some had moved up, some had been let go to create space for a new intake. He assured me it was good and normal and I didn't need to fret, but it sounded pretty brutal and ruthless. It was what I would have done with the men's team, and it was interesting to see what that kind of churn looked like. The rate of change was discombobulating.

Then it was the under-twelves playing seven-a-side with no slide tackles and no headers. Very sensible rules! I was stunned to realise how good those kids were—the starting seven had an average PA of 63, while the backup goalie had a PA of 130. Absolutely mint! And many, many magnitudes better than their opponents. Spectrum was busy managing them, so I sent him a quick email saying we needed to challenge this group with top-level opponents.

Stephen Watson stole the show, as he normally did. He was the kid I'd found when taking Jackie to the knee specialist. His dad, a worrier by na-ture, came up to me after and said it was the first time he realised I'd followed through on my promise to surround his kid with talented peers.

"And," he added, "when you said Stephen would get personal attention from the director of football, I didn't think you'd actually train with them!"

I smiled. "That wasn't really the plan. But I enjoyed it. I learned a turn from him!"

"You did?"

"Yeah. The one where the ball's coming at him, he's got the defender tight, and he lets it come right to him and flicks it round. It's absolutely gorgeous. I can't do it as well as Stephen, but I'm working on it."

"You played in the cup!"

"I played in the cup."

"So . . . are you staying?" He licked his lips.

I put my arm around his shoulders, and we watched as his child played passes to little Simon Black. Simon's passes were a little ragged, but the ones Stephen hit always went to Simon's shoelaces, as though pulled in by a magnet. "If Everton offer me the manager's job, and I'm stupid enough to take it, the first thing I'm going to do is call you and get Stephen decked out in royal blue. Actually, the first thing I'd do would be to buy a house where the walls don't slope and there aren't loads of buttons that don't do anything and there isn't an infestation. And *then* I'd call you."

"I saw you're trying to get Jackie Reaper back. Is that to replace you?"

"No. He can't play right wing."

"What happened between you two?"

"Between us?" I wondered what rumours had been going around. Probably all kinds of improbable and impossible theories. "Honestly, nothing. If I hadn't . . . you know . . . he would have had a break at the end of last season. Let me do the rest of the matches while he rested his knee. He'd have had a lovely summer, Tenerife, maybe, while I scouted and got things ready. He'd have come back refreshed and I'd have gone on a break. It's fucking exhausting doing this all the time."

"I can imagine."

"I'd like him back tomorrow—that'd be great for everyone. But if he needs another couple of months, fine! Good for him. If I could have December off, that'd be incredible. But it's all good. Stephen's in good hands, I promise you that."

"Oh, I know. But I really liked Jackie."

"He'll be back. But if he goes somewhere else, that's good news for you."

"Is it?"

"That'd be two clubs where you know without a shadow of a doubt that your son would get looked after."

That struck a nerve. He visibly relaxed. "Thanks, Max."

The last match featured the under-eighteens and was a bit disappointing. We struggled against a team of randos.

The only player who had a PA higher than 40 was Vivek. His CA wasn't increasing very fast, presumably because his teammates weren't much good and we didn't arrange tough games for them to play because they would only get mullered.

After their matches, the twelves and eighteens got sandwiches and drinks and whatnot. The idea was to keep them in the area for when all the coaches arrived, so we'd have a stock of players available to do whatever drills came up in the coaching event I had advertised.

Learn from THE BEST!

Are you a <u>coach</u> based in <u>Cheshire</u>?

Then you're cordially invited to the King George V Sports Hub on Sunday, September 17, before the **first ever** league fixture of the Chester FC Women's team. There, director of football, manager, and mystery winger **Max Best** will put on a demonstration of his coaching methods and tactical acumen to *amaze* and *delight* all comers. You will SWOON as he demonstrates his famous Art of

Slapping drill. You will GASP as he recreates the motivational speeches that secured vital wins for Chester. You will SCRATCH YOUR HEAD PUZZLED BUT IN A GOOD WAY as he shows how the strategic thinking of Sun Tzu can be applied to a Tuesday evening away tie against, I dunno, Exeter City.

In-game management! Long-term planning! No topic is off limits! Except Brexit lol.

Bring a pencil, trainers, and a smile. (Smile optional.)

There will be food! And drink! Plus <u>free entry</u> to watch Chester Women versus Wythenshawe Women.

BONUS! Chester FC will subsidise the continuing development of one lucky coach! Got a C license? We'll pay for you to do the B.

Chester FC—Committed to Coaches.

The idea was to get a bunch of local coaches into one spot. It was something of a switcheroo—I wouldn't be doing much coaching myself, but scamming anyone who came into coaching our players so I could scout them. After all, if they coached real players for a real club on a matchday, why wouldn't the curse show me their profiles?

MD found the whole thing cringeworthy, but also community-minded, so he was happy to give me a few hundred quid in budget, and he helped with the organising. Of course, me fluttering my eyelashes at Darlington had unnerved him, so he was curt and distant around me. Which was one part understandable to five parts annoying—every time I did something mad, ticket sales bumped up. Fourth in the league, the talk of the town. What more did he want?

About twenty people turned up, which was way better than I would have thought. Eight weren't coaches, but randos who wanted to meet me and be part of the event and get free grub. I quickly filtered them out, but let them hang out in the area as long as they didn't take the piss on the sandwiches. The remaining twelve were a mixed bag, ranging from the tissue-thin transparent bags you put apples in if you could rub them open (coaching outfield players 5 or less), to worn and faded hemp carriers beloved of tofu-eating liberals (coaching outfield players 10 or more).

As an example of my method, I had some cones set out for a passing drill and got some of the kids lined up and explained it to them. Then I pretended to get a phone call "from Bob Geldof" and handed the nearest coach a whistle and asked if they'd get it started. Yep—it was that simple to trick the curse, and it was child's play to make sure every coach got a few seconds of involvement. My favourite was pausing a drill, asking if anyone had any ideas for an upgrade, pretending not to understand the feedback and saying, "Show me."

So I had a lot of fun being a honeybee zooming from flower to flower, and I actually found a couple of decent coaches. One with coaching outfield players 11, and one with 10. I got Jude to take their details so we could let them take half a session here and there for minimum wage. They were beyond ecstatic to be given the chance to get involved with Chester—it was a huge step up from their current levels. And it would help us out, too, by taking the pressure off the existing coaches. At first, the newbies would act like teacher's assistants, putting out cones and helping to give feedback and monitor groups. Later, they'd get the chance to run some drills of their own.

All in all, it was a very fractional gain for the club, that we'd paid for with a fuckton of online mockery aimed at me. Probably not quite worth it, on balance, but you never knew till you tried.

I said as much to MD, who said that a few coaches had called to ask if we'd be running the event again because they worked on Sunday and could we do it again on Saturday?

"Did we get their details?"

"We did."

"Do any of them have any experience dealing with invasive species and or satanic rituals?"

MD sighed and looked towards somewhere he'd rather be. "I don't know."

"Okay. Let's get them here next Saturday, nine in the morning. I'll do this again, then head down to Lincolnshire. Let me know if you want some sausages."

He mumbled something about being fine for sausages, so I asked if he'd let me know when the FA Cup draw was made. He cheered up a tiny fraction, asking who I wanted to play in the next round.

"Anyone except Darlington," I said, smiling. He didn't smile back.

The event was over, and now that I'd gone from fun-loving focal point to brooding and intense football manager, Spectrum came over with a couple of concerns.

"Boss. I finished my research into GPS tracker vests."

"Smack me in the face with knowledge."

"Yeah, well. The basic ones are three hundred pounds a pop. The ones the big clubs use are fifteen grand."

"Holy shit."

"I know. Maybe postpone those till we've got hot water in the bathrooms. So, I need to talk to you about Future."

"How is the little scamp?"

"Still little."

"Aww. Cute."

"There's more lads on their growth spurts, though."

I pulled a face. "Do we have to talk about teenage boys and use the word *spurt*?"

"Other lads are on their growth *gushes*." He laughed. "Future is looking very, very tiny. I want to move him back down."

I had massively promoted the kid because he was just that talented. "Okay."

"Er . . . do I have your permission, then?"

"You don't need my permission. You're in charge of that." Teenage boys grew at different times. Some of it came flooding back to me. Kids in the changing rooms who were suddenly all hairy. Voices breaking. The first day a kid sprayed deodorant after a match, and the eight years it took to get the smell out of my nostrils. "Growth spurts. Wow. So many mad things I need to think about. Okay. The fourteens are pretty shit, though. Can Future deal with going right back to the twelves?"

"He could, but I don't think that's the right move."

"The fourteens, then. That's really not great for him. I'm going to a couple of schools next week. I'll try to find some talented kids his age. Er . . . in the meantime, bump John, Adam, and Big Sam up for a few weeks so Future has some talent around him."

"This is me being in charge, is it?"

I laughed. "Yep! You're in charge of all the things I don't specifically tell you to do. Let me know if any kids freak out about being moved up or down. I'll reassure them if they need it. And I'm thinking of letting Vivek train with the first team every now and then."

"Right," he said, dubious.

I shrugged. "See if we can't shock him into improving. Right, be off with you. I've got to fill in my team sheet."

"You should let your assistant do that."

"My assistant is busy flirting with soccer moms."

Match 1 of 22: Chester Women versus Wythenshawe Women.

Henri turned up to watch the coaching session—he loved a bit of weirdness after breakfast. I volunteered him to be my assistant manager for the day because he knew a lot more than me about the countryside and I had questions for him.

First, I needed to set my team up for the match. My players got changed and came out for their warm-ups. Compared to the nice stadium from last week, this felt pretty shit. We were playing on what was basically a local park with a temporary stand at the side, but their excitement was undimmed.

The other team were Wythenshawe, which you might remember is where Manchester Airport is, and where the Yalleys lived. Pretty close to my heart, in fact, and Shawe had a decent team. An average CA of 22, but very lumpy. Their keeper was terrible—good jumping but handling 2—they had two players with shocking technique and passing, but they had a good spine. They were experienced, too. It was going to be a tough day.

We had a new addition to the squad—Julie McKay. She was the PA 53 striker with good movement I'd tried to sign before crashing into Welly, her much older hooligan boyfriend. I'd recently had the wonderful, philanthropic, utopian idea to see if Julie still wanted to join the team. The Brig and Ruth had gone to talk to her, and they had come to the decision she was a nice girl and a good person who had stumbled into a bad relationship and had tried hard to get out. Ruth said Julie was brave, which shocked me. She normally only used positive adjectives to describe horses.

I hadn't been to training, and the women had been told to turn up at 1 p.m., meaning the first time I'd see Julie since my attack was drawing near. And as it came closer, I felt weirder and weirder. The walls were closing in and there was evil in the ceiling. Soon . . . the screams.

When Julie walked past, I was showing the magic whistle to the referee. The ref had heard about it and was keen to try it. I was holding it out, but I wouldn't let go. My eyes were locked onto Julie's, and that's when I knew.

I knew.

Welly *was* the guy who'd tried to kill me. And it had all happened because of her. The guilt she showed made me nauseous and I started to feel dizzy.

When I came to my senses, the ref had wandered off, holding the armband and blowing the whistle, repeating the trick while her assistants had a go. I was moving. Floating away from our gear and equipment.

Henri's hand was on my back and he was pushing me, easing me, mumbling some sweet nothings. When we were some distance away, he gave me a few seconds to calm down. "What is it?"

I tried to think what I'd told him, and what I hadn't. I think he knew pretty much everything. "Inviting her was a mistake." I shuddered. "When I look at her, I feel there's a big hole in my head. All my brains leaking out."

"I see. Yes, I see. The Brig thinks the older boyfriend did it? Then, yes. I would feel the same. So . . . why did you give her this chance?"

I looked down. "Good question." I took my time. "I thought the worst was over. He'd already tried to get me. Whatever I do now, he'll try again, or he won't. The guy's fucking mental. It's nothing to do with Julie. Right? So I try to think that. But then, why's she got this murderous boyfriend? Why's she attracted to violent dudes? And I'm like, it's none of my business. Except it is, because one of them tried to kill me. So I was right to be wary, I think. But now, is that it, forever? Do I say there's no second chances? How can Mr. Yalley forgive a man who tried to get him put away for the rest of his life, and I can't even look at this girl who did literally nothing to me?" I sighed. "I dunno. It's a mess. Honestly, Henri, I don't wake up every morning trying to make my life more difficult. But she's from Chester, she's talented, she's never done anyone any harm, and if this isn't her home, where is?"

"Oh," he said, in a weird way.

"What?"

"So you're really thinking of leaving."

I frowned. How had he got from what I said to what he said? "Why . . . what makes you say that?"

"She's not a problem to anyone except you. So you bring her in . . . because you might not be here for very long."

"I'll be here longer than you," I said. But I wasn't sure I meant it.

Talking about the situation calmed me down, and I knew Henri would be around to help me if things got a bit intense. I'd have the Morale perk soon. What would it say about Henri? I was sure he'd have a good score—since I'd put myself on the team sheet and had my little cameo, the entire squad had been buzzing.

I filled in the team sheet, mentally totting up their CAs. Hoping to capitalise on their first-ever taste of real, competitive football, I'd asked Jude and Spectrum to join the week's training sessions, and it had paid off. Everyone had increased by a point at least, while Charlotte, my midfield superstar, added two. Our 4-5-1 formation gave us an average CA of exactly 15.

A little bit off the standard, it seemed. Seven points behind Wythenshawe's average. But we'd catch up soonish, so then the question was: were Wythenshawe one of the better teams? And could we afford to lose many games while we got going? Last season's winners had drawn one, lost one, and won the rest. Only one team was promoted, so if there was a team that had something like CA 40, we were screwed.

My pre-match team talk consisted of me picking out three very weak Wythenshawe players and telling my ladies to press the two outfield ones, and to take potshots at the goalie.

"Lots of shots! Imagine you're on a night out in Manchester. Shots shots shots! Bea Pea, get on the rebounds."

The team clapped and Bonnie shouted, "Come on ladies!" and so on, only to pause while Dani started laughing—she had just read the text. She looked at me and signed. It was like two finger guns making a W in front of her chin.

"Good joke?" I said.

Funny, she wrote in the chat.

"Max," said Maddy. "Are we going to talk about you?"

"About me? Er . . . I like canal-side walks and if I ever buy a house I want to cover it from top to bottom in vandal paint."

"You played a match and didn't tell us. We would have come to watch!"

"Oh. Well I didn't realise how bad Tadcaster were until I got there. I thought, now's as good a time as any."

"But you're not ready."

I shrugged. "The first match I played was always going to be terrible. Next one, too, maybe. But it's a shortcut."

Dani waved her hand, indicating she had an important question. I picked up my phone and saw she was being her usual blunt self.

Dani: Everyone said you were shit. People were laughing at you. Don't you feel embarrassed?

Me: No. I'd be embarrassed if I gave up. If I didn't try. I'll play in the next round, too, and I'll be shit again. No one will ever work harder to put in a 4 out of 10 performance.

Dani: You're brave.

Me: I'm not brave. I just know there's only one opinion that matters.

We waited for Dani to reply, but she stared at her screen for a while, then nodded at Bonnie. They left, arm in arm, heading out onto the pitch.

I was offered Bench Boost and Triple Captain, but it didn't seem the right match for those. For a start, my bench options were weak. Erin, Susan, and Julie. The longer I waited in the season, the more useful those players would be. Maybe I'd get lucky and be able to spot who the best team in the league was, and try to surprise them. If we could beat the best team twice, that would make life so much easier.

The first half was tough.

In front of a sizeable crowd of almost 400—which sounds good until you remember entry was free and Brits are pulled towards free food like dust to my copy of *Foucalt's Pendulum*—we went about our business of playing nice passing moves and controlling the ball. When we lost it, Shawe would counter, and fast, but half their breaks would end when one of their shit players got involved.

"We don't have much goal threat," said Henri. "We're struggling to move through the thirds." He meant it was hard for the defence to get the ball to the midfield, who found it hard to get up to the attacking line.

"I know. This is our struggle. We compete well, but find it hard to create chances. Last week, the team went defensive and that helped. If we're a couple of goals down near the end, they might go into their shell and we can have a barnstorming late run. I'd prefer to be more proactive, though."

"Dani isn't the answer?"

"She is, but not yet. At the moment, she's neat and tidy but a bit . . . safe. She looks overcoached, but that's obviously not what it is."

"Coaching. The theme of the day."

"It's the theme of my life. We have talent everywhere. Now we need to unlock it." I stretched. The lack of sleep was kicking in. "It's hard to find good coaches. The ones I meet have all got jobs already. I can find a good player on any park or beach. But coaches don't go to Ibiza and start coaching passers-by."

"You should talk to Raffi."

"Raffi?"

"He's been working one-on-one with a coach. Talk to him about it."

"Huh. Okay. Will do, thanks." We watched as Charlotte tried to get a grip on the midfield. Shawe had quickly spotted that she was our main weapon, though, and were snapping into her as soon as she got the ball. I tried moving her to be the left of the three CMs—maybe it would draw Shawe towards that side of the pitch, leaving a bit more space for Dani and Maddy. "Henri. You know things."

"I do."

"I live in a barn now. There's something in the attic. It fucking screams all night long. It's terrifying. I think it's a fox. Or an eagle."

"*Merde*," said Henri.

"I know. Very, very *merde*."

"I did not say *merde*. I said *merde*."

"I'm sorry, are you taking the piss now?"

He raised his eyes to the heavens, and with a massive show of patience, exhaled. He took out his phone and went to a translation app he very rarely used. "Martin."

I slapped my hips. "Martin. Martin Keown? Martin Sheen. Chris Martin from Coldplay. What's the game? This isn't fun."

Henri showed me his phone. It said: marten. "In French we say, marten of the pines."

"Oh, *pine marten*. Yeah, I've heard of that. Marten. Huh. What is it?"

"Do you know what a weasel is?"

"I know the *word* weasel."

"Max, seriously. You are not equipped for life in the countryside. You are clueless." He huffed and puffed and showed me a picture. "This is what is in your attic."

It was a squirrel with the head of a racoon. I'd probably have found it cute if I didn't know it had a heart of darkness.

We watched quietly for a while. Moving Charlotte to our weaker side had, indeed, drawn Shawe's attention over there, for all the good it did us. "This team needs something."

"A second striker?" he said, glancing at our subs, one of whom was cute but had a heart of darkness.

"Something we don't have on the bench. Our midfield is good. They are technical. I love the effort they put in and it's satisfying to see them improve over time. But it's missing a spark."

"Speed," said Henri. "Dynamism. Exuberance."

"Oh," I said, surprised that he'd come to the same conclusion as me. "Yes, please."

He shook his head. "Those aren't my words, Max. They're yours. The answer you seek is standing over there."

"Where?"

"With her brother. And her father, who saved your life."

At halftime, I skipped the team talk so I could talk to Kisi. And so I wouldn't have to look at Julie for a second longer than I had to. Then I read about martens. They'd nearly been wiped out of the British Isles but had recovered. I texted Ruth and she expressed surprise there were any near her.

So this little guy was branching out. Looking for a safe place to live, just like me.

In the second half, there wasn't much for me to do. I put Erin and Susan on to give us some fresh legs, and then it was simply a case of when I would bring Julie on. Probably five minutes from time—she was CA 3 and would have to catch up to the rest of the group before she was really useful.

"Max. I have an idea."

"Oh? Is it as good as your idea to fix our lack of experience by recruiting a fifteen-year-old?"

Henri smiled. "Kisi will be sixteen soon. No, mine is an off-pitch idea. I found a property in Chester. It is currently used as a bed-and-breakfast but the owner is retiring. Twelve bedrooms, ten bathrooms. Some original features. All surprisingly tasteful except for one room, which— Never mind."

"A French footballer running a B and B sounds like the pitch for a sitcom."

"I would run it as a digs."

"Oh!" A digs. Like where I stayed in Darlington before moving in to Henri's place. "Twelve bedrooms. Twelve horny young footballers. You'd need a Ghostbuster to come once a month to hoover out all the testosterone."

Henri gave me a strange glance. "I am only pitching the idea, you understand? But if my first two tenants were Pascal and Youngster . . . and if I took the biggest room. That would set the tone, so to speak. Serious and professional. Modern and classy. Affordable but civilised. European."

I smiled. "It sounds top."

He shuffled. "I need your approval."

We had a corner and I was wondering if I should use the free hit perk. It took me a second to realise what he'd said. "Approval? What? What for?"

"I believe players like Pascal and Youngster would come quite willingly. The Triplets, too. But you might sign an older player and that player might need a place to stay for a few weeks while he got settled. Or you might invite a player to come for a two-week trial. When you start your refereeing academy, or have one of your many madcap ideas, the participants slash victims will need a roof over their heads. Paid for by the club, of course. The permanent residents, let's say five or six of us, would have the space to ourselves most of the time. Then there would be periods when it was full. Those periods would make the financials stack up in my favour."

"What if I leave and the next manager doesn't want to send you loads of free money?"

"It isn't free money, Max. Hospitality is hard work! Washing the towels. Folding the towels. Unfolding and refolding the towels because there was an inexplicable little bump. Choosing a font. Having dinner with the font designer. Having a torrid affair with the font designer. Tiny bars of soap. Do you know where to buy seven thousand tiny bars of soap, Max? Do you know how to choose a shower gel that is both cost efficient and not repellent to women? Do you hoover behind the door, Max? You strike me as the type of person who regularly sleeps on a damp pillowcase because you threw them in the dryer with the bedsheets and covers. You know less about running a hotel than you know about the planet you live on." He picked up a water bottle, but then immediately dropped it. He wasn't thirsty, but needed to make some kind of gesture. "Of course it would be ideal if you stayed, but the model works without you. It works without me, too. I would simply need to discuss it with MD and the board. Have it all above board, so to speak."

"Well, I don't have a problem with it." I tried to imagine the digs in Darlington, but run by Henri. There certainly wouldn't be fucking Mars bar wrappers everywhere. Maybe he'd teach the kids to cook properly. Like, chopping vegetables dead fast and stuff like that. "I reckon you'd run the best digs in the country." Henri preened so much I couldn't resist a little dig at his motives. "And you'd make a killing."

He sighed. "Money is like an energy. It is attracted to me." He laughed suddenly. "I mentioned this idea to the Brig and Vimsy, to see what they thought, and to see if perhaps the Brig would allow you to stay with us. The Brig approved, but not for you. Vimsy was equally in favour. He said he had heard that I was 'a right property magnet.'"

I smiled. "These guys."

"These guys know the difference between a fox and an eagle."

"Good point."

I think Henri sensed that my mood had dropped when he'd said I couldn't live with him. He gave me a little push. "I'm no expert in martens," he said. "But I know they do not scream every night. They are probably . . . what was that disturbing phrase you used? Porking their brains out. They will stop soon enough. You will hear them scrabbling around up there, but mating season . . . is seasonal."

I wanted to believe him, but I needed something a little more reliable than Henri repeating something he'd learned when he was a kid. The on-pitch action didn't help. The match stats started to really pivot against us, and after sixty minutes, Wythenshawe scored from a corner.

I paced around, beating myself up for having no options. No comebacks. No way to influence the game.

"How much is it?" I asked, meaning the property Henri had found. I wouldn't normally have asked, but I needed a distraction.

"Nine hundred thousand."

I nearly fell over. "Right. Don't panic, Max. He made a mistake. He meant three hundred thousand. He meant four hundred thousand. He's still shaking his head; he really meant nine hundred. And the mortgage is . . ."

"Ten percent deposit, interest-only. Five thousand three hundred."

Over five grand a month! Just on the interest. Pay £5,000 a month for twenty-five years and you'd *still* owe the £900K. It was bonkers. "Mate, no. Come on."

He grinned and slapped me on the back. "No risk, no fun."

"There's risk and there's that." We were coming back into the game now. Pippa had the chance to launch a long-range strike, but thought better of it. She passed to Dani, who dribbled past a defender and hit a good cross that went through everyone, all the way to the other side of the pitch where the right back hacked the ball away.

Henri applauded, remembered that Dani couldn't hear, then applauded anyway. "No, no. It's not such a risk. There is a shortage of homes in this country. The worst case is not so bad—I sell at a loss. Thirty thousand in fees. Another thirty in lost equity. But the best case . . ."

"What?"

"I charge according to a player's means, yes? Youngster pays five hundred a month. You sell him, you buy someone more premium. You pay him double, he pays me double." He grinned. "I'm placing the safest bet in town. I'm betting on you."

"What if I leave?" I said, but then I was pulled by an invisible force to the edge of the pitch. Scanning left and right confirmed what the curse had told me—the other manager had sounded the retreat. I couldn't believe this was happening again! A free invitation to camp in their half.

Seizing the chance to make something happen, I took our right back off and threw Julie up front in a 3-5-2. Suddenly the game came alive—we passed and threatened and pushed opponents out of position. Julie had great movement—she was like a magnet, drawing defenders like I'd asked Wilson to do the first time Henri was my assistant—and that opened space for the midfielders to run onto.

Now that she was finally in range, Charlotte tried out her long shots. The first came back off the goalie and Bea Pea latched onto the rebound. One–all! The second, the keeper got a hand to it again, but made an even bigger mess of it and it dribbled across the line.

We were winning 2–1!

My rival manager fixed her mistake, made a few subs of her own, and tried to bombard us with long balls. My team was relatively short, young, and weak, and the tactic worked. Shawe scored, but Bonnie and Lucy reorganised the defence and our midfielders raced to stop those long balls being hit with any accuracy.

The end of the match came as a relief. Our first league match had finished 2–2.

Henri considered the game. It had been pretty one-sided for eighty of the ninety minutes. "Well done, Max."

"It was all right, wasn't it?"

Henri nodded. "It was more than all right. I'm sure with any other manager, this team would have lost today." He slapped my back again. "Always bet on Max."

He hovered while I gave my post-match debrief. "Ladies, well played. You suffered, you sacrificed, and you earned the right to play your way for ten minutes, and in those ten minutes you slapped. Charlotte, we're going to get that contract signed this week. If City want you back, they'll have to pay. And I'm going to bring another City player in this week. I think some of you know her, and you all know her brother. What else? Yeah . . . Julie." This was the first time I'd really spoken to her. The curse had given her 7 out of 10—not bad for a sub making her debut against much better players. Looking at her was weird— she was attractive, but she'd caused me, inadvertently, so much grief. It'd be a struggle to get past that. I wanted to try, though. "Good job." I thought about the way she'd moved around. "Were you the right of the two forwards in your other team?"

She nodded. She was timid around me. "We mostly played one striker. But when we had two . . ." She pushed her right hand to the right.

"Yeah, Bea Pea has been doing that for us when we've played two. You made the same runs today, sometimes. Coaches will give you some time to work on it this week. You've been on your own, doing well, but you'll have to learn to coexist. That is, if you're going to stay."

She didn't reply. I mentally shrugged. On balance, I wanted her to stay. She was an asset to the club and a chance for me to learn and grow as a person.

"No match next week, so go hard in training. All right? I'm off early. I have a date with someone who might turn out to be a stone-cold fox." I glanced at Henri. He didn't like it. "I have a rendezvous and we'll be up all night?" He shook his head and pushed me away.

Outside, away from the others, he leaned closer and murmured, "You've been on your own but you'll have to learn to coexist. *If you're going to stay.* Did I hear that right?"

"Er . . . yes. Why?"

"Oh, no reason."

He walked off with a very smug look on his face. Nutjob! The Brig's idea was right. I attracted nutjobs because I was so sane and rational. But later I thought—was he comparing the marten to Julie McKay? I bit my thumbnail. Trick Williams had done more harm than Julie, and I'd found a way to coexist with *him*.

MD rushed over, smiling. Finally! The miserable bastard had remembered how to do it. "Max! They're doing the FA Cup draw. We're away to Cray Wanderers. Isthmian League. That's er . . . seventh tier. Down in London. Win that and we're one step away from being in the real cup!"

"And we're fourth in the league and tickets are flying off the shelves. Huh. It's almost as though what I'm doing . . . is working."

He tutted and breathed in through his eyes. "Of course it's working. That's not . . ."

Whatever he was going to say, he never did. I'd stopped him by gripping his wrist. "Mike. You're great at walking around, scuffing your shoes, pretending to be consternated." I smiled from dimple to dimple. "I've just had an amazing idea. Let's put that grumpy, sullen face of yours to good use."

I don't think his morale improved when I told him my idea, but he promised to go along with it.

XP balance: 2,088

Debt repaid: 2,126/3,000

Thanks to the Brig dropping me off early, I could buy Morale. Not a moment too soon—I didn't have good man-management skills. The perk, hopefully, would tell me how to keep my players happy.

But I'd do it in the morning, hopefully after a good night's sleep. Tired people made bad decisions.

I went into Ruth's house, just to satisfy my curiosity about the guest room and the state of her kitchen and whatnot. I found everything feminine and classy. Staying there for one night when she was away would be fine. But using her guest room when she was at home would be catastrophic. We would one hundred percent end up having noisy, wild, fantastic sex, and neither of us wanted *that*.

So after taking one of her premium Marks and Spencer tartlets into the barn, I lay on my bed, dressed like I was going to the arctic, and drifted off a few times. But then—the scrabbling! It was here!

I ran downstairs, grabbed the torch I'd taken from one of Ruth's many horse sheds, and dashed into the garden—AKA the mud around the house.

A hint of evening mist was in the air, and I found myself crouching slightly to make less noise as I walked. I flicked the torch on, shone it around the roof, around the drainpipes, along the gutters. How did this thing get in the roof, and where?

Then—there it was! Two bright eyes, shining down on me.

The thing was much smaller than I'd expected. It was like a long cat. Half the size of a fox. It was pretty majestic. Balanced and agile and way, way smarter than he looked. He'd be fucking amazing on the left wing.

He took a long look at me, decided I was nothing, and walked off, swaying like he owned the place.

"Oi!" I cried.

He paused, then stared at me again.

"I could fuck you up," I said. "Go and live at Ruth's. Seriously. Fuck off my gaff."

He didn't blink, and with one last disdainful glance, pottered to the other side of the roof.

I sprinted round, but by the time I'd got there, he'd vanished. Into the roof, or off on his nightly adventures?

Back inside, I undressed and hopped into bed, and fell into a wonderfully deep and drooly sleep. At 2 a.m. the screaming started again.

In Ruth's guest room, I spent twenty minutes listening hard to every noise, and realised that the countryside was way, way louder than the city. Yeah, in the city you get cars, planes, people outside screaming at each other.

But in the countryside the floor creaks. Just creaks! On its own! And if you aren't scared of that, you're not watching the right movies.

Or a wooden beam will crack, or there will be an ominous rumbling that you can only hear in one little patch of one room and nowhere else. Totally freaky.

I started to get used to it, and drifted off towards sleep.

On my way down, I reflected that I was doing a pretty amazing job. I'd won two FA Cup matches, and the women's team I'd created was up and running. One of our youth teams was jam packed with talent.

But I was still homeless. I was still a million miles away from owning my own house. Meanwhile, Henri had, what, five?

I felt a tiny pang of jealousy and resentment, but only a little bit. Why couldn't I be a property magnet?

What I didn't realise until later was that the events of this week, stressful as the nights had been, had sent me hurtling down a path that would pretty quickly lead to me owning my first property. Not a house, or a barn, or a former B and B. Soon I would own a property that wouldn't have been in my top million guesses. A property I would have to share with a lot of animals.

14

HOMESCHOOLED, PART ONE

Monday, September 18.

Ruth's open-plan upper-middle-class fantasy home was a lot closer to my ideal space than the barn, with its cramped little worker's kitchen and old brown countertops. My kettle cost nineteen pounds from Argos. Ruth's had all *kinds* of buttons and features, including a temperature setting for Oolong. How posh is *that*?

I spent a calm morning enjoying the trappings of other people's wealth. Had a couple of teas, had a big think.

I'd pre-decided to buy the Morale perk—it should help me get the most out of my players, on match days *and* in training, and help me undo some of my relationship mistakes. It could also help me help my friends when they were feeling bad—as long as they played football. It wouldn't help me with Emma, more's the pity, since I could use a few tips there.

So, Morale then.

But . . . there was this tribunal coming up. A hearing to settle the dispute between Blackburn Rovers and Tranmere over how much a player was worth. If I were representing Blackburn at the hearing, I would try to downplay the value of Danny Prince. "We needed a reserve left back and his name came up" kinda thing. If I had the Contracts perk, I might be able to see how much they were paying him. If he was being paid like a top first teamer, they couldn't say they thought he was a reserve! And time was running out to re-scout the player Ian Evans had recommended—when that guy signed a new contract, I wouldn't know for sure if his weekly wage was what Ian Evans had told me.

My suspicions that clubs lied to other clubs about how much their players earned had been confirmed when I read a former club owner's autobiography. Arsenal had loaned him a player, charging £10,000 a week, but the owner later learned the player's salary was only £5,000. The Contracts perk could allow me to help my new besties at Tranmere Rovers, and would insulate me from shady characters.

But helping Tranmere and confirming my suspicions about Ian Evans were neither here nor there in the grand scheme of things. I scanned the perk shop and the only other option that stood out was Finances. That would give me a summary of the club's incomings and expenditures, which I didn't need. I'd previously dismissed the perk completely. But the rivalry with Darlington had made me reconsider—if I could get financial data for *other* clubs—and the curse gave me all kinds of secret shit, so it was possible—that would be an amazing media weapon. I assumed Darlo's total player salaries would be much higher than ours, so I could keep banging on about that in interviews, presenting ourselves as the plucky underdogs. You know, ignoring the fact that we had the sixth biggest budget, or whatever the true number was.

These were passing fancies.

I bought Morale—one small step for one man, one giant leap for one man, delete as appropriate.

I went to Henri's player profile, and there it was!

Morale: Superb

Hooray!
How about Pascal Bochum?

Morale: Very Good

Great!
I had a look at Trick Williams.

Morale: OK

Oh, fuck you, you miserable prick!

I checked everyone, and only saw four different levels: Superb, Very Good, Good, and OK.

It was similar in the women's team, but Julie McKay and Mel Robinson had "Poor." Julie's low morale made some sort of sense—her boyfriend was a murderer who'd gone into hiding. On the other hand, she'd joined a proper football team and had played in a big match. So . . . I assumed there was a level below Poor and she'd been there until the good news had lifted her up. Meanwhile Mel had gone—in her mind—from being our starting right back, expecting to play every minute of every game to finding out I was actively trying to replace her.

Was that how all this worked, then? Things made you happy and your morale went up?

Our levels seemed phenomenally high, all in all. We were somewhere in the region of 4.71 out of 5. Mostly five-star reviews for the Max Best experience. So why had I spent more time thinking about the low numbers than the high ones? It was like they were reviews of me as a *person*.

Silly Max.

Still, without obsessing about how a one-star rating showed that I was a fraud and a hack and all my best work was in the past, I wondered if I could change one of the bad reviews to a positive one.

I sent Mel a text.

Just thinking about the Wythenshawe match. You did great against their left winger!

It took ten minutes to craft that message. Deleted drafts had detailed analysis of her match stats or talked about how she had fit into the overall framework of the team's success. In the end, I decided that simple was best.

She didn't reply, and nothing happened. Well, no reason why my life should get any easier. With a sigh, I went to the barn, got my gear, and chucked it into the passenger seat of a car that cost less than Ruth's fridge. I was driving; the Brig had another day off. As I was about to turn onto the main road, my phone beeped. Mel sent back a thumbs-up emoji. Women with their fucking emojis! Don't they know men need THE WORDS? Pretty sure my morale dropped a level.

I said something along the lines of "ugh" and drove off. But at a traffic light, I dipped into Mel's profile and her morale had changed. Now, in green, it said, OK.

Yes! Yes! Yes!

Training was good. We skipped the team meeting, so Vimsy and Jude had the guys doing some basic running, agility drills, stuff like that. I didn't need my new toy to tell me that the mood was very positive—we'd won five matches in a row, seven of the last eight, were getting better defensively, and were starting to score goals easily. Our fitness was really kicking in at the ends of matches. Belief in my outline for the season, the NostradaMax as everyone should have been calling it, was through the roof.

There was a break before we started doing more intense ball work, and I called the lads over. "Quick team meeting. Won't take long. No Tuesday night game, as you know. We play Boston on Saturday. Watch out, they've got those little robot dogs. Wait, wrong Boston. Boston *United* have got a midfielder called Bostwick and their assistant manager is called Bastock. I'm obsessed with that. They're at home so they'll be confident. We'll teach them a lesson. That's the end of my thoughts about the Boston match. Raffi and Aff, quick word? Raffi first."

Raffi came over, vaguely worried. "Max?"

"Henri told me I should ask you about coaches. I've been trying to find a Jackie replacement. You know someone."

His expression cleared up—no change in morale. "Right. I've been having private lessons. One on one. Not sure how interested he'd be in working here." He looked down, regretting his choice of words. "But come down tomorrow. Join my session and meet him. In Chorlton. Near where you grew up!"

"Oh! Bit of homeschooling." I smiled. "Top. Sorted. Job's a good 'un." I gave him a friendly little shove towards the main pack, then waved Aff over.

His morale was Very Good. "Boss?"

"Yeah. Not trying to mess with your head," I lied, "but you seem pretty happy here."

"At Chester?"

"Yep."

"Yeah, it's deadly. Love it."

"Top. I'd like to give you a new contract. Bit more long-term. Two plus one sort of thing." Two years with an option—for the club, not him—to extend it by another year.

"Oh!"

"No need to say anything. Have a think, and we'll sit down with MD and talk about it. Awight?"

"Yes, boss."

He walked off, beaming. Morale, in green: Superb.

I turned away so the guys wouldn't see me absurdly delighted to be alive on a crisp September morn. Then I thought—happiness is contagious, right? So I let them peer at me, let them wonder what had put me in such a good mood. I went to the squad screen, sorted it by morale, and got an instant overview of how the group as a whole was feeling.

"Right, listen up. Gather round. One last announcement." I pursed my lips, pretending to think about how to word what I needed to say. "Er . . . got a new guy training with you from now on. He's not good, but he's enthusiastic." I pulled off my hoodie, revealing I was wearing my Best 77 away kit. I raised my arms and spun slowly. "Behold! Is this the perfect specimen of a man . . . ager?"

A mighty roar from the lads! A surge! Led by Henri, they came close, and we bounced up and down shouting "Ches-ter! Ches-ter!"

Vimsy blew his whistle and yelled, "Break's over! Back to fucking work!"

I clapped my hands and jogged to position for the next drill. Just one of the boys. A morning like any other.

But one where almost everyone's morale increased by one, sometimes two levels.

Everyone . . . with three exceptions. Three players whose morale *dropped* when they saw I was well enough to train with them. Donny "D-Day" Dorigo. Trick Williams. And, so shocking it almost ruined my day, my captain and defensive rock, Glenn Ryder.

At 3:30 p.m., I was camped out in the car park at Abbey Gate College. Loads of little ruffians were scuffing past, some heading home, most heading to after-school clubs like the Debating Society, the choir, or the Homework Club. That's right, it was a school for posh brats.

I sighed. If I wanted to dedicate my life to giving opportunities to people who already had more than enough, I would have become a Conservative MP. Still, whatever. They were the first school who had set up a match in the way

I'd requested, so here I was. We'd promote the shit out of it on the socials and other schools would be like "oh that's what he meant" and fucking take five minutes to organise it.

Someone tapped on my window, scaring the shit out of me. Steve Alton, our new signing, and one of my two bodyguards for the event. Joe Anka was behind him.

I got out and pushed my hands down, telling someone in the area, possibly me, to calm it. "Steve, someone snuck up on me and tried to kill me. Not that long ago. Thanks for coming but please try to avoid startling me."

"Sorry, boss. How should I do it?"

"Walk in front of the car, back and forth, until I notice you."

"Got it."

"Right, time to watch some rich kids play association football. See if any realise the rules apply to them." This got a laugh.

Joe watched a group of girls go past in their school uniforms—green blazers, crisp shirts, red and black striped ties—and raised his eyebrows. "Boss, you go to a posh school?"

"Did I fuck," I said. "You?"

"Nah."

We looked around us. The place was insane. Surrounded by lush fields, with chunky, Hogwarts castle-type buildings, what looked like an actual hedge maze, and better football facilities than Chester Football Club.

"Anyone going to ask if I went to a posh school?" said Steve Alton.

I laughed and patted him on the back. "No need, mate. We can tell from the way you always lick your plate clean."

"Cheeky bastard," he said.

We set off towards the all-weather pitch. "What's the gig?" said Joe. "Gonna play them some music and see who vibes to it?"

"Nah, it's simple scouting. Remember I said I wanted to scout every schoolkid in Cheshire? This is phase one."

Steve Alton hadn't heard my appearance on *Seals Live*. "Every kid in Cheshire? How many's that?"

"An absurd number," I said. "What I want . . ." I paused as a kid walked past, oblivious to my existence, not bothered that I could hear him. He seemed to be doing grammar drills, in Latin. "Fucketh me-eth. What I want . . . Er . . . yeah *ideally* I'd turn up to a school and every kid would be playing simultaneously. Not really possible, so I'm focusing on the under-sixteens for a few weeks. We've got some good players at that age, but if we can add another ten or fifteen, we can really get impressive. Then I'll do the fourteens, then the twelves."

"What about girls?" said Joe.

"Might have to wait." I stopped walking and cracked my neck. "If I could get a top manager for the women's team, that'd free up a lot of time." I shook my head. There was no one on the horizon. "So, this match today. The school's divided their best fourteen- and fifteen-year-olds into two groups. I guess they did Slytherin plus thingy against you know plus wotsit. Sort of a posh sods all-stars. I've asked them to use as many subs as possible so that it's not just the tall kids who get on the pitch. I mean, the concept won't show me *every* boy in the age group, but if there's a secret star player from the leftovers, I'll have to hope he appears on my radar some other time."

"Right," said Joe. "But if he's not in the first forty best players in one age group in one school, he's probably no good."

I shrugged. "Not sure I would have played in this match. Not sure Youngster would. Dani wouldn't."

"I see your point," he said. "But *you* would have."

I tsked. "Think when you played in school. Anyone decent gets played as a striker. There's defenders in midfield, midfielders up front, wingers in goal." I shook my head. "Anyway, if I got to wear one of those smart green blazers, I'd never have taken it off. Talk about a chick magnet."

"Would you send your kids here?" said Steve.

"Yeah," I said. "It's the irony, isn't it? I don't like this. All schools should look like this, know what I mean? But yeah. I'd send my kid here until he started calling me 'pater.' Then I'd homeschool him." When we walked through to the outdoor sports area, I saw a good couple of hundred people had turned up. "Shit. They've made it into a thing. I was hoping to leave early. Er . . . make sure I behave myself."

"What does that mean?" said Joe, laughing.

"Like . . . the goal is to be invited back to watch the other age groups, then the girls. Right? So if anyone gets in my face, or I get in someone's face, get me out of their face."

"How about you don't get in anyone's face?" suggested Joe.

"You make it sound easy." A thin, desiccated man was making a beeline for me. "Shit, that must be the headmaster. He looks like a vicar. I knew it. This place, seriously. Right, er . . . be charming. If I say I'm getting a call from Bob Geldof, that means I'm about to leave."

"Max, behave," said Joe. "Don't use Bob Geldof, at least. No one knows that name anymore."

We met the headmaster, who introduced himself and was more charming than he looked from afar. He asked if I wanted a tour and I said maybe next time because I was expecting a call from Josh Hartnett. Joe stepped in with a question about the choir, and I stepped onto the next social level down, which included the deputy headmistress and influential parents. The lowest level were the P.E. teachers, who were waiting for His Royal Headness to proclaim kickoff. This school was like a mini kingdom with its own royal family and courtiers. Very hierarchical. My Chester was pretty flat—I had the final word on football matters, but the coaches and physios had a lot of freedom.

"Max!" said a familiar voice.

I turned and saw Tyson Bulldog, wearing one of the green blazers. Of *course* he went to the posh school. He was all excited and whatnot. Annoyingly, his player profile wasn't showing, so I couldn't check his morale. "Sup dog?"

His voice was fifteen percent more snobbish than normal. "Oh, it's amazing. This isn't a football school, but this match is all anyone's been talking about.

And I'm, like, the big expert so people keep asking me who should play and who's going to win. It's amazing. It's like . . . this match is a microcosm of what's happening in the whole of Chester!"

"All right, if you're the expert, get the match started without me appearing rude. After this I've got an appointment with the Chester Illuminati and if I'm late, they won't tell me where the secret pyramid is buried."

"Oh," he said, surprised. "Start the match. Of course."

He strode straight over to the headmaster and said something, and then the head waved at the P.E. teachers and suddenly it was all go. Action stations. Tyson gave me a little thumbs-up. I waved him back. Joe, too.

"Joe, Steve, this is Tyson from our youth system. He's in 'The Wizard of Us.' That article."

"In it? I'm the star of it."

"You'd get an 'introducing' credit, maybe. What did you say to the vicar?"

"The who? Oh!" He laughed. "That's funny. I said we should start."

That simple. "Fuck me. Guys, were either of you that ballsy at school?"

"Nah," said Joe. "It's what they learn here. Treating everyone like they work for them. Act like you know your place in the world, and the world goes along with it."

"So apparently Tyson's the local football expert. Tactics twenty. He's going to stand here and analyse the game for us." Tyson pulled a weird face. Looked like he was in pain. "What?" I said.

"It's just . . . I was with those girls."

We looked over and saw a group of young women whose skirts didn't seem to quite reach regulation length. They saw us looking and smirked. "Christ," I said. "How do you get any work done?"

"I do it at home," said Tyson, apparently in earnest.

"Just checking," I said. "You're going to give up the chance to hear my thoughts about football, about your mates, with two first-team stars, so you can go and flirt with the mean girls?"

"Definitely."

"Joe? Steve?"

"Kid's got his head screwed on right."

Tyson grinned, and sensing that he'd won the conversation, got cocky. "Anyway, you're only tactics seven."

"Ek-fucking-scuse me?"

His grin fixed in place. He'd gone too far. "I mean, that's what *Soccer Supremo* thinks."

"What?"

"You're in the game! They finally put you in. You're player-manager."

Holy shit. I'd put myself in *Champion Manager*, and that had made me a super player. But now I was in the modern version of that game. Wait wait wait—did that mean . . . would it *override*? Would I take on the numbers that the game gave me? That would be absolutely bonkers, but . . . Tactics 7 . . . I mean, I knew seven formations . . .

"Gosh," I said snootily. "I'm in the game? I don't remember selling my image rights. And they put me low on tactics? Oh, dear. I thought they made an effort to get those numbers accurate."

"Yours are pretty dire." He had taken screenshots of my profile, because of course he had. He swung his phone up.

"How many times have I told you not to shove a phone in my face?"

"None."

"You know blue light melts my brain. Sake. Tell me with your *words*. Acceleration?"

"Eight."

"The fuck?" I laughed. I was instantly *fairly* sure the new numbers weren't controlling me. I was speeding up on a daily basis, and could sometimes blast past my opponents in training. But then again . . . most of them were twelve years old. "Pace?"

"Six."

"Handsomeness?"

"That's not in it. I could just show you the—"

"I get it. It's all shit."

"Well, you've got high *xcccccsssss*." The last sound came out all weird and evil. Obviously he'd said one of the attributes I hadn't unlocked yet. No word had ever been censored by the curse in this way, but I supposed it was different if said naturally versus if said in relation to *Soccer Supremo* or *Champion Manager*.

"Finishing."

"Five."

"Huh," I said. So that would explain why I couldn't lash the ball into the goal like I used to. Another explanation was that I'd recently been nearly killed and was learning to use my body again. But but but . . . there *were* days I felt like I'd hit a ceiling . . .

So then who had given me such low numbers? Someone with a grudge like Folke Wester or Bradley Rymarquis could have got to the scouts who sent in player reports and convinced them to give me a bad rating. To annoy me, not realising it could literally determine what level of player I was.

"What's my current ability?"

He swiped through his screenshots. "Sorry, what? What's that? That's not on the player profile."

I pondered. My human adversaries probably didn't think about *Soccer Supremo* more than once a year. It was more likely that Old Nick had given me low attributes to keep my level of fame down. To make me less interesting. If another demon saw me doing crazy tekkers, Nick could say, 'Well these actual football experts think he's shit.' Something like that. But was I limited by these numbers, or not?

"So it's got my manager profile as well. If I remember right there's something like judging player ability."

Tyson swiped. "Yeah, you've got four."

Okay, so that *probably* put paid to the idea that my skills were in any way linked to a new set of numbers. "What a load of bollocks," I said. "Go flirt. Keep it classy."

He was reluctant to leave suddenly. He had something on his mind. "Er . . ." I was pleased to see he hesitated more with me than with his headmaster. "There's a rumour you're going to train with us. The sixteens."

"That a question, bro?"

"Are you going to train with us?"

"That would ruin the illusion, wouldn't it? Pace three, acceleration two, wizarding one. Nah. I'm already training with the first team."

He nodded. Slightly disappointed, he walked off towards the hotties. Halfway there, he smiled at one of them, raised a finger, and turned away to take a phone call. There was no question in my mind that it was fake. I imagined him telling her it was Bob Geldof. The absolute shit.

The referee's shorts and training top were resplendent with the school's logo—a fox or a pine marten or a particularly ferocious squirrel. This guy was almost certainly the head of P.E., though here he was probably called the Games Master. He checked his watch, and suddenly I was getting the player profiles. I nearly burst out laughing. Tyson, loverboy, the smooth operator, wasn't even the best player in his age group at his own school. Crazy stuff.

With nine subs per team, there was a lot to see. There was the usual smattering of PA 2 to 10 players who I mentally assigned to the PA 1 category. And there were a few PA 11 to 20s, who again, I barely looked twice at. All these guys did was clog up my player search database.

There was one great prospect and two lesser lights.

But I was still trying to work out what the Morale perk had brought me, and with all these moody teenagers came a rainbow of emotions. After buying the perk, I'd seen eighty player profiles, and I was pretty sure I had now seen the entire morale spectrum. In addition to the five levels I'd seen, the lowest of which was Poor, I discovered Very Poor and Abysmal.

I briefly wondered if I should tell someone about the kid with abysmal morale. Like, a social worker or something. But how to explain it? *That kid looks a bit depressed, lol!* Yeah, hard pass. The kid was probably sad because someone told him we all live in a simulation and free will doesn't exist. Or because the Liverpool FC club shop was still doing brisk business in the centre of town.

Or, more likely, he was depressed because his idiot P.E. teacher had put him in completely the wrong position for this, his big chance to impress a real football insider.

I made small talk with Joe and Steve for a while, but they felt me getting restless.

"Max, what's up?" said Joe.

"It's all wrong. Players out of positions. These P.E. teachers trying to do funky formations to impress me. Sometimes four-four-two is best, know what I mean? It's not about you, it's about the kids. Holy fuck."

Joe began singing, "Let it go, let it goooo."

"I know! I'm letting it go. Look at me. Look how chill I am. It's impressive." I made some clicking noises while I had a think. "The best player's a sub, though. I want to get him on. How do I do that without being a bull in a china shop?"

"Which one?" said Steve.

"Tall, gangly one." I needed to get the kid's name in a non-curse way. I waved at Tyson, who came over. "How's it going?"

"Oh, pretty dull. They can't move through the thirds. Their positional discipline is pretty dogshit."

I glared at him. "I know. I'm asking how it's going with you and your harem."

"A gentleman does not kiss and tell," he said, and that got him a low five from Steve and Joe. More potential traitors!

"Tall, lanky kid over there. Warming up over on Team Excelsior."

"Team B. Yes, that's Fungus."

"What?"

"Charles Fungrieve. We all call him Fungus."

"Not anymore."

"Oh. Oh, right. Um . . . do you like him? He's . . ."

"What?"

"I mean, he's all right. Not good enough for Chester."

For the first time in a long time, I doubted myself. The stupid *Soccer Supremo* conversation! If I had judging player ability 4, then there was a 16 in 20 chance I'd get a player's PA badly wrong. Right? I couldn't think like that—I had to trust the information I had. So I pretended to be as cocky as always. "Tyson Bulldog, preferred foot right, teamwork twenty, judging player ability one."

He frowned and scratched the back of his head. "Okay. That's . . . I don't see it, but . . ."

I spoke to the three guys. "I could invite him to training, or Tyson could. What's best?"

"You," said everyone.

"Sure?"

"Yes," said everyone.

I sighed. Seemed like something that could be delegated in a fun way. "I suppose I should wait till after the match. Tyson, can you make sure he gets on the pitch at halftime?"

"Yes, I think so." He started to make his way around the pitch. "Oh. What position?"

"Are you joking? Striker."

"Striker? Fun . . . Charles is a striker?"

I slapped my hips, being driven fake-crazy by all this insubordination. "What the fuck is happening right now?" Tyson smiled and scampered away.

While I waited for my prospect to enter the fray, I chatted with Joe and Steve. Asked them how they were doing, tried to remember some details about them so I could chat like a real boy. I nearly texted Emma to get some tips from her, but once I stopped trying so hard, the conversation flowed better.

Joe said he *quite* liked the album I'd talked about and accused me of enjoying "soundscapes." Steve said he was glad he'd joined the club but thought he'd have played more minutes by now. I nodded. He was still three points of CA behind Gerald May, though, and Gerald was taller which meant other teams double-marked him on corners. Which was dumb so I encouraged it.

"Are *you* in *Soccer Supremo?*" I asked him.

"Everyone is," said Steve. "Last time I looked, they'd given me positioning six. That's a piss take. I haven't looked at it since."

I laughed. "If you had positioning six in real life, I never would have signed you."

At halftime we circulated, meeting parents and signing Chester tops and being in selfies and stuff. A whistle signalled the second half would start soon.

"Ah, mint, he's coming on," I said. "Wonder if Tyson learned to sweet-talk people from the school or from his dad."

"Nature versus nurture," said Joe. "But Max, *you* didn't learn it from school, and you didn't get it from, you know, your dad. So why are you good at talking to people?"

Because a demon gave me influence 20. "I think it's because when I talk, I talk from the heart."

He laughed. "You're so full of shit."

I got serious. "I think what it is, is that I really believe if we pull together, towards a common goal, and if we're in a good mood, and there's a good vibe, we can achieve anything."

Steve and Joe took this garbage at face value, and they seemed impressed, but their morale didn't change.

Huh, I thought. If I'm going to try those little speeches, I should save them for guys with bad morale.

Charles Fungrieve was a thin, awkward fourteen-year-old, so tall that he had trained himself to slouch and to bend his neck. The curse said he had good heading, poor jumping, decent technique and passing, plus good finishing. He was CA 1, of course, but PA 83. A PA 83 striker? Local lad? Incredible. If he bulked up, he could become an absolute fucking menace all the way up to League Two. "Lads, every time the ball goes anywhere near that kid, whatever he does, we all look at each other and nod and look impressed. You with me?"

"Yes, boss."

We stuck to the plan, but it was hard—Fungrieve had a nightmare. The ball hated him, when he accelerated it took months for his arms and legs to get coordinated, and when he got the chance to do a header—which should have been his speciality—the ball bounced off at a mad angle.

"Max, you sure about this?" said Joe, as he did an over-the-head clap followed by a thumbs-up.

"He's got a fifty-pee head," said Steve, a reference to one of my top five favourite British coins—the heptagonal fifty-pence piece.

In short, it was literally impossible that someone could have watched Charles play and thought that guy could be twice as good as Tony Hetherington. I probably should have left it and signed him another day, when no one was looking and when I was sure the curse was working properly, but fuck it. Time is money and all that.

After the final whistle, I gestured for Charles to come away from his post-match debrief. "Hey, buddy. I'm Max."

"I know. You're famous."

"I'm both famous and in-famous," I said, saying it wrong. He opened his mouth to correct me but thought better of it. "Good decision. How do you like this school?"

"It's got good facilities," he said diplomatically.

"It's got a star footballer who gets all the girls," I said.

He nodded. Apparently without bitterness, he said, "Tyson. I read that article about you two."

"Whoa!" I said, laughing, holding my hands up. "It was about me, solo. Tyson was like a special guest villain."

"Max," said Joe.

"Chas," I said. "Would you like to be a footballer and get all the girls—respectfully and not problematically, of course—and be famous and be on big posters and be one of the people who gets chosen to go on the escape rocket to Alpha Centauri?"

"Um . . . yes? To some of those. I'd be more excited to go to *Proxima Centauri.*"

"Yeah, that ship's full. Jesus Christ, he's not even a footballer yet and he's making crazy demands. I'm going to get Tyson to bring you to training, all right? Monday, Wednesday, Friday. You'll need to sign a document that says any magazine articles we're both in, you waive the right to call yourself the star."

"Max."

"I mean," said Charles. "Sure. Yes, of course! Yes! Not tonight, sorry. I'm babysitting my little sister. But . . . Chas? Why?"

"Charles is too long. Takes too long to say. Football's fast, dynamic. You need a short name for when your mates are calling you. Ste! Joe! Max! French dude! Chas!"

"Chas and Charles are both one syllable."

"Charl . . . sssssss," I said, ending all discussion.

With a future Chester legend in the bag, I set off in the direction of the other team. They were heading towards the changing rooms, but slowly, in case I wanted to sign one of them too. As luck would have it, I did.

That team actually had two decent players, both fifteen years old. One was a left back slash left mid with PA 29. The other was a PA 25 goalie. Neither would make it as a pro, but they would round out the under-sixteens squad quite nicely. I brought them away from the rest of the kids.

"Lads. You two are good at football. I'd like you to train with our under-sixteens." Their morales both smashed to Superb instantly. "Yep yep yep. Now, listen. Our sixteens are really good. Really good. Even then, half of them won't make it as pros. Right? I don't think either of you are ever going to play for Manchester United." Although the state that club was in, maybe they *would*. "What I'm saying is, come train with us. We'll teach you to play, we'll see how fast you pick things up, whatnot. You'll get some game time, you'll go to tournaments, all that fun stuff. It's a laugh. And whatever happens, for the rest of your lives, you'll boss your Sunday Leagues and your five-a-sides. What do you reckon?"

They reckoned yes, please.

Three new signings! A good day's work. Max Best, morale: superbissimo.

Joe wanted to hang around and do some more networking—he was handing out business cards for his DJ side hustle. Rich kid birthday parties, DJed by a local football star—sounded like a good business model.

Steve hovered around me, doing a good job at being my bodyguard; he was escorting me to my car. "How was that, Steve? Not too bad?"

"Yeah, bit weird. All right, though, yeah. Community service. Knew what I was getting into."

I happened to glance at him as his forehead twitched. "What?"

"Just . . . what you said to those two. That they wouldn't play for Man U. You've got to have hope, though. At that age."

I shrugged. "They've got hope. They won't play for our first team, not while I'm in charge. But they could play for a team like Tadcaster Albion. They could play in the FA Cup." I smiled as I said it, and Steve smiled, too. We didn't know each other too well, but we knew we each had a romantic inside of us. "For players like that, Chester will be a school. Football school. We'll give them an education, and what they do with it is up to them."

"Like Ajax."

"What?"

"Ajax. They do it. They've got, like, a thousand youth teams all over Amsterdam. They teach everyone."

I stopped still, causing Steve's hands to curl into fists. "What? Where?"

I put my hand on his arm, calming him. "Sorry, man. My fault. It's all good. It's all good." He relaxed, and again he got loads of relationship points with me. "No, it was what you said. I . . . I had that same thought ages ago. So much has happened since then. But I had that idea. Hundreds of kids. Thousands. Coaches as far as the eye can see. I'm still looking for the stars, but these other kids. Why not? Why not train them up?"

"Money."

I bit my thumb. "Yeah. Soon, though. Soon." I brightened up. "Hey!"

"What?"

"You know how we can fill our stadium every week?"

"With you playing right wing?"

More relationship points! "If we've got a thousand kids in the youth system, that's two thousand parents probably coming to every home game!"

Steve Alton, CA 34, PA 53, who I bought for eight thousand pounds, who never went to a good school, shook his head. "I'm not sure the economics of that scenario stack up in your favour, boss."

I offered him a hug. Surprised, he took it. "Call me Max. Unless, you know, there's some reason to be formal. And Steve . . . thanks."

"For what?"

"For bodyguarding me! I know it's weird."

He smiled and shook his head. His morale went to Superb. "It's one of the only things about you that makes complete sense." His smile faded ever so slightly as he looked around at the few schoolkids who were still around, their green blazers turning to a dull grey as the clouds came overhead. "So you're going to be all right?"

I smiled. "Yeah. I'll park outside the vegan restaurant. Safest place in Cheshire."

At six, I saw Tyson again, for I had lied to him about going to the under-sixteens training. The new kids weren't there—it was too short notice for that. First, though, I hid at the side, taking in their morale.

I'd started to think numerically, converting the words into numbers.

Superb	7
Very Good	6
Good	5
OK	4
Poor	3
Very Poor	2
Abysmal	1

If my maths was right, the first team squad had an average morale of 6.14 (out of 7). It was hard to imagine that getting much higher, just because there were so many Superbs and Very Goods. The sixteens though, with the drama caused by Noah Harrison's arrival, had an average morale of 4.1. Interestingly, Noah's was the lowest of them all.

When I turned up to train, though, the morale increase was dramatic. Noah, for example, went from Very Poor to Good—a three-point climb.

We did the drills and played a small-sided match at the end. I was starting to reliably do all the basics, and as my fitness was getting better, so was my decision-making. Annoyingly, I was much better defensively than as a creative, attacking force. Getting in someone's way was easy. Chipping a lofted pass between two defenders with a soupçon of side spin so that it'd land on the striker's preferred foot . . . is even more complicated than it sounds. It needs a lot of high-level attributes working in tandem.

During the match, I kept an eye out for any signs of friction between Noah and the others, but couldn't see anything. The quality was really coming along, though. The under-sixteens had Tyson, leading the way on CA 9, Benny, Lucas Friend (the left back who wanted to be a goalie), Dan Badford (who had that strange -1 PA), and, of course, Noah himself.

And after the match, there was no sign of anything untoward—they all ran off, excited and happy, to the showers. Maybe they didn't rush to include Noah in their chats, but they didn't obviously exclude him, either.

Baffling.

I went over to watch the women train. Our new recruit was there.

@ChesterFC

Chester FC are stupendously amazingly ecstatic to announce that Kisi Yalley has joined on a short-term loan from Manchester Actual City. Chief copywriter Max Best says, "Yeah, it's Youngster's little sister. What to expect? Imagine the opposite of Youngster. That's how she plays. Also: she's funny and you're allowed to say Tuesday when you meant Wednesday without your head being bitten off. I shouldn't say this but she's my favourite."

Kisi's effect on morale was almost as good as mine!

Maybe it was her big smile, her on-the-ball skills (she'd eased to CA 14 in her time at City), or the fact that Youngster and Pascal had come to watch her train—whatever it was, she brought the good vibes.

Kisi's arrival added half a point on average to the squad's morale. Half a point! It was still new to me, but half a point across a squad of fourteen seemed like finding-a-twenty-pound-note-in-your-old-jeans levels of happiness.

Knowing what I knew about Kisi, the increase made sense, but now I needed to know exactly what morale did! It would be hard to measure the effect of morale on training, though it made sense to assume players trained better when their morale was high. It also made sense that players with shit morale would play worse in matches. Testing needed.

The vibe was so fun that I decided I'd join in, for my third training session of the day. Burnout? WHAT'S THAT?

But just as I was getting stuck into the first rondos, holding my own against Mel—whose increase in morale had lasted since I texted her in the morning—plus Erin, Kisi, and Bea Pea, my phone rang.

"Max," said Jill. "Your phone."

"Ignore it. It's Bob Geldof asking me to explain K-Pop."

"It's Emma."

"Huh."

Emma had been weird for a while. Obviously busy at work, but also obviously avoiding football matches. Which meant avoiding me. I was giving her time and space and trying not to catastrophise about it. But the way she'd been cool about postponing our anniversary, in retrospect, seemed suss.

I picked up and wandered to the edge of the sports hub. "Hey, bebs."

"Max, we need to talk."

My heart sank. My heart sank to the bottom of the ocean, waved at the *Titanic*, then kept going, down the Mariana Trench, and through a little crevice into the molten core of the earth itself. "Okay."

She took a deep breath. "You know we've been swamped on this Greggs case." Greggs was a wildly popular baker famous for its sausage rolls. I found their stuff a bit dry, but almost everyone I knew went weak at the knees for the sausage rolls. Emma's company had been doing some legal stuff for them. Legal stuff as dry as the flakes of pastry that—you know what? No time for half-baked similes. Emma was about to break up with me.

"So last Monday," she started.

"Our anniversary," I said, aghast that the coming betrayal would start on our special day.

"Yes," she said, matter-of-fact. "I take some papers to the coffee shop, like I always do on my break, and as I look for a good spot, there's a cute guy sitting at the counter."

"I am coping with this conversation very well," I said, as I ate the phone and went to live in a monastery, forever, with my stomach slowly dissolving the memory card that contained every detail of our shared life.

She kept going as though I hadn't said anything, probably because I hadn't actually said anything. "Anyway, I sit, get to work, absorbed in the legal drama, you know."

"Yes." I think I said that. Not sure. It was like she'd slapped my brain into a blender and was turning the speed up and down.

"Suddenly, there's a couple of blokes on my little sofa bit. Couple of lads."

Hold up. Both *blokes* and *lads* were bad. Suddenly, the cute guy at the counter didn't sound so ominous.

"I'm knee deep in enterprise interruption rulings when I realise they're . . . you know . . . overstepping. Like, one guy's way too close and the other takes the doc I was reading out of my hand, starts looking through it, says I have to impress him to get it back. And it reminded me so much of Tranmere and half my head was thinking about how to argue the case and half was thinking, shit, I shouldn't have brought these documents out of the office, if these guys run off with them, Dad's going to kill me."

"What."

"So suddenly the cute guy's there, and he gets all John Smith on them, and they say they were just being friendly and he says maybe they want to be friendly to his friends Fuck and Off and they clear out and I check all the papers are still there and I'm freaking out but it's all fine."

She took a deep breath. The story had gone from blender setting 1 to 3 and back to 1, but I'd turned it all the way up to 4 as soon as she said "we have to talk." So . . . it was nothing. Nothing happened. I could . . . relax?

"I calm down a bit and I'm about to rush back to the office but then it's like fuck no! This is my spot, I won't be ladded out. And the guy's just there at the counter, not even trying to look at me or use it to get my number or any of the usual. So I say thanks and we start chatting."

WHAT BRAIN HAS BEEN BLENDED ON LEVEL SEVEN CAN NEVER BE MADE WHOLE.

"And okay he's cute but he's funny and interesting and all that. You'd like him."

Not a chance in hell I'd like him. "Yes," I said, because women like it when you're positive.

"And we get talking and I mention you and how you played in Darlington." How the fuck did that come up? And wait, Emma mentioned me? The ex-boyfriend. "And he was like, oh what a ride! I'm going there soon, what should I look out for? Turns out he's Australian, doing a tour of the UK. So I tell him about the market and those alleys with the fun shops and stuff like that."

"And then you porked, and you've been porking non-stop for a week and he's your porcupine now and you lied about being busy. I get it. Goodbye forever."

"Max?"

"Still here."

"Oh. So that was that, but when I went back—"

"Wait, what?"

"What what?"

"That was that?"

"Yeah I took my stuff back to the office, forgot all about it. But the next day I thought about going to the coffee shop, stick to my routine, you know? And I went and he wasn't there and neither were the creeps but . . . *He knew who you were.*"

My head was literally in billions of little bits, and I was still trying to process the revelation that—talk about a shit cliffhanger—there WAS no revelation. She went back to the office, end of story? "Rugby's massive in Australia. They probably have streets named after me."

She giggled—the bizarre, discordant twinkling of an angel. "Silly Max." She went right back to the we-have-to-talk voice, and I realised she was going through a morale blender of her own. "But don't you see? The whole thing was a setup. They were trying to get dirt on you, and I gave it to them."

"Er . . . three questions. Who *they*?"

"One of your many enemies. Based on the questions . . . that new Darlington manager."

What? "Question two. They were trying to get dirt on me?"

"Yeah it was so subtle at first, but when I thought about it later he asked me about things that I hadn't told him about. Like when you took over the team at halftime. I only mentioned that match because of the alleys and our first date and you were tired so we went slow and really savoured it. So when he asked what really happened at halftime, I didn't think anything of it. But later, it clicked. If all this was new to him, how did he know about things like that? So . . . yeah. And I know question three. Yeah, I'm afraid I said some indiscreet things. Private things you told me." She took a shuddering breath. "I'm sorry."

Absolutely a billion questions, but only one real one—are we still porcupines? "I'm going to Manchester tomorrow evening. Doing some special training with Raffi, and meeting up with Mateo after. I'm helping him out with a former player on Wednesday morning so he's booked me a nice hotel. Do you want to come?"

"But Max! I've made a big mess. They're coming after you and I've made it easy."

Emma as a traitor? By telling some rando she'd never meet again some funny stories about her awesome boyfriend? It was . . . not ideal, but it was just a cool and chill woman being cool and chill. I was over it almost instantly. "There's a continental breakfast. Just don't eat the scrambled eggs. Heard some shocking things about hotel eggs. On a Tottenham fan podcast, would you believe it."

"Max!"

"Emma. They put me in *Soccer Supremo* with shit stats. It's probably that. But imagine there's a big article that comes out about me. Either it's all true, in which case I can only blame myself. Or it's all lies and then you did nothing wrong. I am having a great week. Let them take their best shot. I'll get through it if you're there with me, dipping croissants into your coffee like an absolute savage."

"So you're not mad at me?"

"I can never get mad at you."

"You got mad at me when I let the handle of the mug poke off the edge of the table."

"Well, yeah, but come on. That's justified."

"And when I overtook that bus."

"We watched a Bond movie and you were so amped up you overtook two buses in one move!" I took a pause. Pottered around—my legs still worked. The blender had shaken me up but left me intact. I was shivering from having been working out and then standing still for so long. "Let me know if you're coming. I'll dress nice if you are."

"I'm coming," she said, suddenly. "We can have it as our anniversary."

"Oh."

"What?"

"Nothing, I was just thinking of what special stuff we could do. What I can show you from Manchester."

"Don't overthink it. Let's see where the wind blows us."

Where the wind blew us was somewhere I'd never set foot before yet was rooted in my past, was filled with important people from my present, and contained a surprising amount of my future.

15

HOMESCHOOLED, PART TWO

Tuesday, September 19.

XP balance: 169

Lung capacity: 3.8 litres (+0.5)

No. of girlfriends: 1

Tartlets eaten: 1

Nights since last pine marten satanic ritual: 0

Properties magnetted: 0

I did training from the start through to the end, even though Vimsy had scheduled some shuffling and sliding practice. I shuffled and slid like a good and diligent boy. It didn't really help solve the mystery of whether I'd been given a new set of attributes, but it definitely helped me integrate with the team. We defended in an Ian Evans style, which differed slightly from the David Cutter style I'd learned at Darlington. The main difference was that Evans was more fearful of crosses, either by instinct or because he knew Gerald May wasn't as good in the air as he looked. To combat that, the wide midfielders stayed a little wider when defending (so they could block crosses). In theory, that weakened us in the centre, but teams in our league didn't have a lot of creative midfielders, plus we usually had a DM.

After lunch, some of the guys wanted to go back to do set pieces training. I didn't want to do headers, and didn't have the power and accuracy to take a free kick or corner, so I went home and got stuck into my year-long UEFA B licence. With all the materials I'd gathered from people who'd already done it, I hoped to breeze through until the practical aspects.

Then it was off to the birthplace of the greatest living Englishman.

Chorlton! South Manchester, got a tram route through it, interesting mix of deprived and hipster. Hough End playing fields, where I'd started my journey towards being a floating megabrain, was in Chorlton, as was the hideous Nell Lane Estate where I grew up.

In fact, let's do a tiny mental map. First, imagine a hell hole with characterless grey-yellow brick houses. That's the Hell Lane Estate. Clamber across the tram line and you're at the vast Hough End playing fields and the enclosed pitch used by the police. Keep going and there's Princess Parkway, one of the main routes through Manchester. And across the road, if a maniac doesn't run you over, is Moss Side. Go the long way back to Nell Lane and you'll see the vast expanse that is Southern Cemetery, where my mum and I will one day be buried.

Raffi Brown had invited me to join one of his private training sessions not far from where most of the early action in this story happened. Fortunately, it was in a much nicer part of Chorlton, near Nell Lane, but much closer to the "village" with all its hipster bars and restaurants.

There were a few football pitches, some basketball and tennis courts, and lots of people jogging through. Perfect conditions for a bit of exercise—gentle sun, light breeze, everyone in a good mood.

The coach Raffi had hired was called Cody Chambers. We didn't talk much before the session but his accent was strange—a little from North America, a little from down south (London, not Brazil), and a lot of those verbal tics people get when they spend a lot of time talking to foreigners, such as using the word *this* instead of *it*. "I like two-footed players. This is a good attribute."

So we put our boots on and got ready to work. While Cody told us what he had prepared, I pondered his coaching profile.

CODY CHAMBERS	
Adaptability	10
Coaching Goalkeepers	12
Coaching Outfield Players	19
Determination	11
Judging Player Ability	15
Judging Player Potential	12
Level of Discipline	6
Man Management	8
Motivating	5
Tactical Knowledge	14
Working with Youngsters	9
Coaching Style	Technique-based
Preferred Formation	4-3-3
Preferred Style	Attractive attacking play
Other	Likes his players to close down the opposition

This guy was by far the best coach I'd met since unlocking the staff profiles, and I had *questions*. The first of which was, will you marry me? Or at least, will you come and be a full-time coach? Name your price.

But I decided to keep my mouth shut and get on with the session he'd planned. That was very hard because every five seconds I wanted to say, why are we doing this? Why don't you put another cone there? What's this for? Why do you do it like this and not that? But Raffi was paying and I'd probably learn more if I kept my gob shut.

Three of Raffi's mates were helping slash hindering. One was recording the sesh on his phone, one was ready to be a goalie, and another was helping to gather the balls and stuff. They copied the drills off to the side, getting a bit of free training when we were taking a breather. None of the three looked familiar, but when we started the warm-up, I got their player profiles, too, and found I already knew them—they were from Raffi's old five-a-side team. "Remembering" their names got me a lot of brownie points.

The warm-up was quite basic—jogging along, rolling a ball as we went, with Cody yelling "Inside outside!" and asking us to keep the ball "straight" as we pushed it along. Then what he called U-turns—dragging the ball back and feeding it to the other foot—with Cody asking for "less V more U." What was interesting, I realised later, was what he *didn't* include in the warm-up. There were no sprints, for example. The only things we did without the ball were a few lunges and crabbing stretches.

After a simple passing drill where we had to manoeuvre left and right behind the mannequin, it was into the meat of the sesh. Cody wanted Raffi to work on his cutbacks. He'd put a mannequin at the edge of the penalty area, and Raffi had to touch it, take a few steps back, control a pass with his right foot, move right, then cut back—basically, turn around really fast—towards the other side of the pitch. After an explosive burst away from an imaginary opponent, Raffi was supposed to flick the ball forward to Cody, run around the mannequin, then take Cody's return pass and hit a low left-footed pass slash shot into either the bottom left or bottom right of the goal.

Raffi did this five times, and each time Cody asked for his movements to be bigger, more dramatic, more dynamic. The more explosive Raffi's movements were, the more praise he got from Cody. At times, they seemed to be talking in code—drills from previous sessions being referenced.

While Raffi rested, I had a go. I did the first couple pretty slowly to get the movements down, then put a bit more effort in, and for the last one tried to add that explosive movement that Cody wanted. "There we go!" he called out in his coaching voice.

To my surprise, we did the whole thing again. Then one more time where we moved to the other side of the mannequin, testing our other feet.

We'd done one tiny drill for what felt like fifteen or twenty minutes about one very specific incident that *might* come up in a match.

Then we had to touch the mannequin, Cody would throw a ball up, and Raffi would head it away as far as possible, and then do the previous drill *again*.

It was crazy to me.

I didn't want to do the headers—didn't feel like blending my brain, so Cody adapted it. His throws to me were chest height. I'd control the ball, volley it back to him, then sprint back five yards to begin the cutback cycle.

What's hard to convey is the fatigue of doing variations of the same drill for an hour. Not the boredom, because it wasn't boring. No, the fatigue in the calves, the way my thighs burned. I could only guess what I looked like, but Cody often shouted things like "Smooth!" and "That's good shape!" But Raffi got very ragged almost immediately. In a set of five, his first would be okay, his second would be flawless, his third sloppy, and his fourth and fifth poor.

We kept at it, kept doing our reps with Cody demanding more technical quality from Raffi and more explosions from me. After three-quarters of an hour, Raffi's CA popped to 43. My eyes narrowed, mate. I made sure I was sucking up *all* the coaching ideas while pushing myself as hard as my body could handle.

All in all, the session was seventy minutes—I guessed Raffi had paid for an hour and Cody had stayed a bit longer to make sure we both had decent workouts. I was only a sixth-tier manager, but I was a manager. No harm in getting on my good side!

After my last set of reps, I sank to the astroturf and lay on my back for a while. I wasn't sure I'd ever played on this exact pitch before, but this was where I'd learned the game. This was my home. What had Jackie said that time? Sometimes you need to go home. I hoped he was in Liverpool, saying 'la' and going to the shell suit history museum. Yeah, home felt good sometimes. I closed my eyes, and felt so at peace I could have slept.

Cody and Raffi were chatting about some technical aspect, Raffi's mates were trying to do the drills—the difference between them and Raffi was astonishing; they were terrible. On other pitches around us, there were games going on. I turned my head and saw a PA 18 midfielder. Local lad. Manc. Little bit of talent. Not enough to be paid to play, but he could be trained up. Would he want to be the best player in almost every game he ever played? Course he would. But who would waste resources on a project like that? Me, maybe.

I turned to the other side and scanned Raffi. He'd come a long way since his first masterclass with Jackie Reaper.

RAFFI BROWN		
Born 8.8.2001	(Age 22)	English
Acceleration 9		
	Handling 1	Stamina 8
	Heading 9	Strength 8
		Tackling 6
	Jumping 9	Teamwork 14
Bravery 6		Technique 10
	Pace 11	preferred foot B

	Passing 14	
Dribbling 8	Positioning 7	
Finishing 7		
CA 43	PA 139	
Midfielder (Centre)		

All his physical stats had gone up. He was faster, stronger, and had more stamina. His technical scores were all better, too. Dribbling, passing, finishing—he was improving in all respects.

And there was much more to come—almost a hundred points of CA! He caught me smiling at him and smiled back. He walked over and held out a hand—I grabbed his wrist and he pulled me up.

"Good, that?"

"Yeah. Top. Loved it. I need to talk Cody's head off before he fucks off."

"Thought you might."

"One thing. What are you paying him?"

"Three-fifty a sesh. Twice a month."

"Holy shit. Three-fifty?" This Cody dude was earning almost what I got in a week . . . in an hour. Not for the first time, I realised I was in the wrong racket.

"Investing in myself. That's a good price. He gave me a discount for this season. Someone told him I was up and coming."

Again, I didn't think to ask who. "Cody," I said, as we stood close by, squirting water into our mouths. "Good sesh. Let's cut to the chase. Are you willing to take an enormous pay cut to work for Chester?"

He laughed. "Sorry, Max. I like a cheeky dollar same as the next fella, but it's not that. I love what I do. Travelling the world teaching. Passing on my skills. Working with elite athletes. Elite athletes and you." He laughed again. It was good banter, but it made me wonder how much he was joking.

"Did you ever play *Champion Manager*?"

"Oh, yeah, back in the day. Not for years, though."

"What about you, Raffi?"

"Nah, Max. That's for *indoor* people." He laughed.

"What's your *Soccer Supremo* technique score?"

"Eight," he said instantly. Cody looked down to help hide his smile.

"Cody, what would you say? Eight out of twenty for Raffi?"

"Technique? It's not a *bad* guess. I think he's a bit better, to be honest. I don't know. Ten." Ooh! Right on the money!

"What about me?"

"You?" he laughed. "I mean, I've seen footage. You're pure twenty."

"Ignore that. What about today?" I realised I was sounding a bit needy. "I want to play on Saturday but I don't know if I'm deluding myself about how fast my recovery's going."

"Right," said Cody, switching into professional mode. "The attack. I can't get my head around this." He switched from the past to the present. "I mean, I don't think in terms of those *Champion Manager* numbers, but from what I saw today you'd be fifteen or so."

"Fifteen?" I said, stupefied. "I was in a coma ten minutes ago."

He pointed to the spot we'd done most of our work. "What you do on the fifth rep is almost identical to what you do on the first. This is not common."

I'd thought enough about *Soccer Supremo* for one season. Time to get to the important stuff. The guys who'd booked the pitch after us started to arrive, so we grabbed our gear and wandered towards the car park. "Why do you do so much repetition? Don't you want to, like, work a few different skills?"

Cody shook his head. "Nah, what we do here is what you can't do in your club training. You can't give such individual attention, really get into the weeds. This is the advantage of what I do. Players hate the repetition, but they love it. Keep coming back. Really work on real-match situations. It's very motivational to work on something you *need* to get good at. This is my USP."

"Why do you do the final pass into the goal? Why not to another mannequin?"

"Goal's more motivational. This is the point of football, no?"

"Why do you want those big, explosive movements? I prefer to keep the ball near me."

"Raffi's athletic. You back him to travel over a distance better than most. Break the press, break the lines, but he's still protecting the ball. Better to go too big than too small. *You* might be better keeping the ball close, but Raffi's better the other way. No defender in the world can beat him over those three yards."

I shook my head. I loved this. Jackie, the traitor, should have been giving me this. "So I can't get you as a coach. How about you manage my women's team?"

"Thanks, but no."

"Annoying. What about private sessions for me? I need to learn, like, fundamentals. Throw-ins. Players grappling me."

"Staying onside," said Raffi, who thought that was the funniest thing anyone had ever said.

"I watched some video of you," said Cody. "You are lazy getting back."

"Me?" I said, astonished.

"Yeah, you walk back. Could be more opportunities if you got onside quicker."

I raised my eyebrows. The guy didn't seem to realise that I was using those moments to check match ratings, switch formations, and order substitutions. But who else was going to give me their honest opinion? Even the Brig wouldn't yell at me if I was dogging the running drills. "Check this out. Raffi does six till seven. I do seven till eight. We pay three hundred each. That's savings for us, double the money for the same travel time for you."

Cody liked it. "Done. You want me to come to Chester?"

I shook my head. "Sometimes it's good to get home. Right, Raffi?" He nodded. "Let's do it here unless I'm super, super rammed."

"Which is always," said Raffi.

"No," I said, in a mock-annoyed tone. "Because I'm actually crushing everything and things are only getting easier. My life is moving rapidly towards simplicity. All right?"

"All right," said Raffi, smirking. For some reason, he didn't believe me.

We had a shower and got changed. I asked what Raffi's plans were—obviously to go and hang out with his five-a-side mates. But he surprised me.

"My cousin's playing for West."

"West?"

"West Didsbury and Chorlton," he said. "Little team here. Then we'll scran up at one of these places."

"Can I come? To the match, I mean."

He looked surprised. "Thought you was gonna meet Emma?"

"She can come here. See where I grew up. It's just down Princess Parkway."

"Huh. Well, come on, then. Hey, Scribe. Go with Max, tell him where to park."

"Aight," said Scribe, who turned out to be a world-class navigator, leading me along Barlow Moor Road and down some side streets. We parked and cut through an alley, coming out into another, leaf-lined alley, that opened onto fields and grass verges and then the River Mersey. I'd never been there before. Never even knew this place existed.

"This is cool" I said, impressed.

"Yeah. Middle class likes it leafy," said Scribe. "It's a conservation area. Got bats and stuff."

"And hedges," I said, running my palm across the leaves of the nearest one like I was nine years old. "I was at a posh school yesterday that had its own hedge maze."

He shook his head. "Eat the rich."

"Totally," I said. "Until I'm rich. Then let's give trickle-down economics another try."

He chuckled. "You been good for Raffi. We all rooting for him."

"He's got the talent," I said. "But he grafts harder than anyone in the squad."

We came to a football pitch with some floodlights around it. To the right there was a little stand. Across was a row of houses—the big semi-detached ones I always used to look at and dream of owning. "Raffi parks over there. He's a creative player, but off the pitch?" He sucked his teeth. "Conventional."

"Suppose it's better to be a bit boring if you're raising a kid."

"Suppose," he said, then lifted himself over the fence.

"Jesus," I said. I was wearing my best suit, and my nicest shoes. "Why?"

"Quicker. And cheaper." Scribe grinned.

"I get in free anyway, you dick." I looked to where he'd stood, where he'd placed his hands, and tentatively copied him. "Been a while since I did a crime."

Vague attempts to sort of daydream my way across the fence didn't work, so I took a couple of steps back, imagined Cody yelling at me to "Explode!" and "Focus on your technique!" And over I went.

Boom!

Nailed it!

Fence hopping 20.

Not quite the perfect crime, though. A player was in the area, retrieving a stray ball. "Oi," he said. "Get fucked. Go round the front or I'll deck you."

"Man, that's Max Best," said Scribe. "Director of football at Chester Football Club. Youngest DoF in Europe, man. Don't be yelling at him now. He's here to scout. Could be scouting you for all you know. Now hush your mouth."

The player wasn't buying it, and if anything had become angrier. Time to defuse the sitch.

"You're Leo Jackson," I said. "You play right mid for Glossop North End. Scored six goals last season."

Well, that fucking floored him. "Yeah, that's me. How the fuck . . . ? But why didn't you come in the front?"

"This prick made me park over there," I said, jabbing my thumb. "Can't be arsed walking all the way round."

"Who are you here to watch?"

"Ah," I said, smiling as I bent to wipe bits of shrub and grass off my legs. "That's confidential."

The player's morale rose one level and he zipped off to tell his mates. I wondered if I'd just won Glossop the game? I smiled. The morale perk had been well fucking worth the grind.

Scribe and I fell into walking down the side of the pitch. He side-eyed me. "Do you know everyone in this league or . . . ?"

"Just some right mids," I said. "Didn't think I'd be able to play this season, right? So we looked at all *kinds* of reprobates."

"That guy any good?"

"He's about as good as you."

"Hey!"

"Next time, we go in the front. Conventional. Okay?"

He sucked his teeth again. But Scribe had one thing right—we were much faster than Raffi, and I had a nice little walk around. The vibe was unbelievably friendly. UnbeLIEVably friendly. On my way round the pitch, five different people had a chat with me, and the queue for drinks was basically the happiest place on earth. The kiosk guy heard it was my first time and offered me a can of beer for free. I accepted and bought a water, then gave the beer to Scribe.

"First time I came here, I thought it was a joke," Scribe told me. "It's all ironic chants. It's all about the laughs and being supportive and inclusive. Not proper football, right?" He opened the can, and we both enjoyed the sound of the fizz. "But I was wrong. It's sweet here. It's like, you invite someone to come they say, 'Who's going?' Not, 'Who's playing?' See what I mean? It's like a rolling party. It's social."

"So pay to get in, you dick."

"Yeah," he said, hoist by his own petard.

"How much is it?"

"Fiver."

That was like being punched on the side of the head. It sent me spinning. Five pounds entry, cheap beer, friendly vibe, watch your local team. Emma hadn't been to a football stadium since the incident at Tranmere. West Didsbury and Chorlton Football Club would ease her back in, I was sure of it.

I texted her, the Brig, and even Mateo, then sent Bulldog a text asking him to ask Tyson what my *Soccer Supremo* technique score was. Then I went to get a snack from the healthiest kiosk I'd ever seen at a football match.

Emma and the Brig arrived just before the second half started, with Mateo and his driver not far behind. I went to get them, then dragged them to the most amazing place in Manchester.

"No time to explain!" I said, like I was in a movie. "Come quick!"

We rushed into the little metal box—smaller than Ruth's living room—that housed West's most vocal fans. I'd only been there for an hour and I knew everything about them.

I gathered my friends around, paused to check the tactics screens—not that the on-pitch action had any real interest for me—then launched into a giddy explanation of what was going on.

"This is West Didsbury and Chorlton Football Club. Their fans call them West. This is Brookburn Road, the Recreation Ground. Used to be an overgrown mess, disused, an eyesore, but now it's the base for a proper community club."

"There's Raffi," said Emma, idiosyncratically looking anywhere but the pitch.

"Yeah, his cousin's playing."

"Is he good?"

"No. This is tier nine. But it doesn't matter. Everyone's having fun. This is the best place, the actual best. The atmosphere is mint. They've got an openly gay goalkeeper. All the work I've done on culture, there's still no chance one of my male players would come out. This club's miles ahead of us. It's five-pound entry, cheap food, the players high-five the fans and you're allowed to drink right here by the pitch." I shook my head, unable to believe how cool this place was. "We're in the Ultras stand."

Mateo burst out laughing—it was probably the most unexpected thing he'd heard all year.

"What's funny?" said Emma.

Mateo explained. "Ultras are the real hard-case fans. Violent, criminal adjacent. You go to Italy and the Ultras are like a paramilitary operation. If the team doesn't play hard enough, they'll lock the players in the stadium and there will be SWAT teams sent in and hostage negotiators." He looked left and right. "These guys look like they work in a restaurant that only serves cereal."

"The Ultras name is *ironic*," said an Ultra who'd been listening. "Our goal is to be the world's first truly post-modern football club." He sighed. "But we also really like kicking the shit out of people."

This line and the deadpan delivery had me in fits. I pushed through to high-five the guy.

"They've got mad songs," I said, arm around my new best friend. "My top five favourite chants are all from West now. Think of a popular song and they've turned it into a chant. It's unreal. You don't normally get this at non-league level. It's . . . it's all the best parts of Manchester in one tiny metal shed. I love it here."

"We love you here, too," said my bestie.

"Emma, it's all posh round this area. Manchester posh, anyway, and they lean into it. They've got a song. *West, West, wherever you may be, we eat hummus and celery! We don't eat meat, we love broccoli, We are Chorlton and West Didsbury.*" My new friend was basking in my enthusiasm. "They're pro EU, anti-fascist, pro-community, pro-sense of humour, and crowds are going up. My dream club was right next to me my whole life, and I never even knew about it! I fucking love this place!"

I gave my friend a shake, then let him get on with his life. The Brig was at the back of the stand, meaning he was about two metres away, chatting with Mateo's driver. They seemed to be friends. Mateo was giving me an amused look. Emma had started out bewildered by my enthusiasm, but now she had something else on her mind. "Max. I haven't seen you in *ages*. Where are your priorities?"

I was so deep in the fantastic, humorous world of ninth-tier football that I struggled to understand what she was saying. "My priorities?"

She sighed, put her arms around my neck, and pulled me down for a kiss. "Priorities."

"Right." I kissed her again.

Satisfied, she examined the nearest West Ultra. He was wearing a Christmas jumper, had a West bobble hat on, and was holding a can of Krombacher beer. The next guy was in a premium hoodie. The next guy owned Tranmere Rovers. "Why is Mateo here? Mateo, why are you here?"

"Max is coming to a transfer tribunal tomorrow. Helping me out," he added, seeing the confusion on her face. "So I'm putting him up for the night in a nice hotel. The tribunal will be in that hotel, in fact, nice and early. We'll present our case, then later they'll decide our fate." The cracks on his face widened. "He said if I wanted him to show me a good time in Manchester, I should get down here. I wasn't expecting—"

Just then, a raucous rendition of "No Limit" by 2 Unlimited broke out, but instead of repeating the words *no* and *limit*, the West fans had replaced every pair of syllables with the word hummus. It worked perfectly. When they'd crescendoed, they went again but with the word *quinoa*.

"What's keen-wah?" said Emma, smiling at the absurdity of it all.

"It's what you call quin-oa," I said.

"Wait. Are you saying it's pronounced keen-wah?"

"Who would know better than a football Ultra?" I said, laughing and the nearest Ultra laughed and clinked his beer against my water. "Now, if you'll excuse me, I have some urgent business to attend to." I turned round, did some little jumps, and sang my heart out.

Around the sixtieth minute, West brought a defender on who reminded me of Henk. Henk was one of the players from Chester's under-fourteens on my fateful first day in charge of those kids. Henk had caught my eye as a promising young defender, and his mother had caught Henri's eye as a promising young defender's hot momma. She followed Henk all over, home and away, and she knew her football.

Henk had moved to Tranmere and I hadn't thought about him since.

"Mateo, you've got one of our former players in your youth system. Henk. He'll be in your fifteens or sixteens now. Can you let me know when they're playing? I want to check up on him."

Mateo pointed at his driver, who nodded and tapped on his phone.

Then I got back to learning the West songs, while Emma chatted away to her new best friends, the Krombacher Ultras, who were telling her about the coolest off-the-beaten-track shops in the city centre.

"Well, that was something," said Mateo, as we settled into our new positions. We'd left early, one of us extremely reluctantly, so we could get a proper meal. Raffi and his mates had stayed, and we'd taken our three cars—environmental disaster—to Green's, the famous vegetarian restaurant in West Didsbury.

"Yes, it was," I agreed, though we'd had totally different experiences. I'd been enchanted, Emma had been cured of football phobia.

Mateo, though, was more practical, and the club's politics didn't move him. "The football was pretty poor, Max."

I grinned at him. "That's the easiest thing to fix." If I'd known about West when I'd got cursed, I'd probably have started there. Ziggy, Raffi, and Youngster would have been playing in that game. Me, too, maybe. How many goals would I score in *that* league? Literally as many as I wanted. But I hadn't known about it, so now I was hanging out with club owners, consulting them on transfer tribunals. I sighed. "Did you bring the things I asked for?" I said.

He nodded. "In the car. We're all set."

"All set for what?" said Emma.

"Justice," said Mateo. "Max is going to help us get a fair price for our former player."

"Your *former* player?"

"Yeah. It's a strange kind of transfer. They take our player then we work out how much they should pay. They tried to pull a fast one, and they'll get away with it unless Max can teach them a lesson." He shook his head. The unfairness of the situation had him stressed and angry.

"Mateo," I said, smiling. I was feeling on top of the world. "I am going to blow the tribunal's socks off. I've got a presentation prepared that will have these fuckers thinking Danny Prince is the second coming of Roberto Carlos."

"You're very confident. I like that. That's reassuring."

"Yeah. It's in the bag. Only . . ."

"What?"

I shrugged. "I mean, I suppose it depends who's on the tribunal. But the case itself is foolproof."

"Case? Are you going to pretend to be a lawyer?" said Emma.

"Max Best QC," I said, then tried to think of what the Q and the C might stand for. "Max Best. Quite . . . convincing." Amazing line! I was absolutely smashing all aspects of my life. I felt two feet taller. Morale 8.

"If Max is doing a courtroom scene, I want to be there," said Emma. "Did he tell you he has a track record of winning the argument but losing the case?"

"Point of fact, he did. But it's all right. It can't get worse than what's on the table, if you see what I mean."

"What can I get you?"

A new voice. I looked up. Astonishingly beautiful redhead waitress! I passed several mental resistance checks. "Oh. Hummus. Keen-wa. Celery."

The tiniest fraction of a smile played around her lips, but I'd have to work a lot harder to impress her than pronouncing keen-wa correctly. "To drink?"

"You don't *drink* hummus?" I smiled at Mateo. "Guess I've been doing it wrong." The redhead's smile was visibly bigger! GOOOOAAAALLLL!!!! "One gallon of Taittinger Blankety-blank Brut 1943, please."

"I'll bring the wine list."

"Max," said Emma. "If you're done being hyper and falling in love with strange football teams you've just met, can we talk about this guy who tricked me into dishing the dirt on you?"

"What?" said the Brig, turning away from his conversation.

I sighed, and tried to cling onto my good mood as the Brig made Emma tell and retell the story, while Mateo and his driver listened in growing horror.

The only interesting part, for me, came when Mateo went to the toilet and the Brig leaned close and asked if Emma thought this incident was related to the one in Tranmere.

"Related how?" said Emma.

"Like, they knew about that and tried it again. If the incidents are *linked* . . ."

Emma gave him an unblinking stare. "Being ogled and harassed by mediocre men all day? That's called being a *woman*, John."

He nodded and shrank back into his seat. "I thought I'd check," he said.

Mateo came back to the table. "Check what?"

My phone pinged. "Just Chester stuff," I said. I looked at the message Bulldog had sent me. It was a screenshot of my *Soccer Supremo* profile. Of course, to my eyes it was all a bubbling tar pit of evil, so I showed it to the Brig and asked him to tell me my technique score.

"Your technique is five," he said. "This is out of twenty, if I understand it correctly?"

"Yeah. They've given me low technique," I said, in an annoyed voice. I *was* annoyed, because *someone* was taking liberties. But I was also relieved—if these new numbers meant nothing, then I could get back to being a mystery winger.

Emma had snapped at the Brig and was remorseful. She tried to smile at him for helping me, then lifted her tall glass to her lips and took sips of water.

"Max has bad technique?" pondered Mateo, and with stupendously good timing, he added, "Poor Emma."

Emma sprayed water all over her tofu.

I stood, hands on head, as everyone else burst into fits of laughter. Had I seen the Brig laugh before? I didn't care. All my work, all my preparations getting Emma to this point, and now someone else had put the ball in the back of the net.

I put my phone to my ear, said it was Bob Geldof, and went outside. I fumed for a while, phone in my pocket, pacing up and down. Then I saw the hot waitress. She gave me the go-ahead to flirt with her, but she was on a cigarette break.

Veto.

Fuck!

This all seemed like some kind of lesson, but one that I wouldn't learn until later. Or it was just a whole load of nothing.

One thing was clear to me—I still had some of my football attributes. My technique, my passing, and my sense of what was going to happen on a football pitch. I intended to show all those in Boston, Lincolnshire at the weekend.

And if I still had those, then I still had influence 20. And the poor saps at the transfer tribunal would get a quadruple dose at 9 a.m. tomorrow.

Because Manchester was my home, and an Englishman's home is his castle, and if this was my castle then I was the king and if you come at the king you best not miss. I gritted my teeth and stared at the future, daring it to defy me.

Also, hummus is dead nice but celery is pretty pointless.

Emma stayed with me in the fancy hotel, built in the days when Manchester was one of the richest cities on earth. I'm guessing they didn't have wi-fi back during the industrial revolution, because the signal in the room was shit. Annoying, because I wanted to research my newest obsession.

I lay in the enormous bed, drawing on Emma's back, tracing vague shapes then rubbing them away and starting again. My thoughts were a few miles away from the city centre. Back where I grew up, in fact. West Didsbury and Chorlton. Operating in the same tier as Tadcaster Albion, who we'd played in the cup. Attendances were going up. That's what you got when you offered something authentic and unrelentingly good-natured. Something that brought people in and made them feel welcome, made them feel part of something bigger.

What about my domain? The pitch. West had lots of players with low CA. One guy was CA 5, but was so experienced he still got in the team. I could find *thirty* PA 30 players who lived near Chorlton in a *week*. What would I need to do? Get to Manchester one Saturday when Chester didn't have a match. Hit the five-a-side leagues after doing my training with Cody. Smash Playdar from Princess Parkway. Finding PA 100 players was hard. Finding PA 50 players was not.

"Don't stop," said Emma.

"Oh, you like that?"

"You know I do." I moved my fingertips across her skin, trying to make as little contact as possible. When I got that right, as I did now, there was a moment when she was in ecstasy, followed by a giggle and a complaint about me tickling her. She turned onto her back and I leaned on my left elbow and admired her. "Max. I wish you'd take this situation more seriously."

I nodded. Everyone at the dinner table had agreed Emma's story was bad news. Someone was out to ruin my reputation. Someone serious. It was a serious situation and I needed to be serious. "Okay," I said, inhaling. "Close your eyes." She did. "I'm putting on my serious face."

Her eyelids shot open and she jiggled in annoyance. "Ugh!"

"I don't want to live in the past," I said. "I've been there. Done that. Gave you the t-shirt, which you wore all the way back to Newcastle and never returned."

"I like how it smells."

"Future. That's where I'm going."

She closed her eyes, sighed, and decided to let it go. "Are you going to manage West Didsbury? My dad will be pissed if you move even further down the ladder."

"Oh, will he? Maybe that's another reason to do it, then."

She didn't laugh. "Why are you helping Mateo?"

"Because I get to see a tribunal. That's interesting. I'm going to have hundreds of talented kids coming through the youth system. Some will get poached. If I can dick people in tribunals, they'll be more willing to negotiate with me. This is only happening because Blackburn didn't offer a fair price, and Mateo wants his day in court, so to speak. It's a mess. But I need to know what goes on in there."

"But you're going to help him out?"

"I'm going to say what I think of the player, yeah. Sort of an independent expert."

"How much are you being paid?"

"I'm being paid in kind."

"No fee?"

I frowned. "I'm helping out a mate."

"You should get something."

"It's not about the money. It's the principle. Blackburn are trying to rip him off. They get away with it, he's not going to be excited about funding his youth team. No, I'll fight this fight for free any day of the week." I brightened up. "Anyway, he has already paid. He paid for dinner. Including what he said was the closest thing to the Taittinger 1943."

"What was *that* all about?"

"James Bond drinks it in one of the books. You want me to dress like Bond, I'm going to drink like him. And he put us up in this swanky hotel. Did you see how big it is? You could do a decent three-a-side in the living room. No head height. No rush goalie. Two touch."

"But Max. You've got value. You shouldn't work for free. Even for Matty."

I ignored her, bounced up, dashed over to the curtains, threw them wide open, and said, "Behold!" The bedroom suite had a view of Central Library, a beautiful round building, one of the best pieces of architecture in the north of England. "Everything there is to know about life, you can learn from those bookshelves in there."

"Does it say how to beat Boston United on Saturday, which is your actual job?"

"Yep. That's in Samuel Pepys's diary. Four-one-four-one, slap down the sides. It's what saved him from the Great Fire of London. I think he used four-three-three against the bubonic plague, though. He had tactics fifteen."

She shook her head. "I still can't believe it's called keen-wa."

I stuck my bottom lip out. "You come to my house, you're gonna get schooled."

We met Mateo and his driver and went through the old, creaky corridors into a modern but tasteful meeting room. Over on the left, the driver began assembling a projector and a stand he'd brought, and connected it to my laptop. In the middle, there was one long table with rounded edges, suitable for twelve participants. Emma was a surprise to all the old men (I was the youngest by perhaps forty years), but shockingly they allowed her to stay and found an extra chair and whatnot. To the right was a drinks table.

The tribunal, properly called the Professional Football Compensation Committee, was five guys, different for every new case. The chairman for this bunch was a respected lawyer who'd worked in football off and on. He was friendly enough, and we scored billions of brownie points with him when Emma said her father was *the* Sebastian Weaver of Weaver, Weaver, and Weaver (not sure I've remembered the whole name, there). There was a representative from the Championship—the division Blackburn played in—and one from League Two—where Tranmere played. There was a nonentity from the Professional Footballers' Association (PFA), and someone looking out for the interests of the League Managers Association (LMA).

Basically, a lot of legal expertise, a lot of bases covered, a lot of years of experience in football.

Oh, maybe I should backtrack just a tiny bit, because when I entered the room, one person's head dropped, and that person went "bloody hell." And that person was the representative from the LMA. His name, drum roll please, was *Ian Evans.*

So when we sat and the chairman went round introducing everyone and he said Ian Evans, former Barnsley, Swindon, and Cambridge manager, I bumped Emma and said, "Oh, I *thought* I remembered him." Which got a little scowl from Evans, and a solicitous smile from the chairman, who didn't know our history. He invited the rest of us to introduce ourselves.

There were three from Blackburn Rovers, but only one mattered. That was the head of recruitment. Next to him, very much on team Blackburn, was someone from the agency who had convinced Danny Prince to leave Tranmere. Which, incidentally, was one hundred percent about making a fast buck and zero percent about developing the player's career. Which, yeah, made me very very slightly despise the prick with all my being. But only slightly.

Mateo introduced himself, his driver said his name was "John," which was just a total no-no if he and the Brig were going to be hanging out all the time. You can't have a friend with the same name as you! That's bonkers. Emma actually put her hand on my arm to calm me down. Or so I thought—in fact, she was just signalling that everyone was waiting for me to introduce myself.

I stood. "I am Max Best, director of football at Chester Football Club. I'm here as an independent consultant, because in addition to running a football club where I'm famous for my scouting ability, I'm also maybe the best right winger in the world, and Danny Prince is a left back. I spend a lot of time analysing left backs, and I'm here today to bless this courtroom with my blistering analysis."

The chairman bowed his head, gracious and amused. "I'm sure we're much obliged, Max. It isn't a courtroom, however. Just a friendly hearing." He raised his eyebrows at the last person on the table.

"I'm Emma," said my girlfriend. "I'm just here to make sure Max doesn't run his mouth off."

"Too bloody late," said Ian Evans, gruffly, scoring the first big laugh of the morning.

The early stages were all pretty routine.

Mateo explained that Danny Prince had been at Tranmere since he was seven years old. They'd coached him, skipped him ahead when he needed more of a challenge, and identified him as a special talent from an early age. He had photocopies of internal documents showing end-of-year coaching assessments all the way up to the end of last season.

He said that the club had offered Prince a new contract, and when it was clear that another club were trying to poach him, Tranmere increased the offer to what Mateo called a "desperate" level. He produced documents showing that they'd offered Prince £4,000 a week to sign a three-year contract. "He would have been the second-highest-paid player at the club. Handing out such contracts is unsustainable, but he was the jewel in the crown of our youth system and every coach, physio, every dinner lady, told me I had to keep him."

He then turned to previous cash offers clubs had made. They ranged from £300,000 to £500,000. He showed copies of the written offers. "We rejected them out of hand, of course. That's insulting for a player so talented, who we'd invested so much in."

I was nodding along. Mateo was killing it. He didn't need me, which was probably best all round given my relationship with Ian Evans. But I gave a brief technical analysis. "Every physical aspect you want from a left back—speed, heading, passing and running through the thirds, ability to overlap, sprints per minute—he's got all that. On the ball, he's very comfortable. Passing, technique, he's very, very solid. But I'm much more interested in his mentality, and I've got a couple of clips I can show that will demonstrate how impressive he is. How well coached he is."

"I look forward to seeing them," said the chairman, and either he really meant it or he was a born diplomat.

Then it was Blackburn's turn. Their job was to downplay how good Prince was so they'd have to pay less money. Understandable, but really fucking weird. He was their player now! Anyway, they pointed out that Prince had never been anywhere near an England youth team setup, hinting that he was perhaps not the bright talent Tranmere thought he was, and that in their more sophisticated assessment criteria, he was one of many young players who had done okay in a lower league that they were willing to "take a punt on."

They also said that Danny Prince had signed for much less than Tranmere's offer. They didn't say the amount aloud but handed over a copy of Prince's contract for the five members of the tribunal to check out.

This annoyed me. If I was going to steal a young player, I would give him a shit contract and then after the tribunal had set the fee, immediately give him a new one. Or I'd make his basic salary very low and give him lots of easily reachable bonuses. Morale had been an amazing purchase, and Injuries *had* to be next. But after that, it was all about Contracts.

The head of recruitment also reiterated that Tranmere thought of Danny Prince in terms of potential, whereas the tribunal needed to apply weight to *evidence*.

The chairman didn't like that, and sarcastically thanked Blackburn for telling him how to do his job. The Blackburn guy had something of a point, though. Danny Prince hadn't played a lot of games, hadn't scored a lot of goals, hadn't won awards for his personal contributions to matches. Most of his value did come from how he might play in the future.

But then the Blackburn guy made a critical mistake—he pissed me off.

"Here, we've got a few screengrabs of Danny Prince's positioning in matches." He smiled. "He's a left back, remember. And, yes, he was playing left back in these games." He tossed out three copies of his printout, but pointedly kept them away from our side of the table. Mateo craned his neck to look, but he was too experienced and sophisticated to do anything as gauche as ask to look at the images. "As you can see," sighed the dude, "Danny Prince has a lot to learn."

I stood up, causing anxiety in my little group, but I simply walked over to the drinks table and helped myself to a water. But then, yeah, I didn't go back to my seat. I went behind the empty suit the PFA had sent. "May I?" I said, as I prised the paper from his hands. I walked around, looking at the pictures, sipping on my water. The first one was an overhead shot showing Tranmere, in white, playing 4-4-2 but with their left back way over, almost playing right midfield. At first glance, it was pretty damning. I allowed myself a little chuckle. "Are you sure you want to do this?" I said to the Blackburn guy.

"What?"

I cracked my head left and right. A few steps took me to my laptop. I opened it and turned on the little projector thing. I jiggled it a bit so that it filled the screen John the Driver had set up. "Ian," I said, talking to my former employee. "These pictures are a black mark against Danny Prince, right? You hate this kind of positional indiscipline."

"I don't *hate* it," he lied. "But it's not a sign the lad's been well trained."

Mateo's head dropped just a fraction. No sooner had I opened my mouth than I'd cost him money. I clicked a couple of times on my laptop, then stood up. "Well, Ian, you know we come at that from a different angle. A guy can be out of position for a good reason. But I think we both hate laziness. And we don't have time for chancers."

"Hey," said the Blackburn dude, but I was just getting warmed up.

I tapped the paper. "Thing is, I know this picture. This is from Danny Prince's Tranmere debut. He must have been buzzing. So excited! Before he met his sleazy new agents, no doubt. An age of innocence, a time—"

The chairman coughed. He didn't mind me putting the Tranmere case across, but he wanted the hearing to be over by eleven so he could get started on his seven-course lunch.

I smiled. "The quick version. Got it. See, I've got that match here. I've got the files of every professional game Danny's played in. So lazy to think we wouldn't have put the effort in. Pisses me off." I glanced down at the scene, trying to remember exactly when it had happened. "This moment . . . pretty sure it was first half. Yeah, Tranmere were attacking the left as the camera sees it. So . . . I think it was nineteen, twenty minutes in." I scrubbed along. "There!"

"Jesus," said the guy from League Two, leaning forward. The image on the projector exactly matched the screengrab.

"So here we go," I said, laughing. "Here's Danny Prince! Left back, but he's way over there. Right-sided central midfielder. Lol! What an idiot!"

"Max," said Emma.

"Let's indulge the silly old professional football player for just a moment, though. Let's rewind. Let's ask *why*." I scrubbed back about a minute. "Gone too far, but you can see him there at left back. Perfectly conventional. Ian, how's his spacing?"

"Looks good."

"You'd better believe it looks good. This kid's sick. Sick means outstanding." I scrubbed a bit to the right. "So, here's a Tranmere goal kick. They're set up in four-four-two like their old manager wanted." I tried to stop myself, but glanced at Ian Evans. He folded his arms and looked at the ceiling. Last time we'd talked about formations I'd been pitching him on a 2-6-2 concept. "So it's four-four-two against four-four-two, like we've all seen a billion times. And . . . here. This is where it starts." I paused the footage and dug a knuckle into my temple. "I *think* what happens is a double transition."

"Sorry," said the guy from the Championship. "Are these the clips you were planning to show us?"

"No."

"But . . . do you remember every minute of every game?"

I smiled. "No, but I did watch this match about five times. And, insane as it sounds, I did have a long look at this very sequence that supposedly demonstrates how shit this player is." It was true. Prince had positioning 15, so when I saw him so far from his zone, it blew my mind. "It's super interesting."

The tribunal member was interested, too. They all were. Even Evans. "Please, go ahead."

I pressed play and let the action go on. "So Tranmere play the ball out . . . ping the ball around . . . quite nice. Walsall, there, press in midfield, ball's loose, they start to transition. See them all go?" I paused, went back five seconds, and pointed at a defender wearing white. "But this centre back here's going to slide in. Watch very carefully."

I let it go five more seconds, then paused. Lots of blank faces, but Ian Evans exhaled and put his hands on his head.

"What?" said the chairman.

"Let's come back to that," I said, and let the scene go on another few seconds. After the centre back's perfectly timed tackle, the ball got played to a Tranmere midfielder. He made a poor choice and tried to chip the ball to one of the strikers. "That was shit. Hate that." I paused. "See Danny Prince? He's gone all the way up the pitch. For a proper midfielder, that's an easy long pass out to the left, and then his team's away. Laughing. But, yeah. I wouldn't know what it's like being a superstar player on a team full of hacks." I coughed, significantly. "Right. Prince is the furthest player up the pitch at this point. Apart from the Walsall goalie. Remember, according to *Blackburn Rovers*, this scene proves that he's shit and worthless. Right?" I pressed play and stopped adding commentary.

What happened next was a quick break from Walsall that got held up for a couple of seconds, before a Walsall player took a shot that the goalie saved.

I went back a little bit. "I'll explain this to Emma, because she doesn't know loads about football." This was an excuse to spell out what to me and Ian Evans was bleeding obvious. I went back and played the move at quarter-speed so I could mention everything I considered relevant. "Prince, remember, is the highest player on the pitch. But he's maxed out on teamwork." That was a white lie. He was teamwork 15. "And so he zooms back. Look at him go! Past the sluggish strikers, overtakes this lazy midfielder. Our left back is haring back to help his mates out. It only takes one little holdup and he's nearly there. Another and he'd have been back in the penalty area. The shot comes in, keeper saves. Prince waits in centre midfield—where he's perfectly comfortable, by the way! The talented little shit. He hangs around there until the next break in play, where he slides back to his position." I looked up, searching for the right words. "So he busts a gut to get back, to help his mates, to affect the game. Does everything you'd ever want in a player. And his own bosses, his own team, take a picture of this, show it out of context, to make him look like he's got no character so they can save a bit of cash." I headed towards the Blackburn lot, jabbing my finger as I went. "Dirty, grubby, cheap."

"Max," said Emma.

I went back to the printout. "Ian, mate. What do you think? Is this kid out of position?"

"No, Best. He ain't." He was folding his arms again, but this time directed at the Blackburn prick.

I was winning. Time to really blow some minds. "Let's talk about what really sets Prince apart. What makes him a shoo-in for the Premier League." I strode to my laptop, closed the match file, and opened a short video. It was a compilation of six clips that showed how Prince used elite cricket psychology to defeat his opponent. I'd added the title "Nature Plus Nurture: the Danny Prince Story." "I already said he's a top athlete, a great technician. But this kid, holy fuck, let's talk about his decision making."

Blackburn's head of recruitment shot to his feet. "Mateo. Can I speak to you, please?"

I watched, dumbfounded, as Mateo got up and left the room, with his enemy, our enemy, holding the door open for him.

The tension left. The five members of the panel relaxed. I held my arms out. "What the shit?"

The chairman gave me a sad smile. "They will come to an amicable agreement. It's better that way. Better for everyone."

"I've got a killer presentation here. In twenty minutes, you'll all be subscribed to Danny Prince's Instagram and TikTok."

"You're very persuasive," said the chairman. "However, I don't think you could persuade me to join TikTok." He pulled out his old flip phone, and there were some chuckles. That was the vibe now. Mild humour. Bunch of friends hanging out.

"Best," said Evans. "You did what you came to do. What you were paid to do."

"Paid? I'm not getting paid." It was always fucking money with Ian Evans. Fuck him. I took a couple of steps towards the agent. "I'm here so Tranmere don't close down their entire fucking academy because of short-sighted parasites." I bent down, got in the guy's face. "Now listen to me, you fucking worm—"

The door opened and Mateo and his counterpart came back in. They announced they'd come to an agreement, and it was all handshakes and laughter and bonhomie. I could not believe what I was seeing.

Pissed, I unplugged my laptop, got the power cable, and gestured at Emma that I wanted to leave.

We stepped outside and someone called my name, but I was storming along the corridor. Emma, the traitor, refused to follow. So I came back a few yards, but no more.

It was the guy from Blackburn. He clapped me on the arm. "Max Best, right? You absolutely mullered me in there." He laughed, but saw that I was fuming. "Hey, come on now. It's just business. You won, I lost. Don't let things fester, or you won't last long in this industry."

I calmed very slightly. "You raided the academy of a smaller team. That isn't business. That's *theft*. Whatever fee you agreed is half what Danny Prince is worth."

He pouted. "Maybe. Maybe not. There are no guarantees." He cheered up again—he could go to his bosses and say he'd saved them millions. "But listen. If you're available for hire, let me know your fee."

"Fee?"

"To do this. To get us a good fee when Liverpool steal one of *our* academy lads."

"How much?"

"Well. What Tranmere paid you."

"Tranmere got a discount because they helped me to learn to *walk* again."

"Oh." His eyes shifted around. He didn't know if I was joking. "Er . . . twenty grand."

"Twenty?"

He misread my shocked expression, thought he'd started too low. "Twenty-five."

Twenty-five thousand pounds? I was no longer mad at the guy. A fuckton of money to get a guy's player profile and get some video that matched what the curse told me about him. Talk about easy money! "Call me when you've got a case. Discount if I get to yell at Liverpool, Newcastle, or Man City."

He was back to smiling, and clapped me on the arm again. "Top lad!"

He fucked off, and I was heading back to the nearest lift. John the Driver hurried along and said Mateo wanted a quick word. I didn't want to talk to the guy—as far as I was concerned he'd snatched defeat from the jaws of victory. But Emma reached up, took my laptop and charger, and jabbed her head back the way we came.

With a sigh, dragging my feet like a fucking toddler, I went halfway down the corridor, then fell against a wall. The driver thought about pleading with me, but went to get Mateo.

He came out, full of beans. It was by far the most animated I'd ever seen him. "Max! You were amazing in there." He took a step back and looked me up and down. "What's up? Are you sick?"

I caught a retort just as it was leaving my mouth and pinched it out of existence. I breathed in. "I was crushing it in there, Mateo. I know Ian Evans, and he was into it. And he was the only one who *totally* understood what I was saying. He would have been in charge of their discussions. He's the real football expert in there. Whatever you negotiated, it wasn't enough."

Mateo's mouth turned rigid like he was about to punch me, but it relaxed almost immediately. He slapped his hands together in a strange way. "You've got the scent of blood in your nostrils and I've taken the fox away just before the kill. Ha! I'm sorry, Max. I should have known you would react like this." He touched me on the arm. "You're an assassin. I'm a businessman. Okay, we could have taken a risk and maybe got more than Blackburn offered. But this was never about the money."

"It wasn't?"

"It was about the principle. You don't take young players away from their home, from where they've been trained and educated, and not pay a price. It was the principle, and it was the respect. You made them treat me with respect, and for that I'm in your debt."

I pinched the bridge of my nose. We were all fighting different fights. Maddeningly, the closest thing to a soulmate I had in that room had been Ian Evans. "How much extra did I get you? I need to know how much to charge if I do this as a side hustle."

"Half a million."

So he'd got £1.2 million. Big money. That'd keep the academy going for another few years. I stuck my bottom lip out. "You'd have got at least three. A year from now he'll be going for ten."

He closed his eyes. "You're so stubborn. That won't end well." He sighed. He looked down the corridor at Emma. He knew we'd not really had an anniversary because we'd been scrabbling around doing our day jobs. "I want to give you a gift."

"Yeah?"

"A percentage."

I knew what he meant. "Ten percent? Fifty grand? In used notes?"

He looked almost blank. "Fifty's fine. You want fifty?"

This was surreal. "I told Emma I was doing it for a friend. For justice. For the principle of small clubs having . . . protection against being used as unpaid player incubators."

"All that can be true and I can pay you for your work. And your time. You watched those matches over and over."

I sighed. "Doesn't feel right." I shook my head. Fifty grand, though. "How about . . . you buy me a new laptop? Mine was struggling in there."

He laughed. "I heard it. It's almost as old as this hotel."

"I'm taking Emma shopping, and we're going to have lunch in Chinatown. I'll send her back on the train. When she's gone, you can give me a big bag of cash and I won't have lied to her."

He was looking at some point on the wall, eyes blazing. Reliving his triumph. He hadn't been listening. "Pardon me, Max? Say that again."

His high morale brought mine all the way back up. With a smile, I said, "Never mind."

I turned to walk away. I hadn't had much for breakfast, and now I was getting pretty hungry. Maybe a nice brunch instead of a Chinese. I began humming the West Didsbury version of "No Limit."

I stopped dead. Turned around. "Mateo. I have an idea. Instead of some cash I never asked for . . . would you consider giving me a loan?"

Emma wanted to stick to the plan, so we shopped, with my stomach complaining nonstop, then went to Chinatown.

While drinking endless green tea from tiny cups, she suddenly frowned. "Max . . . what was the thing? The thing you pointed out that only Ian Evans noticed? I tried really hard, but couldn't tell what it was."

"Ah. You see, about fifteen seconds before the screenshot was taken, when the ball was bouncing around, Danny Prince was sticking to his zone, doing his job at left back. Then his centre back dives into the tackle, Prince gets on his bike, bombs forward."

"So? Isn't he supposed to?"

"He did it, like, half a second early. Before the tackle had started."

"Oh!" she said, teeth showing. Her smile died. "I don't follow."

"He knew what would happen before it happened. Imagine a striker who had that skill—he'd score five, ten goals a season more than his clone who didn't. It's valuable. It's one of *my* superpowers. It's rare. Danny Prince has it." I shook my head. "Evans would have added half a mill for that alone. Fuck!"

"You're frustrated."

"Yes and no. I mean, if you're winning, win big. Right? But on a personal level . . ."

"What?"

"Well, it was amazing being able to talk to Ian Evans about football sort of openly and honestly." No clue why, but saying that made me well up. "And the Blackburn guy didn't like being shown up and he said he'd pay me to be on his side next time. And best of all," I said, but I didn't want to tell her what Mateo and I had agreed. "Best of all, Mateo said he'd buy me a new laptop."

She didn't notice I'd changed tack. "Boys and their toys," she said, sipping on her tea.

When she said that, I brought my cup to my lips to cover a smile. I had a new toy—the Morale perk—and I was going to play with it, hard, on Saturday at 3 p.m.

Match 10 of 46: Boston United versus Chester FC.

This match produced my first-ever football-related appearance on *talk-SPORT*. It was on the radio, of course, but they usually put their phone-in segment on YouTube, so you could see the bored and frankly disrespectful faces of their presenters.

Here's the transcript.

Previous Caller: But I'd just sack him, mate. Bin him off, he's awful. Clueless.

Smug Host 1: Thanks for your call. On line six we've got Paul in Lincolnshire.

Paul: Hi, yeah, I'm a Boston fan.

Smug Host 2: [swinging an imaginary baseball bat] Red Sox, yeah! They're due.

Paul: Boston United.

SH 1: [genuinely incredulous] What's that?

Paul: It's National League North. One step below what we used to call the Conference. So I've been the Jakemans today and I've seen something I've never seen in all my years of watching football.

SH 1: A fit bird? [sniggers merging into a silence so elongated the emergency signal almost kicks in]

SH 2: [giving his mate an okay sign to show approval for the joke] Go on, Paul. Tell us about it.

Paul: Right, well, you probably remember this Max Best lad.

SH 2: [making a "this guy's crazy" sign by spinning his finger around his temple] No.

Paul: Really? He's the one what was nearly killed after a match. Phenomenal player, but he's managing now. I think he's twenty-four. Twenty-five, maybe. His Chester's gone from being one of the worst in the league to the best. He's got them playing top football, like Burnley last year, but at this level it's even more amazing if you ask me. First half today, we're competing. Boston United are, that's my team. Then something funny happens, bit of a strange one, but that's by the by, not why I'm calling. Suffice to say, halftime, we're a goal down. This Max Best kid, remember, he's been in a coma, he's been paralysed, he's played ten minutes in a cup qualifier and stank the place out, people are saying he'll never be the same, but he brings himself on at halftime. Now, we're not a top team, but we're not *bad*. You'd watch us and say we were decent and played the right way. But . . . [laughter] This boy, I'm laughing because I can't believe what I've seen, I really can't. He comes on at half time and . . . there's only one way to put it—all hell breaks loose.

SH 1: [looking up from his phone, which he'd been on the whole time] John, let me stop you there. We're just hearing that Danny Murphy has Pep Guardiola with him after his side's routine two–nil win at home to Nottingham Forest. City very much saving their energy for the midweek game coming up. Over to you, Danny.

16

MAX GO CRAY CRAY

Saturday, October 14.

SealCast: The Official Chester FC Podcast, Episode 36: Max Best Interview!

Boggy: Hello and welcome to SealCast, the monthly Chester FC podcast brought to you by Seals Live. I'm your host, Boggy Marsh, and we've got an unusual episode for you today. Not three guests, not two guests, but one guest!

Max: Subverting expectations. Love it. Good job, Boggy.

Boggy: There he is. Chester's director of football and manager of the men's and women's teams, Max Best.

Max: Do you want to push that mic away from your mouth? You're very plosive.

Boggy: We can fix that in post.

Max: Great. When are you going to start doing that?

Boggy: I know you're pressed for time— Oh, that was a big one. [sound of microphone stand being moved] Peter Piper picked a peck of pickled peppers. That better? I know you don't want to be in here with me all night, so let's get straight into the meat. Since the last pod, we've played twice in the league, had two cup matches, and strangely only played once with the women. Let's go all the way back to the match against Boston United.

Max: No. I want to start with the women's team. Every day someone tells me I need to stop managing the women's team and focus on the men. Even people on the new board have said it. I say if you make me choose, I'll choose the women, except I won't, because put me in that position and I'll be straight out the door.

Boggy: Let's start with the women's team, then.

Max: This is a serious project for me. I'm building something from scratch. It's exciting. It's fulfilling on a personal level. If you don't like it, I don't care. You don't want to hear me talk about it? Fine. Turn off. Go support Liverpool—they don't take their women's team seriously. But don't tell me what to do. It's bonkers you have an opinion on how I should manage my career.

Boggy: Let me check my notes. It was a cup match, wasn't it?

Max: This country drives me absolutely crazy sometimes. I've said it again and again—the women's team matters to me. If it doesn't matter to you, fine. But listen to the words coming out of my mouth. I'm doing it. End of story. You don't get to choose. You don't own me. You don't own me. Get that into your thick skulls.

Boggy: Of course, Max. [loud pen scrape] That was me crossing out a question about your contract. [nervous chuckle]

Max: I hate stupidity, Boggy. Someone comes up to me in the street, says we should play a flat back four because with Lucy we get more height, experience, and leadership on the pitch, love that. Someone says Dani needs to play on the right because she's too right-footed to play left mid—hey! Agree to disagree but nice talking to you, see you on Sunday. Some absolute jellyfish comes up to me, says, you know when they start banging on about women's football, you know what I do? I turn the radio off. All right. So? You want a medal? I check out when people talk about Formula One but I wouldn't say that to Lewis Hamilton. I have the right to like and dislike whatever I want, but going out of my way to say that to his face would be rude and ignorant. And it would be stupid because then he wouldn't want to talk to me and if Darlington offered him a juicy contract, maybe he'd take that just to spite me.

Boggy: You're doing very well at not swearing.

Max: I'm not happy, Boggy.

Boggy: Well, I for one am more than happy to talk about the women's team.

Max: No.

Boggy: Sorry?

Max: It makes no sense to start there. Let's do it chronologically. Let's talk about Boston.

Match 10 of 46: Boston United versus Chester FC.

I didn't go on the team bus to Lincolnshire, because I spent the morning with the coaches who couldn't make my Learn from the Best event. Seven of the eight who'd expressed interest turned up, and again there were two decent ones who I added to our list of "spares." If I ever had the budget for it, I would try letting these coaches do one-to-one skills sessions like Cody had been doing with Raffi. Maybe with the Triplets, or Vivek, to see if I could get them up to CA 20, like, twenty percent faster.

Seven coaches turned up, but I immediately became obsessed with the eighth—the one who'd asked if we would repeat the session but who hadn't shown up. For some reason, I was desperate to meet him. I asked the Brig if he could track the guy down.

Then we drove to Boston, which blew my mind by being halfway between Skegness and Norwich. *How is that possible? Surely Skegness is in Wales?* My mental map of England was still basically a rectangle with Manchester in the centre, represented by a big star, London, bottom-right, depicted as a skull, and Bristol, somewhere near the bottom-left, a question mark.

Boston United play in yellow. Their nickname is the Pilgrims and they've got the Mayflower ship as their logo. The stands at the Jakemans Community Stadium are fully covered, and although it's relatively humble from the inside, from the outside it's impressive. It's all sweeps and curves—even the floodlights bend in a pleasing arc.

I'd been watching clips and they played some nice football. Tidy, attractive passing moves. They had a centre back who liked to dribble into midfield and make things happen, and they had a left-footed midfielder who had a fantastic long shot. In the warm-up, I saw their average CA was 40, but their best player wasn't available, so I guessed they were normally a little bit stronger.

Their average morale was 4.3 out of 7—way lower than ours. The midfielder with the great left foot—let's call him Harry Moodini—had Very Poor morale.

After this, we would have a week to recover before playing a tier-seven team, so I decided to go hard against Boston. That meant using 3-5-2.

Ben in goal had turned silver—CA 40.

Steve, Carl, and Glenn were the three centre backs. Glenn had maxed out his PA of 54, which was a big shame, but Carl's relentless hard work and new focus was paying off big-time. His CA had crept up to 49—almost gold standard! And his default match rating had gone from 6 to 7. Not quite first name on the team sheet, but it was getting to the point I needed to tie him down to a long-term contract.

Then on the wings: Aff, who'd gone gold, and Joe Anka, who was struggling to get to his limit of 40. We had Ryan Jack, Raffi, and Sam Topps in a pretty fearsome centre.

Up front, Henri and Tony. Henri had been improving rapidly and was nearly at platinum level.

Our average CA was 47.8, and average morale was still sky-high at 6.14.

Boston United, then, were a very good mid-table side, but we were already the fourth-best team in the division. They had home advantage, we had the morale edge. And we absolutely slapped when it came to bench options—apart from Robbo, the backup goalie, we had Trick, who would let us switch to a back four, Magnus, who had gone silver and was starting to be hard to leave out of the first eleven, Pascal, who'd give us a burst of speed late in the game, and Max Best.

Before we left the dressing room, I had a surprise for the lads. Normally there was no need for any great tactical input from me. If we played our game, we didn't need to worry about what the other team might do.

"Okay shut the fuck up," I said. I'd arranged some yellow magnets on the board in a 4-4-2. "These guys are all right. They'll come out fighting and try to get ahead, then they'll play around us, tire us out, and in the second half they'll bring on a couple of fast forwards and dick us on counters. They've got a nasty streak, so if things go wrong, they'll dip into their bag of dirty tricks and try to put you off. Right? They're here to battle."

I looked around the changing room. They looked ready to fight. No problems there.

"Glenn tells me you've got a couple of set pieces you're all happy with. Knock yourself out." This thing where I let them try out set pieces they designed was very motivational for them. To me it was like letting a kid choose how to slice his pizza—it ended up ugly, but it kept them busy for a couple of minutes. "This guy," I said, touching the right-sided CB magnet, "loves to dribble up into midfield. It's very beautiful, very elegant, pure class." I slid the magnet to midfield. "Pure class until we transition and their lone centre back has to deal with Henri *and* Tony." I shook my head, smiling, as I imagined the mayhem that would ensue. "I can't believe he'd have the nerve to do that against Henri fucking Lyons, but let's see."

Henri was staring at the tactics board, affronted at the idea that his marker would push up into midfield. I tried not to laugh. Manipulating Henri was one of my favourite parts of the job. I thought I was getting pretty good at it.

"This dude," I said, sliding the left-sided CM around, "has, er . . ." How could I say he had bad morale? I couldn't. I scratched my chin. "Sam and Joe, you'll be closest to him most of the time. Everyone else, pay attention because I don't know who'll be near him on set pieces. What I want . . ." Again I had to stop myself laughing. Mirth was definitely not the right vibe for this. "What I want is for you to talk to him. This doesn't leave this room, except for a couple of comments on the pitch. Got that? But this whole summer, his manager was hawking him around, trying to offload him. I had a look at him before going for Ryan." This was all fabricated, but my players didn't know that. "Basically, Sam, ask him if he knew he was up for sale. Then Joe, you say no, there was no *fee*, the gaffer wanted him off the wages so he would have binned him off for nowt. Right? Third guy, say something like, 'Hey bro, are you still on the transfer list?' Or 'How come you're playing if your boss don't rate you?'"

Sam stood up. "Is that an order?"

Unexpected. Was he about to rebel? Had he grown a moral compass? "Yes."

"Got it." He took a few steps away, then stopped. He took in my posture—I was still in didactic mode. "Sorry, I thought we were done. I need to pee."

"Have at it." I shooed him away, then smiled at Glenn. "Captain."

He stood and clapped his hands. "Come on, lads! Let's warm up. Top quality, now, lads!"

Boggy: The Jakemans Stadium has been a tough place for us to go in recent years. What were you expecting?

Max: Oh, you know. I told the lads to keep it tight first thirty, see if we could snatch a goal on a set piece or something like that.

Boston kicked off, Moodini dribbled forward, Sam Topps took the ball from him, and that was Boston's best move of the half. We fucking crushed them. Suffocated them. Our midfield was so dominant, it was funny. I couldn't remember a more one-sided half—ever.

I was leaning against the dugout, enjoying it. We all were—Ben had the easiest half of his career. Glenn spent more time in Boston's penalty area—going up for corners and free kicks—than in his own. Sam seemed to have challenged Raffi to see who could recover the ball the fastest, and they were both winning. Aff was firing delicious crosses to Henri, and Joe was getting to the byline and doing cutbacks for Tony.

The new free kick and corner routines the lads had cooked up looked fun, but they weren't all that threatening. I liked them as a way to disrupt Boston. Keep them wondering what we might try next.

But the more we dominated and didn't get a goal, the more we snatched at the chances we were creating. Even Henri tried to hit a couple of half-chances too hard, causing them to skyrocket over the bar. Not for the first time, I wondered about using God Save the King on his finishing. Sure, giving the points to Youngster was the only sensible long-term play, but I really wanted to get out of this league.

The Brig came up to me. "Are you worried we haven't scored?"

"Not yet. There's loads of time."

"Whenever I watch a match on the television, the commentator says something like 'Will they rue all these missed chances?'"

"It happens sometimes. You get a match exactly like this, and the better team doesn't win. There was one game, I think it was Arsenal v Bolton or something. Arsenal had thirty shots, Bolton had one and won two–nil."

"How is that possible?"

"One was an own goal. So yeah, mad stuff happens, but Boston look pretty much out of ideas already. They were expecting four-one-four-one. I think their second striker was supposed to be marking our DM."

The Brig checked out the other dugout. It was very, very close and its occupants were losing their minds, screaming at their players and the ref. "Is it possible they can adapt at halftime?"

I shrugged. "Not really bothered what they do. But I've got a surprise for them."

"Oh?"

A breeze blew the toggles of my hoodie around. Cold air dragged along my neck, chilled the back parts of my ears. The pitch was good. The skies were blue. Our fans were in good voice. And as Harry Moodini's morale dropped from Very Poor to Abysmal, so did his match rating, from 7 to 6. "I'm feeling frisky."

Near the end of a first half in which we'd had eleven shots on target, Sam passed back to Glenn Ryder. Some crazy new thought went through his mind, one he'd never had before. Under no pressure, he turned and passed back to Ben. At first, I thought he was simply letting the keeper have a touch of the ball, but the captain ordered his fellow centre backs to retreat with him.

Sam understood instantly, and he brought the midfield line back, too. Ryder was deliberately encouraging his opponents to come closer to his goal! For the first time in his career!

Boston sensed a chance to make something happen—they pushed forward en masse.

Ryder stands with his foot on the ball. He plays it sideways to Alton.

Alton to Carlile.

Carlile chips forward to Joe Anka, who fires a diagonal to Lyons.

Lyons is too strong for his marker.

Lyons brings Jack into the move.

Jack's first-touch pass to the left takes two defenders out of the game!

Chester are flying forward from all angles.

Boston are struggling to get back.

Aff takes a touch, looks up, and pulls the ball back across goal.

Raffi Brown is there! He's unmarked!

GOOOOAAAALLLL!!!!

That was far too easy for Chester.

The team's delight at scoring wasn't just the usual mix of emotions like relief and joy. There was a lot of amused wonderment in there, too. Two things made it taste sweeter.

First, that Ryder had taken it upon himself to play the Youngster role.

Second, that Raffi *should* have been tracked by Harry Moodini, but when my midfielders had surged past him, Moodini had only trotted back. Danny Prince or any of my players would have fucking *sprinted*. Was that a demonstration of what shit morale could do on the pitch? My players had got in this lad's head, he hadn't done his job, and we'd scored from it.

And I knew what my guys were thinking—Max has done it again.

I suppose you have to give credit where credit's due—I basically created and scored that goal myself, in the changing room fifteen minutes before the match even kicked off. Messi never did that. Maradona never did that. It was, conceivably, the single greatest individual achievement in the history of any sport.

Boggy: The celebrations for Raffi Brown's goal were unusually bouncy.

Max: Bouncy? I don't know about that. When the goal went in I was thinking about in-game tweaks we needed to make.

Boggy: From where I was watching, the goal seemed to have a special meaning to the players. Can you tell us what?

Max: Just relief, I think. They'd had a lot of shots and you get those days, right, where the ball just won't go in. Actually, wasn't it just before halftime? The last kick of the half? It's always a buzz to score right before the break.

Boggy: Max, are you being coy? There was a strong rumour that you set the goal up in some way indiscernible to mortal men.

Max: Me? I wasn't playing.

Boggy: Not yet.

Max: Not yet.

Halftime was a laugh. Jokes all round, banter, vibes vibes vibes. There was an unwritten rule that until I engaged them, the players would leave me alone while I played tower defence games on my phone or dicked around with the tactics board, but this was one match where they nearly couldn't restrain themselves. They wanted to know how I'd known about Moodini.

Near the end of the break, Boston's tactics board changed to 3-5-2. Moodini was off, and now they planned to match us up and see if they could get back into the game that way. That meant putting one of their fast forwards on the left wing, where I felt confident he'd be pretty rubbish. It also ended our chance of getting an overload if their centre back went walkies, but you can't have everything.

"All right," I said, surprising the guys. There were halftimes where I didn't say anything at all and they thought this was one of them. "You boys were very mean and cruel to their number eleven. I don't condone that at all. But they're taking him off and switching to three-five-two, so I'm going to bring myself on."

Physio Dean stepped forward. He had been driven crazy by my surprise cameo against Tadcaster and had begged me to get another MRI before launching into real action. "Are you sure?"

"Very, very, very sure." Although Ryder had shown the on-pitch leadership we had needed, I didn't see any harm in getting out there myself. It would accelerate my path back to full fitness, and I thought if I was on the pitch my guys wouldn't stop attacking when we got to 3–0 up. Also, I felt like playing, so whatever. No need for a reason beyond that. "So let's think . . ." It was only a question of which player I'd replace. I stared at the board. It was a choice between two solid guys, but one was faster and speed was all Boston had. "Steve, great game, thanks. Early shower, enjoy the show. Good?"

"You're going to play centre back?" he said.

"How can I play centre back? I'm a mystery winger."

"So . . . what's the plan?" said Vimsy.

"You'll see," I said, smirking, like I was in complete control of the entire universe. (A few minutes later, on the way to the pitch, when no one was looking, I told the Brig what the plan was and what subs to make if I got knocked out. I wasn't a *complete* lunatic.)

"Here you go, boss," said Glenn. He was doing something weird that I couldn't get my head around. It took me a second to realise he was slipping the captain's armband up my wrist.

"The fuck are you doing?" I said.

"You're gonna be the captain when you play, right?"

"What the fuck are you talking about?" Captains had to do all kinds of tedious shit like fine players who were late to team meetings and stuff. It was way too authoritarian for me, but basically everyone I'd ever met had said that kind of discipline was important and without it, my club would spiral out of control faster than a malfunctioning rocket. The only time I *might* put myself as captain was when we used the Triple Captain perk. "Put that back on, and get fucking captaining!"

When I scanned the lads at the start of the half, everything was looking good, but with one notable change—Ryder's morale had gone to Superb. He wasn't a traitor! He just wanted to be the captain and worried he'd lose that honour to me. Well, he could lift the trophies at the end of the season. That didn't motivate me at all. Clearly, it motivated him.

The Morale perk was one of my favourites. Understanding my players was beyond motivational. My own morale must have gone green, because I found I was floating. I scanned the pitch again and found we were primed and ready to drop hand grenades. Just for a second, I felt sorry for Boston United.

Boggy: We came out for the second half with you on the pitch, and you got a standing ovation.

Max: I did?

Boggy: You did. From the home fans, too.

Max: Oh, that's cool. I genuinely didn't hear it. I was super focused.

Boggy: So you were on for your league debut, but Joe Anka was still there. So obviously the plan was for him to play right midfield.

Max: Yep.

Boggy: But then it struck me that we only had two defenders. But two right midfielders.

Max: I've been known to play central midfield, Boggy. I've never been asked to play there, but I have played there.

Boggy: Right, and that would have made four CMs!

Max: You seem upset.

Boggy: I just don't understand what I saw.

Max: Let's say I played as a kind of trainee centre back.

Boggy: Well, you need more training because you played as a defensive midfielder. Spectrum told me, after the match.

Max: So you know. What's the problem?

Boggy: We can't play two-six-two! We can't play away from home with two defenders, Max. That's all kinds of crazy.

Max: Are you sure?

Boggy: No!

Seeing Ian Evans at the tribunal had reminded me of the formation I'd come up with to make the best use of our squad. I'd called it a 4-4-2 killer and Ian Evans had laughed in my face.

All right, well, we were absolutely crushing this match, there was a ten-point difference in CA, we were fitter, and our morale was as high as you could get without pharmaceuticals. What better time to test my theory?

Now, you might be thinking, Max, *bro*, it's a dumb formation but anyway, you didn't *have* 2-6-2 so why do you keep banging on about it? Because, *mate*, I could disobey myself! As long as I was on the pitch, I could switch things around. I could take a 4-4-2 with me as the second striker and turn it into a 5-4-1. The only catch in that hypothetical example was that I would have to play in defence.

At my current level of recovery, I couldn't play in my usual position of right midfield. I didn't have the skill or the acceleration to get past a fullback and if I did, my crosses were weak and my shots had no power. Also, in a 3-5-2 variant, the wide players have to track back as much as they go forward, so it needed more stamina than I had.

But I could play DM. I could play D fucking M! My ability to read the game and guess what was going to happen next was as good as ever, and after intercepting I could play a short pass and get us rocking and rolling.

Yeah. I subbed myself on as the central centre back, and simply walked ten yards farther forward. The tactics screen "broke" and I had my dream formation.

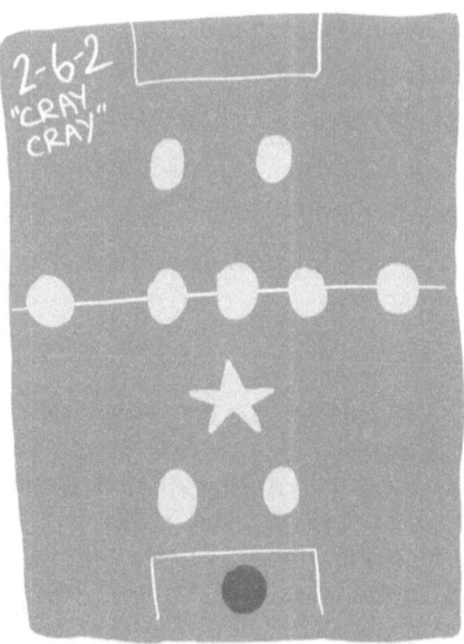

Things started pretty well. Boston came out of the blocks fast and furious, and ran straight into a brick wall. A good-looking brick wall, it has to be said.

Thorpe breaks free down the left. He picks out a pass to Julian.

Julian takes a touch and looks for an option.

But Best nips in and takes the ball.

Best finds Brown and Chester are away!

Wright breaks through the tackle. Boston have a three-on-three break!

He looks left and right. He slides a pass to the right . . .

But it's intercepted. Best was in the right place at the right time.

Julian is first to the second ball!

He turns and scampers towards goal.

But he's wiped out!

A thunderous tackle from Best.

Best has some choice words for the Boston forward.

Boggy: There was an incident where you tackled their striker—very 1980s—and after setting Aff free, you turned and gave the chap a piece of your mind.

Max: Really? Doesn't ring a bell.

Boggy: It was pretty intense.

Max: Huh. Tackles aren't really my thing. You might be misremembering, there.

Boggy: Max! You wiped him out!

Max: Nah. I'm a flair player. I don't get involved in that stuff. Tackles? What's that?

Boston's manager must have given them a fire-and-brimstone halftime speech, because they had upped their intensity, upped their work rate, and upped their level of kicking the shit out of anyone in a different colour shirt.

Twice I got the ball, passed it on, and got hit by a late cheap shot by this Julian prick. So when he tried to dribble to the big open space on my right, I tracked him, calculated, and slid in, hard. I got the ball, yes, clean as a whistle, and then I upended him, clean as a music festival toilet. But my elegant slide slash brutal assault ended with me daintily lifting myself to my feet, and cutting back the way Cody had trained me. It was so beautiful, so controlled, the ref didn't even think about giving a free kick. And when the action had moved on, I suggested to the Julian guy that if he went for me off the ball again, he would find himself being driven to his house in a medical vehicle.

Boggy: It got the Chester fans going, I can tell you that. They were making a fearsome racket. Then came the setbacks.

Max: Setbacks? Against Boston? What?

I did my big tackle and to me, that was that, on with the game, but the Boston manager went cray cray. Joe Anka was over that side of the pitch and heard what was said, as did Vimsy and Physio Dean.

But it was Joe who most completely lost his mind, and there was an enormous melee. The ref tried to calm things down by showing Joe a red card, but it didn't help. If anything, things got even more heated.

While everyone on both teams converged on the home dugout, which was really close to the away dugout, I calmly walked over and waved at Livia to join me on the pitch. She'd been right at the edge of the aggro, trying to stay out of it, but "it" kept coming closer. She was more than happy to escape the scrum.

From our position in the centre circle, I put my hand on her shoulder and she did the same to my waist. We were like a squad watching one of their mates go forward to take a penalty. I sighed. "You okay?"

"Yes, Max."

I glanced at her. No morale help with this relationship. She *seemed* fine. "Look at Vimsy and Dean getting stuck in. What a pair of twats. Christ, all the subs are at it, too. What the fuck?"

She looked up at me. "The manager was trying to gee up his players. To foul you."

"Tell me something I don't know."

"It was the phrasing. He said, 'Oi, Trev, Gaz, put that fucking Nancy boy on a stretcher.' That's when Joe went for him."

I groaned. "So I can't even fine him for getting sent off? Because he was defending my honour? Is that it?"

The flame of the fire had died down enough for a bit of common sense to kick in. The Brig had been pushing players away from the action, and Glenn and Sam had eventually switched from troublemakers to peacemakers.

When things had settled down, I brought Livia back to the dugout. "Vimsy, Dean, all the subs, you're an embarrassment, fuck off to the dressing room. Brig, sit here next to Livia. Do not let any of those fucks within five yards of her."

The Brig was just as pissed as me about the loss of discipline. It might have been the first time I ever heard him swear. "Which fucks? Our fucks or the Boston fucks?"

"The Boston fucks." My guys were still hanging around. Rage flooded me, but I got on top of it instantly. "Ten seconds to get out of sight or it's two week fines all round."

Pascal went first, followed by Magnus, then everyone else headed up the tunnel, leaving our bench empty save for Livia with her medical bag, being guarded by the Brig.

All the time, the referee was trying to peck my head off, talking shit, but I ignored it, just as I ignored everything the Boston twats were saying. Being down to ten men wouldn't stop me humiliating them. I was angrier with my lot than Boston, but that didn't mean I was going to let them off the hook. If they wanted some dark arts, I'd show them how dark this art could get.

I went back onto the pitch. We had a big hole on the right now, and we had three central midfielders who weren't naturals at playing right mid. I had Sam as the right-most of the three CMs, and he was the most solid defensively. I switched him to no forward runs to give us a bit of protection, then made Aff our playmaker and set the team to pass left.

The match restarted, full of spite and menace, and that was not the vibe we needed for this one. We needed to get back to how we'd approached the first half. So when I wasn't scampering around making interceptions, playing one-touch passes into the midfield, or covering our exposed right-hand flank, I was pottering around getting my guys back in the right mental state.

Tony, Raffi, Ryan, and Ben didn't need a calming word. With Aff, it was a simple, small gesture—*focus*. With Henri, instinct told me not to motivate him as such, but to get technical. Bring him back to the match that way.

"Henri, if you and Tony switch, do you think this rampaging centre back will be more likely to push forward?"

"Do you want him to push forward?"

"Absolutely."

Henri thought about it, and the unwanted aggression fell out of him. "Let's keep it this way. I will stop pressing him and appear disinterested. He might become emboldened."

"Amazing."

I jogged back to the DM slot, and we saw off another attack. Boston had renewed energy, and half an hour to play against ten men. But they were utterly predictable, and anything I couldn't deal with on my own, Carl mopped up.

"Carl! Leave some work for Glenn, you greedy prick!" He liked that, and the compliment was enough to achieve my goal. As a Boston player sat down to get treatment on a sore ankle, I went to my captain. "Glenn. I want to get a couple more goals on the board, and then I'm going to repay these pricks in kind. I'll need you to keep a lid on."

"On what?"

"On us. I'm going to act crazy, but we all know I'm not crazy. So you get the lads and bring them over to one side. Do not engage Boston. Do not get into verbals. Do not get involved."

"But *you're* going to?"

"Course," I said, laughing. "But no one else. Right? Set an example. You're my captain. You're my champion. And today your job is to let me do my thing." Calling him captain had been powerful, but calling him my champion went right into his soul. The guy's eyes turned red with all steamy fire coming out. Motivation 9,000.

The physio went off, and the Boston player winced as he tested his foot. He had decided to play on.

I scanned the pitch, and felt a surge of expectation. We were ready to get back to work.

But I'd missed one guy—Sam Topps. Raffi competed for a header, won it, won the second ball, and faked to pass. His opponent slid in, but Raffi did the cutback we'd done in training—very smoothly, I might add—pushed past another midfielder, shovelled the ball to Sam, and sprinted around another player, ready to be fed the ball.

Sam had other ideas—he got the ball out from under his feet and chipped it towards Henri.

I went crazy.

Fake crazy, of course, but maybe with a couple of drops of actual mania.

"The fuck?" I said, storming towards him. "The fuck was that?"

"Henri was free."

"Who gives a shit? We don't fucking hand the ball to the other team, mate! We don't do shit, low-percentage garbage! Just coz we fucking feel like it!" This was fun, being on the pitch to give a constant, rolling bollocking. "Have some fucking *pride* in your performance, mate."

That got him. He bit his lip to stop him giving me shit back—I'd been pretty flawless so he couldn't get me on mistakes I'd made—and he turned away, jaw clenched.

The ball was launched into midfield again, Raffi won the header, again, but this time a Boston dude was there first. Sam sprinted like a maniac towards it, and for a second I was sure he would launch into a reckless, dangerous, red-card tackle. But as he shifted his body weight to do just that, the ball carrier sensed it and turned away from the danger—right into my path. I booped the ball up the way I'd taught Dani, and when it hit the grass I side footed it to Sam.

He scampered away and played a simple pass to Ryan Jack.

I smiled. I was in complete control of my team now, and we were in complete control of this match.

Boggy: I mean, the setbacks! The red card! The injuries.

Max: Not really setbacks, are they? They're just events. Just things that happened.

Boggy: But you must have been worried.

Max: I was worried Boston's manager might pop.

Boston were able to move the ball down their left, our right, with their fast forward going on dribbles with no direct opponent. But as soon as he got into our last third, I'd sprint over and sort him out. It was easy; he was so right-footed he would always try to dribble to the "inside" of the pitch, and not once did he go straight down the line. In the time before I got over there, he could have done all sorts of things, but he looked like a lost little lamb.

"You know," I said to him, helpfully, after he tried to run past me for the fourth time, "it's not your day. You should probably just cross it. You know how to hit a cross, right?"

"Fuck you," he said.

But next time he got clear, he slowed down, took a long, hard look at the ball, and swung his left foot at it. He nudged the ball with his right just before his left arrived, and he blasted the ball at a crazy angle that brought a snide, mocking jeer from the Chester fans, and some angry shouts from the home lot.

I was right next to him, stroking my chin. "Right," I said, like an engineer trying to work out why a machine was broken. "Maybe go back to running into blind alleys. It's still embarrassing, but not as bad as that."

He didn't tell me to get fucked. He didn't say anything. He didn't need to—his morale went red.

And then, with our attacking play starting to crank back into gear:

Best takes the throw-in. All the way back to the keeper.

Cavanagh plays it short to Ryder.

Ryder to Jack. He turns.

Jack to Brown. Brown accelerates.

Suddenly, Chester players are everywhere!

The ball's played to Aff. He gets his head down, shapes to cross.

But he surges to the byline . . .

He cuts back, onto his weaker right foot.

Aff stands the ball up to the far post.

Lyons heads it back into the centre . . .

Hetherington can't miss!

GOOOOAAAALLLL!!!!

The Boston keeper has his head in his hands.

His defence didn't give him much help.

Amazing goal, but it came at a cost. When he'd cut back, Aff had been caught by the defender who slid in, and his acceleration and pace had turned red. These situations were where I needed the Injuries perk. Was this a minor knock? Could Aff run it off? Or would playing on risk making it worse?

Until I had the perk, I intended to play it safe.

I sent him to the dressing room, and told him to send Pascal out.

As I escorted Aff off the pitch, the referee came up to me. "Best, you've got nine players. We can't hold up the match while we wait for your sub to come from the dressing room and warm up!"

"No worries," I said, laughing, making eye contact with the Boston manager. "Nine's enough. This lot are shit."

Well, Boston didn't like that, and they tried to get stuck into a tackle, somewhere, on someone. But Ryan Jack knew what was up, and the two of us played bounce passes off each other while the Boston midfielders ran in a frenzy. When one came too close, we'd pass to Sam or Raffi. We fucking took the piss in midfield, and when Boston ran out of steam, I booted the ball as hard as I could in the general direction of the home dugout. It didn't go *very* near the manager, but he reacted like I'd fired a cannonball at him—one from a ship, not from my boot.

"Bossss," complained Glenn, from behind me, as the Julian guy came up to me and tried to shove me over.

"What?" I said, as much to the referee as to my captain. "It's just so we can bring our sub on!"

Boggy: What do you mean, you thought he might pop?

Max: Didn't you see him? He was screaming so much he looked like the kid in *Willy Wonka and the Chocolate Factory*. You know, the girl who chews the blueberry bubble gum she was told not to try. We were all ignoring him by then, which I think made him even angrier.

Boggy: Sorry, Max, sorry. But did you say . . . you ignored him?

Max: I mean . . . mostly. Right?

I put Pascal on the right and switched us to right passing. As I finished tweaking the settings, I fell to my haunches—a tiny wave of fatigue had hit me. Being player-manager was three times as tiring as doing one or the other. I imagined lining up against Darlington and pushed myself to keep going. If we could just play for five minutes without having to make any tweaks or changes, that would help.

We dicked for a while, and Boston fell further and further back. I switched with Sam Topps—he went to centre back and I played something like a right wing back. Basically, I hugged the touchline and stood fifteen yards behind Pascal, just in front of Boston's manager. When he took a step to the right, so did I. When he took another step, I mean, come on, you know what I did, and if you find that exasperating, imagine how he felt.

In my weird position, the ball wasn't coming to me, so I set myself as playmaker and stopped my guys from making forward runs. I wanted the ball!

It came, and I did some kick-ups. Eight, in fact. As I was going, I did the old counting trick I'd learned as a kid so that I could hyper-inflate my skills. "One, two, skip a few, ninety-nine a hun-dred!"

Well, the manager came at me but stopped himself before he did anything too stupid, which was disappointing. I did get clattered, and their left winger got a yellow card.

I lay on the ground, pretending to be in agony, for a full minute, pausing only to wink at my rival. When the referee's back was turned, I squirmed and saw Glenn Ryder giving an impromptu motivational speech in the centre circle. Keeping the lads away from me. Perfect!

Up on my feet, I took the free kick, and the match settled back into some semblance of normalcy for as long as it took me to jog to the centre spot and back to my new hunting ground in front of the home dugout.

Next time I got the ball, I stopped it dead, mentally switched Pascal to the left wing, set him as playmaker and made all the passes go left, then did one of the most obnoxious, disgusting things ever seen on an English football pitch.

Boggy: You positioned yourself right in front of the home dugout, and you were . . .

Max: What?

Boggy: You were being silly.

Max: Who, me? [laughter] That doesn't sound like me, Boggy.

The tension as I stared at the ball was palpable. Fifteen hundred people knew I was going to do something mad, and even though I was so focused on the match I couldn't hear most of the shouts and songs from the crowd, I felt it.

I bent and touched the ball with my right knee.

The crowd went apoplectic. Seriously, there could have been riots if I'd provoked them any further.

I bent and touched the ball with my left knee.

Multiple Boston players were storming towards me, and three arrived at once. Just in time, I flicked the ball sideways to Sam.

Topps sends the ball forward to Jack.

Jack finds Bochum in acres of space. Where are the defenders?

Bochum looks up. He has multiple options!

He chooses Brown.

Brown only has the keeper to beat . . .

GOOOOAAAALLLL!!!!

Safely into the corner.

And there's some trouble over on the benches.

Boggy: There was a lot of talk after that goal about sportsmanship and things like that.

Max: Seems like a perfectly legitimate goal to me.

Boggy: Well, yes, but it was . . . provocative.

Max: Nah. It was a training ground routine. A set move, in fact.

Boggy: So will we be seeing that one again?

Max: [laughter] No. No no no. [more laughter]

Boston went crazy, and I was surrounded by feral idiots throwing random punches. Most of their anger was because they knew I'd used their emotions against them, but still, I had to be rescued by the Brig. Once he'd got me out of the scrum, he suggested I might want to stop doing *that*. Then when I got a cheeky glint in my eye, he suggested if I did *that* again *he'd* be one of the guys ready to beat the devil out of me.

Boggy: So that was three–nil, with Raffi Brown on a hat trick. Something changed then.

Max: [distantly] Isn't it weird that *on* a hat trick means *close* to a hat trick? [normal] Yeah, the Boston Blueberry realised that his gamesmanship and sanctioned violence was blowing up in his face, so he tried something radical. He tried playing some football. He switched to four-four-two and tried to attack down the flanks.

Boggy: You called for Trick Williams.

Max: Yeah. I wanted to put him at left mid and Pascal on the right, and see how that shaped up. I hadn't seen Trick in that exact position but he's solid defensively and decent going forward. He's not quite at Aff's levels but I thought he might do a job for us. And if he can play there, we can rest Aff more often. I just wanted to try it in a real match, and it was hard to imagine there'd ever be a better time.

Boggy: You weren't worried at all? About saving a substitution for an emergency? About the possibility of a comeback?

Max: From Boston? In the state they were in? With us playing how we were playing? Not in the slightest.

Boggy: But then there was another setback.

Max: You and your setbacks.

The threat from the flanks wasn't going to keep me awake at night, but I was burning stamina getting around the pitch putting out fires. All we needed was to have Trick on the left, Pascal on the right, and that would deal with three-quarters of it.

So who to take off?

A striker? Nah.

One of my three CMs? Bro, why? They're running the game.

So I took Carl off and put Trick in Aff's position at left midfield.

"Boss," said Glenn.

"Oh, captain, my captain."

"Just checking . . . are we playing two-five-two with a right winger as our second centre back?"

"Ooh, I'm first centre back, wouldn't you say? I'm on at least eight out of ten today. You're barely breaking seven."

He laughed. "Okay, but you're not doing headers. That's all right as DM, but back here . . ."

I thought about it. "I will if I have to. Long punts, you get over and get your head on, all right? Don't worry if you need to go out of position. I've got you." I rubbed my hands together. "Now, let's slap."

And for a few minutes, we were right back to looking imperious. Trick slotted into the left mid position pretty well, and the team had a beautiful balance again.

But the universe didn't want me to enjoy my day. Sam challenged for a header, and when he landed, he crumpled to the floor, with his profile turning all kinds of red.

I checked the commentary and the foul count, but it didn't seem like the Boston guy had done anything wrong. Just a bad landing. My guys stayed calm—perfect.

Livia checked Sam out, and after a delay, called for the stretcher.

Sam was carried off. Normally a player who is stretchered off gets a round of applause from the opposition fans. Shows they are classy and it's just a game and all that. But I'd wound them up something rotten, so Sam was taken off to dead silence.

We went over to the side to take on liquid and squeeze marathon paste into our mouths.

"Max," said Henri. "We've made all our subs, yes? We're down to nine men. Will we defend? Three–nil is a good result."

"The best way to defend is to . . . help me finish the sentence . . . is to . . . ? Anybody?"

He shook his head. "You're crazy."

"You know what's crazy?" I said, standing tall and speaking from the heart for the first time that day. I swept my finger around the group. "Crazy is working as hard as you've all done. The fitness, the drills, the early starts, the double sessions. Crazy is doing all that, getting to this position, and saying that's enough. Fuck that! *We're* top, *they're* shit, let's go slap."

"Come on!" screamed Glenn, and the rest joined in.

We strode back onto the pitch, fists clenched.

Boggy: The last ten minutes were quite eventful.

Max: Refresh my memory.

Boggy: Well, we played some astonishing football considering we were down to nine men . . .

Jack passes to Brown.

Brown is pulled back, but lays it off to Bochum.

Bochum finds Jack and scampers away.

Jack feeds it through to Bochum.

His first-time pass is gathered by Lyons.

He combines with Hetherington.

Hetherington lines up a shot!

But it goes just wide!

Scintillating play from the away team.

Boggy: Did you think about taking your foot off the accelerator?

Max: No.

Boggy: Boston had a little purple patch.

Max: What? With their lump of a centre back as an emergency striker?

Boggy: You didn't react to that move.

Max: By what, putting Henri in goal? Come on, Boggy.

Boggy: It helped them get something going. A few corners and throw-ins. Bit of pressure. Their fans were getting really animated. They sensed their chance.

Max: What I think you're saying is that everyone in Lincolnshire who knew about football left on the Mayflower.

Boston fire a long ball forward.

Ryder leaps—he's beaten to it.

Chance here for Boston?

No—Best covers and puts the ball out for a throw.

Boston want to load the penalty area.

Bochum waits on the halfway line.

The long throw comes in.

It's flicked on—danger here!

Best chests the ball on the goal line!

He volleys it out to the left. That looked risky!

Williams is there. He gathers and pumps the ball forward.

Now Chester are one on one!

Bochum beats his man for pace.

He's going through!

But he's fouled!

The referee is going to his pocket.

It's red!

Boggy: They got a red card, and while the referee was dealing with the aftermath of that, we got some good news. Sam Topps declared himself fit to return to the action.

Max: Yeah, well, he said he was fit but he wasn't.

Boggy: You let him on, though.

Max: Just for the change in the vibe, right? It was eleven against nine, then it was ten against ten. They had a player walking off, we had one walking on. That's hard to take. Their morale took a nosedive.

Boggy: You had another altercation with the manager.

Max: Ah, this got blown way out of proportion. I simply, Boggy, simply tried to shake the hand of the player who got a red card. To tell him there were no hard feelings and whatnot.

Boggy: It did sort of look like you were thanking him for costing his team the chance of a comeback, or something like that.

Max: Come on.

Boggy: Then the manager shoved you, and you offered him a handshake, too. Would you like to tell us why?

Max: Just being friendly.

Boggy: Was it to wind him up?

Max: What a thing to say.

Boggy: Can you please tell us what happened next?

Max: Well . . .

Boggy: But, Max, please. I'm burning with curiosity. I know it's the kind of thing football insiders like to keep to themselves, but . . . please.

Max: All right. But that's your please card used for the year, okay? [sound of water being sipped] The referee came over. Asked me to stop winding the Boston guys up. Which, by the way, an outrageous slur. I mean, me? I said I'd stop if Boston stopped trying to cripple me and my players. The ref said yeah but it's not safe. He meant with the crowd, but by then they weren't hopeful. Loads left when we scored the fourth goal and the ones that stayed were stunned. I told the ref my employees weren't safe and if you think I'm going to let that slide you're delusional.

Boggy: I heard you shout, "Don't mess with Chesters."

Max: I'm sure you didn't. I was totally calm. But I did say I intended to run up the score and get this person sacked because he was a disgrace and we'd do it playing fantasy football and after every goal I'd offer the gentleman a handshake and every time he refused we'd score another one.

Boggy: Max . . .

Max: It was really a storm in a teacup. I had quite a lot of exhaustion and frustration that had built up and the guy got pretty much full blast.

Boggy: That explains why he left the dugout after the fifth goal . . . I thought he'd been sent off.

Max: He sent himself off. All right, that was Boston.

Boggy: We've got two more goals and another red card to talk about!

Max: Yeah but, you know. It's boring.

Boggy: It's not boring! Let's recap. We played a tough team, away, red card, used all the subs, down to nine men, you're playing DM, you're playing centre back. And we win six–nil. And those last two goals prove crucial in putting you just slightly ahead of Folke Wester in the race for Manager of the Month. Which you win.

Max: Okay, it's not boring. But we've only talked about one game and there's loads of other stuff to cover. I need a nap. Then a sleep. Then a holiday. Then a mini break to recover from the holiday.

Boggy: I really wanted to spend a good amount of time on the Boston match, Max, because it was . . . There was a good minute where I couldn't talk, there near the end. I pretended the microphone had a problem, but it wasn't that. I was looking around the pitch and it was mostly the same players as last year, but we'd gone from being awful, really terrible, to this. We were passing the ball around, doing whatever we wanted, it looked like. There was a swagger to it. A confidence. I was up there in the stands, biting my nails, worrying, begging you to retreat, to defend, to see it out. But after the fifth goal, I got emotional. It was unprofessional. But I just felt such . . . pride.

Max: Push that mic away a little bit.

Boggy: [tearful laughter] There we go. Ahh. Sorry. Being a silly old sod, here. I really just wanted to say thank you, Max. I work in the entertainment industry and there's a lot of overnight successes. Bands and comedians appear out of nowhere and set the world alight. But I saw them four years ago, playing to empty rooms. I know what it takes to get from mediocre to outstanding. You make it look easy, but I know it's not.

Max: It's a lot of work.

Boggy: I bet.

Max: I appreciate it, Boggy. I really do. Sometimes it feels that people . . . Okay, Boston. It was a great win and what I liked was that it was a culmination of lots of things. The fitness training, the technique drills, the way we build attacks. Even the stupid set pieces. But when the final whistle went, I was completely spent. You can't imagine how draining it is to try to play and monitor the whole team.

Boggy: I can imagine. I have twins.

Max: [laughter] Okay, you win. But I was spent, like I said, and then I have to go to the dressing room and work out what to do with my staff. They let me down and they let the club down. It doesn't matter why they did it. They need to be better than that. So I've done a full day's work, and there's more work to do. And of course, I tell them off and they don't like it. So now they're mad at me for telling them off for something they did wrong. Ugh.

Boggy: Was it—?

Max: Joe's red card makes teams think they can get at us with this dark arts stuff. I thought I'd put that to bed, right? Now the next ten matches, we're going to get it again and again, harder and harder. We're going to lose players to injury because of teams trying to kick us into getting red cards. It's infuriating. We've got to be smarter. The way we play, the way we behave, everything. We can't give advantages to our opponents. It drives me crazy. It's exhausting.

Boggy: Is that why you make the subs wait in the dressing rooms now?

Max: Yeah. I don't trust them.

Boggy: It's quite strange seeing one physio and your assistant manager and realising everyone else is in the naughty corner.

Max: I want to win matches, and they could have stopped me doing that. That's not acceptable. Fans like it when the guys lose their heads. I don't. I want to win. They'll serve their sentence and then get a last chance.

Boggy: Sentence? Did you do a court case? A trial?

Max: No comment.

Boggy: I suppose it was a bittersweet day for you, when you put it into perspective like that. Thanks for the insight, by the way. That's fascinating. But for us fans, it was unfettered joy. Darlington and York slipped up, and that result put us in second place, and really put the cat among the pigeons. Lots of people were taking notice. Raffi's hat trick got him the Player of the Month award, too.

Max: Deserved. Everyone's working hard, but he's on another level.

Boggy: We were all excited about the league, but then it was a few cup matches in a row. First up was Cray Wanderers. All the way down in London.

Max: Yeah, it was a long trip. [sigh]

Boggy: Talk us through the strategy and the lineup and your thoughts going into the match.

Max: Well, no disrespect to Cray, but they're near the bottom of the table in the . . . not sure I can say this right . . . Isthmian League? That's seventh tier, so it's like playing FC United in bad form. Obviously, on their day, they can beat us, but also obviously, on our day, we smash them. I did four-one-four-one, bit of rotation, Robbo in goal, Youngster as DM, Henri rested.

Boggy: You put yourself on the bench.

Max: Sometimes you get people saying such and such a cup isn't important, we should concentrate on the league. So I'm there to give myself fifteen minutes if things are going well, or the whole second half if my guys aren't on it. Obviously, a couple of guys like Trick who are getting minutes but aren't starting every week are keen to impress, and someone like Robbo knows every cup match is another match for him, so all in all, motivation was high and the will to win was there.

Boggy: Is Robbo the cup goalie, then?

Max: Not exactly. But if there's a cup match, he'll play in that or in one of the closest league games.

Boggy: A lot of people—

Max: I'm not interested in discussing that. My goalies rotate. Complain if you want. Get voted onto the board and you'll be able to tell me to my face what a mistake it is. Next.

Boggy: It was a very routine win.

Max: Yes. Really couldn't have gone better. And a little run out for Andrew Harrison, plus fifteen minutes for me.

Boggy: As the defensive midfielder.

Max: Right. I'm treating myself like your bog-standard genius who's recovering from injury. The forty-five minutes against Boston was an exception. I'll be building up to playing the full ninety, but don't expect me to do any mystery winger stuff. Maybe not this whole season.

Boggy: Okay, that's not what I wanted to hear. Wow. That's . . . I should be grateful you're playing, I suppose. I don't really see everything you do in that role but Spectrum's in complete rapture about it. Sometimes he just sighs. It's bad radio. But three–nil, and these wins are starting to feel comfortable.

Max: Why wouldn't they be?

Boggy: It certainly helps that we keep so many clean sheets. The Cray win made five games in a row without conceding, although there were plenty of hairy moments in that period. At the other end, there were lots of goals going in. Most from open play, but with some caused by the chaos of some very unusual set pieces. I'm guessing those are training ground routines?

Max: Every Wednesday morning, the lads get together in those huts, those shaman huts, throw weird mushrooms onto a fire, breathe the fumes, and the most surreal free kick idea gets chosen to be tried in a real, professional football match. That's what I think happens, anyway. It's certainly the best way to explain some of the stuff we do.

Boggy: You don't have input into the set pieces?

Max: My input is to delegate it. It's bonkers, what they think we're capable of, but it has the benefit of making us really quite good at defending set pieces. We're ready for anything, it feels like.

Boggy: The draw for the next round was made the next evening, and we got another Cray!

Max: I had no idea there were so many teams called Cray.

Boggy: Cray Valley Paper Mills FC. Another away tie!

Max: It's really crazy the way that's happening. But I don't care. I'm just thinking, win that and we're in the FA Cup proper. The first round. I mean, we're likely to be big underdogs but if we could win, that'd be forty grand in prize money. It's already starting to add up.

Boggy: Handy in the January transfer window.

Max: No, the prize money's reserved for the players. It's all going on training equipment and medical gadgets and the like. Basically saying to the lads, win and we'll help you win more. When I say it out loud, it sounds stupid. But I think it's working. They're telling us what they want. Stuff they've had at other clubs. And whenever one of us hears a club is doing something to their training ground, Inga calls and asks if they're selling their old gear. We've picked up a few little bargains. We got a load of boxing stuff and the lads are absolutely mad for it. Yeah, it's motivational.

Boggy: So that was September. Manager of the Month, as we said. Congratulations, again. The first match in October was for the women's team.

Max: October first was the FA Cup Qualifying Second Round against Warrington. The same Warrington who are not only in our league, but were our next scheduled opponents. Back-to-back games against the same team—I'm not a fan.

Boggy: Were you prioritising the cup or the league?

Max: Yes.

FA Cup Qualifying Round 2: Warrington Double Question Marks versus Chester Women.

The monthly perk dropped on October 1, a cold Sunday morning. It was called Hot Stuff! For 500 XP it would let me create preset hot buttons with different tactical options to use in matches. It said I could switch formations and individual tactics with one "key press" instead of having to click on individual profiles.

It was a quality of life upgrade I normally would have postponed, but I was starting to get a bit frazzled from making hundreds of decisions and not getting proper sleep. It was also the only perk that would make being player-manager slightly easier. I'd be able to set Aff as the playmaker and make the team pass left, then switch it all over to the right, with a single thought. A little less time in my screens, a little more mental energy for being a player. So while it would delay my getting the Injuries perk, I felt I needed it.

We were away at local rivals Warrington. On all my documents, they were listed as Warrington Wolves, but on the day they called themselves Warrington Town Women, while one website had them as Warrington Town Ladies.

Just annoying, and by the way, don't switch from a cool name to a generic one.

Their average CA was 18, which put me in a great mood, because with a little bit more time on the training pitch and a little bit of tactical cleverness, we could hope to beat them home and away in the league. Our best possible CA, playing a 4-5-1, was a smidge over 16. Tough match, then, and a good chance we'd get knocked out of the cup. So I decided to smash Triple Captain and Bench Boost. To make that more effective, I dropped Bea Pea and Dani to the bench so they'd play great in the second half. I also had Kisi available.

Dani and Kisi had a weird relationship. Kisi was super friendly, of course, and had secretly been learning sign language. Dani, though, was only polite in return.

Bonnie took me aside and explained that my enthusiasm for Kisi made Dani jealous, and I could use that as a motivational tool. So I turned up to training and expressed amazement at Kisi's dribbling, forward thinking, positivity, two-footedness. Basically, anything I wanted Dani to do more of, I praised Kisi for.

And it worked! Dani improved slightly faster than the group on average.

Boggy: You surprised everyone by leaving out Dani and Bea Pea. It was almost as though you were happy to get knocked out. Happy to play a weakened team.

Max: Nah. They only have a match every two weeks so it's important to do well in the cups. That was a tactical plan.

Boggy: Could you explain the plan? Julie McKay struggled on her own in that first half.

Max: The plan was to smash the second half.

Boggy: I suppose that's a pretty good plan.

Max: I didn't think we'd smash quite that hard.

Boggy: From one–nil down to four–one up. Warrington scored two late on to make the match look closer than it was.

Max: The prize money for that was three thousand pounds. Did you know that? That's handy cash.

Boggy: The interchange between all the midfielders was something to behold.

Max: Oh, mate, it was unreal. Dani, Kisi, Maddy, and Bea Pea were like a little whirlwind. I told the defenders to stay back because we didn't need them. So we had that solid base, Pippa and Charlotte bossing the midfield, and then a healthy bit of chaos.

Boggy: A healthy bit of chaos. Could be the name of your autobiography.

Max: I was thinking *Max Best: Starboy.*

Boggy: So we're in good shape, there. There's the league match against the same opponents tomorrow, and then another cup tie.

Max: Stockport County in the Cheshire Cup. They're tier four. I can imagine that'll be tough. And it's another away match! We're crazy unlucky in the cup draws. Did you know Man United have had ten home cup matches in a row? It's like a thousand-to-one odds. Yeah, the women are on track. Unless there's a super team in the league, we'll be all right. It looks, so far, like Altrincham are the best so we'll know more after we've played them.

Boggy: Going back to the first week in October, if I may, we had a little spate of contract announcements. That came as a surprise to a lot of people. I've got the first tweet here. Let me read it out . . . "Chester FC are delighted to announce we've signed a contract extension with Diarmuid Dubhlainn! Manager Max Best says, 'Aff! Aff! Aff!'"

Max: Yep. Two more years, plus an extension if we want it. It's great.

Boggy: There were a few rumours doing the rounds that you didn't like him.

Max: Am I supposed to discuss rumours with you, Boggy? Is that a good use of our time?

Boggy: Why did you start with Aff?

Max: Very important player, still got the potential to improve, works hard, great for the team, gets what we're doing here. There's no particular rhyme or reason to the order. There's loads of great players I want to keep who I haven't spoken with, yet. Some of it depends if we get promoted or not.

Boggy: Next was Ben Cavanagh.

Max: Young goalie, we think he can keep improving.

Boggy: Max, he's three years older than you! You can't call him young.

Max: Channeling my inner dinosaur. Who else? Carl Carlile. I was pleased with that one, especially, because we had a good talk before. I told him he can move up a couple of divisions and I'll help him do that, but he has to knuckle down. Not that he's lazy, but he's a bit, I don't know, disillusioned that he's been stuck at this level. But he feels we're building a head of steam. He feels what's happening here, and he wants to come with us and be part of it, and that's exciting for me. With the women's team, it's all about starting from scratch and every time you add a new player it unlocks all kinds of combos and special moves—I mean, look what happened when we unleashed Kisi Yalley! But the men's team is way more established and it's just thrilling to take someone like Carl and energise him and turn him into a new player.

Boggy: You're really motivated by coaching.

Max: Not me as the coach, not all that much, no, but seeing the potential in someone and getting obstacles out of their way in some cases and beating it out of them in other cases, that's so much fun. That's so satisfying.

Boggy: It's good to see you smile!

Max: I smile, Boggy. I'm just tired.

Boggy: I can see that. On the women's side, you started with Charlotte.

Max: She's quality. Two plus one, but the one comes with a big pay raise so we won't trigger that if we're still in tier six. It protects her. Win-win. Then I offered the same to Bonnie, and that was . . .

Boggy: What?

Max: Nothing. She signed, all good. Big step forward for the group.

I had the Brig in my office at the credit card building as I stared at a computer screen. The rectangle of blue light was squashing and expanding like a psychedelic screen saver. It was fascinating. My head dipped, and that woke me back up for a few seconds, but then it was dipping again.

Bonnie appeared, knocked on the open door, and stepped inside, a bit wary. Her morale was in red—it had plummeted to Ok. She'd come in on her lunch break from whatever garbage job she did because I'd said I had a deal to offer her. I fished in various drawers and found the standard contracts we'd drawn up. I talked her through the terms but it was so boilerplate there wasn't much to say.

"The money's shit. You'll need to keep your day job. It's more about rewarding you for your effort. And getting some stability. I don't want twenty new players every season."

She had this weird, defensive look about her. "Why start with me?"

"I'm not. Charlotte signed. Dani's parents want me to wait. You're up." I wanted her to sign so I could stare at the screen and get back into that headspace of nearly being asleep. That was awesome. I put my hands on my lap and felt their warmth. If I was in bed, I could curl up into a ball. That would be nice.

Bonnie checked out the Brig, who was doing some coaching coursework. He noticed the gap in the conversation and looked up, but Bonnie turned to me again. She turned towards the door, just a fraction. "Why me?"

"Jesus Christ," I said, standing up and pottering around. I paused in front of the photo of young Jackie. I'd decided to keep it. Sort of a warning—don't work so hard you burn out. It wasn't going that well. "You're the captain. You're my best defender. You're essential to everything we're doing. Holy shit. Bonnie, I'm completely out of battery. I'd love one interaction to go smoothly. One per month. Sign, or don't, but don't give me the twenty questions treatment. Please." I sat back down, rubbing my hands all over my face.

"I just want to know," she said, in an unexpected soft-spoken voice, as she stared at her hands, "if it's for me or for Angel."

I slumped against the back of my chair—the Ian Evans chair—and hunted around my memories for someone called Angel. There was nothing in the player database. Nothing in the staff section. My normal, human memories came up blank. I leant forward and put my head on the desk. I felt so, so tired. Dog tired. What did dogs do when they'd had enough? They found somewhere soft and crashed on it, right? "Brig, get me a pillow."

"You have a meeting with the board at one o'clock, sir. Then it's off to a school to watch a match."

"Mate," I said, with half my cheek squashed flat. I made a sad little noise. "You do the board."

"Regrettably, I cannot. They are impertinent." He had been pretty smug when I'd started complaining about the new board. They had some uppity guys who thought they had the right to ask me about my decisions. The fact that I didn't feel like explaining myself to anyone was a source of no little friction. But when they'd dared to press the Brig about his qualifications and suitability for the role, he had reacted just the same as me. Sulkily.

"Max?" said Bonnie.

"Go way," I mumbled.

"So it's really not about Angel?"

"Angel!" I said, briefly flashing wide awake. But that only served to make the next collapse into sleep even more irresistible. "I know a demon. Do you have an angel? That's not fair."

I dreamt that I heard the contracts being signed.

Match 11 of 46: Chester FC versus Peterborough Sports.

Boggy: Next up was the men's home league match against Peterborough.

P Sports. Tenth on my list of the strongest teams. Average CA: 43. Average morale: 4.7. Typical 4-4-2 team with a more technical midfield than most. I went 3-5-2 to try to swamp them, and it worked. Still, they gave us a fright.

Boggy: Were you worried when they went two–nil up?

Max: I mean, only in the sense that if you go crazy looking for a goal and they score a third, you make it really difficult for yourself. But the way we played the ten minutes before their goals and the ten minutes after was exactly the same, which shows the players were really sticking to the plan. Believed in our way of playing. And when we got the goal back before halftime, I did think we'd come out blazing in the second half. So I got a bit more technical than normal at halftime.

Boggy: What like?

Max: Pointing out weaknesses in their players. I really focused on two lads who I thought we could get at, but when we went back out we saw they'd subbed them off. I don't know if you remember they were all laughing their heads off . . .

Boggy: I do remember that! That's why?

Max: Yeah. They thought me wasting my time like that was hilarious. And I suppose it was. But that's the mood in the dressing room. Very confident. You could say that's a setback, right, analysing those players so much and then finding out they're not even playing. Stuff like that makes winning even sweeter. And the guys who came on weren't as good, so whatever.

Boggy: They were taller.

Max: Teams in this league are obsessed with the idea they can score, like, five corners a match against us because we've got a couple of short players. I don't understand why people think of me as some kind of tactical maverick when you've got managers setting up basketball teams against us. I think most of what I do is pretty conventional by comparison. And look at the numbers! There are two teams who are very good at defending corners, two who are very bad, and the rest are in a big statistical blob. And we are one of the most dangerous teams from other teams' corners. We're more likely to score from your corner than from ours. That's the most self-evident thing in the world to me, but they keep finding tall, slow men to throw into the box and they wonder why we keep scoring.

Boggy: We did concede from two corners, though.

Max: I know. I was there. And the board told me. How we defend corners was items eighty to ninety-five on the most recent agenda. Here's the thing about corners: the probabilities are massively in our favour. He had a good left foot, the guy in that match. Got three or four right in the danger zone. Good player. But so what? We get back to two–all, and Ryan Jack's got a little tweak or something. He could play on, but he's so, so important to what we do I don't want to risk it. So I go on for him.

Boggy: I had Spectrum doing co-comms with me, and he promised me—promised me!—that you would play central midfield, that there was no way you'd play DM in front of a back three. But you played DM again! What formation was that?

Max: I suppose you'd call it three-one-four-two.

Boggy: And you practise that, no doubt, assiduously, in the week before you use it.

Max: We don't need to practise it, Boggy. It's three-five-two with one guy a bit deeper. Everyone knows their roles, and the only guy doing something different is me. Why do you worry about these things?

Boggy: Because other teams can't do these things! Because we're the only team that plays two new formations every week!

Max: Come on. Yeah, so with the three centre backs behind me, I decide to interpret my role in a more, kind of, marauding way.

Boggy: Which was a disaster.

Max: Which was a disaster, yes. But one of my moves led to the free kick which—

Boggy: Hold on. Hold on! You played a nice one-two with Raffi, and you were closing in on the penalty box, and Henri and Tony were making runs away from you, and you tried to do a couple of Ronaldo stepovers—

Max: I lost my mind, mate.

Boggy: And you fell over, and the ref gave a free kick.

Max: That's exactly what happened. Thing is, when I'm slapping the ball left and right, doing one-touch passes, hundred percent pass accuracy rate, I sometimes forget that I'm not superhuman anymore. And, yeah, it was a bit embarrassing falling over in front of two thousand people, but guess what? They didn't notice. And neither did you.

Boggy: Spectrum told me.

Max: Right. So Aff clips the free kick to the far post, Henri powers a header down into the goal, three–two, job's a good 'un, and we all had a laugh about it after.

Boggy: Really?

Max: No, Peterborough were livid. They called me a cheat and cast aspersions about my parentage. I mean, I hope they look at the footage because you can see I trip myself up, and I don't even appeal for the free kick. I actually really liked that match and how they played.

Boggy: Okay, so that was another three points. Twenty-five points after eleven games seemed pretty unlikely after losing the first two. And today was the FA Cup Qualifying Fourth Round, down in Greenwich! Which is where we both were, six hours ago. London, again, to play Cray Valley Paper Mills. Oh, Max. You're struggling.

Max: Yeah. Boggy, my goose is cooked. We won. We're in the real FA Cup now. Big achievement. Hope we get a home draw so the fans can get some of that FA Cup magic. Etcetera. But yeah. Six hours there. Manage. Play. Media. Six hours back. Talk to Boggy. Sleep. Another away match tomorrow.

Boggy: So . . . Hmm.

Max: What?

Boggy: I know you don't like hearing it, but . . . No, it's not my place.

Max: Go on. Say it. I'm doing all this for you, mate. When I'm stuck in my chair, trying to convince myself to get up and go to the next thing, I think of you screaming into the microphone, hoping the goalscorer doesn't have the letter P in his name. Your joy and passion, Boggy. That's what's keeping me going. You're the voice of this club. Who else in the world am I going to sit down for an interview with at the end of a long, long day when all I want is to go to bed? No one. So you've got my permission. Speak your mind. This is me pre–absolving you.

Boggy: [sigh] Max, you're doing too much. Are . . . are you getting the support you need?

Max: Yes. When I ask for something, I get it. I asked MD for some cash to send a rando on a scouting course and he huffed and puffed, preening himself up like a big accountant peacock, but he said yes. So I'm hoping we'll get a scout out of that. If she's as good as I suspect, she'll help. She'll be a force multiplier.

Boggy: Oh. That all sounds . . . very Max. You need a proper break, though. I'm not saying you shouldn't manage the women, far from it, but . . .

Max: It's the playing, Boggy. That's the thing. I'm pushing my limits so I can play . . . in a certain match. And so I can help the team when they really need me to go on and make a difference. And I am looking for someone to be a head coach for the women. I told them at the start of the season I was looking for someone. We've had applicants. But, take two examples of managers I've worked under. Ian Evans and David Cutter. Very typical football guys, yeah? But it's four-four-two defensive. I've put together a team full of crafty little midfielders, so I can't have a four-four-two guy. I can't have a defensive guy. That rules out seventy percent of the industry.

Boggy: But—

Max: Look, don't worry about it. I'm not on a mad self-destructive power trip. I know I need help, but it has to be the right help. The wrong help is more tiring than no help.

Boggy: I feel sorry for you, seeing you there on the touchline with just your assistant and one physio, and the other manager has ten people to talk to. And your girlfriend lives so far away. I hate to think you're lonely when you're doing so much for this city.

Max: I'm not lonely, Boggy. I've got you. And listen, I'm working hard, but I love it. I'm very lucky. It's a dream job. Sometimes it's one of those dreams where you're filling in endless paperwork or people are telling you all the mistakes they think you're making based on something they heard a guy say in a pub. And I suppose if I was designing the absolute perfect state of affairs, there wouldn't be a guy who'd made a whole website called has Max signed a proper contract dot co dot uk which is just the word no in big letters.

Boggy: One thing you could do that not a single fan would think less of you for, is put out a weak team in the Cheshire Seniors Cup this Tuesday night.

Max: Absolutely not. We're in it to win it. And we're going for the FA Trophy, too, when that starts.

Boggy: You know, I think you might actually be a little bit crazy.

Max: You might be right.

Boggy: Great win today. There's incredible energy around the place. I got some voice note submissions from the fan buses today. I can't use a single one, but trust me, you've lifted the whole city, Max.

Max: Okay.

Boggy: Join us next month where we'll talk about our various cup runs, league performances, and, first and foremost, the women's team. All right, Max? Oh! Let's end on that smile.

Max: They can't see it, Boggy.

Boggy: They can hear it.

Max: Come on, you Seals.

17

NOTES FROM UNDERGROUND

Monday, October 16. Five days until Kidderminster.

From: Physio Dean
To: Max
Subject: Notes from Underground

I am a sick man, I am a wicked man. I am an unattractive man. My undiagnosed neuroses are legion, but I choose to believe they compete with each other rather than their host, leaving me able to muddle through as a somewhat functional member of society. I lie awake wondering what I'll get wrong next. Daily life with all its mundanity is joyless and solitary. My office is a cave burrowed into the side of another cave. Everyone I meet despises me, and I despise them for being justified.

Long ago, a fellow undergrounder on LinkedIn confessed that he writes scathing, vicious emails to his boss with the To: field filled in. Typed it all out, always a key press away from disaster. Typed it all out, and at 5 p.m. deleted and went home, cleansed and refreshed. Like most advice on LinkedIn, it's gold. It keeps me sane, though I'm too vain to delete my work. The man is my hero. I spend three hours a week trying to rediscover him, but misanthropes don't like and subscribe. My highest ever review was four stars. Uber drivers are one of many groups who rightly spit on me. The others are women, footballers, authority figures, and water park employees.

Today was the usual—a bunch of miserable men asking me to check their aches and pains. Players who start every match, players with fresh ink on their contracts, those players don't come. They have the same aches and strains as the marginalised, but they don't feel it. Donny feels the aches. Joe Anka feels the pain. Gerald May is starting to complain about his back. Max promised to use everyone through the season, and he has, but these three are sliding down the pecking order. Joe, along with Vimsy, along with me, is being punished. Left out of matchday squads, banished from the touchline, pitied and mocked by the others. The others who, to a man, joined in the fight at Boston. The inequity is staggering. Spite is the only logical response, and I came to work today full of spite. Yesterday, so close to catharsis: Max's precious women were losing, losing, losing, then got two jammy late goals. Of course my bitterness lasted only a fleeting moment, then I was happy for the ladies. I can't blame them for what Max does. The dust of understanding comes a microsecond before the collapsed ceiling of self-loathing.

Max. The talent, the looks, the girlfriend, the late goals to save his stupid dreams of winning the league at the first swing. Why does he get everything?

Then he comes in, boss baby himself, drops his bags, and the walking wounded stand up and insist he go to the front of the queue.

"It's just my neck," he says, not for a second thinking to wait his turn. "I bought a tent to sleep in. Try to get some quiet. Have you ever slept in a tent? It's shit. You're lying on the actual ground. Why's that fun?"

We're all looking at each other thinking this is a wind-up, but I sit him down and test his traps. They're rock hard. Doctor voice says, "Hoodie off, get up on here."

"You need a bigger tent," says Gerald, who is tall. We concede more from set pieces when he isn't playing, and there's only one person in the world who can't see that. "Otherwise you get yourself curled up and, yeah, you get cricks and cramps."

"Argh," says Max. I've gone in medium strength but he's so tense it's agony.

I try my soothing voice. It comes easier with the aromas and the plinky plonky music. "We'll get you relaxed, loosen these knots, then later we'll go in for some deep tissue stuff. All right?"

"Yeah," he says, but as I start making circles on his upper body, I feel him sink, through the massage table, through the foundations of the building, into snoresville. The podcast interview that was released yesterday morning had seemed like self-serving claptrap to me, but no. The boy is genuinely wrecked. I keep massaging while I try to think of all the parts I spat at. Scoffed at. Made rude gestures at.

Livia comes in, wondering what's going on.

"It's Max," whispers Joe. "Says he camped out in a tent and now his neck's mangled. Dean found his off button. Lights out. Never seen anything like it."

"Why don't you three go and train?" she murmurs in her most seductive voice. She's got that in her locker, but she only uses it in dire straits. "Tell Glenn no one's to come in."

Annoyed, I stop the massage. Max stirs, Livia notices, and she gestures that I'm to move aside. I obey and she takes over, but she goes straight to his neck and starts a fucking ASMR routine on it. The result is immediate—a deep sigh, slow breaths.

"What about the treatments that are *scheduled*?" I whisper.

"Do it outside," she says in a lullaby voice.

This hits me right in the spleen. Spite and bile bubble up. Livia is not my boss. Livia does not get to make these decisions. Treating players outside is not professional. But she's a thousand percent on Team Max, because Max is a thousand percent on Team Jackie. No one is on Team Dean. Not even Dean.

Joe tugs on my sleeve. "Didn't you hear the podcast?"

I am a few glands short of spitting a globule of acid in his face. "Of course I did." Max is tired? Boo hoo. Stop trying to be an action hero. Easy fix.

"Come on," he whispers. "Let him sleep."

He cajoles me into going outside, explains what's going on to Glenn, and then it's all about finding different solutions. Henri nominates himself as the stealthiest—says he has certain trophies he could show as proof—so he'll sneak in and come back with a massage table without disturbing Max. Glenn asks what else I need. I mention a few things, and twenty guys start explaining where we can get some without stepping foot in the medical room.

"It's not very cosy out here," I suggest, trying to play up the concept that a medical room should look like a spa, so that someone will see sense and wheel Max into the meeting room or something. Something sensible.

Ryan Jack says, "I've got this." He gets his car keys, wanders off, and comes back with a lamp he's got in his boot for some reason. He puts his Christmas tree air freshener on the top, slaps his hands together, says, "Diffuser."

And then it's bedlam. Energy's through the roof and training is paused while they rebuild my medical room, outside. Additions to the "room" get sillier and sillier, with Raffi Brown noisily pouring Powerade from one glass into another—a water feature—and two young players are told to stand apart and lean towards each other, fingertips touching. This is, apparently, the wall art.

I keep waiting for the Brig or Vimsy to get a grip, get on with the actual training, but no. This is our life now. When Henri comes out, with Pascal and Youngster holding the doors open for him, he lifts the massage table over his head like it's a trophy, and the squad goes bananas.

While Carl and Henri, cosplaying as me and Livia, do a reiki treatment on Magnus, who is laughing his head off as they talk about unblocking his "chlamydians", I look at the two kids who are there and say, "Who's this?" even though I know. Why? Some mad power play. Make someone justify their presence to me. I'm filled with bile and self-loathing.

Glenn hasn't noticed. "Vivek from the eighteens, and Tyson from the sixteens. It's half-term at school. Max wants them to get a taste of what professional football looks like."

"When's that going to start?" I say, using one of Max's favourite lines to devastating effect. But far from being hilarious, it bombs. Glenn looks embarrassed that I would say something like that. Tyson looks furious—I've made another enemy. Why am I so shit at life?

"Come on, Viv," Glenn says. "I'll show you the ropes."

There's a bit of a comedown and in the gap I tap the massage table and say, "Who's up first?" but everyone's in such a good mood they shun my therapy and get on with training. I put my foot down, and demand Aff let me do his stretches. He doesn't want to, so I say he needs to get on the table or I'll tell Max.

What have I become?

It never rains, only pours.

I've been in my sub-cave, venting by email. I have a string of emails in draft form describing how much I hate Max. I fantasise about sending them out one day. The day I get my new job. As soon as I find a job that's somehow more of a dream job than working for a football club, and as soon as I fix the many and various character defects that make me unemployable.

I reread today's missive, and while the act of writing it up is mildly therapeutic, the act of reading it brings up the bile and the spite and the loathing. Max is right to keep me in my cave, away from sunlight. Sunlight is the best disinfectant and I am a germ.

"Help! Can you help us?"

I shoot to my feet. Max, snoozing like an old bloodhound, wakes up. I'm spitefully happy to see he gets nap face and drool like the rest of us. "Come in!" I say, and it's my doctor voice. The one I try to use all the time, the one that only comes when it wants.

It's three people from the credit card company. Two young, one old. The old one has had a fall and hit something sharp on the way down. She's in tears, she's in pain, there's blood. Max puts his hoodie back on and offers the massage table. He helps lift her up, and I'm right into action.

I blink, all is quiet, and I've finished the cleanup and assessment and got her patched up. It's a nasty cut but I'm pretty sure nothing's broken. It hurts and it will get worse. I tell her all this, but she refuses to take any tablets I give her. She's shaken, but this suspicion of doctors comes from the pandemic. It's depressing, but there's so many like that I have to ignore it or I'll crack. I recognise her—she's the boss. Head of UK operations at the credit card company. I retrace all my steps. Did I miss anything? Should we send her to the emergency room, if only to cover our backs?

Max doesn't know who she is, and is giving her double barrels of his so-called charm.

"Stop complaining, you big baby," he says. "It hurts. You're fine." The woman's underlings are scandalised, but they're too scared to intervene.

"It's broken! I can't feel my toes!"

"Dean's fixed you, mate. He's a genius. You've probably got *more* toes, if anything. Right. Let's talk about this cover. You've got blood all over it. That's cost me, hasn't it? Hey, what gets red blood stains out? It's white blood, isn't it? Dean, where's the white blood?"

I work for a toddler. "We're out, Max. It's all stuck in the Suez canal."

He gets close to the knee. "Can you make this bruise come up in the shape of Jesus or something? Could make some cash out of that. Try to think holy thoughts. Although you've just seen me topless, so that'll be hard." He shapes his fingers into a square, like a movie director. "That knobbly bit could be his forehead."

"My knees," declares one of Chester's most senior businesswomen, "are not knobbly." She locks eyes with Max, they have some kind of contest, but when Max smiles, she does too. "It hurts like hell."

"Dean, what do we do? Do we need to amputate?"

"Shush, you," says the woman, rolling her eyes.

"Well," I say, and doctor voice is fading. Max is in charge now. "We've cleaned the wound. It's disinfected. Next we bandage it. Then ice and elevation against swelling. Ideally some ibuprofen." Her face says no, no way, like I want her to suck on plutonium. If I keep my sadness off my face, it's a miracle. "It looked horrible but on the whole, I'd say you were lucky. An inch to the side could have been very unpleasant. You might have a tiny, tiny scar."

Max jabs his finger at her. "You heard the man! You're fine. Get back to work! No malingering!" For some reason, she laughs. He grabs a roll of bandage. "What do you do, anyway?"

"I'm a manager," she says, which is something of an understatement.

He makes a dismissive noise. "Nothing important, then." That gets him a playful slap. He looks at the underlings. Now that my tunnel vision is fading, I realise one is attractive. Very attractive. It feels like Max is winking at her, but I know that's the jealousy talking. Winking is what people like me think people like him do. "I'll do the bandage. I'm a *genius* at bandages."

Everyone in the room, including the two underlings, knows where this is going. Max is going to act the maggot. And sure enough, within seconds the boss's entire leg, from knee to ankle, is mummified.

"Beautifully done, Max," I say, as I help the patient lean back on the table and put cushions under her head and under her ankles.

"Keep that on for, what, fifty-two days? Don't worry if there's a kind of rancid smell that develops. That's normal. Shows you're healing." As he babbles, I undo his work and rebind it properly. "Oh," he says, sniffily, "you prefer the Double Thatched Method. Each to their own, I suppose."

"And what are *you*?" says the big boss.

"Me?" says Max, and I'm gobsmacked to realise that just as he is ignorant of her status, she is also unaware of his. "I do a bit of this and that. Some copywriting. I did a TikTok, once. They retweeted it but didn't pay me." He moves my stool and sits on it so she can see him without moving her head too much. "And sometimes I talk a load of shit so people can take their minds off things." He looks at her knee. "How's that working out for you?"

"Good. I'm fine now. I'll go soon. Be out of your hair."

"Nope. You're staying. You're in shock and when you calm down, we'll find out if you've banged some other bits. We're not letting you leave here with a broken collarbone or something mad." He gets up, goes into my cave, writes the number *1* on two post-it notes, and hands one to what I am starting to realise is the woman I'll be fantasising about for the next two years. "Come back in . . ." He looks at me.

I shrug. I'm sure there's no more damage, but Max is right to be cautious. And he has that weird sixth sense about when people are more hurt than they look. I've learned not to gainsay him. "Couple of hours?"

Max finger guns the one holding the note. She looks at it. "What's this for?"

"So we know which one is yours." He places the other post it on the boss's forehead, and she snatches it off, looks at it, laughs, and sticks it to her chest like a name badge.

The underlings leave, and Max sits patiently next to the . . . patient. (Christ. Glad no one will ever read this.) It's not long until she's restless. She squirms around until she spots the diffuser. She relaxes. "It's nice in here." That's it.

That's all she says. But Max's face lights up. He gives me a wide beam and double thumbs-up. It's a bigger celebration than he does for most of our goals.

I don't know what it is, but this tiny moment pushes back the date I will unleash my resignation email storm by a week or two. I realise I'm smiling, too. "Max, can I . . . work in here?"

He muses. "I think your patient would like some action. She's not the type to sit and suffer." He nods at the treatment table. "Do you want to see a fit young man get expertly stretched and bent while both doctor and patient grunt and groan? Don't answer that. Dean, use extra oil. Extra grunting."

The boss laughs more. I get the feeling she doesn't do much of that. "Laughter is the best medicine."

"Ibuprofen works, too," I say.

She grimaces and turns away. Oof. All my good feeling gone in a second. Why did doctors become the enemy?

I go out and wait for a drill to end, then drag Joe out of the session. He's got a long-term calf problem that needs a lot of attention. Max banishing him from the team couldn't have come at a better time—we might be able to get on top of it. Joe is finding it hard to see the silver lining.

When we're about to go in, I get suspicious and block Joe. We both lean forward to eavesdrop.

"Expertise, athleticism, moments of surprise," Max is saying. "Right? And I love that. But my job is to reduce the surprise."

"How exactly do you mean?" says the boss lady. I realise he's never going to ask her name. He's enjoying this little drama, but he's not interested in meeting her again.

"It's like . . . I've got this system of playing that's very, very hard to stop. It's designed to be overpowered for this level, but still within the, like, realm of possibility for our players. They can do it. None of the individual moves are hard. It's just a question of doing it under pressure, and I take away the pressure."

"How?"

"By reframing their jobs so that the only pressure comes from me. Outsiders? They're welcome to their opinion, but no one understands what we're trying to do. So why would you care what they think? No, you do what I want and you get praise, even if we lose. Because do what I want and we'll win almost all the time. We're better than almost everyone we play. It helps that my methods *work*. We're second in the league and on Saturday, we play the team who are top. That could be tricky, but we've basically eliminated the surprise result already. You know, where weaker teams beat us. We're way ahead of schedule. The guys have been really working hard. We have buy-in from most."

"Most?"

"There's a few holdouts. People who think they're on board, but they're not. They understand some specific parts of their roles, but still haven't grasped the, ah, holistic view."

"Why are you laughing?"

"A football outsider used the word holistic a few years ago and everyone laughed at him. His team wins the league every year, now."

"I had no idea your industry was so fascinating. I see you playing on our fields but it all seems . . ."

"Homoerotic?"

"Medieval."

I tap Joe, and we sneak away, then return, noisily clomping our way down the corridor and into the room. Joe hops onto the second massage table and I get to work. Joe, at least, values what I do.

Max and the woman talk about management styles, *The Art of War*, Myers–Briggs. They're very different, chalk and cheese, really, but they've got a strange kinship. They've both got hard jobs, a lot of responsibility, and both are delighted to discover that another Tsar has been in this building the whole time. Max jokes about mentoring her, and she laughs so much it hurts. He's not afraid to make fun of himself. They don't teach that on LinkedIn. Maybe there's a TED Talk about it.

Max says he needs a tea and he'll get "one of the noobs" to make drinks, and does she want a vegan hotdog or something? She's been losing the alpha personality contest, but she's got an ace up her sleeve—a PA who does her coffees just right, and access to all sorts of corporate snacks. She puts her phone on speaker and they place their order, with Max asking what Joe and I want before telling the PA exactly how he wants his tea brewed. Even by the standards of British tea culture, it's so convoluted it has to be a joke, but Joe changes his order to have his tea done the same.

Six minutes later, the PA comes, and I see the very moment when Max decides he needs a hot assistant of his own. It's when she bends to put the tray down and pushes her hair behind her ear. He's briefly on the back foot, but then he sips his tea and says, "By jove, she's done it! God, I'm in the wrong business. There's twenty men outside who can't follow instructions."

"They don't do what you tell them?"

"On the pitch, yeah. But there isn't a single one who can make a cuppa."

The PA slinks away, which unleashes another torrent of manager-bonding, and while I drink my delicious, perfect cappuccino, Joe sips his tea with wide eyes. Then it's back to work on his leg. Soon, I'm in the flow, a state where I barely hear anything. I snap out of it because Max is pacing the room, berating my other patient.

"That's a piss take! You don't seem to know who you're dealing with! We're going up! We've been in the *Daily Mail* twice. Massive photo of me with a future star wearing the club kit with a sponsor who isn't you!"

"You just said you were in the sixth level."

"Yeah, and then fifth. And then fourth. You're talking about paying sixth-tier rates for fourth-tier exposure. You're thinking local. I'm going national. Have you never heard of Ryan Reynolds? You're crazy if you think I'll hand over the family silver. I've told MD we're only doing year-long deals because every year we'll double our money. We're scoring goals, we're playing fantasy football, kids love us, we're in the FA Cup! The draw's this evening. Get on your socials tonight—the whole of Chester will be talking about it. We fucking slap."

"It needs careful consideration."

"Consideration? You're the one who brought it up! We're the sexiest thing in Cheshire. The stadium's capacity is five thousand four hundred. Imagine that! Two years from now, there will be twenty thousand applications for five thousand tickets. Christmas morning, 2026, there'll be some kid who gets a ticket to see us play fucking, I don't know, *Barrow,* and the kid will burst into tears. Tears of joy. Mummy! I got a ticket! Will Max Best be playing? I heard he slaps so hard you can hear it from space! That's right, little Timmy, he does. Now you've had your Christmas present, singular, so get back to work. Break's over. You've got to print a hundred credit cards before lunch or it's half gruel for the whole family."

She smiles. His rant is delightful, somehow. "I'm Ebenezer Scrooge, am I? There are many who would agree."

"Choose a number between one and ten."

"Seven."

"Fine. We're going to win seven–nil tomorrow night. And I'm going to rave about our sponsors. Glendale Logistics. And you're going to be on your bed with massive, swollen knees because you won't listen to Dean, looking at the ceiling, thinking, oh God, that could have been us. I chose the wrong guy to lowball. Okay? Nice chatting to you. Bye."

And then he walks out, and she tries to get up, but she gets a big twinge so she stays there. She calls her PA down.

While we're waiting for the PA, I'm thinking about what to say when she arrives. Something like "What a fucking prick that guy is, am I right?" But then the Brig comes in.

"Marm? I'm under orders to take you home."

She shakes her head. "No, I'm not going home. I'm going back to work."

The Brig looks at me, his face a question. The PA arrives, which makes me want to say something impressive. "She can't work horizontally. She's not a pen designed by NASA." In my head? Great line.

"Sorry, marm. Orders are orders. I'm to take you home, put you, ahem, 'all cosy on a sofa with some pills, cigarettes, and gin, she looks like a gin girl,' that was all a quote, and I'm to fluff up the cushions and make it all relaxing, and then I'm to put on a sponsor-friendly compilation of goals from Chester's season so far, which will be online by the time you get home under the title 'Look What You Could Have Won.'" It suddenly hits me—while he's pretending to say all this with extreme reluctance, the Brig is absolutely loving it. He's revelling in the role, like a ham actor. "The compilation will include a semi-viral dance video in which Max Best, ahem, struts his stuff. And there will be a short clip of our former manager promoting a local food company. This is to showcase 'the many and various possibilities.' He assured me you'd know what all that meant."

A thin smile. She likes the Brig and doesn't mind letting him know it. "It means he is a very strange young man."

"Indeed, marm. But he told me to check you weren't in pain before I tried to move you."

"Currently not."

"I am to encourage you to keep it that way."

The woman looks at me and I realise that between Max's weird charm and the Brig's ladykilling seriousness, she is willing to see sense. I step over to my little bottle of painkillers and the glass of water I'd prepared earlier.

She looks at the pills, the water, and then at the Brig. The pills revolt her.

"The boy trusts this doctor, does he?"

The Brig doesn't blink. The flirting is over. "With his life."

"Go on, then," she says, but I'm frozen. The boss lady, the hot PA, and Joe are looking at me with renewed respect. More respect than I have for myself. Max trusts me with his life, but not to sit behind him during a football match. Somewhere, my career has gone very much off the rails. "Before I change my mind," she says, and it's said kindly, but my brain interprets it as a sharp rebuke. I give her two pills, and she shudders, but takes them. She'll be glad of it in an hour or so.

Half an hour later, everyone's gone. I'm drained.

Max has come in, fallen asleep, promised to win 7–0 in the cup tomorrow, helped then harangued an intimidating CEO who had seemingly done no worse than express interest in sponsoring the team.

I made a few paperwork errors. Caught them in time, nothing serious, but I'm not thinking straight. I'll send Max the injury update and have an early lunch. Maybe a mega dose of B12 will help me make sense of it all.

I'll finish how I always finish: fuck you, you grotesque monster, I quit.

From: Physio Dean
To: Max
Subject: Injury updates

Hey, still looking pretty good. Almost a clean bill of health! Keeping an eye on Robbo's shoulder. Joe's calf is improving. Andrew's groin is sore, but you can use him tomorrow and then we'll assess him after. I did some preventative work with Aff. Since Henri adjusted his car seat, his hamstrings have been much less trouble but if you could encourage him to do the extra stretches I showed him, that'd be very helpful.

From: Physio Dean
To: Max
Subject: Notes from Underground
<UNSEND>

From: Physio Dean
To: John Smith
Subject: Help

John, I sent Max an email that wasn't meant for him. Please can you intercept it. Please.

From: John Smith
To: Physio Dean
Subject: re: Help
He's reading it.

From: Physio Dean
To: Max
Subject: I'm fired, aren't I?
I'm sorry.

From: Max
To: Physio Dean
Subject: re: I'm fired, aren't I?
I believe you sent me that "draft" because subconsciously there's something you very much want but are too afraid to say to my face. But I can read between the lines. So my answer is yes. Yes, you can buy a water feature. I like the ones where there are buckets that pour into other buckets, but I also like the ones that are just a whole wall of dribbling water. Talk to Magnus. If it's going to be more than five hundred quid, let me know.

Voicemail from Secretary Joe.
"Max! Are you watching the FA Cup draw? Home to Salford City! They're owned by your lot! The Man United legends. Beckham and Giggs and Gary Neville and the other one! Bit of a glamour tie. We might get on TV! Chester in the FA Cup on TV, Max! You've brought back the old days. I don't care what anyone says about you, I think you're—"

Tuesday, October 17.

From: Max
To: Inga; MD
Subject: WHERE IS EVERYBODY
Hello. Max here. If you look down from your ivory tower you'll see me on the touchline managing the local football team in its nice stadium. Capacity is over 5,000, I think I remember hearing? So my question is WHERE IS EVERYBODY?
It looks like there are 200 people here.
WHAT THE SHIT IS GOING ON?

From: Inga
To: Max; MD
Subject: re: WHERE IS EVERYBODY

It's the Cheshire Senior Cup. There isn't a great deal of interest in it, and season tickets don't provide entrance to these games.

Would you like to manage the game instead of sending me emails?

p.s. I'm not at the match. Because it's the Cheshire Senior Cup.

From: Max
To: Inga; MD
Subject: re: re: WHERE IS EVERYBODY

I AM managing, Inga. I could manage this one from a barrel over Niagara Falls. We're playing Stockport Town. That's a tenth-tier team, Inga. West Didsbury could beat them. They don't even have ironic chants.

Listen. My team, our team, this city's team, are putting on a MASTER-CLASS right now. This is incredible stuff that's happening. FOUR players are putting on 10 out of 10 performances. I am not motivated by playing in front of 200 people and neither are the superstar players I want to sign. We had more people at the posh school. This is DEMOTIVATIONAL.

Get people in for these matches. Give away tickets. We should have 2,000 screaming schoolkids in tonight. I heard a guy BURP just now.

From: MD
To: Max; Inga
Subject: re: re: re: WHERE IS EVERYBODY

If we let two thousand kids in for free, we'd need more police, more stewards, more everything. We'd lose money.

From: Max
To: MD; Inga
Subject: re: re: re: re: WHERE IS EVERYBODY

Free tickets or I quit.

From: MD
To: Max
Subject: re: re: re: re: re: WHERE IS EVERYBODY

Please don't be so belligerent. Of course you want to play in front of big crowds. I understand. We will do something for the next round, I promise.

That's made easier by recent events. As you know, BoshCard is interested in sponsoring us from next season. It's early in the process but the numbers being discussed are already excellent. Agatha seems to believe she's catching a rising tide. Wonder why. (Well done, Max!)

And a bit of a strange one. We got a donation from a British military foundation. They claim to offer grants for companies that employ ex-servicemen. Apparently, when we hired John Smith that put us on a shortlist, and we "won," so they're sending us £52,000. It's one year of John's salary. Curious, isn't it, Max? Is there anything you'd like to say to me about that?

From: Max
To: MD
Subject: re: re: re: re: re: re: WHERE IS EVERYBODY
Weird timing, dude. I'm trying to manage a football match, here. Don't you know how hard that is?

Also: when the final whistle goes, send Agatha (really? She doesn't look like an Agatha) a smiley face message. No, SEVEN smiley faces. And send her a link to the match report with my post-match interview.

From: MD
To: Max
Subject: re: re: re: re: re: re: re: WHERE IS EVERYBODY
Why? What are you planning? Don't do anything crazy!

Wednesday, October 18.
Chester 7 Stockport Town 0—Stockport Stare into Abyss; Max Best Stares Back

Chester annihilated a willing but limited Stockport Town team in last night's Cheshire Cup match. The poorly attended affair was illuminated by masterful performances from Raffi Brown, Youngster, Donny Dorigo, and Joe Anka. Max Best brought himself on for the last twenty-five minutes, playing in a defensive midfield role from where he could scheme and plot.

The plotting and scheming fell apart in the last ten minutes, however. Chester, leading by seven goals at that time, found that their shooting boots deserted them. Star striker Henry Lyons had a blazing row with Best, seemingly because Lyons, after sending several shots into orbit, crashed a stunning half-volley against the crossbar. It seemed as though Lyons simply gave up after that failure. Best's mania for high standards was further undermined by Pascal Bochum's cameo, which ended when he outpaced two defenders, rounded the goalkeeper, and faced with an open goal, collapsed in stages, clutching his hamstring with the ball waiting to be pushed across the goal line.

Best was all smiles at the final whistle, and was unusually garrulous in the post-match interview.

"Great performance, very happy with that. Before the match I gave a team talk in which we looked at an internal PowerPoint from Glendale Logistics, our main club sponsor this season, and we talked about what high performance really means. It isn't just about delivering, it's about delivering on time, with a smile, and exceeding customer expectations. Glendale Logistics have a great motto. *We truly recognise the needs of manufacturers and adapt our business around yours.* I said that to the lads before the match and there was a lot of emotion. We talk a lot about recognising needs. In our case, it's the needs of the other players, of the fans, of the community. For Glendale Logistics it's about warehousing and storage, but it's much more than that. I'm obviously oversimplifying, but if there's one thing you learn as a manager it's that amateurs talk tactics, professionals talk logistics, and the real wise men leave it to Glendale! Anyway, we're happy to be in the next round, and if it's an away match, we can count on Glendale to help get us there."

Thursday, October 19.

Voicemail from Fleur (Henk's mum).

"Hi Max. This is Fleur. Henk's mum. I went to watch Kidderminster's league match on Saturday and their friendly on Tuesday. Kidderminster Harriers. You know that. Sorry. I still can't believe you've asked me to do this. I'm trying hard not to fuck this up like I did the first time we met. Deep breath."

[audibly reading from her notes] "Bob Horseman likes to set his team up in an unambitious four-four-two formation. Christian Fierce is a rock at the back. Kidderminster's defence is very physical. You won't have much luck if you try long balls or crosses. I know that's not how you play, but I'm just saying. They all go up for set pieces, too. The two central midfielders stay on the halfway line when they've got corners. To me it looked like Kidderminster were going to score from every corner they had, and I never felt they'd concede from one. I know that's 'eye stuff' but I looked at the stats and it seems true.

"The midfield is just all right—from what I've seen you'll dominate the middle. But the strikers are fast and dynamic. Peabody and Craddock. Can you play Carlile in the middle? This pair are a real handful. You need mobility and a bit of devil.

"What else?

"To me, it's clear why they're top of the league. They're a unit in everything they do. There are no silly mistakes. There's a lot of talking. It will be a very tough match. They're not fast, which is something.

"One last thing. Probably not worth mentioning, but in the second half of the friendly, they took the strikers off and played five-five-oh. Men behind the ball, shape, closing down space. It looked to me like they were practising what to do when they got a man sent off, but with all their players on the pitch. Not everyone has the you-know-whats to take a player off just to do an experiment. Or it was a punishment from Horseman for something they'd done wrong. Which is not something you'd be overly familiar with. Fuck. Why am I being passive aggressive? Sorry.

"Their three best players are Christian Fierce (centre back), Peabody (striker), Craddock (striker).

"Let me know if there's anything else you need to know.

"Oh, and thanks again for giving me this chance. I mean it. Let's just say it came at a good time."

From: Max

To: Fleur (Henk's mum)

Amazing. You're hired.

(This is an expression of extreme satisfaction, not an actual job offer. You still have to finish the scouting course. But this is super helpful. Thanks!)

From: Spectrum
To: Max
Subject: MYSTERY SOLVED

Wow. Okay. I KNOW. I can't believe it. Hahaha. It's like Das Tournament when everything came together. But without Bethany to spin it into a masterpiece. Are you still in touch with her? Never mind that.

So you invited Tyson to train with the first team. And Noah found out on Monday. He was like, "Where's Tyson?" and people said, "With the firsts," and he flat out didn't believe it. So obvs he goes home, asks his brothers, they say yeah, new kid was with us today. Noah takes this . . . NOT WELL.

Yesterday at training he's zooming around, full sprint into tackles and being reckless. Acting out. I say he might want to calm down. He keeps doing it. I tell him to take a time out. He grabs all his stuff and flounces!

I'm on my own doing the sesh so I can't do anything about it. I'm packing up, thinking about if I should call Andrew. I don't know him that well, really, but it's probably my best move because I'm clueless. Like: WHAT IS GOING ON.

But before I can even do anything, Noah appears and helps me put the stuff away. He's sort of crying the whole time, and doesn't say a word.

Eventually, we're all packed up and I'm thinking okay it was good when we had something to do because now what? So I walk back to the pitch and sit on the bench and he does, too, and he vents.

First up, he's all, "It's not fair, I'm way better than Tyson. Tyson's only been sent up because his dad's a sponsor. It's an actual scandal." I'm trying not to laugh because I know your history with Tyson and the idea you'd—never mind. You know all that. So I'm being stoic, it looks like, which makes him have to do all the talking.

"Spectrum!" he says. "Max only signed my brothers to get to me. He's paying a grand a week to two guys he doesn't rate because he wants me. So why would he promote Tyson?"

"Did he tell you that?"

"No. He hinted, though. My brothers think the same."

"I don't know if there's one of you he rates higher. What I know of Max is it's all about the football. If Tyson's training with the firsts, there's a football reason. Meaning Tyson deserves it."

He doesn't speak for ages. I start to get cold. Then he goes, "I fucked up."

And I think, what would Max do? I decide you would pretend you already knew the answer and be sort of amused.

It pours out of him. His first day with the group, he's so excited the only way he can deal with it is to get cocky. So he gets all Charlie Big Bollocks, telling the group he's their new star player, he's gonna score all the goals, get all the boot deals and that. And they're just rolling their eyes so he doubles down and he's like, "I'm only gonna be at Chester for a year then I'll get scouted by a proper team and you'll all be begging me for tickets to watch me play Premier League." And that's a slap in the face to the club, a slap in the face to you, and that's what does it. He's done a *treason*. He's out.

Ever since then he's been manic depressive, trying to be super cool one day, not talking to anyone the next, because he knows he can't get it back, but he wants to. He's desperate, but how? He didn't give himself a chance.

So that's it! That's the mystery. All that loyalty you wizarded up has turned the group into a bunch of white blood cells, and along comes an infection and they do. Not. Like it.

It's just us and if you're one of us you get on the bus. He got on the bus, but with no ticket.

Poor Noah!

Whoo. I'm hyper. Now that we know what happened, we can do something. I'm going to think what. I think I can deal with it. I just wanted to tell you. Might be a tiny weight off your shoulders. You're not to blame for once! (Well, you are, but only in a good way.) Maybe I'll talk to Andrew just to be sure.

From: Max
To: Spectrum
Subject: re: MYSTERY SOLVED
Very happy to let you deal with this any way you want but it seems obvious. Get them in a room. Noah says he was trying to be cocky to impress them. They ask questions. They talk. There are tears. When they are on the floor emotionally, you say that Max Actual Best has sent you a letter to be opened in the event of any unexpected team building.

And you open the envelope and you say:
YOUR MISSION
SHOULD YOU CHOOSE TO ACCEPT IT
IS
WIN THE FA YOUTH CUP
And when they say it's impossible, you say, "Yeah but he means next year though when you're 17."

And they say, "No that's still bonkers." You sort of look into the distance and smile, and you go, "Is it?"

I'm only writing it out because it seems self-evident. It's hard to think there's a better way to handle it. Seriously, though, your call.

To: Max
From: MD
Subject: Programme notes
The match programme editor has just called me. You know we'd never spoken, ever, before you turned up? Now we have regular chats. I spend more time talking to this guy than my nieces.

His latest complaint is pretty much everything about your latest manager notes.

From what he says, you have written "ALL WORK AND NO PLAY MAKES JACK A DULL BOY" seventy times in different fonts and with letters missing sometimes and the spacings slightly different on some lines. And I'm actually tempted to let it go in like that because programme sales are way up and people talk about them and this one sounds like a classic of the subgenre you've invented—the "terrifying insight into a broken psyche" notes.

I just want to be sure this is what you want people talking about during the match where we go top of the league. I know it's a movie thing but it's the Jack part. People will think you're laughing at Jackie Reaper.

From: Max
To: MD
Subject: re: Programme notes
    You're right. I didn't think of that. I'll do something else. Dostoevsky maybe.

From: MD
To: Max
Subject: re: re: Programme notes
    But what can a decent man speak of with most pleasure?
    Answer: Of himself.
    So I will talk about myself.

From: Max
To: MD
Subject: re: re: re: Programme notes
    are you ok bro

Friday, October 20. One day until Kidderminster.

From: Anonymous
To: Max
Subject: Sponsored swim 1
    Max. Check out Eddie Moore at Sutton United when you get a chance. If you like what you see, there's more tips to come. I'll identify myself on Saturday with the password *I gave you that tip that'll be a hundred pounds please.*

From: Max
To: Fleur (Henk's mum); Inga
Subject:

Can you watch Sutton United next? Special eye on Eddie Moore. Talk to Inga about your tickets, as usual.

From: J Planter (Groundsman)
To: Max
Subject: The Pitch

She's holding up well. Couple of bare patches in and around the penalty area. That will happen if you let teams warm up there, which you'll recall I've said to you many a time. You'll certainly be pleased to know I've been tracking the growth potential, rainfall, temps, and base nitrogen. I know you've said you don't want to hear it but base nitrogen of 4kg per week at this time of year is pretty staggering. We've used the warm weather to repair and improve fertility. That said, I'd repeat my previous request for more budget for the bio stimulants I saw demonstrated at GroundsFest 23. Especially what with the TV people likely coming. We would like to present ourselves shipshape and Bristol fashion, I am sure you will agree.

From: Max
To: J Planter (Groundsman)
Subject: Re: The Pitch

Jonny, what have I told you about nitrogen? I don't understand it. I don't understand any of the words you use. For me, grass will always be TIME + SUN = GRASS.

I also don't understand why you talk like you're the embittered groundsman of a country estate and you've lived there for sixty years man and boy and you're a suspect in the murder of Lord Baguette since you possess the only key to the shed in which the BASE NITROGEN is stored. I feel it's my job to remind you that you are THIRTY YEARS OLD. I know for a fact you go to CONCERTS.

If you wish it, smother yourself with bio stimulants and roll around on the bare patches. If it costs more than five hundred pounds, talk to MD first.

Also, you get very shifty when I ask about zigzag mowing effects. They are so cool and no one does them anymore. Let's buy a fucking specialist lawnmowing robot that puts those patterns on the grass. How much is a zigzag robot?

Also, I asked for comically long corner flags. I want corner flags the length of a pole vault pole and I DON'T think you tried very hard to find them.

Also, I know you don't want to think about digging up your precious turf, but I want to go underground. I want to dig it all up, put drainage, undersoil heating, maybe an ice rink that we can slide in and out, anything else that's cool. And to plan for that I need a price. So stop counting nitrogens for ten minutes and talk to a person who likes digging things to find out how much the digging will cost me. All right?

p.s. The pitch is very nice. From what I've seen so far, it's the best in the league. Keep up the good work.

From: MD

To: Max
Subject: Super-please

Max, I'm stressed. It's worse than the relegation battle. No, that's not true.

It's a different kind of stress. Second versus first. If we win, we go top of the table. When was the last time we were top? Years. I can't stand the hope! What if we do it, though? As long as I can remember it's been a dour struggle. How am I supposed to feel about this all-conquering, attacking, winning football?

Please just tell me you've got a plan or something up your sleeve or something. Please. I promised to keep the new board off your back. You owe me. No, I don't mean that. But please, though. Boggy gets a super-please once a year. This is my super-please.

From: Max
To: MD
Subject: re: Super-please

Don't waste your super-please on something so trivial.

We are fit and fresh. No injuries. Morale is high. We've scored 32 goals in 7 games. That's a preposterous number of goals. While a couple of players have hit their personal ceilings, and a couple have hit the limit of what we seem able to do for them, we're at least 20% better than we were when we played York.

We're not underestimating Kidderminster. The players know what to expect from the number one team in the league, and we sent our new scout to watch them. Her report confirms what we knew and gave us some extra insight. Worth the small fee!

It'll be a tough game, then, but I'm confident. Don't be so stressed you forget to talk to your fellow directors. Trick Williams is our most important player. We couldn't possibly replace him. etc etc

From: MD
To: Max
Subject: re: re: Super-please

I've been doing that.

Okay. I'm still nervous, but I do feel better. Thanks. I'd take a draw to be honest. Our new sponsors (fingers crossed) will be with me in the box.

From: Max
To: MD
Subject: re: re: re: Super-please

This is Chester. We don't play for draws. This time tomorrow, we'll be top of the league. You can take that to the bank. Now if you'll excuse me, I have an enormous tent to assemble.

18

KIDDERMINSTER HARRIERS

Saturday, October 21.

At the start of the season, I thought everything would build up to the Darlington match, but one of my post-match interviews had rocked their boat, as I'd hoped it would. By insinuating that referees were giving them an easy ride, I'd brought more focus on their hard tackling. A couple of red cards had cost them wins, and from what I'd heard Folke Wester had been forced to modify his tactics. *My* tactics. They were still winning, but it was a few percent harder than before. Destabilising Darlo had cost me something in terms of my relationships in Chester, but at the time I thought it had been worth it.

York City had also been slightly erratic, leaving Kidderminster Harriers with an easy ride to the top of the league. They had the meanest defence in the division, and their two strikers were near the top of the goalscoring charts. An hour before kickoff, after I'd handed in my team sheet, I saw that Kidderminster had named their strongest team, with an average CA of 51. Our starting eleven would be CA 48.8.

The Triple Captain and Bench Boost options loomed in my vision, but I swiped them away. Yes, the stakes were high—win and we would go top of the league, impress our potential new sponsors, lay down a marker, lift the city. But we were at home, we were flying, we had a slight morale advantage. My once-per-season perks were still earmarked for Darlo away. No, our secret weapon today was me. I would play the final thirty minutes as a DM, and Harriers wouldn't get a kick in our half.

I had almost 2,000 XP. Enough to buy Attributes 5, but the plan was to get Injuries next, which was 3,000. It'd happen soon enough, though playing was slowing me down.

The Brig was with me in the manager's room, cosy, seemingly unaffected by the nerves and excitement that had spread through the city. He sipped on a cup of tea and picked his newspaper back up. Instead of reading his usual *Daily Telegraph*, he'd gone out of his way to buy *The Socialist Worker*, which was his version of a prank.

"You seem to actually be reading that."

"Yes, sir. I recently learned about filter bubbles. I am endeavouring to pop mine."

"Once you pop . . . How's it going?"

He squirmed. "This periodical reads like it was written by your friends at West Didsbury and Chorlton." Slight twitch around the mouth. "I don't agree with what's written here, but it is interesting to read different perspectives."

"Are you trying to say something?"

He frowned and tilted his head. "Sir? No. No, I don't think so. You are receptive to new ideas, though you have a blind spot when it comes to menswear. The scout suggested you use Carl as a centre back today, and you're doing that."

"She meant as one of a back four." I stretched. "I *hope* I listen to people. Don't want to end up as a dinosaur." I pointed to the paper. "Those guys don't listen. They'd call you a warmonger. That's where I lose patience with them."

He closed the paper and folded it neatly. He gave it an almost affectionate flattening rub. "We'll always need an army. But I don't resent them for dreaming."

We enjoyed a minute of dreaming of our own.

The Brig sighed and reached into his coat pocket. He withdrew a little notebook. "May I ask some questions?"

"Absolutely."

"Vivek and Tyson spent a week training with the first team. How did that go, do you think?"

"Superb. A new tradition is born. They were overawed, but I don't mind that. They have time to think about it, now. First shot of the vaccine, isn't it? When we do it again, they'll be way more ready."

"Who is closer to playing for the first team?"

"Tyson."

"Though he is two years younger?"

"Vivek's only just started playing the sport. I'm thinking about loaning him out to a small club so he can get a crash course."

He made a little note. "You watched several matches in schools while I was otherwise engaged this week. I believe that makes six school visits in total."

"I think that's right."

"Any players of note?"

"Fungrieve is still the best, but I found another couple of okay guys." A sixteen- and a fifteen-year-old, both PA 33. "There's talent out there. But I've asked Inga to stop booking more until further notice. For now, I'll dial down the scouting and hit it hard over the winter when our matches are postponed."

"Won't the school matches be postponed, too?"

"Indoor games, all-weather pitches, five-a-sides. There's enough to keep me busy. You'll help me find places to go."

"Very good, sir." He made another note. "You extended Sam's contract, but not Tony's."

"Yes." He waited. "Next season we can improve on Tony. And several others." Gerald. D-Day. Trick. Joe. Robbo. "And if we can't, we can offer a new deal in March or April. Save a bit of money on the pay raises." I wasn't often dishonest with the Brig, but I didn't see the benefit in outright telling him

I planned to cut six players next season. It could filter through to the players themselves and affect their morale. The Brig didn't have Super Scout, so in this way he was more of a socialist than me. He wanted to believe in the best version of every young man he ever met. In the army, anyone could turn out to be Audie Murphy. In football, there was only one Messi.

"Why do you think Glenn Ryder is hesitant about signing his extension?"

I sighed. Glenn had been a rare disappointment. "I don't need to think. He told me. He thinks he can get a bit more base salary elsewhere. But also . . . he likes it here, but he doesn't want to stay if I'm going to leave ten minutes later." I shook my head. "I still think hinting that I'd go to Darlington if they asked me was a net positive. But it has made a lot of people kind of lose their minds. MD has only recently stopped treating me like Typhoid Mary. And being doubted by MD, by Glenn, by the fans . . . it doesn't bring out the best in me. Bit childish maybe, but that's how it is."

"If I may be esoteric . . . I feel I've seen you staring at Ryan Jack and Henri a lot recently. While biting your nails."

"They're not improving. I didn't really expect Ryan to improve, but he's sort of . . ." He was fluctuating between CA 60 and 61. "Sort of threatening to get better, but also threatening to get worse. It's perplexing. And Henri's simply stalled." He'd hit CA 58 weeks and weeks ago, and there was no sign of any further improvement.

That was distressing, not only because having a CA 90 striker would make my life a lot less stressful. No, it all implied that CA 60 was about the limit of where we could take players. What was causing the ceiling? Our coaches? Our facilities? The league itself? If we got promoted, would that automatically let us get another 20 points out of every player?

The Brig made another note. "MD has implied he'd like to whisk you up to the director's box after the match and to facilitate that, I might do the post-match interviews."

"Do you mind when he gives you little tasks?"

"It's always very clear that it's a suggestion. In which case, I'm happy to oblige. It's not my place to suggest that Agatha would be happier to see me than you."

I rubbed my lip to hide my smile. "Right."

He tried to stare me out, but it became a twinkling contest. When we stopped having fun, he tapped his pencil against the paper. "I made notes in case you suddenly asked me to do the interview. Themes from recent media coverage . . . Goalkeeper rotation. Vulnerability at set pieces. Our own powderpuff set pieces. No goals or assists for Max Best. You taking minutes from Youngster. Lack of harmony in the group. Pascal too short."

"Are they still on that?" I said. "How many guys has he got sent off with his pace? Is it two or three? Lack of harmony? We're not at the absolute high mark of a few weeks ago, but we're still way happier on average than any other team I've seen. Even West Didsbury."

"Would you like me to be uncontroversial?"

"Probably best that way," I said. I looked up at the wall clock. There was still ages to go. "I'm bored. Let's do the Dean thing now."

We found Dean out on the pitch, monitoring the lads as they did some light jogs and stretches and whatnot under the watchful eye of Vimsy and Jude.

I motioned for him to come away from the others so the three of us could have a chat.

"Dean," I said. "I was so excited last night I couldn't sleep. So I read your email again." He shrank. Got a hunted kind of look. We hadn't talked about it face to face. I suppose he'd been wishing I would never bring it up. I nodded. "Yeah, it's pretty intense stuff. You write loads of these, right?"

He looked left and right as he shifted his weight from foot to foot. Flight animal. "I do one on Monday, one on Friday. But, you know, it's just—"

"The Brig's been encouraging me to get out of my echo chamber and seek out new perspectives. And the thing is, I loved your email. I know that makes me a bit of a crazy person. I genuinely think I'd pay ten dollars a month to get these sent to my inbox twice a week. And I'd understand if you needed to take a break every now and then to keep the quality up." Dean looked at the Brig to see if he was the only one not enjoying this conversation. I continued. "Anyway, last night I had weird dreams that I was turning into an insect or something, but when I woke up, there was this thought nagging at me." I took my phone out and got the screenshot I'd taken. I turned my phone to show him the screen, then flipped it round and read it aloud anyway. *"I'm too vain to delete my work.* Mate. Have you got a *stash* of these email drafts going back years?"

"No," he said. We waited. "Yes," he said. "But, Max—"

"Did you write one the Monday after my murder?"

He stopped jiggling. "Oh. I'm . . . No. But . . . The Tuesday or the Wednesday, maybe. But I wasn't slagging you off, then. I promise!"

I raised my eyes to the sky. The forecast was for some rain in the second half. "Mate. You're allowed to slag me off. In private. You think I don't know I'm annoying? I annoy myself! I annoy you, don't I, Brig?"

"I find your antics charming, sir."

"Dean, let's cut the shit. You were one of the first on the crime scene. I've learned this week that you're highly observant. *Highly* observant. Do you get where this is going?"

"Yes. No."

"I want you to let the Brig read the email you wrote after the attack. I'd love to read it myself but we talked about it and you probably wouldn't want that. Frustrating, but if the roles were reversed, I wouldn't want my boss reading my diary either."

"But, then, why?"

"Because someone tried to kill me, mate! And the Brig's out of leads. Maybe you noticed something and you wrote it down and you don't think it's important but the Brig can use it."

"Oh."

"Look, the Brig's going to read it. And I'll say, 'Well?' And he'll puff out his cheeks and say, 'Physio Dean is batshit crazy.' And I'll say, 'Yes but is there anything we didn't know?'" Dean bit his bottom lip while looking at his shoes. "And there won't be anything useful or new or relevant to the case. But maybe there *will* be. And maybe you'll be the guy who caught my murderer. Know what I mean? I just . . . what if? Right? What if that's *it*?" I could tell he was thinking about what sociopathic things he'd written that day. "Brig, tell Dean how many people you've killed."

"That's classified."

I raised my thumb. "See? Army secrets. Don't ask, don't tell. Right?"

The Brig did a tiny shake of the head while he smiled. "That's a different thing altogether, but yes. I won't repeat anything, Dean."

Dean rubbed the back of his neck. "It's humiliating."

I stretched my arms. "I'll take a yes or a no, mate."

"Yes," he mumbled.

"Give us a second," I said to the Brig. He went over to chat to Vimsy. I looked at Dean. Proper eye contact for the first time this week. "I should probably keep my mouth shut because I'm not good at this sort of thing." I inhaled. "How many football physiotherapists do you think have saved someone's life?"

"In this country? I don't know. Fifty?"

"Fifty? I thought the answer was one. You."

"Footballers are always collapsing on the pitch and getting resuscitated. There are players who have heart attacks."

"Right. Okay. How many football physios have saved a CEO's leg from being amputated and ended up getting their club a massive new sponsorship deal?"

"That one is zero. Including me."

I made a harsh buzzing noise. "Nope. You made the room nice. You made it so the credit card people—what did you call them? The underlings—thought to come to us first. They walk past it all the time, probably talk about how nice it smells, talk about how everyone's always laughing in there. You know what? It's probably not even that. It's probably your reputation."

"My reputation?"

"You fucking unsmashed my head, you dick! You think everyone in that building doesn't know you're the guy to see if their skull's been cracked open? Anyway, look, I know what it's like to be hard on yourself. I just think you're being a bit *too* hard. Most people think you're pretty top. In fact," I added, in a warm voice, "some people are saying you're the Max Best of football physiotherapy."

Microexpressions came and went—pride, rage, doubt, hope. In a flat voice, he said, "Yes, Max."

I laughed. "I want to read *this* chapter."

That's when he knew I was taking the piss. He untensed and shook his head, annoyed at himself. "The Max Best of physiotherapy. Where do you come up with this stuff?" I tensed, and he noticed. His neck swivelled like an owl's "What? What is it?"

Kidderminster were on the pitch, doing similar things to us. Craddock, one of their two great strikers, CA 58, same as Henri, had been taking shots on an empty goal. His acceleration had turned red and he was feeling his hamstring. Dean followed my gaze, saw it, too. "I wonder if he'll tell his physio," I said.

"They could swap him out for free, right? If they do it now, it won't cost them a substitution."

"Right. But he's desperate to play. I bet you a million pounds he doesn't say anything."

We watched as he went on a little jog. He went up and down, then got a ball and did a few kick-ups. He stood still for a while, then wandered over to his team's head physio and they had a chat. Bob Horseman, Kidderminster's manager, was summoned and informed. Horseman put his arm around Craddock. Thanking him for being honest, I reckoned.

"You owe me a million pounds," said Dean.

I barely heard him. Horseman's manager stats were merely all right. His highest attributes were motivating and man management. I hadn't been worried about him. Until now.

Dean had seen a lot more of Kidderminster than me. "Isn't that one of their good strikers? If he can't play, that's great for us. Why are you worried?"

I bit my nail. "Something's happening."

Dean looked around. All he saw was excited, nervous fans and players. "What?"

Henk's mum had said Harriers had been practising for going down to ten men. I took it to mean they would go in hard against us, maybe try to take one of our best players out of the game. Would you take a red card if it meant Henri was off the pitch? Yeah, but you wouldn't set out to actually break his leg or something like that. I went into the tactics screens and saw Harriers were set to normal tackling. What the fuck? Could you have normal tackling and still be out for blood? "I don't know," I said, but before I could get any further, it was time to go back to the dressing room for our final preparations. "Dean. Stay on the bench today. Stay calm. I need my best people."

"Yes, Max."

This was our biggest game of the season so far, so I took the pre-match team talk seriously. Went through the Harriers player by player. The goalie, the formidable defence, the weak midfield. As I got to the forwards, I paid attention to the guys I had picked to oppose them.

We had Ben in goal, with a back three of Glenn, Carl, and Steve Alton. Alton still had slightly lower CA than Gerald May, but May was maxed at 38. Alton, if he kept improving, could be my third gold defender by the end of the season. He was better than May on the ball, too. Literally the only benefit of May was a bit of height. The choice, really, was between Steve and Magnus. I started with the specialist defender.

"Craddock," I said, coming to the last two Harriers, "tweaked his hamstring in the warm-up. It looks like he's going to play anyway, so Carl, if you are one on one with him, don't beat him for pace too soon. Okay? Let him make sprints. Is it a risk? Yes. But that's what I want. Understood?"

"Yes, Max."

"It might be they'll see how he goes for ten minutes and reassess it, because this is a big game for them, too. My instinct is they'll sub him off, and they don't have much attacking quality on the bench. If he goes off, Carl will man-mark the other one."

"Peabody," said the Brig.

"Right. We're going to dick them in midfield, so we'll have most of the ball and these fucks won't get many chances." Four of our midfield five were awesome. Aff on the left, then Raffi, Ryan, and Sam Topps. Mwah! Chef's kiss. The right of midfield was becoming an issue. Joe had done well against Stockport Town, as had D-Day, but showing off against a tier-ten side didn't impress me much. Joe was CA 38, D-Day 34. Increasingly looking out of place as the rest of the team improved around them. Joe had a better cross, while D-Day, if he was in the mood, had more individual skill. Both had OK morale. "Obviously, their main thing is corners and free kicks. Jude's been showing you the tapes and that. We think we've nailed their signals. Last refresh, Jude?"

He stepped away from the wall. He raised two hands. "Far post," called out six or seven players. He raised one hand. The same players and more said, "Near post."

I looked at the tactics board. We'd analysed Kidderminster's players. We'd talked about their set pieces. I had a vague sense of disquiet that I couldn't put my finger on. But we *had* prepared well. We were in incredible form, we had a great system, we had options on the bench.

And as for me—when I trained, I slotted in with the defenders. I'd never be a great defender—I didn't have the temperament for it. Didn't want to concentrate and be disciplined for ninety minutes. Didn't want to suffer and sacrifice and throw my body in front of shots. Didn't want to play a forty-six-game season and finish with one goal and no Man of the Match awards.

But I had the *toolkit* of a great defender. Especially the awareness, the sense of danger, the ability to make calm decisions with players running at me. Over one thirty-minute period that could decide our season, I'd concentrate, and if I concentrated, I'd snuff out attacks and get the ball forward where our system would do the rest.

I was confident about one thing: the last thirty minutes of this match would be one-way traffic.

I left the changing room and walked down the tunnel, slowly, with my forehead slightly creased. Something was off. Some thought nagging at the back of my mind.

When I got to the side of the pitch, I understood the feeling better. The stadium was resonating at the same frequency as the Southport game last season. You might remember I mentioned that one. It was the one where someone tried to kill me.

"Brig," I said. "*John.* Stay close to me."

"Yes, sir." He gestured and the six nearest stewards moved closer. One of the on-duty policemen noticed, stood more erect, spoke into his walkie-talkie.

I looked around the stands. I thought I saw the women's team supporting me from behind the goal to our right. To the left, the away fans, bouncing, chanting "We are top of the league!" Was Ian Evans in there with them? Across the other side, were the Yalleys surrounded by Man City players?

I didn't want to turn and look at the stands behind me, but I forced myself. Bravery 20. I saw scouts dotted around. No Bradley Rymarquis this time. He hadn't shown his face since my attack. In the director's box, I knew the guys from Glendale Logistics were there, along with Agatha and some bigwigs from BoshCard. MD's plan was to play them off against each other. Seemed like he'd be having fun, at least.

A dazzling flash of blonde hair appeared at a window, and suddenly Emma was bursting out the door and coming down the steps.

"Bebs," I said, delighted. She'd surprised me against Southport, too, but I hadn't known about it. We kissed.

"Mum and Dad are here. Dad wants to talk about Newcastle United's winning streak. Apparently they tore Mbappé a new one? Ever since you got gobby about their bad start, they've been playing amazing." She bit her lip. "He says."

I pulled her close, face to face, let her hair tickle my cheeks. She was deliciously warm; I could have stayed like that for hours. I peeled myself away and smiled. "I don't suppose you've seen the helicopter twat from Sheffield?"

"Oh," she said, surprised. "Yes." The hairs on my neck went haywire. "He's right there. Oh." She pointed to five empty seats. Nick and the imps had gone to get a vegan hotdog, no doubt. "Why is he here? Getting involved with the sale of Man United one day, ten billion dollars, the day after, keeping an eye on Max Best?"

I shrugged. "Guess he thinks I'm worth more than ten billion."

It was like all the floodlights in the stadium turned on and shone directly onto her face. "I think he's right. I got you a present." She unzipped her puffy coat, revealing a blue and white Chester home kit. She handed me the coat, turned around and jabbed two thumbs at the name and number on the back. BEST 77.

"Seems more like a gift to the universe than to me."

"This isn't the present," she said. "I'll send it at halftime. It's not finished, but . . . it nearly is. What's the plan today?"

"Keep it tight first ninety, try to snatch something in injury time."

"Are you going to play?"

"Probably."

"Are you going to score a hat trick for me?"

"Me? I won't be going anywhere near their goal. I'm a defensive hard man now."

"A what man?"

"A hard man."

"Gosh." Her lips twisted and she slunk back up the stairs. She was so busy being a temptress she forgot her coat.

The match kicked off. In the first minute, it became clear that Craddock wasn't interested in sprinting. Peabody stepped up his work rate—apparently he'd been told to do the pressing for both of them.

We very quickly got a grip of the ball, passing it neatly around midfield, making triangles, bringing it towards the corners of our attacking third, looking for overlaps and slaps, but being patient. I'd told Joe and Aff not to hit crosses unless conditions were absolutely perfect, since Christian Fierce and his fellow beefy boys would gobble up any aimless high balls.

While the "feeling out" phase was happening, I took the temperature of the away dugout—very calm, very professional, very disciplined. There would be no foolishness today. So I went to the tactics screens and checked my new Hot Stuff! perk. It allowed me to create hotkeys that would appear in my vision that I could use to quickly change formations or tactics.

For example, I had my seven formations floating on the upper left of my vision. When I wasn't thinking about them, they became completely transparent. But now I could instantly switch from the 3-5-2 we were using to 4-2-4 or whatever I wanted and save myself a couple of clicks.

Then I had three icons linking to strategies I'd designed that simply told everyone to play left, to play right, or to play through the centre.

Underneath was a slightly more advanced version of that, where it was play left *and* set the left mid as playmaker.

And after lots of experimenting, I'd found I could make more elaborate hotkeys. For example, 3-5-2 with the starting left mid and right mid switching sides. That was more useful in the women's matches because there were times I'd want Dani and Maddy to swap sides. It gave their opponents a new challenge, and had led to our frankly undeserved equaliser in the most recent Warrington match, which had led to our win.

Yeah, the hotkeys perk wasn't a *massive* step forward, but when I was on the pitch trying to do twenty things at once, it was a time saver. I normally regretted my perk buys, at least at first, but this time, nah. Absolute banger.

Five minutes passed. We had sixty percent possession. Ten minutes. Sixty-three percent. The ball was ours and we were starting to make chances. We got to the sides and worked our way closer to the goal line. Joe or Aff fired in low passes that Henri and Tony tried to turn into goals. So far, so normal.

Why had Kiddie been practising 5-5-0? I looked at the match ratings. Raffi, Sam, and Ryan were all on 8 out of 10. You couldn't foul one out of the game and hope to achieve anything. I could play CM. Surely even the dinosaurs at National League North level knew not to get me on the pitch too early? Surely they watched at least the highlights of our most recent games?

Henri, then? But he was struggling in his battle against Christian Fierce. No need for Bob Horseman to do anything special. Tony Hetherington was a journeyman striker. Aff? Yes, hurting Aff would make sense. That would make a *lot* of sense. He was over on the far side of the pitch from me, but things seemed perfectly normal over there.

I looked at my bench. Who could help me with this? "Dean, do you know where Vimsy is?"

"Yes." He pointed to a spot a little farther down the stand—right next to the action, then, but far enough from the away dugout he couldn't possibly get up to mischief.

"Will you get him, please?"

Dean scampered off, and they came back together. "Max?" said the old, defensive, easily provoked coach whose most recent outburst had been perceived by some as a resignation letter.

"Can you do me a weird favour? Go round to the other side and keep an eye on Aff."

He nodded like an eager-to-please puppy, which made me feel bad about having mentally sacked him already. "Anything in particular?"

"I don't know," I said. "I just have a weird feeling that they're going to try to kick him out of the game or something. I . . . I don't know. Just call Livia if you see anything weird." Livia, as the most junior, was the one person on the bench who always had her phone handy.

Vimsy nodded and jogged away.

"What's happening, Max?" said the Brig, sensitive to changes in my tone.

"I don't know," I said, getting frustrated. "It's a perfectly normal match. Perfectly normal in every way. Exactly as I predicted. So what am I . . . ?"

I spun on a dime and for the first time, saw Old Nick and his imps were in place. Nick was pretty bored, it seemed. One of the imps waved at me, and Nick slapped his hand down. Nick checked the time, rolled his eyes, and picked up some kind of glossy brochure or magazine. If I had to guess, I'd say it was a private jet catalogue.

I looked away, then instantly back again. The tactics imp raised the thumb and index finger of both hands, shaping them into the letter *W*.

W for Wibwob.

I copied the gesture, but let my fingers flop down. Wibwob wilting.

The imp looked frustrated, but glanced at Nick and kept his mouth shut.

Around the twenty-five-minute mark, I started to pace around my technical area. Things were . . . fine. But there's almost never a match against a team of your level where you dominate for ninety minutes. Your players get tired or distracted or your opponents smell their chance, and the momentum shifts. With our higher technique, these phases didn't normally last too long. We'd simply wait for the fire to die down, then with a few crisp touches we'd be back to our midfielders running the show.

So now came ten minutes where Kidderminster were in the ascendency. Craddock and Peabody started to hold the ball up better, started to bring their midfield into the game. They moved up the pitch. They competed for the morsels that were on offer. Worked hard at throw-ins. Made the game scrappy, broke up our tempo, earned the right to play in our half for a while.

They got a corner. Two hands raised. Far post. Their tallest players shifted that way—it was subtle, but blindingly obvious when you knew about it. Glenn, Raffi, and Henri moved to the far post. The penalty area was jam packed. Only Ryan Jack was on the edge for us, and Harriers had kept two players on the halfway line.

The cross was hit hard, high, and flat. Not bad, not good. Ben Cavanagh raced out to punch it away, ran into Sam Topps who was turning to follow the flight of the ball, and they both went tumbling.

The ball went into an area with five or six tall men competing, heads up, eyes closed, fearlessly putting their skulls in harm's way. The ball bounced against the side of Craddock's head and floated, slowly, into our goal.

One–nil.

"What the fuck's Ben doing?" I said, borderline shouted. "Why's he come for that?"

"I couldn't say, sir."

"Where's Angles?"

"In the naughty corner, sir. Where Vimsy was."

"Fuck me," I said, fuming as I paced around. "If he stays on his line that's the easiest catch in the world. We've got enough height. Enough quality. No one's going to get a good header against us. Just stay on your fucking line!" I re-read the match commentary in disbelief. "And he's smashed into Sam! At least run into one of their players! What the fuck."

Ben's match rating dropped to 5.

I paced around some more, mumbling angrily. Then I stopped, looked up, and let it go. Shit happens. We had a process. We'd wear them down with our passing, get our rewards in the second half.

And that's how it went for the next five minutes. Pass pass pass. Zip zip zip. Raffi's sudden changes of direction made the entire defence have to shuffle and slide, again and again. They would tire.

Ryan Jack played a rare loose pass, and the ball was fired up to Craddock. He didn't trust himself to run flat out, but he was fast enough to get between the ball and Carl. Carl did his job, stopped Craddock from getting anywhere dangerous. Craddock found his strike partner, Peabody, who soon had Steve Alton smothering him. Peabody did exceptionally well to buy his team a few seconds. Enough time to play a pass to the right midfielder. But Aff, being Aff, had tracked his man in a way most left-wingers didn't, so the pass turned out to be a mistake.

Except the right mid, in desperation, tried to slide tackle the ball back to Peabody.

A jolt of electricity went through me—this would be the moment! The moment Aff was injured. But no—the guy tackled the ball into Aff's stride, from mere inches away. The ball bounced off Aff's foot, travelled no less than forty yards, straight down the line, and out for a corner.

"Oh, shit." I knew what was going to happen.

Kidderminster did, too. They sent everyone up, including one of the two covering guys. This was their chance to win this game, and they were willing to take the risk.

Their players waited on the edge of the box—all our guys had a clear view of the corner-taker. One hand was raised. Near post. Ben took a few steps that way. Too obvious. The Harriers surged forward, and one guy bounced in front of Ben, annoying him, getting in his way, being a dick. Ben pushed him. The corner-taker raised both arms. Far post! But Ben hadn't seen the signal. He was too busy defending his territory. Too busy being a twat.

I turned away and watched Old Nick's face while Christian Fierce rose at the far post and bumped a header into that unguarded side of the goal. Two–nil.

Nick raised his head, clocked that there had been a goal, then went back to his brochure.

Whatever was going on, it wasn't him.

My goalkeeper's match rating fell to 4 out of 10. That happened some-times—especially with temperamental players like D-Day. He'd start shit, something would go right for him, and it was fifty-fifty if he'd end up with decent stats and 7 out of 10. If Ben made a good save, there was still a chance he could finish with a good rating. If he let the next one in, he was toast, and so were we.

"Brig," I said. "Get Robbo."

Chester are making an early change.

Ben Cavanagh will be replaced by Robbie Robson.

As he trudged past me and went down the tunnel, Ben's morale collapsed, hitting Abysmal.

I think he didn't dare look at me, but I was too furious to look at *him*.

As calmly as I could, I explained to the Brig where Ben had gone wrong. Spectrum would get the footage clipped up, and the coaches would go through it with Ben. He would learn from this, or he'd be binned in the summer.

The Brig's jaw tightened. He didn't like it when I talked like that. In the army, you had to do a lot worse than lose your head at two corners to be kicked out.

But I'd put my trust in Ben and he'd repaid me by shitting the bed in our biggest game of the season. He'd made me look like a dick, and every interview I did for the rest of my life would include a question about whether I'd realised you can't trust young goalkeepers.

Somewhere in the north of England, Ian Evans was laughing his head off.

"Fuck!"

We continued to have quarter-chances. Moves that nearly went somewhere, but not quite. The guys were working hard, fighting their duels, carrying out their roles. Most players on both teams were getting 6 or 7 out of ten. Fierce and Craddock, the goalscorers, were on 9. Raffi, Sam, and Ryan were on 8. Overall, advantage Kidderminster.

The away team pushed forward, got another corner. They did the same trick where they made one signal, then changed it when the goalie was distracted. But Robbo, instead of getting involved with the guy who was harassing him, kept himself behind the goal line so he could see. And when the cross came in, he realised immediately he wouldn't get to it, stayed on his goal line, and easily collected a header that was blooped up into the air.

Glenn and the rest of the defence took heart from that, and went about their business with renewed confidence. Harriers didn't get a sniff for the rest of the half, but we just couldn't get the ball to Henri in a position where he could get a shot away.

At halftime, I let the guys decompress as I normally did. They were very quiet. They knew they were up against it.

Vimsy sidled up to me, loath to interrupt me while I was plotting, and mumbled that he couldn't see anything strange about Aff's personal battle. I said thanks and he could sit on the bench for the rest of the game. Then I got back into my head.

What could I do? I looked at my hotkeys. Formation switches. Four-four-two? If we turned the match into a caveman contest, we'd lose. Four-one-four-one? That meant putting Trick on, which would weaken us in terms of CA, and we'd lose one of our three central midfielders. No, I couldn't switch away from 3-5-2 because the only thing we were really crushing was the midfield. If we were going to get back into this match, it would be through having one place we were utterly dominant.

Just as I was about to get their attention and tell them to stick to the plan, I remembered what Emma had said about sending me a present. I got my phone out. There was a video file and a comment: *It's nearly finished!*

I clicked it and saw myself, looking like shit, looking grumpy. The camera panned down to my feet. There was a ball.

"Do a tekkers," says Emma from behind the camera.

"I can't."

"Try."

I try. It is pitiful. I look up and see I am being filmed. "What are you doing?"

"Doing a progress video so people can see what hard work can get you. Today, no tekkers. We'll try every day and edit it into a video. See where you are in . . . a while."

My face hardens. "That's inspirational is it? To whom?"

"To me."

I take a slow breath, get the ball, and try again.

Cut to: me doing one kick-up.

Cut to: me doing one kick-up in different clothes.

Cut to: me doing three, looking a bit more perky. Four. Eight. *Many* kick-ups, with a faraway look on my healthy, tanned face.

Cut to: me training with Cody, doing explosive bursts and a pass forward.

Cut to: me playing for Chester, killing a high pass dead with one touch, waiting for an opponent to come to me, and passing the ball through their legs to a teammate.

The video ended abruptly.

I got the point—there was one more clip to add on. From today, perhaps. A clip of me doing something mad on a football pitch. The thrilling ending that would make it go viral. Come for the recovery montage, stay for the game-winning no-look backheel nutmeg.

"What's that, boss?" asked Sam.

I'd left the sound on. Emma had put a snippet from "Let It Happen" over it, though I supposed the final choice of music would depend on the nature of the last clip. "Emma was filming me doing kick-ups in Tenerife. She's stuck them together with some recent stuff. She wants to make an inspirational video."

Sam smiled at someone on the opposite bench. Henri, maybe. "We could use some inspiration, boss."

Everyone was listening. I took a couple of beats. "I made a bit of a promise to myself that I wouldn't use what happened to me to motivate you. That always felt like it would be . . . tawdry. Or something. I don't feel like learning to walk again is very inspirational, anyway. Every one of you would have done the same. Some faster, some slower. There were plenty of days I didn't feel like doing it, and someone like Dean had to fucking bully me into walking two metres holding the bannisters." I shook my head. "This video is fake. I love movie montages, but this doesn't make me feel good."

I put my phone away.

"The only thing I'd say is that . . . I had a goal and most of the time I worked at it. I know it's hard out there today. They're a really good side. But we're a little bit better. You don't need to be inspired, you just need to let your technique do the work for you. Which is exactly what you *are* doing. You're doing everything I wanted, and if we stick to the plan, we'll cause them all sorts of problems. Stick to the plan. Overloads, overlaps, slaps. Fifteen minutes, then I'll come on and we'll push them even further back. We will get five amazing chances this half, even if they defend as well as they did in the first half. All right?"

In these situations I was normally pretty fidgety, but this time I was motionless. A memory resurfaced.

"Remember we all watched England versus Spain? England huffed and puffed, but Spain won on technical quality. We're Spain. Yeah, we play fast. We play with heart. But we play technical football. We move the ball faster than they can deal with. We get into tighter situations than anyone else in this league, we make sudden breakthroughs, and we attack from angles they've never seen before. Stick to the plan and we will slap. Okay? You don't need inspiration."

Henri leaned back with a big smile on his face. "I'm quite inspired anyway, Max. Is that all right with you?"

"It's all right with me," I said. "Now get to the corners, worm your way into the box, slap, score, and we'll be home in time for Christmas. Let's go."

"Come on, lads!" yelled Glenn, and they clomped out.

For five minutes, we were rampant. Fast, dynamic thrusts down the sides. Overloads on the left, overlaps on the right. It was beautiful. We upgraded our quarter chances to half chances. For the first time, Harriers looked ragged. You could see where the goals were coming from.

But they were top of the league for a reason. They surged back at us, and they had five minutes where they got a few crosses in, had a couple of corners and long throws.

We resisted, turned the tide, and had five minutes back on top.

It was going to be a mad last thirty minutes, and if we kept slugging at each other, anything could happen. I was confident; Bob Horseman was stressed off his tits, barely able to stand the tension. He kept berating one of his members of staff. A young guy, a Spectrum type. He was telling his boss it was going to be okay.

Yeah. Good luck with that.

It was time for 2-6-2.

I subbed Steve off, and theoretically took his place as the third centre back, though of course I was free to go anywhere I wanted.

We passed the ball around a little bit. Matches sometimes felt different when seen from the middle. Liberated from the narratives you told yourself, you could get a truer sense of the action. The curse didn't agree—it only gave me 1 XP per minute when playing, versus the 4 I'd get if I stuck to the sideline. I wondered what Old Nick was thinking right now.

I took a pass from Ryan and was about to turn back to Glenn when Peabody barged me off my feet. It was so unexpected, I went flying.

"Ref," called Craddock. "Sub."

The ref acknowledged him. Peabody helped me up. "Sorry, lad."

"The fuck?"

He shrugged and walked away. I mean, it seemed to confirm my fears that Kidderminster were out to hurt someone. Why me, though? I hadn't scored or assisted the whole season.

The thought they would target me was breaking my brain. What was happening?

What happened next didn't help.

Both Craddock and Peabody left the pitch, and Bob Horseman sent on another left back and another right back.

I got down on my haunches and stared at their goal.

It wasn't 5-5-0. Close, but not quite. Fleur's mistake was understandable. No, Kidderminster Harriers, top of the league, were playing 6-4-0 against us.

Two left backs. Two right backs. Insane. Why?

I had warmed up, but felt chills all over my body. They wanted to lock down the sides of the penalty area. Stop us overloading. Stop us overlapping. Cut out our main source of attacks. Force us to hit hopeful crosses into the box, which Christian Fierce, his centre back partner, or any of the four DMs would head away.

Why wait till I came on?

Because I would shut down all their attacks, draw players out of position, and start quick counterattacks. But the way they were playing now, we *couldn't* counter. They were doing a low block, which is a fancy way of saying they were parking the bus. There would be eleven defenders between me and the goal at all times.

We couldn't slap, cross, counter, we were shit at long shots, the penalty area would be too crowded for crafty through balls, chips, or dribbles. Their goalie had been playing as a sweeper, coming off his line almost like an extra defender. Our goalie was simply taking up space, Glenn and Carl would sit on the halfway line like decorations, and I was useless in an attacking sense. Horseman had turned this match into seven attackers against eleven defenders.

So how were we going to score?

We weren't.

The ref was blowing his whistle again and again. Trying to get me to take the free kick. I stood up and bashed the ball to the side of the pitch, miles over Glenn's head. It went out for a throw-in to Kidderminster. My players started to jog back, and I yelled at them to stay.

I got back on my haunches and watched as the Kidderminster guys looked at each other. They didn't know what to do. Bob Horseman and his Spectrum guy were in deep conversation. Horseman yelled something, and one Harrier walked forward, slowly, fifty yards, to where the throw-in would be taken.

He picked up the ball, threw it away down the line, not really bothered about where it landed, and jogged back to his position in the low block.

They were not going to try to attack us. Not even with a ribbon-tied invitation.

Holy fucking shit.

While Robbo and Glenn moved the ball up the pitch, I stared at Horseman and his bench.

He wasn't all that impressive himself, but he had his Spectrum guy with tactics 15, and his assistant manager had judging player ability 16. Horseman had one ability not rated by the curse: hiring great staff and trusting them. He'd assembled a top team, good enough to win most matches at this level, and his brains trust had the ability to pull tactical rabbits out of hats. And he himself knew how to motivate.

"Max!" called Glenn. He wanted to pass to me. I stood, collected the pass, and stood in the middle of the pitch with the ball underfoot. Nobody ahead of me moved. I frantically, desperately searched for options.

But all I got was a rising sense of shame. My Maxterplan for the season was built on a foundation of sand. Mistake after mistake had piled up, and I'd gotten away with it until I'd hit the first opponent with a brain. And his solution would be passed around the National League North, just as the secret of how to beat Jackie had been. The solution was: the low block. Men behind ball. Park the bus. An idea so obvious I'd used it against Manchester City and thought myself clever. My cheeks were burning. I felt tears behind my eyes.

I'd rotated the goalies, trusting the young, talented, inexperienced one against the advice of everyone in the sport. The Art of Slapping was the art of being predictable. In God Save the King, I had a way to get more goals out of Henri, but I'd been too indecisive to use it, and now it was too late. In front of Emma, her dad, the sponsors, in front of thousands of people, a little boy had shouted, "The Emperor's got no clothes on!"

I felt my whole face blazing red. My stomach churning.

As the rain started to come in a light drizzle, I thought of Emma's inane "inspirational" video. The first change in the scene for at least fifteen seconds—a lifetime in the fast-moving world of professional sports—was me flicking the ball up and keeping it aloft with little flicks of my right foot.

The day was lost, the season was lost. The drawbridge would be pulled up. Chester would have no route to the top.

Donk, donk, donk, went the ball. No one from Kidderminster moved a muscle.

So many people believed in me. Benny and Tyson, the Knights, Sam and Aff, Emma. And all it took to fuck me up was the most predictable thing in the entire world of football. Men behind ball. Don't even try to attack. Just shut us down.

Donk, donk, as a new wave of self-loathing rippled through me. Team Dean all the way. How could I have been so stupid?

But hang on. I couldn't have imagined the fucking best team in the league would have done this to us. No, but I *could.* Henk's mum had *told* me. She'd fucking told me, but I was too stupid, too arrogant to take it for what it was—a team practicing the low block.

I took half a step forward. *Donk, donk*, another step, another *donk*.

I'd been complacent. But no! I'd seen this coming. I'd predicted this the first time I watched Pascal Bochum play. I knew we'd have days like this, and he was the type of player who could help out.

But he wasn't on the bench. So my only option for my remaining substitution was switching Joe Anka to D-Day. Wow.

I was gritting my teeth, making myself furious. Close to two and a half thousand people were about to get drenched watching a farce. I was sure they would be screaming their heads off, screaming at me to fucking do something, but all I could hear was the fear and shame and rage that my heart was pumping out.

A stray thought—if I got one good long shot away, their fucking keeper would stay on his fucking line. That was the first thing I'd learned in Darlington. Pin the bastard keeper back and things got easier. One shot. All I needed was one shot on target.

I bent my knees, and that was the signal for my team to start making moves. Aff sprinted down the left, taking two guys with him. Henri and Tony crossed paths, giving their markers something to think about. Ryan came near then spun away, Raffi jogged backwards towards the penalty area, then sideways like a receiver in motion.

My kick-ups got bigger, I pushed on faster, and when a Harrier took a tentative step towards me, I took it personally.

Donk, donk, donk—I was close enough to goal he had to do *something*—*donk*—he ran to stop me moving right—*donk*—I lifted the ball across my body onto my left foot—two left donks, the second a big, looping one, back over the defender's head—as he spun, completely lost, I donked the ball farther right, threatened to boop it to the right, to Joe, then pushed my left leg far forward and ripped my right as hard as I thought I could go. Too hard and the ball would go into orbit. But with it dipping from the kick-ups, if I caught it *just so*, it would arc and dip like one of my cannonballs.

We were shooting towards the away fans—a piece of bad luck from the start of the match I hadn't noticed until now. As I made contact and the ball flew towards the goal, a hundred spectators with a great view of the shot put their hands to their heads. They had probably been laughing at me when I was stationary. They weren't laughing now.

The goalie stepped, stepped, and flapped at the ball as it dipped below the crossbar. He got some fingers to it, it hit the crossbar, came back out, and Christian Fierce smashed it away for a corner.

Noise tried to assault me, but I didn't give a shit. The goalie would stay on his line from now on. It wasn't much, but it was fucking something. I ran over to demand the corner. I hadn't switched the takers yet. Ryan Jack sent the ball to me. I took a touch and thrashed it towards the penalty spot. Henri and Tony both launched themselves at it. Somehow, the ball went through everyone, but we got another corner. I set myself as the taker of all corners and free kicks, and ran over to the other side.

I dabbed the ball left-footed to Joe, ran diagonally past him, and took the return pass. I feinted to shoot, then, left-footed, clipped a cross between the defenders and goal. My eyes widened with hope—Henri was going to get there! But just before he could control it on his thigh, Christian Fierce launched himself horizontally, and did an acrobatic kick to clear the ball.

It went out to the left, where Aff collected. I was there, legs pumping, mind blank, and I overlapped. He passed to me and I held the ball up. The two right backs weren't sure what to do. I faked a return pass to Aff, faked a dribble, passed back to Raffi, and burst forward. He chipped it into my path and I lashed it, left-footed, a metre in front of the goalie. Legs went flying. Henri slid towards it, as did Fierce, as did Tony, as did everyone. No one got a decisive touch, and the ball went through to Joe Anka all the way on the right of the box. He steadied himself and hit a curling cross. A defender headed it away, but only to Ryan Jack. I ran around him and he touched the ball into my path. It was too delicious an invitation to ignore. I took a breath and focused on my technique as I leathered it—it started going straight at the goalie, but then exploded, curling away to the right. The keeper threw his hands up as he dived, batting it away, hoping for the best. One of his mates got there and hacked the ball away, anywhere will do.

It went out for a throw-in, and Joe took it. I received the ball with my back to goal, and a Harrier came charging at me from behind. I sensed him coming, set myself, and let him crash into my shoulder. It bumped me backwards, but I touched the ball to Joe, turned, got it back, and was powering towards the edge of the box. Another defender came at me. I dipped my shoulder left, surged right, and yet another guy was there. I feinted to cut into the box, he came with me, and I'd done enough to leave Joe wide open. I touched the ball towards the byline for him to run onto. He absolutely smashed the ball low across goal, and this time the forest of legs paid off—Tony got a toe to it. It deflected off one Harrier, and another, and Henri was able to stab at the ball—the goalie dived—but yet another deflection made it boop up. It went straight into the keeper's arms. He lay there for twenty seconds, unable to believe his luck.

I ambled back to my DM slot and fell on my haunches again. I rubbed my hair, covered my ears, then my eyes. Hear no evil, see no evil. "FUCK!" I yelled.

I got up and walked around. My head was complete jelly. I didn't know what to think, what to feel, what to do.

The ball came to me. Why? What's the point? I lashed it right-footed over a defender, right onto Aff's left foot. He tried a few moves, got past one, found another, turned, played it back to Raffi. He touched it to Ryan, who thought I might have a better idea than him. Why? I smashed the ball as hard as I could, left-footed, onto Joe Anka's right toes. He sorted his feet out, crossed, and it came back out. Sam won it, and after touches from Raffi and Ryan, Aff had it. He thrashed in a cross which was headed behind for a corner.

"Robbo," I said, waving our goalie up, while setting Ryan as the corner-taker again. I would patrol the halfway line and clear any danger. It was all I was good for.

"Max," complained Glenn as he jogged forward. "There's twenty minutes left. No need for that, yet."

"Attack," I said, but I didn't mean it. I didn't feel it.

The corner was sent in, cleared, a cross was sent in again, it was punched away by their keeper, sent in again, and finally a Harrier took the ball on his chest and calmly booped it out for a guy. He only had me ahead of him, and with Robbo stranded, if he could get a shot away, he'd score. He took a touch as he sprinted, looked up, saw me absolutely motionless, panicked, tried to push the ball past me and beat me in a foot race. I simply stepped to the side, took the ball into my ownership, and let the guy crash into my left shoulder. He went spinning, his attributes turned red, but I turned and played a long pass out to Aff again. I was thinking *this is it* when the ref stopped the game and came running to check on the guy who had fouled me. He summoned the physios, urging them to hurry.

Clearly it was going to be a long break in play. I got down on my arse, held my head. My defeat was so overwhelming, so complete, it was hard to comprehend.

Henri was bent next to me, hand on my shoulder. It hurt like hell—they both did—but I was too stunned to worry about that just then. "Max," he said. "Max."

"What?" Sulky teenager voice.

"When did you turn into Al Capone?"

Lots of laughs. The whole gang was there. Looking at me like I was *somebody*. They'd soon realise I was the traitor. I nearly burst into tears. "Is he all right?" I said.

"Who gives a shit?" said Robbo. "Shouldn't have run into you, should he?" His morale had gone to Superb.

"Max, what do we do?" said Henri. He'd seen enough of me to think I would have a magic word to say. A genie's wish held in reserve for this moment. All I had to offer was 3-5-2 with a roving centre back.

"Our only option is to swap Sam for D-Day," I said. I looked up at Sam. He'd been a dick at first, but when I'd gotten to know him better, I found I liked him more and more. "But no offence to Donny, if we're gonna sink, I'd rather wake up on a desert island with Sam."

Plenty of nodding. These guys knew exactly what I meant. Carl bent down next to Henri, right in my eyeline. "Max. *Boss*," he said. "You've got something, though. You've got the winning move, you just haven't played it yet. You've sent the Brig to break into Langley and you've got a flux capacitor. Right?"

I stared at the grass below me for way too long. "No, mate. I've got nothing. We attack until we drop. That's it. That's all I've got."

The referee broke the long silence with his whistle. We'd get a drop ball over on the left.

We stayed a couple of beats longer than we should. Glenn Ryder took his armband off and slid it up my arm. "You heard him, lads! Attack until we drop! Come on!"

Most of the guys ran off, shouting, leaving me there with Glenn and Carl lifting me to my feet. Robbo slapped me on the back and walked home.

"I'm with you, boss," said Carl. He went to the right of the centre circle.

I looked from Glenn to the armband. "Why did you do that?"

"I'm not a genius, but I know a captain's performance when I see one."

"Inspirational, is it?"

"I can never tell if you're joking. But do that for five more minutes, I'll sign your contract."

He wandered off, and I bent, hands on knees, thinking, *What's the point?*

But when the ball came to me, I sucked in a breath and burst forward.

I popped up on the left, connecting Aff and Raffi. I scooted right, combining with Joe. And from the centre, I let Ryan and Sam buy me space before trying chips, reversed passes, dinks, lobs, and if there were enough bodies in the way, long shots. What I wanted, the only thing I could offer, was pressure.

Relentless pressure.

Not mad shots into row Z. Not zero-percent-probability passes or dribbles into blind alleys. Simple things that I could do. Sometimes I tried things that were slightly above my current skill level. Sometimes I tried unexpected passes between the goalie and the last defender, hoping that Henri or Tony would be able to create something.

Corners? No point firing them into the box. We did short passes, worked through our little triangles, drawing defenders away from the penalty area, then I'd slash a cross-cum-shot, always keeping the ball low since the defenders were so tall.

We attacked from all angles, relentless, tireless, but fruitless. Christian Fierce put in the single most dominant display I'd ever seen, from anyone, ever, including me. And he didn't seem bothered. He was a piece of iron. He had an aura around him, a demotivational field that got bigger and bigger the closer we got to full time.

I had to take him on head-to-head. So I moved to a third striker position. We were playing 2-5-3, and it was only my lack of Wibwob that was stopping me going even more attacking.

As I suspected, Fierce latched onto me when I appeared in the area. If I could get the better of him, we'd have a chance. Henri, surely, would have the beating of his new marker. And Tony would be there, too.

Ryan, Raffi, and Sam pinged the ball around in front of the low block. Ten defenders, shuffling and sliding, trying to stop balls coming forward. I sprinted away from Fierce, going to be an extra man for the build-up, and there was a point near the edge of the box where Fierce passed me on to his midfielders.

Noted! I took a step back and hung around that area. It took a while, but Raffi fired a pass at my feet, hard, knowing I could deal with it. I took a touch, feinted right, moved left, and put my foot on the ball in the penalty area.

The game now was—touch me and I fall over and we get a penalty. Christian Fierce was blocking me, too clever to dive in and make my life easy. With hundreds of tiny body feints, weight shifts, fake passes, leg pumps, the entirety of the match came down to me, surrounded by red shirts, all afraid to make a challenge, trying to create something out of nothing. Raffi came storming through, across me, and as I faked to pass to him, a fake so good even Fierce bought it, I clipped the ball with a little bit of side spin, headed towards the inside of the goal.

The goalie scrambled sideways, water flying up around his boots in slow motion, threw himself at the ball, and pushed my shot behind for a corner.

I wandered back to the halfway line, done. Absolutely done. Couldn't even be bothered sending our goalkeeper up. No matter what we did, we'd fall short.

I'd been so drained I hadn't even checked the time—still five minutes plus injury time left. Another ten minutes or more. A lot could happen in ten minutes. We could score four goals. But not today.

Ryan Jack sent in a tired corner, it was cleared by a Harriers defender, fresh as a daisy. A mad scramble, Raffi sliding in, the ball bouncing around, winding up at the feet of Sam Topps.

Don't pass to me, I thought. Don't you dare fucking pass to me, I cried with all my being.

He fizzed it towards me, turned, head bobbing, exhausted but nowhere near giving up, and ran forward. He'd fight to the end.

My whole body sagged as the ball came towards me. I was so done with this shit. I flopped like a badly controlled marionette, and popped back up all of a sudden, the ball spinning up from my standing foot. I snarled as I did kick-ups, walking towards the opposition goal, gnashing my teeth, rabid, mad, literally driven mad, Tommy Tekkers, *donk donk donk*. A Harrier pushed his mate towards me, but I realised—the shock was so great I missed a kick—I realised he didn't *want* to come. He was knackered. He was spent. He was spent and he was afraid of me. I faked a long shot, drove forward, keen to see what mischief I could manage in the time that was left.

Kidderminster: 6 shots, 2 goals.

Chester Football Club: 31 shots, 0 goals.

I had the last kick of the game. I put every last calorie, every last mote of myself into a move that bought me half a centimetre, which was all that Christian Fierce was willing to let me have, and I smacked the ball towards goal. It was going top-left, top bins, top banana, and at least we'd have that. At least we'd leave the pitch with something.

But Fierce blocked it. Don't ask me how, but he blocked it.

The final whistle went. *Peep peep peep*, and some of the sound came back. The roar of the away fans. They were ecstatic. Top of the league. They had a team of warriors fighting for the badge, a top manager, top coaches, a floating megabrain.

I flopped to my back. Knees up, hands covering my eyes. I was too tired to dwell on my mistakes, all the people I'd lied to, all the people I'd let down. I didn't need the Live Tables perk to know we'd slumped to fourth in the league. No chance we'd finish above Kidderminster. No chance we'd finish above Darlo.

We're dogshit, mate.

As the tears finally came, I was cheered by the thought that, as well as the away fans, someone in the stadium would have been enjoying this. Physio Dean's next email draft would be more uplifting than *Holes* by Louis Sachar.

I stayed there for approximately eight hours, but when I finally moved my hands onto the grass behind my head, I realised there were loads of bodies near me. Henri was on the ground. Tony was. So was Aff.

And I was gobsmacked to see the guy closest to me was none other than Christian Fierce. He was making weird moaning noises. The ecstasy of victory? No—he'd got mega cramp but couldn't get attention. It was like the Battle of Gettysburg out there. I rolled over, clambered to one knee—I was attacked by a wave of dizziness; it passed—and I got to Fierce's leg. I lifted it and pressed it forward. He wailed with the pain and the relief. I switched legs and he groaned. We were a bottle of oil away from securing the UK's biggest ever non-league sponsorship—Wrexham included.

Job done, I decided it was time to go home, and strode off to the tunnel. Forget the media, the sponsors, the fans. I was going home. I got there and I was legitimately stupefied to realise there was no tunnel. No tunnel. Where's the fucking tunnel?

I realised I was on the wrong side of the stadium. *Mate.*

The tears nearly came again. I did my best to get to the other side of the pitch, but I knew there was no way I'd make it. It was miles away. I wanted to stop and take a break, but I knew if I did, I'd never be able to get going again. I wobbled, Schrödinger's Max, half dead on the grass, half staring at the tunnel that was receding into the distant distance.

Arms grabbed me, I was floating, being carried, hovering, falling, I was holding someone, I was dizzy, they were holding me. *There's* the tunnel. Goodbye, tunnel! I was being placed on a table. Someone was squirting paste into my mouth. Hey! Not on a first date! I lay there, face down, and someone was rubbing my neck, whispering, and it seemed like I was allowed to close my eyes.

So I closed my eyes.

19

PURPOSING THE DEFEAT

My ten minutes of rest was followed by an Henri-length cold shower and half an hour staring at the ceiling of my windowless little bed-office. There was no point leaving the stadium until the traffic had cleared. I got cursemail immediately after the final whistle, but was in absolutely no mood to open it. In fact, I didn't want to talk about football for the foreseeable future—a task made tricky by the fact that I'd be managing the women's team the next afternoon. I turned my phone off, lay still, and counted ceiling tiles.

Emma spent her first-ever night in the barn. I hadn't prepared or shopped accordingly, but she was patient and somehow rustled up a nice, simple dinner like the first one she'd made for me in Darlington.

"We can watch a movie if you want. Your choice."

"My choice? Even *Predator?*"

"Is it scary? Nothing scary."

"It's scary how there's always a residue of testosterone on the screen when it's over. How about *Spirited Away?*"

The living room wasn't set up for two people, so we spooned on the bed with my new laptop turned sideways.

Emma liked the film but fell asleep after about half an hour. I watched the rest, had a hot shower, and hoped I'd fall right to sleep after. Nope. Hard as I tried, I couldn't stop going over and over the chain of events, before and during the match, that had led to disaster.

But finally I crashed, and when I opened my eyes it was bright and Emma was gone. I threw some clothes on and got slightly more panicky as every space I checked proved to be Emmaless. I went through the stables, thinking that maybe she'd gone to look at the ponies. Eventually, Ruth appeared and pulled me into her house, into the kitchen. Emma was there along with a posh buffet of breads, butters (yes, plural), jams, meats, cheeses, grapes, and mueslis.

"Hey, babes," she said.

"We saw you darting around in a panic," said Ruth. "Scaring the horses."

"I was worried."

"I sent you a text," said Emma.

"Phone's off." The women looked at each other.

"Max lost yesterday," said Emma, as though Ruth might somehow have missed it. "So he has to wear sackcloth and ashes and isolate himself."

Ruth rang an imaginary bell. "Unclean! Unclean!" The pair of them thought that was hilarious. Ruth looked me up and down. "Are you going to manage the women today?"

"Of course," I said.

She shrugged. If I wanted a pity party, I was welcome to it. She sat down, picked up an iPad, and popped a grape into her mouth. Emma was texting away while sipping on coffee.

"Can I have a tea?" I said.

Ruth gave me a look. "If you think I'm going to wait on you hand and foot, you've got another thing coming."

"Oh. It's self-service, then." That earned me a tiny smile. I looked at what was on offer. All very nice, but I was in the mood for something sweet. "Have you got any tartlets?"

"No," said Ruth. "Never eat them."

I nodded. Maybe I'd try the jams. I went to fill the kettle. For a second, I thought Ruth had frozen—she was absolutely motionless, not chewing, not scrolling on the tablet. Then I blinked and she was back to normal. Must have been my imagination.

After a nice brunchy breakfast, I announced my intention to go for a walk. Emma announced her intention to stay flopped on Ruth's sofa.

So I walked alone on the paths around the area. Sometimes there were horse riders, joggers, dog walkers, but this morning it was completely isolated. Just me and my thoughts.

There was a spot where, if the sun was right, there was a spectacular view of the countryside. Rolling hills, hedges, a couple of cute farms, a small lake. The path just before and just after were always in shade, which added to the sense that you were turning into a secret garden. Cold, cold, warm, what a view!

This morning was exceptional—the sun defrosted me, and a little bird dude alighted on a nearby hedge to see what I was looking at.

The bird flew off, unimpressed, and I finally felt alive enough to check my cursemail.

New achievements: You Arrogant Ass, You've Killed Us!; Failed Audition; Raise the Roof; Tinkerman 5; Life Begins at Fifty.

I'd been getting achievements pretty consistently, and had been all but ignoring them. Most seemed to be ways for Nick to poke fun at me. There was 1 XP for being Tommy Transfers, 1 XP for Make Up Your Mind (for using a different starting formation in three consecutive matches), and 0 XP for Know You Are, Said You Are, So What Am I? That came when I'd "childishly" provoked an opposition manager.

Achievements were useless in themselves, and only interesting in that they sometimes led to new perks becoming available. In that respect, this latest batch of five were highly significant. But as I stood there, I found I envied the little bird. If he didn't like where he was, he could easily go and find somewhere better.

I left the beauty spot and walked in the direction of a stile that separated two fields. My habit was to go there, climb the two steps, and proclaim myself the King of the World before turning back.

I recognised the name of the first new achievement. It was from the film *The Hunt for Red October.* A submarine captain removes the safety protocols from his torpedoes and one of those torpedoes ends up circling around, powering towards his own vessel. His right-hand dude says, "You arrogant ass, you've killed *us!*" It's awesome. The curse awarded me 1 XP for having one of my tactics successfully used against me. Bit of a weird one—why not give me this achievement when someone beat me using 4-4-2? The only tactic I used that was uniquely mine was the Two Jackies Trick.

Failed Audition came with 0 XP and was given because I had lost a match when given the opportunity to impress a VIP spectator.

Now, *that* got my brain fizzing. I became convinced that the imps had persuaded Old Nick to come and watch the match just so I'd get this achievement. Which meant they'd fixed it so I'd lose!

I dismissed the idea—I'd lost fair and square and had no one to blame but myself.

My initial thought was compelling, though. Otherwise, why had Nick turned up? He wasn't interested in the match in the slightest.

Raise the Roof came with 1 XP and the description said the stadium had been "uncommonly loud." I tuned out most of the noise when I was on the pitch—I'd have to check with Crackers.

Tinkerman 5 was for my continued tactical tweaks and changes.

And then Life Begins at Fifty. It came with 50 XP—by far the most the achievements system had ever given me. It was awarded because I had unlocked 49 achievements.

Now I had 50 in total, and the cursemail ended with a few words that got my pulse racing.

New perks are available to buy.

The stile was just ahead, so I jogged there, and hopped on to the first climbing post. I went to the perk shop and saw all the usual options: Injuries, Contracts, Form, Player Comparison. And two new ones!

Future

Unlocks the Future area of a player's profile.

Cost: 900 XP

With Ball/Without Ball

Unlocks the With Ball/Without Ball tabs in the tactics screens. Deformation range is limited but can be extended by unlocking achievements.

Cost: 10,000 XP

Ten thousand! But wait . . . where was Wibwob? It seemed obvious this was all leading to Wibwob. I took a closer look.

With Ball . . . WIB.

Without Ball . . . WOB.

Okay! But what *was* it? What did it do? I felt pretty sure it would let me put players wherever I wanted them, limited by this "deformation range" guff.

I stared down at the stile. This was the boundary between one plot of land and another. I could cross it and follow the footpath, but I wasn't supposed to stray onto the farmer's working land. If I did, either the farmer or one of his guard cows would come and shoo me away.

I opened the men's team page and looked at the 3-5-2 graphic. I hoped Wibwob would let me push one of the CBs forward into DM, or drop the second striker in a 4-4-2 into an attacking midfield role. But this "deformation range" suggested I wouldn't be able to drop a midfielder all the way back into the rear-guard—that would be a two-slot jump. And the right mids could go one slot up, one slot down, but I couldn't turn them into fullbacks or actual forwards.

That made sense, actually, otherwise I wouldn't need to buy any more formations. There had to be some limits. All I wanted, really, was to make little tweaks.

So, yes, I was pretty confident I knew what Wibwob would do. And it made sense that the tactics imp would encourage me to go for it. It was a powerful tool and in the right hands—mine—there could be some fairly entertaining exploits. But I wished the curse had spelled it all out. Based on the description alone, I probably wouldn't have looked twice at such an expensive, mysterious perk. It was only the imps constantly nagging me about it that made me want it. It would take ages to save up for this thing, and in the meantime I'd be missing out on unlocking more attributes and more tactics.

I started walking home.

Should I skip Injuries and Contracts and go straight for Wibwob?

Manchester United had four left backs injured, including the one they'd signed to cover for the other three. Chelsea had thirteen first-team players in the medical room. Wibwob would help me win matches, but not as much as having my best players on the pitch. And I was pretty sure Contracts would give me the skills to find great players to bring in during the transfer window.

Stick to the plan, then, but Wibwob was now third on the list. In the meantime, I'd keep trying to unlock new achievements so that one day I'd be able to reduce the deformation limit.

When I got back to the barn, I found a post-it note that said Emma had gone "riding out" with Ruth. I took it to mean they had gone out riding.

So I watched a bit more footage of today's Cheshire Ladies Cup opponents—Stockport County. They were well-established, competing well in the fourth tier. They would probably smash us to bits, but there was a chance they'd put out a weaker team and we'd at least be able to leave the pitch with our heads held high.

I thought about what I'd say to the ladies before the match, and nothing came.

I got to the sports centre early and waited in the men's changing rooms while Jill and Terry did all the preparations. It was a surprise to see our Chester Knights coach helping with the women's team. I didn't interrogate it further—it was more proof that I needed to hire another coach ASAP to take the burden off the ones I already had. Sighing, I thought about the Finances perk that was available. It would show me that while I needed more coaches, more players, and more scouts, I didn't have the money for all three.

I filled in the team sheet with our usual 4-5-1. We'd crept up to an average CA of just over 18. Lucy, who was in her forties, had stopped improving at CA 17, leaving Bonnie as the only one of our defenders with growth potential. The midfielders were more talented, and with some league and cup experience under their belt, had kicked on a little bit. Pippa and Dani were CA 20, with Bea Pea and Maddy just behind. Julie McKay was still only CA 7, but catching up fast, and as she came out of her shell was proving to have a wicked sense of humour.

Which left Kisi. She'd added a couple of points in CA thanks to getting a taste of real first-team action. I'd talked to her and told her I'd keep her for another month or two and when she stopped improving, I'd kick her back to Man City. She pretended to agree, but I knew what she was thinking. *I won't stop improving.*

"So it's true!" my star striker had come into the sweaty room, surrounded by an actual vortex of fragrant top notes. "You're really in here. Sulking!"

"I'm not sulking," I lied.

Henri laughed. "We can talk about this later. First, do your job."

I handed the team sheet over. He scanned it and disappeared. A couple of minutes later, he came back and gestured that I needed to follow him. I obeyed and found myself walking the one metre across the corridor and into the women's changing room.

"The financier doesn't like seeing you do the team talks on the pitch like some Sunday League team," he told me. He was terrible at giving nicknames—they never caught on. The financier was Ruth. "So she's booked this room for us. Like a proper team."

"Us?"

"Us. We are us, Max. A wise man once told me that. In between sulks. Ladies, may I have your attention?" They were very happy to offer it. "I have found your manager. His girlfriend tells me he has switched his phone off and does not wish to engage with the rest of the human race. So I am here to be his assistant manager for the day. I see you are pleased. That is good. That is one of the correct reactions. Another is euphoria. Now, Max. What is your plan for the match?"

He pushed me towards the tactics board with its multi-coloured magnets. I sighed. "Goalie," I said. "Defenders." I moved four magnets in a line just below the keeper. "Midfield." Another four, touching the defenders. "Forwards." Two more. 4-4-2, all squashed into the penalty area. "Low block. Keep it tight. Nothing silly. Win second balls. Defend for ninety, win on penalties."

Some of the women were frowning like I was really serious, but Henri clapped his hands with delight. "Amazing. Your humour when you are in a black mood is drier than the Gobi. But why on earth are you in a bad mood? Because the Brig took some of your limelight?"

"What?"

He stopped smiling. "Why are you grumpy? Tell me now. Come on. I insist."

I swept my gaze around the room. Twenty women were watching us in a state of great interest. Another bonkers scene. Just how Henri liked it. I didn't have the energy to obfuscate or delay. "Yesterday was dispiriting. It came out of nowhere. Sucker punch. I let everyone down. The team, the fans. MD was showing us off to new sponsors. I . . . I don't know what I'm supposed to do now. I need to go and lick my wounds but I have to do this. Tier six against tier four. I normally turn up with a trick up my sleeve, some mad idea I'd like to try. But today I'm empty. I've had the stuffing knocked out of me, is how I feel."

Someone snorted. Charlotte. "What, have you never lost before?"

Henri answered for me. "Not when he's been playing."

Charlotte's eyes widened. "What, seriously?"

"Seriously. Why should he have lost? He could score whenever he wanted. The Darlington players called it God Mode. Now? Now, he's merely a demi-god." He rubbed my upper arm, with affection. "My friend. You need time to process your feelings. That is true. But a wise man once said, 'Life can only be understood backwards but it must be lived forwards.'" He paused. Frowned. "That was a very good line. I said something exceptionally helpful, there. I expected more of a reaction."

I smiled from one side of my mouth. "Round of applause for Henri." The ladies obliged. Kisi threw in a few *whoops*. When the merriment subsided, I asked a ludicrously pleased Henri to repeat the phrase.

"Life can only be understood backwards but it must be lived forwards. Tonight you will think. Tomorrow you will think. By Saturday, you will have seventeen solutions to a low block. But today you have a job. So do your job." He looked around the room. "It is a cup match, yes? Against a very good side. So, tell us what to do."

I closed my eyes and thought about what he had said. Life can only be understood backwards . . . "Four-five-one," I said, snapping out of battery-saving mode and into something resembling normal operations. "We will have to do a lot of defending. Suffer, sacrifice, shuffle, slide, spacing. Now, this lot are going to take one look around, wonder how they've ended up in a shithole like this, and they'll be walking around with a big sneer. So . . ." I looked down, suddenly ashamed.

"Go on, Max," murmured Henri.

"So . . . pretend to be shit for five minutes. You have to defend well. But when you get the ball, Charlotte, Bea Pea, make a big mess of it. Someone send a long pass to the left and Dani, make a big deal of how you didn't hear that the ball was coming." I looked at my feet. Another half-baked idea. Another piece of deception that had no right to work. That *wouldn't* work. Because I didn't even believe in it myself.

"Why is no one asking why?" said Henri.

"Because it's obvious," said Bea Pea. "Get them to underestimate us. Even more."

I gave her a tiny smile that died on my face like a snowflake landing on a hot car. "Do that for five minutes. They'll relax. Then close the trap. Our first piece of quality needs to lead to a goal. Do you get me? Shit, shit, shit, goal. Hopefully that's one–nil."

"And then?" said Henri.

This was it. The moment I didn't want to face. The moment I had to tell them they had absolutely no chance of winning. Stockport's average CA was in the 40s, and their bench was even stronger. "Then whatever. Just do your best or whatever."

Henri rubbed his palms down his sides. He looked worried suddenly. "I see."

Dani got up and went to Henri. Showed him something on her phone. "Dani says to turn your phone on."

I looked at the ceiling. "Yeah. Later."

Henri mimed. Dani responded. Typed, her thumbs a blur. "Dani says turn your phone on and read what Bethany sent you." I was about to complain when he glanced down at her screen. "Do it now."

With a grunt, I sat in the corner, and held the power button down. While I waited for my home screen to load, I tried understanding life backwards or whatever. I didn't get very far.

My phone finished loading and I found I had been bombarded with texts, calls, voicemails, and emails. Messages from Beth begged me to read an email she'd sent. I opened it.

From: Beth

To: Max

Subject: The DM Podcast

Max. I've got the chance to record something for my newspaper's daily sport podcast. It's called *Our Jackboot, Your Neck*. Short snippets of sport from around the world. Mostly football but anything with a fun little story. This is what I'll read and submit—it could be great for my career. Another string to my bow if I can get audio work as well as written. Journalists have to hustle like crazy. It's grim. You might consider being nicer to your local guy.

I'm not asking for your approval, but I don't want you getting all Max on me so here's what I've got planned and if there's anything you don't like I *might* change it.

Purposing the Defeat, written and read by Bethany Alban
What does it mean to lose?

Don't ask Max Best. He likes to overcomplicate *everything*.

Max is, among many complicated things, the manager of Chester FC men's first team. Earlier today, his men had the chance to go top of the National League North in a match against the current leaders, Kidderminster Harriers.

All very simple so far, but Max doesn't do simple.

Since taking over as manager, he has done a lot of *stirring*. Not only whacking hornets' nests and running away, but also planting nests for future use.

Take one example. He suggested he could easily be tempted to return to his former club as player-manager. That club's form dipped just enough for Chester to overtake them in the table. Annoyed at his decisions being questioned by the club's board, Max hinted they were contributing to a feeling of burnout. The club recently took steps to relieve Max of the terrible burden of explaining himself. And while Max gets whatever he wants, Chester's fans don't get the one thing they crave—for Max to sign a long-term contract. A move they say will show that he is committed.

All this chaos is intended to strengthen Chester's position. Most observers think it defeats the purpose. Every time Max flutters his lashes at a rival team, every time he adds another floor to his ivory tower or sends his minions to communicate with the media, he creates a wedge between him and the fans who pay him. They want a king for their castle; he wants to be a jester.

Why would any club put up with such a complicated person?

[leave a pause here]

Because Max Best is a winner.

The last thirteen results for the men's team? Won twelve, drawn one. Goals galore, delightful football, and playing time for Max Best himself as he recovers from a serious injury.

Enter top-of-the-table Kidderminster. They came to Max's fortress armed to the teeth and carrying an enchanted item—the Sword of Superior Set Pieces. As Chester pressed and probed, Kidderminster slashed their way to a two–nil lead. Max Best, habitual winner, brought himself on for the last half hour. His opponents reacted by revealing their second magical item—the Shield of the Legendary Low Block.

Max knew he had no answer to the Shield. He gave up. He wilted like old lettuce.

But he kept fighting.

Standing unopposed on the halfway line, Max did kick-ups, a challenge, a challenge that went unanswered until he reached the edge of the D, when finally he found an opponent willing to face him. Facing the goal, facing defeat, Max flicked the ball left and right until the defender was facing the wrong way. His shot arced to the top corner, and though it was saved, there came the first stirrings from the crowd. The first audible recognition that they might be witnessing something special.

Joining the dots, playing one-twos, recovering the ball, Max was everywhere on the pitch, a man possessed, but one too many shots went wide, were blocked, were saved, and he quit. He gave up.

But he kept fighting.

He ran, he dribbled, he passed long and short, he tried everything, threw the kitchen sink at the problem. As one by one his considerable bag of tricks failed him, he kept fighting, kept banging his head against the enchanted shield, and amazingly, as the volume from the crowd hit eleven, the shield cracked. Surely one more charge would break it?

The next charge came, and the next, and the next, and each time more players fell with cramp, more players begged the referee to stop the contest, and still the jester king mounted his horse and gathered his lance. One final tilt! And another!

Kidderminster's defenders had never seen anything like it, nor had the Chester fans. Oh, perhaps in the old days, in the eighties, but not recently. Certainly not in the age of Max Best. This aloof, process-driven cipher, this chaotic neutral character, me first, you second, this boy so arrogant he doesn't even celebrate his own goals, was smashing himself into a brick wall, time and time again, and the wall was finally starting to wobble.

The walls of Jericho fell when the horns and the shouts of the enemy brought them down—perhaps history would have repeated in Chester, such was the noise generated by the home supporters. Whatever distance had come between them and Max in the past few months was cut away. Many Chester players contributed to a performance full of heart and quality, but two thousand Chester fans lived every second of the last ten minutes as though they were controlling Max in a video game. Perhaps one might say Best was controlling *them*. When a pass went astray and he had to break stride to collect it, his two thousand mouths groaned. When he was patiently building play on the right in order to work an opening, they fell to a patient, nodding hush. When he ran to the left to add his weight to that thrust, they swayed left, then swayed right as he cut into the box, then bobbed up and down as his shot crashed back off the shield. And in the final, frantic few minutes where Chester did everything but score, as Max orchestrated incessant attacks, they roared their approval, roared in a stupefying, endlessly overlapping series of waves.

[pause]

The shield held.

Max Best was dragged to the dressing room, disconsolate, apparently unaware that he was receiving a standing ovation of biblical proportions. Unaware that, in valiant defeat, he'd formed an eternal bond with every Chester fan present. They understand him better now. He likes to project an image of being all style, no substance, because being underestimated helps him win football matches. He likes to keep those around him in suspense, likes to put on an air of sophisticated detachment. But today there was no hiding his commitment. From jester to king in thirty inspirational minutes.

What does it mean to lose?

For a complicated man, losing is just another way to win.

I read it again before replying, fact-checking that I did in fact have a contract with Chester and suggesting she change the word *minions*, but saying she had my blessing.

Something had *happened* the day before. Something I couldn't understand through the lens of my own experience. I needed Beth, and Boggy, and to hear from the fans. Like Henri had said, it could wait.

I got to my feet and smashed Triple Captain and Bench Boost.

"All right, shut the fuck up. It's going to be fucking hard today. Do my little scam and you might get an early goal out of it. If we have insane luck, we might get a second. Then what? Do you want to do a low block, hope to survive? Or do you want to do what I did yesterday? Attack until you drop and get dragged off the pitch because you've left your mind, body, and soul out there?"

"Yeah!" cried Bonnie, not realising that I'd proposed a multiple-choice question.

"Attack until you drop!" called Maddy, clapping her hands.

They went out to do their final warm-ups and all that. "Maybe you should wait here," said Henri.

"Why?"

He was staring at something. "Just a feeling."

I shrugged and lay with my back on the hard slats of the bench until it was time to go out and start the match.

What happened next was like a dream. It was a series of madnesses joined by the loose connective tissue of a football match.

I left the dressing room and there was a burst of applause. The spectators around the pitch were two, sometimes three deep. To my right, families and players and randos. To my left, along the length, a lot of aggressive-looking young men. For a second I was scared—my skull, except for the part that had been operated on—tingled. But they were doing most of the clapping. Half a second after that tiny burst of anxiety came the realisation that they were Chester fans. The hardcore. The proto gammons.

I waved at them as I passed.

"What's going on?" I said, but Emma and Henri were busy bickering about who was going to be my assistant manager. I laid my hand on Jill's shoulder. Long-suffering Jill, always the bridesmaid, never the bride, except I supposed at her own wedding. "Jill's my assistant manager. You guys can be cheerleaders."

"You've got enough of those," said Emma, but before I could ask what she meant, the match was underway.

Stockport County passed the ball around, very neat and tidy. Their team was lumpy—pockets of very good players, with some who were overrated. It didn't help us much, but it did mean some of their moves were sloppy. Some instinct made me man-mark their number 10 right away, even before I'd fully processed why.

When we got the ball first, Charlotte smashed a low pass . . . almost to the corner flag. She held her hand up, yelling sorry.

We defended for a while, then got the ball again. A nice combination between Pippa and Charlotte ended with a pass being pinged out to Dani. As the ball zipped past her, she ran in quite the wrong direction. Hundreds of people had inexplicably turned up to watch, and along with the Stockport players, looked slightly embarrassed as Dani bent and pretended to fiddle with a hearing aid. Stockport's two centre backs turned away. One said something to the other and there was laughter.

"Oh my God, oh my God," I said, practically hopping around.

"Max," hissed Jill. "Don't ruin it."

I got my poker face back on and watched, feeling like I was slowly unwrapping an enormous Christmas present, as my players waited for the right moment.

The long ball comes to nothing.

Bonnie heads clear.

It's gathered by Lucy. She has no one to pass to.

She's furious! She points to where Pippa should be.

Stockport sense a chance to press.

They're pushing forward.

Lucy plays it over the top.

Dani chases . . . and gets there!

She shapes to shoot . . .

But drags the ball onto her left. She powers forward . . .

Draws the keeper . . .

Oh, that's a clever pass.

Bea Pea can't miss!

The roar from the crowd told me what had happened even before the curse did. I lost my mind, running up and down in a four-metre rut.

The crowd! They were into it. Really into it!

When the match resumed, there was a real crackle around the place. It was almost hostile. They really wanted to see Chester win, and the Stockport players felt it. They were good, though, and they snapped out of the complacency. They'd learned the hard way that Chester Women could play. Time to step up.

And step up they did. A few minutes of pressure led to an equaliser.

I sighed. This was inevitable. At least we'd scored. At least we'd had that moment. But a CA 18 team wasn't going to beat a CA 43 one.

A cheer came up from the far corner flag. The crowd parted, briefly, and someone hopped over the railing and walked along the touchline. The fans yelled something, a single syllable, but it wasn't until the man came closer that I realised what they were chanting.

"Brig! Brig! Brig!"

I laughed. "What now?"

My assistant manager offered me a handshake, all smiles. "Can I have a quick word, sir?"

"Yes. Tell me why you've got a chant. That's new."

He frowned. Emma replied. "He doesn't know what happened. He turned his phone off and he's been feeling sorry for himself since the match ended."

The Brig grinned, but then got serious. "That's why I've come. The chant, I mean. You instructed me to be uncontroversial in the post-match interview. But I'm afraid your display was too much for me to take and I . . . spoke my mind. I have come to tender my resignation."

"No!" said Emma, pushing me angrily as though *I* had done something wrong.

"Er . . . maybe I'd better know what you said."

"Let me," said Henri, first to his phone. He tapped and I heard a whooshing noise. My phone pinged.

"Excuse me," I said, fishing my earbuds out of my pocket and popping them in my ears. I took a quick glance at the match ratings. Stockport's talented number 10 was on 5. She did not like being man marked. How had I spotted that so fast? I noticed what the link was. "This is the post-match interview? Why's it on YouTube?"

Jill knew. "Gary's been filming them for a while but he doesn't upload the ones where you bully him."

I pressed play. It wasn't a long clip. I could watch it while keeping an eye on the match.

Gary kept himself out of frame, so all we saw was the Brig, his eyes shining, shark-like. He didn't bully Gary, but surely this was more terrifying than what he got from me?

Gary: John, that's a tough loss to take. What's the mood in the dressing room?

Brig: Professional footballers are competitive. They play to win, and if they don't win, they react badly. There were some shouts, some thrown drink bottles. I believe it was performative.

Gary: Sorry, what?

Brig: The players don't like losing, of course. But I'd say the overall mood is one of euphoria.

Gary: Euphoria?

Brig: Football players go to work every day, the same as everyone else, and they work hard, clock off, and do it all again the next day. They worry about their mortgages and providing for their family, the same as everyone else. There's one difference between a footballer and most people—everyone dreams of being a sports star. Sam Topps didn't grow up wanting to be an accountant. He wanted to play football in a noisy stadium. Even more than that, he didn't grow up wanting to shuffle and slide and keep proper spacing. He dreamed of attacking, of taking shots, scoring goals. Today was, I believe, the closest he has ever got to living out his childhood dreams.

Gary: What did you think of the referee?

Brig: The referee refereed the game to the best of his ability.

Gary: Would the result have been different if we had played a weak team in the Cheshire Cup on Tuesday?

Brig: Yes, because in that alternate reality, Max Best would not be the manager of Chester Football Club.

Gary: Some players who played in that match didn't look at their best today. Perhaps they were tired.

Brig: On Tuesday night, eleven men plus substitutes were asked to pull on a Chester shirt and represent the club. There's a badge on the front of the shirt. I'm an outsider to this club, but I like to believe someone made a choice to depict a lion and a crown because they hoped it would inspire the players to fight like lions and play like kings. If you want us to play like mice and cowards, you must give us a different shirt with a different badge and find us a new manager because the one we have wants to win every game.

Gary: What about the goalkeeper situation? Many people are saying—

Brig: Ben Cavanagh is a king. Robbo Robson is a lion. Max trusts them both. Demands more from them both. The same as with Sam. The same as with Henri. The same as with me. But there is no one Max demands more of than himself. If there's a player at this club who feels harshly treated, he can ask himself if he's ever had to be peeled off the pitch like Max was just now. If there's a fan who thinks this manager and this team aren't sufficiently committed, I'd like to see what state they're in when *they* clock off from work. If this team, this lineup, this formation, is not exactly how you want it, not exactly how you'd do it, then I have news for you. You are wrong. Max knows best. Goodbye.

I popped the earbuds out and put them in their case. I treated myself to a few seconds of staring at the backs of my hands.

A few seconds later, after telling the Brig I didn't accept his resignation, I found myself prowling up and down the touchline, jaw set, eyes sucking in all the data that was available to me. I barked out a few orders. Tweaked some settings. Waved my arms around, trying to push my rekindled passion into the players.

It was hopeless. It was a lost cause. But defeats could be glorious, too.

The crowd responded. Maybe Beth was right. Maybe I could control them.

I stopped what I was doing, amazed, disbelieving. Stockport had been pushed back. Not quite into a low block, but they'd gone defensive. I checked the screens—their tactics were the same as at the start.

It wasn't the tactics; it was the crowd! Pushed right up against the sides of the pitch, closer than in any real stadium, they were yelling and screaming and generally being fucking intimidating. And Stockport, though they must have been used to playing in front of bigger crowds, were used to playing in front of women's football crowds. Raucous, sure. But, let's face it, wholesome.

This bunch of pricks weren't wholesome. They were rabid Chester fans. High on the drama from yesterday, come to inject more into their veins.

I grinned savagely. Holy shit!

The more I pranced up and down the touchline, yelling mindless shit, the more the fans responded. They fucking loved it!

And as Stockport sat back, waiting for this unexpected fire to go out, Dani exchanged passes with her fellow midfielders and worked her way to the centre circle.

Where she started doing kick-ups.

The reaction was electric.

Kick-ups in a match? Pointless. Stupid. What kind of idiot does that?

She moved forward. A Stockport player ran to do something about this upstart, and Dani flicked the ball over her head, much as I had done. The second defender came faster, but Dani was smarter than me, and she passed the ball to Charlotte. Who, in turn, passed it back so that Dani could flick the ball up again, laughing at her own talent. Was that an impression of *me*?

Stockport's number 10, who Pippa had tracked and followed almost wherever she went, depriving her of contact with the ball, went into meltdown. She lunged at Dani, who crumpled into a heap. I saw from her attributes that she wasn't seriously hurt, but the swan dive was so convincing that I was racing onto the pitch almost before she'd screamed.

I got there, did some fake sign language, and as she writhed and made weird noises, Dani signed back. "Ambulance!" I screamed. "Fucking ambulance!"

The crowd had gone feral, and now they bayed for blood. It would have been legit concerning, but I knew I had control of the mob. The mob and I were besties.

As I pretended to mourn for Dani's broken bones, I saw the referee flash a card at the vile number 10. Red.

"Sub!" I yelled, jogging back to the touchline, and four hundred people expected me to replace Dani.

There was tremendous surprise when, in fact, I replaced a defender, Mo, with a striker, Julie.

"Attack!" I yelled. There was a strange moment when all my players turned to me, confused. I'd already changed the formation to 3-5-2, and now I clicked various hotkeys. Make forward runs: yes. Try through balls: yes. Crosses: yes. Pressing: yes.

I sucked in air, ready to try again. It was for the benefit of the fans, really. "Attack! Attack! Attack attack attack!"

I repeated the chant, and this time, all the fans on my length of the pitch joined in. One more time, and it was everyone.

Charlotte passed to Susan, who went wide to Maddy, whose first touch bamboozled the defender. Maddy's run brought Bea Pea across and they tried a one-two. It wasn't quite right, so Maddy had to turn back. She found Charlotte had made a darting run, and when the ball was played to her, she hit a fast, high, spinning pass that went over all the defenders, all the way to Julie, who tried to redirect the ball at goal. Supremely difficult, but she made good contact. It hit the post.

I celebrated like we'd scored. It was thrilling to see them play like this!

And that's when it happened. Other people said the defeat to Kidderminster had been magical for them. Some said they'd had out-of-body experiences. But for me, this was the most magical moment. In the first half of our heroic 4–2 defeat to Stockport County in the Cheshire Ladies Cup, as I punched the air and jumped around like a hyperactive kitten because my players had put together a half-decent sequence, the fans sang something I never thought I'd hear sung in earnest.

"Max Best's blue and white army!
Max Best's blue and white army!"

Monday, October 23.

The guys were jogging around the training ground at BoshCard HQ. I was ready for action, but Physio Dean had ordered me not to play until he'd checked me out. I had said something like, "You're not the boss of me." And he had said something like, "I'm the Max Best of physios so sit the fuck down." And I couldn't argue with that.

So I sat on a football, thinking. Trying and failing to understand my life. I got so many things backwards. So . . . if I thought backwards, shouldn't I have seen the backwards parts . . . forwards?

"Henri!" I cried. He looked over. "I need a crash course in philosophy."

He shook his head. "And chess. And fashion. And car maintenance." The rest of the players loved this exchange. They liked that someone was allowed to talk shit to me.

The Brig strode into the area and blew his whistle. He summoned everyone, ordered them to form a circle. Intrigued, I joined in, with my arms around Henri and Ben Cavanagh. I gave the goalie a smile and ruffled the back of his training top. His morale increased from Very Poor to Poor.

"Men!" barked the Brig. "A few months ago, your director of football laid out how the season would go. He said there were three dangerous teams. Today, those teams fill the top three places in the league. He said if we trained hard, we'd soon be the fourth-best team. We're fourth in the league. He said if we kept training hard, we'd overtake those bastards by January." This got him some laughs, some cheers. "Your director of football took Saturday's result to heart, but by his own admission we're ahead of schedule. We're doing what he told us we would do, including progressing in every cup competition. As soon as he stops sighing and asking Henri to comfort him, he will soon realise that." More laughs. "He *will* realise that. I'm no football expert, but what I saw on Saturday was clearly the best team in this league. And I don't mean Kidderminster." Nods. Nods from pretty much everyone.

"I agree," said a new voice. The circle opened a fraction, revealing MD and someone with their hood pulled over their head. MD looked curiously stern.

"Me too," said the man in the hood. He pulled it down, revealing he was as bald as the day he was born. The squad cheered. "Not bad for a Manc," he said in his languid Scouse accent. It was none other than Jackie Actual Reaper.

Vimsy smiled at his mate. "You're looking well. How you feeling?"

"Never better," said Jackie. He was, indeed, looking well-rested and healthy. "Ready to get back to work."

Lots of smiles, especially from players like Trick and D-Day. With a flicker of his eyes in my direction, Sam risked a cheeky comment. "Are you going to teach us how to beat a low block?"

"Nothing like that, no, lad. I've come to apply for the manager's job."

20

EPILOGUE

Euphoria was the word of the hour.

The men's, women's and youth teams were, on the whole, in high spirits. Our employees, admins, and sponsors were over the moon. The fan base was as united as it was realistically possible to get in the age of social media.

Emma and I walked around town, popping into shops, stopping for selfies, soaking up the vibe.

I checked the morale of the first team. Since we'd appointed Jackie as manager, almost everyone was happier. A record number of players were on Superb. Vimsy had spent the whole morning beaming. I thought a miserable Livia was beautiful, but a happy Livia was something to behold.

"What are you smiling at?" said Emma. How did she always know when I was thinking about other women?

"Just excited. I've never met a property magnet before."

"What?" she said, laughing at my mistake.

"I think it's *this* road," I said, slowly, trying to put all the landmarks together. "And then to the right."

"Check the app," she whined.

"I don't want to check the app. I want to find it using my brain. And my intuition."

"Christ. Aren't you tired? You pushed yourself on the weekend and you've been going nonstop today."

"I feel fucking amazing," I said, and it was true. "Look, it's more fun this way. What you do is you ask yourself, if I was Henri, where would I live?"

She shook her head, but she squeezed my hand. "You're a bit of a nutjob sometimes."

"Like what?" I said, mock offended.

"Like not looking at a map when you go somewhere the first time. Like being really super happy when you lose a job."

"I didn't lose a job. I gained a friend."

She took her hand away so she could laugh properly—it took over her whole body. She looked up at me with great affection, then slipped her arm through mine. "I think Henri would live *this* way."

After a pleasant, meandering walk, and a quick final bicker about the use of technology, we arrived, guided *most* of the way by my splendid intuition, at

Henri's new house, and the club's unofficial new digs. From the front it was a large but unremarkable building. When we went inside, Henri gave us the tour. The thing was enormous. It went back and back and back—it had merged with the house behind at some point in the past.

"Henri," said Emma. "It's amazing. I'm impressed. But Max made me walk in a loop and I'm hungry. Take me to your hams."

They departed, and I pottered through the fire doors—until recently the property had been a B and B and had to conform to modern regulations. Charlotte was in the farthest room. "Hey," I said, poking my head in. She looked up from her task—she was getting ready for training. A few suitcases and boxes showed that she was still very much moving in. "Everything okay?"

"Yes, Max."

I worried about her. She was a top talent and she'd put her trust in me when, like her friends, she could have hitched a ride with more of a sure thing. "Well played yesterday."

"Thanks." She checked her studs and put her boots into their private little carry case. She picked up her training socks and glanced up, surprised that I was still there. She smiled. "I know that face. You've been watching old movies and need to tell someone about it."

I smiled back, then looked at the carpeted floors. How long until Henri ripped out the carpet and put parquet down? "Are we good?"

She blinked. "Yes, Max. We're good."

"You put a lot of faith in me. I want . . . I need . . ."

"I know. We're good." She dropped the socks into her kit bag and pushed her fringe away. It fell back instantly. "There have been times when I've had doubts. But not anymore."

"What? Because I ran around like a headless chicken?"

She rolled her eyes. "Don't talk like that. I know what you did." She glared at me until I gave her a little nod. "No, it was Henri. He's letting me rent this room for a quarter of my salary."

I knew what she was on. Three hundred and fifty pounds a month for this room in this location was dirt cheap. "Huh. I don't get it."

"He thinks we'll get promoted. Thinks I'll get a new contract. Thinks we'll get promoted again. Get a new contract again. Always a quarter. He'll get paid in the end."

I tried—not very hard—to hide a smile. "So you believe in our little project because Henri's not very good at calculating risk versus return?"

She didn't smile. "Yes. I think he's exceptional at it."

"He missed the part when you wake up one day and realise you don't want to live with Pascal and Youngster."

"And the Triplets," she said.

"Oh, are they here, too? Henri moves fast."

Charlotte zipped up her bag. "We've got a striker. Loads of midfielders. What this house needs," she said, hands on hips like a bossy toddler, "is some defenders. A goalie. Get on it."

"How come you're allowed to boss me around?"

"Because you're in my bedroom."

I looked down and took two careful steps back. I was outside the frame of the door. "How about now?"

"It's a grey area." She hauled up her bag and gestured that I should get out of her way. She closed the door, locked it, and as she was about to head down the corridor, she paused. She looked around, leaned close to me, and whispered, "Can you talk to Henri about the carpets?"

I was astonished. "You want to change them to wooden floors?"

"No," she said, shaking her head violently. "But Henri does. Pascal, too. Apparently they don't have carpet in their countries. That's mad, innit? No carpet. Your feet would freeze. I need my feet, Max. Youngster doesn't think it's his right to have a vote. The Triplets are happy to be here. So it's me on me own holding back the tide."

A smile played around the edges of my lips. This kind of caper used to get my juices flowing, but I'd been squeezed and squeezed by the demands of all my jobs. I had one less now, and felt the old brain cogs clicking into gear. "Henri's stubborn, and surprisingly ruthless. If you approach him head on, you will lose. You have to disarm him and charm him. Watch."

Hope came into her eyes, and she followed me through the many fire doors. She put her bag down in the huge shared living room. Emma was on a bean bag, eating from a plate while reading what turned out to be the menu from a local Portuguese restaurant. I briefly imagined how fun it would be to live here with loads of cool people. Oh, and it spilled out onto a massive patio. Holy shit, this was top!

"Max," said Charlotte.

"Right." We went to the kitchen where Henri was desalinating his peanuts or whatever these super-hosts did. "Oh!" I said, and his head snapped up, already smiling. I made my face go big. "This place! It's top! The more I look, the more I see. I'm jealous, mate. Jealous."

"No, really?"

"Mate! Just everything. The cornicing! The high ceilings. The carpets. They're so thick and lush. I just want to take my shoes and socks off and squirm around. So cosy in the winter. Yeah, the carpets are the cherry on top. Gives the place a real premium vibe. Sort of classy. Ahh . . . Oh, food, nice. I'm quite hungry. What do you recommend?"

Henri, euphoric, helped me choose between all the cheeses and hams and nuts. I turned and Charlotte did a funny, wide-eyed, unblinking exit.

MD came next. He took me aside ted said he had good news.

"BoshCard want to sponsor us from next season. Great terms. But Glendale were, well, the only word I can think of is euphoric, about that interview you did. They knew you were being sarcastic, but they loved it anyway. They had two weeks where their customers talked of nothing else. So the plan is, Glendale will sponsor the women's team, Bosh the men's. How does that sound?"

"Yeah. Sounds ace."

"Good."

"Can I have some of that money already?"

"Glendale want to start soon, this season, so yes. For transfers? It's not much."

I popped a blob of cheese into my mouth. "Any player we could realistically sign, I could get with the budget I already have. And I don't feel like paying fees when great players are around every corner." I munched for a few seconds. "The men, though. Our scout went to see Eddie Moore on the weekend. Sutton United are terrible, they're going down, but he caught the eye. I will scout him myself, but I have a suspicion he'll be what the team needs. *Part* of what the team needs."

"What is he?"

"Left back. But we can't sign him as a left back. We'll have to say he's a right mid or something."

"What are you talking about?"

I laughed. "Don't worry about it! It's part of a wider scheme. Have any of my schemes ever gone wrong?"

"Yes."

"Look. If we sign a left back, our other plan doesn't work. But we need a left back. So we'll sign a left back and tell the world he's something else. Bet you a million pounds no one will ever check."

MD pinched his nose. "You give me a headache. Anyway, there's no money. The women's money has to be used for the women's team."

"Mate," I said. "You just said the men are getting loads of money. Soon! Loan it to me from next year! And we'll get forty thousand if we beat Salford City in the cup. And how much will we get if we're on TV? I'm not trying to bankrupt the club. Just trying to be a good director of football."

He shook his head for ages, then froze while his thoughts moved from *no* to *maybe*. "I suppose . . . we could bring in one player."

"Nah," I said. "The men need two."

"Max . . ."

"All these chumps are going to do low blocks against us. We need a battering ram."

"A battering ram? That doesn't sound very Max Best. Have you got anyone in mind?"

I rubbed my lips as you might do if you were trying to hide a smile. "Remember we played Banbury? They had that guy everyone calls Goliath? Imagine if he played for us."

MD's face was incredibly funny, but I wasn't allowed to laugh. Life's so unfair sometimes. "Are you joking? You're joking. You wouldn't . . ." His distress cleared. The vision of a world where my awesome midfield was firing cross after cross towards Goliath and Henri came into focus. "But . . . It'd make sense, though, wouldn't it? He'd win headers even against those Kidderminster guys. If you do a low block with him on the pitch, you're just letting him walk all the way up to the goal." He pinched his nose again. "He'd score by the dozen. Max. Why do you do this to me?"

I slipped to his side and put my arm around him. "Because we're going to give you another expense. Another bill to pay." With my free left hand, I drew a rainbow in front of us. "We're going to need a bigger trophy cabinet."

The Brig came in. For a moment, I thought he looked flustered, but the impression passed. Emma was delighted to see him and took it upon herself to give the tour.

"Henri," I said. "Got any good trees?"

This was me inviting myself into his garden, and he understood that. "I'll show you."

We slid open the patio doors and slipped outside. I closed the door behind me. One of Henri's eyebrows shot up. I checked no one was around. "Tell me about trees later," I said. "I need to talk as your director of football."

"Oh?" He stood straighter.

"I have decided to loan you out."

His face hardened, just for a second, but it passed. "It is not logical. You would loan me to another club in January? Then who will score the goals to win Chester the title?"

I smirked. "You will. I won't loan you in January. That would be fucking mental."

He frowned, then relaxed. "I see. You are creating some football." He exhaled. "If I go along with it, I'll probably enjoy it. Does that sound right?"

"Yep."

"But explain it to me. You can't loan me out *until* January, but you won't loan me *in* January. And anyway, who benefits from this?"

"Me. You. The club. And I *can* loan you. I've found a loophole. You start on Wednesday."

"Wednesday! We have a match on Saturday."

"Which you will play in."

He threw his arms up. "Max!" He laughed. "Explain it to me."

"Explain it to the world's greatest detective?"

"You're right. Give me a moment." He sat on a comfy-looking outdoor sofa. Sat like *The Thinker* for a few minutes while I pottered around looking at his slightly overgrown garden trying to imagine how it'd look when Henri was finished with it. He shook his head a few times. "I give up."

I explained it to him. It didn't take long. He stared at me, blankly, and laughed a single time. "Absurd. But why?"

"Because I need to know."

He shook his head and mumbled, almost to himself. "That's no kind of reason. It must be something else. I will do it, of course. Why not?" Louder, he said, "You know this has never been done before in the entire history of football?"

"It probably has," I said. "It's obvious if you think about it."

Another laugh. "No, my friend. It is not obvious and no one would ever think about it. Come on. After hearing that, I need a drink."

Emma and the Brig were now chatting merrily with MD, Youngster, Pascal, and the older Triplets. Noah was at training.

I brought Emma a little flute of prosecco and clinked my glass against hers.

The Brig tried to get my attention. I separated from Emma but was enjoying the conversation and didn't want to leave it. The Brig kept bobbling his head as if to say, *Let's go over there.* Why? I saw him all the time. What could be so urgent? I indicated I was happy to stay put.

He leaned close and whispered the only word that could convey how urgent and serious the matter was. "Dude."

Stunned to my core, I followed him to one of the empty rooms. He closed the door behind us, put some music on his phone and let that play while we talked. Not taking any risks!

There were two hard-backed chairs in the room, and we sat facing each other. "Max," he said, which was less shocking than "dude", but was still reserved for serious moments. I realised my mouth was dry. "I know who tried to kill you."

He let that bombshell explode, and while my jaw was still dropped, he glanced at the door and pulled something out of his jacket pocket. It was a clear plastic bag. An evidence bag as used by the police. Inside were my car keys and some flecks of soil. I made some incoherent noises. As I reached out, automatically, for my property, he shook his head and put the bag back in his pocket.

"Who?" I said. He shook his head again. The song came to a quiet part, so he scooched forward on his chair, and so did I. We were speaking softly. "Who?" I repeated. Again, he struggled with the answer. Why? It was fucking simple! Two syllables, probably! "Was it Welly?"

"Before we discuss this further, I need to know how you want to proceed."

"Proceed?"

He looked into my soul, then his expression softened. "If I may change the subject completely, sir."

"No you may not! Are you crazy?"

"Ahem. One of the reasons I fell into the Android ecosystem is that it had dark mode and the iPhone did not. Do you have dark mode on your phone, sir?"

"Er . . . yes. I think so. Yes."

"So the dark mode option is available to you. That's good. It's good to have options."

"Are you saying . . . ?" All right. It had taken me a few seconds to get up to speed, and when you're travelling at those speeds, it's better to shut your mouth. He'd found the murderer and wanted to know what I thought should happen next. The obvious answer was prison. But a dark option was available. Holy *shit*. "I see."

"That's good, sir. Unfortunately, it is a binary choice. Light mode or dark mode."

"Can we discuss the pros and cons of the modes?"

"When you choose dark mode, you are kept in the dark."

"Light mode would be more . . . how do I say it? More in line with the spirit and ethos I try to live by. But with light mode, the problem might return in fifteen to twenty years. And I'd need another Brig."

He smiled and brushed some crumbs from my sleeve. "You will always need a Brig."

"Is this a free choice? You won't think less of me if I choose one or the other?"

"If I felt strongly either way, I wouldn't offer a choice."

I narrowed my eyes and imagined what dark mode would mean. A hole being dug in the middle of a forest in Wales, Scotland, or Cornwall. A body that would perhaps never be found. One less thing keeping me awake at night. It was tempting. "Light mode."

"I thought so, sir. If you don't mind, I'll keep you in the dark for a while longer."

"So it's light mode but with added darkness?"

"Just so, sir. I assume you do not wish DI Barton to get the credit for the arrest."

"Right."

"So I have to proceed methodically. I assure you, it will go well."

I nodded. The sequence of events that led to this moment suddenly became clear. "I should thank Dean."

He winced. "Perhaps it's best if you keep your mouth shut, sir. When the time comes to thank Dean, I will do it. Nonverbally. Long after your attacker is in prison."

"Right. I keep my mouth shut. I pretend to be surprised when the news breaks. All that stuff."

"All that stuff."

I bit my thumbnail while I thought. "Amazing. I mean . . . amazing. This is . . . It's a weight off my shoulders."

He inhaled. "Undoubtedly."

"How do we tell Emma?"

"We don't. She will find out at the same time as you."

"Right. Riiiigggght. But," I started, now that my mind was moving away from the immediate repercussions. "If that's as good as wrapped up, you won't need to stay."

"I have a contract to the summer, sir."

"But after that. I don't want you to go."

He smiled. "I could be persuaded to continue, sir. However, my peers who specialise in dark mode earn much, much more."

"I just allocated our future money to a human siege weapon. How about a promotion? What's above a brigadier?"

"Major general."

"Majjy. May-gen. The maggo."

"I like the Brig. It has grown on me."

"Great. You're hired."

"Let's discuss my large salary increase when the season is over. And sir . . ."

"Yes?"

"Dark mode is a lot cheaper than light mode."

"With dark mode you just need to buy a spade."

He looked around and gave me a slightly exasperated look. "Light mode will come with expenses."

I thought about it. Tried to guess what sort of expenses he meant. Hiring some of his army mates to do things. Which things? He didn't want me to know. Maybe he'd tell me in a couple of years. He wouldn't rip me off, though. Not over this. How much would I pay to make sure the guy who killed me went to prison? A whole fucking lot. "I've got about seven grand." He did a microexpression. "If it's more, I'll get it. Are we talking . . . hundreds?"

"No, nothing like that."

"Okay. I think I'm good for it."

He analysed me. "I think so, too." He raised his glass, intending for me to clink it. But he hesitated. "It could happen quickly, but as the net closes in, animals become wild. I encourage you to be sensible. No surprises."

I laughed. "Right. Bad news for you on that one . . . But I understand. I'll be good."

We clinked our glasses together, and I took a big swig. Justice was coming. I bathed in the moment.

"Shall we return?" said the Brig.

"Wait. Why can't I have my keys?"

The Brig's exasperated look returned. He made his eyes go big, and speaking at something close to his normal volume—it sounded like a shout after we'd been so quiet—he said, "What keys, sir?"

Right. He needed them for some reason. A thought struck me, then. Maybe I would be bad at that *Traitors* TV show, after all. I could plot, but I couldn't follow the plots of others. I smiled. "Cheese. Why can't I have my cheese?"

"You must have left it somewhere, sir. Shall we go find it?"

The soirée was going great. Curious first teamers popped in to say hello and to check out the new digs. Dean came for a look. Jackie and Livia stopped by with a bottle of red wine that Henri lost his mind over.

But things turned, not sour exactly, but . . . less euphoric. I was mingling, trying to give some quality time to as many people as possible. But I realised the bad vibes were centred around . . . drum roll . . . Emma.

"What's going on?" I said finally. I didn't say it very loudly, but somehow the entire room stopped what they were doing to listen.

Emma took a deep breath. "We're worried about this reporter who was digging dirt on you and when that bomb is going to drop. It has to be soon. Before the Darlington match. If it's really bad and there's a big brouhaha and you can't play . . ."

When she'd said "digging dirt," my shoulders had slumped. Not this again! But I was in such a good mood I was soon smiling once more. "I'm sorry, did you say . . . brouhaha?"

"Why don't you take this seriously?"

Henri tapped her on the shoulder and offered her a glass of this superb red wine Jackie had brought. It wasn't very full, but there was only one bottle and many who wanted to try it.

I sighed and pointed to a footstool. "Do you mind?"

"Go ahead," said Henri.

I stood on it and looked around the room. The people I worked with. A very high proportion of whom I could call friends. I didn't want them worrying. I wanted them euphoric!

"Listen up. No one can destabilise this football club better than me." Some laughs. "I take great pride in that." Lots of head shakes from MD, but he was smiling. Emma took an exploratory sip of her wine. Seemed to hit the spot. "If Darlington want to stop us winning the league, it'll take a lot more than one scurrilous newspaper article. All right?" Nods. Approval. Smiles. "Now, there *could* be some pretty weird things in there." I scratched my ear. "I wonder if they've got access to my search history." Lots of people turned to Emma, which made her take another nervous, embarrassed sip of wine. "I'm joking because I'm not worried about it. Not in the slightest. On the whole, I think I make good and fair decisions. You could describe me as upstanding. Generous. Noble."

"Max," said Emma.

I smiled, but the hairs on the back of my neck went haywire. If I got the timing of this right, I could finally achieve my lifelong ambition of making Emma spray out her drink. I'd read that a spit take was more likely to happen in real life through laughter, but shock might do it, too. I licked my lips. My heart was suddenly beating faster. I needed a cool head, though. Like trying to beat a low block with a clever series of passes, timing was everything.

I held my hands up, making sure I had everyone's attention. "There is one thing that won't be in that article, because no one knows about it. I haven't told Emma, or Henri, or anyone. It's something that, taken out of context, could destabilise the club. Could give some people the wrong idea about my intentions." I glanced at the Brig. He looked panicked. *Was I going to . . . ?* I looked at MD. He was staring in horror. *What has he done now?*

I gulped. "The thing is," I said, pausing, and I felt electricity shoot up my spine as Emma took a nervous sip of wine. "The thing is, I bought a football club."

NATIONAL LEAGUE NORTH STANDINGS (CHESTER MEN)

	TEAM	P	W	D	L	F	A	GD	PTS
1	Kidderminster	13	8	5	0	25	9	16	29
2	York	14	7	6	1	22	14	8	27
3	Darlington	13	7	5	1	19	12	7	26
4	Chester	12	8	1	3	31	15	16	25

NORTH WEST REGIONAL FOOTBALL LEAGUE DIVISION 1 SOUTH (CHESTER WOMEN)

	TEAM	P	W	D	L	F	A	GD	PTS
1	Altrincham	2	2	0	0	9	0	9	6
2	Runcorn	2	2	0	0	3	1	2	6
3	Wythenshawe	2	1	1	0	6	3	3	4
4	Chester	2	1	1	0	4	3	1	4

XP balance: 2,596

Debt repaid: 2,458/3000

2023/24 to October 23rd

Max Best player stats

Played 7, goals 0, assists 0

Man of the Match awards: 1

Average rating (curse-assessed): 7.43

Max Best manager stats

Chester Men: P16 W12 D1 L3

Chester Women: P5 W3 D1 L1

Manager of the Month awards: 1

Players bought: 2

Traitors unmasked: 0

Triplets scouted: 3. Or 1. Wait, what?

Cars found: 1

Car keys found: 1

Dream sequences: 1

Cliffhangers: 0

ABOUT THE AUTHOR

Ted Steel is the author of the Player Manager series, which features a charming but secretive main character. He also wrote Nerves of Steel, a LitRPG featuring a charming but secretive main character. When asked to provide a bit of color for his biography, Steel was charming but . . . secretive. Learn more at www.ted-steel.com.

Podium